Agatha Christie is known th[...] Her books have sold over a billion copies in English with another billion in foreign languages. She is the most widely published author of all time and in any language, outsold only by the Bible and Shakespeare. She is the author of 80 crime novels and short story collections, 20 plays, and six novels written under the name of Mary Westmacott.

Agatha Christie's first novel, *The Mysterious Affair at Styles*, was written towards the end of the First World War, in which she served as a VAD. In it she created Hercule Poirot, the little Belgian detective who was destined to become the most popular detective in crime fiction since Sherlock Holmes. It was eventually published by The Bodley Head in 1920.

In 1926, after averaging a book a year, Agatha Christie wrote her masterpiece. *The Murder of Roger Ackroyd* was the first of her books to be published by Collins and marked the beginning of an author–publisher relationship which lasted for 50 years and well over 70 books. *The Murder of Roger Ackroyd* was also the first of Agatha Christie's books to be dramatized – under the name *Alibi* – and to have a successful run in London's West End. *The Mousetrap*, her most famous play of all, opened in 1952 and is the longest-running play in history.

Agatha Christie was made a Dame in 1971. She died in 1976, since when a number of books have been published posthumously: the bestseller novel *Sleeping Murder* appeared later that year, followed by her autobiography and the short story collections *Miss Marple's Final Cases, Problem at Pollensa Bay* and *While the Light Lasts*. In 1998 *Black Coffee* was the first of her plays to be novelized by another author, Charles Osborne.

THE AGATHA CHRISTIE COLLECTION

The Man in the Brown Suit
The Secret of Chimneys
The Seven Dials Mystery
The Mysterious Mr Quin
The Sittaford Mystery
The Hound of Death
The Listerdale Mystery
Why Didn't They Ask Evans?
Parker Pyne Investigates
Murder is Easy
And Then There Were None
Towards Zero
Death Comes as the End
Sparkling Cyanide
Crooked House
They Came to Baghdad
Destination Unknown
Ordeal by Innocence
The Pale Horse
Endless Night
Passenger to Frankfurt
Problem at Pollensa Bay
While the Light Lasts

Poirot
The Mysterious Affair at Styles
The Murder on the Links
Poirot Investigates
The Murder of Roger Ackroyd
The Big Four
The Mystery of the Blue Train
Peril at End House
Lord Edgware Dies
Murder on the Orient Express
Three-Act Tragedy
Death in the Clouds
The ABC Murders
Murder in Mesopotamia
Cards on the Table
Murder in the Mews
Dumb Witness
Death on the Nile
Appointment With Death
Hercule Poirot's Christmas
Sad Cypress
One, Two, Buckle My Shoe
Evil Under the Sun
Five Little Pigs
The Hollow
The Labours of Hercules
Taken at the Flood
Mrs McGinty's Dead
After the Funeral
Hickory Dickory Dock

Dead Man's Folly
Cat Among the Pigeons
The Adventure of the Christmas Pudding
The Clocks
Third Girl
Hallowe'en Party
Elephants Can Remember
Poirot's Early Cases
Curtain: Poirot's Last Case

Marple
The Murder at the Vicarage
The Thirteen Problems
The Body in the Library
The Moving Finger
A Murder is Announced
They Do It With Mirrors
A Pocket Full of Rye
4.50 from Paddington
The Mirror Crack'd from Side to Side
A Caribbean Mystery
At Bertram's Hotel
Nemesis
Sleeping Murder
Miss Marple's Final Cases

Tommy & Tuppence
The Secret Adversary
Partners in Crime
N or M?
By the Pricking of My Thumbs
Postern of Fate

Published as Mary Westmacott
Giant's Bread
Unfinished Portrait
Absent in the Spring
The Rose and the Yew Tree
A Daughter's a Daughter
The Burden

Memoirs
An Autobiography
Come, Tell Me How You Live

Play Collections
The Mousetrap and Selected Plays
Witness for the Prosecution
and Selected Plays

Play Adaptations by Charles Osborne
Black Coffee (Poirot)
Spider's Web
The Unexpected Guest

Agatha Christie

1930s

OMNIBUS

•

THE SITTAFORD MYSTERY

•

WHY DIDN'T THEY ASK EVANS?

•

MURDER IS EASY

•

AND THEN THERE WERE NONE

•

HarperCollins*Publishers*

HarperCollins*Publishers*
77–85 Fulham Palace Road,
Hammersmith, London W6 8JB
www.harpercollins.co.uk

This edition first published 2006
4

The Sittaford Mystery © Agatha Christie Limited 1931
Why Didn't They Ask Evans? © Agatha Christie Limited 1934
Murder is Easy © Agatha Christie Limited 1939
And Then There Were None © Agatha Christie Limited 1939

ISBN 0 00 720863 4

Typeset in Plantin Light and Gill Sans by
Palimpsest Book Production Limited,
Polmont, Stirlingshire

Printed and bound in Great Britain by
Clays Ltd, St Ives plc

CONTENTS

THE SITTAFORD MYSTERY

CHAPTER I
SITTAFORD HOUSE

Major Burnaby drew on his gum boots, buttoned his overcoat collar round his neck, took from a shelf near the door a hurricane lantern, and cautiously opened the front door of his little bungalow and peered out.

The scene that met his eyes was typical of the English countryside as depicted on Xmas cards and in old-fashioned melodramas. Everywhere was snow, deep drifts of it – no mere powdering an inch or two thick. Snow had fallen all over England for the last four days, and up here on the fringe of Dartmoor it had attained a depth of several feet. All over England householders were groaning over burst pipes, and to have a plumber friend (or even a plumber's mate) was the most coveted of all distinctions.

Up here, in the tiny village of Sittaford, at all times remote from the world, and now almost completely cut off, the rigours of winter were a very real problem.

Major Burnaby, however, was a hardy soul. He snorted twice, grunted once, and marched resolutely out into the snow.

His destination was not far away. A few paces along a winding lane, then in at a gate, and so up a drive partially swept clear of snow to a house of some considerable size built of granite.

The door was opened by a neatly clad parlourmaid. The Major was divested of his British Warm, his gum boots and his aged scarf.

A door was flung open and he passed through it into a room which conveyed all the illusion of a transformation scene.

Although it was only half past three the curtains had been drawn, the electric lights were on and a huge fire blazed cheerfully on the hearth. Two women in afternoon frocks rose to greet the staunch old warrior.

'Splendid of you to turn out, Major Burnaby,' said the elder of the two.

'Not at all, Mrs Willett, not at all. Very good of you to ask me.' He shook hands with them both.

'Mr Garfield is coming,' went on Mrs Willett, 'and Mr Duke, and Mr Rycroft *said* he would come – but one can hardly expect him at his age in such weather. Really, it is *too* dreadful. One feels one *must* do something to keep oneself cheerful. Violet, put another log on the fire.'

The Major rose gallantly to perform this task.

'Allow me, Miss Violet.'

He put the log expertly in the right place and returned once more to the armchair his hostess had indicated. Trying not to appear as though he were doing so, he cast surreptitious glances round the room. Amazing how a couple of women could alter the whole character of a room – and without doing anything very outstanding that you could put your finger on.

Sittaford House had been built ten years ago by Captain Joseph Trevelyan, R.N., on the occasion of his retirement from the Navy. He was a man of substance, and he had always had a great hankering to live on Dartmoor. He had placed his choice on the tiny hamlet of Sittaford. It was not in a valley like most of the villages and farms, but perched right on the shoulder of the moor under the shadow of Sittaford Beacon. He had purchased a large tract of ground, had built a comfortable house with its own electric light plant and an electric pump to save labour in pumping water. Then, as a speculation, he had built six small bungalows, each in its quarter acre of ground, along the lane.

The first of these, the one at his very gates, had been allotted to his old friend and crony, John Burnaby – the others had by degrees been sold, there being still a few people who from choice or necessity like to live right out of the world. The village itself consisted of three picturesque but dilapidated cottages, a forge and a combined post office and sweet shop. The nearest town was Exhampton, six miles away, a steady descent which necessitated the sign, 'Motorists engage your lowest gear', so familiar on the Dartmoor roads.

Captain Trevelyan, as has been said, was a man of substance.

In spite of this – or perhaps because of it – he was a man who was inordinately fond of money. At the end of October a house agent in Exhampton wrote to him asking if he would consider letting Sittaford House. A tenant had made inquiries concerning it, wishing to rent it for the winter.

Captain Trevelyan's first impulse was to refuse, his second to demand further information. The tenant in question proved to be a Mrs Willett, a widow with one daughter. She had recently arrived from South Africa and wanted a house on Dartmoor for the winter.

'Damn it all, the woman must be mad,' said Captain Trevelyan. 'Eh, Burnaby, don't you think so?'

Burnaby did think so, and said so as forcibly as his friend had done.

'Anyway, you don't want to let,' he said. 'Let the fool woman go somewhere else if she wants to freeze. Coming from South Africa too!'

But at this point Captain Trevelyan's money complex asserted itself. Not once in a hundred times would you get a chance of letting your house in mid-winter. He demanded what rent the tenant was willing to pay.

An offer of twelve guineas a week clinched matters. Captain Trevelyan went into Exhampton, rented a small house on the outskirts at two guineas a week, and handed over Sittaford House to Mrs Willett, half the rent to be paid in advance.

'A fool and her money are soon parted,' he growled.

But Burnaby was thinking this afternoon as he scanned Mrs Willett covertly, that she did not look a fool. She was a tall woman with a rather silly manner – but her physiognomy was shrewd rather than foolish. She was inclined to overdress, had a distinct Colonial accent, and seemed perfectly content with the transaction. She was clearly very well off and that – as Burnaby had reflected more than once – really made the whole affair more odd. She was not the kind of woman one would credit with a passion for solitude.

As a neighbour she had proved almost embarrassingly friendly. Invitations to Sittaford House were rained on everybody. Captain Trevelyan was constantly urged to 'Treat the house as though we hadn't rented it.' Trevelyan, however, was not fond of women.

Report went that he had been jilted in his youth. He persistently refused all invitations.

Two months had passed since the installation of the Willetts and the first wonder at their arrival had passed away.

Burnaby, naturally a silent man, continued to study his hostess, oblivious to any need for small talk. Liked to make herself out a fool, but wasn't really. So he summed up the situation. His glance shifted to Violet Willett. Pretty girl – scraggy, of course – they all were nowadays. What was the good of a woman if she didn't look like a woman? Papers said curves were coming back. About time too.

He roused himself to the necessity of conversation.

'We were afraid at first that you wouldn't be able to come,' said Mrs Willett. 'You said so, you remember. We were so pleased when you said that after all you would.'

'Friday,' said Major Burnaby, with an air of being explicit.

Mrs Willett looked puzzled.

'Friday?'

'Every Friday go to Trevelyan's. Tuesday he comes to me. Both of us done it for years.'

'Oh! I see. Of course, living so near –'

'Kind of habit.'

'But do you still keep it up? I mean now that he is living in Exhampton –'

'Pity to break a habit,' said Major Burnaby. 'We'd both of us miss those evenings.'

'You go in for competitions, don't you?' asked Violet. 'Acrostics and crosswords and all those things.'

Burnaby nodded.

'I do crosswords. Trevelyan does acrostics. We each stick to our own line of country. I won three books last month in a crossword competition,' he volunteered.

'Oh! really. How nice. Were they interesting books?'

'Don't know. Haven't read them. Looked pretty hopeless.'

'It's the winning them that matters, isn't it?' said Mrs Willett vaguely.

'How do you get to Exhampton?' asked Violet. 'You haven't got a car.'

'Walk.'

'What? Not really? Six miles.'

'Good exercise. What's twelve miles? Keeps a man fit. Great thing to be fit.'

'Fancy! Twelve miles. But both you and Captain Trevelyan were great athletes, weren't you?'

'Used to go to Switzerland together. Winter sports in winter, climbing in summer. Wonderful man on ice, Trevelyan. Both too old for that sort of thing nowadays.'

'You won the Army Racquets Championship, too, didn't you?' asked Violet.

The Major blushed like a girl.

'Who told you that?' he mumbled.

'Captain Trevelyan.'

'Joe should hold his tongue,' said Burnaby. 'He talks too much. What's the weather like now?'

Respecting his embarrassment, Violet followed him to the window. They drew the curtain aside and looked out over the desolate scene.

'More snow coming,' said Burnaby. 'A pretty heavy fall too, I should say.'

'Oh! how thrilling,' said Violet. 'I do think snow is so romantic. I've never seen it before.'

'It isn't romantic when the pipes freeze, you foolish child,' said her mother.

'Have you lived all your life in South Africa, Miss Willett?' asked Major Burnaby.

Some of the girl's animation dropped away from her. She seemed almost constrained in her manner as she answered.

'Yes – this is the first time I've ever been away. It's all most frightfully thrilling.'

Thrilling to be shut away like this in a remote moorland village? Funny ideas. He couldn't get the hang of these people.

The door opened and the parlourmaid announced:

'Mr Rycroft and Mr Garfield.'

There entered a little elderly, dried-up man and a fresh-coloured, boyish young man. The latter spoke first.

'I brought him along, Mrs Willett. Said I wouldn't let him be buried in a snowdrift. Ha, ha. I say, this all looks simply marvellous. Yule logs burning.'

'As he says, my young friend very kindly piloted me here,' said Mr Rycroft as he shook hands somewhat ceremoniously. 'How do you do, Miss Violet? Very seasonable weather – rather too seasonable, I fear.'

He moved to the fire talking to Mrs Willett. Ronald Garfield buttonholed Violet.

'I say, can't we get up any skating anywhere? Aren't there some ponds about?'

'I think path digging will be your only sport.'

'I've been at it all the morning.'

'Oh! you he-man.'

'Don't laugh at me. I've got blisters all over my hands.'

'How's your aunt?'

'Oh! she's always the same – sometimes she says she's better and sometimes she says she's worse, but I think it's all the same really. It's a ghastly life, you know. Each year, I wonder how I can stick it – but there it is – if one doesn't rally round the old bird for Xmas – why, she's quite capable of leaving her money to a Cat's Home. She's got five of them, you know. I'm always stroking the brutes and pretending I dote upon them.'

'I like dogs much better than cats.'

'So do I. Any day. What I mean is a dog is – well, a dog's a dog, you know.'

'Has your aunt always been fond of cats?'

'I think it's just a kind of thing old maids grow into. Ugh! I hate the brutes.'

'Your aunt's very nice, but rather frightening.'

'I should think she was frightening. Snaps my head off sometimes. Thinks I've got no brains, you know.'

'Not really?'

'Oh! look here, don't say it like that. Lots of fellows look like fools and are laughing underneath.'

'Mr Duke,' announced the parlourmaid.

Mr Duke was a recent arrival. He had bought the last of the six bungalows in September. He was a big man, very quiet and devoted to gardening. Mr Rycroft who was an enthusiast on birds and who lived next door to him had taken him up, overruling the section of thought which voiced the opinion that of course Mr Duke was a very nice man, quite unassuming, but was he, after all, quite – well, quite? Mightn't he, just possibly, be a retired tradesman?

But nobody liked to ask him – and indeed it was thought better not to know. Because if one did know, it might be awkward, and really in such a small community it was best to know everybody.

'Not walking to Exhampton in this weather?' he asked of Major Burnaby.

'No, I fancy Trevelyan will hardly expect me tonight.'

'It's awful, isn't it?' said Mrs Willett with a shudder. 'To be buried up here, year after year – it must be ghastly.'

Mr Duke gave her a quick glance. Major Burnaby too stared at her curiously.

But at that moment tea was brought in.

CHAPTER 2
···
THE MESSAGE

After tea, Mrs Willett suggested bridge.

'There are six of us. Two can cut in.'

Ronnie's eyes brightened.

'You four start,' he suggested. 'Miss Willett and I will cut in.'

But Mr Duke said that he did not play bridge.

Ronnie's face fell.

'We might play a round game,' said Mrs Willett.

'Or table-turning,' suggested Ronnie. 'It's a spooky evening. We spoke about it the other day, you remember. Mr Rycroft and I were talking about it this evening as we came along here.'

'I am a member of the Psychical Research Society,' explained Mr Rycroft in his precise way. 'I was able to put my young friend right on one or two points.'

'Tommy rot,' said Major Burnaby very distinctly.

'Oh! but it's great fun, don't you think?' said Violet Willett. 'I mean, one doesn't believe in it or anything. It's just an amusement. What do you say, Mr Duke?'

'Anything you like, Miss Willett.'

'We must turn the lights out, and we must find a suitable table. No – not that one, Mother. I'm sure it's much too heavy.'

Things were settled at last to everyone's satisfaction. A small round table with a polished top was brought from an adjoining room. It was set in front of the fire and everyone took his place round it with the lights switched off.

Major Burnaby was between his hostess and Violet. On the other side of the girl was Ronnie Garfield. A cynical smile creased the Major's lips. He thought to himself:

'In my young days it was Up Jenkins.' And he tried to recall the name of a girl with fluffy hair whose hand he had held beneath the table at considerable length. A long time ago that was. But Up Jenkins had been a good game.

There were all the usual laughs, whispers, stereotyped remarks.

'The spirits are a long time.'

'Got a long way to come.'

'Hush – nothing will happen unless we are serious.'

'Oh! do be quiet – everyone.'

'Nothing's happening.'

'Of course not – it never does at first.'

'If only you'd all be quiet.'

At last, after some time, the murmur of talk died away.

A silence.

'This table's dead as mutton,' murmured Ronnie Garfield disgustedly.

'Hush.'

A tremor ran through the polished surface. The table began to rock.

'Ask it questions. Who shall ask? You, Ronnie.'

'Oh – er – I say – what do I ask it?'

'Is a spirit present?' prompted Violet.

'Oh! Hullo – is a spirit present?'

A sharp rock.

'That means yes,' said Violet.

'Oh! er – who are you?'

No response.

'Ask it to spell its name.'

The table started rocking violently.

'*A B C D E F G H I* – I say, was that *I* or *J*?'

'Ask it. Was that I?'

One rock.

'Yes. Next letter, please.'

The spirit's name was Ida.

'Have you a message for anyone here?'

'Yes.'

'Who is it for? Miss Willett?'

'No.'

'Mrs Willett?'

'No.'

'Mr Rycroft?'

'No.'

'Me?'

'Yes.'

'It's for you, Ronnie. Go on. Make it spell it out.'

The table spelt 'Diana'.

'Who's Diana? Do you know anyone called Diana?'

'No, I don't. At least –'

'There you are. He does.'

'Ask her if she's a widow?'

The fun went on. Mr Rycroft smiled indulgently. Young people must have their jokes. He caught one glance of his hostess's face in a sudden flicker of the firelight. It looked worried and abstracted. Her thoughts were somewhere far away.

Major Burnaby was thinking of the snow. It was going to snow again this evening. Hardest winter he ever remembered.

Mr Duke was playing very seriously. The spirits, alas, paid very little attention to him. All the messages seemed to be for Violet and Ronnie.

Violet was told she was going to Italy. Someone was going with her. Not a woman. A man. His name was Leonard.

More laughter. The table spelt the name of the town. A Russian jumble of letters – not in the least Italian.

The usual accusations were levelled.

'Look here, Violet,' ('Miss Willett' had been dropped) 'you are shoving.'

'I'm not. Look, I take my hands right off the table and it rocks just the same.'

'I like raps. I'm going to ask it to rap. Loud ones.'

'There should be raps.' Ronnie turned to Mr Rycroft. 'There ought to be raps, oughtn't there, sir?'

'Under the circumstances, I should hardly think it likely,' said Mr Rycroft drily.

There was a pause. The table was inert. It returned no answer to questions.

'Has Ida gone away?'

One languid rock.

'Will another spirit come, please?'

Nothing. Suddenly the table began to quiver and rock violently.

'Hurrah. Are you a new spirit?'

'Yes.'

'Have you a message for someone?'

'Yes.'

'For me?'

'No.'

'For Violet?'

'No.'

'For Major Burnaby?'

'Yes.'

'It's for you, Major Burnaby. Will you spell it out, please?'

The table started rocking slowly.

'*T R E V* – are you sure it's *V*? It can't be. *T R E V* – it doesn't make sense.'

'Trevelyan, of course,' said Mrs Willett. 'Captain Trevelyan.'

'Do you mean Captain Trevelyan?'

'Yes.'

'You've got a message for Captain Trevelyan?'

'No.'

'Well, what is it then?'

The table began to rock – slowly, rhythmically. So slowly that it was easy to count the letters.

'*D* –' a pause. '*E – A D*.'

'Dead.'

'Somebody is dead?'

Instead of Yes or No, the table began to rock again till it reached the letter *T*.

'*T* – do you mean Trevelyan?'

'Yes.'

'You don't mean Trevelyan is dead?'

'Yes.'

A very sharp rock. 'Yes.'

Somebody gasped. There was a faint stir all round the table.

Ronnie's voice as he resumed his questions held a different note – an awed uneasy note.

'You mean – that Captain Trevelyan is dead?'

'Yes.'

There was a pause. It was as though no one knew what to ask next, or how to take this unexpected development.

And in the pause, the table started rocking again.

Rhythmically and slowly, Ronnie spelled out the letters aloud . . .

M-U-R-D-E-R . . .

Mrs Willett gave a cry and took her hands off the table.

'I won't go on with this. It's horrible. I don't like it.'

Mr Duke's voice rang out, resonant and clear. He was questioning the table.

'Do you mean – that Captain Trevelyan has been murdered?'

The last word had hardly left his lips when the answer came. The table rocked so violently and assertively that it nearly fell over. One rock only.

'Yes . . .'

'Look here,' said Ronnie. He took his hands from the table. 'I call this a rotten joke.' His voice trembled.

'Turn up the lights,' said Mr Rycroft.

Major Burnaby rose and did so. The sudden glare revealed a company of pale uneasy faces.

Everyone looked at each other. Somehow – nobody quite knew what to say.

'All rot, of course,' said Ronnie with an uneasy laugh.

'Silly nonsense,' said Mrs Willett. 'Nobody ought to – to make jokes like that.'

'Not about people dying,' said Violet. 'It's – oh! I don't like it.'

'I wasn't shoving,' said Ronnie, feeling unspoken criticism levelled at him. 'I swear I wasn't.'

'I can say the same,' said Mr Duke. 'And you, Mr Rycroft?'

'Certainly not,' said Mr Rycroft warmly.

'You don't think I'd make a joke of that kind, do you?' growled Major Burnaby. 'Rotten bad taste.'

'Violet dear –'

'I didn't, Mother. Indeed, I didn't. I wouldn't do such a thing.'

The girl was almost tearful.

Everyone was embarrassed. A sudden blight had come over the cheerful party.

Major Burnaby pushed back his chair, went to the window and pulled aside the curtain. He stood there looking out with his back to the room.

'Twenty-five minutes past five,' said Mr Rycroft glancing up at the clock. He compared it with his own watch and somehow everyone felt the action was significant in some way.

'Let me see,' said Mrs Willett with forced cheerfulness. 'I think we'd better have cocktails. Will you ring the bell, Mr Garfield?'

Ronnie obeyed.

Ingredients for cocktails were brought and Ronnie was appointed mixer. The situation grew a little easier.

'Well,' said Ronnie, raising his glass. 'Here's how.'

The others responded – all but the silent figure by the window.

'Major Burnaby. Here's your cocktail.'

The Major roused himself with a start. He turned slowly.

'Thank you, Mrs Willett. Not for me.' He looked once more out into the night, then came slowly back to the group by the fire. 'Many thanks for a very pleasant time. Good night.'

'You're not going?'

'Afraid I must.'

'Not so soon. And on a night like this.'

'Sorry, Mrs Willett – but it's got to be done. If there were only a telephone.'

'A telephone?'

'Yes – to tell you the truth – I'm – well. I'd like to be sure that Joe Trevelyan's all right. Silly superstition and all that – but there it is. Naturally, I don't believe in this tommy rot – but –'

'But you can't telephone from anywhere. There's not such a thing in Sittaford.'

'That's just it. As I can't telephone, I'll have to go.'

'Go – but you couldn't get a car down that road! Elmer wouldn't take his car out on such a night.'

Elmer was the proprietor of the sole car in the place, an aged

Ford, hired at a handsome price by those who wished to go into Exhampton.

'No, no – car's out of the question. My two legs will take me there, Mrs Willett.'

There was a chorus of protest.

'Oh! Major Burnaby – it's *impossible*. You said yourself it was going to snow.'

'Not for an hour – perhaps longer. I'll get there, never fear.'

'Oh! you can't. We can't allow it.'

She was seriously disturbed and upset.

But argument and entreaty had no more effect on Major Burnaby than if he were a rock. He was an obstinate man. Once his mind was made up on any point, no power on earth could move him.

He had determined to walk to Exhampton and see for himself that all was well with his old friend, and he repeated that simple statement half a dozen times.

In the end they were brought to realize that he meant it. He wrapped himself up in his overcoat, lighted the hurricane lantern, and stepped out into the night.

'I'll just drop in to my place for a flask,' he said cheerily, 'and then push straight on. Trevelyan will put me up for the night when I get there. Ridiculous fuss, I know. Everything sure to be all right. Don't worry, Mrs Willett. Snow or no snow – I'll get there in a couple of hours. Good night.'

He strode away. The others returned to the fire.

Rycroft had looked up at the sky.

'It *is* going to snow,' he murmured to Mr Duke. 'And it will begin long before he gets to Exhampton. I – I hope he gets there all right.'

Duke frowned.

'I know. I feel I ought to have gone with him. One of us ought to have done so.'

'Most distressing,' Mrs Willett was saying, 'most distressing. Violet, I will not have that silly game ever played again. Poor Major Burnaby will probably plunge into a snowdrift – or if he doesn't he'll die of the cold and exposure. At his age, too. Very foolish of him to go off like that. Of course, Captain Trevelyan is perfectly all right.'

Everyone echoed:

'Of course.'

But even now they did not feel really too comfortable.

Supposing something *had* happened to Captain Trevelyan . . .

Supposing . . .

CHAPTER 3

FIVE AND TWENTY PAST FIVE

Two and a half hours later, just before eight o'clock, Major Burnaby, hurricane lantern in hand, his head dropped forward so as not to meet the blinding drive of snow, stumbled up the path to the door of 'Hazelmoor', the small house tenanted by Captain Trevelyan.

The snow had begun to fall about an hour ago – great blinding flakes of it. Major Burnaby was gasping, emitting the loud sighing gasps of an utterly exhausted man. He was numbed with cold. He stamped his feet, blew, puffed, snorted and applied a numbed finger to the bell push.

The bell trilled shrilly.

Burnaby waited. After a pause of a few minutes, as nothing happened, he pushed the bell again.

Once more there was no stir of life.

Burnaby rang a third time. This time he kept his finger on the bell.

It trilled on and on – but there was still no sign of life in the house.

There was a knocker on the door. Major Burnaby seized it and worked it vigorously, producing a noise like thunder.

And still the little house remained silent as the dead.

The Major desisted. He stood for a moment as though perplexed – then he slowly went down the path and out at the gate, continuing on the road he had come towards Exhampton. A hundred yards brought him to the small police station.

He hesitated again, then finally made up his mind and entered.

Constable Graves, who knew the Major well, rose in astonishment.

'Well, I never, sir, fancy you being out on a night like this.'

'Look here,' said Burnaby curtly. 'I've been ringing and knocking at the Captain's house and I can't get any answer.'

'Why, of course, it's Friday,' said Graves who knew the habits of the two pretty well. 'But you don't mean to say you've actually come down from Sittaford on a night like this? Surely the Captain would never expect you.'

'Whether he's expected me or not, I've come,' said Burnaby testily. 'And as I'm telling you, I can't get in. I've rung and knocked and nobody answers.'

Some of his uneasiness seemed to communicate itself to the policeman.

'That's odd,' he said, frowning.

'Of course it's odd,' said Burnaby.

'It's not as though he's likely to be out – on a night like this.'

'Of course he's not likely to be out.'

'It *is* odd,' said Graves again.

Burnaby displayed impatience at the man's slowness.

'Aren't you going to do something?' he snapped.

'Do something?'

'Yes, do something.'

The policeman ruminated.

'Think he might have been taken bad?' His face brightened. 'I'll try the telephone.' It stood at his elbow. He took it up and gave the number.

But to the telephone, as to the front door bell, Captain Trevelyan gave no reply.

'Looks as though he *has* been taken bad,' said Graves as he replaced the receiver. 'And all alone in the house, too. We'd best got hold of Dr Warren and take him along with us.'

Dr Warren's house was almost next door to the police station. The doctor was just sitting down to dinner with his wife and was not best pleased at the summons. However, he grudgingly agreed to accompany them, drawing on an aged British Warm and a pair of rubber boots and muffling his neck with a knitted scarf.

The snow was still falling.

'Damnable night,' murmured the doctor. 'Hope you haven't brought me out on a wild goose chase. Trevelyan's as strong as a horse. Never has anything the matter with him.'

Burnaby did not reply.

Arriving at Hazelmoor once more, they rang again and knocked, but elicited no response.

The doctor then suggested going round the house to one of the back windows.

'Easier to force than the door.'

Graves agreeing, they went round the back. There was a side door which they tried on the way, but it too was locked, and presently they emerged on the snow-covered lawn that led up to the back windows. Suddenly, Warren uttered an exclamation.

'The window of the study – it's open.'

True enough, the window, a French one, was standing ajar. They quickened their steps. On a night like this, no one in his senses would open a window. There was a light in the room that streamed out in a thin yellow band.

The three men arrived simultaneously at the window – Burnaby was the first man to enter, the constable hard on his heels.

They both stopped dead inside and something like a muffled cry came from the ex-soldier. In another moment Warren was beside them, and saw what they had seen.

Captain Trevelyan lay on the floor, face downwards. His arms sprawled widely. The room was in confusion – drawers of the bureau pulled out, papers lying about the floor. The window beside them was splintered where it had been forced near the lock. Beside Captain Trevelyan was a dark green baize tube about two inches in diameter.

Warren sprang forward. He knelt down by the prostrate figure.

One minute sufficed. He rose to his feet, his face pale.

'He's dead?' asked Burnaby.

The doctor nodded.

Then he turned to Graves.

'It's for you to say what's to be done. I can do nothing except examine the body and perhaps you'd rather I didn't do that until the Inspector comes. I can tell you the cause of death now. Fracture of the base of the skull. And I think I can make a guess at the weapon.'

He indicated the green baize tube.

'Trevelyan always had them along the bottom of the door – to keep the draught out,' said Burnaby.

His voice was hoarse.

'Yes – a very efficient form of sandbag.'

'My God!'

'But this here –' the constable broke in, his wits arriving at the point slowly. 'You mean – this here is murder.'

The policeman stepped to the table on which stood a telephone.

Major Burnaby approached the doctor.

'Have you any idea,' he said, breathing hard, 'how long he's been dead?'

'About two hours, I should say, or possibly three. That's a rough estimate.'

Burnaby passed his tongue over dry lips.

'Would you say,' he asked, 'that he might have been killed at five twenty-five?'

The doctor looked at him curiously.

'If I had to give a time definitely, that's just about the time I would suggest.'

'Oh my God,' said Burnaby.

Warren stared at him.

The Major felt his way blindly to a chair, collapsed on to it and muttered to himself whilst a kind of staring terror overspread his face.

'*Five and twenty past five* – Oh my God, then it *was* true after all.'

CHAPTER 4

INSPECTOR NARRACOTT

It was the morning after the tragedy, and two men were standing in the little study of Hazelmoor.

Inspector Narracott looked round him. A little frown appeared upon his forehead.

'Ye-es,' he said thoughtfully. 'Ye-es.'

Inspector Narracott was a very efficient officer. He had a quiet persistence, a logical mind and a keen attention to detail which brought him success where many another man might have failed.

He was a tall man with a quiet manner, rather far-away grey eyes, and a slow soft Devonshire voice.

Summoned from Exeter to take charge of the case, he had arrived on the first train that morning. The roads had been impassable for cars, even with chains, otherwise he would have arrived the night before. He was standing now in Captain Trevelyan's study having just completed his examination of the room. With him was Sergeant Pollock of the Exhampton police.

'Ye-es,' said Inspector Narracott.

A ray of pale wintry sunshine came in through the window. Outside was the snowy landscape. There was a fence about a hundred yards from the window and beyond it the steep ascending slope of the snow-covered hillside.

Inspector Narracott bent once more over the body which had been left for his inspection. An athletic man himself, he recognized the athlete's type, the broad shoulders, narrow flanks, and the good muscular development. The head was small and well set on the shoulders, and the pointed naval beard was carefully trimmed. Captain Trevelyan's age, he had ascertained, was sixty, but he looked not much more than fifty-one or two.

'Ah!' said Sergeant Pollock.

The other turned on him.

'What is your view of it?'

'Well –' Sergeant Pollock scratched his head. He was a cautious man, unwilling to advance further than necessary.

'Well,' he said, 'as I see it, sir, I should say that the man came to the window, forced the lock, and started rifling the room. Captain Trevelyan, I suppose, must have been upstairs. Doubtless the burglar thought the house was empty –'

'Where is Captain Trevelyan's bedroom situated?'

'Upstairs, sir. Over this room.'

'At the present time of year it is dark at four o'clock. If Captain Trevelyan was up in his bedroom the electric light would have been on, the burglar would have seen it as he approached this window.'

'You mean he'd have waited.'

'No man in his senses would break into a house with a light in it. If anyone forced this window – he did it because he thought the house was empty.'

Sergeant Pollock scratched his head.

'Seems a bit odd, I admit. But there it is.'

'We'll let it pass for the moment. Go on.'

'Well, suppose the Captain hears a noise downstairs. He comes down to investigate. The burglar hears him coming. He snatches up that bolster arrangement, gets behind the door, and as the Captain enters the room strikes him down from behind.'

Inspector Narracott nodded.

'Yes, that's true enough. He was struck down when he was facing the window. But all the same, Pollock, I don't like it.'

'No, sir?'

'No, as I say, I don't believe in houses that are broken into at five o'clock in the afternoon.'

'We-ell, he may have thought it a good opportunity –'

'It is not a question of opportunity – slipping in because he found a window unlatched. It was deliberate house-breaking – look at the confusion everywhere – what would a burglar go for first? The pantry where the silver is kept.'

'That's true enough,' admitted the Sergeant.

'And this confusion – this chaos,' continued Narracott, 'these drawers pulled out and their contents scattered. Pah! It's bunkum.'

'Bunkum?'

'Look at the window, Sergeant. *That window was not locked and forced open!* It was merely shut and then splintered from the outside to give the appearance of forcing.'

Pollock examined the latch of the window closely, uttering an ejaculation to himself as he did so.

'You are right, sir,' he said with respect in his voice. 'Who'd have thought of that now!'

'Someone who wishes to throw dust in our eyes – and hasn't succeeded.'

Sergeant Pollock was grateful for the 'our'. In such small ways did Inspector Narracott endear himself to his subordinates.

'Then it wasn't burglary. You mean, sir, it was an inside job.'

Inspector Narracott nodded. 'Yes,' he said. 'The only curious thing is, though, that I think the murderer did actually enter by the window. As you and Graves reported, and as I can still see for myself, there are damp patches still visible where the snow melted and was trodden in by the murderer's boots. These damp patches are only in this room. Constable Graves was quite positive that there was nothing of the kind in the hall when he and Dr Warren passed through it. In this room he noticed them immediately. In that case it seems clear that the murderer was admitted by Captain Trevelyan through the window. Therefore it must have been someone whom Captain Trevelyan knew. You are a local man, Sergeant, can you tell me if Captain Trevelyan was a man who made enemies easily?'

'No, sir, I should say he hadn't an enemy in the world. A bit keen on money, and a bit of a martinet – wouldn't stand for any slackness or incivility – but bless my soul, he was respected for that.'

'No enemies,' said Narracott thoughtfully.

'Not here, that is.'

'Very true – we don't know what enemies he may have made during his naval career. It's my experience, Sergeant, that a man who makes enemies in one place will make them in another, but I agree that we can't put that possibility entirely aside. We come logically now to the next motive – the most common motive for every crime – gain. Captain Trevelyan was, I understand, a rich man?'

'Very warm indeed by all accounts. But close. Not an easy man to touch for a subscription.'

'Ah!' said Narracott thoughtfully.

'Pity it snowed as it did,' said the Sergeant. 'But for that we'd have had his footprints as something to go on.'

'There was no one else in the house?' asked the Inspector.

'No. For the last five years Captain Trevelyan has only had one servant – retired naval chap. Up at Sittaford House a woman came in daily, but this chap, Evans, cooked and looked after his master. About a month ago he got married – much to the Captain's annoyance. I believe that's one of the reasons he let Sittaford House to this South African lady. He wouldn't have any woman living in the house. Evans lives just round the corner here in Fore Street with his wife, and comes in daily to do for his master. I've got him here now for you to see. His statement is that he left here at half past two yesterday afternoon, the Captain having no further need for him.'

'Yes, I shall want to see him. He may be able to tell us something – useful.'

Sergeant Pollock looked at his superior officer curiously. There was something so odd about his tone.

'You think –' he began.

'I think,' said Inspector Narracott deliberately, 'that there's a lot more in this case than meets the eye.'

'In what way, sir?'

But the Inspector refused to be drawn.

'You say this man, Evans, is here now?'

'He's waiting in the dining-room.'

'Good. I'll see him straightaway. What sort of a fellow is he?'

Sergeant Pollock was better at reporting facts than at descriptive accuracy.

'He's a retired naval chap. Ugly customer in a scrap, I should say.'

'Does he drink?'

'Never been the worse for it that I know of.'

'What about this wife of his? Not a fancy of the Captain's or anything of that sort?'

'Oh! no, sir, nothing of that kind about Captain Trevelyan. He wasn't that kind at all. He was known as a woman hater, if anything.'

'And Evans was supposed to be devoted to his master?'

'That's the general idea, sir, and I think it would be known if he wasn't. Exhampton's a small place.'

Inspector Narracott nodded.

'Well,' he said, 'there's nothing more to be seen here. I'll interview Evans and I'll take a look at the rest of the house and after that we will go over to the Three Crowns and see this Major Burnaby. That remark of his about the time was curious. Twenty-five past five, eh? He must know something he hasn't told, or why should he suggest the time of the crime so accurately?'

The two men moved towards the door.

'It's a rum business,' said Sergeant Pollock, his eye wandering to the littered floor. 'All this burglary fake!'

'It's not that that strikes me as odd,' said Narracott, 'under the circumstances it was probably the natural thing to do. No – what strikes me as odd is the window.'

'The window, sir?'

'Yes. Why should the murderer go to the window? Assuming it was someone Trevelyan knew and admitted without question, why not go to the front door? To get round to this window from the road on a night like last night would have been a difficult and unpleasant proceeding with the snow lying as thick as it does. Yet there must have been some reason.'

'Perhaps,' suggested Pollock, 'the man didn't want to be seen turning in to the house from the road.'

'There wouldn't be many people about yesterday afternoon to see him. Nobody who could help it was out of doors. No – there's some other reason. Well, perhaps it will come to light in due course.'

CHAPTER 5
EVANS

They found Evans waiting in the dining-room. He rose respectfully on their entrance.

He was a short thick-set man. He had very long arms and a habit of standing with his hands half clenched. He was clean shaven with small, rather piglike eyes, yet he had a look of cheerfulness and efficiency that redeemed his bulldog appearance.

Inspector Narracott mentally tabulated his impressions.

'Intelligent. Shrewd and practical. Looks rattled.'

Then he spoke:

'You're Evans, eh?'

'Yes, sir.'

'Christian names?'

'Robert Henry.'

'Ah! Now what do you know about this business?'

'Not a thing, sir. It's fair knocked me over. To think of the Capting being done in!'

'When did you last see your master?'

'Two o'clock I should say it was, sir. I cleared away the lunch things and laid the table here as you see for supper. The Capting, he told me as I needn't come back.'

'What do you usually do?'

'As a general rule, I come back about seven for a couple of hours. Not always – sometimes the Capting would say as I needn't.'

'Then you weren't surprised when he told you that yesterday you wouldn't be wanted again?'

'No, sir. I didn't come back the evening before either – on account of the weather. Very considerate gentleman, the Capting was, as long as you didn't try to shirk things. I knew him and his ways pretty well.'

'What exactly did he say?'

'Well, he looked out of the window and he says, "Not a hope of Burnaby today". "Shouldn't wonder," he says, "if Sittaford isn't cut off altogether. Don't remember such a winter since I was a boy." That was his friend Major Burnaby over to Sittaford that he was referring to. Always comes on a Friday, he does, he and the Capting play chess and do acrostics. And on Tuesdays the Capting would go to Major Burnaby's. Very regular in his habits was the Capting. Then he said to me: "You can go now, Evans, and you needn't come till tomorrow morning."'

'Apart from his reference to Major Burnaby, he didn't speak of expecting anyone that afternoon?'

'No, sir, not a word.'

'There was nothing unusual or different in any way in his manner?'

'No, sir, not that I could see.'

'Ah! Now I understand, Evans, that you have lately got married.'

'Yes, sir. Mrs Belling's daughter at the Three Crowns. Matter of two months ago, sir.'

'And Captain Trevelyan was not overpleased about it.'

A very faint grin appeared for a moment on Evans's face.

'Cut up rough about it, he did, the Capting. My Rebecca is a fine girl, sir, and a very good cook. And I hoped we might have been able to do for the Capting together, but he – he wouldn't hear of it. Said he wouldn't have women servants about his house. In fact, sir, things were rather at a deadlock when this

South African lady came along and wanted to take Sittaford House for the winter. The Capting he rented this place, I came in to do for him every day, and I don't mind telling you, sir, that I had been hoping that by the end of the winter the Capting would have come round to the idea; and that me and Rebecca would go back to Sittaford with him. Why, he would never even know she was in the house. She would keep to the kitchen, and she would manage so that he would never meet her on the stairs.'

'Have you any idea what lay behind Captain Trevelyan's dislike of women?'

'Nothing to it, sir. Just an 'abit, sir, that's all. I have seen many a gentleman like it before. If you ask me, it's nothing more or less than shyness. Some young lady or other gives them a snub when they are young – and they gets the 'abit.'

'Captain Trevelyan was not married?'

'No, indeed, sir.'

'What relations had he? Do you know?'

'I believe he had a sister living at Exeter, sir, and I think I have heard him mention a nephew or nephews.'

'None of them ever came to see him?'

'No, sir. I think he quarrelled with his sister at Exeter.'

'Do you know her name?'

'Gardner, I think, sir, but I wouldn't be sure.'

'You don't know her address?'

'I'm afraid I don't, sir.'

'Well, doubtless we shall come across that in looking through Captain Trevelyan's papers. Now, Evans, what were you yourself doing from four o'clock onwards yesterday afternoon?'

'I was at home, sir.'

'Where's home?'

'Just round the corner, sir, 85 Fore Street.'

'You didn't go out at all?'

'Not likely, sir. Why, the snow was coming down a fair treat.'

'Yes, yes. Is there anyone who can support your statement?'

'Beg pardon, sir.'

'Is there anyone who knows that you were at home during that time?'

'My wife, sir.'

'She and you were alone in the house?'

'Yes, sir.'

'Well, well, I have no doubt that's all right. That will be all for the present, Evans.'

The ex-sailor hesitated. He shifted from one foot to the other.

'Anything I can do here, sir – in the way of tidying up?'

'No – the whole place is to be left exactly as it is for the present.'

'I see.'

'You had better wait, though, until I have had a look round,' said Narracott, 'in case there might be any question I want to ask you.'

'Very good, sir.'

Inspector Narracott transferred his gaze from Evans to the room.

The interview had taken place in the dining-room. On the table an evening meal was set out. A cold tongue, pickles, a Stilton cheese and biscuits, and on a gas ring by the fire a saucepan containing soup. On the sideboard was a tantalus, a soda water siphon, and two bottles of beer. There was also an immense array of silver cups and with them – a rather incongruous item – three very new-looking novels.

Inspector Narracott examined one or two of the cups and read the inscriptions on them.

'Bit of a sportsman, Captain Trevelyan,' he observed.

'Yes, indeed, sir,' said Evans. 'Been an athlete all his life, he had.'

Inspector Narracott read the titles of the novels. 'Love Turns the Key', 'The Merry Men of Lincoln', 'Love's Prisoner'.

'H'm,' he remarked. 'The Captain's taste in literature seems somewhat incongruous.'

'Oh! that, sir.' Evans laughed. 'That's not for reading, sir. That's the prizes he won in these Railway Pictures Names Competitions. Ten solutions the Capting sent in under different names, including mine, because he said 85 Fore Street was a likely address to give a prize to! The commoner your name and address the more likely you were to get a prize in the Capting's opinion. And sure enough a prize I got – but not the £2,000, only three new novels – and the kind of novels, in my opinion, that no one would ever pay money for in a shop.'

Narracott smiled, then again mentioning that Evans was to wait, he proceeded on his tour of inspection. There was a large kind of cupboard in one corner of the room. It was almost a small room in itself. Here, packed in unceremoniously, were two pairs of skis, a pair of sculls mounted, ten or twelve hippopotamus tusks, rods and lines and various fishing tackle including a book of flies, a bag of golf clubs, a tennis racquet, an elephant's foot stuffed and mounted and a tiger skin. It was clear that, when Captain Trevelyan had let Sittaford House furnished, he had removed his most precious possessions, distrustful of female influence.

'Funny idea – to bring all this with him,' said the Inspector. 'The house was only let for a few months, wasn't it?'

'That's right, sir.'

'Surely these things could have been locked up at Sittaford House?'

For the second time in the course of the interview, Evans grinned.

'That would have been much the easiest way of doing it,' he agreed. 'Not that there *are* many cupboards at Sittaford House. The architect and the Capting planned it together, and it takes a female to understand the value of cupboard room. Still, as you say, sir, that would have been the common sense thing to do. Carting them down here was a job – I should say it was a job! But there, the Capting couldn't bear the idea of anyone messing around with his things. And lock things up as you will, he says, a woman will always find a way of getting in. It's curiosity, he says. Better not lock them up at all if you don't want her to handle them, he says. But best of all, take them along, and then you're sure to be on the safe side. So take 'em along we did, and as I say, it was a job, and came expensive too. But there, those things of the Capting's was like his children.'

Evans paused, out of breath.

Inspector Narracott nodded thoughtfully. There was another point on which he wanted information, and it seemed to him that this was a good moment when the subject had arisen naturally.

'This Mrs Willett,' he said casually. 'Was she an old friend or acquaintance of the Captain's?'

'Oh no, sir, she was quite a stranger to him.'

'You are sure of that?' said the Inspector, sharply.

'Well –' the sharpness took the old sailor aback. 'The Capting never actually said so – but – Oh yes, I'm sure of it.'

'I ask,' explained the Inspector, 'because it is a very curious time of year for a let. On the other hand, if this Mrs Willett was acquainted with Captain Trevelyan and knew the house, she might have written to him and suggested taking it.'

Evans shook his head.

'Twas the agents – Williamsons – that wrote, said they had an offer from a lady.'

Inspector Narracott frowned. He found this business of letting Sittaford House distinctly odd.

'Captain Trevelyan and Mrs Willett met, I suppose?' he asked.

'Oh! yes. She came to see the house and he took her over it.'

'And you're positive they hadn't met before?'

'Oh! quite, sir.'

'Did they – er –' the Inspector paused, as he tried to frame the question naturally. 'Did they get on well together? Were they friendly?'

'The lady was.' A faint smile crossed Evans's lips. 'All over him, as you might say. Admiring the house, and asking him if he'd planned the building of it. Altogether laying it on thick, as you might say.'

'And the Captain?'

The smile broadened.

'That sort of gushing lady wasn't likely to cut any ice with him. Polite he was, but nothing more. And declined her invitations.'

'Invitations?'

'Yes, to consider the house as his own any time, and drop in, that's how she put it – drop in. You don't drop in to a place when you're living six miles away.'

'She seemed anxious to – well – to see something of the Captain?'

Narracott was wondering. Was that the reason for the taking of the house? Was it only a prelude to the making of Captain Trevelyan's acquaintance? Was that the real game? It would probably not have occurred to her that the Captain would have gone as far as Exhampton to live. She might have calculated on his moving into one of the small bungalows, perhaps sharing Major Burnaby's.

Evans's answer was not very helpful.

'She's a very hospitable lady, by all accounts. Someone in to lunch or dinner every day.'

Narracott nodded. He could learn no more here. But he determined to seek an interview with this Mrs Willett at an early date. Her abrupt arrival needed looking into.

'Come on, Pollock, we'll go upstairs now,' he said.

They left Evans in the dining-room and proceeded to the upper story.

'All right, do you think?' asked the Sergeant in a low voice, jerking his head over his shoulder in the direction of the closed dining-room door.

'He seems so,' said the Inspector. 'But one never knows. He's no fool, that fellow, whatever else he is.'

'No, he's an intelligent sort of chap.'

'His story seems straightforward enough,' went on the Inspector. 'Perfectly clear and above board. Still, as I say, one never knows.'

And with this pronouncement, very typical of his careful and suspicious mind, the Inspector proceeded to search the rooms on the first floor.

There were three bedrooms and a bathroom. Two of the bedrooms were empty and had clearly not been entered for some weeks. The third, Captain Trevelyan's own room, was in exquisite and apple-pie order. Inspector Narracott moved about in it, opening drawers and cupboards. Everything was in its right place. It was the room of a man almost fanatically tidy and neat in his habits. Narracott finished his inspection and glanced into the adjoining bathroom. Here, too, everything was in order. He gave a last glance at the bed, neatly turned down, with folded pyjamas laid ready.

Then he shook his head.

'Nothing here,' he said.

'No, everything seems in perfect order.'

'There are the papers in the desk in the study. You had better go through those, Pollock. I'll tell Evans that he can go. I may call round and see him at his own place later.'

'Very good, sir.'

'The body can be removed. I shall want to see Warren, by the way. He lives near here, doesn't he?'

'Yes, sir.'

'This side of the Three Crowns or the other?'

'The other, sir.'

'Then I'll take the Three Crowns first. Carry on, Sergeant.'

Pollock went to the dining-room to dismiss Evans. The Inspector passed out of the front door and walked rapidly in the direction of the Three Crowns.

CHAPTER 6

AT THE THREE CROWNS

Inspector Narracott was not destined to see Major Burnaby until he had had a protracted interview with Mrs Belling – licensed proprietor of the Three Crowns. Mrs Belling was fat and excitable, and so voluble that there was nothing to be done but to listen patiently until such time as the stream of conversation should dry up.

'And such a night as never was,' she ended up. 'And little did any of us think what was happening to the poor dear gentleman. Those nasty tramps – if I've said it once, I've said it a dozen times, I can't abear those nasty tramps. Do anybody in they would. The Captain had not so much as a dog to protect him. Can't abear a dog, tramps can't. Ah, well, you never know what is happening within a stone's throw.

'Yes, Mr Narracott,' she proceeded in answer to his question, 'the Major is having his breakfast now. You will find him in the coffee-room. And what kind of a night he has passed with no pyjamas or anything, and me a widow woman with nothing to lend him, I can't say, I am sure. Said it made no matter he did – all upset and queer he was – and no wonder with his best friend murdered. Very nice gentlemen the two of them, though the Captain had the reputation of being close with his money. Ah, well, well, I have always thought it dangerous to live up to Sittaford, miles away from anywhere, and here's the Captain struck down in Exhampton itself. It's always what you don't expect in this life that happens, isn't it, Mr Narracott?'

The Inspector said that undoubtedly it was. Then he added:

'Who did you have staying here yesterday, Mrs Belling? Any strangers?'

'Now let me see. There was Mr Moresby and Mr Jones – commercial gentlemen they are, and there was a young gentleman from London. Nobody else. It stands to reason there wouldn't be this time of year. Very quiet here in the winter. Oh, and there was another young gentleman – arrived by the last train. Nosey young fellow I call him. He isn't up yet.'

'The last train?' said the Inspector. 'That gets in at ten o'clock, eh? I don't think we need trouble ourselves about him. What about the other – the one from London? Did you know him?'

'Never seen him before in my life. Not a commercial gentle-man, oh, no – a cut above that. I can't remember his name for the moment – but you'll find it in the register. Left on the first train to Exeter this morning, he did. Six ten. Rather curious. What did he want down here anyway, that's what I'd like to know.'

'He didn't mention his business?'

'Not a word.'

'Did he go out at all?'

'Arrived at lunch time, went out about half past four and came in about twenty past six.'

'Where did he go when he went out?'

'I haven't the remotest idea, sir. May have been just for a stroll like. That was before the snow came, but it wasn't what you might call a pleasant day for walking.'

'Went out at half past four and returned about twenty past six,' said the Inspector thoughtfully. 'That's rather odd. He didn't mention Captain Trevelyan?'

Mrs Belling shook her head decisively.

'No, Mr Narracott, he didn't mention anybody at all. Kept himself to himself he did. A nice looking young fellow – but worried, I should say.'

The Inspector nodded and stepped across to inspect the register.

'James Pearson, London,' said the Inspector. 'Well – that doesn't tell us much. We'll have to make a few inquiries about Mr James Pearson.'

Then he strode off to the coffee-room in search of Major Burnaby.

The Major was the only occupant of the room. He was drinking some rather muddy-looking coffee and *The Times* was propped up in front of him.

'Major Burnaby?'

'That's my name.'

'I am Inspector Narracott from Exeter.'

'Good morning, Inspector. Any forrarder?'

'Yes, sir. I think we are a little forrarder. I think I can safely say that.'

'Glad to hear it,' said the Major drily. His attitude was one of resigned disbelief.

'Now there are just one or two points I would like some information on, Major Burnaby,' said the Inspector, 'and I think you can probably tell me what I want to know.'

'Do what I can,' said Burnaby.

'Had Captain Trevelyan any enemies to your knowledge?'

'Not an enemy in the world.' Burnaby was decisive.

'This man, Evans – do you yourself consider him trustworthy?'

'Should think so. Trevelyan trusted him, I know.'

'There was no ill feeling about this marriage of his?'

'Not ill feeling, no. Trevelyan was annoyed – didn't like his habits upset. Old bachelor, you know.'

'Talking of bachelors, that's another point. Captain Trevelyan was unmarried – do you know if he made a will? And in the event of there being no will, have you any idea who would inherit his estate?'

'Trevelyan made a will,' said Burnaby promptly.

'Ah – you know that?'

'Yes. Made me executor. Told me so.'

'Do you know how he left his money?'

'That I can't say.'

'I understand he was very comfortably off?'

'Trevelyan was a rich man,' replied Burnaby. 'I should say he was much better off than anyone around here suspected.'

'What relations had he – do you know?'

'He'd a sister and some nephews and nieces, I believe. Never saw much of any of them, but there was no quarrel.'

'About this will, do you know where he kept it?'

'It's at Walters & Kirkwood – the solicitors here in Exhampton. They drew it up for him.'

'Then perhaps, Major Burnaby, as you are executor, I wonder if you would come round to Walters & Kirkwood with me now. I should like to have an idea of the contents of that will as soon as possible.'

Burnaby looked up alertly.

'What's in the wind?' he said. 'What's the will got to do with it?'

Inspector Narracott was not disposed to show his hand too soon.

'The case isn't such plain sailing as we thought,' he said. 'By the way, there's another question I want to ask you. I understand, Major Burnaby, that you asked Dr Warren whether death had occurred at five and twenty minutes past five?'

'Well,' said the Major gruffly.

'What made you select that exact time, Major?'

'Why shouldn't I?' said Burnaby.

'Well – something must have put it into your head.'

There was quite a pause before Major Burnaby replied. Inspector Narracott's interest was aroused. The Major had something he quite patently wished to conceal. To watch him doing so was almost ludicrous.

'Why shouldn't I say twenty-five past five?' he demanded truculently, 'or twenty-five to six – or twenty past four, for that matter?'

'Quite so, sir,' said Inspector Narracott soothingly.

He did not wish to antagonize the Major just at this moment. He promised himself that he would get to the bottom of the matter before the day was out.

'There's one thing that strikes me as curious, sir,' he went on.

'Yes?'

'This business of the letting of Sittaford House. I don't know what you think about it, but it seems to me a curious thing to have happened.'

'If you ask me,' said Burnaby, 'it's damned odd.'

'That's your opinion?'

'It's everyone's opinion.'

'In Sittaford?'

'In Sittaford and Exhampton too. The woman must be mad.'

'Well, I suppose there's no accounting for tastes,' said the Inspector.

'Damned odd taste for a woman of that kind.'

'You know the lady?'

'I know her. Why, I was at her house when –'

'When what?' asked Narracott as the Major came to an abrupt halt.

'Nothing,' said Burnaby.

Inspector Narracott looked at him keenly. There was something here he would have liked to get at. The Major's obvious confusion and embarrassment did not escape him. He had been on the point of saying – what?

'All in good time,' said Narracott to himself. 'Now isn't the moment to rub him up the wrong way.'

Aloud he said innocently:

'You were at Sittaford House, you say, sir. The lady has been there now – about how long?'

'A couple of months.'

The Major was eager to escape the result of his imprudent words. It made him more loquacious than usual.

'A widow lady with her daughter?'

'That's it.'

'Does she give any reason for her choice of residence?'

'Well –' the Major rubbed his nose dubiously. 'She talks a lot, she's that kind of woman – beauties of nature – out of the world – that sort of thing. But –'

He paused rather helplessly. Inspector Narracott came to his rescue.

'It didn't strike you as natural on her part?'

'Well, it's like this. She's a fashionable sort of woman. Dressed up to the nines – daughter's a smart, pretty girl. Natural thing would be for them to be staying at the Ritz or Claridge's, or some other big hotel somewhere. You know the sort.'

Narracott nodded.

'They don't keep themselves to themselves, do they?' he asked. 'You don't think they are – well – hiding?'

Major Burnaby shook his head positively.

'Oh! no, nothing of that kind. They're very sociable – a bit too sociable. I mean, in a little place like Sittaford, you can't have previous engagements, and when invitations are showered on you it's a bit awkward. They're exceedingly kind, hospitable people, but a bit too hospitable for English ideas.'

'The Colonial touch,' said the Inspector.

'Yes, I suppose so.'

'You've no reason to think they were previously acquainted with Captain Trevelyan?'

'Sure they weren't.'

'You seem very positive?'

'Joe would have told me.'

'And you don't think their motive could have been – well – to scrape acquaintance with the Captain?'

This was clearly a new idea to the Major. He pondered over it for some minutes.

'Well, I never thought of that. They were very gushing to him, certainly. Not that they got any change out of Joe. But no, I think it was just their usual manner. Over friendly, you know, like Colonials are,' added the super-insular soldier.

'I see. Now, as to the house itself. Captain Trevelyan built that, I understand?'

'Yes.'

'And nobody else has ever lived in it? I mean, it's not been let before?'

'Never.'

'Then it doesn't seem as though it could be anything in the house itself that was the attraction. It's a puzzle. Ten to one it's got nothing to do with the case, but it just struck me as an odd coincidence. This house that Captain Trevelyan took, Hazelmoor, whose property was that?'

'Miss Larpent's. Middle-aged woman, she's gone to a boarding house at Cheltenham for the winter. Does every year. Usually shuts the house up, but lets it if she can, which isn't often.'

There seemed nothing promising there. The Inspector shook his head in a discouraged fashion.

'Williamsons were the agents, I understand?' he said.

'Yes.'

'Their office is in Exhampton?'

'Next door to Walters & Kirkwood.'

'Ah! then, perhaps, if you don't mind, Major, we might just drop in on our way.'

'Not at all. You won't find Kirkwood at his office before ten anyway. You know what lawyers are.'

'Then, shall we go?'

The Major, who had finished his breakfast some time ago, nodded assent and rose.

CHAPTER 7

THE WILL

An alert-looking young man rose to receive them in the office of Messrs Williamson.

'Good morning, Major Burnaby.'

'Morning.'

'Terrible business, this,' said the young man chattily. 'Not been such a thing in Exhampton for years.'

He spoke with gusto and the Major winced.

'This is Inspector Narracott,' he said.

'Oh! yes,' said the young man pleasurably excited.

'I want some information that I think you can give me,' said the Inspector. 'I understand that you put through this let of Sittaford House.'

'To Mrs Willett? Yes, we did.'

'Can you give me full details, please, of how that came about. Did the lady apply personally, or by letter?'

'By letter. She wrote, let me see –' He opened a drawer and turned up a file. 'Yes, from the Carlton Hotel, London.'

'Did she mention Sittaford House by name?'

'No, she merely said she wanted to rent a house for the winter, it must be right on Dartmoor and have at least eight bedrooms. Being near a railway station or town was of no consequence.'

'Was Sittaford House on your books?'

'No, it was not. But as a matter of fact it was the only house in the neighbourhood that at all fulfilled the requirements. The lady mentioned in her letter that she would be willing to go to twelve guineas, and in these circumstances I thought it worth while writing to Captain Trevelyan and asking whether he would consider letting. He replied in the affirmative, and we fixed the thing up.'

'Without Mrs Willett seeing the house?'

'She agreed to take it without seeing it, and signed the agreement. Then she came down here one day, drove up to Sittaford, saw Captain Trevelyan, arranged with him about plate and linen, etc., and saw over the house.'

'She was quite satisfied?'

'She came in and said she was delighted with it.'

'And what did you think?' asked Inspector Narracott, eyeing him keenly.

The young man shrugged his shoulders.

'You learn never to be surprised at anything in the house business,' he said.

On this note of philosophy they left, the Inspector thanking the young man for his help.

'Not at all, a pleasure, I'm sure.'

He accompanied them politely to the door.

The offices of Messrs Walters and Kirkwood were, as Major Burnaby had said, next door to the estate agents. On reaching there, they were told that Mr Kirkwood had just arrived and they were shown into his room.

Mr Kirkwood was an elderly man with a benign expression. He was a native of Exhampton and had succeeded his father and grandfather in the firm.

He rose, put on his mourning face, and shook hands with the Major.

'Good morning, Major Burnaby,' he said. 'This is a very shocking affair. Very shocking indeed. Poor Trevelyan.'

He looked inquiringly at Narracott and Major Burnaby explained his presence in a few succinct words.

'You are in charge of the case, Inspector Narracott?'

'Yes, Mr Kirkwood. In pursuance of my investigations, I have come to ask you for certain information.'

'I shall be happy to give you any information if it is proper for me to do so,' said the lawyer.

'It concerns the late Captain Trevelyan's will,' said Narracott. 'I understand the will is here in your office.'

'That is so.'

'It was made some time ago?'

'Five or six years ago. I cannot be sure of the exact date at the moment.'

'Ah! I am anxious, Mr Kirkwood, to know the contents of that will as soon as possible. It may have an important bearing on the case.'

'Indeed?' said the lawyer. 'Indeed! I should not have thought that, but naturally you know your own business best, Inspector. Well –' he glanced across at the other man. 'Major Burnaby and myself are joint executors of the will. If he has no objection –'

'None.'

'Then I see no reason why I should not accede to your request, Inspector.'

Taking a telephone that stood on his desk he spoke a few words down it. In two or three minutes a clerk entered the room and laid a sealed envelope in front of the lawyer. The clerk left the room, Mr Kirkwood picked up the envelope, slit it open with a paper knife and drew out a large and important-looking document, cleared his throat and began to read –

'I, Joseph Arthur Trevelyan, of Sittaford House, Sittaford, in the County of Devon, declare this to be my last will and testament which I make this thirteenth day of August nineteen hundred and twenty-six.

'(1) I appoint John Edward Burnaby of 1 The Cottages, Sittaford, and Frederick Kirkwood of Exhampton, to be the executors and trustees of this, my will.

'(2) I give to Robert Henry Evans, who has served me long and faithfully, the sum of £100 (one hundred pounds) free of legacy duty for his own benefit absolutely, provided that he is in my service at the time of my death and not under notice to leave whether given or received.

'(3) I give the said John Edward Burnaby, as a token of our friendship and of my affection and regard for him, all my trophies of sport, including my collection of heads and pelts of big game as well as any challenge cups and prizes awarded to

me in any department of sport and any spoils of the chase in my possession.

'(4) I give all my real and personal property, not otherwise disposed of by this, my will, or any codicil hereto, to my Trustees upon Trust that my Trustees shall sell, call in and convert the same into money.

'(5) My Trustees shall out of the moneys to arise out of such sale, calling in and conversion pay any funeral and testamentary expenses and debts, and the legacies given by this, my will, or any codicil hereto and all death duties and other moneys.

'(6) My Trustees shall hold the residue of such moneys or the investments for the time being, representing the same upon Trust to divide the same into four equal parts or shares.

'(7) Upon such division as aforesaid my Trustees shall hold one such equal fourth part or share upon Trust to pay the same to my sister Jennifer Gardner for her own use and enjoyment absolutely.

'And my Trustees shall hold the remaining three such equal fourth parts or shares upon Trust to pay one such equal fourth part or share to each of the three children of my deceased sister, Mary Pearson, for the benefit of each such child absolutely.

'In Witness whereof I, the said Joseph Arthur Trevelyan, have hereunto set my hand the day and year first above written.

'Signed by the above names Testator as his last will in the presence of us both present at the same time, who in his presence and at his request and in the presence of each other have hereunto subscribed our names as witness.'

Mr Kirkwood handed the document to the Inspector.

'Witnessed by two of my clerks in this office.'

The Inspector ran his eye over the will thoughtfully.

'My deceased sister, Mary Pearson,' he said. 'Can you tell me anything about Mrs Pearson, Mr Kirkwood?'

'Very little. She died about ten years ago, I believe. Her husband, a stockbroker, had predeceased her. As far as I know, she never visited Captain Trevelyan here.'

'Pearson,' said the Inspector again. Then he added: 'One thing more. The amount of Captain Trevelyan's estate is not mentioned. To what sum do you think it will amount?'

'That is difficult to say exactly,' said Mr Kirkwood, enjoying, like all lawyers, making the reply to a simple question difficult. 'It is a question of real or personal estate. Besides Sittaford House, Captain Trevelyan owns some property in the neighbourhood of Plymouth, and various investments he made from time to time have fluctuated in value.'

'I just want an approximate idea,' said Inspector Narracott.

'I should not like to commit myself –'

'Just the roughest estimate as a guide. For instance would twenty thousand pounds be out of the way?'

'Twenty thousand pounds. My dear sir! Captain Trevelyan's estate will be worth at least four times as much as that. Eighty or even ninety thousand pounds will be much nearer the mark.'

'I told you Trevelyan was a rich man,' said Burnaby.

Inspector Narracott rose.

'Thank you very much, Mr Kirkwood,' he said, 'for the information you have given me.'

'You think you will find it helpful, eh?'

The lawyer very clearly was agog with curiosity, but Inspector Narracott was in no mood to satisfy it at present.

'In a case like this we have to take everything into account,' he said, noncommittally. 'By the way, have you the names and addresses of this Jennifer Gardner and of the Pearson family?'

'I know nothing of the Pearson family. Mrs Gardner's address is The Laurels, Waldon Road, Exeter.'

The Inspector noted it down in his book.

'That will do to get on with,' he said. 'You don't know how many children the late Mrs Pearson left?'

'Three, I fancy. Two girls and a boy – or possibly two boys and a girl – I cannot remember which.'

The Inspector nodded and put away his notebook and thanked the lawyer once more and took his departure.

When they had reached the street, he turned suddenly and faced his companion.

'And now, sir,' he said, 'we'll have the truth about the twenty-five past five business.'

Major Burnaby's face reddened with annoyance.

'I have told you already –'

'That won't go down with me. Withholding information, that is what you are doing, Major Burnaby. You must have had some idea in mentioning that specific time to Dr Warren – and I think I have a very good idea of what that something is.'

'Well, if you know about it, why ask me?' growled the Major.

'I take it that you were aware that a certain person had an appointment with Captain Trevelyan somewhere about that time. Now, isn't that so?'

Major Burnaby stared at him in surprise.

'Nothing of the kind,' he snarled, 'nothing of the kind.'

'Be careful, Major Burnaby. What about Mr James Pearson?'

'James Pearson? James Pearson, who's he? Do you mean one of Trevelyan's nephews?'

'I presume it would be a nephew. He had one called James, hadn't he?'

'Not the least idea. Trevelyan had nephews – I know that. But what their names were, I haven't the vaguest idea.'

'The young man in question was at the Three Crowns last night. You probably recognized him there.'

'I didn't recognize anybody,' growled the Major. 'Shouldn't anyway – never saw any of Trevelyan's nephews in my life.'

'But you knew that Captain Trevelyan was expecting a nephew to call upon him yesterday afternoon?'

'I did not,' roared the Major.

Several people in the street turned round to stare at him.

'Damn it, won't you take plain truth! I knew nothing about any appointment. Trevelyan's nephews may have been in Timbuctoo for all I knew about them.'

Inspector Narracott was a little taken aback. The Major's vehement denial bore the mark of truth too plainly for him to be deceived.

'Then why this twenty-five past five business?'

'Oh! well – I suppose I had better tell you,' the Major coughed in an embarrassed fashion. 'But mind you – the whole thing is damned foolishness! Tommy rot, sir. How any thinking man can believe such nonsense!'

Inspector Narracott looked more and more surprised. Major Burnaby was looking more uncomfortable and ashamed of himself every minute.

'You know what it is, Inspector. You have to join in these

things to please a lady. Of course, I never thought there was anything in it.'

'In what, Major Burnaby?'

'Table-turning.'

'*Table-turning?*'

Whatever Narracott had expected he had not expected this. The Major proceeded to explain himself. Haltingly, and with many disclaimers of his own belief in the thing, he described the events of the previous afternoon and the message that had purported to come through for himself.

'You mean, Major Burnaby, that the table spelt out the name of Trevelyan and informed you that he was dead – murdered?'

Major Burnaby wiped his forehead.

'Yes, that's what happened. I didn't believe in it – naturally, I didn't believe in it.' He looked ashamed. 'Well – it was Friday and I thought after all I would make sure and go along and see if everything was all right.'

The Inspector reflected on the difficulties of that six mile walk, with the piled-up snowdrifts and the prospect of a heavy snowfall, and he realized that deny it as he would Major Burnaby must have been deeply impressed by the spirit message. Narracott turned it over in his mind. A queer thing to happen – a very queer thing to happen. The sort of thing you couldn't explain satisfactorily. There might be something in this spirit business after all. It was the first well-authenticated case he had come across.

A very queer business altogether but, as far as he could see, though it explained Major Burnaby's attitude, it had no practical bearing on the case as far as he himself was concerned. He had to deal with the physical world and not the psychic.

It was his job to track down the murderer.

And to do that he required no guidance from the spirit world.

CHAPTER 8

MR CHARLES ENDERBY

Glancing at his watch, the Inspector realized he could just catch the train for Exeter if he hurried off. He was anxious to interview the late Captain Trevelyan's sister as soon as possible and obtain from her the addresses of the other members of the family. So, with a hurried word of farewell to Major Burnaby, he raced off to the station. The Major retraced his steps to the Three Crowns. He had hardly put a foot across the doorstep when he was accosted by a bright young man with a very shiny head and a round, boyish face.

'Major Burnaby?' said the young man.

'Yes.'

'Of No. 1 Sittaford Cottages?'

'Yes,' said Major Burnaby.

'I represent the *Daily Wire*,' said the young man, 'and I –'

He got no further. In true military fashion of the old school, the Major exploded.

'Not another word,' he roared. 'I know you and your kind. No decency. No reticence. Clustering round a murder like vultures round a carcass, but I can tell you, young man, you will get no information from me. Not a word. No story for your damned paper. If you want to know anything, go and ask the police, and have the decency to leave the friends of the dead man alone.'

The young man seemed not a whit taken aback. He smiled more encouragingly than ever.

'I say, sir, you know you have got hold of the wrong end of the stick. I know nothing about this murder business.'

This was not, strictly speaking, the truth. No one in Exhampton could pretend ignorance of the event that had shaken the quiet moorland town to its core.

'I am empowered on behalf of the *Daily Wire*,' went on the young man, 'to hand you this cheque for £5,000 and congratulate you on sending in the only correct solution of our football competition.'

Major Burnaby was completely taken aback.

'I have no doubt,' continued the young man, 'that you have already received our letter yesterday morning informing you of the good news.'

'Letter?' said Major Burnaby. 'Do you realize, young man, that Sittaford is about ten feet deep in snow? What chance do you think we have had in the last few days of a regular delivery of letters?'

'But doubtless you saw your name announced as winner in the *Daily Wire*, this morning?'

'No,' said Major Burnaby. 'I haven't glanced at the paper this morning.'

'Ah! of course not,' said the young man. 'This sad business. The murdered man was a friend of yours, I understand.'

'My best friend,' said the Major.

'Hard lines,' said the young man tactfully averting his eyes. Then he drew from his pocket a small folded piece of mauve paper and handed it to Major Burnaby with a bow.

'With the compliments of the *Daily Wire*,' he said.

Major Burnaby took it and said the only thing possible under the circumstances.

'Have a drink, Mr – er –?'

'Enderby, Charles Enderby my name is. I got here last night,' he explained. 'Made inquiries about getting to Sittaford. We make it a point to hand cheques to winners personally. Always publish a little interview. Interests our readers. Well, everyone told me it was out of the question – the snow was falling and it simply couldn't be done, and then with the greatest good luck I find you are actually here, staying at the Three Crowns.' He smiled. 'No difficulty about identification. Everybody seems to know everybody else in this part of the world.'

'What will you have?' said the Major.

'Beer for me,' said Enderby.

The Major ordered two beers.

'The whole place seems off its head with this murder,' remarked Enderby. 'Rather a mysterious business by all accounts.'

The Major grunted. He was in something of a quandary. His sentiments towards journalists remained unchanged, but a man who has just handed you a cheque for £5,000 is in a privileged position. You cannot very well tell him to go to the devil.

'No enemies, had he?' asked the young man.

'No,' said the Major.

'But I hear the police don't think it is robbery,' went on Enderby.

'How do you know that?' asked the Major.

Mr Enderby, however, did not reveal the source of his information.

'I hear it was you who actually discovered the body, sir,' said the young man.

'Yes.'

'It must have been an awful shock.'

The conversation proceeded. Major Burnaby was still determined to give no information, but he was no match for the adroitness of Mr Enderby. The latter made statements with which the Major was forced to agree or disagree, thereby providing the information the young man wanted. So pleasant was his manner, however, that the process was really not painful at all and the Major found himself taking quite a liking to the ingenuous young man.

Presently, Mr Enderby rose and observed that he must go along to the post office.

'If you will just give me a receipt for that cheque, sir.'

The Major went across to the writing table, wrote a receipt and handed it to him.

'Splendid,' said the young man and slipped it into his pocket.

'I suppose,' said Major Burnaby, 'that you are off back to London today?'

'Oh! no,' said the young man. 'I want to take a few photographs, you know, of your cottage at Sittaford, and of you feeding the pigs, or hoeing up the dandelions, or doing anything characteristic that you fancy. You have no idea how our readers appreciate that sort of thing. Then I would like to have a few words from you on "What I intend to do with the £5,000". Something snappy. You have no idea how disappointed our readers would be if they didn't get that sort of thing.'

'Yes, but look here – it's impossible to get to Sittaford in this weather. The fall of snow was exceptionally heavy. No vehicle has been able to take the road for three days anyway, and it may be another three before the thaw sets in properly.'

'I know,' said the young man, 'it *is* awkward. Well, well, one will just have to resign oneself to kicking up one's heels in Exhampton. They do you pretty well at the Three Crowns. So long, sir, see you later.'

He emerged into the main street of Exhampton and made his way to the post office and wired his paper that by the greatest of good luck he would be able to supply them with tasty and exclusive information on the Exhampton Murder Case.

He reflected on his next course of action and decided on interviewing the late Captain Trevelyan's servant, Evans, whose name Major Burnaby had incautiously let slip during their conversation.

A few inquiries brought him to 85 Fore Street. The servant of the murdered man was a person of importance today. Everyone was willing and anxious to point out where he lived.

Enderby beat a smart rat-tat on the door. It was opened by a man so typically an ex-sailor that Enderby had no doubt of his identity.

'Evans, isn't it?' said Enderby cheerfully. 'I have just come along from Major Burnaby.'

'Oh –' Evans hesitated a moment. 'Will you come in, sir.'

Enderby accepted the invitation. A buxom young woman with dark hair and red cheeks hovered in the background. Enderby judged her as the newly-wed Mrs Evans.

'Bad thing about your late master,' said Enderby.

'It's shocking, sir, that's what it is.'

'Who do you think did it?' demanded Enderby with an ingenuous air of seeking information.

'One of those low-down tramps, I suppose,' said Evans.

'Oh! no, my dear man. That theory is quite exploded.'

'Eh?'

'That's all a put-up job. The police saw through that at once.'

'Who told you that, sir?'

Enderby's real informant had been the housemaid at the Three Crowns whose sister was the legal spouse of Constable Graves, but he replied:

'Had a tip from headquarters. Yes, the burglary idea was all a put-up job.'

'Who do they think did it then?' demanded Mrs Evans, coming forward. Her eyes looked frightened and eager.

'Now, Rebecca, don't you take on so,' said her husband.

'Cruel stupid the police are,' said Mrs Evans. 'Don't mind who they take up as long as they get hold of someone.' She cast a quick glance at Enderby.

'Are you connected with the police, sir?'

'Me? Oh! no. I am from a newspaper, the *Daily Wire*. I came down to see Major Burnaby. He has just won our Free Football Competition for £5,000.'

'What?' cried Evans. 'Damn it all, then those things are square after all.'

'Didn't you think they were?' asked Enderby.

'Well, it's a wicked world, sir.' Evans was a little confused, feeling that his exclamation had been wanting in tact. 'I have heard there's a lot of trickery concerned. The late Capting used to say that a prize never went to a good address. That's why he used mine time and again.'

With a certain naïveté he described the Captain's winning of three new novels.

Enderby encouraged him to talk. He saw a very good story being made out of Evans. The faithful servant – old sea dog touch. He wondered just a little why Mrs Evans seemed so nervous, he put it down to the suspicious ignorance of her class.

'You find the skunk that done it,' said Evans. 'Newspapers can do a lot, they say, in hunting down criminals.'

'It was a burglar,' said Mrs Evans. 'That's what it was.'

'Of course, it was a burglar,' said Evans. 'Why, there's no one in Exhampton would want to harm the Capting.'

Enderby rose.

'Well,' he said. 'I must be going. I will run in now and then and have a little chat if I may. If the Captain won three new novels in a *Daily Wire* Competition, the *Daily Wire* ought to make it a personal matter to hunt down his murderer.'

'You can't say fairer than that, sir. No, you can't say fairer than that.'

Wishing them a cheery good day, Charles Enderby took his leave.

'I wonder who really did the beggar in?' he murmured to himself. 'I don't think our friend Evans. Perhaps it *was* a burglar! Very disappointing, if so. Doesn't seem any woman in the case, which is a pity. We've got to have some sensational development soon or the case will fade into insignificance. Just my luck, if so. First time I have ever been on the spot in a matter of this kind. I must make good. Charles, my boy, your chance in life has come. Make the most of it. Our military friend will, I see, soon be eating out of my hand if I remember to be sufficiently respectful and call him "sir" often enough. Wonder if he was in the Indian Mutiny. No, of course not, not old enough for that. The South African War, that's it. Ask him about the South African War, that will tame him.'

And pondering these resolutions in his mind Mr Enderby sauntered back to the Three Crowns.

CHAPTER 9

THE LAURELS

It takes about half an hour from Exhampton to Exeter by train. At five minutes to twelve Inspector Narracott was ringing the front door bell of The Laurels.

The Laurels was a somewhat dilapidated house, badly in need of a new coat of paint. The garden round it was unkempt and weedy and the gate hung askew on its hinges.

'Not too much money about here,' thought Inspector Narracott to himself. 'Evidently hard up.'

He was a very fair-minded man, but inquiries seemed to indicate that there was very little possibility of the Captain's having been done to death by an enemy. On the other hand, four people, as far as he could make out, stood to gain a considerable sum by the old man's death. The movements of each of these four people had got to be inquired into. The entry in the hotel register was suggestive, but after all Pearson was quite a common name. Inspector Narracott was anxious not to come to any decision too rapidly and to keep a perfectly open mind whilst covering the preliminary ground as rapidly as possible.

A somewhat slatternly-looking maid answered the bell.

'Good afternoon,' said Inspector Narracott. 'I want to see Mrs Gardner, please. It is in connection with the death of her brother, Captain Trevelyan, at Exhampton.'

He purposely did not hand his official card to the maid. The mere fact of his being a police officer, as he knew by experience, would render her awkward and tongue-tied.

'She's heard of her brother's death?' asked the Inspector casually as the maid drew back to let him into the hall.

'Yes, got a telegram she did. From the lawyer, Mr Kirkwood.'

'Just so,' said Inspector Narracott.

The maid ushered him into the drawing-room – a room which, like the outside of the house, was badly in need of a little money spent upon it, but yet had, with all that, an air of charm which the Inspector felt without being able to particularize the why and wherefore of it.

'Must have been a shock to your mistress,' he observed.

The girl seemed a little vague about that, he noticed.

'She didn't see much of him,' was her answer.

'Shut the door and come here,' said Inspector Narracott.

He was anxious to try the effect of a surprise attack.

'Did the telegram say that it was murder?' he asked.

'Murder!'

The girl's eyes opened wide, a mixture of horror and intense enjoyment in them. 'Murdered was he?'

'Ah!' said Inspector Narracott, 'I thought you hadn't heard that. Mr Kirkwood didn't want to break the news too abruptly to your mistress, but you see, my dear – what is your name, by the way?'

'Beatrice, sir.'

'Well, you see, Beatrice, it will be in the evening papers tonight.'

'Well, I never,' said Beatrice. 'Murdered. 'orrible, isn't it? Did they bash his head in or shoot him or what?'

The Inspector satisfied her passion for detail, then added casually, 'I believe there was some idea of your mistress going over to Exhampton yesterday afternoon. But I suppose the weather was too bad for her.'

'I never heard anything about it, sir,' said Beatrice. 'I think you must have made a mistake. The mistress went out in the afternoon to do some shopping and then she went to the Pictures.'

'What time did she get in?'

'About six o'clock.'

So that let Mrs Gardner out.

'I don't know much about the family,' he went on in a casual tone. 'Is Mrs Gardner a widow?'

'Oh, no, sir, there's master.'

'What does he do?'

'He doesn't do anything,' said Beatrice staring. 'He can't. He's an invalid.'

'An invalid, is he? Oh, I'm sorry. I hadn't heard.'

'He can't walk. He lies in bed all day. Got a nurse always in the house we have. It isn't every girl what stays on with an 'ospital nurse in the house the whole time. Always wanting trays carried up and pots of tea made.'

'Must be very trying,' said the Inspector soothingly. 'Now, will you go and tell your mistress, please, that I am here from Mr Kirkwood of Exhampton?'

Beatrice withdrew, and a few minutes later the door opened and a tall, rather commanding woman came into the room. She had an unusual-looking face, broad about the brows, and black hair with a touch of grey at the temples, which she wore combed straight back from her forehead. She looked at the Inspector inquiringly.

'You have come from Mr Kirkwood at Exhampton?'

'Not exactly, Mrs Gardner. I put it that way to your maid. Your brother, Captain Trevelyan, was murdered yesterday afternoon and I am Divisional Inspector Narracott in charge of the case.'

Whatever else Mrs Gardner might be she was certainly a woman of iron nerve. Her eyes narrowed and she drew in her breath sharply, then motioning the Inspector to a chair and sitting down herself she said:

'Murdered! How extraordinary! Who in the world would want to murder Joe?'

'That is what I'm anxious to find out, Mrs Gardner.'

'Of course. I hope I shall be able to help you in some way, but I doubt it. My brother and I have seen very little of each other in the last ten years. I know nothing of his friends or of any ties he has formed.'

'You'll excuse me, Mrs Gardner, but had you and your brother quarrelled?'

'No – not quarrelled. I think estranged would be a better word to describe the position between us. I don't want to go into family details, but my brother rather resented my marriage. Brothers, I think, seldom approve of their sisters' choice, but usually, I fancy, they conceal it better than my brother did. My brother, as perhaps you know, had a large fortune left him by an aunt. Both my sister and myself married poor men. When my husband was invalided out of the army after the war with shell shock, a little financial assistance would have been a wonderful relief – would have enabled me to give him an expensive course of treatment which was otherwise denied to him. I asked my brother for a loan which he refused. That, of course, he was perfectly entitled to do. But since then we have met at very rare intervals, and hardly corresponded at all.'

It was a clear succinct statement.

An intriguing personality, this Mrs Gardner's, the Inspector thought. Somehow, he couldn't quite make her out. She seemed unnaturally calm, unnaturally ready with her recital of facts. He also noticed that, with all her surprise, she asked for no details of her brother's death. That struck him as extraordinary.

'I don't know if you want to hear what exactly occurred – at Exhampton,' he began.

She frowned.

'Must I hear it? My brother was killed – painlessly, I hope.'

'Quite painlessly, I should say.'

'Then please spare me any revolting details.'

'Unnatural,' thought the Inspector, 'decidedly unnatural.'

As though she had read his mind she used the word that he had spoken to himself.

'I suppose you think that very unnatural, Inspector, but – I have heard a good many horrors. My husband has told me things when he has had one of his bad turns –' she shivered. 'I think you would understand if you knew my circumstances better.'

'Oh! quite so, quite so, Mrs Gardner. What I really came for was to get a few family details from you.'

'Yes?'

'Do you know how many relatives living your brother has besides yourself?'

'Of near relations, only the Pearsons. My sister Mary's children.'

'And they are?'

'James, Sylvia and Brian.'

'James?'

'He is the eldest. He works in an Insurance Office.'

'What age is he?'

'Twenty-eight.'

'Is he married?'

'No, but he is engaged – to a very nice girl, I believe. I've not yet met her.'

'And his address?'

'21 Cromwell Street, S.W.3.'

The Inspector noted it down.

'Yes, Mrs Gardner?'

'Then there's Sylvia. She's married to Martin Dering – you may have read his books. He's a moderately successful author.'

'Thank you, and their address?'

'The Nook, Surrey Road, Wimbledon.'

'Yes?'

'And the youngest is Brian – but he is out in Australia. I am afraid I don't know his address, but either his brother or sister would know.'

'Thank you, Mrs Gardner. Just a matter of form, do you mind my asking you how you spent yesterday afternoon?'

She looked surprised.

'Let me see. I did some shopping – yes – then I went to the Pictures. I came home about six and lay down on my bed until dinner, as the Pictures had given me rather a headache.'

'Thank you, Mrs Gardner.'

'Is there anything else?'

'No, I don't think I have anything further to ask you. I will now get into communication with your nephew and niece. I don't know if Mr Kirkwood has informed you of the fact yet, but you and the three young Pearsons are the joint inheritors of Captain Trevelyan's money.'

The colour came into her face in a slow, rich blush.

'That will be wonderful,' she said quietly. 'It has been so difficult – so terribly difficult – always skimping and saving and wishing.'

She started up as a man's rather querulous voice came floating down the stairs.

'Jennifer, Jennifer, I want you.'

'Excuse me,' she said.

As she opened the door the call came again, louder and more imperiously.

'Jennifer, where are you? I want you, Jennifer.'

The Inspector had followed her to the door. He stood in the hall looking after her as she ran up the stairs.

'I am coming, dear,' she called.

A hospital nurse who was coming down the stairs stood aside to let her pass up.

'Please go to Mr Gardner, he is getting very excited. You always manage to calm him.'

Inspector Narracott stood deliberately in the nurse's way as she reached the bottom of the stairs.

'May I speak to you for a moment?' he said. 'My conversation with Mrs Gardner was interrupted.'

The nurse came with alacrity into the drawing-room.

'The news of the murder has upset my patient,' she explained, adjusting a well-starched cuff. 'That foolish girl, Beatrice, came running up and blurted it all out.'

'I am sorry,' said the Inspector. 'I am afraid that was my fault.'

'Oh, of course, you couldn't be expected to know,' said the nurse graciously.

'Is Mr Gardner dangerously ill?' inquired the Inspector.

'It's a sad case,' said the nurse. 'Of course, in a manner of speaking, there's nothing the matter with him really. He's lost the use of his limbs entirely through nervous shock. There's no visible disability.'

'He had no extra strain or shock yesterday afternoon?' inquired the Inspector.

'Not that I know of,' the nurse looked somewhat surprised.

'You were with him all the afternoon?'

'I intended to be, but, well – as a matter of fact, Captain Gardner was very anxious for me to change two books for him at the library. He had forgotten to ask his wife before she went out. So, to oblige him I went out with them, and he asked me at the same time to get one or two little things for him – presents for his wife as a matter of fact. Very nice about it he was, and told me I was to have tea at his expense at Boots. He said nurses never liked missing their tea. His little joke, you know. I didn't get out until past four, and what with the shops being so full just before Christmas, and one thing and another, I didn't get back until after six, but the poor fellow had been quite comfortable. In fact, he told me he had been asleep most of the time.'

'Mrs Gardner was back by then?'

'Yes, I believe she was lying down.'

'She's very devoted to her husband, isn't she?'

'She worships him. I really do believe that woman would do anything in the world for him. Quite touching, and very different from some of the cases I have attended. Why, only last month –'

But Inspector Narracott fended off the impending scandal of last month with considerable skill. He glanced at his watch and gave a loud exclamation.

'Goodness gracious,' he cried, 'I shall miss my train. The station is not far away, is it?'

'St David's is only three minutes' walk, if it's St David's you want, or did you mean Queen Street?'

'I must run,' said the Inspector, 'tell Mrs Gardner I am sorry not to have seen her to say goodbye. Very pleased to have had this little chat with you, nurse.'

The nurse bridled ever so slightly.

'Rather a good-looking man,' she said to herself as the front door shut after the Inspector. 'Really quite good-looking. Such a nice sympathetic manner.'

And with a slight sigh she went upstairs to her patient.

CHAPTER 10

THE PEARSON FAMILY

Inspector Narracott's next move was to report to his superior, Superintendent Maxwell.

The latter listened with interest to the Inspector's narrative.

'It's going to be a big case,' he said thoughtfully. 'There'll be headlines in the papers over this.'

'I agree with you, sir.'

'We've got to be careful. We don't want to make any mistake. But I think you're on the right track. You must get after this James

Pearson as soon as possible – find out where he was yesterday afternoon. As you say, it's a common enough name, but there's the Christian name as well. Of course, his signing his own name openly like that shows there wasn't any premeditation about it. He'd hardly have been such a fool otherwise. It looks to me like a quarrel and a sudden blow. If it is the man, he must have heard of his uncle's death that night. And if so, why did he sneak off by the six train in the morning without a word to anyone? No, it looks bad. Always granting that the whole thing's not a coincidence. You must clear that up as quickly as possible.'

'That's what I thought, sir. I'd better take the 1.45 to town. Some time or other I want to have a word with this Willett woman who rented the Captain's house. There's something fishy there. But I can't get to Sittaford at present, the roads are impassable with snow. And anyway, she can't have any direct connection with the crime. She and her daughter were actually – well – table-turning at the time the crime was committed. And, by the way, rather a queer thing happened –'

The Inspector narrated the story he had heard from Major Burnaby.

'That's a rum go,' ejaculated the Superintendent. 'Think this old fellow was telling the truth? That's the sort of story that gets cooked up afterwards by those believers in spooks and things of that kind.'

'I fancy it's true all right,' said Narracott with a grin. 'I had a lot of difficulty getting it out of him. *He's* not a believer – just the opposite – old soldier, all damned nonsense attitude.'

The Superintendent nodded his comprehension.

'Well, it's odd, but it doesn't get us anywhere,' was his conclusion.

'Then I'll take the 1.45 to London.'

The other nodded.

On arrival in town Narracott went straight to 21 Cromwell Street. Mr Pearson, he was told, was at the office. He would be back for certain about seven o'clock.

Narracott nodded carelessly as though the information were of no value to him.

'I'll call back if I can,' he said. 'It's nothing of importance,' and departed quickly without leaving a name.

He decided not to go to the Insurance Office, but to visit Wimbledon instead and have an interview with Mrs Martin Dering, formerly Miss Sylvia Pearson.

There were no signs of shabbiness about The Nook. 'New and shoddy,' was how Inspector Narracott described it to himself.

Mrs Dering was at home. A rather pert-looking maid dressed in lilac colour showed him into a rather over-crowded drawing-room. He gave her his official card to take to her mistress.

Mrs Dering came to him almost immediately, his card in her hand.

'I suppose you have come about poor Uncle Joseph,' was her greeting. 'It's shocking – really shocking! I am so dreadfully nervous of burglars myself. I had two extra bolts put on the back door last week, and new patent catches on the windows.'

Sylvia Dering, the Inspector knew from Mrs Gardner, was only twenty-five, but she looked considerably over thirty. She was small and fair and anaemic-looking, with a worried and harassed expression. Her voice had that faintly complaining note in it which is about the most annoying sound a human voice can contain. Still not allowing the Inspector to speak, she went on:

'If there's anything I can do to help you in any way, of course, I shall be only too glad to do so, but one hardly ever saw Uncle Joseph. He wasn't a very nice man – I am sure he couldn't have been. Not the sort of person one could go to in trouble, always carping and criticizing. Not the sort of man who had any knowledge of what literature meant. Success – true success is not always measured in terms of money, Inspector.'

At last she paused, and the Inspector, to whom those remarks had opened certain fields of conjecture, was given his turn to speak.

'You've heard of the tragedy very quickly, Mrs Dering.'

'Aunt Jennifer wired it to me.'

'I see.'

'But I suppose it will be in the evening papers. Dreadful, isn't it?'

'I gather you've not seen your uncle of late years.'

'I have only seen him twice since my marriage. On the second occasion he was really very rude to Martin. Of course he was a regular philistine in every way – devoted to sport. No appreciation, as I said just now, of literature.'

'Husband applied to him for a loan and got refused,' was Inspector Narracott's private comment on the situation.

'Just as a matter of form, Mrs Dering, will you tell me what your movements were yesterday afternoon?'

'My movements? What a very queer way of putting it, Inspector. I played bridge most of the afternoon and a friend came in and spent the evening with me, as my husband was out.'

'Out, was he? Away from home altogether?'

'A literary dinner,' explained Mrs Dering with importance. 'He lunched with an American publisher and had this dinner in the evening.'

'I see.'

That seemed quite fair and above board. He went on.

'Your younger brother is in Australia, I believe, Mrs Dering?'

'Yes.'

'You have his address?'

'Oh, yes, I can find it for you if you wish – rather a peculiar name – I've forgotten it for the minute. Somewhere in New South Wales.'

'And now, Mrs Dering, your elder brother?'

'Jim?'

'Yes. I shall want to get in touch with him.'

Mrs Dering hastened to supply him with the address – the same as that which Mrs Gardner had already given him.

Then, feeling there was no more to be said on either side, he cut the interview short.

Glancing at his watch, he noted that by the time he had returned to town it would be seven o'clock – a likely time, he hoped, for finding Mr James Pearson at home.

The same superior-looking, middle-aged woman opened the door of No. 21. Yes, Mr Pearson was at home now. It was on the second floor, if the gentleman would walk up.

She preceded him, tapped at a door, and in a murmured and apologetic voice said: 'The gentleman to see you, sir.' Then, standing back, she allowed the Inspector to enter.

A young man in evening dress was standing in the middle of the room. He was good-looking, indeed handsome, if you took no account of the rather weak mouth and the irresolute slant of the eye. He had a haggard, worried look and an air of not having had much sleep of late.

He looked inquiringly at the Inspector as the latter advanced.

'I am Detective Inspector Narracott,' he began – but got no further.

With a hoarse cry the young man dropped on to a chair, flung his arms out in front of him on the table, bowing his head on them and muttering:

'Oh! my God! It's come.'

After a minute or two he lifted his head and said, 'Well, why don't you get on with it, man?'

Inspector Narracott looked exceedingly stolid and unintelligent.

'I am investigating the death of your uncle, Captain Joseph Trevelyan. May I ask you, sir, if you have anything to say?'

The young man rose slowly to his feet and said in a low strained voice:

'Are you – arresting me?'

'No, sir, I am not. If I was arresting you I would give you the customary caution. I am simply asking you to account for your movements yesterday afternoon. You may reply to my questions or not as you see fit.'

'And if I don't reply to them – it will tell against me. Oh, yes, I know your little ways. You've found out then that I was down there yesterday?'

'You signed your name in the hotel register, Mr Pearson.'

'Oh, I suppose there's no use denying it. I *was* there – why shouldn't I be?'

'Why indeed?' said the Inspector mildly.

'I went down there to see my uncle.'

'By appointment?'

'What do you mean, by appointment?'

'Did your uncle know you were coming?'

'I – no – he didn't. It – it was a sudden impulse.'

'No reason for it?'

'I – reason? No – no, why should there be? I – I just wanted to see my uncle.'

'Quite so, sir. And you did see him?'

There was a pause – a very long pause. Indecision was written on every feature of the young man's face. Inspector Narracott felt a kind of pity as he watched him. Couldn't the boy see that his palpable indecision was as good as an admission of the fact?

At last Jim Pearson drew a deep breath. 'I – I suppose I had better make a clean breast of it. Yes – I did see him. I asked at the station how I could get to Sittaford. They told me it was out of the question. The roads were impassable for any vehicle. I said it was urgent.'

'Urgent?' murmured the Inspector.

'I – I wanted to see my uncle very much.'

'So it seems, sir.'

'The porter continued to shake his head and say that it was impossible. I mentioned my uncle's name and at once his face cleared up, and he told me my uncle was actually in Exhampton, and gave me full directions as to how to find the house he had rented.'

'This was at what time, sir?'

'About one o'clock, I think. I went to the Inn – the Three Crowns – booked a room and had some lunch there. Then afterwards I – I went out to see my uncle.'

'Immediately afterwards?'

'No, not immediately.'

'What time was it?'

'Well, I couldn't say for certain.'

'Half past three? Four o'clock? Half past four?'

'I – I –' he stammered worse than ever. 'I don't think it could have been as late as that.'

'Mrs Belling, the proprietress, said you went out at half past four.'

'Did I? I – I think she's wrong. It couldn't have been as late as that.'

'What happened next?'

'I found my uncle's house, had a talk with him and came back to the Inn.'

'How did you get into your uncle's house?'

'I rang the bell and he opened the door to me himself.'

'Wasn't he surprised to see you?'

'Yes – yes – he was rather surprised.'

'How long did you remain with him, Mr Pearson?'

'A quarter of an hour – twenty minutes. But look here, he was perfectly all right when I left him. Perfectly all right. I swear it.'

'And what time *did* you leave him?'

The young man lowered his eyes. Again, the hesitation was palpable in his tone, 'I don't know exactly.'

'I think you do, Mr Pearson.'

The assured tone had its effect. The boy replied in a low tone.

'It was a quarter past five.'

'You returned to the Three Crowns at a quarter to six. At most it could only take you seven or eight minutes to walk over from your uncle's house.'

'I didn't go straight back. I walked about the town.'

'In that icy weather – in the snow!'

'It wasn't actually snowing then. It came on to snow later.'

'I see. And what was the nature of your conversation with your uncle?'

'Oh! nothing in particular. I – I just wanted to talk to the old boy, look him up, that sort of thing, you know.'

'He's a poor liar,' thought Inspector Narracott to himself. 'Why, I could manage better than that myself.'

Aloud he said:

'Very good, sir. Now, may I ask you why, on hearing of your uncle's murder, you left Exhampton without disclosing your relationship to the murdered man?'

'I was scared,' said the young man frankly. 'I heard he had been murdered round about the time I left him. Now, dash it all, that's enough to scare anyone, isn't it? I got the wind up and left the place by the first available train. Oh, I dare say I was a fool to do anything of the sort. But you know what it is when you are rattled. And anyone might have been rattled under these circumstances.'

'And that's all you have to say, sir?'

'Yes – yes, of course.'

'Then, perhaps you'll have no objection, sir, to coming round with me and having this statement taken down in writing, after which you will have it read over to you, and you will sign it.'

'Is – is that all?'

'I think it possible, Mr Pearson, that it may be necessary to detain you until after the inquest.'

'Oh! my God,' said Jim Pearson. 'Can nobody help me?'

At that moment the door opened and a young woman walked into the room.

She was, as the observant Inspector Narracott noted at once, a very exceptional kind of young woman. She was not strikingly beautiful, but she had a face which was arresting and unusual, a face that having once seen you could not forget. There was about her an atmosphere of common sense, *savoir faire*, invincible determination and a most tantalizing fascination.

'Oh! Jim,' she exclaimed. 'What's happened?'

'It's all over, Emily,' said the young man. 'They think I murdered my uncle.'

'Who thinks so?' demanded Emily.

The young man indicated his visitor by a gesture.

'This is Inspector Narracott,' he said, and he added with a dismal attempt at introduction, 'Miss Emily Trefusis.'

'Oh!' said Emily Trefusis.

She studied Inspector Narracott with keen hazel eyes.

'Jim,' she said, 'is a frightful idiot. But he doesn't murder people.'

The Inspector said nothing.

'I expect,' said Emily, turning to Jim, 'that you've been saying the most frightfully imprudent things. If you read the papers a little better than you do, Jim, you would know that you must never talk to policemen unless you have a strong solicitor sitting beside you making objections to every word. What's happened? Are you arresting him, Inspector Narracott?'

Inspector Narracott explained technically and clearly exactly what he was doing.

'Emily,' cried the young man, 'you won't believe I did it? You never will believe it, will you?'

'No, darling,' said Emily kindly. 'Of course not.' And she added in a gentle meditative tone, 'You haven't got the guts.'

'I don't feel as if I had a friend in the world,' groaned Jim.

'Yes, you have,' said Emily. 'You've got me. Cheer up, Jim, look at the winking diamonds on the third finger of my left hand.

Here stands the faithful fiancée. Go with the Inspector and leave everything to me.'

Jim Pearson rose, still with a dazed expression on his face. His overcoat was lying over a chair and he put it on. Inspector Narracott handed him a hat which was lying on a bureau near by. They moved towards the door and the Inspector said politely:

'Good evening, Miss Trefusis.'

'Au revoir, Inspector,' said Emily sweetly.

And if he had known Miss Emily Trefusis better he would have known that in these three words lay a challenge.

CHAPTER 11
EMILY SETS TO WORK

The inquest on the body of Captain Trevelyan was held on Monday morning. From the point of view of sensation it was a tame affair, for it was almost immediately adjourned for a week, thus disappointing large numbers of people. Between Saturday and Monday, Exhampton had sprung into fame. The knowledge that the dead man's nephew had been detained in connection with the murder made the whole affair spring from a mere paragraph in the back pages of the newspapers to gigantic headlines. On the Monday, reporters had arrived at Exhampton in large numbers. Mr Charles Enderby had reason once more to congratulate himself on the superior position he had obtained from the purely fortuitous chance of the football competition prize.

It was the journalist's intention to stick to Major Burnaby like a leech, and under the pretext of photographing the latter's cottage, to obtain exclusive information of the inhabitants of Sittaford and their relationship with the dead man.

It did not escape Mr Enderby's notice that at lunch time a small table near the door was occupied by a very attractive girl. Mr Enderby wondered what she was doing in Exhampton. She was well dressed in a demure and provocative style, and did not appear to be a relation of the deceased, and still less could be labelled as one of the idle curious.

'I wonder how long she's staying?' thought Mr Enderby.

'Rather a pity I am going up to Sittaford this afternoon. Just my luck. Well, you can't have it both ways, I suppose.'

But shortly after lunch, Mr Enderby received an agreeable surprise. He was standing on the steps of the Three Crowns observing the fast melting snow, and enjoying the sluggish rays of wintry sunshine, when he was aware of a voice, an extremely charming voice, addressing him.

'I beg your pardon – but could you tell me – if there is anything to see in Exhampton?'

Charles Enderby rose to the occasion promptly.

'There's a castle, I believe,' he said. 'Not much to it – but there it is. Perhaps you would allow me to show you the way to it.'

'That would be frightfully kind of you,' said the girl. 'If you are sure you are not too busy –'

Charles Enderby disclaimed immediately the notion of being busy.

They set out together.

'You are Mr Enderby, aren't you?' said the girl.

'Yes. How did you know?'

'Mrs Belling pointed you out to me.'

'Oh, I see.'

'My name is Emily Trefusis. Mr Enderby – I want you to help me.'

'To help you?' said Enderby. 'Why, certainly – but –'

'You see, I am engaged to Jim Pearson.'

'Oh!' said Mr Enderby, journalistic possibilities rising before his mind.

'And the police are going to arrest him. I know they are. Mr Enderby, I *know* that Jim didn't do this thing. I am down here to prove he didn't. But I must have someone to help me. One can't do anything without a man. Men know so much, and are able to get information in so many ways that are simply impossible to women.'

'Well – I – yes, I suppose that is true,' said Mr Enderby complacently.

'I was looking at all these journalists this morning,' said Emily. 'Such a lot of them I thought had such stupid faces. I picked you out as the one really clever one among them.'

'Oh! I say. I don't think that's true, you know,' said Mr Enderby still more complacently.

'What I want to propose,' said Emily Trefusis, 'is a kind of partnership. There would, I think, be advantages on both sides. There are certain things I want to investigate – to find out about. Where you in your character of journalist can help me. I want –'

Emily paused. What she really wanted was to engage Mr Enderby as a kind of private sleuth of her own. To go where she told him, to ask the questions she wanted asked, and in general to be a kind of bond slave. But she was aware of the necessity of couching these proposals in terms at once flattering and agreeable. The whole point was that she was to be the boss, but the matter needed managing tactfully.

'I want,' said Emily, 'to feel that I can *depend* upon you.'

She had a lovely voice, liquid and alluring. As she uttered the last sentence a feeling rose in Mr Enderby's bosom that this lovely helpless girl could depend upon him to the last ditch.

'It must be ghastly,' said Mr Enderby, and taking her hand he squeezed it with fervour.

'But you know,' he went on with a journalistic reaction, 'my time is not entirely my own. I mean, I have got to go where I am sent, and all that.'

'Yes,' said Emily. 'I have thought of that, and that you see is where I come in. Surely I am what you call a "scoop", aren't I? You can do an interview with me every day, you can make me say anything that you think your readers will like. *Jim Pearson's fiancée. Girl who believes passionately in his innocence. Reminiscences of his childhood which she supplies*. I don't really know about his childhood, you know,' she added, 'but that doesn't matter.'

'I think,' said Mr Enderby, 'that you are marvellous. You really are marvellous.'

'And then,' said Emily pursuing her advantage, 'I have access naturally to Jim's relations. I can get you in there as a friend of mine, where quite possibly you might have the door shut in your face any other way.'

'Don't I know that only too well,' said Mr Enderby with feeling, recalling various rebuffs of the past.

A glorious prospect opened out before him. He had been in luck over this affair all round. First the lucky chance of the football competition, and now this.

'It's a deal,' he said fervently.

'Good,' said Emily becoming brisk and business-like. 'Now, what's the first move?'

'I'm going up to Sittaford this afternoon.'

He explained the fortunate circumstance which had put him in such an advantageous position with regard to Major Burnaby. 'Because, mind you, he is the kind of old buffer that hates newspapermen like poison. But you can't exactly push a chap in the face who has just handed you £5,000, can you?'

'It would be awkward,' said Emily. 'Well, if you are going to Sittaford, I am coming with you.'

'Splendid,' said Mr Enderby. 'I don't know, though, if there's anywhere to stay up there. As far as I know there's only Sittaford House and a few old cottages belonging to people like Burnaby.'

'We shall find something,' said Emily. 'I always find something.'

Mr Enderby could well believe that. Emily had the kind of personality that soars triumphantly over all obstacles.

They had arrived by now at the ruined castle, but paying no attention to it, they sat down on a piece of wall in the so-called sunshine and Emily proceeded to develop her ideas.

'I am looking at this, Mr Enderby, in an absolutely unsentimental and business-like way. You've got to take it from me to begin with that Jim didn't do the murder. I'm not saying that simply because I am in love with him, or believe in his beautiful character or anything like that. It's just well – knowledge. You see I have been on my own pretty well since I was sixteen. I have never come into contact with many women and I know very little about them, but I know a lot about men. And unless a girl can size up a man pretty accurately, and know what she's got to deal with, she will never get on. I have got on. I work as a mannequin at Lucie's, and I can tell you, Mr Enderby, that to arrive there is a Feat.

'Well, as I was saying, I can size up men pretty accurately. Jim is rather a weak character in many ways. I am not sure,' said Emily, forgetting for a moment her role of admirer of strong men, 'that that's not why I like him. The feeling that I can run him and make something of him. There are quite a lot of – well – even criminal things that I can imagine him doing if pushed to it – but not murder. He simply couldn't pick up a sandbag and hit an old man on the back of the neck with it. He would make a bosh shot and hit him in the wrong place if he did. He is a – he is a *gentle* creature, Mr Enderby. He doesn't even like killing wasps. He always tries to put them out of a window without hurting them and usually gets stung. However, it's no good my going on like this. You've got to take my word for it and start on the assumption that Jim is innocent.'

'Do you think that somebody is deliberately trying to fasten the crime on him?' asked Charles Enderby in his best journalistic manner.

'I don't think so. You see nobody knew about Jim coming down to see his uncle. Of course, one can't be certain, but I should put that down as just a coincidence and bad luck. What we have to find is someone else with a motive for killing Captain Trevelyan. The police are quite certain that this is not what they call an "outside job" – I mean, it wasn't a burglar. The broken open window was faked.'

'Did the police tell you all this?'

'Practically,' said Emily.

'What do you mean by practically?'

'The chambermaid told me, and her sister is married to Constable Graves, so, of course, she knows everything the police think.'

'Very well,' said Mr Enderby, 'it wasn't an outside job. It was an inside one.'

'Exactly,' said Emily. 'The police – that is Inspector Narracott, who, by the way, I should think is an awfully sound man, have started investigating to find who benefits by Captain Trevelyan's death, and with Jim sticking out a mile, so to speak, they won't bother to go on with other investigations much. Well, that's got to be our job.'

'What a scoop it would be,' said Mr Enderby, 'if you and I discovered the real murderer. The crime expert of the *Daily Wire* – that's the way I should be described. But it's too good to be true,' he added despondently. 'That sort of thing only happens in books.'

'Nonsense,' said Emily, 'it happens with me.'

'You're simply marvellous,' said Enderby again.

Emily brought out a little notebook.

'Now let's put things down methodically. Jim himself, his brother and sister, and his Aunt Jennifer benefit equally by Captain Trevelyan's death. Of course Sylvia – that's Jim's sister – wouldn't hurt a fly, but I wouldn't put it past her husband, he's what I call a nasty kind of brute. You know – the artistic nasty kind, has affairs with women – all that sort of thing. Very likely to be in a hole financially. The money they'd come into would actually be Sylvia's, but that wouldn't matter to him. He would soon manage to get it out of her.'

'He sounds a most unpleasant person,' said Mr Enderby.

'Oh! yes. Good-looking in a bold sort of way. Women talk about sex with him in corners. Real men hate him.'

'Well, that's suspect No. 1,' said Mr Enderby, also writing in a little book. 'Investigate his movements on Friday – easily done under the guise of interview with popular novelist connected with the crime. Is that all right?'

'Splendid,' said Emily. 'Then there's Brian, Jim's younger brother. He's supposed to be in Australia, but he might quite easily have come back. I mean, people do sometimes without saying.'

'We could send him a cable.'

'We will. I suppose Aunt Jennifer is out of it. From all I've heard she's a rather wonderful person. She's got character. Still, after all, she wasn't very far away, she was only at Exeter. She *might* have come over to see her brother, and he *might* have said something nasty about her husband whom she adores, and she *might* have seen red and snatched up a sandbag and biffed him one.'

'Do you really think so?' said Mr Enderby dubiously.

'No, not really. But one never *knows*. Then, of course, there's the batman. He only gets £100 under the will and he seems all right. But there again, one never knows. His wife is Mrs Belling's niece. You know Mrs Belling who keeps the Three Crowns. I think I shall weep on her shoulder when I get back. She looks rather a motherly and romantic soul. I think she would be terribly sorry for me with my young man probably going to prison, and she might let slip something useful. And then, of course, there's Sittaford House. Do you know what struck me as queer?'

'No, what?'

'These people, the Willetts. The ones that took Captain Trevelyan's house furnished in the middle of winter. It's an awfully queer thing to do.'

'Yes, it is odd,' agreed Mr Enderby. 'There might be something at the bottom of that – something to do with Captain Trevelyan's past life.

'That *séance* business was queer too,' he added. 'I'm thinking of writing that up for the paper. Get opinions from Sir Oliver Lodge and Sir Arthur Conan Doyle and a few actresses and people about it.'

'What *séance* business?'

Mr Enderby recounted it with gusto. There was nothing connected with the murder that he had not managed somehow or other to hear.

'Bit odd, isn't it?' he finished. 'I mean, it makes you think and all that. May be something in these things. First time I've really ever come across anything authentic.'

Emily gave a slight shiver. 'I hate supernatural things,' she said. 'Just for once, as you say, it does look as though there was something in it. But how – how gruesome!'

'This *séance* business never seems very practical, does it? If the old boy could get through and say he was dead, why couldn't he say who murdered him? It ought to be all so simple.'

'I feel there may be a clue in Sittaford,' said Emily thoughtfully.

'Yes, I think we ought to investigate there thoroughly,' said Enderby. 'I've hired a car and I'm starting there in about half an hour's time. You had better come along with me.'

'I will,' said Emily. 'What about Major Burnaby?'

'He's going to tramp it,' said Enderby. 'Started immediately after the inquest. If you ask me, he wanted to get out of having my company on the way there. Nobody could like trudging there through all this slush.'

'Will the car be able to get up all right?'

'Oh! yes. First day a car has been able to get through though.'

'Well,' said Emily rising to her feet. 'It's about time we went back to the Three Crowns, and I will pack my suitcase and do a short weeping act on Mrs Belling's shoulder.'

'Don't you worry,' said Mr Enderby rather fatuously. 'You leave everything to me.'

'That's just what I mean to do,' said Emily with a complete lack of truth. 'It's so wonderful to have someone you can really rely on.'

Emily Trefusis was really a very accomplished young woman.

CHAPTER 12
THE ARREST

On her return to the Three Crowns, Emily had the good fortune to run right into Mrs Belling who was standing in the hallway.

'Oh! Mrs Belling,' she exclaimed. 'I am leaving this afternoon.'

'Yes, Miss. By the four ten train to Exeter, Miss?'

'No, I am going up to Sittaford.'

'To Sittaford?'

Mrs Belling's countenance showed the most lively curiosity.

'Yes, and I wanted to ask you if you knew of anywhere there where I could stay.'

'You want to stay up there?'

The curiosity was heightened.

'Yes, that is – Oh! Mrs Belling, is there somewhere I could speak to you privately for a moment?'

With something like alacrity Mrs Belling led the way to her own private sanctum. A small comfortable room with a large fire burning.

'You won't tell anyone, will you?' began Emily, knowing well that of all openings on earth this one is the most certain to provoke interest and sympathy.

'No, indeed, Miss, that I won't,' said Mrs Belling her dark eyes aglitter with interest.

'You see, Mr Pearson – you know –'

'The young gentleman that stayed here on Friday? And that the police have arrested?'

'Arrested? Do you mean really arrested?'

'Yes, Miss. Not half an hour ago.'

Emily had gone very white.

'You – you're sure of that?'

'Oh! yes, Miss. Our Amy had it from the Sergeant.'

'It's too awful!' said Emily. She had been expecting this, but it was none the better for that. 'You see, Mrs Belling, I – I'm engaged to him. And he didn't do it, and, oh dear, it's all too dreadful!'

And here Emily began to cry. She had, earlier in the day, announced her intention to Charles Enderby of doing so, but what appalled her so was with what ease the tears came. To cry at will is not an easy accomplishment. There was something much too real about these tears. It frightened her. She mustn't really give way. Giving way wasn't the least use to Jim. To be resolute, logical and clear-sighted – these were the qualities that were going to count in this game. Sloppy crying had never helped anyone yet.

But it was a relief all the same, to let yourself go. After all she had meant to cry. Crying would be an undeniable passport to Mrs Belling's sympathy and help. So why not have a good cry while she was about it? A real orgy of weeping in which all her troubles, doubts and unacknowledged fears might find vent and be swept away.

'There, there, my dear, don't ee take on so,' said Mrs Belling.

She put a large motherly arm round Emily's shoulders and patted her consolingly.

'Said from the start I have that he didn't do it. A regular nice young gentleman. A lot of chuckle-heads the police are, and so I've said before now. Some thieving tramp is a great deal more likely. Now, don't ee fret, my dear, it'll all come right, you see if it don't.'

'I am so dreadfully fond of him,' wailed Emily.

Dear Jim, dear, sweet, boyish, helpless, impractical Jim. So utterly to be depended on to do the wrong thing at the wrong moment. What possible chance had he got against that steady, resolute Inspector Narracott?

'We *must* save him,' she wailed.

'Of course, we will. Of course, we will,' Mrs Belling consoled her.

Emily dabbed her eyes vigorously, gave one last sniff and gulp, and raising her head demanded fiercely:

'Where can I stay at Sittaford?'

'Up to Sittaford? You're set on going there, my dear?'

'Yes,' Emily nodded vigorously.

'Well, now,' Mrs Belling cogitated the matter. 'There's only one place for ee to stay. There's not much to Sittaford. There's the big house, Sittaford House, which Captain Trevelyan built, and that's let now to a South African lady. And there's the six cottages he built, and No. 5 of them cottages has got Curtis, what used to be gardener at Sittaford House, in it, and Mrs Curtis. She lets rooms in the summer time, the Captain allowing her to do so. There's nowhere else you could stay and that's a fact. There's the blacksmith's and the post office, but Mary Hibbert, she's got six children and her sister-in-law living with her, and the blacksmith's wife she's expecting her eighth, so there won't be so much as a corner there. But how are you going to get up to Sittaford, Miss? Have you hired a car?'

'I am going to share Mr Enderby's.'

'Ah, and where will he be staying, I wonder?'

'I suppose he will have to be put up at Mrs Curtis's too. Will she have room for both of us?'

'I don't know that that will look quite right for a young lady like you,' said Mrs Belling.

'He's my cousin,' said Emily.

On no account, she felt, must a sense of propriety intervene to work against her in Mrs Belling's mind.

The landlady's brow cleared. 'Well, that may be all right then,' she allowed grudgingly, 'and likely as not if you're not comfortable with Mrs Curtis they would put you up at the big house.'

'I'm sorry I've been such an idiot,' said Emily mopping once more at her eyes.

'It's only natural, my dear. And you feel better for it.'

'I do,' said Emily truthfully. 'I feel much better.'

'A good cry and a cup of tea – there's nothing to beat them, and a nice cup of tea you shall have at once, my dear, before you start off on that cold drive.'

'Oh, thank you, but I don't think I really want –'

'Never mind what you want, it's what you're going to have,' said Mrs Belling rising with determination and moving towards the door. 'And you tell Amelia Curtis from me that she's to look after you and see you take your food proper and see you don't fret.'

'You *are* kind,' said Emily.

'And what's more I shall keep my eyes and ears open down here,' said Mrs Belling entering with relish into her part of the romance. 'There's many a little thing that I hear that never goes to the police. And anything I do hear I'll pass on to you, Miss.'

'Will you really?'

'That I will. Don't ee worry, my dear, we'll have your young gentleman out of his trouble in no time.'

'I must go and pack,' said Emily rising.

'I'll send the tea up to you,' said Mrs Belling.

Emily went upstairs, packed her few belongings into her suit-case, sponged her eyes with cold water and applied a liberal allowance of powder.

'You *have* made yourself look a sight,' she apostrophized herself in the glass. She added more powder and a touch of rouge.

'Curious,' said Emily, 'how much better I feel. It's worth the puffy look.'

She rang the bell. The chambermaid (the sympathetic sister-in-law of Constable Graves) came promptly. Emily presented her with a pound note and begged her earnestly to pass on any information she might acquire in roundabout ways from police circles. The girl promised readily.

'Mrs Curtis's up to Sittaford? I will indeed, Miss. Do anything, that I will. We all feel for you, Miss, more than I can say. All the time I keep saying to myself, "Just fancy if it was you and Fred," I keep saying. I would be distracted – that I would. The least thing I hears I'll pass it on to you, Miss.'

'You angel,' said Emily.

'Just like a sixpenny I got at Woolworth's the other day, The Syringa Murders it was called. And do you know what led them to find the real murderer, Miss. Just a bit of common sealing wax. Your gentleman *is* good-looking, Miss, isn't he? Quite unlike his picture in the papers. I'm sure I'll do anything I can, Miss, for you and for him.'

Thus the centre of romantic attention, Emily left the Three Crowns, having duly gulped down the cup of tea prescribed by Mrs Belling.

'By the way,' she said to Enderby as the aged Ford sprang forward, 'you are my cousin, don't forget.'

'Why?'

'They've got such pure minds in the country,' said Emily. 'I thought it would be better.'

'Splendid. In that case,' said Mr Enderby rising to his opportunities, 'I had better call you Emily.'

'All right, cousin – what's your name?'

'Charles.'

'All right, Charles.'

The car went upwards on the Sittaford road.

CHAPTER 13

SITTAFORD

Emily was rather fascinated by her first view of Sittaford. Turning off the main road about two miles from Exhampton, they went upwards over a rough moorland road until they reached a village that was situated right on the edge of the moor. It consisted of a smithy, and a combined post office and sweet shop. From there they followed a lane and came to a row of newly built small granite bungalows. At the second of these the car stopped and the driver volunteered the information that this was Mrs Curtis's.

Mrs Curtis was a small, thin, grey-haired woman, energetic and shrewish in disposition. She was all agog with the news of the murder which had only penetrated to Sittaford that morning.

'Yes, of course I can take you in, Miss, and your cousin too, if he can just wait until I shift a few duds. You won't mind having your meals along of us, I don't suppose? Well, who would have believed it! Captain Trevelyan murdered and an inquest and all! Cut off from the world we've been since Friday morning, and this morning when the news came you could have knocked me down with a feather. "The Captain's dead," I said to Curtis, "that *shows* you the wickedness there is in the world nowadays." But I'm keeping you talking here, Miss. Come away in and the gentleman too. I have got the kettle on and you shall have a cup of tea immediately, for you must be perished by the drive up, though of course, it's warmer today after what it's been. Eight and ten feet the snow has been hereabout.'

Drowned in this sea of talk, Emily and Charles Enderby were shown their new quarters. Emily had a small square room, scrupulously clean, looking out and up to the slope of Sittaford Beacon. Charles's room was a small slit facing the front of the house and the lane, containing a bed and a microscopic chest of drawers and washstand.

'The great thing is,' he observed after the driver of the car had disposed his suitcase upon the bed, and had been duly paid and thanked, 'that we are here. If we don't know all there is to be known about everyone living in Sittaford within the next quarter of an hour, I'll eat my hat.'

Ten minutes later, they were sitting downstairs in the comfortable kitchen being introduced to Curtis, a rather gruff-looking, grey-haired old man, and being regaled with strong tea, bread and butter, Devonshire cream and hard-boiled eggs. While they ate and drank they listened. Within half an hour they knew everything there was to be known about the inhabitants of the small community.

First there was a Miss Percehouse, who lived in No. 4, The Cottages, a spinster of uncertain years and temper who had come down here to die, according to Mrs Curtis, six years ago.

'But believe it or not, Miss, the air of Sittaford is that healthy that she picked up from the day she came. Wonderfully pure air for lungs it is.

'Miss Percehouse has a nephew who occasionally comes down to see her,' she went on, 'and indeed he's staying with her at the present time. Seeing to it that the money doesn't go out of the family, that's what he's doing. Very dull for a young gentleman at this time of year. But there, there's more ways than one of amusing yourself, and his coming has been a providence for the young lady at Sittaford House. Poor young thing, the idea of bringing her to that great barrack of a house in the winter time. Selfish is what some mothers are. A very pretty young lady, too. Mr Ronald Garfield is up there as often as he can be without neglecting Miss Percehouse.'

Charles Enderby and Emily exchanged glances. Charles remembered that Ronald Garfield had been mentioned as one of the party present at the table-turning.

'The cottage this side of mine, No. 6,' continued Mrs Curtis, 'has only just been took. Gentleman of the name of Duke. That is if you would call him a gentleman. Of course, he may be and he may not. There's no saying, folks aren't so particular nowadays as they used to be. He's been made free of the place in the heartiest manner. A bashful sort of gentleman he is – might be a military gentleman from the look of him, but somehow he hasn't got the manner. Not like Major Burnaby, that you would know as a military gentleman the first time you clapped eyes on him.

'No. 3, that's Mr Rycroft's, little elderly gentleman. They do say that he used to go after birds to outlandish parts for the British Museum. What they call a naturalist he is. Always out and roaming over the moor when the weather permits. And he has a very fine library of books. His cottage is nearly all bookcases.

'No. 2, is an invalid gentleman's, a Captain Wyatt with an Indian servant. And poor fellow he does feel the cold, he does. The servant I mean, not the Captain. Coming from warm outlandish parts, it's no wonder. The heat they keep up inside the house would frighten you. It's like walking into an oven.

'No. 1, is Major Burnaby's cottage. Lives by himself he does, and I go in to do for him early mornings. He is a very neat gentleman, he is, and very particular. He and Captain Trevelyan were as thick as thieves. Friends of a lifetime they were. And they both have the same kind of outlandish heads stuck up on the walls.

'As for Mrs Willett and Miss Willett, that's what no one can make out. Plenty of money there. Amos Parker at Exhampton they deal with, and he tells me their weekly book comes to well over eight pounds or nine pounds. You wouldn't believe the eggs that goes into that house! Brought their maidservants from Exeter with them, they did, but they don't like it and want to leave, and I'm sure I don't blame them. Mrs Willett, she sends them into Exeter twice a week in her car, and what with that and the living being so good, they agreed to stop on, but if you ask me it's a queer business, burying yourself in the country like this, a smart lady like that. Well, well, I suppose I had better be clearing away these tea things.'

She drew a deep breath and so did Charles and Emily. The flow of information loosened with so little difficulty had almost overwhelmed them.

Charles ventured to put a question.

'Has Major Burnaby got back yet?' he asked.

Mrs Curtis paused at once, tray in hand. 'Yes, indeed, sir, came tramping in just the same as ever about half an hour before you arrived. "Why, sir," I cried to him. "You've never walked all the way from Exhampton?" And he says in his stern way, "Why not? If a man has got two legs he doesn't need four wheels. I do it once a week anyway as you know, Mrs Curtis." "Oh, yes, sir, but this is different. What with the shock and the murder and the inquest it's wonderful you've got the strength to do it." But he only grunted like and walked on. He looks bad though. It's a miracle he ever got through on Friday night. Brave I call it at his age. Tramping off like that and three miles of it in a snowstorm. You may say what you like, but nowadays the young gentlemen aren't a patch on the old ones. That Mr Ronald Garfield he would never have done it, and it's my opinion, and it's the opinion of Mrs Hibbert at the post office, and it's the opinion of Mr Pound, the blacksmith, that Mr Garfield ought never to have let him go off alone the way he did. He should have gone with him. If Major Burnaby had been lost in a snowdrift, everybody would have blamed Mr Garfield. And that's a fact.'

She disappeared triumphantly into the scullery amid a clatter of tea things.

Mr Curtis thoughtfully removed an aged pipe from the right side of his mouth to the left side.

'Women,' he said, 'talk a lot.'

He paused and then murmured.

'And half the time they don't know the truth of what they are talking about.'

Emily and Charles received this announcement in silence. Seeing that no more was coming, however, Charles murmured approvingly.

'That's very true – yes, very true.'

'Ah!' said Mr Curtis, and relapsed into a pleasant and contemplative silence.

Charles rose. 'I think I'll go round and see old Burnaby,'

he said, 'tell him the camera parade will be tomorrow morning.'

'I'll come with you,' said Emily. 'I want to know what he really thinks about Jim and what ideas he has about the crime in general.'

'Have you got any rubber boots or anything? It's awfully slushy.'

'I bought some Wellingtons in Exhampton,' said Emily.

'What a practical girl you are. You think of everything.'

'Unfortunately,' said Emily, 'that's not much help to you in finding out who's done a murder. It might help one to do a murder,' she added reflectively.

'Well, don't murder me,' said Mr Enderby.

They went out together. Mrs Curtis immediately returned.

'They be gone round to the Major's,' said Mr Curtis.

'Ah!' said Mrs Curtis. 'Now, what do you think? Are they sweethearting, or are they not? A lot of harm comes of cousins marrying, so they say. Deaf and dumbs and half wits and a lot of other evils. He's sweet on her, that you can see easily enough. As for her, she's a deep one like my Great Aunt Sarah's Belinda, she is. Got a way with her and with the men. I wonder what she's after now? Do you know what I think, Curtis?'

Mr Curtis grunted.

'This young gentleman that the police are holding on account of the murder, it's my belief that he's the one she's set on. And she's come up here to nose about and see what she can find out. And mark my words,' said Mrs Curtis, rattling china, 'if there's anything *to* find out she will find it!'

CHAPTER 14

THE WILLETTS

At the same moment that Charles and Emily started out to visit Major Burnaby, Inspector Narracott was seated in the drawing-room of Sittaford House, trying to formulate an impression of Mrs Willett.

He had not been able to interview her sooner as the roads had been impassable until this morning. He had hardly known what he had expected to find, but certainly not what he had found. It was Mrs Willett who had taken charge of the situation, not he.

She had come rushing into the room, thoroughly business-like and efficient. He saw a tall woman, thin-faced and keen-eyed. She was wearing rather an elaborate knitted silk jumper suit that was just over the border line of unsuitability for country wear. Her stockings were of very expensive gossamer silk, her shoes high-heeled patent leather. She wore several valuable rings and rather a large quantity of very good and expensive imitation pearls.

'Inspector Narracott?' said Mrs Willett. 'Naturally, you want to come over the house. What a shocking tragedy! I could hardly believe it. We only heard about it this morning, you know. We were terribly shocked. Sit down, won't you, Inspector? This is my daughter, Violet.'

He had hardly noticed the girl who had followed her in, and yet, she was a very pretty girl, tall and fair with big blue eyes.

Mrs Willett herself took a seat.

'Is there any way in which I can help you, Inspector? I knew very little of poor Captain Trevelyan, but if there is anything you can think of –'

The Inspector said slowly:

'Thank you, madam. Of course, one never knows what may be useful or what may not.'

'I quite understand. There may possibly be something in the house that may throw light upon this sad business, but I rather doubt it. Captain Trevelyan removed all his personal belongings. He even feared I should tamper with his fishing rods, poor, dear man.'

She laughed a little.

'You were not acquainted with him?'

'Before I took the house, you mean? Oh! no. I've asked him here several times since, but he never came. Terribly shy, poor dear. That was what was the matter with him. I've known dozens of men like it. They are called women haters and all sorts of silly things, and really all the time it's only shyness. If I could have got at him,' said Mrs Willett with determination, 'I'd soon have got over all that nonsense. That sort of man only wants bringing out.'

Inspector Narracott began to understand Captain Trevelyan's strongly defensive attitude towards his tenants.

'We both asked him,' continued Mrs Willett. 'Didn't we, Violet?'

'Oh! yes, Mother.'

'A real simple sailor at heart,' said Mrs Willett. 'Every woman loves a sailor, Inspector Narracott.'

It occurred to Inspector Narracott at this juncture that the interview so far had been run entirely by Mrs Willett. He was convinced that she was an exceedingly clever woman. She might be as innocent as she appeared. On the other hand she might not.

'The point I am anxious to get information about is this,' he said and paused.

'Yes, Inspector?'

'Major Burnaby, as you doubtless know, discovered the body. He was led to do so by an accident that occurred in this house.'

'You mean?'

'I mean, the table-turning. I beg your pardon –'

He turned sharply.

A faint sound had come from the girl.

'Poor Violet,' said her mother. 'She was terribly upset – indeed we all were! Most unaccountable. I'm not superstitious, but really it was the most unaccountable thing.'

'It did occur then?'

Mrs Willett opened her eyes very wide.

'Occur? Of course it occurred. At the time I thought it was a joke – a most unfeeling joke and one in very bad taste. I suspected young Ronald Garfield –'

'Oh! no, Mother. I'm sure he didn't. He absolutely swore he didn't.'

'I'm saying what I thought at the time, Violet. What could one think it but a joke?'

'It was curious,' said the Inspector slowly. 'You were very upset, Mrs Willett?'

'We all were. Up to then it had been, oh, just light-hearted fooling. You know the sort of thing. Good fun on a winter's evening. And then suddenly – this! I was very angry.'

'Angry?'

'Well, naturally. I thought someone was doing it deliberately – for a joke, as I say.'

'And now?'

'Now?'

'Yes, what do you think now?'

Mrs Willett spread her hands out expressively.

'I don't know what to think. It – it's uncanny.'

'And you, Miss Willett?'

'I?'

The girl started.

'I – I don't know. I shall never forget it. I *dream* of it. I shall never dare to do table-turning again.'

'Mr Rycroft would say it was genuine, I suppose,' said her mother. 'He believes in all that sort of thing. Really I'm inclined to believe in it myself. What other explanation is there except that it was a genuine message from a spirit?'

The Inspector shook his head. The table-turning had been his red herring. His next remark was most casual sounding.

'Don't you find it very bleak here in winter, Mrs Willett?'

'Oh, we love it. Such a change. We're South Africans, you know.'

Her tone was brisk and ordinary.

'Really? What part of South Africa?'

'Oh! the Cape. Violet has never been in England before. She is enchanted with it – finds the snow most romantic. This house is really most comfortable.'

'What led you to come to this part of the world?'

There was just gentle curiosity in his voice.

'We've read so many books on Devonshire, and especially on Dartmoor. We were reading one on the boat – all about Widdecombe Fair. I've always had a hankering to see Dartmoor.'

'What made you fix on Exhampton? It's not a very well known little town.'

'Well – we were reading these books as I told you, and there was a boy on board who talked about Exhampton – he was so enthusiastic about it.'

'What was his name?' asked the Inspector. 'Did he come from this part of the world?'

'Now, what was his name? Cullen – I think. No – it was Smythe. How stupid of me. I really can't remember. You know how it is on board ship, Inspector, you get to know people so well and plan to meet again – and a week after you've landed, you can't even be sure of their names!'

She laughed.

'But he was such a nice boy – not good-looking, reddish hair, but a delightful smile.'

'And on the strength of that you decided to take a house in these parts?' said the Inspector smiling.

'Yes, wasn't it mad of us?'

'Clever,' thought Narracott. 'Distinctly clever.' He began to realize Mrs Willett's methods. She always carried the war into the enemy's country.

'So you wrote to the house agents and inquired about a house?'

'Yes – and they sent us particulars of Sittaford. It sounded just what we wanted.'

'It wouldn't be my taste at this time of year,' said the Inspector with a laugh.

'I daresay it wouldn't be ours if we lived in England,' said Mrs Willett brightly.

The Inspector rose.

'How did you know the name of a house agent to write to in Exhampton?' he asked. 'That must have presented a difficulty.'

There was a pause. The first pause in the conversation. He thought he caught a glimpse of vexation, more, of anger in Mrs Willett's eyes. He had hit upon something to which she had not thought out the answer. She turned towards her daughter.

'How did we, Violet? I can't remember.'

There was a different look in the girl's eyes. She looked frightened.

'Why, of course,' said Mrs Willett. 'Delfridges. Their information bureau. It's too wonderful. I always go and inquire there about everything. I asked them the name of the best agent here and they told me.'

'Quick,' thought the Inspector. 'Very quick. But not quite quick enough. I had you there, madam.'

He made a cursory examination of the house. There was nothing there. No papers, no locked drawers or cupboards.

Mrs Willett accompanied him talking brightly. He took his leave, thanking her politely.

As he departed he caught a glimpse of the girl's face over her shoulder. There was no mistaking the expression on her face.

It was fear he saw on her countenance. Fear written there plainly at this moment when she thought herself unobserved.

Mrs Willett was still talking.

'Alas. We have one grave drawback here. The domestic problem, Inspector. Servants will not stand these country places. All of mine have been threatening to leave us for some time, and the news of the murder seems to have unsettled them utterly. I don't know what I shall do. Perhaps men servants would answer the case. That is what the Registry Office in Exeter advised.'

The Inspector answered mechanically. He was not listening to her flow of talk. He was thinking of the expression he had surprised on the girl's face.

Mrs Willett had been clever – but not quite clever enough.

He went away cogitating on his problem.

If the Willetts had nothing to do with Captain Trevelyan's death, why was Violet Willett afraid?

He fired his last shot. With his foot actually over the threshold of the front door he turned back.

'By the way,' he said, 'you know young Pearson, don't you?'

There was no doubt of the pause this time. A dead silence of about a second. Then Mrs Willett spoke:

'Pearson?' she said. 'I don't think –'

She was interrupted. A queer sighing breath came from the room behind her and then the sound of a fall. The Inspector was over the threshold and into the room in a flash.

Violet Willett had fainted.

'Poor child,' cried Mrs Willett. 'All this strain and shock. That dreadful table-turning business and the murder on the top of it. She isn't strong. Thank you so much, Inspector. Yes, on the sofa please. If you would ring the bell. No, I don't think there is anything more you can do. Thank you so much.'

The Inspector went down the drive with his lips set in a grim line.

Jim Pearson was engaged, he knew, to that extremely charming-looking girl he had seen in London.

Why then should Violet Willett faint at the mention of his name? What was the connection between Jim Pearson and the Willetts?

He paused indecisively as he emerged from the front gate. Then he took from his pocket a small notebook. In it was entered a list of the inhabitants of the six bungalows built by Captain Trevelyan with a few brief remarks against each name. Inspector Narracott's stubby forefinger paused at the entry against No. 6 The Cottages.

'Yes,' he said to himself. 'I'd better see him next.'

He strode briskly down the lane and beat a firm rat-tat on the knocker of No. 6 – the bungalow inhabited by Mr Duke.

CHAPTER 15

VISIT TO MAJOR BURNABY

Leading the way up the path to the Major's front door, Mr Enderby rapped upon it in a cheery fashion. The door was flung open almost immediately and Major Burnaby, red in the face, appeared on the threshold.

'It's you, is it?' he observed with no very great fervour in his voice, and was about to go on in the same strain when he caught sight of Emily and his expression altered.

'This is Miss Trefusis' said Charles with the air of one producing the ace of trumps. 'She was very anxious to see you.'

'May I come in?' said Emily with her sweetest smile.

'Oh! yes. Certainly. Of course – Oh, yes, of course.'

Stumbling in his speech the Major backed into the living-room of his cottage and began pulling forward chairs and pushing aside tables.

Emily, as was her fashion, came straight to the point.

'You see, Major Burnaby, I am engaged to Jim – Jim Pearson, you know. And naturally I am terribly anxious about him.'

In the act of pushing a table the Major paused with his mouth open.

'Oh dear,' he said, 'that's a bad business. My dear young lady, I am more sorry about it than I can say.'

'Major Burnaby, tell me honestly. Do you yourself believe he is guilty? Oh, you needn't mind saying if you do. I would a hundred times rather people didn't lie to me.'

'No, I do *not* think him guilty,' said the Major in a loud assertive voice. He hit a cushion once or twice vigorously, and then sat down facing Emily. 'The chap is a nice young chap. Mind you, he might be a bit weak. Don't be offended if I say that he's the kind of young fellow that might easily go wrong if temptation came in his way. But murder – no. And mind you, I know what I am talking about – a lot of subalterns have passed through my hands in my time. It's the fashion to poke fun at retired army officers nowadays, but we know a thing or two all the same, Miss Trefusis.'

'I'm sure you do,' said Emily. 'I'm awfully grateful to you for saying what you've done.'

'Have – have a whisky and soda?' said the Major. 'I'm afraid there's nothing else,' he said apologetically.

'No, thank you, Major Burnaby.'

'Some plain soda then?'

'No, thank you,' said Emily.

'I ought to be able to produce tea,' said the Major with a touch of wistfulness.

'We've had it,' said Charles. 'At Mrs Curtis's,' he added.

'Major Burnaby,' said Emily, 'who do you think did it – have you any idea at all?'

'No. I am damned – er – bother – if I have,' said the Major. 'Took it for granted it was some chap that broke in, but now the police say that can't be so. Well, it's their job, and I suppose they know best. They say nobody broke in, so I suppose nobody did break in. But all the same it beats me, Miss Trefusis. Trevelyan hadn't an enemy in the world as far as I know.'

'And *you* would know if anybody did,' said Emily.

'Yes, I suppose I knew more of Trevelyan than many of his relations did.'

'And you can't think of anything – anything that would help, in any way?' asked Emily.

The Major pulled at his short moustache.

'I know what you're thinking. Like in books there ought to be some little incident that I should remember that would be a clue. Well, I'm sorry, but there isn't any such thing. Trevelyan just led an ordinary life. Got very few letters and wrote less. There were no female complications in his life, I am sure of that. No, it beats me, Miss Trefusis.'

All three were silent.

'What about that servant of his?' asked Charles.

'Been with him for years. Absolutely faithful.'

'He had married lately,' said Charles.

'Married a perfectly decent respectable girl.'

'Major Burnaby,' said Emily, 'forgive me putting it this way – but didn't you get the wind up rather easily about him?'

The Major rubbed his nose with the embarrassed air that always came over him when the table-turning was mentioned.

'Yes, there's no denying it, I did. I knew the whole thing was tommy rot and yet –'

'You felt somehow it wasn't,' said Emily helpfully.

The Major nodded.

'That's why I wonder –' said Emily.

The two men looked at her.

'I can't quite put what I mean in the way I want,' said Emily. 'What I mean is this: You say that you don't believe in all this table-turning business – and yet, in spite of the awful weather and what must have seemed to you the absurdity of the whole thing – you felt so uneasy that you had to set out, no matter what the weather conditions, and see for yourself that Captain Trevelyan was all right. Well, don't you think that may have been because – because there was something in the atmosphere?

'I mean,' she continued desperately as she saw no trace of comprehension in the Major's face, 'that there was something in someone else's mind as well as yours. And that somehow or other you felt it.'

'Well, I don't know,' said the Major. He rubbed his nose again. 'Of course,' he added hopefully, 'women do take these things seriously.'

'Women!' said Emily. 'Yes,' she murmured softly to herself, 'I believe somehow or other that's it.'

She turned abruptly to Major Burnaby.

'What are they like, these Willetts?'

'Oh, well,' Major Burnaby cast about in his mind, he was clearly no good at personal description. 'Well – they are very kind you know – very helpful and all that.'

'Why do they want to take a house like Sittaford House at this time of year?'

'I can't imagine,' said the Major. 'Nobody does,' he added.

'Don't you think it's very queer?' persisted Emily.

'Of course, it's queer. However, there's no accounting for tastes. That's what the Inspector said.'

'That's nonsense,' said Emily. 'People don't do things without a reason.'

'Well, I don't know,' said Major Burnaby cautiously. 'Some people don't. You wouldn't, Miss Trefusis. But some people –' He sighed and shook his head.

'You are sure they hadn't met Captain Trevelyan before?'

The Major scouted the idea. Trevelyan would have said something to him. No, he was as astonished himself as anyone could be.

'So *he* thought it queer?'

'Of course, I've just told you we all did.'

'What was Mrs Willett's attitude towards Captain Trevelyan?' asked Emily. 'Did she try and avoid him?'

A faint chuckle came from the Major.

'No, indeed she didn't. Pestered the life out of him always asking him to come and see them.'

'Oh!' said Emily thoughtfully. She paused and then said. 'So she might – just possibly she might have taken Sittaford House just on purpose to get acquainted with Captain Trevelyan.'

'Well,' the Major seemed to turn it over in his mind. 'Yes, I suppose she might have. Rather an expensive way of doing things.'

'I don't know,' said Emily. 'Captain Trevelyan wouldn't have been an easy person to get to know otherwise.'

'No, he wouldn't,' agreed the late Captain Trevelyan's friend.

'I wonder,' said Emily.

'The Inspector thought of that too,' said Burnaby.

Emily felt a sudden irritation against Inspector Narracott. Everything that she thought of seemed to have already been thought of by the Inspector. It was galling to a young woman who prided herself on being sharper than other people.

She rose and held out her hand.

'Thank you very much,' she said simply.

'I wish I could help you more,' said the Major. 'I'm rather an obvious sort of person – always have been. If I were a clever chap I might be able to hit upon something that might be a clue. At any rate count on me for anything you want.'

'Thank you,' said Emily. 'I will.'

'Good-bye, sir,' said Enderby. 'I shall be along in the morning with my camera, you know.'

Burnaby grunted.

Emily and Charles retraced their steps to Mrs Curtis's.

'Come into my room, I want to talk to you,' said Emily.

She sat on the one chair and Charles sat on the bed. Emily plucked off her hat and sent it spinning into a corner of the room.

'Now, listen,' she said. 'I think I've got a kind of starting point. I may be wrong and I may be right, at any rate it's an idea. I think a lot hinges on this table-turning business. You've done table-turning, haven't you?'

'Oh, yes, now and then. Not serious, you know.'

'No, of course not. It's the kind of thing one does on a wet afternoon, and everyone accuses everyone else of shoving. Well, if you've played it you know what happens. The table starts spelling out, say, a name, well, it's a name somebody knows. Very often they recognize it at once and hope it isn't going to be that, and all the time unconsciously they are what one calls shoving. I mean sort of recognizing things makes one give an involuntary jerk when the next letter comes and stops the thing. And the less you want to do that sometimes the more it happens.'

'Yes, that's true,' agreed Mr Enderby.

'I don't believe for a moment in spirits or anything like that. But supposing that one of those people who were playing knew that Captain Trevelyan was being murdered at that minute –'

'Oh, I say,' protested Charles, 'that's awfully far fetched.'

'Well, it needn't be quite so crude as that. Yes, I think it must be. We are just taking a hypothesis – that's all. We are asserting that somebody knew that Captain Trevelyan was dead and absolutely couldn't hide their knowledge. The table betrayed them.'

'It's awfully ingenious,' said Charles, 'but I don't believe for a minute it's true.'

'We'll assume that it is true,' said Emily firmly. 'I am sure that in detection of crime you mustn't be afraid to assume things.'

'Oh, I'm quite agreeable,' said Mr Enderby. 'We'll assume that it is true – anything you like.'

'So what we have to do,' said Emily, 'is to consider very carefully the people who were playing. To begin with there's Major Burnaby and Mr Rycroft. Well, it seems wildly unlikely that either of them should have an accomplice who was the murderer. Then there is this Mr Duke. Well, for the moment we know nothing about him. He has only just arrived here lately and of course, he might be a sinister stranger – part of a gang or something. We will put X against his name. And now we come to the Willetts. Charles, there is something awfully mysterious about the Willetts.'

'What on earth have they got to gain from Captain Trevelyan's death?'

'Well, on the face of it, nothing. But if my theory is correct there must be a connection somewhere. We've got to find what is the connection.'

'Right,' said Mr Enderby. 'And supposing it's all a mare's nest?'

'Well, we'll have to start all over again,' said Emily.

'Hark!' cried Charles suddenly.

He held up his hand. Then he went over to the window and opened it, and Emily too, heard the sound which had aroused his attention. It was the far-off booming of a great bell.

As they stood listening, Mrs Curtis's voice called excitedly from below:

'Do you hear the bell, Miss – do you hear it?'

Emily opened the door.

'D'you hear it? Plain as plain, isn't it? Well now, now, to think of that!'

'What is it?' asked Emily.

'It's the bell at Princetown, Miss, near to twelve mile away. It means that a convict's escaped. George, George, where is the man? D'you hear the bell? There's a convict loose.'

Her voice died away as she went through the kitchen.

Charles shut the window and sat down on the bed again.

'It's a pity that things happen all wrong,' he said dispassionately. 'If only this convict had escaped on Friday, why, there would be our murderer nicely accounted for. No farther to look. Hungry man, desperate criminal breaks in. Trevelyan defends his Englishman's castle – and desperate criminal biffs him one. All so simple.'

'It would have been,' said Emily with a sigh.

'Instead of which,' said Charles, 'he escapes three days too late. It's – it's hopelessly inartistic.'

He shook his head sadly.

CHAPTER 16

MR RYCROFT

Emily woke early the next morning. Being a sensible young woman, she realized there was little possibility of Mr Enderby's collaboration until the morning was well advanced. So, feeling restless and unable to lie still she set out for a brisk walk along the lane in the opposite direction from which they had come last night.

She passed the gates of Sittaford House on her right and shortly after that the lane took a sharp turn to the right and ran steeply up hill and came out on the open moor where it degenerated into a grass track and soon petered out altogether. The morning was a fine one, cold and crisp, and the view was lovely. Emily ascended to the very top of Sittaford Tor, a pile of grey rock of a fantastic shape. From this height she looked down over an expanse of moorland, unbroken as far as she could see without any habitation or any road. Below her, on the opposite side of the Tor, were grey masses of granite boulders and rocks. After considering the scene for a minute or two she turned to view the prospect to the north from which she had come. Just below her lay Sittaford, clustering on the flank of the hill, the square grey blob of Sittaford House, and the dotted cottages beyond it. In the valley below she could see Exhampton.

'One ought,' thought Emily confusedly, 'to see things better when you are high up like this. It ought to be like lifting off the top of a doll's house and peering in.'

She wished with all her heart that she had met the dead man even if only once. It was so hard to get an idea of people you had never seen. You had to rely on other people's judgment, and Emily had never yet acknowledged that any other person's judgment was superior to her own. Other people's impressions were no good to you. They might be just as true as yours but you couldn't act on them. You couldn't, as it were, use another person's angle of attack.

Meditating vexedly on these questions, Emily sighed impatiently and shifted her position.

She had been so lost in her own thoughts that she had been oblivious to her immediate surroundings. It was with a shock of surprise that she realized that a small elderly gentleman was standing a few feet away from her, his hat held courteously in his hand, while he breathed rather fast.

'Excuse me,' he said. 'Miss Trefusis, I believe?'

'Yes,' said Emily.

'My name is Rycroft. You must forgive me speaking to you, but in this little community of ours the smallest detail is known, and your arrival here yesterday has naturally gone the round. I can assure you that everyone feels a deep sympathy with your position, Miss Trefusis. We are all, one and all, anxious to assist you in any way we can.'

'That's very kind of you,' said Emily.

'Not at all, not at all,' said Mr Rycroft. 'Beauty in distress, you will pardon my old-fashioned manner of putting it. But seriously, my dear young lady, do count on me if there is any way in which I can possibly assist you. Beautiful view from up here, is it not?'

'Wonderful,' agreed Emily. 'The moor is a wonderful place.'

'You know that a prisoner must have escaped last night from Princetown.'

'Yes. Has he been recaptured?'

'Not yet, I believe. Ah, well, poor fellow, he will no doubt be recaptured soon enough. I believe I am right in saying that no one has escaped successfully from Princetown for the last twenty years.'

'Which direction is Princetown?'

Mr Rycroft stretched out his arm and pointed southwards over the moor.

'It lies over there, about twelve miles as the crow flies over unbroken moorland. It's sixteen miles by road.'

Emily gave a faint shiver. The idea of a desperate hunted man impressed her powerfully. Mr Rycroft was watching her and gave a little nod.

'Yes,' he said. 'I feel the same myself. It's curious how one's instincts rebel at the thought of a man being hunted down, and yet, these men at Princetown are all dangerous and violent criminals, the kind of men whom probably you and I would do our utmost to put there in the first place.'

He gave a little apologetic laugh.

'You must forgive me, Miss Trefusis, I am deeply interested in the study of crime. A fascinating study. Ornithology and criminology are my two subjects.' He paused and then went on:

'That's the reason why, if you will allow me to do so, I should like to associate myself with you in this matter. To study a crime at first hand has long been an unrealized dream of mine. Will you place your confidence in me, Miss Trefusis, and allow me to place my experience at your disposal? I have read and studied this subject deeply.'

Emily was silent for a minute. She was congratulating herself on the way events were playing into her hands. Here was first-hand knowledge being offered her of life as it had been lived at Sittaford. 'Angle of attack,' Emily repeated the phrase that had crept into her mind so short a time before. She had had Major Burnaby's angle – matter of fact – simple – direct. Taking cognizance of facts and completely oblivious of subtleties. Now, she was being offered another angle which she suspected might open up a very different field of vision. This little, shrivelled, dried-up gentleman had read and studied deeply, was well versed in human nature, had that devouring interested curiosity in life displayed by the man of reflection as opposed to the man of action.

'Please help me,' she said simply. 'I am so very worried and unhappy.'

'You must be, my dear, you must be. Now, as I understand the position, Trevelyan's eldest nephew has been arrested or detained – the evidence against him being of a somewhat simple and obvious nature. I, of course, have an open mind. You must allow me that.'

'Of course,' said Emily. 'Why should you believe in his innocence when you know nothing about him?'

'Most reasonable,' said Mr Rycroft. 'Really, Miss Trefusis, you yourself are a most interesting study. By the way, your name – is it Cornish like our poor friend Trevelyan?'

'Yes,' said Emily. 'My father was Cornish, my mother was Scottish.'

'Ah!' said Mr Rycroft, 'very interesting. Now to approach our little problem. On the one hand we assume that young Jim – the name is Jim, is it not? We assume that young Jim had a pressing need of money, that he came down to see his uncle, that he asked for money, that his uncle refused, that in a moment of passion he picked up a sandbag that was lying at the door and that he hit his uncle over the head. The crime was unpremeditated – was in fact a foolish irrational affair most deplorably conducted. Now, all that may be so; on the other hand he may have parted with his uncle in anger and some other person may have stepped in shortly afterwards and committed the crime. That is what you believe – and to put it a little differently, that is what I hope. I do not want your fiancé to have committed the crime, for from my point of view it is so uninteresting that he should have done so. I am therefore backing the other horse. The crime was committed by someone else. We will assume that and go at once to a most important point. Was that someone else aware of the quarrel that had just taken place? Did that quarrel, in fact, actually precipitate the murder? You see my point? Someone is meditating doing away with Captain Trevelyan and seized this opportunity, realizing that suspicion is bound to fall on young Jim.'

Emily considered the matter from this angle.

'In that case,' she said slowly –

Mr Rycroft took the words out of her mouth.

'In that case,' he said briskly, 'the murderer would have to be a person in close association with Captain Trevelyan. He would have to be domiciled in Exhampton. In all probability he would have to be in the house, either during or after the quarrel. And since we are not in a court of law and can bandy about names freely, the name of the servant, Evans, leaps to our minds as a person who could satisfy our conditions. A man who quite possibly might have been in the house, have overheard the quarrel and seized the opportunity. Our next point is to discover whether Evans benefits in any way from his master's death.'

'I believe he gets a small legacy,' said Emily.

'That may or may not constitute a sufficient motive. We shall have to discover whether or not Evans had a pressing need of money. We must also consider Mrs Evans – there is a Mrs Evans of recent date, I understand. If you had studied criminology, Miss Trefusis, you would realize the curious effect caused by inbreeding, especially in country districts. There are at least four young women in Broadmoor, pleasant in manner, but with that curious kink in their dispositions that human life is of little or no account to them. No – we must not leave Mrs Evans out of account.'

'What do you think about this table-turning business, Mr Rycroft?'

'Now, that is very strange. Most strange. I confess, Miss Trefusis, that I am powerfully impressed by it. I am, as perhaps you may have heard, a believer in psychic things. To a certain degree I am a believer in spiritualism. I have already written out a full account and sent it up to the Society of Psychical Research. A well-authenticated and amazing case. Five people present, none of whom could have the least idea or suspicion that Captain Trevelyan was murdered.'

'You don't think –'

Emily stopped. It was not so easy to suggest her own idea to Mr Rycroft that one of the five people might have guilty foreknowledge, as he himself had been one of them. Not that she suspected for a moment that there was anything whatever to connect Mr Rycroft with the tragedy. Still she felt that the suggestion might not be wholly tactful. She pursued her object in a more roundabout manner.

'It all interested me very much, Mr Rycroft; it is, as you say, an amazing occurrence. You don't think that any of the people present, with the exception of yourself of course, were in any way psychic?'

'My dear young lady, I myself am not psychic. I have no

powers in that direction. I am only a very deeply interested observer.'

'What about this Mr Garfield?'

'A nice lad,' said Mr Rycroft, 'but not remarkable in any way.'

'Well off, I suppose,' said Emily.

'Stony broke, I believe,' said Mr Rycroft. 'I hope I am using that idiom correctly. He comes down here to dance attendance on an aunt, from whom he has what I call "expectations". Miss Percehouse is a very sharp lady and I think she knows what these attentions are worth. But as she has a sardonic form of humour of her own she keeps him dancing.'

'I should like to meet her,' said Emily.

'Yes, you must certainly meet her. She will no doubt insist on meeting you. Curiosity – alas, my dear Miss Trefusis – curiosity.'

'Tell me about the Willetts,' said Emily.

'Charming,' said Mr Rycroft, 'quite charming. Colonial, of course. No real poise, if you understand me. A little too lavish in their hospitality. Everything a shade on the ornate side. Miss Violet is a charming girl.'

'A funny place to come for the winter,' said Emily.

'Yes, very odd, is it not? But after all it is only logical. We ourselves living in this country long for the sunshine, hot climates, waving palm trees. People who live in Australia or South Africa are enchanted with the idea of an old-fashioned Christmas with snow and ice.'

'I wonder which of them,' said Emily to herself, 'told him that.'

She reflected that it was not necessary to bury yourself in a moorland village in order to obtain an old-fashioned Christmas with snow and ice. Clearly, Mr Rycroft did not see anything suspicious in the Willetts' choice of a winter resort. But that, she reflected, was perhaps natural in one who was an ornithologist and a criminologist. Sittaford clearly appeared an ideal residence to Mr Rycroft, and he could not conceive of it as an unsuitable environment to someone else.

They had been slowly descending the slope of the hillside and were now wending their way down the lane.

'Who lives in that cottage?' asked Emily abruptly.

'Captain Wyatt – he is an invalid. Rather unsociable I fear.'

'Was he a friend of Captain Trevelyan's?'

'Not an intimate friend in any way. Trevelyan merely made a formal visit to him every now and then. As a matter of fact Wyatt doesn't encourage visitors. A surly man.'

Emily was silent. She was reviewing the possibility of how she herself might become a visitor. She had no intention of allowing any angle of attack to remain unexplored.

She suddenly remembered the hitherto unmentioned member of the *séance*.

'What about Mr Duke?' she asked brightly.

'What about him?'

'Well, who is he?'

'Well,' said Mr Rycroft slowly, 'that is what nobody knows.'

'How extraordinary,' said Emily.

'As a matter of fact,' said Mr Rycroft, 'it isn't. You see, Duke is such an entirely unmysterious individual. I should imagine that the only mystery about him was his social origin. Not – not quite, if you understand me. But a very solid good fellow,' he hastened to add.

Emily was silent.

'This is my cottage,' said Mr Rycroft pausing, 'perhaps you will do me the honour of coming in and inspecting it.'

'I should like to,' said Emily.

They went up the small path and entered the cottage. The interior was charming. Bookcases lined the walls.

Emily went from one to the other glancing curiously at the titles of the books. One section dealt with occult phenomena, another with modern detective fiction, but by far the greater part of the bookcase was given up to criminology and to the world's famous trials. Books on ornithology held a comparatively small portion.

'I think, it's all delightful,' said Emily. 'I must get back now. I expect Mr Enderby will be up and waiting for me. As a matter of fact I haven't had breakfast yet. We told Mrs Curtis half past nine, and I see it's ten o'clock. I shall be dreadfully late – that's because you've been so interesting – and so very helpful.'

'Anything I can do,' burbled Mr Rycroft as Emily turned a bewitching glance on him. 'You can count on me. We are collaborators.'

Emily gave him her hand and squeezed his warmly.

'It's so wonderful,' she said, using the phrase that in the course of her short life she had found so effectual, 'to feel that there's someone on whom one can really rely.'

CHAPTER 17

MISS PERCEHOUSE

Emily returned to find eggs and bacon, and Charles, waiting for her.

Mrs Curtis was still agog with excitement over the escape of the convict.

'Two years it is since last one escaped,' she said, 'and three days it was before they found him. Near to Moretonhampstead he was.'

'Do you think he'll come this way?' asked Charles.

Local knowledge vetoed this suggestion.

'They never comes this way, all bare moorland it is and only small towns when you do come off the moor. He'll make for Plymouth, that's the most likely. But they'll catch him long before that.'

'You could find a good hiding place among these rocks on the other side of the Tor,' said Emily.

'You're right, Miss, and there *is* a hiding place there, the Pixie's Cave they call it. As narrow an opening between two rocks as you could find, but it widens out inside. They say one of King Charles's men hid there once for a fortnight with a serving maid from a farm bringing him food.'

'I must take a look at that Pixie's Cave,' said Charles.

'You'll be surprised how hard it is to find, sir. Many a picnic party in summer looks for it the whole afternoon and doesn't find it, but if you do find it be sure you leave a pin inside it for luck.'

'I wonder,' said Charles when breakfast was over and he and Emily had strolled out into the small bit of garden, 'if I ought to go off to Princetown? Amazing how things pile up once you have a bit of luck. Here I am – I start with a simple football competition prize, and before I know where I am I run straight into an escaped convict and a murderer. Marvellous!'

'What about this photographing of Major Burnaby's cottage?' Charles looked up at the sky.

'H'm,' he said. 'I think I shall say the weather is wrong. I have got to hang on to my *raison d'être* of being in Sittaford as long as possible, and it's coming over misty. Er – I hope you don't mind, I have just posted off an interview with you?'

'Oh! that's all right,' said Emily mechanically. 'What have you made me say?'

'Oh, the usual sort of things people like to hear,' said Mr Enderby. 'Our special representative records his interview with Miss Emily Trefusis, the fiancée of Mr James Pearson who has been arrested by the police and charged with the murder of Captain Trevelyan – Then my impression of you as a high-spirited, beautiful girl.'

'Thank you,' said Emily.

'Shingled,' went on Charles.

'What do you mean by shingled?'

'You are,' said Charles.

'Well, of course I am,' said Emily. 'But why mention it?'

'Women readers always like to know,' said Charles Enderby. 'It was a splendid interview. You've no idea what fine womanly touching things you said about standing by your man, no matter if the whole world was against him.'

'Did I really say that?' said Emily wincing slightly.

'Do you mind?' said Mr Enderby anxiously.

'Oh! no,' said Emily. 'Enjoy yourself, darling.' Mr Enderby looked slightly taken aback.

'It's all right,' said Emily. 'That's a quotation. I had it on my bib when I was small – my Sunday bib. The weekday one had "Don't be a glutton" on it.'

'Oh! I see. I put in a very good bit about Captain Trevelyan's sea career and just a hint at foreign idols looted and a possibility of a strange priest's revenge – only a hint you know.'

'Well, you seem to have done your day's good deed,' said Emily.

'What have you been up to? You were up early enough, heaven knows.'

Emily described her meeting with Mr Rycroft.

She broke off suddenly and Enderby, glancing over his shoulder and following the direction of her eyes, became aware of a pink, healthy-looking young man leaning over the gate and making various apologetic noises to attract attention.

'I say,' said the young man, 'frightfully sorry to butt in and all that. I mean, it is awfully awkward, but my aunt sent me along.'

Emily and Charles both said, 'Oh,' in an inquiring tone, not being much the wiser for the explanation.

'Yes,' said the young man. 'To tell the truth my aunt's rather a Tartar. What she says *goes*, if you know what I mean. Of course, I think it's frightfully bad form coming along at a time like this, but if you knew my aunt – and if you do as she wants, you will know her in a few minutes –'

'Is your aunt Miss Percehouse?' broke in Emily.

'That's right,' said the young man much relieved. 'So you know all about her? Old Mother Curtis has been talking, I suppose. She can wag a tongue, can't she? Not that she's a bad sort, mind you. Well, the fact is, my aunt said she wanted to see you, and I was to come along and tell you so. Compliments, and all that, and would it be troubling you too much – she was an invalid and quite unable to get out and it would be a great kindness – well, you know the sort of thing. I needn't say it all. It's curiosity really, of course, and if you say you've got a headache, or have got letters to write, it will be quite all right and you needn't bother.'

'Oh, but I should like to bother,' said Emily. 'I'll come with you at once. Mr Enderby has got to go along and see Major Burnaby.'

'Have I?' said Enderby in a low voice.

'You have,' said Emily firmly.

She dismissed him with a brief nod and joined her new friend in the road.

'I suppose you're Mr Garfield,' she said.

'That's right. I ought to have told you.'

'Oh, well,' said Emily, 'it wasn't very difficult to guess.'

'Splendid of you coming along like this,' said Mr Garfield. 'Lots of girls would have been awfully offended. But you know what old ladies are.'

'You don't live down here, do you, Mr Garfield?'

'You bet your life I don't.' said Ronnie Garfield with fervour. 'Did you ever see such a god-forsaken spot? Not so much as the Pictures to go to. I wonder someone doesn't commit a murder to –'

He paused, appalled by what he had said.

'I say, I *am* sorry. I am the most unlucky devil that ever lived. Always coming out with the wrong thing. I never meant it for a moment.'

'I'm sure you didn't,' said Emily soothingly.

'Here we are,' said Mr Garfield. He pushed open a gate, and Emily passed through and went up the path leading to a small cottage identical with the rest. In the living-room giving on the garden was a couch, and on it was lying an elderly lady with a thin wrinkled face and with one of the sharpest and most interrogative noses that Emily had ever seen. She raised herself on an elbow with a little difficulty.

'So you've brought her,' she said. 'Very kind of you, my dear, to come along to see an old woman. But you know what it is when you are an invalid. You must have a finger in every pie going and if you can't go to the pie, then the pie has got to come to you. And you needn't think it's all curiosity – it's more than that. Ronnie, go out and paint the garden furniture. In the shed at the end of the garden. Two basket chairs and a bench. You'll find the paint there all ready.'

'Right oh, Aunt Caroline.'

The obedient nephew disappeared.

'Sit down,' said Miss Percehouse.

Emily sat on the chair indicated. Strange to say she had immediately felt conscious of a distinct liking and sympathy for this rather sharp-tongued middle-aged invalid. She felt indeed a kind of kinship with her.

'Here is someone,' thought Emily, 'who goes straight to the point and means to have her own way and bosses everybody she can. Just like me, only I happen to be rather good-looking, and she has to do it all by force of character.'

'I understand you are the girl who is engaged to Trevelyan's nephew,' said Miss Percehouse. 'I've heard all about you and now I have seen you I understand exactly what you are up to. And I wish you good luck.'

'Thank you,' said Emily.

'I hate a slobbering female,' said Miss Percehouse. 'I like one who gets up and does things.'

She looked at Emily sharply.

'I suppose you pity me – lying here never able to get up and walk about?'

'No,' said Emily thoughtfully. 'I don't know that I do. I suppose that one can, if one has the determination, always get something out of life. If you can't get it in one way you get it in another.'

'Quite right,' said Miss Percehouse. 'You've got to take life from a different angle, that's all.'

'Angle of attack,' murmured Emily.

'What's that you say?'

As clearly as she was able, Emily outlined the theory that she had evolved that morning and the application of it she had made to the matter in hand.

'Not bad,' said Miss Percehouse nodding her head. 'Now, my dear – we will get down to business. Not being a born fool, I suppose you've come up to this village to find out what you can about the people here, and to see if what you find out has any bearing on the murder. Well, if there's anything you want to know about the people here, I can tell it to you.'

Emily wasted no time. Concise and business-like she came to the point.

'Major Burnaby?' she asked.

'Typical retired army officer, narrow-minded and limited in outlook, jealous disposition. Credulous in money matters. Kind of man who invests in a South Sea Bubble because he can't see a yard in front of his own nose. Likes to pay his debts promptly and dislikes people who don't wipe their feet on the mat.'

'Mr Rycroft?' said Emily.

'Queer little man, enormous egotist. Cranky. Likes to think himself a wonderful fellow. I suppose he has offered to help you solve the case aright owing to his wonderful knowledge of criminology.'

Emily admitted that that was the case.

'Mr Duke?' she asked.

'Don't know a thing about the man – and yet I ought to. Most ordinary type. I ought to know – and yet I don't. It's queer. It's like a name on the tip of your tongue and yet for the life of you, you can't remember it.'

'The Willetts?' asked Emily.

'Ah! the Willetts!' Miss Percehouse hoisted herself up on an elbow again in some excitement. 'What about the Willetts indeed? Now, I'll tell you something about them, my dear. It may be useful to you, or it may not. Go over to my writing table there and pull out the little top drawer – the one to the left – that's right. Bring me the blank envelope that's there.'

Emily brought the envelope as directed.

'I don't say it's important – it probably isn't,' said Miss Percehouse. 'Everybody tells lies one way or another, and Mrs Willett is perfectly entitled to do the same as everybody else.'

She took the envelope and slipped her hand inside.

'I will tell you all about it. When the Willetts arrived here, with their smart clothes and their maids and their innovation trunks, she and Violet came up in Forder's car and the maids and the innovation trunks came by the station bus. And naturally, the whole thing being an event as you might say, I was looking out as they passed, and I saw a coloured label blow off from one of the trunks and dive down on to one of my borders. Now, if there is one thing I hate more than another it is a litter of paper or mess of any kind, so I sent Ronnie out to pick it up, and I was going to throw it away when it struck me it was a bright, pretty thing, and I might as well keep it for the scrapbooks I make for the children's hospital. Well, I wouldn't have thought about it again except for Mrs Willett deliberately mentioning on two or three occasions that Violet had never been out of South Africa and that she herself had only been to South Africa, England, and the Riviera.'

'Yes?' said Emily.

'Exactly. Now – look at this.'

Miss Percehouse thrust a luggage label into Emily's hand. It bore the inscription, Mendle's Hotel, Melbourne.

'Australia,' said Miss Percehouse, 'isn't South Africa – or it wasn't in my young days. I daresay it isn't important, but there it is for what it is worth. And I'll tell you another thing. I have heard Mrs Willett calling to her daughter, and she called Cooee, and that again is more typical of Australia than South Africa. And what I say is, it is queer. Why shouldn't you wish to admit that you come from Australia if you do?'

'It's certainly curious,' said Emily. 'And it's curious that they should come to live here in winter time as they have.'

'That leaps to the eye,' said Miss Percehouse. 'Have you met them yet?'

'No. I thought of going there this morning. Only I didn't know quite what to say.'

'I'll provide you with an excuse,' said Miss Percehouse briskly. 'Fetch me my fountain pen and some notepaper and an envelope. That's right. Now, let me see.' She paused deliberately, then without the least warning raised her voice in a hideous scream.

'Ronnie, Ronnie, Ronnie! Is the boy deaf? Why can't he come when he's called? Ronnie! Ronnie!'

Ronnie arrived at a brisk trot, paint brush in hand.

'Is there anything the matter, Aunt Caroline?'

'What should be the matter? I was calling you, that was all. Did you have any particular cake for tea when you were at the Willetts' yesterday?'

'Cake?'

'Cake, sandwiches – anything. How slow you are, boy. What did you have to eat for tea?'

'There was coffee cake,' said Ronnie very much puzzled, 'and some *pâté* sandwiches –'

'Coffee cake,' said Miss Percehouse. 'That'll do.' She began to write briskly. 'You can go back to your painting, Ronnie. Don't hang about, and don't stand there with your mouth open. You had your adenoids out when you were eight years old, so there is no excuse for it.'

She continued to write:

Dear Mrs Willett, – I hear you had the most delicious coffee cake for tea yesterday afternoon. Will you be so very kind as to give me the recipe for it? I know you'll not mind my asking you this – an invalid has so little variety except in her diet. Miss Trefusis has kindly promised to take this note for me as Ronnie is busy this morning. Is not this news about the convict too dreadful?

Yours very sincerely,
Caroline Percehouse.

She put it in an envelope, sealed it down and addressed it.

'There you are, young woman. You will probably find the doorstep littered with reporters. A lot of them passed along the lane in Forder's charabanc. I saw them. But you ask for Mrs Willett and say you have brought a note from me and you'll sail in. I needn't tell you to keep your eyes open and make the most you can of your visit. You will do that anyway.'

'You are kind,' said Emily. 'You really are.'

'I help those who can help themselves,' said Miss Percehouse. 'By the way, you haven't asked me what I think of Ronnie yet. I presume he is on your list of the village. He is a good lad in his way, but pitifully weak. I am sorry to say he would do almost anything for money. Look at what he stands from me! And he hasn't got the brains to see that I would like him just ten times better if he stood up to me now and again, and told me to go to the devil.

'The only other person in the village is Captain Wyatt. He smokes opium, I believe. And he's easily the worst-tempered man in England. Anything more you want to know?'

'I don't think so,' said Emily. 'What you have told me seems pretty comprehensive.'

CHAPTER 18

EMILY VISITS SITTAFORD HOUSE

As Emily walked briskly along the lane she noticed once more how the character of the morning was changing. The mist was closing up and round.

'What an awful place to live in England is,' thought Emily. 'If it isn't snowing or raining or blowing it's misty. And if the sun does shine it's so cold that you can't feel your fingers or toes.'

She was interrupted in these reflections by a rather hoarse voice speaking rather close to her right ear.

'Excuse me,' it said, 'but do you happen to have seen a bull terrier?'

Emily started and turned. Leaning over a gate was a tall thin man with a very brown complexion, bloodshot eyes and grey hair. He was propped up with a crutch one side, and was eyeing Emily with enormous interest. She had no difficulty in identifying him as Captain Wyatt, the invalid owner of No. 2 The Cottages.

'No, I haven't,' said Emily.

'She's got out,' said Captain Wyatt. 'An affectionate creature, but an absolute fool. With all these cars and things –'

'I shouldn't think many motors come up this lane,' said Emily.

'Charabancs do in the summer time,' said Captain Wyatt grimly. 'It's the three and sixpenny morning run from Exhampton. Ascent of Sittaford Beacon with a halt halfway up from Exhampton for light refreshments.'

'Yes, but this isn't summer time,' said Emily.

'All the same a charabanc came along just now. Reporters, I suppose, going to have a look at Sittaford House.'

'Did you know Captain Trevelyan well?' asked Emily.

She was of the opinion that the incident of the bull terrier had been a mere subterfuge on Captain Wyatt's part dictated by a very natural curiosity. She was, she was well aware, the principal object of attention in Sittaford at present, and it was only natural that Captain Wyatt should wish to have a look at her as well as everyone else.

'I don't know about well,' said Captain Wyatt. 'He sold me this cottage.'

'Yes,' said Emily encouragingly.

'A skinflint, that's what he was,' said Captain Wyatt. 'The arrangement was that he was to do the place up to suit the purchaser's taste, and just because I had the window sashes in chocolate picked out in lemon, he wanted me to pay half. Said the arrangement was for uniform colour.'

'You didn't like him,' said Emily.

'I was always having rows with him,' said Captain Wyatt. 'But

I always have rows with everyone,' he added as an afterthought. 'In a place like this you have to teach people to leave a man alone. Always knocking at the door and dropping in and chattering. I don't mind seeing people when I am in the mood – but it has got to be my mood, not theirs. No good Trevelyan giving me his Lord of the Manor airs and dropping in whenever he felt like it. There's not a soul in the place comes near me now,' he added with satisfaction.

'Oh!' said Emily.

'That's the best of having a native servant,' said Captain Wyatt. 'They understand orders. Abdul!' he roared.

A tall Indian in a turban came out of the cottage and waited attentively.

'Come in and have something,' said Captain Wyatt. 'And see my little cottage.'

'I'm sorry,' said Emily, 'but I have to hurry on.'

'Oh, no, you haven't,' said Captain Wyatt.

'Yes, I have,' said Emily. 'I've got an appointment.'

'Nobody understands the art of living nowadays,' said Captain Wyatt. 'Catching trains, making appointments, fixing times for everything – all nonsense. Get up with the sun, I say, have your meals when you feel like it, and never tie yourself to a time or a date. I could teach people how to live if they would listen to me.'

The results of this exalted way of living were not too hopeful, Emily reflected. Anything more like a battered wreck of a man than Captain Wyatt she had never seen. However, feeling that his curiosity had been sufficiently satisfied for the time being, she insisted once more on her appointment and went on her way.

Sittaford House had a solid oak front door, a neat bell pull, an immense wire mat, and a brilliantly polished brass letter box. It represented, as Emily could not fail to see, comfort and decorum. A neat and conventional parlourmaid answered the bell.

Emily deduced the journalist evil had been before her as the parlourmaid said at once in a distant tone, 'Mrs Willett is not seeing anyone this morning.'

'I have brought a note from Miss Percehouse,' said Emily.

This clearly altered matters. The parlourmaid's face expressed indecision, then she shifted her ground.

'Will you come inside, please.'

Emily was ushered into what house agents describe as 'a well-appointed hall', and from there into a large drawing-room. A fire was burning brightly and there were traces of feminine occupation in the room. Some glass tulips, an elaborate workbag, a girl's hat, and a Pierrot doll with very long legs, were lying about. There were, she noticed, no photographs.

Having taken in all there was to see, Emily was warming her hands in front of the fire when the door opened and a girl about her own age came in. She was a very pretty girl, Emily noticed, smartly and expensively dressed, and she also thought that she had never seen a girl in a greater state of nervous apprehension. Not that this was apparent on the surface, however. Miss Willett was making a gallant appearance of being entirely at her ease.

'Good morning,' she said advancing and shaking hands. 'I'm so sorry Mother isn't down, but she's spending the morning in bed.'

'Oh, I am sorry, I'm afraid I have come at an unfortunate time.'

'No, of course not. The cook is writing out the recipe for that cake now. We are only too delighted for Miss Percehouse to have it. Are you staying with her?'

Emily reflected with an inward smile that this was perhaps the only house in Sittaford whose members were not exactly aware of who she was and why she was there. Sittaford House had a definite regime of employers and employed. The employed might know about her – the employers clearly did not.

'I am not exactly staying with her,' said Emily. 'In fact, I'm at Mrs Curtis's.'

'Of course the cottage is terribly small, and she has her nephew, Ronnie, with her, hasn't she? I suppose there wouldn't be room for you too. She's a wonderful person, isn't she? So much character, I always think, but I am rather afraid of her really.'

'She's a bully, isn't she?' agreed Emily cheerfully. 'But it's an awful temptation to be a bully, especially if people won't stand up to you.'

Miss Willett sighed.

'I wish I could stand up to people,' she said. 'We've had the most awful morning absolutely pestered by reporters.'

'Oh, of course,' said Emily. 'This is Captain Trevelyan's house really, isn't it? – the man who was murdered at Exhampton.'

She was trying to determine the exact cause of Violet Willett's nervousness. The girl was clearly on the jump. Something was frightening her – and frightening her badly. She mentioned Captain Trevelyan's name bluntly on purpose. The girl didn't noticeably react to it in any way, but then she was probably expecting some such reference.

'Yes, wasn't it dreadful?'

'Do tell me – that's if you don't mind talking about it?'

'No – no – of course not – why should I?'

'There's something very wrong with this girl,' thought Emily. 'She hardly knows what she's saying. What has made her get the wind up this morning particularly?'

'About that table-turning,' went on Emily. 'I heard about it in a casual sort of way and it seemed to me so frightfully interesting – I mean so absolutely gruesome.'

'Girlish thrills,' she thought to herself, 'that's my line.'

'Oh, it was horrid,' said Violet. 'That evening – I shall never forget it! We thought, of course, that it was somebody just fooling – only it seemed a very nasty kind of joke.'

'Yes?'

'I shall never forget when we turned the lights on – everybody looked so queer. Not Mr Duke and Major Burnaby – they are the stolid kind, they would never like to admit that they were impressed by anything of that kind. But you could see that Major Burnaby was really awfully rattled by it. I think that actually he believed in it more than anybody else. But I thought poor little Mr Rycroft was going to have a heart attack or something, yet he must be used to that kind of thing because he does a lot of psychic research, and as for Ronnie, Ronnie Garfield you know – he looked as though he had seen a ghost – actually seen one. Even Mother was awfully upset – more than I have ever seen her before.'

'It must have been most spooky,' said Emily. 'I wish I had been there to see.'

'It was rather horrid really. We all pretended that it was – just fun, you know, but it didn't seem like that. And then Major Burnaby suddenly made up his mind to go over to Exhampton and we all tried to stop him, and said he would be buried in a snowdrift, but he would go. And there we sat, after he had gone, all feeling dreadful and worried. And then, last night – no, yesterday morning, we got the news.'

'You think it was Captain Trevelyan's spirit?' said Emily in an awed voice. 'Or do you think it was clairvoyance or telepathy?'

'Oh, I don't know. But I shall never, never laugh at these things again.'

The parlourmaid entered with a folded piece of paper on a salver which she handed to Violet.

The parlourmaid withdrew and Violet unfolded the paper, glanced over it and handed it to Emily.

'There you are,' she said. 'As a matter of fact you are just in time. This murder business has upset the servants. They think it's dangerous to live in this out of the way part. Mother lost her temper with them yesterday evening and has sent them all packing. They are going after lunch. We are going to get two men instead – a houseparlourman and a kind of butler-chauffeur. I think it will answer much better.'

'Servants are silly, aren't they?' said Emily.

'It isn't even as if Captain Trevelyan had been killed in this house.'

'What made you think of coming to live here?' asked Emily, trying to make the question sound artless and girlishly natural.

'Oh, we thought it would be rather fun,' said Violet.

'Don't you find it rather dull?'

'Oh, no, I love the country.'

But her eyes avoided Emily's. Just for a moment she looked suspicious and afraid.

She stirred uneasily in her chair and Emily rose rather reluctantly to her feet.

'I must be going now,' she said. 'Thank you so much, Miss Willett. I do hope your mother will be all right.'

'Oh, she's quite well really. It's only the servants – and all the worry.'

'Of course.'

Adroitly, unperceived by the other, Emily managed to discard her gloves on a small table. Violet Willett accompanied her to the front door and they took leave of each other with a few pleasant remarks.

The parlourmaid who had opened the door to Emily had unlocked it, but as Violet Willett closed it behind her retreating guest Emily caught no sound of the key being turned. When she reached the gate, therefore, she retraced her steps slowly.

Her visit had more than confirmed the theories she held about Sittaford House. There was something queer going on here. She didn't think Violet Willett was directly implicated – that is unless she was a very clever actress indeed. But there was something wrong, and that something *must* have a connection with the tragedy. There *must* be some link between the Willetts and Captain Trevelyan, and in that link there might lie the clue to the whole mystery.

She came up to the front door, turned the handle very gently and passed across the threshold. The hall was deserted. Emily paused, uncertain what to do next. She had her excuse – the gloves left thoughtfully behind in the drawing-room. She stood stock still listening. There was no sound anywhere except a very faint murmur of voices from upstairs. As quietly as possible Emily crept to the foot of the stairs and stood looking up. Then, very gingerly she ascended a step at a time. This was rather more risky. She could hardly pretend that her gloves had walked of their own accord to the first floor, but she had a burning desire to overhear something of the conversation that was going on upstairs. Modern builders never made their doors fit well, in Emily's opinion. You could hear a murmur of voices down here. Therefore, if you reached the door itself you would hear plainly the conversation that was going on inside the room. Another step – one more again . . . Two women's voices – Violet and her mother without doubt.

Suddenly there was a break in the conversation – a sound of a footstep. Emily retreated rapidly.

When Violet Willett opened her mother's door and came down the stairs she was surprised to find her late guest standing in the hall peering about her in a lost dog kind of way.

'My gloves,' she explained. 'I must have left them. I came back for them.'

'I expect they are in here,' said Violet.

They went into the drawing-room and there, sure enough, on a little table near where Emily had been sitting lay the missing gloves.

'Oh, thank you,' said Emily. 'It's so stupid of me. I am always leaving things.'

'And you want gloves in this weather,' said Violet. 'It's so cold.' Once again they parted at the hall door, and this time Emily heard the key being turned in the lock.

She went down the drive with plenty to think about, for, as that door on the upper landing had opened, she had heard distinctly one sentence spoken in an older woman's fretful and plaintive voice.

'*My God,*' the voice had wailed, '*I can't bear it. Will tonight never come?*'

CHAPTER 19
THEORIES

Emily arrived back at the cottage to find her boy friend absent. He had, Mrs Curtis explained, gone off with several other young gentlemen, but two telegrams had come for the young lady. Emily took them, opened them, and put them in the pocket of her sweater, Mrs Curtis eyeing them hungrily the while.

'Not bad news, I hope?' said Mrs Curtis.

'Oh, no,' said Emily.

'Always gives me a turn, a telegram does,' said Mrs Curtis.

'I know,' said Emily. 'Very disturbing.'

At the moment she felt disinclined for anything but solitude. She wanted to sort out and arrange her own ideas. She went up to her own room, and taking pencil and notepaper she set to work on a system of her own. After twenty minutes of this exercise she was interrupted by Mr Enderby.

'Hullo, hullo, hullo, there you are. Fleet Street has been hard on your tracks all morning but they have just missed you everywhere. Anyway they have had it from me that you are not to be worried. As far as you're concerned, I am the big noise.'

He sat down on the chair – Emily was occupying the bed – and chuckled.

'Envy and malice isn't in it!' he said. 'I have been handing them out the goods. I know everyone and I am right in it. It's too good to be true. I keep pinching myself and feeling I will wake up in a minute. I say, have you noticed the fog?'

'It won't stop me going to Exeter this afternoon, will it?' said Emily.

'Do you want to go to Exeter?'

'Yes. I have to meet Mr Dacres there. My solicitor, you know – the one who is undertaking Jim's defence. He wants to see me. And I think I shall pay a visit to Jim's Aunt Jennifer, while I am there. After all, Exeter is only half an hour away.'

'Meaning she might have nipped over by train and batted her brother over the head and nobody would have noticed her absence.'

'Oh, I know it sounds rather improbable, but one has to go into everything. Not that I want it to be Aunt Jennifer – I don't. I would much rather it was Martin Dering. I hate the sort of man who presumes on going to be a brother-in-law and does things in public that you can't smack his face for.'

'Is he that kind?'

'Very much that kind. He's an ideal person for a murderer – always getting telegrams from bookmakers and losing money on horses. It's annoying that he's got such a good *alibi*. Mr Dacres told me about it. A publisher and a literary dinner seems so very unbreakable and respectable.'

'A literary dinner,' said Enderby. 'Friday night. Martin Dering – let me see – Martin Dering – why, yes – I am almost sure of it. Dash it all, I am quite sure of it, but I can clinch things by wiring to Carruthers.'

'What are you talking about?' said Emily.

'Listen. You know I came down to Exhampton on Friday evening. Well, there was a bit of information I was going to get from a pal of mine, another newspaperman, Carruthers his name is. He was coming round to see me about half past six if he could – before he went on to some literary dinner – he is rather a big bug, Carruthers, and if he couldn't make it he would send me a line to Exhampton. Well, he didn't make it and he did send me a line.'

'What *has* all this got to do with it?' said Emily.

'Don't be so impatient, I am coming to the point. The old chap was rather screwed when he wrote it – done himself well at the dinner – after giving me the item I wanted, he went on to waste a good bit of juicy description on me. You know – about the speeches, and what asses so and so, a famous novelist and a famous playwright, were. And he said he had been rottenly placed at dinner. There was an empty seat on one side of him where Ruby McAlmott, that awful best-seller woman, ought to have sat and an empty place on the other side of him where the sex specialist, Martin Dering, ought to have been, but he moved up nearer to a poet, who is very well known in Blackheath, and tried to make the best of things. Now, do you see the point?'

'Charles! Darling!' Emily became lyrical with excitement. 'How marvellous. Then the brute wasn't at the dinner at all?'

'Exactly.'

'You are sure you've remembered the name right?'

'I'm positive. I have torn up the letter, worse luck, but I can always wire to Carruthers to make sure. But I absolutely know that I'm not mistaken.'

'There's the publisher still, of course,' said Emily. 'The one he spent the afternoon with. But I rather think it was a publisher who was just going back to America, and if so, that looks fishy. I mean it looks as though he had selected someone who couldn't be asked without rather a lot of trouble.'

'Do you really think we have hit it?' said Charles Enderby.

'Well, it looks like it. I think the best thing to be done is – to go straight to that nice Inspector Narracott and just tell him these new facts. I mean, we can't tackle an American publisher who is on the *Mauretania* or the *Berengaria* or somewhere. That's a job for the police.'

'My word if this comes off. What a scoop!' said Mr Enderby. 'If it does, I should think the *Daily Wire* couldn't offer me less than –'

Emily broke ruthlessly into his dreams of advancement.

'But we mustn't lose our heads,' she said, 'and throw everything else to the wind. I must go to Exeter. I don't suppose I shall be able to be back here until tomorrow. But I've got a job for you.'

'What kind of a job?'

Emily described her visit to the Willetts and the strange sentence she had overheard on leaving.

'We have got absolutely and positively to find out what is going to happen tonight. There's something in the wind.'

'What an extraordinary thing!'

'Wasn't it? But of course it may be a coincidence. Or it may not – but you observe that the servants are being cleared out of the way. Something queer is going to happen there tonight, and *you* have to be on the spot to see what it is.'

'You mean I have to spend the whole night shivering under a bush in the garden?'

'Well, you don't mind that, do you? Journalists don't mind what they do in a good cause.'

'Who told you that?'

'Never mind who told me, I know it. You will do it, won't you?'

'Oh, rather,' said Charles. 'I am not going to miss anything. If anything queer goes on at Sittaford House tonight, I shall be in it.'

Emily then told him about the luggage label.

'It's odd,' said Mr Enderby. 'Australia is where the third Pearson is, isn't it? – the youngest one. Not, of course, that that means anything, but still it – well, there might be a connection.'

'H'm,' said Emily. 'I think that's all. Have you anything to report on your side?'

'Well,' said Charles, 'I've got an idea.'

'Yes?'

'The only thing is I don't know how you'll like it.'

'What do you mean – how I'll like it?'

'You won't fly out over it, will you?'

'I don't suppose so. I mean I hope I can listen sensibly and quietly to anything.'

'Well, the point is,' said Charles Enderby eyeing her doubtfully, 'don't think I mean to be offensive or anything like that, but do you think that lad of yours is to be depended on for the strict truth?'

'Do you mean,' said Emily, 'that he did murder him after all? You are quite welcome to that view if you like. I said to you at the beginning that that was the natural view to take, but I said we had to work on the assumption that he didn't.'

'I don't mean that,' said Enderby. 'I am with you in assuming that he didn't do the old boy in. What I mean is, how far is his own story of what happened true? He says that he went there, had a chat with the old fellow, and came away leaving him alive and well.'

'Yes.'

'Well, it just occurred to me, you don't think it's possible that he went there and actually found the old man dead? I mean, he might have got the wind up and been scared and not like to say so.'

Charles had propounded this theory rather dubiously, but he was relieved to find that Emily showed no signs of flying out at him over it. Instead, she frowned and creased her brow in thought.

'I am not going to pretend,' she said. 'It *is* possible. I hadn't thought of it before. I know Jim wouldn't murder anyone, but he might quite well get rattled and tell a silly lie and then, of course, he would have to stick to it. Yes, it is quite possible.'

'The awkward thing is that you can't go and ask him about it now. I mean they wouldn't let you see him alone, would they?'

'I can put Mr Dacres on to him,' said Emily. 'You see your solicitor alone, I believe. The worst of Jim is that he is frightfully obstinate, if he has once said a thing he sticks to it.'

'That's my story and I'm going to stick to it,' said Mr Enderby comprehendingly.

'Yes. I am glad you mentioned that possibility to me, Charles, it hadn't occurred to me. We have been looking for someone who came in *after* Jim had left – but if it was *before* –'

She paused, lost in thought. Two very different theories stretched out in opposite directions. There was the one suggested by Mr Rycroft, in which Jim's quarrel with his uncle was the determining point. The other theory, however, took no cognizance of Jim whatsoever. The first thing to do, Emily felt, was to see the doctor who had first examined the body. If it were possible that Captain Trevelyan had been murdered at – say – four o'clock, it might make a considerable difference to the question of alibis. And the other thing to do was to make Mr

Dacres urge most strongly on his client the absolute necessity of speaking the truth on this point.

She rose from the bed.

'Well,' she said, 'you had better find out how I can get to Exhampton. The man at the smithy has a car of a kind, I believe. Will you go and settle with him about it? I'll start immediately after lunch. There's a train at three ten to Exeter. That will give me time to see the doctor first. What's the time now?'

'Half past twelve,' said Mr Enderby, consulting his watch.

'Then we will both go up and fix up about that car,' said Emily. 'And there's just one other thing I want to do before leaving Sittaford.'

'What's that?'

'I am going to pay a call on Mr Duke. He's the only person in Sittaford I haven't seen. And he was one of the people at the table-turning.'

'Oh, we'll pass his cottage on the way to the smithy.'

Mr Duke's cottage was the last of the row. Emily and Charles unlatched the gate and walked up the path. And then something rather surprising occurred. For the door opened and a man came out. And that man was Inspector Narracott.

He, too, looked surprised and, Emily fancied, embarrassed.

Emily abandoned her original intention.

'I am so glad to have met you, Inspector Narracott,' she said. 'There are one or two things I want to talk to you about if I may.'

'Delighted, Miss Trefusis.' He drew out a watch. 'I'm afraid you will have to look sharp. I've a car waiting. I've got to go back to Exhampton almost immediately.'

'How extraordinarily fortunate,' said Emily. 'You might give me a lift, will you, Inspector?'

The Inspector said rather woodenly that he would be very pleased to do so.

'You might go and get my suitcase, Charles,' said Emily. 'It's packed up and ready.'

Charles departed immediately.

'It's a great surprise meeting you here, Miss Trefusis,' said Inspector Narracott.

'I said *au revoir*,' Emily reminded him.

'I didn't notice it at the time.'

'You've not seen the last of me by a long way,' said Emily candidly. 'You know, Inspector Narracott, you've made a mistake. Jim's not the man you're after.'

'Indeed!'

'And what's more,' said Emily, 'I believe in your heart that you agree with me.'

'What makes you think that, Miss Trefusis?'

'What were you doing in Mr Duke's cottage?' retaliated Emily.

Narracott looked embarrassed, and she was quick to follow it up.

'You're doubtful, Inspector – that's what you are – doubtful. You thought you had got the right man and now you are not so sure, and so you are making a few investigations. Well, I have got something to tell you that may help. I'll tell it to you on the way to Exhampton.'

Footsteps sounded down the road, and Ronnie Garfield appeared. He had the air of a truant, breathless and guilty.

'I say, Miss Trefusis,' he began. 'What about a walk this afternoon? While my aunt has a nap, you know.'

'Impossible,' said Emily. 'I'm going away. To Exeter.'

'What, not really! For good you mean?'

'Oh, no,' said Emily. 'I shall be back again tomorrow.'

'Oh, that's splendid.'

Emily took something from the pocket of her sweater and handed it to him. 'Give that to your aunt, will you? It's a recipe for coffee cake, and tell her that she was just in time, the cook is leaving today and so are the other servants. Be sure to tell her, she will be interested.'

A far-off scream was borne on the breeze. 'Ronnie,' it said, 'Ronnie, Ronnie.'

'There's my aunt,' said Ronnie starting nervously. 'I had better go.'

'I think you had,' said Emily. 'You've got green paint on your left cheek,' she called after him. Ronnie Garfield disappeared through his aunt's gate.

'Here's my boy friend with my suitcase,' said Emily. 'Come on, Inspector. I'll tell you everything in the car.'

CHAPTER 20

VISIT TO AUNT JENNIFER

At half past two Dr Warren received a call from Emily. He took an immediate fancy to this business-like and attractive girl. Her questions were blunt and to the point.

'Yes, Miss Trefusis, I see exactly what you mean. You'll understand that contrary to the popular belief in novels it is extremely difficult to fix the time of death accurately. I saw the body at eight o'clock. I can say decidedly that Captain Trevelyan had been dead at least two hours. How much longer than that would be difficult to say. If you were to tell me that he was killed at four o'clock, I should say that it was possible, though my own opinion inclines to a later time. On the other hand he could certainly not have been dead for much longer than that. Four and a half hours would be the outside limit.'

'Thank you,' said Emily, 'that's all I wanted to know.'

She caught the three ten train at the station and drove straight to the hotel where Mr Dacres was staying.

Their interview was business-like and unemotional. Mr Dacres had known Emily since she was a small child and had managed her affairs for her since she came of age.

'You must prepare yourself for a shock, Emily,' he said. 'Things are much worse for Jim Pearson than we imagined.'

'Worse?'

'Yes. It's no good beating about the bush. Certain facts have come to light which are bound to show him up in a most unfavourable light. It is those facts which led the police actually to charge him with the crime. I should not be acting in your interests if I withheld these facts from you.'

'Please tell me,' said Emily.

Her voice was perfectly calm and composed. Whatever the inward shock she might have felt, she had no intention of making an outward display of her feelings. It was not feelings that were going to help Jim Pearson, it was brains. She must keep all her wits about her.

'There is no doubt that he was in urgent and immediate need of money. I am not going to enter into the ethics of the situation at the moment. Pearson had apparently before now occasionally borrowed money – to use a euphemism – from his firm – I may say without their knowledge. He was fond of speculating in shares, and on one occasion previously, knowing that certain dividends were to be paid into his account in a week's time, he anticipated them by using the firm's money to buy certain shares which he had pretty certain knowledge were bound to go up. The transaction was quite satisfactory, the money was replaced and Pearson really doesn't seem to have had any doubts as to the honesty of the transaction. Apparently he repeated this just over a week ago. This time an unforeseen thing occurred. The books of the firm were examined at certain stated times, but for some reason or other this date was advanced, and Pearson was faced with a very unpleasant dilemma. He was quite aware of the construction that would be put on his action and he was quite unable to raise the sum of money involved. He admits himself that he had tried in various quarters and failed when as a last resource he rushed down to Devonshire to lay the matter before his uncle and persuade him to help him. This Captain Trevelyan absolutely refused to do.

'Now, my dear Emily, we shall be quite unable to prevent these facts from being brought to light. The police have already unearthed the matter. And you see, don't you, that we have here a very pressing and urgent motive for the crime? The moment Captain Trevelyan was dead Pearson could easily have obtained the necessary sum as an advance from Mr Kirkwood and saved himself from disaster and possibly criminal prosecution.'

'Oh, the idiot,' said Emily helplessly.

'Quite so,' said Mr Dacres dryly. 'It seems to me that our only chance lies in proving that Jim Pearson was quite unaware of the provisions of his uncle's will.'

There was a pause while Emily considered the matter. Then she said quietly:

'I'm afraid that's impossible. All three of them knew – Sylvia, Jim and Brian. They often discussed it and laughed and joked about the rich uncle in Devonshire.'

'Dear, dear,' said Mr Dacres. 'That's unfortunate.'

'You don't think him guilty, Mr Dacres?' asked Emily.

'Curiously enough I do not,' replied the lawyer. 'In some

ways Jim Pearson is a most transparent young man. He hasn't, if you will allow me to say so, Emily, a very high standard of commercial honesty, but I do not believe for one minute that his hand sandbagged his uncle.'

'Well, that's a good thing,' said Emily. 'I wish the police thought the same.'

'Quite so. Our own impressions and ideas are of no practical use. The case against him is unfortunately strong. I am not going to disguise from you, my dear child, that the outlook is bad. I should suggest Lorimer, K.C., as the defence. Forlorn hope man they call him,' he added cheerfully.

'There is one thing I should like to know,' said Emily. 'You have, of course, seen Jim?'

'Certainly.'

'I want you to tell me honestly if you think he has told the truth in other respects.' She outlined to him the idea that Enderby had suggested to her.

The lawyer considered the matter carefully before replying.

'It's my impression,' he said, 'that he is speaking the truth when he describes his interview with his uncle. But there is little doubt that he has got the wind up badly, and if he went round to the window, entered that way and came across his uncle's dead body – he might just possibly be too scared to admit the fact and have concocted this other story.'

'That's what I thought,' said Emily. 'Next time you see him, Mr Dacres, will you urge him to speak the truth? It may make the most tremendous difference.'

'I will do so. All the same,' he said after a moment or two's pause, 'I think you are mistaken in this idea. The news of Captain Trevelyan's death was bandied around in Exhampton about eight thirty. At that time the last train had left for Exeter, but Jim Pearson got the first train available in the morning – a thoroughly unwise proceeding, by the way, as it called attention to his movements which otherwise would not have been aroused if he had left by a train at a more conventional hour. Now if, as you suggest, he discovered his uncle's dead body some time after half past four, I think he would have left Exhampton straight away. There's a train which leaves shortly after six and another at a quarter to eight.'

'That's a point,' admitted Emily, 'I didn't think of that.'

'I have questioned him narrowly about his method of entering his uncle's house,' went on Mr Dacres. 'He says that Captain Trevelyan made him remove his boots, and leave them on the doorstep. That accounts for no wet marks being discovered in the hall.'

'He doesn't speak of having heard any sound – anything at all – that gives him the idea that there might have been someone else in the house?'

'He didn't mention it to me. But I will ask him.'

'Thank you,' said Emily. 'If I write a note can you take it to him?'

'Subject to its being read, of course.'

'Oh, it will be a very discreet one.'

She crossed to the writing table and scribbled a few words.

Dearest Jim, – Everything's going to be all right, so cheer up. I am working like the worst kind of slave to find out the truth. What an idiot you've been, darling.

Love from
Emily.'

'There,' she said.

Mr Dacres read it but made no comment.

'I have taken pains with my handwriting,' said Emily, 'so that the prison authorities can read it easily. Now, I must be off.'

'You will allow me to offer you a cup of tea.'

'No, thank you, Mr Dacres. I have no time to lose. I am going to see Jim's Aunt Jennifer.'

At The Laurels, Emily was informed that Mrs Gardner was out but would be home shortly.

Emily smiled upon the parlourmaid.

'I'll come in and wait then.'

'Would you like to see Nurse Davis?'

Emily was always ready to see anybody. 'Yes,' she said promptly.

A few minutes later Nurse Davis, starched and curious, arrived.

'How do you do,' said Emily. 'I am Emily Trefusis – a kind of niece of Mrs Gardner's. That is, I am going to be a niece, but my fiancé, Jim Pearson, has been arrested, as I expect you know.'

'Oh, it's been too dreadful,' said Nurse Davis. 'We saw it all in the papers this morning. What a terrible business. You seem to be bearing up wonderfully, Miss Trefusis – really wonderfully.'

There was a faint note of disapproval in the nurse's voice. Hospital nurses, she implied, were able to bear up owing to their force of character, but lesser mortals were expected to *give way*.

'Well, one mustn't sag at the knees,' said Emily. 'I hope you don't mind very much. I mean, it must be awkward for you to be associated with a family that has got a murder in it.'

'It's very unpleasant, of course,' said Nurse Davis, unbending at this proof of consideration. 'But one's duty to one's patient comes before everything.'

'How splendid,' said Emily. 'It must be wonderful for Aunt Jennifer to feel she has somebody upon whom she can rely.'

'Oh, really,' said the nurse simpering, 'you are too kind. But, of course, I have had curious experiences before this. Why, at the last case I attended –' Emily listened patiently to a long and scandalous anecdote comprising complicated divorce and paternity questions. After complimenting Nurse Davis on her tact, discretion and *savoir faire*, Emily slid back to the topic of the Gardners.

'I don't know Aunt Jennifer's husband at all,' she said. 'I've never met him. He never goes away from home, does he?'

'No, poor fellow.'

'What exactly is the matter with him?'

Nurse Davis embarked on the subject with professional gusto.

'So, really he might get well again any minute,' Emily murmured thoughtfully.

'He would be terribly weak,' said the nurse.

'Oh, of course. But it makes it seem more hopeful, doesn't it?'

The nurse shook her head with firm professional despondency.

'I don't suppose there will be any cure in his case.'

Emily had copied down in her little notebook the timetable of what she called Aunt Jennifer's *alibi*. She now murmured tentatively:

'How queer it seems to think that Aunt Jennifer was actually at the Pictures when her brother was being killed.'

'Very sad, isn't it?' said Nurse Davis. 'Of course, she couldn't tell – but it gives one such a shock afterwards.'

Emily cast about in her mind to find out what she wanted to know without asking a direct question.

'Didn't she have some queer kind of vision or premonition?' she inquired. 'Wasn't it you who met her in the hall when she came in and exclaimed that she looked quite queer?'

'Oh, no,' said the nurse. 'It wasn't me. I didn't see her until we were sitting down to dinner together, and she seemed quite her ordinary self then. How very interesting.'

'I expect I am mixing it up with something else,' said Emily.

'Perhaps it was some other relation,' suggested Nurse Davis. 'I came in rather late myself. I felt rather guilty about leaving my patient so long, but he himself had urged me to go.'

She suddenly looked at her watch.

'Oh, dear. He asked me for another hot water bottle. I must see about it at once. Will you excuse me, Miss Trefusis?'

Emily excused her and going over to the fireplace she put her finger on the bell.

The slipshod maid came with rather a frightened face.

'What's your name?' said Emily.

'Beatrice, Miss.'

'Oh, Beatrice, I may not be able to wait to see my aunt, Mrs Gardner, after all – I wanted to ask her about some shopping she did on Friday. Do you know if she brought a big parcel back with her?'

'No, Miss, I didn't see her come in.'

'I thought you said she came in at six o'clock.'

'Yes, Miss, she did. I didn't see her come in, but when I went to take some hot water to her room at seven o'clock it gave me a shock to find her lying in the dark on the bed. "Well, ma'am," I said to her, "You gave me quite a shock." "I came in quite a long time ago. At six o'clock," she said. I didn't see a big parcel anywhere,' said Beatrice trying her hardest to be helpful.

'It's all very difficult,' thought Emily. 'One has to invent so many things. I've already invented a premonition and a big parcel, but so far as I can see one has to invent something if one doesn't want to sound suspicious.' She smiled sweetly and said:

'That's all right, Beatrice, it doesn't matter.'

Beatrice left the room. Emily took a small local time-table out of her handbag and consulted it.

'Leave Exeter, St David's, three ten,' she murmured, 'arrive Exhampton, three forty-two. Time allowed for going to brother's house and murdering him – how beastly and cold-blooded it sounds – and such nonsense too – say half an hour to three quarters. What are the trains back? There's one at four twenty-five and there's one Mr Dacres mentioned at six ten, that gets in at twenty-three minutes to seven. Yes, it's actually possible either way. It's a pity there's nothing to suspect the nurse for. She was out all the afternoon and nobody knows where she was. Of course, I don't really believe anybody in this house murdered Captain Trevelyan, but in a way it's comforting to know that they could have. Hello – there's the front door.'

There was a murmur of voices in the hall and the door opened and Jennifer Gardner came into the room.

'I'm Emily Trefusis,' said Emily. 'You know – the one who is engaged to Jim Pearson.'

'So you are Emily,' said Mrs Gardner shaking hands. 'Well, this is a surprise.'

Suddenly Emily felt very weak and small. Rather like a little girl in the act of doing something very silly. An extraordinary person, Aunt Jennifer. Character – that was what it was. Aunt Jennifer had about enough character for two and three quarter people instead of one.

'Have you had tea, my dear? No? Then we'll have it here. Just a moment – I must go up and see Robert first.'

A strange expression flitted over her face as she mentioned her husband's name. The hard, beautiful voice softened. It was like a light over dark ripples of water.

'She adores him,' thought Emily, left alone in the drawing-room. 'All the same there's something frightening about Aunt Jennifer. I wonder if Uncle Robert likes being adored quite as much as that.'

When Jennifer Gardner returned, she had taken off her hat.

Emily admired the smooth sweep of the hair back from her forehead.

'Do you want to talk about things, Emily, or don't you? If you don't I shall quite understand.'

'It isn't much good talking about them, is it?'

'We can only hope,' said Mrs Gardner, 'that they will find the real murderer quickly. Just press the bell, will you, Emily? I'll send nurse's tea up to her. I don't want her chattering down here. How I hate hospital nurses.'

'Is she a good one?'

'I suppose she is. Robert says she is anyway. I dislike her intensely and always have. But Robert says she's far and away the best nurse we've had.'

'She's rather good-looking,' said Emily.

'Nonsense. With her ugly beefy hands?'

Emily watched her aunt's long white fingers as they touched the milk jug and the sugar tongs.

Beatrice came, took the cup of tea and a plate of eatables and left the room.

'Robert has been very upset over all this,' said Mrs Gardner. 'He works himself into such curious states. I suppose it's all part of his illness really.'

'He didn't know Captain Trevelyan well, did he?'

Jennifer Gardner shook her head.

'He neither knew him nor cared about him. To be honest, I myself can't pretend any great sorrow over his death. He was a cruel grasping man, Emily. He knew the struggle we have had. The poverty! He knew that a loan of money at the right time might have given Robert special treatment that would have made all the difference. Well, retribution has overtaken him.'

She spoke in a deep brooding voice.

'What a strange woman she is,' thought Emily. 'Beautiful and terrible, like something out of a Greek play.'

'It may still not be too late,' said Mrs Gardner. 'I wrote to the lawyers at Exhampton today, to ask them if I could have a certain sum of money in advance. The treatment I am speaking of is in some respects what they would call a quack remedy, but it has been successful in a large number of cases. Emily – how wonderful it will be if Robert is able to walk again.'

Her face was glowing, lit up as though by a lamp.

Emily was tired. She had had a long day, little or nothing to eat, and she was worn out by suppressed emotion. The room kept going away and coming back again.

'Aren't you feeling well, dear?'

'It's all right,' gasped Emily, and to her own surprise, annoyance and humiliation burst into tears.

Mrs Gardner did not attempt to rise and console her, for which Emily was grateful. She just sat silently until Emily's tears should subside. She murmured in a thoughtful voice:

'Poor child. It's very unlucky that Jim Pearson should have been arrested – very unlucky. I wish – something could be done about it.'

CHAPTER 21

CONVERSATIONS

Left to his own devices Charles Enderby did not relax his efforts. To familiarize himself with life as lived in Sittaford village he had only to turn on Mrs Curtis much as you would turn on the tap of a hydrant. Listening slightly dazed to a stream of anecdote, reminiscence, rumours, surmise and meticulous detail he endeavoured valiantly to sift the grain from the chaff. He then mentioned another name and immediately the force of the water was directed in that direction. He heard all about Captain Wyatt, his tropical temper, his rudeness, his quarrels with his neighbours, his occasional amazing graciousness, usually to personable young women. The life he led his Indian servant, the peculiar times he had his meals and the exact diet that composed them. He heard about Mr Rycroft's library, his hair tonics, his insistence on strict tidiness and punctuality, his inordinate curiosity over other people's doings, his recent selling of a few old prized personal possessions, his inexplicable fondness for birds, and the prevalent idea that Mrs Willett was setting her cap at him. He heard about Miss Percehouse and her tongue and the way she bullied her nephew, and of the rumours of the gay life that same nephew led in London. He heard all over again of Major Burnaby's friendship with Captain Trevelyan, their reminiscences of the past and their fondness for chess. He heard everything that was known about the Willetts, including the belief that Miss Violet Willett was leading on Mr Ronnie Garfield and that she didn't really mean to have him. It was hinted that she made mysterious excursions to the moor and that she had been seen walking there with a young man. And it was doubtless for that reason, so Mrs Curtis had surmised, that they had come to this desolate spot. Her mother had taken her right away, 'to get right over it like'. But there – 'girls can be far more artful than ladies ever dream of'. About Mr Duke, there was curiously little to hear. He had been there only a short time and his activities seemed to be solely horticultural.

It was half past three, and, with his head spinning from the effects of Mrs Curtis's conversation, Mr Enderby went out for a stroll. His intention was to cultivate the acquaintance of Miss Percehouse's nephew more closely. Prudent reconnaissance in the neighbourhood of Miss Percehouse's cottage proved unavailing, but by a stroke of good fortune he ran into that young man just as he was emerging disconsolately from the gates of Sittaford House. He had all the appearance of having been sent away with a flea in his ear.

'Hello,' said Charles. 'I say, isn't that Captain Trevelyan's house?'

'That's right,' said Ronnie.

'I was hoping to get a snapshot of it this morning. For my paper, you know,' he added. 'But this weather is hopeless for photography.'

Ronnie accepted this statement in all good faith without reflecting that if photography was only possible on days of brilliant sunshine, the pictures appearing in the daily papers would be few.

'It must be a very interesting job – yours,' he said.

'A dog's life,' said Charles faithful to the convention of never showing enthusiasm about one's work. He looked over his shoulder at Sittaford House. 'Rather a gloomy place I should imagine.'

'No end of a difference there since the Willetts moved in,' said Ronnie. 'I was down here last year about the same time, and really you would hardly take it for the same place, and yet, I don't know quite what they have done. Moved the furniture about a bit, I suppose, got cushions and things of that sort about. It's been a godsend to me their being there, I can tell you.'

'Can't be a very jolly spot as a rule, I suppose,' said Charles.

'Jolly? If I lived here a fortnight I should pass out altogether. How my aunt manages to cling on to life in the way she does beats me. You haven't seen her cats, have you? I had to comb one of them this morning and look at the way the brute scratched me.' He held out a hand and an arm for inspection.

'Rather rough luck,' said Charles.

'I should say it was. I say, are you doing any sleuthing? If so, can I help? Be the Watson to your Sherlock, or anything of that kind?'

'Any clues in Sittaford House?' inquired Charles casually. 'I mean did Captain Trevelyan leave any of his things there?'

'I don't think so. My aunt was saying he moved lock, stock and barrel. Took his elephant's trotters and his hippopotamus's toothy pegs and all the sporting rifles and what nots.'

'Almost as though he didn't mean to come back,' said Charles.

'I say – that's an idea. You don't think it was suicide, do you?'

'A man who can hit himself correctly on the back of the head with a sandbag would be something of an artist in the suicide world,' said Charles.

'Yes, I thought there wasn't much in that idea. Looks as if he had a premonition though,' Ronnie's face brightened. 'Look here, what about this? Enemies on his track, he knows they're coming, so he clears out and passes the buck, as it were, to the Willetts.'

'The Willetts were a bit of a miracle by themselves,' said Charles.

'Yes, I can't make it out. Fancy planting yourself down here in the country like this. Violet doesn't seem to mind – actually says she likes it. I don't know what's the matter with her today. I suppose it's the domestic trouble. I can't think why women worry so about servants. If they cut up nasty, just push them out.'

'That's just what they have done, isn't it?' said Charles.

'Yes, I know. But they are in a great stew about it all. Mother lying down with screaming hysterics or something and daughter snapping like a turtle. Fairly pushed me out just now.'

'They haven't had the police here, have they?'

Ronnie stared.

'The police, no, why would they?'

'Well, I wondered. Seeing Inspector Narracott in Sittaford this morning.'

Ronnie dropped his stick with a clatter and stooped to pick it up.

'Who did you say was in Sittaford this morning – Inspector Narracott?'

'Yes.'

'Is he – is he the man in charge of the Trevelyan case?'

'That's right.'

'What was he doing in Sittaford? Where did you see him?'

'Oh, I suppose he was just nosing about,' said Charles, 'checking up Captain Trevelyan's past life so to speak.'

'You think that's all?'

'I suppose so.'

'He doesn't think anyone in Sittaford had anything to do with it?'

'That would be very unlikely, wouldn't it?'

'Oh, frightfully. But then you know what the police are – always butting in on the wrong tack. At least that's what it says in detective novels.'

'I think they are really rather an intelligent body of men,' said Charles. 'Of course, the Press does a lot to help them,' he added. 'But if you really read a case carefully it's amazing the way they track down murderers with practically no evidence to go on.'

'Oh – well – it's nice to know that, isn't it? They have certainly got on to this man Pearson pretty quick. It seems a pretty clear case.'

'Crystal clear,' said Charles. 'A good thing it wasn't you or me, eh? Well, I must be sending off a few wires. They don't seem very used to telegrams in this place. If you send more than half a crown's worth at one go they seem to think you are an escaped lunatic.'

Charles sent his telegrams, bought a packet of cigarettes, a few doubtful-looking bull's eyes and two very aged paper-backed novelettes. He then returned to the cottage, threw himself on his bed and slept peacefully, blissfully unaware that he and his affairs, particularly Miss Emily Trefusis, were being discussed in various places all around him.

It is fairly safe to say that there were only three topics of conversation at present in Sittaford. One was the murder, one was the escape of the convict, and the other was Miss Emily Trefusis and her cousin. Indeed at a certain moment, four separate conversations were going on with her as their main theme.

Conversation No. 1 was at Sittaford House, where Violet Willett and her mother had just washed up their own tea things owing to the domestic retreat.

'It was Mrs Curtis who told me,' said Violet.

She still looked pale and wan.

'It's almost a disease the way that woman talks,' said her mother.

'I know. It seems the girl is actually stopping there with a cousin or something. She did mention this morning that she was at Mrs Curtis's, but I thought that that was simply because Miss Percehouse hadn't room for her. And now it seems that she'd never even seen Miss Percehouse till this morning!'

'I dislike that woman intensely,' said Mrs Willett.

'Mrs Curtis?'

'No, no, the Percehouse woman. That kind of woman is dangerous. They live for what they can find out about other people. Sending that girl along here for a recipe for coffee cake! I'd like to have sent her a poisoned cake. That would have stopped her interfering for good and all!'

'I suppose I ought to have realized –' began Violet. But her mother interrupted her.

'How could you, my dear! And anyway what harm is done?'

'Why do you think she came here?'

'I don't suppose she had anything definite in mind. She was just spying out the land. Is Mrs Curtis sure about her being engaged to Jim Pearson?'

'That girl told Mr Rycroft so, I believe. Mrs Curtis said she suspected it from the first.'

'Well, then the whole thing's natural enough. She's just looking about aimlessly for something that might help.'

'You didn't see her, Mother,' said Violet. 'She isn't aimless.'

'I wish I had seen her,' said Mrs Willett. 'But my nerves were all to pieces this morning. Reaction, I suppose, after that interview with the police inspector yesterday.'

'You were wonderful, Mother. If only I hadn't been such an utter fool – to go and faint. Oh! I'm ashamed of myself for giving the whole show away. And there were you perfectly calm and collected – not turning a hair.'

'I'm in pretty good training,' said Mrs Willett in a hard dry voice. 'If you'd been through what I've been through – but there, I hope you never will, my child. I trust and believe that you've got a happy, peaceful life ahead of you.'

Violet shook her head.

'I'm afraid – I'm afraid –'

'Nonsense – and as for saying you gave the show away by fainting yesterday – nothing of the kind. Don't worry.'

'But that Inspector – he's bound to think –'

'That it was the mention of Jim Pearson made you faint? Yes – he'll think that all right. He's no fool, that Inspector Narracott. But what if he does? He'll suspect a connection – and he'll look for it – *and he won't find it.*'

'You think not?'

'Of course not! How can he? Trust me, Violet dear. That's cast-iron certainty and, in a way, perhaps that faint of yours was a lucky happening. We'll think so anyway.'

Conversation No. 2 was in Major Burnaby's cottage. It was a somewhat one-sided one, the brunt of it being borne by Mrs Curtis, who had been poised for departure for the last half hour, having dropped in to collect Major Burnaby's laundry.

'Like my Great Aunt Sarah's Belinda, that's what I said to Curtis this morning,' said Mrs Curtis triumphantly. 'A deep one – and one that can twist all the men round her little finger.'

A great grunt from Major Burnaby.

'Engaged to one young man and carrying on with another,' said Mrs Curtis. 'That's my Great Aunt Sarah's Belinda all over. And not for the fun of it, mark you. It's not just flightiness – she's a deep one. And now young Mr Garfield – she'll have him roped in before you can say knife. Never have I seen a young gentleman look more like a sheep than he did this morning – and that's a sure sign.'

She paused for breath.

'Well, well,' said Major Burnaby. 'Don't let me keep you, Mrs Curtis.'

'Curtis will be wanting his tea and that's a fact,' said Mrs Curtis without moving. 'I was never one to stand about gossiping. Get on with your job – that's what I say. And talking about jobs, what do you say, sir, to a good turn out?'

'No!' said Major Burnaby with force.

'It's a month since it's been done.'

'No. I like to know where to lay my hand on everything. After one of these turn outs nothing's ever put back in its place.'

Mrs Curtis sighed. She was an impassioned cleaner and turner out.

'It's Captain Wyatt as could do with a spring cleaning,' she observed. 'That nasty native of his – what does he know about cleaning, I should like to know? Nasty black fellow.'

'Nothing better than a native servant,' said Major Burnaby. 'They know their job and they don't talk.'

Any hint the last sentence might have contained was lost on Mrs Curtis. Her mind had reverted to a former topic.

'Two telegrams she got – two arriving in half an hour. Gave me quite a turn it did. But she read them as cool as anything. And then she told me she was going to Exeter and wouldn't be back till tomorrow.'

'Did she take her young man with her?' inquired the Major with a gleam of hope.

'No, he's still here. A pleasant spoken young gentleman. He and she'd make a nice pair.'

Grunt from Major Burnaby.

'Well,' said Mrs Curtis. 'I'll be getting along.'

The Major hardly dared breathe for fear he might distract her from her purpose. But this time Mrs Curtis was as good as her word. The door closed behind her.

With a sigh of relief the Major drew forth a pipe and began to peruse a prospectus of a certain mine which was couched in terms so blatantly optimistic that it would have aroused suspicion in any heart but that of a widow or a retired soldier.

'Twelve per cent,' murmured Major Burnaby. 'That sounds pretty good . . .'

Next door Captain Wyatt was laying down the law to Mr Rycroft.

'Fellows like you,' he said, 'don't know anything of the world. You've never lived. You've never roughed it.'

Mr Rycroft said nothing. It was so difficult not to say the wrong thing to Captain Wyatt that it was usually safer not to reply at all.

The Captain leaned over the side of his invalid chair.

'Where's that bitch got to? Nice-looking girl,' he added.

The association of ideas in his mind was quite natural. It was less so to Mr Rycroft, who looked at him in a scandalized fashion.

'What's she doing here? That's what I want to know?' demanded Captain Wyatt. 'Abdul!'

'Sahib?'

'Where's Bully? Has she got out again?'

'She in kitchen, Sahib.'

'Well, don't feed her.' He sank back in his chair again and proceeded on his second tack. 'What does she want here? Who's she going to talk to in a place like this? All you old fogies will bore her stiff. I had a word with her this morning. Expect she was surprised to find a man like me in a place like this.'

He twisted his moustache.

'She's James Pearson's fiancée,' said Mr Rycroft. 'You know – the man who has been arrested for Trevelyan's murder.'

Wyatt dropped a glass of whisky he was just raising to his lips with a crash upon the floor. He immediately roared for Abdul and cursed him in no measured terms for not placing a table at a convenient angle to his chair. He then resumed the conversation.

'So that's who she is. Too good for a counter-jumper like that. A girl like that wants a real man.'

'Young Pearson is very good-looking,' said Mr Rycroft.

'Good-looking – good-looking – a girl doesn't want a barber's block. What does that sort of young man who works in an office every day know of life? What experience has he had of reality?'

'Perhaps the experience of being tried for murder will be sufficient reality to last him for some time,' said Mr Rycroft dryly.

'Police sure he did it, eh?'

'They must be fairly sure or they wouldn't have arrested him.'

'Country bumpkins,' said Captain Wyatt contemptuously.

'Not quite,' said Mr Rycroft. 'Inspector Narracott struck me this morning as an able and efficient man.'

'Where did you see him this morning?'

'He called at my house.'

'He didn't call at mine,' said Captain Wyatt in an injured fashion.

'Well, you weren't a close friend of Trevelyan's or anything like that.'

'I don't know what you mean. Trevelyan was a skinflint and I told him so to his face. He couldn't come bossing it over me. I didn't kowtow to him like the rest of the people here. Always dropping in – dropping in – too much dropping in. If I don't choose to see anyone for a week, or a month, or a year, that's my business.'

'You haven't seen anyone for a week now, have you?' said Mr Rycroft.

'No, and why should I?' The irate invalid banged the table. Mr Rycroft was aware, as usual, of having said the wrong thing. 'Why the bloody hell should I? Tell me that?'

Mr Rycroft was prudently silent. The Captain's wrath subsided.

'All the same,' he growled, 'if the police want to know about Trevelyan I'm the man they should have come to. I've knocked about the world, and I've got judgment. I can size a man up for what he's worth. What's the good of going to a lot of dodderers and old women? What they want is a *man's* judgment.'

He banged the table again.

'Well,' said Mr Rycroft, 'I suppose they think they know themselves what they are after.'

'They inquired about me,' said Captain Wyatt. 'They would naturally.'

'Well – er – I don't quite remember,' said Mr Rycroft cautiously.

'Why can't you remember? You're not in your dotage yet.'

'I expect I was – er – rattled,' said Mr Rycroft soothingly.

'Rattled, were you? Afraid of the police? I'm not afraid of the police. Let 'em come here. That's what I say. I'll show them. Do you know I shot a cat at a hundred yards the other night?'

'Did you?' said Mr Rycroft.

The Captain's habit of letting off a revolver at real or imaginary cats was a sore trial to his neighbours.

'Well, I'm tired,' said Captain Wyatt suddenly. 'Have another drink before you go?'

Rightly interpreting this hint, Mr Rycroft rose to his feet. Captain Wyatt continued to urge a drink upon him.

'You'd be twice the man if you drank a bit more. A man who can't enjoy a drink isn't a man at all.'

But Mr Rycroft continued to decline the offer. He had already consumed one whisky and soda of most unusual strength.

'What tea do you drink?' asked Wyatt. 'I don't know anything about tea. Told Abdul to get some. Thought that girl might like to come in to tea one day. Darned pretty girl. Must do something for her. She must be bored to death in a place like this with no one to talk to.'

'There's a young man with her,' said Mr Rycroft.

'The young men of the present day make me sick,' said Captain Wyatt. 'What's the good of them?'

This being a difficult query to answer suitably, Mr Rycroft did not attempt it, he took his departure.

The bull terrier bitch accompanied him to the gate and caused him acute alarm.

In No. 4 The Cottages, Miss Percehouse was speaking to her nephew, Ronald.

'If you like to moon about after a girl who doesn't want you, that is your affair, Ronald,' she was saying. 'Better stick to the Willett girl. You may have a chance there, though I think it is extremely unlikely.'

'Oh, I say,' protested Ronnie.

'The other thing I have to say is, that if there was a police officer in Sittaford I should have been informed of it. Who knows, I might have been able to give him valuable information.'

'I didn't know about it myself till after he had gone.'

'That is so like you, Ronnie. Absolutely typical.'

'Sorry, Aunt Caroline.'

'And when you are painting the garden furniture, there is no need to paint your face as well. It doesn't improve it and it wastes the paint.'

'Sorry, Aunt Caroline.'

'And now,' said Miss Percehouse closing her eyes, 'don't argue with me any more. I'm tired.'

Ronnie shuffled his feet and looked uncomfortable.

'Well?' said Miss Percehouse sharply.

'Oh! nothing – only –'

'Yes?'

'Well, I was wondering if you'd mind if I blew in to Exeter tomorrow.'

'Why?'

'Well, I want to meet a fellow there.'

'What kind of a fellow?'

'Oh! just a fellow.'

'If a young man wishes to tell lies, he should do so well,' said Miss Percehouse.

'Oh! I say – but –'

'Don't apologize.'

'It's all right then? I can go?'

'I don't know what you mean by saying, "I can go?" as though you were a small child. You are over twenty-one.'

'Yes, but what I mean is, I don't want –'

Miss Percehouse closed her eyes again.

'I have asked you once before not to argue. I am tired and wish to rest. If the "fellow" you are meeting in Exeter wears skirts and is called Emily Trefusis, more fool you – that is all I have to say.'

'But look here –'

'I am tired, Ronald. That's enough.'

CHAPTER 22

NOCTURNAL ADVENTURES OF CHARLES

Charles was not looking forward with any relish to the prospect of his night's vigil. He privately considered that it was likely to be a wild goose chase. Emily, he considered, was possessed of a too vivid imagination.

He was convinced that she had read into the few words she had overheard a meaning that had its origin in her own brain. Probably sheer weariness had induced Mrs Willett to yearn for night to come.

Charles looked out of his window and shivered. It was a piercingly cold night, raw and foggy – the last night one would wish to spend in the open hanging about and waiting for something, very nebulous in nature, to happen.

Still he dared not yield to his intense desire to remain comfortably indoors. He recalled the liquid melodiousness of Emily's voice as she said, 'It's wonderful to have someone you can really rely on.'

She relied on him, Charles, and she should not rely in vain. What? Fail that beautiful, helpless girl? Never.

Besides, he reflected as he donned all the spare underclothes he possessed before encasing himself in two pullovers and his overcoat, things were likely to be deucedly unpleasant if Emily on her return found out that he had not carried out his promise.

She would probably say the most unpleasant things. No, he couldn't risk it. But as for anything happening –

And anyway, when and how was it going to happen? He couldn't be everywhere at once. Probably whatever was going to happen would happen inside Sittaford House and he would never know a thing about it.

'Just like a girl,' he grumbled to himself, 'waltzing off to Exeter and leaving me to do the dirty work.'

And then he remembered once more the liquid tones of Emily's voice as she expressed her reliance on him, and he felt ashamed of his outburst.

He completed his toilet, rather after the model of Tweedledee, and effected a surreptitious exit from the cottage.

The night was even colder and more unpleasant than he had thought. Did Emily realize all he was about to suffer on her behalf? He hoped so.

His hand went tenderly to a pocket and caressed a hidden flask concealed in a near pocket.

'The boy's best friend,' he murmured. 'It *would* be a night like this of course.'

With suitable precautions he introduced himself into the

grounds of Sittaford House. The Willetts kept no dog, so there was no fear of alarm from that quarter. A light in the gardener's cottage showed that it was inhabited. Sittaford House itself was in darkness save for one lighted window on the first floor.

'Those two women are alone in the house,' thought Charles. 'I shouldn't care for that myself. A bit creepy!'

He supposed Emily had really overheard that sentence, '*Will tonight never come?*' What did it really mean?

'I wonder,' he thought to himself, 'if they mean to do a flit? Well, whatever happens, little Charles is going to be here to see it.'

He circled the house at a discreet distance. Owing to the foggy nature of the night he had no fears of being observed. Everything as far as he could see appeared to be as usual. A cautious visiting of the outbuildings showed them to be locked.

'I hope something does happen,' said Charles as the hours passed. He took a prudent sip from his flask. 'I've never known anything like this cold. "What did you do in the Great War, Daddy?" can't have been any worse than this.'

He glanced at his watch and was surprised to find that it was still only twenty minutes to twelve. He had been convinced that it must be nearly dawn.

An unexpected sound made him prick up his ears excitedly. It was the sound of a bolt being very gently drawn back in its socket, and it came from the direction of the house. Charles made a noiseless sprint from bush to bush. Yes, he had been quite right, the small side door was slowly opening. A dark figure stood on the threshold. It was peering anxiously out into the night.

'Mrs or Miss Willett,' said Charles to himself. 'The fair Violet, I think.'

After waiting a minute or two, the figure stepped out on the path and closed the door noiselessly behind her and started to walk away from the house in the opposite direction to the front drive. The path in question led up behind Sittaford House, passing through a small plantation of trees and so out on to the open moor.

The path wound quite near the bushes where Charles was concealed, so near that Charles was able to recognize the woman as she passed. He had been quite right, it was Violet Willett.

She was wearing a long dark coat and had a beret on her head.

She went on up, and as quietly as possible Charles followed her. He had no fears of being seen, but he was alive to the danger of being overheard. He was particularly anxious not to alarm the girl. Owing to his care in this respect she outdistanced him. For a moment or two he was afraid lest he should lose her, but as he in his turn wound his way anxiously through the plantation of trees he saw her standing a little way ahead of him. Here the low wall which surrounded the estate was broken by a gate. Violet Willett was standing by this gate, leaning over it peering out into the night.

Charles crept up as near as he dared and waited. The time passed. The girl had a small pocket torch with her and once she switched it on for a moment or two, directing it, Charles thought, to see the time by the wrist watch she was wearing, then she leant over the gate again in the same attitude of expectant interest. Suddenly, Charles heard a low whistle twice repeated.

He saw the girl start to sudden attention. She leant farther over the gate and from her lips came the same signal – a low whistle twice repeated.

Then with startling suddenness a man's figure loomed out of the night. A low exclamation came from the girl. She moved back a pace or two, the gate swung inward and the man joined her. She spoke to him in a low hurried voice. Unable to catch what they said, Charles moved forward somewhat imprudently. A twig snapped beneath his feet. The man swung round instantly.

'What's that?' he said.

He caught sight of Charles's retreating figure.

'Hie, you stop! What are you doing here?'

With a bound he sprang after Charles. Charles turned and tackled him adroitly. The next moment they were rolling over and over together locked in a tight embrace.

The tussle was a short one. Charles's assailant was by far the heavier and stronger of the two. He rose to his feet jerking his captive with him.

'Switch on that light, Violet,' he said, 'let's have a look at this fellow.'

The girl who had been standing terrified a few paces away came forward and switched on the torch obediently.

'It must be the man who is staying in the village,' she said. 'A journalist.'

'A journalist, eh?' exclaimed the other. 'I don't like the breed. What are you doing, you skunk, nosing round private grounds at this time of night?'

The torch wavered in Violet's hand. For the first time Charles was given a full view of his antagonist. For a few minutes he had entertained the wild idea that the visitor might have been the escaped convict. One look at the other dispelled any such fancy. This was a young man not more than twenty-four or -five years of age. Tall, good-looking and determined, with none of the hunted criminal about him.

'Now then,' he said sharply, 'what's your name?'

'My name is Charles Enderby,' said Charles. 'You haven't told me yours,' he continued.

'Confound your cheek!'

A sudden flash of inspiration came to Charles. An inspired guess had saved him more than once. It was a long shot, but he believed that he was right.

'I think, however,' he said quietly, 'that I can guess it.'

'Eh?'

The other was clearly taken aback.

'I think,' said Charles, 'that I have the pleasure of addressing Mr Brian Pearson from Australia. Is that so?'

There was a silence – rather a long silence. Charles had a feeling that the tables were turned.

'How the devil you knew that I can't think,' said the other at last, 'but you're right. My name *is* Brian Pearson.'

'In that case,' said Charles, 'supposing we adjourn to the house and talk things over!'

CHAPTER 23

AT HAZELMOOR

Major Burnaby was doing his accounts or – to use a more Dickens-like phrase – he was looking into his affairs. The Major was an extremely methodical man. In a calf-bound book he kept a record of shares bought, shares sold and the accompanying loss or profit – usually a loss, for in common with most retired army men the Major was attracted by a high rate of interest rather than a modest percentage coupled with safety.

'These oil wells looked all right,' he was muttering. 'Seems as though there ought to have been a fortune in it. Almost as bad as that diamond mine! Canadian land, that ought to be sound now.'

His cogitations were interrupted as the head of Mr Ronald Garfield appeared at the open window.

'Hello,' said Ronnie cheerfully, 'I hope I'm not butting in?'

'If you are coming in go round to the front door,' said Major Burnaby. 'Mind the rock plants. I believe you are standing on them at the moment.'

Ronnie retreated with an apology and presently presented himself at the front door.

'Wipe your feet on the mat, if you don't mind,' cried the Major.

He found young men extremely trying. Indeed, the only young man towards whom he had felt any kindliness for a long time was the journalist, Charles Enderby.

'A nice young chap,' the Major had said to himself. 'And very interested, too, in what I have told him about the Boer War.'

Towards Ronnie Garfield the Major felt no such kindliness. Practically everything that the unfortunate Ronnie said or did managed to rub the Major up the wrong way. Still, hospitality is hospitality.

'Have a drink?' said the Major, loyal to that tradition.

'No thanks. As a matter of fact I just dropped in to see if we couldn't get together. I wanted to go to Exhampton today and I hear Elmer is booked to take you in.'

Burnaby nodded.

'Got to go over Trevelyan's things,' he explained. 'The police have done with the place now.'

'Well, you see,' said Ronnie rather awkwardly, 'I particularly wanted to go into Exhampton today. I thought if we could get together and share and share alike as it were. Eh? What about it?'

'Certainly,' said the Major. 'I am agreeable. Do you a lot more good to walk,' he added. 'Exercise. None of you young chaps nowadays take any exercise. A brisk six miles there and a brisk six miles back would do you all the good in the world. If it weren't that I needed the car to bring some of Trevelyan's things back here, I should be walking myself. Getting soft – that's the curse of the present day.'

'Oh, well,' said Ronnie, 'I don't believe in being strenuous myself. But I'm glad we've settled that all right. Elmer said you were starting at eleven o'clock. Is that right?'

'That's it.'

'Good. I'll be there.'

Ronnie was not quite so good as his word. His idea of being on the spot was to be ten minutes late, and he found Major Burnaby fuming and fretting and not at all inclined to be placated by a careless apology.

'What a fuss old buffers make,' thought Ronnie to himself. 'They have no idea what a curse they are to everybody with their punctuality, and everything done on the dot of the minute, and their cursed exercise and keeping fit.'

His mind played agreeably for a few minutes with the idea of a marriage between Major Burnaby and his aunt. Which, he wondered, would get the better of it? He thought his aunt every time. Rather amusing to think of her clapping her hands and uttering piercing cries to summon the Major to her side.

Banishing these reflections from his mind he proceeded to enter into cheerful conversation.

'Sittaford has become a pretty gay spot – what? Miss Trefusis and this chap Enderby and the lad from Australia – by the way, when did he blow in? There he was as large as life this morning and nobody knew where he had come from. It's been worrying my aunt blue in the face.'

'He is staying with the Willetts,' said Major Burnaby tartly.

'Yes, but where did he blow in from? Even the Willetts haven't got a private aerodrome. You know, I think there's something deuced mysterious about this lad Pearson. He's got what I call a nasty gleam in his eye – a very nasty glint. It's my impression that he's the chap who did in poor old Trevelyan.'

The Major made no reply.

'The way I look at it is this,' continued Ronnie, 'fellows that go off to the Colonies are usually bad hats. Their relations don't like them and push them out there for that reason. Very well then – there you are. The bad hat comes back, short of money, visits wealthy uncle in the neighbourhood of Christmas time, wealthy relative won't cough up to impecunious nephew – and impecunious nephew bats him one. That's what I call a theory.'

'You should mention it to the police,' said Major Burnaby.

'I thought you might do that,' said Mr Garfield. 'You're Narracott's little pal, aren't you? By the way he hasn't been nosing about Sittaford again, has he?'

'Not that I know about.'

'Not meeting you at the house today, is he?'

The shortness of the Major's answers seemed to strike Ronnie at last.

'Well,' he said vaguely, 'that's that,' and relapsed into a thoughtful silence.

At Exhampton the car drew up outside the Three Crowns. Ronnie alighted and after arranging with the Major that they would rendezvous there at half past four for the return journey, he strode off in the direction of such shops as Exhampton offered.

The Major went first to see Mr Kirkwood. After a brief conversation with him, he took the keys and started off for Hazelmoor.

He had told Evans to meet him there at twelve o'clock, and he found the faithful retainer waiting on the doorstep. With a rather grim face, Major Burnaby inserted the key into the front door and passed into the empty house, Evans at his heels. He had not been in it since the night of the tragedy, and in spite of his iron determination to show no weakness, he gave a slight shiver as he passed the drawing-room.

Evans and the Major worked together in sympathy and silence.

When either of them made a brief remark it was duly appreciated and understood by the other.

'Unpleasant job this, but it has to be done,' said Major Burnaby, and Evans, sorting out socks into neat piles, and counting pyjamas, responded.

'It seems rather unnatural like, but as you say, sir, it's got to be done.'

Evans was deft and efficient at his work. Everything was neatly sorted and arranged and classified in heaps. At one o'clock they repaired to the Three Crowns for a short mid-day meal. When they returned to the house the Major suddenly caught Evans by the arm as the latter closed the front door behind him.

'Hush,' he said. 'Do you hear that footstep overhead? It's – it's in Joe's bedroom.'

'My Gawd, sir. So it is.'

A kind of superstitious terror held them both for a minute, and then, breaking loose from it, and with an angry squaring of the shoulders, the Major strode to the foot of the stairs and shouted in a stentorian voice:

To his intense surprise and annoyance and yet, be it confessed, to his slight relief, Ronnie Garfield appeared at the top of the stairs. He looked embarrassed and sheepish.

'Hello,' he said. 'I have been looking for you.'

'What do you mean, looking for me?'

'Well, I wanted to tell you that I shan't be ready at half past four. I've got to go into Exeter. So don't wait for me. I'll have to get a car up from Exhampton.'

'How did you get into this house?' asked the Major.

'The door was open,' exclaimed Ronnie. 'Naturally I thought you were here.'

The Major turned to Evans sharply.

'Didn't you lock it when you came out?'

'No, sir, I hadn't got the key.'

'Stupid of me,' muttered the Major.

'You don't mind, do you?' said Ronnie. 'I couldn't see anyone downstairs so I went upstairs and had a look round.'

'Of course, it doesn't matter,' snapped the Major, 'you startled me, that's all.'

'Well,' said Ronnie airily. 'I shall be pushing along now. So long.'

The Major grunted. Ronnie came down the stairs.

'I say,' he said boyishly, 'do you mind telling me – er – er – where it happened?'

The Major jerked a thumb in the direction of the drawing-room.

'Oh, may I look inside?'

'If you like,' growled the Major.

Ronnie opened the drawing-room door. He was absent a few minutes and then returned.

The Major had gone up the stairs, but Evans was in the hall. He had the air of a bulldog on guard; his small deep-set eyes watched Ronnie with a somewhat malicious scrutiny.

'I say,' said Ronnie. 'I thought you could never wash out blood stains. I thought, however much you washed them, they always came back. Oh, of course – the old fellow was sandbagged, wasn't he? Stupid of me. It was one of these, wasn't it?' He took up a long narrow bolster that lay against one of the other doors. He weighed it thoughtfully and balanced it in his hand. 'Nice little toy, eh?' He made a few tentative swings with it in the air.

Evans was silent.

'Well,' said Ronnie, realizing that the silence was not a wholly appreciative one, 'I'd better be getting along. I'm afraid I've been a bit tactless, eh?' He jerked his head towards the upper story. 'I forgot about them being such pals and all that. Two of a kind, weren't they? Well, I'm really going now. Sorry if I've said all the wrong things.'

He walked across the hall and out through the front door. Evans stayed impassively in the hall, and only when he had heard the latch of the gate close behind Mr Garfield did he mount the stairs and rejoin Major Burnaby. Without any word or comment he resumed where he had left off, going straight across the room and kneeling down in front of the boot cupboard.

At half past three their task was finished. One trunk of clothes and underclothes was allotted to Evans, and another was strapped up ready to be sent to the Seamen's Orphanage. Papers and bills were packed into an attaché case and Evans was given instructions to see a local firm of removers about the storage of the various sporting trophies and heads, as there was no room for them in Major Burnaby's cottage. Since Hazelmoor was only rented furnished no other questions arose.

When all this was settled Evans cleared his throat nervously once or twice and then said:

'Beg pardon, sir, but – I'll be wanting a job to look after a gentleman, same as I did to look after the Capting.'

'Yes, yes, you can tell anyone to apply to me for a recommendation. That will be quite all right.'

'Begging your pardon, sir, that wasn't quite what I meant. Rebecca and me, sir, we've talked it over and we was wondering if, sir – if maybe you would give us a trial?'

'Oh! but – well – I look after myself as you know. That old what's her name comes in and cleans for me once a day and cooks a few things. That's – er – about all I can afford.'

'It isn't the money that matters so much, sir,' said Evans quickly. 'You see, sir, I was very fond of the Capting and – well, if I could do for you, sir, the same as I did for him, well, it would be almost like the same thing, if you know what I mean.'

The Major cleared his throat and averted his eyes.

'Very decent of you, 'pon my word. I'll – I'll think about it.' And escaping with alacrity he almost bolted down the road. Evans stood looking after him, an understanding smile upon his face.

'Like as two peas, him and the Capting,' he murmured.

And then a puzzled expression came over his face.

'Where can they have got to?' he murmured. 'It's a bit queer that. I must ask Rebecca what she thinks.'

CHAPTER 24
INSPECTOR NARRACOTT DISCUSSES THE CASE

'I am not entirely happy about it, sir,' said Inspector Narracott.

The Chief Constable looked at him inquiringly.

'No,' said Inspector Narracott. 'I'm not nearly as happy about it as I was.'

'You don't think we've got the right man?'

'I'm not satisfied. You see, to start with, everything pointed the one way but now – it's different.'

'The evidence against Pearson remains the same.'

'Yes, but there's a good deal of further evidence come to light, sir. There's the other Pearson – Brian. Feeling that we had no further to look I accepted the statement that he was in Australia. Now, it turns out that he was in England all the time. It seems he arrived back in England two months ago – travelled on the same boat as these Willetts apparently. Looks as though he had got sweet on the girl on the voyage. Anyway, for whatever reason he didn't communicate with any of his family. Neither his sister nor his brother had any idea he was in England. On Thursday of last week he left the Ormsby Hotel in Russell Square and drove to Paddington. From there until Tuesday night, when Enderby ran across him, he refuses to account for his movements in any way.'

'You pointed out to him the gravity of such a course of action?'

'Said he didn't give a damn. He had had nothing to do with the murder and it was up to us to prove he had. The way he had employed his time was his own business and none of ours, and he declined definitely to state where he had been and what he had been doing.'

'Most extraordinary,' said the Chief Constable.

'Yes, sir. It's an extraordinary case. You see, there's no use getting away from the facts, this man's far more the type than the other. There's something incongruous about James Pearson hitting an old man on the head with a sandbag – but in a manner of speaking it might be all in the day's work to Brian Pearson. He's a hot-tempered, high-handed young man – and he profits to exactly the same extent, remember?'

'Yes – he came over with Mr Enderby this morning, very bright and breezy, quite square and above-board, that was his attitude. But it won't wash, sir, it won't wash.'

'H'm – you mean –'

'It isn't borne out by the facts. Why didn't he come forward before? His uncle's death was in the papers Saturday. His brother was arrested Monday. And he doesn't give a sign of life. And he wouldn't have either, if that journalist hadn't run across him in the garden of Sittaford House at midnight last night.'

'What was he doing there? Enderby, I mean?'

'You know what journalists are,' said Narracott, 'always nosing round. They're uncanny.'

'They are a darned nuisance very often,' said the Chief Constable. 'Though they have their uses too.'

'I fancy it was the young lady put him up to it,' said Narracott.

'The young lady?'

'Miss Emily Trefusis.'

'How did she know anything about it?'

'She was up at Sittaford nosing around. And she's what you'd call a sharp young lady. There's not much gets past her.'

'What was Brian Pearson's own account of his movements?'

'Said he came to Sittaford House to see his young lady, Miss Willett, that is. She came out of the house to meet him when everyone was asleep because she didn't want her mother to know about it. That's their story.'

Inspector Narracott's voice expressed distinct disbelief.

'It's my belief, sir, that if Enderby hadn't run him to earth, he never would have come forward. He'd have gone back to Australia and claimed his inheritance from there.'

A faint smile crossed the Chief Constable's lips.

'How he must have cursed these pestilential prying journalists,' he murmured.

'There's something else come to light,' continued the Inspector. 'There are three Pearsons, you remember, and Sylvia Pearson is married to Martin Dering, the novelist. He told me that he lunched and spent the afternoon with an American publisher and went to a literary dinner in the evening, but now it seems that he wasn't at the dinner at all.'

'Who says so?'

'Enderby again.'

'I think I must meet Enderby,' said the Chief Constable. 'He appears to be one of the live wires of this investigation. No doubt about it, the *Daily Wire* does have some bright young men on their staff.'

'Well, of course, that may mean little or nothing,' continued the Inspector. 'Captain Trevelyan was killed before six o'clock, so where Dering spent his evening is really of no consequence – but why should he have deliberately lied about it? I don't like it, sir.'

'No,' agreed the Chief Constable. 'It seems a little unnecessary.'

'It makes one think that the whole thing may be false. It's a far-fetched supposition, I suppose, but Dering *might* have left Paddington by the twelve ten train – arrived at Exhampton some time after five, have killed the old man, got the six ten train and been back home again before midnight. At any rate it's got to be looked into, sir. We've got to investigate his financial position, see if he was desperately hard up. Any money his wife came into he would have the handling of – you've only got to look at her to know that. We've got to make perfectly sure that the afternoon alibi holds water.'

'The whole thing is extraordinary,' commented the Chief Constable. 'But I still think the evidence against Pearson is pretty conclusive. I see that you don't agree with me – you've a feeling you've got hold of the wrong man.'

'The evidence is all right,' admitted Inspector Narracott, 'circumstantial and all that, and any jury ought to convict on it. Still, what you say is true enough – I don't see him as a murderer.'

'And his young lady is very active in the case,' said the Chief Constable.

'Miss Trefusis, yes, she's a one and no mistake. A real fine young lady. And absolutely determined to get him off. She's got hold of that journalist, Enderby, and she's working him for all she's worth. She's a great deal too good for Mr James Pearson. Beyond his good looks I wouldn't say there was much to him in the way of character.'

'But if she's a managing young woman that's what she likes,' said the Chief Constable.

'Ah well,' said Inspector Narracott, 'there's no accounting for tastes. Well, you agree, sir, that I had better take up this alibi of Dering's without any more delay.'

'Yes, get on to it at once. What about the fourth interested party in the will? There's a fourth, isn't there?'

'Yes, the sister. That's perfectly all right. I have made inquiries there. She was at home at six o'clock all right, sir. I'll get right on with the Dering business.'

It was about five hours later that Inspector Narracott found himself once more in the small sitting-room of The Nook. This time Mr Dering was at home. He couldn't be disturbed as he was writing, the maid had said at first, but the Inspector had produced an official card and bade her take it to her master without delay. Whilst waiting he strode up and down the room. His mind was working actively. Every now and then he picked up a small object from a table, looked at it almost unseeingly, and then replaced it. The cigarette box of Australian fiddleback – a present from Brian Pearson possibly. He picked up a rather battered old book. 'Pride and Prejudice.' He opened the cover and saw scrawled on the fly-leaf in rather faded ink the name, Martha Rycroft. Somehow, the name of Rycroft seemed familiar, but he could not for the moment remember why. He was interrupted as the door opened and Martin Dering came into the room.

The novelist was a man of middle height with thick rather heavy chestnut hair. He was good-looking in a somewhat heavy fashion, with lips that were rather full and red.

Inspector Narracott was not prepossessed by his apppearance.

'Good morning, Mr Dering. Sorry to trouble you all here again.'

'Oh, it doesn't matter, Inspector, but really I can't tell you any more than you've been told already.'

'We were led to understand that your brother-in-law, Mr Brian Pearson, was in Australia. Now, we find that he has been in England for the last two months. I might have been given an inkling of that, I think. Your wife distinctly told me that he was in New South Wales.'

'Brian in England!' Dering seemed genuinely astonished. 'I can assure you, Inspector, that I had no knowledge of that fact – nor, I'm sure, had my wife.'

'He has not communicated with you in any way?'

'No, indeed, I know for a fact that Sylvia has twice written him letters to Australia during that time.'

'Oh, well, in that case I apologize, sir. But naturally I thought he would have communicated with his relations and I was a bit sore with you for holding out on me.'

'Well, as I tell you we knew nothing. Have a cigarette, Inspector? By the way, I see you've recaptured your escaped convict.'

'Yes, got him late Tuesday night. Rather bad luck for him the mist coming down. He walked right round in a circle. Did about twenty miles to find himself about half a mile from Princetown at the end of it.'

'Extraordinary how everyone goes round in circles in a fog. Good thing he didn't escape on the Friday. I suppose he would have had this murder put down to him as a certainty.'

'He's a dangerous man. Fremantle Freddy, they used to call him. Robbery with violence, assault – led the most extraordinary double life. Half the time he passed as an educated, respectable wealthy man. I am not at all sure myself that Broadmoor wasn't the place for him. A kind of criminal mania used to come over him from time to time. He would disappear and consort with the lowest characters.'

'I suppose many people don't escape from Princetown?'

'It's well-nigh impossible, sir. But this particular escape was extraordinarily well planned and carried out. We haven't nearly got to the bottom of it yet.'

'Well,' Dering rose and glanced at his watch, 'if there's nothing more, Inspector – I'm afraid I am rather a busy man –'

'Oh, but there *is* something more, Mr Dering. I want to know why you told me that you were at a literary dinner at the Cecil Hotel on Friday night?'

'I – I don't understand you, Inspector.'

'I think you do, sir. You weren't at that dinner, Mr Dering.'

Martin Dering hesitated. His eyes ran uncertainly from the Inspector's face, up to the ceiling, then to the door, and then to his feet.

The Inspector waited calm and stolid.

'Well,' said Martin Dering at last, 'supposing I wasn't. What the hell has that got to do with you? What have my movements, five hours after my uncle was murdered, got to do with you or anyone else?'

'You made a certain statement to us, Mr Dering, and I want that statement verified. Part of it has already proved to be untrue. I've got to check up on the other half. You say you lunched and spent the afternoon with a friend.'

'Yes – my American publisher.'

'His name?'

'Rosenkraun, Edgar Rosenkraun.'

'Ah, and his address?'

'He's left England. He left last Saturday.'

'For New York?'

'Yes.'

'Then he'll be on the sea at the present moment. What boat is he on?'

'I – I really can't remember.'

'You know the line? Was it a Cunard or White Star?'

'I – I really don't remember.'

'Ah well,' said the Inspector, 'we'll cable his firm in New York. They'll know.'

'It was the *Gargantua*,' said Dering sullenly.

'Thank you, Mr Dering, I thought you could remember if you tried. Now, your statement is that you lunched with Mr Rosenkraun and that you spent the afternoon with him. At what time did you leave him?'

'About five o'clock I should say.'

'And then?'

'I decline to state. It's no business of yours. That's all you want surely.'

Inspector Narracott nodded thoughtfully. If Rosenkraun confirmed Dering's statement then any case against Dering must fall to the ground. Whatever his mysterious activities had been that evening could not affect the case.

'What are you going to do?' demanded Dering uneasily.

'Wireless Mr Rosenkraun on board the *Gargantua*.'

'Damn it all,' cried Dering, 'you'll involve me in all sorts of publicity. Look here –'

He went across to his desk, scribbled a few words on a bit of paper, then took it to the Inspector.

'I suppose you've got to do what you're doing,' he said ungraciously, 'but at least you might do it in my way. It's not fair to run a chap in for a lot of trouble.'

On the sheet of paper was written:

Rosenkraun S.S. 'Gargantua.' Please confirm my statement I was with you lunch-time until five o'clock Friday 14th. Martin Dering.

'Have the reply sent straight to you – I don't mind. But don't have it sent to Scotland Yard or a Police Station. You don't know what these Americans are like. Any hint of me being mixed up in a police case and this new contract that I've been discussing will go to the winds. Keep it a private matter, Inspector.'

'I've no objection to that, Mr Dering. All I want is the truth. I'll send this reply paid, the reply to be sent to my private address in Exeter.'

'Thank you, you are a good chap. It's not such easy going earning your living by literature, Inspector. You'll see the answer will be all right. I did tell you a lie about the dinner, but as a matter of fact I had told my wife that that was where I had been, and I thought I might as well stick to the same story to you. Otherwise I would have let myself in for a lot of trouble.'

'If Mr Rosenkraun confirms your statement, Mr Dering, you will have nothing else to fear.'

'An unpleasant character,' the Inspector thought, as he left the house. 'But he seems pretty certain that this American publisher will confirm the truth of his story.'

A sudden remembrance came to the Inspector, as he hopped into the train which would take him back to Devon.

'Rycroft,' he said, 'of course – that's the name of the old gentleman who lives in one of the cottages at Sittaford. A curious coincidence.'

CHAPTER 25

AT DELLER'S CAFÉ

Emily Trefusis and Charles Enderby were seated at a small table in Deller's Café in Exeter. It was half past three, and at that hour there was comparative peace and quiet. A few people were having a quiet cup of tea, but the restaurant on the whole was deserted.

'Well,' said Charles, 'what do you think of him?'

Emily frowned.

'It's difficult,' she said.

After his interview with the police, Brian Pearson had lunched with them. He had been extremely polite to Emily, rather too polite in her opinion.

To that astute girl it seemed a shade unnatural. Here was a young man conducting a clandestine love affair and an officious stranger butts in. Brian Pearson had taken it like a lamb; had fallen in with Charles's suggestion of having a car and driving over to see the police. Why this attitude of meek acquiescence? It seemed to Emily entirely untypical of the natural Brian Pearson as she read his character.

'I'll see you in hell first!' would, she felt sure, have been far more his attitude.

This lamb-like demeanour was suspicious. She tried to convey something of her feelings to Enderby.

'I get you,' said Enderby. 'Our Brian has got something to conceal, therefore he can't be his natural high-handed self.'

'That's it exactly.'

'Do you think he might possibly have killed old Trevelyan?'

'Brian,' said Emily thoughtfully, 'is – well, a person to be reckoned with. He is rather unscrupulous, I should think, and if he wanted anything, I don't think he would let ordinary conventional standards stand in his way. He's not plain tame English.'

'Putting all personal considerations on one side, he's a more likely starter than Jim?' said Enderby.

Emily nodded.

'Much more likely. He would carry a thing through well – because he would never lose his nerve.'

'Honestly, Emily, do you think he did it?'

'I – I don't know. He fulfils the conditions – the only person who does.'

'What do you mean by fulfils the conditions?'

'Well, (1) *Motive*.' She ticked off the items on her fingers. 'The same motive. Twenty thousand pounds. (2) *Opportunity*. Nobody knows where he was on Friday afternoon, and if he was anywhere that he could say – well – surely he would say it? So we assume that he was actually in the neighbourhood of Hazelmoor on Friday.'

'They haven't found anyone who saw him in Exhampton,' Charles pointed out, 'and he's a fairly noticeable person.'

Emily shook her head scornfully.

'He wasn't in Exhampton. Don't you see, Charles, if he

committed the murder; he planned it beforehand. It's only poor innocent Jim who came down like a mug and stayed there. There's Lydford and Chagford or perhaps Exeter. He might have walked over from Lydford – that's a main road and the snow wouldn't have been impassable. It would have been pretty good going.'

'I suppose we ought to make inquiries all round.'

'The police are doing that,' said Emily, 'and they'll do it a lot better than we shall. All public things are much better done by the police. It's private and personal things like listening to Mrs Curtis and picking up a hint from Miss Percehouse and watching the Willetts – that's where we score.'

'Or don't, as the case may be,' said Charles.

'To go back to Brian Pearson fulfilling the conditions,' said Emily. 'We've done two, motive and opportunity, and there's the third – the one that in a way I think is the most important of all.'

'What's that?'

'Well, I have felt from the beginning that we couldn't ignore that queer business of the table-turning. I have tried to look at it as logically and clear-sightedly as possible. There are just three solutions of it. (1) That it was supernatural. Well, of course, that may be so, but personally I am ruling it out. (2) That it was deliberate – someone did it on purpose, but as one can't arrive at any conceivable reason, we can rule that out also. (3) Accidental. Someone gave himself away without meaning to do so – indeed quite against his will. An unconscious piece of self-revelation. If so, someone among those six people either knew definitely that Captain Trevelyan was going to be killed at a certain time that afternoon, or that someone was having an interview with him from which violence might result. None of those six people could have been the actual murderer, but one of them must have been in collusion with the murderer. There's no link between Major Burnaby and anybody else, or Mr Rycroft and anybody else, or Ronald Garfield and anybody else, but when we come to the Willetts it's different. There's a link between Violet Willett and Brian Pearson. Those two are on very intimate terms and that girl was all on the jump after the murder.'

'You think she knew?' said Charles.

'She or her mother – one or other of them.'

'There's one person you haven't mentioned,' said Charles. 'Mr Duke.'

'I know,' said Emily. 'It's queer. He's the one person we know absolutely nothing about. I've tried to see him twice and failed. There seems no connection between him and Captain Trevelyan, or between him and any of Captain Trevelyan's relations, there's absolutely nothing to connect him with the case in any way, and yet –'

'Well?' said Charles Enderby as Emily paused.

'And yet we met Inspector Narracott coming out of his cottage. What does Inspector Narracott know about him that we don't? I wish I knew.'

'You think –'

'Supposing Duke is a suspicious character and the police know it. Supposing Captain Trevelyan had found out something about Duke. He was particular about his tenants, remember, and supposing he was going to tell the police what he knew. And Duke arranges with an accomplice to have him killed. Oh, I know it all sounds dreadfully melodramatic put like that, and yet, after all, something of the kind might be possible.'

'It's an idea certainly,' said Charles slowly.

They were both silent, each one deep in thought.

Suddenly Emily said:

'Do you know that queer feeling you get when somebody is looking at you? I feel now as though someone's eyes were burning the back of my neck. Is it all fancy or is there really someone staring at me now?'

Charles moved his chair an inch or two and looked round the café in a casual manner.

'There's a woman at a table in the window,' he reported. 'Tall, dark and handsome. She's staring at you.'

'Young?'

'No, not very young. Hello!'

'What is it?'

'Ronnie Garfield. He has just come in and he's shaking hands with her and he's sitting down at her table. I think she's saying something about us.'

Emily opened her handbag. Rather ostentatiously she powdered her nose, adjusting the small pocket mirror to a convenient angle.

'It's Aunt Jennifer,' she said softly. 'They are getting up.'

'They are going,' said Charles. 'Do you want to speak to her?'

'No,' said Emily. 'I think it's better for me to pretend that I haven't seen her.'

'After all,' said Charles, 'why shouldn't Aunt Jennifer know Ronnie Garfield and ask him to tea?'

'Why should she?' said Emily.

'Why shouldn't she?'

'Oh, for goodness sake, Charles, don't let's go on and on like this, *should – shouldn't – should – shouldn't*. Of course it's all nonsense, and it doesn't mean anything! But we *were* just saying that nobody else at that *séance* had any relation with the family, and not five minutes later we see Ronnie Garfield having tea with Captain Trevelyan's sister.'

'It shows,' said Charles, 'that you never know.'

'It shows,' said Emily, 'that you are always having to begin again.'

'In more ways than one,' said Charles.

Emily looked at him.

'What do you mean?'

'Nothing at present,' said Charles.

He put his hand over hers. She did not draw it away.

'We've got to put this through,' said Charles. 'Afterwards –'

'Afterwards?' said Emily softly.

'I'd do anything for you, Emily,' said Charles. 'Simply anything –'

'Would you?' said Emily. 'That's rather nice of you, Charles dear.'

CHAPTER 26
ROBERT GARDNER

It was just twenty minutes later when Emily rang the front door bell of The Laurels. It had been a sudden impulse.

Aunt Jennifer, she knew, would be still at Deller's with Ronnie

Garfield. She smiled beamingly on Beatrice when the latter opened the door to her.

'It's me again,' said Emily. 'Mrs Gardner's out, I know, but can I see Mr Gardner?'

Such a request was clearly unusual. Beatrice seemed doubtful.

'Well, I don't know. I'll go up and see, shall I?'

'Yes, do,' said Emily.

Beatrice went upstairs, leaving Emily alone in the hall. She returned in a few minutes to ask the young lady to please step this way.

Robert Gardner was lying on a couch by the window in a big room on the first floor. He was a big man, blue-eyed and fair-haired. He looked, Emily thought, as Tristan ought to look in the third act of *Tristan and Isolde* and as no Wagnerian tenor has ever looked yet.

'Hello,' he said. 'You are the criminal's spouse to be, aren't you?'

'That's right, Uncle Robert,' said Emily. 'I suppose I *do* call you Uncle Robert, don't I?' she asked.

'If Jennifer will allow it. What's it like having a young man languishing in prison?'

A cruel man, Emily decided. A man who would take a malicious joy in giving you sharp digs in painful places. But she was a match for him. She said smilingly:

'Very thrilling.'

'Not so thrilling for Master Jim, eh?'

'Oh, well,' said Emily, 'it's an experience, isn't it?'

'Teach him life can't be all beer and skittles,' said Robert Gardner maliciously. 'Too young to fight in the Great War, wasn't he? Able to live soft and take it easily. Well, well . . . He got it in the neck from another source.'

He looked at her curiously.

'What did you want to come and see me for, eh?'

There was a tinge of something like suspicion in his voice.

'If you are going to marry into a family it's just as well to see all your relations-in-law beforehand.'

'Know the worst before it's too late. So you really think you are going to marry young Jim, eh?'

'Why not?'

'In spite of this murder charge?'

'In spite of this murder charge.'

'Well,' said Robert Gardner, 'I have never seen anybody less cast down. Anyone would think you were enjoying yourself.'

'I am. Tracking down a murderer is frightfully thrilling,' said Emily.

'Eh?'

'I said tracking down a murderer is frightfully thrilling,' said Emily.

Robert Gardner stared at her, then he threw himself back on his pillows.

'I am tired,' he said in a fretful voice. 'I can't talk any more. Nurse, where's Nurse? Nurse, I'm tired.'

Nurse Davis had come swiftly at his call from an adjoining room. 'Mr Gardner gets tired very easily. I think you had better go now if you don't mind, Miss Trefusis.'

Emily rose to her feet. She nodded brightly and said:

'Good-bye, Uncle Robert. Perhaps I'll come back some day.'

'What do you mean?'

'Au revoir,' said Emily.

She was going out of the front door when she stopped.

'Oh!' she said to Beatrice. 'I have left my gloves.'

'I will get them, Miss.'

'Oh, no,' said Emily. 'I'll do it.' She ran lightly up the stairs and entered without knocking.

'Oh,' said Emily. 'I beg your pardon. I am so sorry. It was my gloves.' She took them up ostentatiously, and smiling sweetly at the two occupants of the room who were sitting hand in hand ran down the stairs and out of the house.

'This glove leaving is a terrific scheme,' said Emily to herself. 'This is the second time it's come off. Poor Aunt Jennifer, does she know, I wonder? Probably not. I must hurry or I'll keep Charles waiting.'

Enderby was waiting in Elmer's Ford at the agreed rendezvous.

'Any luck?' he asked as he tucked the rug round her.

'In a way, yes. I'm not sure.'

Enderby looked at her inquiringly.

'No,' said Emily in answer to his glance, 'I'm not going to tell you about it. You see, it may have nothing whatever to do with it – and if so, it wouldn't be fair.'

Enderby sighed.

'I call that hard,' he observed.

'I'm sorry,' said Emily firmly. 'But there it is.'

'Have it your own way,' said Charles coldly.

They drove on in silence – an offended silence on Charles's part – an oblivious one on Emily's.

They were nearly at Exhampton when she broke the silence by a totally unexpected remark.

'Charles,' she said, 'are you a bridge player?'

'Yes, I am. Why?'

'I was thinking. You know what they tell you to do when you're assessing the value of your hand? If you're defending – count the winners – but if you're attacking count the losers. Now, we're attacking in this business of ours – but perhaps we have been doing it the wrong way.'

'How do you mean?'

'Well, we've been counting the winners, haven't we? I mean going over the people who *could* have killed Captain Trevelyan, however improbable it seems. And that's perhaps why we've got so terribly muddled.'

'I haven't got muddled,' said Charles.

'Well, I have then. I'm so muddled I can't think at all. Let's look at it the other way round. Let's count the losers – the people who can't possibly have killed Captain Trevelyan.'

'Well, let's see –' Enderby reflected. 'To begin with there's the Willetts and Burnaby and Rycroft and Ronnie – Oh! and Duke.'

'Yes,' agreed Emily. 'We know none of them can have killed him. Because at the time he was killed they were all at Sittaford House and they all saw each other and they can't all be lying. Yes, they're all out of it.'

'As a matter of fact everyone in Sittaford is out of it,' said Enderby. 'Even Elmer,' he lowered his voice in deference to the possibility of the driver hearing him. 'Because the road to Sittaford was impassable for cars on Friday.'

'He could have walked,' said Emily in an equally low voice. 'If Major Burnaby could have got there that evening Elmer could have started at lunch time – got to Exhampton at five, murdered him, and walked back again.'

Enderby shook his head.

'I don't think he could have walked back again. Remember the snow started to fall about half past six. Anyway, you're not accusing Elmer, are you?'

'No,' said Emily, 'though, of course, he might be a homicidal maniac.'

'Hush,' said Charles. 'You'll hurt his feelings if he hears you.'

'At any rate,' said Emily, 'you can't say definitely that he couldn't have murdered Captain Trevelyan.'

'Almost,' said Charles. 'He couldn't walk to Exhampton and back without all Sittaford knowing about it and saying it was queer.'

'It certainly is a place where everyone knows everything,' agreed Emily.

'Exactly,' said Charles, 'and that's why I say that everyone in Sittaford is out of it. The only ones that weren't at the Willetts – Miss Percehouse and Captain Wyatt are invalids. They couldn't go ploughing through snowstorms. And dear old Curtis and Mrs C. If any of them did it, they must have gone comfortably to Exhampton for the week-end and come back when it was all over.'

Emily laughed.

'You couldn't be absent from Sittaford for the week-end without its being noticed, certainly,' she said.

'Curtis would notice the silence if Mrs C was,' said Enderby.

'Of course,' said Emily, 'the person it ought to be is Abdul. It would be in a book. He'd be a Lascar really, and Captain Trevelyan would have thrown his favourite brother overboard in a mutiny – something like that.'

'I decline to believe,' said Charles, 'that that wretched depressed-looking native ever murdered anybody.'

'I know,' he said suddenly.

'What?' said Emily eagerly.

'The blacksmith's wife. The one who's expecting her eighth. The intrepid woman despite her condition walked all the way to Exhampton and batted him one with the sandbag.'

'And why, pray?'

'Because, of course, although the blacksmith was the father of the preceding seven, Captain Trevelyan was the father of her coming che-ild.'

'Charles,' said Emily. 'Don't be indelicate.

'And anyway,' she added, 'it would be the blacksmith who did it, not her. A really good case there. Think how that brawny arm could wield a sandbag! And his wife would never notice his absence with seven children to look after. She wouldn't have time to notice a mere man.'

'This is degenerating into mere idiocy,' said Charles.

'It is rather,' agreed Emily. 'Counting losers hasn't been a great success.'

'What about you?' said Charles.

'Me?'

'Where were you when the crime was committed?'

'How extraordinary! I never thought of that. I was in London, of course. But I don't know that I could prove it. I was alone in my flat.'

'There you are,' said Charles. 'Motive and everything. Your young man coming into twenty thousand pounds, what more do you want?'

'You are clever, Charles,' said Emily. 'I can see that really I'm a most suspicious character. I never thought of it before.'

CHAPTER 27

NARRACOTT ACTS

Two mornings later Emily was seated in Inspector Narracott's office. She had come over from Sittaford that morning.

Inspector Narracott looked at her appraisingly. He admired Emily's pluck, her courageous determination not to give in and her resolute cheerfulness. She was a fighter, and Inspector Narracott admired fighters. It was his private opinion that she was a great deal too good for Jim Pearson, even if that young man was innocent of the murder.

'It's generally understood in books,' he said, 'that the police are intent on having a victim and don't in the least care if that victim is innocent or not as long as they have enough evidence to convict him. That's not the truth, Miss Trefusis, it's only the guilty man we want.'

'Do you honestly believe Jim to be guilty, Inspector Narracott?'

'I can't give you an official answer to that, Miss Trefusis. But I'll tell you this – that we are examining not only the evidence against him but the evidence against other people very carefully.'

'You mean against his brother – Brian?'

'A very unsatisfactory gentleman, Mr Brian Pearson. Refused to answer questions or to give any information about himself, but I think –' Inspector Narracott's slow Devonshire smile widened, 'I think I can make a pretty good guess at some of his activities. If I am right I shall know in another half hour. Then there's the lady's husband, Mr Dering.'

'You've seen him?' asked Emily curiously.

Inspector Narracott looked at her vivid face, and felt tempted to relax official caution. Leaning back in his chair he recounted his interview with Mr Dering, then from a file at his elbow he took out a copy of the wireless message he had dispatched to Mr Rosenkraun. 'That's what I sent,' he said. 'And here's the reply.'

Emily read it.

Narracott 2 Drysdale Road Exeter. Certainly confirm Mr Dering's statement. He was in my company all Friday afternoon. Rosenkraun.

'Oh! – bother,' said Emily, selecting a milder word than she had meant to use, knowing that the police force was old-fashioned and easily shocked.

'Ye-es,' said Inspector Narracott reflectively. 'It's annoying, isn't it?'

And his slow Devonshire smile broke out again.

'But I am a suspicious man, Miss Trefusis. Mr Dering's reasons sounded very plausible – but I thought it a pity to play into his hands too completely. So I sent another wireless message.'

Again he handed her two pieces of paper.

The first ran:

Information wanted re murder of Captain Trevelyan. Do you

support Martin Dering's statement of alibi for Friday afternoon. Divisional Inspector Narracott Exeter.

The return message showed agitation and a reckless disregard for expense.

Had no idea it was criminal case did not see Martin Dering Friday Agreed support his statement as one friend to another believed his wife was having him watched for divorce proceedings.

'Oh,' said Emily. 'Oh! – you *are* clever, Inspector.'

The Inspector evidently thought that he *had* been rather clever. His smile was gentle and contented.

'How men do stick together,' went on Emily looking over the telegrams. 'Poor Sylvia. In some ways I really think that men are beasts. That's why,' she added, 'it's so nice when one finds a man on whom one can really rely.'

And she smiled admiringly at the Inspector.

'Now, all this is very confidential, Miss Trefusis,' the Inspector warned her. 'I have gone further than I should in letting you know about this.'

'I think it's adorable of you,' said Emily. 'I shall never *never* forget it.'

'Well, mind,' the Inspector warned her. 'Not a word to *anybody*.'

'You mean that I am not to tell Charles – Mr Enderby.'

'Journalists will be journalists,' said Inspector Narracott. 'However well you have got him tamed, Miss Trefusis – well, news is news, isn't it?'

'I won't tell him then,' said Emily. 'I think I've got him muzzled all right, but as you say newspapermen will be newspapermen.'

'Never part with information unnecessarily. That's my rule,' said Inspector Narracott.

A faint twinkle appeared in Emily's eyes, her unspoken thought being that Inspector Narracott had infringed this rule rather badly during the last half hour.

A sudden recollection came into her mind, not of course that it probably mattered now. Everything seemed to be pointing in a totally different direction. But still it would be nice to know.

'Inspector Narracott!' she said suddenly. 'Who is Mr Duke?'

'Mr Duke?'

She thought the Inspector was rather taken aback by her question.

'You remember,' said Emily, 'we met you coming out of his cottage in Sittaford.'

'Ah, yes, yes, I remember. To tell you the truth, Miss Trefusis, I thought I would like to have an independent account of that table-turning business. Major Burnaby is not a first-rate hand at description.'

'And yet,' said Emily thoughtfully, 'if I had been you, I should have gone to somebody like Mr Rycroft for it. Why Mr Duke?'

There was a silence and then the Inspector said:

'Just a matter of opinion.'

'I wonder. I wonder if the police know something about Mr Duke.'

Inspector Narracott didn't answer. He had got his eyes fixed very steadily on the blotting paper.

'The man who leads a blameless life!' said Emily, 'that seems to describe Mr Duke awfully accurately, but perhaps he hasn't always led a blameless life? Perhaps the police know that?'

She saw a faint quiver on Inspector Narracott's face as he tried to conceal a smile.

'You like guessing, don't you, Miss Trefusis?' he said amiably.

'When people don't tell you things you have to guess!' retaliated Emily.

'If a man, as you say, is leading a blameless life,' Inspector Narracott said, 'and if it would be an annoyance and an inconvenience for him to have his past life raked up, well, the police are capable of keeping their own counsel. We have no wish to give a man away.'

'I see,' said Emily, 'but all the same – you went to see him, didn't you? That looks as though you thought, to begin with at any rate, that he might have had a hand in it. I wish – I wish I knew who Mr Duke really was? And what particular branch of criminology he indulged in in the past?'

She looked appealingly at Inspector Narracott but the latter preserved a wooden face, and realizing that on this point she could not hope to move him, Emily sighed and took her departure.

When she had gone the Inspector sat staring at the blotting pad, a trace of a smile still lingering on his lips. Then he rang the bell and one of his underlings entered.

'Well?' demanded Inspector Narracott.

'Quite right, sir. But it wasn't the Duchy at Princetown, it was the hotel at Two Bridges.'

'Ah!' The Inspector took the papers the other handed to him.

'Well,' he said. 'That settles it all right. Have you followed up the other young chap's movements on Friday?'

'He certainly arrived at Exhampton by the last train, but I haven't found out yet what time he left London. Inquiries are being made.'

Narracott nodded.

'Here is the entry from Somerset House, sir.'

Narracott unfolded it. It was the record of a marriage in 1894 between William Martin Dering and Martha Elizabeth Rycroft.

'Ah!' said the Inspector, 'anything else?'

'Yes, sir. Mr Brian Pearson sailed from Australia on a Blue Funnel Boat, the *Phidias*. She touched at Cape Town but no passengers of the name of Willett were aboard. No mother and daughter at all from South Africa. There was a Mrs and Miss Evans and a Mrs and Miss Johnson from Melbourne – the latter answer the description of the Willetts.'

'H'm,' said the Inspector – 'Johnson. Probably neither Johnson nor Willett is the right name. I think I've got them taped out all right. Anything more?'

There was nothing else it seemed.

'Well,' said Narracott, 'I think we have got enough to go on with.'

CHAPTER 28

BOOTS

'But, my dear young lady,' said Mr Kirkwood, 'what can you possibly expect to find at Hazelmoor? All Captain Trevelyan's effects have been removed. The police have made a thorough search of the house. I quite understand your position and your anxiety that Mr Pearson shall be – er – cleared if possible. But what can you do?'

'I don't expect to find anything,' Emily replied, 'or to notice anything that the police have overlooked. I can't explain to you, Mr Kirkwood. I want – I want to get the *atmosphere* of the place. Please let me have the key. There's no harm in it.'

'Certainly there's no harm in it,' said Mr Kirkwood with dignity.

'Then please be kind,' said Emily.

So Mr Kirkwood was kind and handed over the key with an indulgent smile. He did his best to come with her, which catastrophe was only averted by great tact and firmness on Emily's part.

That morning Emily had received a letter. It was couched in the following terms:

'Dear Miss Trefusis,' – wrote Mrs Belling. 'You said as how you would like to hear if anything at all should happen that was in any way out of the common even if not important, and, as this is peculiar, though not in any way important, I thought it my duty Miss to let you know at once, hoping this will catch you by the last post tonight or the first post tomorrow. My niece she came round and said it wasn't of any importance but peculiar which I agreed with her. The police said, and it was generally agreed that nothing was taken from Captain Trevelyan's house and nothing was in a manner of speaking nothing that is of any value, but something there is missing though not noticed at the time being unimportant. But it seems Miss that a pair of the Captain's boots is missing which Evans noticed when he went over the things with Major Burnaby. Though I don't suppose it is of any importance Miss I thought you would like to know. It was a pair of boots Miss the thick kind you

rubs oil into and which the Captain would have worn if he had gone out in the snow but as he didn't go out in the snow it doesn't seem to make sense. But missing they are and who took them nobody knows and though I well know it's of no importance I felt it my duty to write and hoping this finds you as it leaves me at present and hoping you are not worrying too much about the young gentleman I remain Miss Yours truly – Mrs J. Belling.'

Emily had read and re-read this letter. She had discussed it with Charles.

'Boots,' said Charles thoughtfully. 'It doesn't seem to make sense.'

'It must mean something,' Emily pointed out. 'I mean – why should a pair of boots be missing?'

'You don't think Evans is inventing?'

'Why should he? And after all if people do invent, they invent something sensible. Not a silly pointless thing like this.'

'Boots suggests something to do with footprints,' said Charles thoughtfully.

'I know. But footprints don't seem to enter into this case at all. Perhaps if it hadn't come on to snow again –'

'Yes, perhaps, but even then.'

'Could he have given them to some tramp,' suggested Charles, 'and then the tramp did him in.'

'I suppose that's possible,' said Emily, 'but it doesn't sound very like Captain Trevelyan. He might perhaps have found a man some work to do or given him a shilling, but he wouldn't have pressed his best winter boots on him.'

'Well, I give it up,' said Charles.

'I'm not going to give it up,' said Emily. 'By hook or by crook I'm going to get to the bottom of it.'

Accordingly she came to Exhampton and went first to the Three Crowns, where Mrs Belling received her with great enthusiasm.

'And your young gentleman still in prison, Miss! Well, it's a cruel shame and none of us don't believe it was him at least I would like to hear them say so when I am about. So you got my letter? You'd like to see Evans? Well, he lives right round the corner, 85 Fore Street it is. I wish I could come with you, but I can't leave the place, but you can't mistake it.'

Emily did not mistake it. Evans himself was out, but Mrs Evans received her and invited her in. Emily sat down and induced Mrs Evans to do so also and plunge straight into the matter on hand.

'I've come to talk about what your husband told Mrs Belling. I mean about a pair of Captain Trevelyan's boots being missing.'

'It's an odd thing, to be sure,' said the girl.

'Your husband is quite certain about it?'

'Oh, yes. Wore these boots most of the time in winter, the Captain did. Big ones they were, and he wore a couple of pairs of socks inside them.'

Emily nodded.

'They can't have gone to be mended or anything like that?' she suggested.

'Not without Evans knowing, they couldn't,' said his wife boastfully.

'No, I suppose not.'

'It's queer like,' said Mrs Evans, 'but I don't suppose it had anything to do with the murder, do you, Miss?'

'It doesn't seem likely,' agreed Emily.

'Have they found out anything new, Miss?' The girl's voice was eager.

'Yes, one or two things – nothing very important.'

'Seeing as that the Inspector from Exeter was here again today, I thought as though they might.'

'Inspector Narracott?'

'Yes, that's the one, Miss.'

'Did he come by train?'

'No, he came by car. He went to the Three Crowns first and asked about the young gentleman's luggage.'

'What young gentleman's luggage?'

'The gentleman you go about with, Miss.'

Emily stared.

'They asked Tom,' went on the girl, 'I was passing by just after and he told me about it. He's a one for noticing is Tom. He remembered there were two labels on the young gentleman's luggage, one to Exeter and one to Exhampton.'

A sudden smile illuminated Emily's face as she pictured the crime being committed by Charles in order to provide a scoop for himself. One could, she decided, write a gruesome little story on that theme. But she admired Inspector Narracott's thoroughness in checking every detail to do with anyone, however remote their connection with the crime. He must have left Exeter almost immediately after his interview with her. A fast car would easily beat the train, and in any case she had lunched in Exeter.

'Where did the Inspector go afterwards?' she asked.

'To Sittaford, Miss. Tom heard him tell the driver.'

'To Sittaford House?'

Brian Pearson was, she knew, still staying at Sittaford House with the Willetts.

'No, Miss, to Mr Duke's.'

Duke again. Emily felt irritated and baffled. Always Duke – the unknown factor. She ought, she felt, to be able to deduce him from the evidence, but he seemed to have produced the same effect on everyone – a normal, ordinary, pleasant man.

'I've got to see him,' said Emily to herself. 'I'll go straight there as soon as I get back to Sittaford.'

Then she had thanked Mrs Evans, gone on to Mr Kirkwood's and obtained the key, and was now standing in the hall of Hazelmoor and wondering how and what she had expected to feel there.

She mounted the stairs slowly and went into the first room at the top of the stairs. This was quite clearly Captain Trevelyan's bedroom. It had, as Mr Kirkwood had said, been emptied of personal effects. Blankets were folded in a neat pile, the drawers were empty, there was not so much as a hanger left in the cupboard. The boot cupboard showed a row of bare shelves.

Emily sighed and then turned and went downstairs. Here was the sitting-room where the dead man had lain, the snow blowing in from the open window.

She tried to visualize the scene. Whose hand had struck Captain Trevelyan down, and why? Had he been killed at five and twenty past five as everyone believed – or had Jim really lost his nerve and lied? Had he failed to make anyone hear at the front door and gone round to the window, looked in and seen his dead uncle's body and dashed away in an agony of fear? If only she knew. According to Mr Dacres, Jim stuck to his story. Yes – but Jim might have lost his nerve. She couldn't be sure.

Had there been, as Mr Rycroft had suggested, someone else in the house – someone who had overheard the quarrel and seized his chance?

If so – did that throw any light on the boot problem? Had someone been upstairs – perhaps in Captain Trevelyan's bedroom? Emily passed through the hall again. She took a quick look into the dining-room; there were a couple of trunks there neatly strapped and labelled. The sideboard was bare. The silver cups were at Major Burnaby's bungalow.

She noticed, however, that the prize of three new novels, an account of which Charles had had from Evans and had reported with amusing embellishments to her, had been forgotten and lay dejectedly on a chair.

She looked round the room and shook her head. There was nothing here.

She went up the stairs again and once more entered the bedroom.

She *must* know why these boots were missing! Until she could concoct some theory reasonably satisfactory to herself which would account for their disappearance, she felt powerless to put them out of her mind. They were soaring to ridiculous proportions, dwarfing everything else to do with the case. Was there *nothing* to help her?

She took each drawer out and felt behind it. In detective stories there was always an obliging scrap of paper. But evidently in real life one could not expect such fortunate accidents, or else Inspector Narracott and his men had been wonderfully thorough. She felt for loose boards, she felt round the edge of the carpet with her fingers. She investigated the spring mattress. What she expected to find in all these places she hardly knew, but she went on looking with dogged perseverance.

And then, as she straightened her back and stood upright, her eye was caught by the one incongruous touch in this room of apple-pie order, a little pile of soot in the grate.

Emily looked at it with the fascinated gaze of a bird for a snake. She drew nearer, eyeing it. It was no logical deduction, no reasoning of cause and effect, it was simply that the sight of soot as such suggested a certain possibility. Emily rolled up her sleeves and thrust both arms up the chimney.

A moment later she was staring with incredulous delight at a parcel wrapped neatly in newspaper. One shake detached the newspaper and there, before her, were the missing pair of boots.

'But why?' said Emily. 'Here they are. But why? Why? Why? Why?'

She stared at them. She turned them over. She examined them outside and inside and the same question beat monotonously in her brain. Why?

Granted that someone had removed Captain Trevelyan's boots and hidden them up the chimney. Why had they done so?

'Oh!' cried Emily desperately, 'I shall go mad!'

She put the boots carefully in the middle of the floor, and drawing up a chair opposite them she sat down. And then deliberately she set herself to think out things from the beginning, going over every detail that she knew herself or had learned by hearsay from other people. She considered every actor in the drama and outside the drama.

And suddenly, a queer nebulous idea began to take shape – an idea suggested by that pair of innocent boots that stood there dumbly on the floor.

'But if so,' said Emily, – 'if so –'

She picked up the boots in her hand and hurried downstairs. She pushed open the dining-room door and went to the cupboard in the corner. Here was Captain Trevelyan's motley array of sporting trophies and sporting outfits, all the things he had not trusted within reach of the female tenants. The skis, the sculls, the elephant's foot, the tusks, the fishing rods – everything still waiting for Messrs Young and Peabody to pack them expertly for store.

Emily bent down boots in hand.

In a minute or two she stood upright, flushed, incredulous.

'So that was it,' said Emily. 'So that was it.'

She sank into a chair. There was still much that she did not understand.

After some minutes she rose to her feet. She spoke aloud.

'I know who killed Captain Trevelyan,' she said. 'But I don't know *why*. I still can't think *why*. But I mustn't lose time.'

She hurried out of Hazelmoor. To find a car to drive her to

Sittaford was the work of a few minutes. She ordered it to take her to Mr Duke's bungalow. Here she paid the man and then walked up the path as the car drove away.

She lifted the knocker and gave a loud rat-tat.

After a moment or two's interval the door was opened by a big burly man with a rather impassive face.

For the first time, Emily met Mr Duke face to face.

'Mr Duke?' she asked.

'Yes.'

'I am Miss Trefusis. May I come in, please?'

There was a momentary hesitation. Then he stood aside to let her pass. Emily walked into the living-room. He closed the front door and followed her.

'I want to see Inspector Narracott,' said Emily. 'Is he here?'

Again there was a pause. Mr Duke seemed uncertain how to answer. At last he appeared to make up his mind. He smiled – a rather curious smile.

'Inspector Narracott is here,' he said. 'What do you want to see him about?'

Emily took the parcel she was carrying and unwrapped it. She took out a pair of boots and placed them on the table in front of him.

'I want,' she said, 'to see him about those boots.'

CHAPTER 29
THE SECOND SÉANCE

'Hullo, hullo, hullo,' said Ronnie Garfield.

Mr Rycroft, slowly ascending the steep slope of the lane from the post office, paused, till Ronnie overtook him.

'Been to the local Harrods, eh?' said Ronnie. 'Old Mother Hibbert.'

'No,' said Mr Rycroft. 'I have been for a short walk along past the forge. Very delightful weather today.'

Ronnie looked up at the blue sky.

'Yes, a bit of a difference from last week. By the way, you're going to the Willetts', I suppose?'

'I am. You also?'

'Yes. Our bright spot in Sittaford – the Willetts. Mustn't let yourself get downhearted, that's their motto. Carry on as usual. My aunt says it is unfeeling of them to ask people to tea so soon after the funeral and all that, but that's all bunkum. She just says that because she's feeling rattled about the Emperor of Peru.'

'The Emperor of Peru?' said Mr Rycroft surprised.

'One of the blinking cats. It's turned out to be an Empress instead and Aunt Caroline's naturally annoyed about it. She doesn't like these sex problems – so, as I say, she got her feelings off her chest by making catty remarks about the Willetts. Why shouldn't they ask people to tea? Trevelyan wasn't a relation, or anything like that.'

'Very true,' said Mr Rycroft turning his head and examining a bird which flew past and in which he thought he recognized a rare species.

'How annoying,' he murmured. 'I haven't got my glasses with me.'

'Eh! I say, talking of Trevelyan, do you think Mrs Willett can have known the old boy better than she says?'

'Why do you ask that?'

'Because of the change in her. Have you ever seen anything like it? She's aged about twenty years in the last week. You must have noticed it.'

'Yes,' said Mr Rycroft. 'I have noticed it.'

'Well, there you are. Trevelyan's death must have been the most frightful shock to her in some way or other. Queer if she turned out to be the old man's long lost wife whom he deserted in his youth and didn't recognize.'

'I hardly think that likely, Mr Garfield.'

'Bit too much of a movie stunt, eh? All the same very odd things happen. I've read some really amazing things in the *Daily Wire* – things you wouldn't credit if a newspaper didn't print them.'

'Are they any more to be credited on that account?' inquired Mr Rycroft acidly.

'You have got a down on young Enderby, haven't you?' said Ronnie.

'I dislike ill-bred nosing into affairs that do not concern you,' said Mr Rycroft.

'Yes, but then they do concern him,' Ronnie persisted. 'I mean nosing about is the poor chap's job. He seems to have tamed old Burnaby all right. Funny, the old boy can hardly bear the sight of me. I'm like a red rag to a bull to him.'

Mr Rycroft did not reply.

'By Jove,' said Ronnie again glancing up at the sky. 'Do you realize it's Friday? Just a week ago today at about this time we were trudging up to the Willetts' just as we are now. But a bit of a change in the weather.'

'A week ago,' said Mr Rycroft. 'It seems infinitely longer.'

'More like a bally year, doesn't it? Hullo, Abdul.'

They were passing Captain Wyatt's gate over which the melancholy Indian was leaning.

'Good afternoon, Abdul,' said Mr Rycroft. 'How's your master?'

The Indian shook his head.

'Master bad today, Sahib. Not see anyone. Not see anyone for long time.'

'You know,' said Ronnie as they passed on, 'that chap could murder Wyatt quite easily and no one would know. He could go on for weeks shaking his head and saying the master wouldn't see anyone and no one would think it the least odd.'

Mr Rycroft admitted the truth of the statement.

'But there would still be the problem of the disposal of the body,' he pointed out.

'Yes, that's always the snag, isn't it? Inconvenient thing, a human body.'

They passed Major Burnaby's cottage. The Major was in his garden looking sternly at a weed which was growing where no weed should be.

'Good afternoon, Major,' said Mr Rycroft. 'Are you also coming to Sittaford House?'

Burnaby rubbed his nose.

'Don't think so. They sent a note asking me. But – well – I don't feel like it. Expect you'll understand.'

Mr Rycroft bowed his head in token of understanding.

'All the same,' he said. 'I wish you'd come. I've got a reason.'

'A reason. What sort of reason?'

Mr Rycroft hesitated. It was clear that the presence of Ronnie

Garfield constrained him. But Ronnie, completely oblivious of the fact, stood his ground listening with ingenuous interest.

'I'd like to try an experiment,' he said at last slowly.

'What sort of experiment?' demanded Burnaby. Mr Rycroft hesitated.

'I'd rather not tell you beforehand. But if you come I'll ask you to back me up in anything I suggest.'

Burnaby's curiosity was aroused.

'All right,' he said. 'I'll come. You can count on me. Where's my hat?'

He rejoined them in a minute, hat on head, and all three turned in at the gates of Sittaford House.

'Hear you are expecting company, Rycroft,' said Burnaby conversationally.

A shade of vexation passed over the older man's face.

'Who told you that?'

'That chattering magpie of a woman, Mrs Curtis. She's clean and she's honest, but her tongue never stops, and she pays no attention to whether you listen or whether you don't.'

'It's quite true,' admitted Mr Rycroft. 'I am expecting my niece, Mrs Dering, and her husband, tomorrow.'

They had arrived at the front door by now, and on pressing the bell it was opened to them by Brian Pearson.

As they removed their overcoats in the hall, Mr Rycroft observed the tall broad-shouldered young man with an interested eye.

'Fine specimen,' he thought. 'Very fine specimen. Strong temper. Curious angle of the jaw. Might be a nasty customer to tackle in certain circumstances. What you might call a dangerous young man.'

A queer feeling of unreality stole over Major Burnaby as he entered the drawing-room, and Mrs Willett rose to greet him.

'Splendid of you to turn out.'

The same words as last week. The same blazing fire on the hearth. He fancied, but was not sure, the same gowns on the two women.

It did give one a queer feeling. As though it were last week again – as though Joe Trevelyan hadn't died – as though nothing had happened or were changed. Stop, that was wrong. The Willett woman had changed. A wreck, that was the only way of describing her. No longer the prosperous determined woman of the world, but a broken nervy creature making an obvious and pathetic effort to appear as usual.

'But I'm hanged if I can see what Joe's death meant to her,' thought the Major.

For the hundredth time he registered the impression that there was something deuced odd about the Willetts.

As usual, he awoke to the realization that he was being silent and that someone was speaking to him.

'Our last little gathering, I am afraid,' Mrs Willett was saying.

'What's that?' Ronnie Garfield looked up suddenly.

'Yes.' Mrs Willett shook her head with a would-be smile. 'We have got to forego the rest of the winter in Sittaford. Personally, of course, I love it – the snow and the tors and the wildness of it all. But the domestic problem! The domestic problem is too difficult – it defeats me!'

'I thought you were going to get a chauffeur-butler and a handyman,' said Major Burnaby.

A sudden shiver shook Mrs Willett's frame.

'No,' she said, 'I – I have to give up that idea.'

'Dear, dear,' said Mr Rycroft. 'This is a great blow to us all. Very sad indeed. We will sink back into our little rut after you have gone. When do you go, by the way?'

'On Monday, I expect,' said Mrs Willett. 'Unless I can get away tomorrow. It's so very awkward with no servants. Of course, I must arrange things with Mr Kirkwood. I took the house for four months.'

'You are going to London?' inquired Mr Rycroft.

'Yes, probably, to start with anyway. Then I expect we shall go abroad to the Riviera.'

'A great loss,' said Mr Rycroft bowing gallantly.

Mrs Willett gave a queer aimless little titter.

'Too kind of you, Mr Rycroft. Well, shall we have tea?'

Tea was laid ready. Mrs Willett poured out. Ronnie and Brian handed things. A queer kind of embarrassment lay over the party.

'What about you?' said Burnaby abruptly to Brian Pearson. 'You off too?'

'To London, yes. Naturally I shan't go abroad till this business is over.'

'This business?'

'I mean until my brother is cleared of this ridiculous charge.'

He flung the words at them defiantly in such a challenging manner that nobody knew quite what to say. Major Burnaby relieved the situation.

'Never have believed he did it. Not for a moment,' he said.

'*None* of us think so,' said Violet, flinging him a grateful glance.

The tinkle of a bell broke the ensuing pause.

'That's Mr Duke,' said Mrs Willett. 'Let him in, Brian.'

Young Pearson had gone to the window.

'It's not Duke,' he said. 'It's that damned journalist.'

'Oh! dear,' said Mrs Willett. 'Well, I suppose we must let him in all the same.'

Brian nodded and reappeared in a few minutes with Charles Enderby.

Enderby entered with his usual ingenuous air of beaming satisfaction. The idea that he might not be welcome did not seem to occur to him.

'Hullo, Mrs Willett, how are you? Thought I'd just drop in and see how things were. I wondered where everyone in Sittaford had got to. Now, I see.'

'Have some tea, Mr Enderby?'

'Awfully kind of you. I will. I see Emily isn't here. I suppose she's with your aunt, Mr Garfield.'

'Not that I know of,' said Ronnie staring. 'I thought she'd gone to Exhampton.'

'Ah! but she's back from there. How do I know? A little bird told me. The Curtis bird, to be accurate. Saw the car pass the post office and go up the lane and come back empty. She is not in No. 5 and she's not in Sittaford House. Puzzle – where is she? Failing Miss Percehouse, she must be sipping tea with that determined lady killer, Captain Wyatt.'

'She may have gone up Sittaford Beacon to see the sunset,' suggested Mr Rycroft.

'Don't think so,' said Burnaby. 'Should have seen her pass. I've been in the garden for the last hour.'

'Well, I don't think it's a very vital problem,' said Charles cheerfully. 'I mean I don't think she's been kidnapped or murdered or anything.'

'That's a pity from the point of view of your paper, isn't it?' sneered Brian.

'Even for copy, I wouldn't sacrifice Emily,' said Charles. 'Emily,' he added thoughtfully, 'is unique.'

'Very charming,' said Mr Rycroft. 'Very charming. We are – er – collaborators, she and I?'

'Has everyone finished?' said Mrs Willett. 'What about some bridge?'

'Er – one moment,' said Mr Rycroft.

He cleared his throat importantly. Everyone looked at him.

'Mrs Willett, I am, as you know, deeply interested in psychic phenomena. A week ago today, in this very room, we had an amazing, indeed an awe-inspiring experience.'

There was a faint sound from Violet Willett. He turned to her.

'I know, my dear Miss Willett, I know. The experience upset you, it was upsetting. I do not deny it. Now, ever since the crime the police force have been seeking the murderer of Captain Trevelyan. They have made an arrest. But some of us, at least, in this room, do not believe that Mr James Pearson is the guilty party. What I propose is this, that we repeat the experiment of last Friday, though approaching it this time in a rather different spirit.'

'No,' cried Violet.

'Oh! I say,' said Ronnie. 'That's a bit too thick. I'm not going to join in anyway.'

Mr Rycroft took no notice of him.

'Mrs Willett, what do you say?'

She hesitated.

'Frankly, Mr Rycroft, I do not like the idea. I don't like it at all. That miserable business last week made a most disagreeable impression on me. It will take me a long time to forget it.'

'What are you getting at exactly?' asked Enderby interestedly. 'Do you propose that the spirits should tell us the name of Captain Trevelyan's murderer? That seems a pretty tall order.'

'It was a pretty tall order, as you call it, when last week

a message came through saying that Captain Trevelyan was dead.'

'That's true,' agreed Enderby. 'But – well – you know this idea of yours might have consequences you haven't considered.'

'Such as?'

'Supposing a name was mentioned? Could you be sure that someone present did not deliberately –'

He paused and Ronnie Garfield tendered the word.

'Shove. That's what he means. Supposing somebody goes and shoves.'

'This is a serious experiment, sir,' said Mr Rycroft warmly. 'Nobody would do such a thing.'

'I don't know,' said Ronnie dubiously. 'I wouldn't put it past them. I don't mean myself. I swear I wouldn't, but suppose everyone turns on me and says I have. Jolly awkward, you know.'

'Mrs Willett, I am in earnest,' the little old gentleman disregarded Ronnie. 'I beg of you, let us make the experiment.'

She wavered.

'I don't like it. I really don't. I –' She looked round her uneasily, as though for a way of escape. 'Major Burnaby, you were Captain Trevelyan's friend. What do you say?'

The Major's eyes met those of Mr Rycroft. This, he understood, was the contingency which the latter had foreshadowed.

'Why not?' he said gruffly.

It had all the decision of a casting vote.

Ronnie went into the adjoining room and brought the small table which had been used before. He set it in the middle of the floor and chairs were drawn up round it. No one spoke. The experiment was clearly not popular.

'That is correct, I think,' said Mr Rycroft. 'We are about to repeat the experiment of last Friday under precisely similar conditions.'

'Not precisely similar,' objected Mrs Willett. 'Mr Duke is missing.'

'True,' said Mr Rycroft. 'A pity he is not here. A great pity. Well – er – we must consider him as replaced by Mr Pearson.'

'Don't take part in it, Brian. I beg of you. Please don't,' cried Violet.

'What does it matter? It's all nonsense anyway.'

'That is quite the wrong spirit,' said Mr Rycroft severely.

Brian Pearson did not reply, but took his place beside Violet.

'Mr Enderby,' began Mr Rycroft, but Charles interrupted him.

'I was not in on this. I'm a journalist and you mistrust me. I'll take notes in shorthand of any phenomena – that's the word, isn't it? – that occur.'

Matters were settled like that. The other six took their places round the table. Charles turned off the lights and sat down on the fender.

'One minute,' he said. 'What's the time?' He peered at his wrist watch in the firelight.

'That's odd,' he said.

'What's odd?'

'It's just twenty-five minutes past five.'

Violet uttered a little cry.

Mr Rycroft said severely:

'Silence.'

The minutes passed. A very different atmosphere this to the one a week ago. There was no muffled laughter, no whispered comments – only silence, broken at last by a slight crack from the table.

Mr Rycroft's voice rose.

'Is there any one there?'

Another faint crack – somehow an eerie sound in that darkened room.

'Is there anyone there?'

Not a crack this time but a deafening tremendous rap.

Violet screamed and Mrs Willett gave a cry.

Brian Pearson's voice rose reassuringly.

'It's all right. That's a knock at the front door. I'll go and open it.'

He strode from the room.

Still nobody spoke.

Suddenly the door flew open, the lights were switched on.

In the doorway stood Inspector Narracott. Behind him were Emily Trefusis and Mr Duke.

Narracott took a step into the room and spoke.

'John Burnaby I charge you with the murder of Joseph

Trevelyan on Friday the 14th instant, and I hereby warn you that anything you may say will be taken down and may be used in evidence.'

CHAPTER 30

EMILY EXPLAINS

It was a crowd of people almost too surprised for words that crowded round Emily Trefusis.

Inspector Narracott had led his prisoner from the room.

Charles Enderby found his voice first.

'For heaven's sake, cough it up, Emily,' he said. 'I want to get to the telegraph office. Every moment's vital.'

'It was Major Burnaby who killed Captain Trevelyan.'

'Well, I saw Narracott arrest him. And I suppose Narracott's sane – hasn't gone off his nut suddenly. But how *can* Burnaby have killed Trevelyan? I mean how is it humanly possible? If Trevelyan was killed at five and twenty past five –'

'He wasn't. He was killed at about a quarter to six.'

'Well, but even then –'

'I know. You'd never guess unless you just happened to think of it. *Skis* – that's the explanation – *skis*.'

'Skis?' repeated everyone.

Emily nodded.

'Yes. He deliberately engineered that table-turning. It wasn't an accident and done unconsciously as we thought, Charles. It was the second alternative that we rejected – done on purpose. He saw it was going to snow before very long. That would make it perfectly safe and wipe out all tracks. He created the impression that Captain Trevelyan was dead – got everyone all worked up. Then he pretended to be very upset and insisted on starting off for Exhampton.

'He went home, buckled on his skis (they were kept in a shed in the garden with a lot of other tackle) and started. He was an expert on skis. It's all down hill to Exhampton – a wonderful run. It would only take about ten minutes.

'He arrived at the window and rapped. Captain Trevelyan let him in, all unsuspecting. Then, when Captain Trevelyan's back was turned he seized his opportunity, picked up that sand-bag thing and – and killed him. Ugh! It makes me sick to think of it.'

She shuddered.

'It was all quite easy. He had plenty of time. He must have wiped and cleaned the skis and then put them into the cupboard in the dining-room, pushed in among all the other things. Then, I suppose he forced the window and pulled out all the drawers and things – to make it look as though someone had broken in.

'Then just before eight o'clock, all he had to do was to go out, make a detour on to the road higher up and come puffing and panting into Exhampton as though he'd walked all the way from Sittaford. So long as no one suspected about the skis, he'd be perfectly safe. The doctor couldn't fail to say that Captain Trevelyan had been dead at least two hours. And, as I say, so long as no one thought of skis, Major Burnaby would have a perfect alibi.'

'But they were friends – Burnaby and Trevelyan,' said Mr Rycroft. 'Old friends – they've always been friends. It's incredible.'

'I know,' said Emily. 'That's what I thought. I couldn't see *why*. I puzzled and I puzzled and at last I had to come to Inspector Narracott and Mr Duke.'

She paused and looked at the impassive Mr Duke.

'May I tell them?' she said.

Mr Duke smiled.

'If you like, Miss Trefusis.'

'Anyway – no, perhaps you'd rather I didn't. I went to them, and we got the thing clear. Do you remember telling me, Charles, that Evans mentioned that Captain Trevelyan used to send in solutions of competitions in his name? He thought Sittaford House was too grand an address. Well – that's what he did in the Football Competition that you gave Major Burnaby five thousand pounds for. It was Captain Trevelyan's solution really, and he sent it in in Burnaby's name. No. 1, The Cottages, Sittaford, sounded much better, he thought. Well, you see what happened? On Friday morning Major Burnaby got the letter saying he'd won five thousand pounds (and by the way, that ought to have made us suspicious. He told you he never got the letter – that nothing had come through on Friday owing to the weather. That was a lie. Friday morning was the last day things did come through). Where was I? Oh! – Major Burnaby getting the letter. He wanted that five thousand – wanted it badly. He'd been investing in some rotten shares or other and had lost a terrible lot of money.

'The idea must have come into his head quite suddenly, I should think. Perhaps when he realized it was going to snow that evening. *If Trevelyan were dead* – he could keep that money and no one would ever know.'

'Amazing,' murmured Mr Rycroft. 'Quite amazing. I never dreamed – But my dear young lady, how did you learn all this? What put you on the right track?'

For answer, Emily explained Mrs Belling's letter, and told how she had discovered the boots in the chimney.

'It was looking at them that put it into my mind. They were ski boots, you see, and they made me think of skis. And suddenly I wondered if perhaps – I rushed downstairs to the cupboard, and sure enough there were *two* pairs of skis there. One pair was longer than the other. And the boots fitted the long pair – *but they didn't fit the other*. The toe-clip things were adjusted for a much smaller pair of boots. The shorter pair of skis belonged to a different person.'

'He ought to have hidden the skis somewhere else,' said Mr Rycroft with artistic disapproval.

'No – no,' said Emily. 'Where else could he hide them? It was a very good place really. In a day or two the whole collection would have been stored, and in the meantime it wasn't likely that the police would bother whether Captain Trevelyan had had one or two pairs of skis.'

'But why did he hide the boots?'

'I suppose,' said Emily, 'that he was afraid the police might do exactly what I did – The sight of ski boots might have suggested skis to them. So he stuffed them up the chimney. And that's really, of course, where he made his mistake, because Evans noticed that they'd gone and I got to know of it.'

'Did he deliberately mean to fasten the crime on Jim?' demanded Brian Pearson angrily.

'Oh! no. That was just Jim's usual idiotic luck. He *was* an idiot, poor lamb.'

'He's all right now,' said Charles. 'You needn't worry about him. Have you told me everything, Emily, because if so, I want to rush to the telegraph office. You'll excuse me, everybody.'

He dashed out of the room.

'The live wire,' said Emily.

Mr Duke spoke in his deep voice.

'You've been rather a live wire yourself, Miss Trefusis.'

'You have,' said Ronnie admiringly.

'Oh! dear,' said Emily suddenly and dropped limply on a chair.

'What you need is a pick-me-up,' said Ronnie. 'A cocktail, eh?'

Emily shook her head.

'A little brandy,' suggested Mr Rycroft solicitously.

'A cup of tea,' suggested Violet.

'I'd like a spot of face powder,' said Emily wistfully. 'I've left my powder puff in the car. And I know I'm simply shining with excitement.'

Violet led her upstairs in search of this sedative to the nerves.

'That's better,' said Emily dabbing her nose firmly. 'What a nice kind. I feel much better now. Have you got any lipstick? I feel almost human.'

'You've been wonderful,' said Violet. 'So brave.'

'Not really,' said Emily. 'Underneath this camouflage I've been as wobbly as a jelly, with a sort of sick feeling in my middle.'

'I know,' said Violet. 'I've felt much the same myself. I have been so terrified this last few days – about Brian, you know. They couldn't hang him for murdering Captain Trevelyan, of course, but if once he had said where he was during that time, they would soon have ferreted out that it was he who engineered Father's escape.'

'What's that?' said Emily pausing in her facial repairs.

'Father was the convict who escaped. That's why we came here. Mother and I. Poor Father, he's always – been queer at times. Then he does these dreadful things. We met Brian on the way over from Australia, and he and I – well – he and I –'

'I see,' said Emily helpfully. 'Of course you did.'

'I told him everything and between us we concocted a plan. Brian was wonderful. We had got plenty of money fortunately, and Brian made all the plans. It's awfully hard to get away from Princetown, you know, but Brian engineered it. Really it was a kind of miracle. The arrangement was that after Father got away he was to go straight across country here and hide in the Pixie's Cave and then later he and Brian were to be our two men servants. You see with our arriving so long beforehand we imagined we would be quite free from suspicion. It was Brian who told us about this place, and suggested us offering a big rent to Captain Trevelyan.'

'I'm awfully sorry,' said Emily – 'I mean that it all went wrong.'

'It's broken Mother up completely,' said Violet. 'I think Brian's wonderful. It isn't everybody who would want to marry a convict's daughter. But I don't think it's really Father's fault, he had an awful kick on the head from a horse about fifteen years ago, and since then he has been a bit queer. Brian says if he had a good counsel he would have got off. But don't let's talk about me any more.'

'Can't anything be done?'

Violet shook her head.

'He's very ill – the exposure, you know. That awful cold. It's pneumonia. I can't help feeling that if he dies – well – it may be best for him really. It sounds dreadful to say so, but you know what I mean.'

'Poor Violet,' said Emily. 'It *is* a rotten shame.'

The girl shook her head.

'I've got Brian,' she said. 'And you've got –'

She stopped embarrassed.

'Ye-es,' said Emily thoughtfully, 'That's just it.'

CHAPTER 31

THE LUCKY MAN

Ten minutes later Emily was hurrying down the lane. Captain Wyatt, leaning over his gate, tried to arrest her progress.

'Hi,' he said, 'Miss Trefusis. What's all this I hear?'

'It's all true,' said Emily hurrying on.

'Yes, but look here. Come in – have a glass of wine or a cup of tea. There's plenty of time. No need to hurry. That's the worst of you civilized people.'

'We're awful, I know,' said Emily and sped on.

She burst in on Miss Percehouse with the explosive force of a bomb.

'I've come to tell you all about it,' said Emily.

And straightaway she poured forth the complete story. It was punctuated by various ejaculations of 'Bless us,' 'You don't say so?' 'Well, I declare,' from Miss Percehouse.

When Emily had finished her narrative, Miss Percehouse raised herself on her elbow and wagged a finger portentously.

'What did I say?' she demanded. 'I told you Burnaby was a jealous man. Friends indeed! For more than twenty years Trevelyan has done everything a bit better than Burnaby. He skied better, and he climbed better, and he shot better, and he did crossword puzzles better. Burnaby wasn't a big enough man to stand it. Trevelyan was rich and he was poor.

'It's been going on a long time. I can tell you it's a difficult thing to go on really liking a man who can do everything just a little bit better than you can. Burnaby was a narrow-minded, small-natured man. He let it get on his nerves.'

'I expect you're right,' said Emily. 'Well, I had to come and tell you. It seemed so unfair you should be out of everything. By the way, did you know that your nephew knew my Aunt Jennifer? They were having tea together at Deller's on Wednesday.'

'She's his godmother,' said Miss Percehouse. 'So that's the "fellow" he wanted to see in Exeter. Borrowing money, if I know Ronnie. I'll speak to him.'

'I forbid you to bite anyone on a joyful day like this,' said Emily. 'Good-bye. I must fly. I've got a lot to do.'

'What have you got to do, young woman? I should say you'd done your bit.'

'Not quite. I must go up to London and see Jim's Insurance Company people and persuade them not to prosecute him over that little matter of the borrowed money.'

'H'm,' said Miss Percehouse.

'It's all right,' said Emily. 'Jim will keep straight enough in future. He's had his lesson.'

'Perhaps. And you think you'll be able to persuade them?'

'Yes,' said Emily firmly.

'Well,' said Miss Percehouse. 'Perhaps you will. And after that?'

'After that,' said Emily. 'I've finished. I'll have done all I can for Jim.'

'Then suppose we say – what next?' said Miss Percehouse.

'You mean?'

'What next? Or if you want it put clearer: *Which of them?*'

'Oh!' said Emily.

'Exactly. That's what I want to know. Which of them is to be the unfortunate man?'

Emily laughed. Bending over she kissed the old lady.

'Don't pretend to be an idiot,' she said. 'You know perfectly well which it is.'

Miss Percehouse chuckled.

Emily ran lightly out of the house and down to the gate just as Charles came racing up the lane.

He caught her by both hands.

'Emily darling!'

'Charles! Isn't everything marvellous?'

'I shall kiss you,' said Mr Enderby, and did.

'I'm a made man, Emily,' he said. 'Now, look here, darling, what about it?'

'What about what?'

'Well – I mean – well, of course, it wouldn't have been playing the game with poor old Pearson in prison and all the rest of it. But he's cleared now and – well, he has got to take his medicine just like anybody else.'

'What *are* you talking about?' said Emily.

'You know well enough I am crazy about you,' said Mr Enderby, 'and you like me. Pearson was just a mistake. What I mean is – well – you and I, we are made for each other. All this time, we have known it, both of us, haven't we? Do you like a Registry Office or a Church, or what?'

'If you are referring to marriage,' said Emily, 'there's nothing doing.'

'What – but I say –'

'No,' said Emily.

'But – Emily –'

'If you will have it,' said Emily. 'I love Jim. Passionately!'

Charles stared at her in speechless bewilderment.

'You can't!'

'I can! And I do! And I always have! And I always shall!'

'You – you made me think –'

'I said,' said Emily demurely, 'that it was wonderful to have someone one could rely on.'

'Yes, but I thought –'

'I can't help what you thought.'

'You *are* an unscrupulous devil, Emily.'

'I know, Charles darling. I know. I'm everything you like to call me. But never mind. Think how great you are going to be. You've got your scoop! Exclusive news for the *Daily Wire*. You're a made man. What's a woman anyway? Less than the dust. No really strong man wants a woman. She only hampers him by clinging to him like the ivy. Every great man is one who is independent of women. A career – there's nothing so fine, so absolutely satisfying to a man, as a great career. You are a strong man, Charles, one who can stand alone –'

'Will you stop talking, Emily? It's like a talk to Young Men on the Wireless! You've broken my heart. You don't know how lovely you looked as you came into that room with Narracott. Just like something triumphant and avenging off an arch.'

A footstep crunched on the lane, and Mr Duke appeared.

'Oh! There you are, Mr Duke,' said Emily. 'Charles, I want to tell you. This is Ex-Chief-Inspector Duke of Scotland Yard.'

'What?' cried Charles recognizing the famous name. 'Not *the* Inspector Duke?'

'Yes,' said Emily. 'When he retired, he came here to live, and being nice and modest he didn't want his renown to get about. I see now why Inspector Narracott twinkled so when I wanted him to tell me what kind of crimes Mr Duke had committed.'

Mr Duke laughed.

Charles wavered. There was a short tussle between the lover and the journalist. The journalist won.

'I'm delighted to meet you, Inspector,' he said. 'Now, I wonder if we could persuade you to do us a short article, say eight hundred words, on the Trevelyan case.'

Emily stepped quickly up the lane and into Mrs Curtis's

cottage. She ran up to her bedroom and pulled out her suitcase. Mrs Curtis had followed her up.

'You're not going, Miss?'

'I am. I've got a lot to do – London, and my young man.'

Mrs Curtis drew nearer.

'Just tell me, Miss, which of 'em is it?'

Emily was throwing clothes haphazard into the suitcase.

'The one in prison, of course. There's never been any other.'

'Ah! You don't think, Miss, that maybe you're making a mistake. You're sure the other young gentleman is worth as much as this one?'

'Oh! no,' said Emily. 'He isn't. This one will get on.' She glanced out of the window where Charles was still holding Ex-Chief-Inspector Duke in earnest parley. 'He's the kind of young man who's simply born to get on – but I don't know what would happen to the other one if I weren't there to look after him. Look where he would be now if it weren't for me!'

'And you can't say more than that, Miss,' said Mrs Curtis.

She retreated downstairs to where her lawful spouse was sitting and staring into vacancy.

'The living image of my Great Aunt Sarah's Belinda she is,' said Mrs Curtis. 'Threw herself away she did on that miserable George Plunket down at the Three Cows. Mortgaged and all it was. And in two years she had the mortgage paid off and the place a going concern.'

'Ah!' said Mr Curtis, and shifted his pipe slightly.

'He was a handsome fellow, George Plunket,' said Mrs Curtis reminiscently.

'Ah!' said Mr Curtis.

'But after he married Belinda he never so much as looked at another woman.'

'Ah!' said Mr Curtis.

'She never gave him the chance,' said Mrs Curtis.

'Ah!' said Mr Curtis.

•

WHY DIDN'T THEY ASK EVANS?

•

To Christopher Mallock
in memory of Hinds

CHAPTER I

THE ACCIDENT

Bobby Jones teed up his ball, gave a short preliminary waggle, took the club back slowly, then brought it down and through with the rapidity of lightning.

Did the ball fly down the fairway straight and true, rising as it went and soaring over the bunker to land within an easy mashie shot of the fourteenth green?

No, it did not. Badly topped, it scudded along the ground and embedded itself firmly in the bunker!

There were no eager crowds to groan with dismay. The solitary witness of the shot manifested no surprise. And that is easily explained – for it was not the American-born master of the game who had played the shot, but merely the fourth son of the Vicar of Marchbolt – a small seaside town on the coast of Wales.

Bobby uttered a decidedly profane ejaculation.

He was an amiable-looking young man of about eight and twenty. His best friend could not have said that he was handsome, but his face was an eminently likeable one, and his eyes had the honest brown friendliness of a dog's.

'I get worse every day,' he muttered dejectedly.

'You press,' said his companion.

Dr Thomas was a middle-aged man with grey hair and a red cheerful face. He himself never took a full swing. He played short straight shots down the middle, and usually beat more brilliant but more erratic players.

Bobby attacked his ball fiercely with a niblick. The third time was successful. The ball lay a short distance from the green which Dr Thomas had reached with two creditable iron shots.

'Your hole,' said Bobby.

They proceeded to the next tee.

The doctor drove first – a nice straight shot, but with no great distance about it.

Bobby sighed, teed his ball, reteed it, waggled his club a long time, took back stiffly, shut his eyes, raised his head, depressed his right shoulder, did everything he ought not to have done – and hit a screamer down the middle of the course.

He drew a deep breath of satisfaction. The well-known golfer's gloom passed from his eloquent face to be succeeded by the equally well-known golfer's exultation.

'I know now what I've been doing,' said Bobby – quite untruthfully.

A perfect iron shot, a little chip with a mashie and Bobby lay dead. He achieved a birdie four and Dr Thomas was reduced to one up.

Full of confidence, Bobby stepped on to the sixteenth tee. He again did everything he should not have done, and this time no miracle occurred. A terrific, a magnificent, an almost superhuman slice happened! The ball went round at right angles.

'If that had been straight – whew!' said Dr Thomas.

'*If*,' said Bobby bitterly. 'Hullo, I thought I heard a shout! Hope the ball didn't hit anyone.'

He peered out to the right. It was a difficult light. The sun was on the point of setting, and, looking straight into it, it was hard to see anything distinctly. Also there was a slight mist rising from the sea. The edge of the cliff was a few hundred yards away.

'The footpath runs along there,' said Bobby. 'But the ball can't possibly have travelled as far as that. All the same, I did think I heard a cry. Did you?'

But the doctor had heard nothing.

Bobby went after his ball. He had some difficulty in finding it, but ran it to earth at last. It was practically unplayable – embedded in a furze bush. He had a couple of hacks at it, then picked it up and called out to his companion that he gave up the hole.

The doctor came over towards him since the next tee was right on the edge of the cliff.

The seventeenth was Bobby's particular bugbear. At it you had to drive over a chasm. The distance was not actually so great, but the attraction of the depths below was overpowering.

They had crossed the footpath which now ran inland to their left, skirting the very edge of the cliff.

The doctor took an iron and just landed on the other side.

Bobby took a deep breath and drove. The ball scudded forward and disappeared over the lip of the abyss.

'Every single dashed time,' said Bobby bitterly. 'I do the same dashed idiotic thing.'

He skirted the chasm, peering over. Far below the sea sparkled, but not every ball was lost in its depths. The drop was sheer at the top, but below it shelved gradually.

Bobby walked slowly along. There was, he knew, one place where one could scramble down fairly easily. Caddies did so, hurling themselves over the edge and reappearing triumphant and panting with the missing ball.

Suddenly Bobby stiffened and called to his companion.

'I say, doctor, come here. What do you make of that?'

Some forty feet below was a dark heap of something that looked like old clothes.

The doctor caught his breath.

'By Jove,' he said. 'Somebody's fallen over the cliff. We must get down to him.'

Side by side the two men scrambled down the rock, the more athletic Bobby helping the other. At last they reached the ominous dark bundle. It was a man of about forty, and he was still breathing, though unconscious.

The doctor examined him, touching his limbs, feeling his pulse, drawing down the lids of his eyes. He knelt down beside him and completed his examination. Then he looked up at Bobby, who was standing there feeling rather sick, and slowly shook his head.

'Nothing to be done,' he said. 'His number's up, poor fellow. His back's broken. Well, well. I suppose he wasn't familiar with the path, and when the mist came up he walked over the edge. I've told the council more than once there ought to be a railing just here.'

He stood up again.

'I'll go off and get help,' he said. 'Make arrangements to have the body got up. It'll be dark before we know where we are. Will you stay here?'

Bobby nodded.

'There's nothing to be done for him, I suppose?' he asked.

The doctor shook his head.

'Nothing. It won't be long – the pulse is weakening fast. He'll last another twenty minutes at most. Just possible he may recover consciousness before the end; but very likely he won't. Still –'

'Rather,' said Bobby quickly. 'I'll stay. You get along. If he does come to, there's no drug or anything –' he hesitated.

The doctor shook his head.

'There'll be no pain,' he said. 'No pain at all.'

Turning away, he began rapidly to climb up the cliff again. Bobby watched him till he disappeared over the top with a wave of his hand.

Bobby moved a step or two along the narrow ledge, sat down on a projection in the rock and lit a cigarette. The business had shaken him. Up to now he had never come in contact with illness or death.

What rotten luck there was in the world! A swirl of mist on a fine evening, a false step – and life came to an end. Fine healthy-looking fellow too – probably never known a day's illness in his life. The pallor of approaching death couldn't disguise the deep tan of the skin. A man who had lived an out-of-door life – abroad, perhaps. Bobby studied him more closely – the crisp curling chestnut hair just touched with grey at the temples, the big nose, the strong jaw, the white teeth just showing through the parted lips. Then the broad shoulders and the fine sinewy hands. The legs were twisted at a curious angle. Bobby shuddered and brought his eyes up again to the face. An attractive face, humorous, determined, resourceful. The eyes, he thought, were probably blue –

And just as he reached that point in his thoughts, the eyes suddenly opened.

They *were* blue – a clear deep blue. They looked straight at Bobby. There was nothing uncertain or hazy about them. They seemed completely conscious. They were watchful and at the same time they seemed to be asking a question.

Bobby got up quickly and came towards the man. Before he got there, the other spoke. His voice was not weak – it came out clear and resonant.

'*Why didn't they ask Evans?*' he said.

And then a queer little shudder passed over him, the eyelids dropped, the jaw fell . . .

The man was dead.

CHAPTER 2

CONCERNING FATHERS

Bobby knelt down beside him, but there was no doubt. The man was dead. A last moment of consciousness, that sudden question, and then – the end.

Rather apologetically, Bobby put his hand into the dead man's pocket and, drawing out a silk handkerchief, he spread it reverently over the dead face. There was nothing more he could do.

Then he noticed that in his action he had jerked something else out of the pocket. It was a photograph and in the act of replacing it he glanced at the pictured face.

It was a woman's face, strangely haunting in quality. A fair woman with wide-apart eyes. She seemed little more than a girl, certainly under thirty, but it was the arresting quality of her beauty rather than the beauty itself that seized upon the boy's imagination. It was the kind of face, he thought, not easy to forget.

Gently and reverently, he replaced the photograph in the pocket from which it had come, then he sat down again to wait for the doctor's return.

The time passed very slowly – or at least so it seemed to the waiting boy. Also, he had just remembered something. He had promised his father to play the organ at the evening service at six o'clock and it was now ten minutes to six. Naturally, his father would understand the circumstances, but all the same he wished that he had remembered to send a message by the doctor. The Rev. Thomas Jones was a man of extremely nervous temperament. He was, *par excellence*, a fusser, and when he fussed, his digestive apparatus collapsed and he suffered agonizing pain. Bobby, though he considered his father a pitiful old ass, was nevertheless extremely fond of him. The Rev. Thomas, on the other hand, considered his fourth son a pitiful *young* ass, and with less tolerance than Bobby sought to effect improvement in the young man.

'The poor old gov'nor,' thought Bobby. 'He'll be ramping up and down. He won't know whether to start the service or not. He'll work himself up till he gets that pain in the tummy, and then he won't be able to eat his supper. He won't have the sense to realize that I wouldn't let him down unless it were quite unavoidable – and, anyway, what does it matter? But he'll never see it that way. Nobody over fifty has got any sense – they worry themselves to death about tuppeny-ha'penny things that don't matter. They've been brought up all wrong, I suppose, and now they can't help themselves. Poor old Dad, he's got less sense than a chicken!'

He sat there thinking of his father with mingled affection and exasperation. His life at home seemed to him to be one long sacrifice to his father's peculiar ideas. To Mr Jones, the same time seemed to be one long sacrifice on *his* part, ill understood or appreciated by the younger generation. So may ideas on the same subject differ.

What an age the doctor was! Surely he might have been back by this time?

Bobby got up and stamped his feet moodily. At that moment he heard something above him and looked up, thankful that help was at hand and his own services no longer needed.

But it was not the doctor. It was a man in plus fours whom Bobby did not know.

'I say,' said the newcomer. 'Is anything the matter? Has there been an accident? Can I help in any way?'

He was a tall man with a pleasant tenor voice. Bobby could not see him very clearly for it was now fast growing dusk.

He explained what had happened whilst the stranger made shocked comments.

'There's nothing I can do?' he asked. 'Get help or anything?'

Bobby explained that help was on the way and asked if the other could see any signs of its arriving.

'There's nothing at present.'

'You see,' went on Bobby, 'I've got an appointment at six.'

'And you don't like to leave –'

'No, I don't quite,' said Bobby. 'I mean, the poor chap's dead and all that, and of course one can't do anything, but all the same –'

He paused, finding it, as usual, difficult to put confused emotions into words.

The other, however, seemed to understand.

'I know,' he said. 'Look here, I'll come down – that is, if I can see my way – and I'll stay till these fellows arrive.'

'Oh, would you?' said Bobby gratefully. 'You see, it's my father. He's not a bad sort really, and things upset him. Can you see your way? A bit more to the left – now to the right – that's it. It's not really difficult.'

He encouraged the other with directions until the two men were face to face on the narrow plateau. The newcomer was a man of about thirty-five. He had a rather indecisive face which seemed to be calling for a monocle and a little moustache.

'I'm a stranger down here,' he explained. 'My name's Bassington-ffrench, by the way. Come down to see about a house. I say, what a beastly thing to happen! Did he walk over the edge?'

Bobby nodded.

'Bit of mist got up,' he explained. 'It's a dangerous bit of path. Well, so long. Thanks very much. I've got to hurry. It's awfully good of you.'

'Not at all,' the other protested. 'Anybody would do the same. Can't leave the poor chap lying – well, I mean, it wouldn't be decent somehow.'

Bobby was scrambling up the precipitous path. At the top he waved his hand to the other then set off at a brisk run across country. To save time, he vaulted the churchyard wall instead of going round to the gate on the road – a proceeding observed by the Vicar from the vestry window and deeply disapproved of by him.

It was five minutes past six, but the bell was still tolling.

Explanations and recriminations were postponed until after the service. Breathless, Bobby sank into his seat and manipulated the stops of the ancient organ. Association of ideas led his fingers into Chopin's funeral march.

Afterwards, more in sorrow than in anger (as he expressly pointed out), the Vicar took his son to task.

'If you cannot do a thing properly, my dear Bobby,' he said, 'it is better not to do it at all. I know that you and all your young friends seem to have no idea of time, but there is One whom we should not keep waiting. You offered to play the organ of your own accord. I did not coerce you. Instead, faint-hearted, you preferred playing a game –'

Bobby thought he had better interrupt before his father got too well away.

'Sorry, Dad,' he said, speaking cheerfully and breezily as was his habit no matter what the subject. 'Not my fault this time. I was keeping guard over a corpse.'

'You were what?'

'Keeping guard over a blighter who stepped over the cliff. You know – the place where the chasm is – by the seventeenth tee. There was a bit of mist just then, and he must have gone straight on and over.'

'Good heavens,' cried the Vicar. 'What a tragedy! Was the man killed outright?'

'No. He was unconscious. He died just after Dr Thomas had gone off. But of course I felt I had to squat there – couldn't just push off and leave him. And then another fellow came along so I passed the job of chief mourner on to him and legged it here as fast as I could.'

The Vicar sighed.

'Oh, my dear Bobby,' he said. 'Will nothing shake your deplorable callousness? It grieves me more than I can say. Here you have been brought face to face with death – with sudden death. And you can joke about it! It leaves you unmoved. Everything – everything, however solemn, however sacred, is merely a joke to your generation.'

Bobby shuffled his feet.

If his father couldn't see that, of course, you joked about a thing because you had felt badly about it – well, he couldn't see it! It wasn't the sort of thing you could explain. With death and tragedy about you had to keep a stiff upper lip.

But what could you expect? Nobody over fifty understood anything at all. They had the most extraordinary ideas.

'I expect it was the War,' thought Bobby loyally. 'It upset them and they never got straight again.'

He felt ashamed of his father and sorry for him.

'Sorry, Dad,' he said with a clear-eyed realization that explanation was impossible.

The Vicar felt sorry for his son – he looked abashed – but he also felt ashamed of him. The boy had no conception of the seriousness of life. Even his apology was cheery and impenitent.

They moved towards the Vicarage, each making enormous efforts to find excuses for the other.

The Vicar thought: 'I wonder when Bobby will find something to do . . . ?'

Bobby thought: 'Wonder how much longer I can stick it down here . . . ?'

Yet they were both extremely fond of each other.

CHAPTER 3

A RAILWAY JOURNEY

Bobby did not see the immediate sequel of his adventure. On the following morning he went up to town, there to meet a friend who was thinking of starting a garage and who fancied Bobby's co-operation might be valuable.

After settling things to everybody's satisfaction, Bobby caught the 11.30 train home two days later. He caught it, true, but only by a very narrow margin. He arrived at Paddington when the clock announced the time to be 11.28, dashed down the subway, emerged on No. 3 Platform just as the train was moving and hurled himself at the first carriage he saw, heedless of indignant ticket collectors and porters in his immediate rear.

Wrenching open the door, he fell in on his hands and knees, picked himself up. The door was shut with a slam by an agile porter and Bobby found himself looking at the sole occupant of the compartment.

It was a first-class carriage and in the corner facing the engine sat a dark girl smoking a cigarette. She had on a red skirt, a short green jacket and a brilliant blue beret, and despite a certain resemblance to an organ grinder's monkey (she had long sorrowful dark eyes and a puckered-up face) she was distinctly attractive.

In the midst of an apology, Bobby broke off.

'Why, it's you, Frankie!' he said. 'I haven't seen you for ages.'

'Well, I haven't seen you. Sit down and talk.'

Bobby grinned.

'My ticket's the wrong colour.'

'That doesn't matter,' said Frankie kindly. 'I'll pay the difference for you.'

'My manly indignation rises at the thought,' said Bobby. 'How could I let a lady pay for me?'

'It's about all we seem to be good for these days,' said Frankie.

'I will pay the difference myself,' said Bobby heroically as a burly figure in blue appeared at the door from the corridor.

'Leave it to me,' said Frankie.

She smiled graciously at the ticket collector, who touched his hat as he took the piece of white cardboard from her and punched it.

'Mr Jones has just come in to talk to me for a bit,' she said. 'That won't matter, will it?'

'That's all right, your ladyship. The gentleman won't be staying long, I expect.' He coughed tactfully. 'I shan't be round again till after Bristol,' he added significantly.

'What can be done with a smile,' said Bobby as the official withdrew.

Lady Frances Derwent shook her head thoughtfully.

'I'm not so sure it's the smile,' she said. 'I rather think it's father's habit of tipping everybody five shillings whenever he travels that does it.'

'I thought you'd given up Wales for good, Frankie.'

Frances sighed.

'My dear, you know what it is. You know how mouldy parents can be. What with that and the bathrooms in the state they are, and nothing to do and nobody to see – and people simply won't come to the country to stay nowadays! They say they're economizing and they can't go so far. Well, I mean, what's a girl to do?'

Bobby shook his head, sadly recognizing the problem.

'However,' went on Frankie, 'after the party I went to last night, I thought even home couldn't be worse.'

'What was wrong with the party?'

'Nothing at all. It was just like any other party, only more so. It was to start at the Savoy at half-past eight. Some of us rolled up about a quarter-past nine and, of course, we got entangled with other people, but we got sorted out about ten. And we had dinner and then after a bit we went on to the Marionette – there was a rumour it was going to be raided, but nothing happened

– it was just moribund, and we drank a bit and then we went on to the Bullring and that was even deader, and then we went to a coffee stall, and then we went to a fried-fish place, and then we thought we'd go and breakfast with Angela's uncle and see if he'd be shocked, but he wasn't – only bored, and then we sort of fizzled home. Honestly, Bobby, it isn't good enough.'

'I suppose not,' said Bobby, stifling a pang of envy.

Never in his wildest moments did he dream of being able to be a member of the Marionette or the Bullring.

His relationship with Frankie was a peculiar one.

As children, he and his brothers had played with the children at the Castle. Now that they were all grown up, they seldom came across each other. When they did, they still used Christian names. On the rare occasions when Frankie was at home, Bobby and his brothers would go up and play tennis. But Frankie and her two brothers were not asked to the Vicarage. It seemed to be tacitly recognized that it would not be amusing for them. On the other hand, extra men were always wanted for tennis. There may have been a trace of constraint in spite of the Christian names. The Derwents were, perhaps, a shade more friendly than they need have been as though to show that 'there was no difference'. The Jones, on their side, were a shade formal, as though determined not to claim more friendship than was offered them. The two families had now nothing in common save certain childish memories. Yet Bobbie was very fond of Frankie and was always pleased on the rare occasions when Fate threw them together.

'I'm so tired of everything,' said Frankie in a weary voice. 'Aren't you?'

Bobby considered.

'No, I don't think I am.'

'My dear, how wonderful,' said Frankie.

'I don't mean I'm hearty,' said Bobby, anxious not to create a painful impression. 'I just can't stand people who are hearty.'

Frankie shuddered at the mere mention of the word.

'I know,' she murmured. 'They're dreadful.'

They looked at each other sympathetically.

'By the way,' said Frankie suddenly. 'What's all this about a man falling over the cliffs?'

'Dr Thomas and I found him,' said Bobby. 'How did you know about it, Frankie?'

'Saw it in the paper. Look.'

She indicated with her finger a small paragraph headed: 'Fatal Accident in Sea Mist.'

The victim of the tragedy at Marchbolt was identified late last night by means of a photograph which he was carrying. The photograph proved to be that of Mrs Leo Cayman. Mrs Cayman was communicated with and journeyed at once to Marchbolt, where she identified the deceased as her brother, Alex Pritchard. Mr Pritchard had recently returned from Siam. He had been out of England for ten years and was just starting upon a walking tour. The inquest will be held at Marchbolt tomorrow.

Bobby's thoughts flew back to the strangely haunting face of the photograph.

'I believe I shall have to give evidence at the inquest,' he said.

'How thrilling. I shall come and hear you.'

'I don't suppose there will be anything thrilling about it,' said Bobby. 'We just found him, you know.'

'Was he dead?'

'No, not then. He died about a quarter of an hour later. I was alone with him.'

He paused.

'Rather grim,' said Frankie with that immediate understanding that Bobby's father had lacked.

'Of course he didn't feel anything –'

'No?'

'But all the same – well – you see, he looked awfully alive – that sort of person – rather a rotten way to finish – just stepping off a cliff in a silly little bit of mist.'

'I get you, Steve,' said Frankie, and again the queer phrase represented sympathy and understanding.

'Did you see the sister?' she asked presently.

'No. I've been up in town two days. Had to see a friend of mine about a garage business we're going in for. You remember him. Badger Beadon.'

'Do I?'

'Of course you do. You must remember good old Badger. He squints.'

Frankie wrinkled her brows.

'He's got an awfully silly kind of laugh – haw haw haw – like that,' continued Bobby helpfully.

Still Frankie wrinkled her brows.

'Fell off his pony when we were kids,' continued Bobby. 'Stuck in the mud head down, and we had to pull him out by the legs.'

'Oh!' said Frankie in a flood of recollection. 'I know now. He stammered.'

'He still does,' said Bobby proudly.

'Didn't he run a chicken farm and it went bust?' inquired Frankie.

'That's right.'

'And then he went into a stockbroker's office and they fired him after a month?'

'That's it.'

'And then they sent him to Australia and he came back?'

'Yes.'

'Bobby,' said Frankie. 'You're not putting any money into this business venture, I hope?'

'I haven't got any money to put,' said Bobby.

'That's just as well,' said Frankie.

'Naturally,' went on Bobby. 'Badger has tried to get hold of someone with a little capital to invest. But it isn't so easy as you'd think.'

'When you look round you,' said Frankie, 'you wouldn't believe people had any sense at all – but they have.'

The point of these remarks seemed at last to strike Bobby.

'Look here, Frankie,' he said. 'Badger's one of the best – one of the very best.'

'They always are,' said Frankie.

'Who are?'

'The ones who go to Australia and come back again. How did he get hold of the money to start this business?'

'An aunt or something died and left him a garage for six cars with three rooms over and his people stumped up a hundred pounds to buy second-hand cars with. You'd be surprised what bargains there are to be had in second-hand cars.'

'I bought one once,' said Frankie. 'It's a painful subject. Don't let's talk of it. What did you want to leave the Navy for? They didn't axe you, did they? Not at your age.'

Bobby flushed.

'Eyes,' he said gruffly.

'You always had trouble with your eyes, I remember.'

'I know. But I just managed to scrape through. Then foreign service – the strong light, you know – that rather did for them. So – well – I had to get out.'

'Grim,' murmured Frankie, looking out of the window.

There was an eloquent pause.

'All the same, it's a shame,' burst out Bobby. 'My eyes aren't really bad – they won't get any worse, they say. I could have carried on perfectly.'

'They look all right,' said Frankie.

She looked straight into their honest brown depths.

'So you see,' said Bobby, 'I'm going in with Badger.'

Frankie nodded.

An attendant opened the door and said, 'First luncheon.'

'Shall we?' said Frankie.

They passed along to the dining car.

Bobby made a short strategic retreat during the time when the ticket collector might be expected.

'We don't want him to strain his conscience too much,' he said.

But Frankie said she didn't expect ticket collectors had any consciences.

It was just after five o'clock when they reached Sileham, which was the station for Marchbolt.

'The car's meeting me,' said Frankie. 'I'll give you a lift.'

'Thanks. That will save me carrying this beastly thing for two miles.'

He kicked his suitcase disparagingly.

'Three miles, not two,' said Frankie.

'Two miles if you go by the footpath over the links.'

'The one where –'

'Yes – where that fellow went over.'

'I suppose nobody pushed him over, did they?' asked Frankie as she handed her dressing-case to her maid.

'Pushed him over? Good Lord, no. Why?'

'Well, it would make it much more exciting, wouldn't it?' said Frankie idly.

CHAPTER 4
THE INQUEST

The inquest on the body of Alex Pritchard was held on the following day. Dr Thomas gave evidence as to the finding of the body.

'Life was not then extinct?' asked the coroner.

'No, deceased was still breathing. There was, however, no hope of recovery. The –'

Here the doctor became highly technical. The coroner came to the rescue of the jury:

'In ordinary everyday language, the man's back was broken?'

'If you like to put it that way,' said Dr Thomas sadly.

He described how he had gone off to get help, leaving the dying man in Bobby's charge.

'Now as to the cause of this disaster, what is your opinion, Dr Thomas?'

'I should say that in all probability (failing any evidence as to his state of mind, that is to say) the deceased stepped inadvertently over the edge of the cliff. There was a mist rising from the sea, and at that particular point the path turns abruptly inland. Owing to the mist the deceased may not have noticed the danger and walked straight on – in which case two steps would take him over the edge.'

'There were no signs of violence? Such as might have been administered by a third party?'

'I can only say that all the injuries present are fully explained by the body striking the rocks fifty or sixty feet below.'

'There remains the question of suicide?'

'That is, of course, perfectly possible. Whether the deceased walked over the edge or threw himself over is a matter on which I can say nothing.'

Robert Jones was called next.

Bobby explained that he had been playing golf with the doctor and had sliced his ball towards the sea. A mist was rising at the time and it was difficult to see. He thought he heard a cry, and for a moment wondered if his ball could have hit anybody coming along the footpath. He had decided, however, that it could not possibly have travelled so far.

'Did you find the ball?'

'Yes, it was about a hundred yards short of the footpath.'

He then described how they had driven from the next tee and how he himself had driven into the chasm.

Here the coroner stopped him since his evidence would have been a repetition of the doctor's. He questioned him closely, however, as to the cry he had heard or thought he heard.

'It was just a cry.'

'A cry for help?'

'Oh, no. Just a sort of shout, you know. In fact I wasn't quite sure I heard it.'

'A startled kind of cry?'

'That's more like it,' said Bobby gratefully. 'Sort of noise a fellow might let out if a ball hit him unexpectedly.'

'Or if he took a step into nothingness when he thought he was on a path?'

'Yes.'

Then, having explained that the man actually died about five minutes after the doctor left to get help, Bobby's ordeal came to an end.

The coroner was by now anxious to get on with a perfectly straightforward business.

Mrs Leo Cayman was called.

Bobby gave a gasp of acute disappointment. Where was the face of the photo that had tumbled from the dead man's pocket? Photographers, thought Bobby disgustedly, were the worst kind of liars. The photo obviously must have been taken some years ago, but even then it was hard to believe that that charming wide-eyed beauty could have become this brazen-looking woman with plucked eyebrows and obviously dyed hair. Time, thought Bobby suddenly, was a very frightening thing. What would Frankie, for instance, look like in twenty years' time? He gave a little shiver.

Meanwhile, Amelia Cayman, of 17 St Leonard's Gardens, Paddington, was giving evidence.

Deceased was her only brother, Alexander Pritchard. She had last seen her brother the day before the tragedy when he had announced his intention of going for a walking tour in Wales. Her brother had recently returned from the East.

'Did he seem in a happy and normal state of mind?'

'Oh, quite. Alex was always cheerful.'

'So far as you know, he had nothing on his mind?'

'Oh! I'm sure he hadn't. He was looking forward to his trip.'

'There have been no money troubles – or other troubles of any kind in his life recently?'

'Well, really I couldn't say as to that,' said Mrs Cayman. 'You see, he'd only just come back, and before that I hadn't seen him for ten years and he was never one much for writing. But he took me out to theatres and lunches in London and gave me one or two presents, so I don't think he could have been short of money, and he was in such good spirits that I don't think there could have been anything else.'

'What was your brother's profession, Mrs Cayman?'

The lady seemed slightly embarrassed.

'Well, I can't say I rightly know. Prospecting – that's what he called it. He was very seldom in England.'

'You know of no reason which should cause him to take his own life?'

'Oh, no; and I can't believe that he did such a thing. It must have been an accident.'

'How do you explain the fact that your brother had no luggage with him – not even a knapsack?'

'He didn't like carrying a knapsack. He meant to post parcels alternate days. He posted one the day before he left with his night things and a pair of socks, only he addressed it to Derbyshire instead of Denbighshire, so it only got here today.'

'Ah! That clears up a somewhat curious point.'

Mrs Cayman went on to explain how she had been communicated with through the photographers whose name was on the photo her brother had carried. She had come down with her husband to Marchbolt and had at once recognized the body as that of her brother.

As she said the last words she sniffed audibly and began to cry.

The coroner said a few soothing words and dismissed her.

Then he address the jury. Their task was to state how this man came by his death. Fortunately, the matter appeared to be quite simple. There was no suggestion that Mr Pritchard had been worried or depressed or in a state of mind where he would be likely to take his own life. On the contrary, he had been in good health and spirits and had been looking forward to his holiday. It was unfortunately the case that when a sea mist was rising the path along the cliff was a dangerous one and possibly they might agree with him that it was time something was done about it.

The jury's verdict was prompt.

'We find that the deceased came to his death by misadventure and we wish to add a rider that in our opinion the Town Council should immediately take steps to put a fence or rail on the sea side of the path where it skirts the chasm.'

The coroner nodded approval.

The inquest was over.

CHAPTER 5

MR AND MRS CAYMAN

On arriving back at the Vicarage about half an hour later, Bobby found that his connection with the death of Alex Pritchard was not yet quite over. He was informed that Mr and Mrs Cayman had called to see him and were in the study with his father. Bobby made his way there and found his father bravely making suitable conversation without, apparently, much enjoying his task.

'Ah!' he said with some slight relief. 'Here is Bobby.'

Mr Cayman rose and advanced towards the young man with outstretched hand. Mr Cayman was a big florid man with a would-be hearty manner and a cold and somewhat shifty eye that rather belied the manner. As for Mrs Cayman, though she might be considered attractive in a bold, coarse fashion, she had little now in common with that early photograph of herself, and no trace of that wistful expression remained. In fact, Bobby reflected, if she had not recognized her own photograph, it seemed doubtful if anyone else would have done so.

'I came down with the wife,' said Mr Cayman, enclosing Bobby's hand in a firm and painful grip. 'Had to stand by, you know; Amelia's naturally upset.'

Mrs Cayman sniffed.

'We came round to see you,' continued Mr Cayman. 'You see, my poor wife's brother died, practically speaking, in your arms. Naturally, she wanted to know all you could tell her of his last moments.'

'Absolutely,' said Bobby unhappily. 'Oh, absolutely.'

He grinned nervously and was immediately aware of his father's sigh – a sigh of Christian resignation.

'Poor Alex,' said Mrs Cayman, dabbing her eyes. 'Poor, poor Alex.'

'I know,' said Bobby. 'Absolutely grim.'

He wriggled uncomfortably.

'You see,' said Mrs Cayman, looking hopefully at Bobby, 'if he left any last words or messages, naturally I want to know.'

'Oh, rather,' said Bobby. 'But as a matter of fact he didn't.'

'Nothing at all?'

Mrs Cayman looked disappointed and incredulous. Bobby felt apologetic.

'No – well – as a matter of fact, nothing at all.'

'It was best so,' said Mr Cayman solemnly. 'To pass away unconscious – without pain – why, you must think of it as a mercy, Amelia.'

'I suppose I must,' said Mrs Cayman. 'You don't think he felt any pain?'

'I'm sure he didn't,' said Bobby.

Mrs Cayman sighed deeply.

'Well, that's something to be thankful for. Perhaps I did hope he'd left a last message, but I can see that it's best as it is. Poor Alex. Such a fine out-of-door man.'

'Yes, wasn't he?' said Bobby. He recalled the bronze face, the deep blue eyes. An attractive personality, that of Alex Pritchard, attractive even so near death. Strange that he should be the brother of Mrs Cayman and the brother-in-law of Mr Cayman. He had been worthy, Bobby felt, of better things.

'Well, we're very much indebted to you, I'm sure,' said Mrs Cayman.

'Oh, that's all right,' said Bobby. 'I mean – well, couldn't do anything else – I mean –'

He floundered hopelessly.

'We shan't forget it,' said Mr Cayman. Bobby suffered once more that painful grip. He received a flabby hand from Mrs Cayman. His father made further adieus. Bobby accompanied the Caymans to the front door.

'And what do you do with yourself, young man?' inquired Cayman. 'Home on leave – something of that kind?'

'I spend most of my time looking for a job,' said Bobby. He paused. 'I was in the Navy.'

'Hard times – hard times nowadays,' said Mr Cayman, shaking his head. 'Well, I wish you luck, I'm sure.'

'Thank you very much,' said Bobby politely.

He watched them down the weed-grown drive.

Standing there, he fell into a brown study. Various ideas flashed chaotically through his mind – confused reflections – the photograph – that girl's face with the wide-apart eyes and the misty hair – and ten or fifteen years later Mrs Cayman with her heavy make-up, her plucked eyebrows, those wide-apart eyes sunk in between folds of flesh till they looked like pig's eyes, and her violent henna-tinted hair. All traces of youth and innocence had vanished. The pity of things! It all came, perhaps, of marrying a hearty bounder like Mr Cayman. If she had married someone else she might possibly have grown older gracefully. A touch of grey in her hair, eyes still wide apart looking out from a smooth pale face. But perhaps anyway –

Bobby sighed and shook his head.

'That's the worst of marriage,' he said gloomily.

'What did you say?'

Bobby awoke from meditation to become aware of Frankie, whose approach he had not heard.

'Hullo,' he said.

'Hullo. Why marriage? And whose?'

'I was making a reflection of a general nature,' said Bobby.

'Namely –?'

'On the devasting effects of marriage.'

'Who is devastated?'

Bobby explained. He found Frankie unsympathetic.

'Nonsense. The woman's exactly like her photograph.'

'When did you see her? Were you at the inquest?'

'Of course I was at the inquest. What do you think? There's little enough to do down here. An inquest is a perfect godsend. I've never been to one before. I was thrilled to the teeth. Of course, it would have been better if it had been a mysterious poisoning case, with the analyst's reports and all that sort of thing; but one mustn't be too exacting when these simple pleasures come one's way. I hoped up to the end for a suspicion of foul play, but it all seemed most regrettably straightforward.'

'What blood-thirsty instincts you have, Frankie.'

'I know. It's probably atavism (however do you pronounce it? – I've never been sure). Don't you think so? I'm sure I'm atavistic. My nickname at school was Monkey Face.'

'Do monkeys like murder?' queried Bobby.

'You sound like a correspondence in a Sunday paper,' said Frankie. 'Our correspondents' views on this subject are solicited.'

'You know,' said Bobby, reverting to the original topic, 'I don't agree with you about the female Cayman. Her photograph was lovely.'

'Touched up – that's all,' interrupted Frankie.

'Well, then, it was so much touched up that you wouldn't have known them for the same person.'

'You're blind,' said Frankie. 'The photographer had done all that the art of photography could do, but it was still a nasty bit of work.'

'I absolutely disagree with you,' said Bobby coldly. 'Anyway, where did you see it?'

'In the local *Evening Echo*.'

'It probably reproduced badly.'

'It seems to me you're absolutely batty,' said Frankie crossly, 'over a painted-up raddled bitch – yes, I said *bitch* – like the Cayman.'

'Frankie,' said Bobby, 'I'm surprised at you. In the Vicarage drive, too. Semi-holy ground, so to speak.'

'Well, you shouldn't have been so ridiculous.'

There was a pause, then Frankie's sudden fit of temper abated.

'What *is* ridiculous,' she said, 'is to quarrel about the damned woman. I came to suggest a round of golf. What about it?'

'OK, chief,' said Bobby happily.

They set off amicably together and their conversation was of such things as slicing and pulling and how to perfect a chip shot on to the green.

The recent tragedy passed quite out of mind until Bobby, holing a long putt at the eleventh to halve the hole, suddenly gave an exclamation.

'What is it?'

'Nothing. I've just remembered something.'

'What?'

'Well, these people, the Caymans – they came round and asked if the fellow had said anything before he died – and I told them he hadn't.'

'Well?'

'And now I've just remembered that he did.'

'Not one of your brightest mornings, in fact.'

'Well, you see, it wasn't the sort of thing they meant. That's why, I suppose, I didn't think of it.'

'What did he say?' asked Frankie curiously.

'He said: "*Why didn't they ask Evans?*"'

'What a funny thing to say. Nothing else?'

'No. He just opened his eyes and said that – quite suddenly – and then died, poor chap.'

'Oh, well,' said Frankie, turning it over in her mind. 'I don't see that you need worry. It wasn't important.'

'No, of course not. Still, I wish I'd just mentioned it. You see, I said he'd said nothing at all.'

'Well, it amounts to the same thing,' said Frankie. 'I mean, it isn't like – "Tell Gladys I always loved her", or "The will is in the walnut bureau", or any of the proper romantic Last Words there are in books.'

'You don't think it's worth writing about it to them?'

'I shouldn't bother. It couldn't be important.'

'I expect you're right,' said Bobby and turned his attention with renewed vigour to the game.

But the matter did not really dismiss itself from his mind. It was a small point but it fretted him. He felt very faintly uncomfortable about it. Frankie's point of view was, he felt sure, the right and sensible one. The thing was of no importance – let it go. But his conscience continued to reproach him faintly. He had said that the dead man had said nothing. That wasn't true. It was all very trivial and silly but he couldn't feel quite comfortable about it.

Finally, that evening, on an impulse, he sat down and wrote to Mr Cayman.

> *Dear Mr Cayman, I have just remembered that your brother-in-law did actually say something before he died. I think the exact words were, 'Why didn't they ask Evans?' I apologize for not mentioning this this morning, but I attached no importance to the words at the time and so, I suppose, they slipped my memory.*
> *Yours truly,*
> *Robert Jones.*

On the next day but one he received a reply:

> *Dear Mr Jones* (wrote Mr Cayman), *Your letter of 6th instant to hand. Many thanks for repeating my poor brother-in-law's last words so punctiliously in spite of their trivial character. What my wife hoped was that her brother might have left her some last message. Still, thank you for being so conscientious.*
> *Yours faithfully,*
> *Leo Cayman.*

Bobby felt snubbed.

CHAPTER 6

END OF A PICNIC

On the following day Bobby received a letter of quite a different nature:

> *It's all fixed, old boy,* (wrote Badger in an illiterate scrawl which

reflected no credit on the expensive public school which had educated him). *Actually got five cars yesterday for fifteen pounds the lot – an Austin, two Morrises and a couple of Rovers. At the moment they won't actually go, but we can tinker them up sufficiently, I think. Dash it all, a car's a car, after all. So long as it takes the purchaser home without breaking down, that's all they can expect. I thought of opening up Monday week and am relying on you, so don't let me down, will you, old boy? I must say old Aunt Carrie was a sport. I once broke the window of an old boy next door to her who'd been rude to her about her cats and she never got over it. Sent me a fiver every Christmas – and now this.*

We're bound to succeed. The thing's a dead cert. I mean, a car's a car after all. You can pick 'em up for nothing. Put a lick of paint on and that's all the ordinary fool notices. The thing will go with a Bang. Now don't forget. Monday week. I'm relying on you.

Yours ever,

Badger.

Bobby informed his father that he would be going up to town on Monday week to take up a job. The description of the job did not rouse the Vicar to anything like enthusiasm. He had, it may be pointed out, come across Badger Beadon in the past. He merely treated Bobby to a long lecture on the advisability of not making himself liable for anything. Not an authority on fianancial or business matters, his advice was technically vague, but its meaning unmistakable.

On the Wednesday of that week Bobby received another letter. It was addressed in a foreign slanting handwriting. Its contents were somewhat surprising to the young man.

It was from the firm of Henriquez and Dallo in Buenos Aires and, to put it concisely, it offered Bobby a job in the firm with a salary of a thousand a year.

For the first minute or two the young man thought he must be dreaming. A thousand a year. He reread the letter more carefully. There was mention of an ex-Naval man being preferred. A suggestion that Bobby's name had been put forward by someone (someone not named). That acceptance must be immediate, and that Bobby must be prepared to start for Buenos Aires within a week.

'Well, I'm damned!' said Bobby, giving vent to his feelings in a somewhat unfortunate manner.

'Bobby!'

'Sorry, Dad. Forgot you were there.'

Mr Jones cleared his throat.

'I should like to point out to you –'

Bobby felt that this process – usually a long one – must at all costs be avoided. He achieved this course by a simple statement:

'Someone's offered me a thousand a year.'

The Vicar remained open-mouthed, unable for the moment to make any comment.

'That's put him off his drive all right,' thought Bobby with satisfaction.

'My dear Bobby, did I understand you to say that someone had offered you a thousand a year? *A thousand?*'

'Holed it in one, Dad,' said Bobby.

'It's impossible,' said the Vicar.

Bobby was not hurt by this frank incredulity. His estimate of his own monetary value differed little from that of his father.

'They must be complete mutts,' he agreed heartily.

'Who – er – are these people?'

Bobby handed him the letter. The Vicar, fumbling for his pince-nez, peered at it suspiciously. Finally he perused it twice.

'Most remarkable,' he said at last. '*Most* remarkable.'

'Lunatics,' said Bobby.

'Ah! my boy,' said the Vicar. 'It is after all, a great thing to be in Englishman. Honesty. That's what we stand for. The Navy has carried that ideal all over the world. An Englishman's world! This South American firm realizes the value of a young man whose integrity will be unshaken and of whose fidelity his employers will be assured. You can always depend on an Englishman to play the game –'

'And keep a straight bat,' said Bobby.

The Vicar looked at his son doubtfully. The phrase, an excellent one, had actually been on the tip of his tongue, but there was something in Bobby's tone that struck him as not quite sincere.

The young man, however, appeared to be perfectly serious.

'All the same, Dad,' he said, 'why me?'

'What do you mean – why you?'

'There are a lot of Englishmen in England,' said Bobby. 'Hearty fellows, full of cricketing qualities. Why pick on me?'

'Probably your late commanding officer may have recommended you.'

'Yes, I suppose that's true,' said Bobby doubtfully. 'It doesn't matter, anyway, since I can't take the job.'

'Can't take it? My dear boy, what do you mean?'

'Well, I'm fixed up, you see. With Badger.'

'Badger? Badger Beadon. Nonsense, my dear Bobby. This is serious.'

'It's a bit hard, I own,' said Bobby with a sigh.

'Any childish arrangement you have made with young Beadon cannot count for a moment.'

'It counts with me.'

'Young Beadon is completely irresponsible. He has already, I understand, been a source of considerable trouble and expense to his parents.'

'He's not had much luck. Badger's so infernally trusting.'

'Luck – luck! I should say that young man had never done a hand's turn in his life.'

'Nonsense, Dad. Why, he used to get up at five in the morning to feed those beastly chickens. It wasn't his fault they all got the roop or the croup, or whatever it was.'

'I have never approved of this garage project. Mere folly. You must give it up.'

'Can't sir. I've promised. I can't let old Badger down. He's counting on me.'

The discussion proceeded. The Vicar, biased by his views on the subject of Badger, was quite unable to regard any promise made to that young man as binding. He looked on Bobby as obstinate and determined at all costs to lead an idle life in company with one of the worse possible companions. Bobby, on the other hand, stolidly repeated without originality that he 'couldn't let old Badger down'.

The Vicar finally left the room in anger and Bobby then and there sat down to write to the firm of Henriquez and Dallo, refusing their offer.

He sighed as he did so. He was letting a chance go here

which was never likely to occur again. But he saw no alternative.

Later, on the links, he put the problem to Frankie. She listened attentively.

'You'd have had to go to South America?'

'Yes.'

'Would you have liked that?'

'Yes, why not?'

Frankie sighed.

'Anyway,' she said with decision. 'I think you did quite right.'

'About Badger, you mean?'

'Yes.'

'I couldn't let the old bird down, could I?'

'No, but be careful the old bird, as you call him, doesn't let you in.'

'Oh! I shall be careful. Anyway, I shall be all right. I haven't got any assets.'

'That must be rather fun,' said Frankie.

'Why?'

'I don't know why. It just sounded rather nice and free and irresponsible. I suppose, though, when I come to think of it, that I haven't got any assets much, either. I mean, Father gives me an allowance and I've got lots of houses to live in and clothes and maids and some hideous family jewels and a good deal of credits at shops; but that's all the family really. It's not *me*.'

'No, but all the same –' Bobby paused.

'Oh, it's quite different, I know.'

'Yes,' said Bobby. 'It's quite different.'

He felt suddenly very depressed.

They walked in silence to the next tee.

'I'm going to town tomorrow,' said Frankie, as Bobby teed up his ball.

'Tomorrow? Oh – and I was going to suggest you should come for a picnic.'

'I'd have liked to. However, it's arranged. You see, Father's got the gout again.'

'You ought to stay and minister to him,' said Bobby.

'He doesn't like being ministered to. It annoys him frightfully. He likes the second footman best. He's sympathetic and doesn't mind having things thrown at him and being called a damned fool.'

Bobby topped his drive and it trickled into the bunker.

'Hard lines,' said Frankie and drove a nice straight ball that sailed over it.

'By the way,' she remarked. 'We might do something together in London. You'll be up soon?'

'On Monday. But – well – it's no good, is it?'

'What do you mean – no good?'

'Well, I mean I shall be working as a mechanic most of the time. I mean –'

'Even then,' said Frankie, 'I suppose you're just as capable of coming to a cocktail party and getting tight as any other of my friends.'

Bobby merely shook his head.

'I'll give a beer and sausage party if you prefer it,' said Frankie encouragingly.

'Oh, look here, Frankie, what's the good? I mean, you can't mix your crowds. Your crowd's a different crowd from mine.'

'I assure you,' said Frankie, 'that my crowd is a very mixed one.'

'You're pretending not to understand.'

'You can bring Badger if you like. There's friendship for you.'

'You've got some sort of prejudice against Badger.'

'I daresay it's his stammer. People who stammer always make me stammer, too.'

'Look here, Frankie, it's no good and you know it isn't. It's all right down here. There's not much to do and I suppose I'm better than nothing. I mean you're always awfully decent to me and all that, and I'm grateful. But I mean I know I'm just nobody – I mean –'

'When you've quite finished expressing your inferiority complex,' said Frankie coldly, 'perhaps you'll try getting out of the bunker with a niblick instead of a putter.'

'Have I – oh! damn!' He replaced the putter in his bag and took out the niblick. Frankie watched with malicious satisfaction as he hacked at the ball five times in succession. Clouds of sand rose round them.

'Your hole,' said Bobby, picking up the ball.

'I think it is,' said Frankie. 'And that gives me the match.'

'Shall we play the bye?'

'No, I don't think so. I've got a lot to do.'

'Of course. I suppose you have.'

They walked together in silence to the clubhouse.

'Well,' said Frankie, holding out her hand. 'Goodbye, my dear. It's been too marvellous to have you to make use of while I've been down here. See something of you again, perhaps, when I've nothing better to do.'

'Look here, Frankie –'

'Perhaps you'll condescend to come to my coster party. I believe you can get pearl buttons quite cheaply at Woolworth's.'

'Frankie –'

His words were drowned in the noise of the Bentley's engine which Frankie had just started. She drove away with an airy wave of her hand.

'Damn!' said Bobby in a heartfelt tone.

Frankie, he considered, had behaved outrageously. Perhaps he hadn't put things very tactfully, but, dash it all, what he had said was true enough.

Perhaps, though, he shouldn't have put it into words.

The next three days seemed interminably long.

The Vicar had a sore throat which necessitated his speaking in a whisper when he spoke at all. He spoke very little and was obviously bearing his fourth son's presence as a Christian should. Once or twice he quoted Shakespeare to the effect that a serpent's tooth, etc.

On Saturday Bobby felt that he could bear the strain of home life no longer. He got Mrs Roberts, who, with her husband, 'ran' the Vicarage, to give him a packet of sandwiches, and, supplementing this with a bottle of beer which he bought in Marchbolt, he set off for a solitary picnic.

He had missed Frankie abominably these last few days. These older people were the limit . . . They harped on things so.

Bobby stretched himself out on a brackeny bank and debated with himself whether he should eat his lunch first and go to sleep afterwards, or sleep first and eat afterwards.

While he was cogitating, the matter was settled for him by his falling asleep without noticing it.

When he awoke it was half-past three! Bobby grinned as he thought how his father would disapprove of this way of spending a day. A good walk across country – twelve miles or so – that was the kind of thing that a healthy young man should do. It led inevitably to that famous remark: 'And now, I think, I've earned my lunch.'

'Idiotic,' thought Bobby. 'Why earn lunch by doing a lot of walking you don't particularly want to do? What's the merit in it? If you enjoy it, then it's pure self-indulgence, and if you don't enjoy it you're a fool to do it.'

Whereupon he fell upon his unearned lunch and ate it with gusto. With a sigh of satisfaction he unscrewed the bottle of beer. Unusually bitter beer, but decidedly refreshing . . .

He lay back again, having tossed the empty beer bottle into a clump of heather.

He felt rather god-like lounging there. The world was at his feet. A phrase, but a good phrase. He could do anything – anything if he tried! Plans of great splendour and daring initiative flashed through his mind.

Then he grew sleepy again. Lethargy stole over him.

He slept . . .

Heavy, numbing sleep . . .

CHAPTER 7
AN ESCAPE FROM DEATH

Driving her large green Bentley, Frankie drew up to the kerb outside a large old-fashioned house over the doorway of which was inscribed 'St Asaph's'.

Frankie jumped out and, turning, extracted a large bunch of lilies. Then she rang the bell. A woman in nurse's dress answered the door.

'Can I see Mr Jones?' inquired Frankie.

The nurse's eyes took in the Bentley, the lilies and Frankie with intense interest.

'What name shall I say?'

'Lady Frances Derwent.'

The nurse was thrilled and her patient went up in her estimation.

She guided Frankie upstairs into a room on the first floor.

'You've a visitor to see you, Mr Jones. Now, who do you think it is? Such a nice surprise for you.'

All this is the 'bright' manner usual to nursing homes.

'Gosh!' said Bobby, very much surprised. 'If it isn't Frankie!'

'Hullo, Bobby, I've brought the usual flowers. Rather a grave-yard suggestion about them, but the choice was limited.'

'Oh, Lady Frances,' said the nurse, 'they're lovely. I'll put them into water.'

She left the room.

Frankie sat down in an obvious visitor's chair.

'Well, Bobby,' she said. 'What's all this?'

'You may well ask,' said Bobby. 'I'm the complete sensation of this place. Eight grains of morphia, no less. They're going to write about me in the *Lancet* and the *BMJ*.'

'What's the *BMJ*?' interrupted Frankie.

'*The British Medical Journal.*'

'All right. Go ahead. Rattle off some more initials.'

'Do you know, my girl, that half a grain is a fatal dose? I ought to be dead about sixteen times over. It's true that recovery has been known after sixteen grains – still, eight is pretty good, don't you think? I'm the hero of this place. They've never had a case like me before.'

'How nice for them.'

'Isn't it? Gives them something to talk about to all the other patients.'

The nurse re-entered, bearing lilies in vases.

'It's true, isn't it, nurse?' demanded Bobby. 'You've never had a case like mine?'

'Oh! you oughtn't to be here at all,' said the nurse. 'In the churchyard you ought to be. But it's only the good die young, they say.' She giggled at her own wit and went out.

'There you are,' said Bobby. 'You'll see, I shall be famous all over England.'

He continued to talk. Any signs of inferiority complex that he had displayed at his last meeting with Frankie had now quite disappeared. He took a firm and egotistical pleasure in recounting every detail of his case.

'That's enough,' said Frankie, quelling him. 'I don't really care terribly for stomach pumps. To listen to you one would think nobody had ever been poisoned before.'

'Jolly few have been poisoned with eight grains of morphia and got over it,' Bobby pointed out. 'Dash it all, you're not sufficiently impressed.'

'Pretty sickening for the people who poisoned you,' said Frankie.

'I know. Waste of perfectly good morphia.'

'It was in the beer, wasn't it?'

'Yes. You see, someone found me sleeping like the dead, tried to wake me and couldn't. Then they got alarmed, carried me to a farmhouse and sent for a doctor –'

'I know all the next part,' said Frankie hastily.

'At first they had the idea that I'd taken the stuff deliberately. Then when they heard my story, they went off and looked for the beer bottle and found it where I'd thrown it and had it analysed – the dregs of it were quite enough for that, apparently.'

'No clue as to how the morphia got in the bottle?'

'None whatever. They've interviewed the pub where I bought it and opened other bottles and everything's been quite all right.'

'Someone must have put the stuff in the beer while you were asleep?'

'That's it. I remember that the paper across the top wasn't still sticking properly.'

Frankie nodded thoughtfully.

'Well,' she said. 'It shows that what I said in the train that day was quite right.'

'What did you say?'

'That that man – Pritchard – had been pushed over the cliff.'

'That wasn't in the train. You said that at the station,' said Bobby feebly.

'Same thing.'

'But why –'

'Darling – it's obvious. Why should anyone want to put *you* out of the way? You're not the heir to a fortune or anything.'

'I may be. Some great aunt I've never heard of in New Zealand or somewhere may have left me all her money.'

'Nonsense. Not without knowing you. And if she didn't know you, why leave money to a fourth son? Why, in these hard times even a clergyman mightn't have a fourth son! No, it's all quite clear. No one benefits by your death, so that's ruled out. Then there's revenge. You haven't seduced a chemist's daughter, by any chance?'

'Not that I can remember,' said Bobby with dignity.

'I know. One seduces so much that one can't keep count. But I should say offhand that you've never seduced anyone at all.'

'You're making me blush, Frankie. And why must it be a chemist's daughter, anyway?'

'Free access to morphia. It's not so easy to get hold of morphia.'

'Well, I haven't seduced a chemist's daughter.'

'And you haven't got any enemies that you know of?'

Bobby shook his head.

'Well, there you are,' said Frankie triumphantly. 'It must be the man who was pushed over the cliff. What do the police think?'

'They think it must have been a lunatic.'

'Nonsense. Lunatics don't wander about with unlimited supplies of morphia looking for odd bottles of beer to put it into. No, somebody pushed Pritchard over the cliff. A minute or two later you come along and he thinks you saw him do it and so determines to put you out of the way.'

'I don't think that will hold water, Frankie.'

'Why not?'

'Well, to begin with, I didn't see anything.'

'Yes, but he didn't know that.'

'And if I had seen anything, I should have said so at the inquest.'

'I suppose that's so,' said Frankie unwillingly.

She thought for a minute or two.

'Perhaps he thought you'd seen something that you didn't think was anything but which really was something. That sounds pure gibberish, but you get the idea?'

Bobby nodded.

'Yes, I see what you mean, but it doesn't seem very probable, somehow.'

'I'm sure that cliff business had something to do with this. You were on the spot – the first person to be there –'

'Thomas was there, too,' Bobby reminded her. 'And nobody's tried to poison him.'

'Perhaps they're going to,' said Frankie cheerfully. 'Or perhaps they've tried and failed.'

'It all seems very far-fetched.'

'I think it's logical. If you get two out of the way things happening in a stagnant pond like Marchbolt – wait – there's a third thing.'

'What?'

'That job you were offered. That, of course, is quite a small thing, but it was odd, you must admit. I've never heard of a foreign firm that specialized in seeking out undistinguished ex-Naval officers.'

'Did you say undistinguished?'

'You hadn't got into the *BMJ*, then. But you see my point. You've seen something you weren't meant to see – or so they (whoever they are) think. Very well. They first try to get rid of you by offering you a job abroad. Then, when that fails, they try to put you out of the way altogether.'

'Isn't that rather drastic? And anyway a great risk to take?'

'Oh! but murderers are always frightfully rash. The more murders they do, the more murders they want to do.'

'Like *The Third Bloodstain*,' said Bobby, remembering one of his favourite works of fiction.

'Yes, and in real life, too – Smith and his wives and Armstrong and people.'

'Well, but, Frankie, what on earth is it I'm supposed to have seen?'

'That, of course, is the difficulty,' admitted Frankie. 'I agree that it can't have been the actual pushing, because you would have told about that. It must be something about the man himself. Perhaps he had a birthmark or double-jointed fingers or some strange physical peculiarity.'

'Your mind is running on Dr Thorndyke, I see. It couldn't be anything like that because whatever I saw the police would see as well.'

'So they would. That was an idiotic suggestion. It's very difficult, isn't it?'

'It's a pleasing theory,' said Bobby. 'And it makes me feel important, but all the same, I don't believe it's much more than a theory.'

'I'm sure I'm right.' Frankie rose. 'I must be off now. Shall I come and see you again tomorrow?'

'Oh! Do. The arch chatter of the nurses gets very monotonous. By the way, you're back from London very soon?'

'My dear, as soon as I heard about you, I tore back. It's most exciting to have a romantically poisoned friend.'

'I don't know whether morphia is so very romantic,' said Bobby reminiscently.

'Well, I'll come tomorrow. Do I kiss you or don't I?'

'It's not catching,' said Bobby encouragingly.

'Then I'll do my duty to the sick thoroughly.'

She kissed him lightly.

'See you tomorrow.'

The nurse came in with Bobby's tea as she went out.

'I've seen her pictures in the papers often. She's not so very like them, though. And, of course, I've seen her driving about in her car, but I've never seen her before close to, so to speak. Not a bit haughty, is she?'

'Oh, no!' said Bobby. 'I should never call Frankie haughty.'

'I said to Sister, I said, she's as natural as anything. Not a bit stuck up. I said to Sister, she's just like you or me, I said.'

Silently dissenting violently from this view, Bobby returned no reply. The nurse, disappointed by his lack of response, left the room.

Bobby was left to his own thoughts.

He finished his tea. Then he went over in his mind the possibilities of Frankie's amazing theory, and ended by deciding reluctantly against it. He then cast about for other distractions.

His eye was caught by the vases of lilies. Frightfully sweet of Frankie to bring him all these flowers, and of course they were lovely, but he wished it had occurred to her to bring him a few detective stories instead. He cast his eye over the table beside him. There was a novel of Ouida's and a copy of *John Halifax, Gentleman* and last week's *Marchbolt Weekly Times*. He picked up *John Halifax, Gentleman*.

After five minutes he put it down. To a mind nourished on *The Third Bloodstain*, *The Case of the Murdered Archduke* and *The Strange Adventure of the Florentine Dagger*, *John Halifax, Gentleman*, lacked pep.

With a sigh he picked up last week's *Marchbolt Weekly Times*.

A moment or two later he was pressing the bell beneath his pillow with a vigour which brought a nurse into the room at a run.

'Whatever's the matter, Mr Jones? Are you taken bad?'

'Ring up the Castle,' cried Bobby. 'Tell Lady Frances she must come back here at once.'

'Oh, Mr Jones. You can't send a message like that.'

'Can't I?' said Bobby. 'If I were allowed to get up from this blasted bed you'd soon see whether I could or couldn't. As it is, you've got to do it for me.'

'But she'll hardly be back.'

'You don't know that Bentley.'

'She won't have had her tea.'

'Now look here, my dear girl,' said Bobby, 'don't stand there arguing with me. Ring up as I tell you. Tell her she's got to come here at once because I've got something very important to say to her.'

Overborne, but unwilling, the nurse went. She took some liberties with Bobby's message.

If it was no inconvenience to Lady Frances, Mr Jones wondered if she would mind coming as he had something he would like to say to her, but, of course, Lady Frances was not to put herself out in any way.

Lady Frances replied curtly that she would come at once.

'Depend upon it,' said the nurse to her colleagues, 'she's sweet on him! That's what it is.'

Frankie arrived all agog.

'What's this desperate summons?' she demanded.

Bobby was sitting up in bed, a bright red spot in each cheek. In his hand he waved the copy of the *Marchbolt Weekly Times*.

'Look at this, Frankie.'

Frankie looked.

'Well,' she demanded.

'This is the picture you meant when you said it was touched up but quite like the Cayman woman.'

Bobby's finger pointed to a somewhat blurred reproduction of a photograph. Underneath it were the words: 'PORTRAIT FOUND ON THE DEAD MAN AND BY WHICH HE WAS IDENTIFIED. MRS AMELIA CAYMAN, THE DEAD MAN'S SISTER.'

'That's what I said, and it's true, too. I can't see anything to rave over in it.'

'No more than I.'

'But you said –'

'I know I said. But you see, Frankie' – Bobby's voice became very impressive – '*this isn't the photograph that I put back in the dead man's pocket . . .*'

They looked at each other.

'Then in that case,' began Frankie slowly.

'Either there must have been two photographs –'

'– Which isn't likely –'

'Or else –'

They paused.

'*That man* – what's his name?' said Frankie.

'Bassington-ffrench!' said Bobby.

'*I'm* quite sure!'

CHAPTER 8

RIDDLE OF A PHOTOGRAPH

They stared at each other as they tried to adjust themselves to the altered situation.

'It couldn't be anyone else,' said Bobby. 'He was the only person who had the chance.'

'Unless, as we said, there were *two* photographs.'

'We agreed that that wasn't likely. If there had been two photographs they'd have tried to identify him by means of both of them – not only one.'

'Anyway, that's easily found out,' said Frankie. 'We can ask the police. We'll assume for the moment that there was just the one photograph, the one you saw that you put back again in his pocket. It was there when you left him, and it wasn't there when the police came, therefore the only person who *could* have taken it away and put the other one in its place was this man Bassington-ffrench. What was he like, Bobby?'

Bobby frowned in the effort of remembrance.

'A sort of nondescript fellow. Pleasant voice. A gentleman and all that. I really didn't notice him particularly. He said that he was a stranger down here – and something about looking for a house.'

'We can verify that, anyway,' said Frankie. 'Wheeler & Owen are the only house agents.' Suddenly she gave a shiver. 'Bobby, have you thought? If Pritchard was pushed over – *Bassington-ffrench must be the man who did it . . .*'

'That's pretty grim,' said Bobby. 'He seemed such a nice pleasant sort of fellow. But you know, Frankie, we can't be sure he really was pushed over.'

'You have been all along.'

'No, I just wanted it to be that way because it made things more exciting. But now it's more or less proved. If it was murder everything fits in. Your unexpected appearance which upsets the murderer's plans. Your discovery of the photograph and, in consequence, the need to put you out of the way.'

'There's a flaw there,' said Bobby.

'Why?' You were the only person who saw that photograph. As soon as Bassington-ffrench was left alone with the body he changed the photograph which only you had seen.'

But Bobby continued to shake his head.

'No, that won't do. Let's grant for the moment that that photograph was so important that I had to be "got out of the way", as you put it. Sounds absurd but I suppose it's just possible. Well, then, whatever was going to be done would have to be done *at once*. The fact that I went to London and never saw the *Marchbolt Weekly Times* or the other papers with the photograph in it was just pure chance – a thing nobody could count on. The probability was that I should say at once, "That isn't the photograph I saw." Why wait till after the inquest when everything was nicely settled?'

'There's something in that,' admitted Frankie.

'And there's another point. I can't be absolutely sure, of course, but I could almost swear that when I put the photograph back in the dead man's pocket Bassington-ffrench wasn't there. He didn't arrive till about five or ten minutes later.'

'He might have been watching you all the time,' argued Frankie.

'I don't see very well how he could,' said Bobby slowly. 'There's really only one place where you can see down to exactly the spot we were. Farther round, the cliff bulges and then recedes underneath, so that you can't see over. There's just the one place and when Bassington-ffrench did arrive there I heard him at once. Footsteps echo down below. He may have been near at hand, but he wasn't looking over till then – I'll swear.'

'Then you think that he didn't know about your seeing the photograph?'

'I don't see how he could have known.'

'And he can't have been afraid you'd seen him doing it – the murder, I mean – because, as you say, that's absurd. You'd never have held your tongue about it. It looks as though it must have been something else altogether.'

'Only I don't see what it could have been.'

'Something they didn't know about till after the inquest. I don't know why I say "*they*".'

'Why not? After all, the Caymans must have been in it, too. It's probably a gang. I like gangs.'

'That's a low taste,' said Frankie absently. 'A single-handed murder is much higher class. Bobby!'

'Yes?'

'What was it Pritchard said – just before he died? You know, you told me about it that day on the links. That funny question?'

'"*Why didn't they ask Evans?*"'

'Yes. Suppose *that* was it?'

'But that's ridiculous.'

'It sounds so, but it might be important, really. Bobby, I'm *sure* it's that. Oh, no, I'm being an idiot – you never told the Caymans about it?'

'I did, as a matter of fact,' said Bobby slowly.

'You *did*?'

'Yes. I wrote to them that evening. Saying, of course, that it was probably quite unimportant.'

'And what happened?'

'Cayman wrote back, politely agreeing, of course, that there was nothing in it, but thanking me for taking the trouble. I felt rather snubbed.'

'And two days later you got this letter from a strange firm bribing you to go to South America?'

'Yes.'

'Well,' said Frankie, 'I don't know what more you want. They try that first; you turn it down, and the next thing is that they follow you round and seize a good moment to empty a lot of morphia into your bottle of beer.'

'Then the Caymans *are* in it?'

'Of course the Caymans are in it!'

'Yes,' said Bobby thoughtfully. 'If your reconstruction is correct, they must be in it. According to our present theory, it goes like this. Dead man X is deliberately pushed over cliff – presumably by BF (pardon these initials). It is important that X should not be correctly identified, so portrait of Mrs C is put in his pocket and portrait of fair unknown removed. (Who was she, I wonder?)'

'Keep to the point,' said Frankie sternly.

'Mrs C waits for photographs to appear and turns up as grief-stricken sister and identifies X as her brother from foreign parts.'

'You don't believe he could really have been her brother?'

'Not for a moment! You know, it puzzled me all along. The Caymans were a different class altogether. The dead man was – well, it sounds a most awful thing to say and just like some deadly old retired Anglo-Indian, but the dead man was a pukka sahib.'

'And the Caymans most emphatically weren't?'

'*Most* emphatically.'

'And then, just when everything has gone off well from the Caymans' point of view – body successfully identified, verdict of accidental death, everything in the garden lovely – *you* come along and mess things up,' mused Frankie.

'"*Why didn't they ask Evans?*"' Bobby repeated the phrase thoughtfully. 'You know, I can't see what on earth there can be in that to put the wind up anybody.'

'Ah! that's because you don't know. It's like making crossword puzzles. You write down a clue and you think it's too idiotically simple and that everyone will guess it straight off, and you're frightfully surprised when they simply can't get it in the least. "*Why didn't they ask Evans?*" must have been a most frightfully significant phrase to them, and they couldn't realize that it meant nothing at all to you.'

'More fools they.'

'Oh, quite so. But it's just possible they thought that if Pritchard said that, he might have said something more which would also recur to you in due time. Anyway, they weren't going to take chances. You were safer out of the way.'

'They took a lot of risk. Why didn't they engineer another "accident"?'

'No, no. That would have been stupid. Two accidents within a week of each other? It might have suggested a connection between the two, and then people would have begun inquiring into the first one. No, I think there's a kind of bald simplicity about their method which is really rather clever.'

'And yet you said just now that morphia wasn't easy to get hold of.'

'No more it isn't. You have to sign poison books and things. Oh! of course, that's a clue. Whoever did it had easy access to supplies of morphia.'

'A doctor, a hospital nurse, or a chemist,' suggested Bobby.

'Well, I was thinking more of illicitly imported drugs.'

'You can't mix up too many different sorts of crime,' said Bobby.

'You see, the strong point would be the absence of motive. Your death doesn't benefit anyone. So what will the police think?'

'A lunatic,' said Bobby. 'And that's what they do think.'

'You see? It's awfully simple, really.'

Bobby began to laugh suddenly.

'What's amusing you?'

'Just the thought of how sick-making it must be for them! All that morphia – enough to kill five or six people – and here I am still alive and kicking.'

'One of Life's little ironies that one can't foresee,' agreed Frankie.

'The question is – what do we do next?' said Bobby practically.

'Oh! lots of things,' said Frankie promptly.

'Such as . . . ?'

'Well – finding out about the photograph – that there was only one, not two. And about Bassington-ffrench's house hunting.'

'That will probably be quite all right and above board.'

'Why do you say that?'

'Look here, Frankie, think a minute. Bassington-ffrench *must* be above suspicion. He *must* be all clear and above board. Not only must there be nothing to connect him in any way with the dead man, but he must have a proper reason for being down here. He may have invented house hunting on the spur of the moment, but I bet he carried out something of the kind. There must be no suggestion of a "mysterious stranger seen in the neighbourhood of the accident". I fancy that Bassington-ffrench is his own name and that he's the sort of person who would be quite above suspicion.'

'Yes,' said Frankie thoughtfully. 'That's a very good deduction. There will be nothing whatever to connect Bassington-ffrench with Alex Pritchard. Now, if we knew who the dead man really was –'

'Ah, then it might be different.'

'So it was very important that the body should not be recognized – hence all the Cayman camouflage. And yet it was taking a big risk.'

'You forget that Mrs Cayman identified him as soon as was humanly possible. After that, even if there had been pictures of him in the papers (you know how blurry these things are) people would only say: "Curious, this man Pritchard, who fell over a cliff, is really extraordinarily like Mr X."'

'There must be more to it than that,' said Frankie shrewdly. 'X must have been a man who wouldn't easily be missed. I mean, he couldn't have been the sort of family man whose wife or relations would go to the police at once and report him missing.'

'Good for you, Frankie. No, he must have been just going abroad or perhaps just come back (he was marvellously tanned – like a big-game hunter – he looked that sort of person) and he can't have had any very near relations who knew all about his movements.'

'We're deducing beautifully,' said Frankie. 'I hope we're not deducing all wrong.'

'Very likely,' said Bobby. 'But I think what we've said so far is fairly sound sense – granted, that is, the wild improbability of the whole thing.'

Frankie waved away the wild improbability with an airy gesture.

'The thing is – what to do next,' she said. 'It seems to me we've got three angles of attack.'

'Go on, Sherlock.'

'The first is *you*. They've made one attempt on your life. They'll probably try again. This time we might get what they call "a line" on them. Using you as a decoy, I mean.'

'No thank you, Frankie,' said Bobby with feeling. 'I've been very lucky this time, but I mightn't be so lucky again if they changed the attack to a blunt instrument. I was thinking of taking a great deal of care of myself in the future. The decoy idea can be washed out.'

'I was afraid you'd say that,' said Frankie with a sigh. 'Young men are sadly degenerate nowadays. Father says so. They don't enjoy being uncomfortable and doing dangerous and unpleasant things any longer. It's a pity.'

'A great pity,' said Bobby, but he spoke with firmness. 'What's the second plan of campaign?'

'Working from the "*Why didn't they ask Evans?*" clue,' said Frankie. 'Presumably the dead man came down here to see Evans, whoever he was. Now, if we could find Evans –'

'How many Evanses,' Bobby interrupted, 'do you think there are in Marchbolt?'

'Seven hundred, I should think,' admitted Frankie.

'At least! We might do something that way, but I'm rather doubtful.'

'We could list all the Evanses and visit the likely ones.'

'And ask them – what?'

'That's the difficulty,' said Frankie.

'We need to know a little more,' said Bobby. 'Then that idea of yours might come in useful. What's No. 3?'

'This man Bassington-ffrench. There we *have* got something tangible to go upon. It's an uncommon name. I'll ask Father. He knows all these county family names and their various branches.'

'Yes,' said Bobby. 'We might do something that way.'

'At any rate, we are going to do something?'

'Of course we are. Do you think I'm going to be given eight grains of morphia and do nothing about it?'

'That's the spirit,' said Frankie.

'And besides that,' said Bobby, 'there's the indignity of the stomach pump to be washed out.'

'That's enough,' said Frankie. 'You'll be getting morbid and indecent again if I don't stop you.'

'You have no true womanly sympathy,' said Bobby.

CHAPTER 9

CONCERNING MR BASSINGTON-FFRENCH

Frankie lost no time in setting to work. She attacked her father that same evening.

'Father,' she said, 'do you know any Bassington-ffrenches?'

Lord Marchington, who was reading a political article, did not quite take in the question.

'It's not the French so much as the Americans,' he said severely. 'All this tomfoolery and conferences – wasting the nation's time and money –'

Frankie abstracted her mind until Lord Marchington, running like a railway train along an accustomed line, came, as it were, to a halt at a station.

'The Bassington-ffrenches,' repeated Frankie.

'What about 'em?' said Lord Marchington.

Frankie didn't know what about them. She made a statement, knowing well enough that her father enjoyed contradiction.

'They're a Yorkshire family, aren't they?'

'Nonsense – Hampshire. There's the Shropshire branch, of course, and then there's the Irish lot. Which are your friends?'

'I'm not sure,' said Frankie, accepting the implication of friendship with several unknown people.

'Not sure? What do you mean? You must be sure.'

'People drift about so nowadays,' said Frankie.

'Drift – drift – that's about all they do. In my days we asked people. Then one knew where one was – fellow said he was the Hampshire branch – very well, your grandmother married my second cousin. It made a link.'

'It must have been too sweet,' said Frankie, 'But there really isn't time for genealogical and geographical research nowadays.'

'No – you've no time nowadays for anything but drinking these poisonous cocktails.'

Lord Marchington gave a sudden yelp of pain as he moved his gouty leg, which some free imbibing of the family port had not improved.

'Are they well off?' asked Frankie.

'The Bassington-ffrenches? Couldn't say. The Shropshire lot have been hard hit, I believe – death duties, and one thing or another. One of the Hampshire ones married an heiress. An American woman.'

'One of them was down here the other day,' said Frankie. 'Looking for a house, I believe.'

'Funny idea. What should anyone want with a house down here?'

That, thought Frankie, was the question.

On the following day she walked into the office of Messrs. Wheeler & Owen, House and Estate Agents.

Mr Owen himself sprang up to receive her. Frankie gave him a gracious smile and dropped into a chair.

'And what can we have the pleasure of doing for you, Lady Frances? You don't want to sell the Castle, I suppose. Ha! Ha!' Mr Owen laughed at his own wit.

'I wish we could,' said Frankie. 'No, as a matter of fact, I believe a friend of mine was down here the other day – a Mr Bassington-ffrench. He was looking for a house.'

'Ah! yes, indeed. I remember the name perfectly. Two small f's.'

'That's right,' said Frankie.

'He was making inquiries about various small properties with a view to purchase. He was obliged to return to town the next day, so could not view many of the houses, but I understand he is in no great hurry. Since he left, one or two suitable properties have come into the market and I have sent him on particulars, but have had no reply.'

'Did you write to London – or to the – er – country address?' inquired Frankie.

'Let me see now.' He called to a junior clerk. 'Frank, Mr Bassington-ffrench's address.'

'Roger Bassington-ffrench, Esq., Merroway Court, Staverley, Hants,' said the junior clerk glibly.

'Ah!' said Frankie. 'Then it wasn't my Mr Bassington-ffrench. This must be his cousin. I thought it was odd his being here and not looking me up.'

'Quite so – quite so,' said Mr Owen intelligently.

'Let me see, it must have been the Wednesday he came to see you.'

'That's right. Just before six-thirty. We close at six-thirty. I remember particularly because it was the day when that sad accident happened. Man fell over the cliff. Mr Bassington-ffrench had actually stayed by the body till the police came. He looked quite upset when he came in here. Very sad tragedy, that, and high time something was done about that bit of path. The Town Council have been criticized very freely, I can tell you, Lady Frances. Most dangerous. Why we haven't had more accidents than we have I can't imagine.'

'Extraordinary,' said Frankie.

She left the office in a thoughtful mood. As Bobby had prophesied, all Mr Bassington-ffrench's actions seemed clear and above aboard. He was one of the Hampshire Bassington-ffrenches, he had given his proper address, he had actually mentioned his part in the tragedy to the house agent. Was it possible that, after all, Mr Bassington-ffrench was the completely innocent person he seemed?

Frankie had a qualm of doubt. Then she refused it.

'No,' she said to herself. 'A man who wants to buy a little place would either get here earlier in the day, or else stay over the next day. You wouldn't go into a house agent's at six-thirty in the evening and go up to London the following day. Why make the journey at all? Why not write?'

No, she decided, Bassington-ffrench was the guilty party.

Her next call was the police station.

Inspector Williams was an old acquaintance, having succeeded in tracking down a maid with a false reference who had absconded with some of Frankie's jewellery.

'Good afternoon, Inspector.'

'Good afternoon, your Ladyship. Nothing wrong, I hope.'

'Not as yet, but I'm thinking of holding up a bank soon, because I'm getting so short of money.'

The inspector gave a rumbling laugh in acknowledgement of this witticism.

'As a matter of fact, I've come to ask questions out of sheer curiosity,' said Frankie.

'Is that so, Lady Frances?'

'Now do tell me this, Inspector – the man who fell over the cliff – Pritchard, or whatever his name was –'

'Pritchard, that's right.'

'He had only *one* photograph on him, didn't he? Somebody told me he had *three*!'

'One's right,' said the inspector. 'Photograph of his sister it was. She came down and identified him.'

'How absurd to say there were three!'

'Oh! That's easy, your Ladyship. These newspaper reporters don't mind how much they exaggerate and as often as not they get the whole thing wrong.'

'I know,' said Frankie. 'I've heard the wildest stories.' She paused a moment then drew freely on her imagination. 'I've heard that his pockets were stuffed with papers proving him to be a Bolshevik agent, and there's another story that his pockets were full of dope, and another again about his having pockets full of counterfeit bank notes.'

The inspector laughed heartily.

'That's a good one.'

'I suppose really he had just the usual things in his pockets?'

'And very few at that. A handkerchief, not marked. Some loose change, a packet of cigarettes and a couple of treasury notes – loose, not in a case. No letters. We'd have had a job to identify him if it hadn't been for the photo. Providential, you might call it.'

'I wonder,' said Frankie.

In view of her private knowledge, she considered providential a singularly inappropriate word. She changed the conversation.

'I went to see Mr Jones, the Vicar's son, yesterday. The one who's been poisoned. What an extraordinary thing that was.'

'Ah!' said the inspector. 'Now that is extraordinary, if you like. Never heard of anything like it happening before. A nice young gentleman without an enemy in the world, or so you'd say. You know, Lady Frances, there are some queer customers going about. All the same, I never heard of a homicidal maniac who acted just this way.'

'Is there any clue at all to who did it?'

Frankie was all wide-eyed inquiry.

'It's so interesting to hear all this,' she added.

The inspector swelled with gratification. He enjoyed this friendly conversation with an Earl's daughter. Nothing stuck up or snobbish about Lady Frances.

'There was a car seen in the vicinity,' said the inspector. 'Dark-blue Talbot saloon. A man on Lock's Corner reported dark-blue Talbot, No. GG 8282, passed going direction St Botolph's.'

'And you think?'

'GG 8282 is the number of the Bishop of Botolph's car.'

Frankie toyed for a minute or two with the idea of a homicidal bishop who offered sacrifices of clergymen's sons, but rejected it with a sigh.

'You don't suspect the Bishop, I suppose?' she said.

'We've found out that the Bishop's car never left the Palace garage that afternoon.'

'So it was a false number.'

'Yes. We've got that to go on all right.'

With expressions of admiration, Frankie took her leave. She made no damping remark, but she thought to herself:

'There must be a large number of dark-blue Talbots in England.'

On her return home she took a directory of Marchbolt from its place on the writing-table in the library and removed it to her own room. She worked over it for some hours.

The result was not satisfactory.

There were four hundred and eighty-two Evanses in Marchbolt.

'Damn!' said Frankie.

She began to make plans for the future.

CHAPTER 10

PREPARATIONS FOR AN ACCIDENT

A week later Bobby had joined Badger in London. He had received several enigmatical communications from Frankie, most in such an illegible scrawl that he was quite unable to do more than guess at their meaning. However, their general purport seemed to be that Frankie had a plan and that he (Bobby) was to do nothing until he heard from her. This was as well, for Bobby would certainly have had no leisure to do anything, since the unlucky Badger had already succeeded in embroiling himself and his business in every way ingenuity could suggest, and Bobby was kept busy disentangling the extraordinary mess his friend seemed to have got into.

Meanwhile, the young man remained very strictly on his guard. The effect of eight grains of morphia was to render their taker extremely suspicious of food and drink and had also induced him to bring to London a Service revolver, the possession of which was extremely irksome to him.

He was just beginning to feel that the whole thing had been an extravagant nightmare when Frankie's Bentley roared down the Mews and drew up outside the garage. Bobby, in grease-stained overalls, came out to receive it. Frankie was at the wheel and beside her sat a rather gloomy-looking young man.

'Hullo, Bobby,' said Frankie. 'This is George Arbuthnot. He's a doctor, and we shall need him.'

Bobby winced slightly as he and George Arbuthnot made faint recognitions of each other's presence.

'Are you sure we're going to need a doctor?' he asked. 'Aren't you being a bit pessimistic?'

'I didn't mean we should need him in that way,' said Frankie. 'I need him for a scheme that I've got on. Look here, is there anywhere we can go and talk?'

Bobby looked round him.

'Well, there's my bedroom,' he said doubtfully.

'Excellent,' said Frankie.

She got out of the car and she and George Arbuthnot followed Bobby up some outside steps and into a microscopic bedroom.

'I don't know,' said Bobby, looking round dubiously, 'if there's anywhere to sit.'

There was not. The only chair was loaded with, apparently, the whole of Bobby's wardrobe.

'The bed will do,' said Frankie.

She plumped down on it. George Arbuthnot did the same and the bed groaned protestingly.

'I've got everything planned out,' said Frankie. 'To begin with, we want a car. One of yours will do.'

'Do you mean you want to buy one of our cars?'

'Yes.'

'That's really very nice of you, Frankie,' said Bobby, with warm appreciation. 'But you needn't. I really do draw the line at sticking my friends.'

'You've got it all wrong,' said Frankie. 'It isn't like that at all. I know what you mean – it's like buying perfectly appalling clothes and hats from one's friends who are just starting in business. A nuisance, but it's got to be done. But this isn't like that at all. I really need a car.'

'What about the Bentley?'

'The Bentley's no good.'

'You're mad,' said Bobby.

'No, I'm not. The Bentley's no good for what I want it for.'

'What's that?'

'Smashing it up.'

Bobby groaned and put a hand to his head.

'I don't seem very well this morning.'

George Arbuthnot spoke for the first time. His voice was deep and melancholy.

'She means,' he said, 'that's she going to have an accident.'

'How does she know?' said Bobby wildly.

Frankie gave an exasperated sigh.

'Somehow or other,' she said, 'we seem to have started wrong. Now just listen quietly, Bobby, and try and take in what I'm going to say. I know your brains are practically negligible, but you ought to be able to understand if you really concentrate.'

She paused, then resumed.

'I am on the trail of Bassington-ffrench.'

'Hear, hear.'

'Bassington-ffrench – our particular Bassington-ffrench – lives at Merroway Court at the village of Staverley in Hampshire. Merroway Court belongs to Bassington-ffrench's brother, and our Bassington-ffrench lives there with his brother and his wife.'

'Whose wife?'

'The brother's wife, of course. That isn't the point. The point is how are you or I or both of us is going to worm ourselves into the household. I've been down and reconnoitred the ground. Staverley's a mere village. Strangers arriving there to stay would stick out a mile. It would be the sort of thing that simply isn't done. So I've evolved a plan. This is what is going to happen: Lady Frances Derwent, driving her car more recklessly than well, crashes into the wall near the gates of Merroway Court. Complete wreckage of the car, less complete wreckage of Lady Frances, who is carried to the house, suffering from concussion and shock and must emphatically not be moved.'

'Who says so?'

'George. Now you see where George comes in. We can't risk a strange doctor saying there is nothing the matter with me. Or perhaps some officious person might pick up my prostrate form and take it to some local hospital. No, what happens is this: George is passing, also in a car (you'd better sell us a second one), sees the accident, leaps out and takes charge. "I am a doctor. Stand back, everybody" (That is, if there is anybody to stand back). "We must take her into that house – what is it, Merroway Court? That will do. I must be able to make a thorough examination." I am carried to the best spare room, the Bassington-ffrenches either sympathetic or bitterly resisting, but in any case, George will overbear them. George makes his examination and emerges with his verdict. Happily, it is not as serious as he thought. No bones broken, but danger of concussion. I must on no account be moved for two or three days. After that, I shall be able to return to London.

'And then George departs and it's up to me to ingratiate myself with the household.'

'And where do I come in?'

'You don't.'

'But look here –'

'My dear child, do remember that Bassington-ffrench knows

you. He doesn't know me from Adam. And I'm in a frightfully strong position, because I've got a title. You see how useful that is. I'm not just a stray young woman gaining admission to the house for mysterious purposes. I am an earl's daughter and therefore highly respectable. And George is a real doctor and everything is quite above suspicion.'

'Oh! I suppose it's all right,' said Bobby unhappily.

'It's a remarkably well-planned scheme, I think,' said Frankie with pride.

'And I don't do anything at all?' asked Bobby.

He still felt injured – much like a dog who has been unexpectedly deprived of a bone. This, he felt, was his own particular crime, and now he was being ousted.

'Of course you do, darling. You grow a moustache.'

'Oh! I grow a moustache, do I?'

'Yes. How long will it take?'

'Two or three weeks, I expect.'

'Heavens! I'd no idea it was such a slow process. Can't you speed it up?'

'No. Why can't I wear a false one?'

'They always look so false and they twist or come off or smell of spirit gum. Wait a minute, though, I believe there is a kind you can get stuck on hair by hair, so to speak, that absolutely defies detection. I expect a theatrical wigmaker would do it for you.'

'He'd probably think I was trying to escape from justice.'

'It doesn't matter what he thinks.'

'Once I've got the moustache, what do I do?'

'Put on a chauffeur's uniform and drive the Bentley down to Staverley.'

'Oh, I see.'

Bobby brightened.

'You see my idea is this,' said Frankie: 'Nobody looks at a chauffeur in the way they look at a *person*. In any case, Bassington-ffrench only saw you for a minute or two and he must have been too rattled wondering if he could change the photograph in time to look at you much. You were just a young golfing ass to him. It isn't like the Caymans who sat opposite you and talked to you and who were deliberately trying to sum you up. I'd bet anything that seeing you in chauffeur's uniform,

Bassington-ffrench wouldn't recognize you even without the moustache. He might just possibly think that your face reminded him of somebody – no more than that. And with the moustache it ought to be perfectly safe. Now tell me, what do you think of the plan?'

Bobby turned it over in his mind.

'To tell you the truth, Frankie,' he said generously, 'I think it's pretty good.'

'In that case,' said Frankie briskly. 'Let's go and buy some cars. I say, I think George has broken your bed.'

'It doesn't matter,' said Bobby hospitably. 'It was never a particularly good bed.'

They descended to the garage, where a nervous-looking young man with a curious lack of chin and an agreeable smile greeted them with a vague 'Haw, haw, haw!' His general appearance was slightly marred by the fact that his eyes had a distinct disinclination to look in the same direction.

'Hullo, Badger,' said Bobby. 'You remember Frankie, don't you?'

Badger clearly didn't, but he said, 'Haw, haw, haw!' again in an amiable manner.

'Last time I saw you,' said Frankie, 'you were head downward in the mud and we had to pull you out by the legs.'

'No, not really?' said Badger. 'Why, that m-m-must have been W-w-w-wales.'

'Quite right,' said Frankie. 'It was.'

'I always was a p-p-putrid r-r-r-rider,' said Badger. 'I s-s-s-still am,' he added mournfully.

'Frankie wants to buy a car,' said Bobby.

'Two cars,' said Frankie. 'George has got to have one, too. He's crashed his at the moment.'

'We can hire him one,' said Bobby.

'Well, come and look at what we've got in s-s-stock,' said Badger.

'They look very smart,' said Frankie, dazzled by lurid hues of scarlet and apple-green.

'They *look* all right,' said Bobby darkly.

'That's r-r-r-remarkably good value in a s-s-second-hand Chrysler,' said Badger.

'No, not that one,' said Bobby. 'Whatever she buys has got to go at least forty miles.'

Badger cast his partner a look of reproach.

'The Standard is pretty much on its last legs,' mused Bobby. 'But I think it would just get you there. The Essex is a bit too good for the job. She'll go at least two hundred before breaking down.'

'All right,' said Frankie. 'I'll have the Standard.'

Badger drew his colleague a little aside.

'W-w-what do you think about p-p-price?' he murmured. 'Don't want to s-s-stick a friend of yours too much. T-t-t-ten pounds?'

'Ten pounds is all right,' said Frankie, entering the discussion. 'I'll pay for it now.'

'Who is she really?' asked Badger in a loud whisper.

Bobby whispered back.

'F-f-f-first time I ever knew anyone with a t-t-t-title who c-c-could pay cash,' said Badger with respect.

Bobby followed the other two out to the Bentley.

'When is this business going to take place?' he demanded.

'The sooner the better,' said Frankie. 'We thought tomorrow afternoon.'

'Look here, can't I be there? I'll put on a beard if you like.'

'Certainly not,' said Frankie. 'A beard would probably ruin everything by falling off at the wrong moment. But I don't see why you shouldn't be a motor-cyclist – with a lot of cap and goggles. What do you think, George?'

George Arbuthnot spoke for the second time:

'All right,' he said, 'the more the merrier.'

His voice was even more melancholy than before.

CHAPTER 11
THE ACCIDENT HAPPENS

The rendezvous for the great accident party was fixed at a spot about a mile from Staverley village where the road to Staverley branched off from the main road to Andover.

All three arrived there safely, though Frankie's Standard had shown unmistakable signs of decrepitude at every hill.

The time fixed had been one o'clock.

'We don't want to be interrupted when we're staging the thing,' Frankie had said. 'Hardly anything ever goes down this road, I should imagine, but at lunch time we ought to be perfectly safe.'

They proceeded for half a mile on the side road and then Frankie pointed out the place she had selected for the accident to take place.

'It couldn't be better in my opinion,' she said. 'Straight down this hill and then, as you see, the road gives a sudden very sharp turn round that bulging bit of wall. The wall is actually the wall of Merroway Court. If we start the car and let it run down the hill it will crash straight into the wall and something pretty drastic ought to happen to it.'

'I should say so,' Bobby agreed. 'But someone ought to be on the lookout at the corner to be sure someone isn't coming round it in the opposite direction.'

'Quite right,' said Frankie. 'We don't want to involve anybody else in a mess and perhaps maim them for life. George can take his car down there and turn it as though he were coming from the other direction. Then when he waves a handkerchief it will show that all is clear.'

'You're looking very pale, Frankie,' said Bobby anxiously. 'Are you sure you're all right?'

'I'm made up pale,' explained Frankie. 'Ready for the concussion. You don't want me to be carried into the house blooming with health.'

'How wonderful women are,' said Bobby appreciatively. 'You look exactly like a sick monkey.'

'I think you're very rude,' said Frankie. 'Now, then, I shall go and prospect at the gate into Merroway Court. It's just this side of the bulge. There's no lodge, fortunately. When George waves his handkerchief and I wave mine, you start her off.'

'Right,' said Bobby. 'I'll stay on the running board to guide her until the pace gets too hot and then I'll jump off.'

'Don't hurt yourself,' said Frankie.

'I shall be extremely careful not to. It would complicate matters to have a real accident on the spot of the faked one.'

'Well, start off, George,' said Frankie.

George nodded, jumped into the second car and ran slowly down the hill. Bobby and Frankie stood looking after him.

'You'll – look after yourself, won't you, Frankie?' said Bobby with a sudden gruffness. 'I mean – don't go doing anything foolish.'

'I shall be all right. Most circumspect. By the way, I don't think I'd better write to you direct. I'll write to George or my maid or someone or other to pass on to you.'

'I wonder if George is going to be a success in his profession.'

'Why shouldn't he?'

'Well, he doesn't seem to have acquired a chatty bedside manner yet.'

'I expect that will come,' said Frankie. 'I'd better be going now. I'll let you know when I want you to come down with the Bentley.'

'I'll get busy with the moustache. So long, Frankie.'

'They looked at each other for a moment, and then Frankie nodded and began to walk down the hill.

George had turned the car and then backed it round the bulge.

Frankie disappeared for a moment then reappeared in the road, waving a handkerchief. A second handkerchief waved from the bottom of the road at the turn.

Bobby put the car into third gear, then, standing on the footboard, he released the brake. The car moved grudgingly forward, impeded by being in gear. The slope, however, was sufficiently steep. The engine started. The car gathered way. Bobby steadied the steering wheel. At the last possible moment he jumped off.

The car went on down the hill and crashed into the wall with considerable force. All was well – the accident had taken place successfully.

Bobby saw Frankie run quickly to the scene of the crime and plop down amid the wreckage. George in his car came round the corner and pulled up.

With a sigh Bobby mounted his motor cycle and rode away in the direction of London.

At the scene of the accident things were busy.

'Shall I roll about in the road a bit,' asked Frankie, 'to get myself dusty?'

'You might as well,' said George. 'Here, give me your hat.'

He took it and inflicted a terrific dent on it. Frankie gave a faint anguished cry.

'That's the concussion,' explained George. 'Now, then, lie doggo just where you are. I think I heard a bicycle bell.'

Sure enough, at that moment, a boy of about seventeen came whistling round the corner. He stopped at once, delighted with the pleasurable spectacle that met his eyes.

'Ooer!' he ejaculated, ''as there been an accident?'

'No,' said George sarcastically. 'The young lady ran her car into the wall on purpose.'

Accepting, as he was meant to do, this remark as irony rather than the simple truth which it was, the boy said with relish:

'Looks bad, don't she? Is she dead?'

'Not yet,' said George. 'She must be taken somewhere at once. I'm a doctor. What's this place in here?'

'Merroway Court. Belongs to Mr Bassington-ffrench. He's a JP, he is.'

'She must be carried there at once,' said George authoritatively. 'Here, leave your bicycle and lend me a hand.'

Only too willing, the boy propped his bicycle against the wall and came to assist. Between them George and the boy carried Frankie up the drive to a pleasant old-fashioned-looking manor house.

Their approach had been observed, for an elderly butler came out to meet them.

'There's been an accident,' said George curtly. 'Is there a room I can carry this lady into? She must be attended to at once.'

The butler went back into the hall in a flustered way. George and the boy followed him up closely, still carrying the limp body of Frankie. The butler had gone into a room on the left and from there a woman emerged. She was tall, with red hair, and about thirty years of age. Her eyes were a light clear blue.

She dealt with the situation quickly.

'There is a spare bedroom on the ground floor,' she said. 'Will you bring her in there? Ought I to telephone for a doctor?'

'I am a doctor,' explained George. 'I was passing in my car and saw the accident occur.'

'Oh! how very fortunate. Come this way, will you?'

She showed them the way into a pleasant bedroom with windows giving on the garden.

'Is she badly hurt?' she inquired.

'I can't tell yet.'

Mrs Bassington-ffrench took the hint and retired. The boy accompanied her and launched out into a description of the accident as though he had been an actual witness of it.

'Run smack into the wall she did. Car's all smashed up. There she was lying on the ground with her hat all dinted in. The gentleman, he was passing in his car –'

He proceeded *ad lib* till got rid of with a half-crown.

Meanwhile Frankie and George were conversing in careful whispers.

'George, darling, this won't blight your career, will it? They won't strike you off the register, or whatever it is, will they?'

'Probably,' said George gloomily. 'That is, if it ever comes out.'

'It won't,' said Frankie. 'Don't worry, George. I shan't let you down.' She added thoughtfully: 'You did it very well. I've never heard you talk so much before.'

George sighed. He looked at his watch.

'I shall give my examination another three minutes,' he said.

'What about the car?'

'I'll arrange with a garage to have that cleared up.'

'Good.'

George continued to study his watch. Finally he said with an air of relief:

'Time.'

'George,' said Frankie, 'you've been an angel. I don't know why you did it.'

'No more do I,' said George. 'Damn fool thing to do.'

He nodded to her.

'Bye bye. Enjoy yourself.'

'I wonder if I shall,' said Frankie.

She was thinking of that cool impersonal voice with the slight American accent.

George went in search of the owner of it, whom he found waiting for him in the drawing-room.

'Well,' he said abruptly. 'I'm glad to say it's not so bad as I feared. Concussion very slight and already passing off. She ought to stay quietly where she is for a day or so, though.' He paused. 'She seems to be a Lady Frances Derwent.'

'Oh, fancy!' said Mrs Bassington-ffrench. 'Then I know some cousins of hers – the Draycotts – quite well.'

'I don't know if it's inconvenient for you to have her here,' said George. 'But if she *could* stay where she is for a day or two . . .' Here George paused.

'Oh, of course. That will be all right, Dr –?'

'Arbuthnot. By the way, I'll see to the car business. I shall be passing a garage.'

'Thank you very much, Dr Arbuthnot. How very lucky you happened to be passing. I suppose a doctor ought to see her tomorrow just to see she's getting on all right.'

'Don't think it's necessary,' said George. 'All she needs is quiet.'

'But I should feel happier. And her people ought to know.'

'I'll attend to that,' said George. 'And as to the doctoring business – well, it seems she's a Christian Scientist and won't have doctors at any price. She wasn't too pleased at finding me in attendance.'

'Oh, dear!' said Mrs Bassington-ffrench.

'But she'll be quite all right,' said George reassuringly. 'You can take my word for it.'

'If you really think so, Dr Arbuthnot,' said Mrs Bassington-ffrench rather doubtfully.

'I do,' said George. 'Goodbye. Dear me. I left one of my instruments in the bedroom.'

He came rapidly into the room and up to the bedside.

'Frankie,' he said in a quick whisper. 'You're a Christian Scientist. Don't forget.'

'But why?'

'I had to do it. Only way.'

'All right,' said Frankie. 'I won't forget.'

CHAPTER 12

....

IN THE ENEMY'S CAMP

'Well, here I am,' thought Frankie. 'Safely in the enemy's camp. Now, it's up to me.'

There was a tap on the door and Mrs Bassington-ffrench entered.

Frankie raised herself a little on her pillows.

'I'm so frightfully sorry,' she said in a faint voice. 'Causing you all this bother.'

'Nonsense,' said Mrs Bassington-ffrench. Frankie heard anew that cool attractive drawling voice with a slight American accent, and remembered that Lord Marchington had said that one of the Hampshire Bassington-ffrenches had married an American heiress. 'Dr Arbuthnot says you will be quite all right in a day or two if you just keep quiet.'

Frankie felt that she ought at this point to say something about 'error' or 'mortal mind', but was frightened of saying the wrong thing.

'He seems nice,' she said. 'He was very kind.'

'He seemed a most capable young man,' said Mrs Bassington-ffrench. 'It was very fortunate that he just happened to be passing.'

'Yes, wasn't it? Not, of course, that I really needed him.'

'But you mustn't talk,' continued her hostess. 'I'll send my maid along with some things for you and then she can get you properly into bed.'

'It's frightfully kind of you.'

'Not at all.'

Frankie felt a momentary qualm as the other woman withdrew.

'A nice kind creature,' she said to herself. 'And beautifully unsuspecting.'

For the first time she felt that she was playing a mean trick on her hostess. Her mind had been so taken up with the vision of a murderous Bassington-ffrench pushing an unsuspecting victim over a precipice that lesser characters in the drama had not entered her imagination.

'Oh, well,' thought Frankie, 'I've got to go through with it now. But I wish she hadn't been so nice about it.'

She spent a dull afternoon and evening lying in her darkened room. Mrs Bassington-ffrench looked in once or twice to see how she was but did not stay.

The next day, however, Frankie admitted the daylight and expressed a desire for company and her hostess came and sat with her for some time. They discovered many mutual acquaintances and friends and by the end of the day, Frankie felt, with a guilty qualm, that they had become friends.

Mrs Bassington-ffrench referred several times to her husband and to her small boy, Tommy. She seemed a simple woman, deeply attached to her home, and yet, for some reason or other, Frankie fancied that she was not quite happy. There was an anxious expression in her eyes sometimes that did not agree with a mind at peace with itself.

On the third day Frankie got up and was introduced to the master of the house.

He was a big man, heavy jowled, with a kindly but rather abstracted air. He seemed to spend a good deal of his time shut up in his study. Yet Frankie judged him to be very fond of his wife, though interesting himself very little in her concerns.

Tommy, the small boy, was seven, and a healthy, mischievous child. Sylvia Bassington-ffrench obviously adored him.

'It's so nice down here,' said Frankie with a sigh.

She was lying out on a long chair in the garden.

'I don't know whether it's the bang on the head, or what it is, but I just don't feel I want to move. I'd like to lie here for days and days.'

'Well, do,' said Sylvia Bassington-ffrench in her calm, incurious tones. 'No, really, I mean it. Don't hurry back to town. You see,' she went on, 'it's a great pleasure to me to have you here. You're so bright and amusing. It quite cheers me up.'

'So she needs cheering up,' flashed across Frankie's mind.

At the same time she felt ashamed of herself.

'I feel we really have become friends,' continued the other woman.

Frankie felt still more ashamed.

It was a mean thing she was doing – mean – mean – mean. She would give it up! Go back to town –

Her hostess went on:

'It won't be too dull here. Tomorrow my brother-in-law is coming back. You'll like him, I'm sure. Everyone likes Roger.'

'He lives with you?'

'Off and on. He's a restless creature. He calls himself the ne'er-do-well of the family, and perhaps it's true in a way. He never sticks to a job for long – in fact I don't believe he's ever done any real work in his life. But some people just are like that – especially in old families. And they're usually people with a great charm of manner. Roger is wonderfully sympathetic. I don't know what I should have done without him this spring when Tommy was ill.'

'What was the matter with Tommy?'

'He had a bad fall from the swing. It must have been tied on to a rotten branch and the branch gave way. Roger was very upset because he was swinging the child at the time – you know, giving him high ones, such as children love. We thought at first Tommy's spine was hurt, but it turned out to be a very slight injury and he's quite all right now.'

'He certainly looks it,' said Frankie, smiling, as she heard faint yells and whoops in the distance.

'I know. He seems in perfect condition. It's such a relief. He's had bad luck in accidents. He was nearly drowned last winter.'

'Was he really?' said Frankie thoughtfully.

She no longer meditated returning to town. The feeling of guilt had abated.

Accidents!

Did Roger Bassington-ffrench specialize in accidents, she wondered.

She said:

'If you're sure you mean it, I'd love to stay a little longer. But won't your husband mind my butting in like this?'

'Henry?' Mrs Bassington-ffrench's lips curled in a strange expression. 'No, Henry won't mind. Henry never minds anything – nowadays.'

Frankie looked at her curiously.

'If she knew me better she'd tell me something,' she thought to herself. 'I believe there are lots of odd things going on in this household.'

Henry Bassington-ffrench joined them for tea and Frankie studied him closely. There was certainly something odd about the man. His type was an obvious one – a jovial, sport-loving, simple country gentleman. But such a man ought not to sit twitching nervously, his nerves obviously on edge, now sunk in an abstraction from which it was impossible to rouse him, now giving out bitter and sarcastic replies to anything said to him. Not that he was always like that. Later that evening, at dinner, he showed out in quite a new light. He joked, laughed, told stories, and was, for a man of his abilities, quite brilliant. Too brilliant, Frankie felt. The brilliance was just as unnatural and out of character.

'He has such queer eyes,' she thought. 'They frighten me a little.'

And yet surely she did not suspect *Henry* Bassington-ffrench of anything? It was his brother, not he, who had been in Marchbolt on that fatal day.

As to the brother, Frankie looked forward to seeing him with eager interest. According to her and to Bobby, the man was a murderer. She was going to meet a murderer face to face.

She felt momentarily nervous.

Yet, after all, how could he guess?

How could he, in any way, connect her with a successfully accomplished crime?

'You're making a bogey for yourself out of nothing,' she said to herself.

Roger Bassington-ffrench arrived just before tea on the following afternoon.

Frankie did not meet him till tea time. She was still supposed to 'rest' in the afternoon.

When she came out on to the lawn where tea was laid, Sylvia said smiling:

'Here is our invalid. This is my brother-in-law, Lady Frances Derwent.'

Frankie saw a tall, slender young man of something over thirty with very pleasant eyes. Although she could see what Bobby meant by saying he ought to have a monocle and a toothbrush moustache, she herself was more inclined to notice the intense blue of his eyes. They shook hands.

He said: 'I've been hearing all about the way you tried to break down the park wall.'

'I'll admit,' said Frankie, 'that I'm the world's worst driver. But I was driving an awful old rattle-trap. My own car was laid up and I bought a cheap one second-hand.'

'She was rescued from the ruins by a very good-looking young doctor,' said Sylvia.

'He was rather sweet,' agreed Frankie.

Tommy arrived at this moment and flung himself upon his uncle with squeaks of joy.

'Have you brought me a Hornby train? You said you would. You said you would.'

'Oh, Tommy! You mustn't ask for things,' said Sylvia.

'That's all right, Sylvia. It was a promise. I've got your train all right, old man.' He looked casually at his sister-in-law. 'Isn't Henry coming to tea?'

'I don't think so.' The constrained note was in her voice. 'He isn't feeling awfully well today, I imagine.'

Then she said impulsively:

'Oh, Roger, I'm glad you're back.'

He put his hand on her arm for a minute.

'That's all right, Sylvia, old girl.'

After tea, Roger played trains with his nephew.

Frankie watched them, her mind in a turmoil.

Surely this wasn't the sort of man to push people over cliffs! This charming young man couldn't be a cold-blooded murderer!

But, then – she and Bobby must have been wrong all along. Wrong, that is, about this part of it.

She felt sure now that it wasn't Bassington-ffrench who had pushed Pritchard over the cliff.

Then who was it?

She was still convinced he had been pushed over. Who had done it? And who had put the morphia in Bobby's beer?

With the thought of morphia suddenly the explanation of Henry Bassington-ffrench's peculiar eyes came to her, with their pin-point pupils.

Was Henry Bassington-ffrench *a drug fiend*?

CHAPTER 13

ALAN CARSTAIRS

Strangely enough, she received confirmation of this theory no later than the following day, and it came from Roger.

They had been playing a single at tennis against each other and were sitting afterwards sipping iced drinks.

They had been talking about various indifferent subjects and Frankie had become more and more sensible of the charm of someone who had, like Roger Bassington-ffrench, travelled about all over the world. The family ne'er-do-well, she could not help thinking, contrasted very favourably with his heavy, serious-minded brother.

A pause had fallen while these thoughts were passing through Frankie's mind. It was broken by Roger – speaking this time in an entirely different tone of voice.

'Lady Frances, I'm going to do a rather peculiar thing. I've known you less than twenty-four hours, but I feel instinctively that you're the one person I can ask advice from.'

'Advice?' said Frankie, surprised.

'Yes. I can't make up my mind between two different courses of action.'

He paused. He was leaning forward, swinging a racquet between his knees, a light frown on his forehead. He looked worried and upset.

'It's about my brother, Lady Frances.'

'Yes?'

'He is taking drugs. I am sure of it.'

'What makes you think so?' asked Frankie.

'Everything. His appearance. His extraordinary changes of mood. And have you noticed his eyes? The pupils are like pinpoints.'

'I had noticed that,' admitted Frankie. 'What do you think it is?'

'Morphia or some form of opium.'

'Has it been going on for long?'

'I date the beginning of it from about six months ago. I remember that he complained of sleeplessness a good deal.

How he first came to take the stuff, I don't know, but I think it must have begun soon after then.'

'How does he get hold of it?' inquired Frankie practically.

'I think it comes to him by post. Have you noticed that he is particularly nervous and irritable some days at tea time?'

'Yes, I have.'

'I suspect that that is when he has finished up his supply and is waiting for more. Then, after the six o'clock post has come, he goes into his study and emerges for dinner in quite a different mood.'

Frankie nodded. She remembered that unnatural brilliance of conversation sometimes at dinner.

'But where does the supply come from?' she asked.

'Ah, that I don't know. No reputable doctor would give it to him. There are, I suppose, various sources where one could get it in London by paying a big price.'

Frankie nodded thoughtfully.

She was remembering having said to Bobby something about a gang of drug smugglers and his replying that one could not mix up too many crimes. It was queer that so soon in their investigations they should have come upon the traces of such a thing.

It was queerer that it should be the chief suspect who should draw her attention to the fact. It made her more inclined than ever to acquit Roger Bassington-ffrench of the charge of murder.

And yet there was the inexplicable matter of the changed photograph. The evidence against him, she reminded herself, was still exactly what it had been. On the other side was only the personality of the man himself. And everyone always said that murderers were charming people!

She shook off these reflections and turned to her companion.

'Why exactly are you telling me this?' she asked frankly.

'Because I don't know what to do about Sylvia,' he said simply.

'You think she doesn't know?'

'Of course she doesn't know. Ought I to tell her?'

'It's very difficult –'

'It *is* difficult. That's why I thought you might be able to help me. Sylvia has taken a great fancy to you. She doesn't care much for any of the people round about, but she liked you at once, she tells me. What ought I to do, Lady Frances? By telling her I shall add a great burden to her life.'

'If she knew she might have some influence,' suggested Frankie.

'I doubt it. When it's a case of drug-taking, nobody, even the nearest and dearest, has any influence.'

'That's rather a hopeless point of view, isn't it?'

'It's a fact. There are ways, of course. If Henry would only consent to go in for a cure – there's a place actually near here. Run by a Dr Nicholson.'

'But he'd never consent, would he?'

'He might. You can catch a morphia taker in a mood of extravagant remorse sometimes when they'd do anything to cure themselves. I'm inclined to think that Henry might be got to that frame of mind more easily if he thought Sylvia didn't know – if her knowing was held over him as a kind of threat. If the cure was successful (they'd call it "nerves", of course) she never need know.'

'Would he have to go away for the cure?'

'The place I mean is about three miles from here, the other side of the village. It's run by a Canadian – Dr Nicholson. A very clever man, I believe. And, fortunately, Henry likes him. Hush – here comes Sylvia.'

Mrs Bassington-ffrench joined them, observing:

'Have you been very energetic?'

'Three sets,' said Frankie. 'And I was beaten every time.'

'You play a very good game,' said Roger.

'I'm terribly lazy about tennis,' said Sylvia. 'We must ask the Nicholsons over one day. She's very fond of a game. Why – what is it?' She had caught the glance the other two had exchanged.

'Nothing – only I happened to be talking about the Nicholsons to Lady Frances.'

'You'd better call her Frankie like I do,' said Sylvia. 'Isn't it odd how whenever one talks of any person or thing, somebody else does the same immediately afterwards?'

'They are Canadians, aren't they?' inquired Frankie.

'He is, certainly. I rather fancy she is English, but I'm not sure. She's a very pretty little thing – quite charming with the most lovely big wistful eyes. Somehow or other, I fancy she isn't terribly happy. It must be a depressing life.'

'He runs a kind of sanatorium, doesn't he?'

'Yes – nerve cases and people who take drugs. He's very successful, I believe. He's rather an impressive man.'

'You like him?'

'No,' said Sylvia abruptly, 'I don't.' And rather vehemently, after a moment or two, she added: 'Not at all.'

Later on, she pointed out to Frankie a photograph of a charming large-eyed woman which stood on the piano.

'That's Moira Nicholson. An appealing face, isn't it? A man who came down here with some friends of ours some time ago was quite struck with it. He wanted an introduction to her, I think.'

She laughed.

'I'll ask them to dinner tomorrow night. I'd like to know what you think of him.'

'Him?'

'Yes. As I told you, I dislike him, and yet he's quite an attractive-looking man.'

Something in her tone made Frankie look at her quickly, but Sylvia Bassington-ffrench had turned away and was taking some dead flowers out of a vase.

'I must collect my ideas,' thought Frankie, as she drew a comb through her thick dark hair when dressing for dinner that night. 'And,' she added resolutely, 'it's time I made a few experiments.'

Was, or was not, Roger Bassington-ffrench the villain she and Bobby assumed him to be?

She and Bobby had agreed that whoever had tried to put the latter out of the way must have easy access to morphia. Now in a way this held good for Roger Bassington-ffrench. If his brother received supplies of morphia by post, it would be easy enough for Roger to abstract a packet and use it for his own purposes.

'Mem.,' wrote Frankie on a sheet of paper: '(1) Find out where Roger was on the 16th – day when Bobby was poisoned.'

She thought she saw her way to doing that fairly clearly.

'(2),' she wrote. 'Produce picture of dead man and observe reactions if any. Also note if R.B.F. admits being in Marchbolt then.'

She felt slightly nervous over the second resolution. It meant coming out into the open. On the other hand, the tragedy had happened in her own part of the world, and to mention it casually would be the most natural thing in the world.

She crumpled up the sheet of paper and burnt it.

She managed to introduce the first point fairly naturally at dinner.

'You know,' she said frankly to Roger. 'I can't help feeling that we've met before. And it wasn't very long ago, either. It wasn't, by any chance, at that party of Lady Shane's at Claridges. On the 16th it was.'

'It couldn't have been on the 16th,' said Sylvia quickly. 'Roger was here then. I remember, because we had a children's party that day and what I should have done without Roger I simply don't know.'

She gave a grateful glance at her brother-in-law and he smiled back at her.

'I don't feel I've ever met you before,' he said thoughtfully to Frankie, and added: 'I'm sure if I had I'd remember it.'

He said it rather nicely.

'One point settled,' thought Frankie. 'Roger Bassington-ffrench was not in Wales on the day that Bobby was poisoned.'

The second point came up fairly easily later. Frankie led the talk to country places, the dullness thereof, and the interest aroused by any local excitement.

'We had a man fall over the cliff last month,' she remarked. 'We were all thrilled to the core. I went to the inquest full of excitement, but it was all rather dull, really.'

'Was that a place called Marchbolt?' asked Sylvia suddenly.

Frankie nodded.

'Derwent Castle is only about seven miles from Marchbolt,' she explained.

'Roger, that must have been your man,' cried Sylvia.

Frankie looked inquiringly at him.

'I was actually in at the death,' said Roger. 'I stayed with the body till the police came.'

'I thought one of the Vicar's sons did that,' said Frankie.

'He had to go off to play the organ or something – so I took over.'

'How perfectly extraordinary,' said Frankie. 'I did hear somebody else had been there, too, but I never heard the name. So it was *you*?'

There was a general atmosphere of 'How curious. Isn't the world small?' Frankie felt she was doing this rather well.

'Perhaps that's where you saw me before – in Marchbolt?' suggested Roger.

'I wasn't there actually at the time of the accident,' said Frankie. 'I came back from London a couple of days afterwards. Were you at the inquest?'

'No. I went back to London the morning after the tragedy.'

'He had some absurd idea of buying a house down there,' said Sylvia.

'Utter nonsense,' said Henry Bassington-ffrench.

'Not at all,' said Roger good-humouredly.

'You know perfectly well, Roger, that as soon as you'd bought it, you'd get a fit of wanderlust and go off abroad again.'

'Oh, I shall settle down some day, Sylvia.'

'When you do you'd better settle down near us,' said Sylvia. 'Not go off to Wales.'

Roger laughed. Then he turned to Frankie.

'Any points of interest about the accident? It didn't turn out to be suicide or anything?'

'Oh, no, it was all painfully above board and some appalling relations came and identified the man. He was on a walking tour, it seems. Very sad, really, because he was awfully good-looking. Did you see his picture in the papers?'

'I think I did,' said Sylvia vaguely. 'But I don't remember.'

'I've got a cutting upstairs from our local paper.'

Frankie was all eagerness. She ran upstairs and came down with the cutting in her hand. She gave it to Sylvia. Roger came and looked over Sylvia's shoulder.

'Don't you think he's good-looking?' she demanded in a rather school-girl manner.

'He is, rather,' said Sylvia. 'He looks very like that man, Alan Carstairs, don't you think so, Roger? I believe I remembered saying so at the time.'

'He's got quite a look of him here,' agreed Roger. 'But there wasn't much real resemblance, you know.'

'You can't tell from newspaper pictures, can you?' said Sylvia, as she handed the cutting back.

Frankie agreed that you couldn't.

The conversation passed to other matters.

Frankie went to bed undecided. Everyone seemed to have reacted with perfect naturalness. Roger's house-hunting stunt had been no secret.

The only thing she had succeeded in getting was a name. The name of Alan Carstairs.

CHAPTER 14

DR NICHOLSON

Frankie attacked Sylvia the following morning.

She started by saying carelessly:

'What was that man's name you mentioned last night? Alan Carstairs, was it? I feel sure I've heard that name before.'

'I daresay you have. He's rather a celebrity in his way, I believe. He's a Canadian – a naturalist and big game hunter and explorer. I don't really know him. Some friends of ours, the Rivingtons, brought him down here one day for lunch. A very attractive man – big and bronzed and nice blue eyes.'

'I was sure I'd heard of him.'

'He'd never been over to this country before, I believe. Last year he went on a tour through Africa with that millionaire man, John Savage – the one who thought he had cancer and killed himself in that tragic way. Carstairs has been all over the world. East Africa, South America – simply everywhere, I believe.'

'Sounds a nice adventurous person,' said Frankie.

'Oh, he was. Distinctly attractive.'

'Funny – his being so like the man who fell over the cliff at Marchbolt,' said Frankie.

'I wonder if everyone has a double.'

They compared instances, citing Adolf Beck and referring lightly to the Lyons Mail. Frankie was careful to make no further references to Alan Carstairs. To show too much interest in him would be fatal.

In her own mind, however, she felt she was getting on now. She was quite convinced that Alan Carstairs had been the victim of the cliff tragedy at Marchbolt. He fulfilled all the conditions. He had no intimate friends or relations in this country and his disappearance was unlikely to be noticed for some time. A man who frequently ran off to East Africa and South America was not likely to be missed at once. Moreover, Frankie noted, although Sylvia Bassington-ffrench had commented on the resemblance in the newspaper reproduction, it had not occurred to her for a moment that it actually *was* the man.

That, Frankie thought, was rather an interesting bit of psychology.

We seldom suspect people who are 'news' of being people we have usually seen or met.

Very good, then. Alan Carstairs was the dead man. The next step was to learn more about Alan Carstairs. His connection with the Bassington-ffrenches seemed to have been of the slightest. He had been brought down there quite by chance by friends. What was the name? Rivington. Frankie stored it in her memory for future use.

That certainly was a possible avenue of inquiry. But it would be well to go slowly. Inquiries about Alan Carstairs must be very discreetly made.

'I don't want to be poisoned or knocked on the head,' thought Frankie with a grimace. 'They were ready enough to bump off Bobby for practically nothing at all –'

Her thoughts flew off at a tangent to that tantalizing phrase that had started the whole business.

Evans! Who was Evans? Where did Evans fit in?

'A dope gang,' decided Frankie. Perhaps some relation of Carstairs was victimized, and he was determined to bust it up. Perhaps he came to England for that purpose. Evans may have been one of the gang who had retired and gone to Wales to live. Carstairs had bribed Evans to give the others away and Evans had consented and Carstairs went there to see him, and someone followed him and killed him.

Was that somebody Roger Bassington-ffrench? It seemed very unlikely. The Caymans, now, were far more what Frankie imagined a gang of dope smugglers would be likely to be.

And yet – that photograph. If only there was some explanation of that photograph.

That evening, Dr Nicholson and his wife were expected to dinner. Frankie was finishing dressing when she heard their car drive up to the front door. Her window faced that way and she looked out.

A tall man was just alighting from the driver's seat of a dark-blue Talbot.

Frankie withdrew her head thoughtfully.

Carstairs had been a Canadian. Dr Nicholson was a Canadian. And Dr Nicholson had a dark-blue Talbot.

Absurd to build anything upon that, of course, but wasn't it just faintly suggestive?

Dr Nicholson was a big man with a manner that suggested great reserves of power. His speech was slow, on the whole he said very little, but contrived somehow to make every word sound significant. He wore strong glasses and behind them his very pale-blue eyes glittered reflectively.

His wife was a slender creature of perhaps twenty-seven, pretty, indeed beautiful. She seemed, Frankie, thought, slightly nervous and chattered rather feverishly as though to conceal the fact.

'You had an accident, I hear, Lady Frances,' said Dr Nicholson as he took his seat beside her at the dinner table.

Frankie explained the catastrophe. She wondered why she should feel so nervous doing so. The doctor's manner was simple and interested. Why should she feel as though she were rehearsing a defence to a charge that had never been made. Was there any earthly reason why the doctor should disbelieve in her accident?

'That was too bad,' he said, as she finished, having, perhaps, made a more detailed story of it than seemed strictly necessary. 'But you seem to have made a very good recovery.'

'We won't admit she's cured yet. We're keeping her with us,' said Sylvia.

The doctor's gaze went to Sylvia. Something like a very faint smile came to his lips but passed almost immediately.

'I should keep her with you as long as possible,' he said gravely.

Frankie was sitting between her host and Dr Nicholson. Henry

Bassington-ffrench was decidedly moody tonight. His hands twitched, he ate next to nothing and he took no part in the conversation.

Mrs Nicholson, opposite, had a difficult time with him, and turned to Roger with obvious relief. She talked to him in a desultory fashion, but Frankie noticed that her eyes were never long absent from her husband's face.

Dr Nicholson was talking about life in the country.

'Do you know what a culture is, Lady Frances?'

'Do you mean book learning?' asked Frankie, rather puzzled.

'No, no. I was referring to germs. They develop, you know, in specially prepared serum. The country, Lady Frances, is a little like that. There is time and space and infinite leisure – suitable conditions, you see, for development.'

'Do you mean bad things?' asked Frankie puzzled.

'That depends, Lady Frances, on the kind of germ cultivated.'

Idiotic conversation, thought Frankie, and why should it make me feel creepy, but it does!

She said flippantly:

'I expect I'm developing all sorts of dark qualities.'

He looked at her and said calmly:

'Oh, no, I don't think so, Lady Frances. I think you would always be on the side of law and order.'

Was there a faint emphasis on the word *law*?

Suddenly, across the table, Mrs Nicholson said:

'My husband prides himself on summing up character.'

Dr Nicholson nodded his head gently.

'Quite right, Moira. Little things interest me.' He turned to Frankie again. 'I had heard of your accident, you know. One thing about it intrigued me very much.'

'Yes?' said Frankie, her heart beating suddenly.

'The doctor who was passing – the one who brought you in here.'

'Yes?'

'He must have had a curious character – to turn his car before going to the rescue.'

'I don't understand.'

'Of course not. You were unconscious. But young Reeves, the

message boy, came from Staverley on his bicycle and no car passed him, yet he comes round the corner, finds the smash, and the doctor's car pointing the same way he was going – towards London. You see the point? The doctor did not come from the direction of Staveley so he must have come the other way, down the hill. But in that case his car should have been pointing towards Staverley. But it wasn't. Therefore he must have turned it.'

'Unless he had come from Staverley some time before,' said Frankie.

'Then his car would have been standing there as you came down the hill. Was it?'

The pale-blue eyes were looking at her very intently through the thick glasses.

'I don't remember,' said Frankie. 'I don't think so.'

'You sound like a detective, Jasper,' said Mrs Nicholson. 'And all about nothing at all.'

'Little things interest me,' said Nicholson.

He turned to his hostess, and Frankie drew a breath of relief. Why had he catechized her like that? How had he found out all about the accident? 'Little things interest me,' he had said. Was that all there was to it?

Frankie remembered the dark-blue Talbot saloon, and the fact that Carstairs had been a Canadian. It seemed to her that Dr Nicholson was a sinister man.

She kept out of his way after dinner, attaching herself to the gentle, fragile Mrs Nicholson. She noticed that all the time Mrs Nicholson's eyes still watched her husband. Was it love, Frankie wondered, or fear?

Nicholson devoted himself to Sylvia and at half-past ten he caught his wife's eye and they rose to go.

'Well,' said Roger after they had gone, 'what do you think of our Dr Nicholson? A very forceful personality, hasn't he?'

'I'm like Sylvia,' said Frankie. 'I don't think I like him very much. I like her better.'

'Good-looking, but rather a little idiot,' said Roger. 'She either worships him or is scared to death of him – I don't know which.'

'That's just what I wondered,' agreed Frankie.

'I don't like him,' said Sylvia, 'but I must admit that he's got a lot of – of *force*. I believe he's cured drug takers in the most marvellous way. People whose relations despaired utterly. They've gone there as a last hope and come out absolutely cured.'

'Yes,' cried Henry Bassington-ffrench suddenly. 'And do you know what goes on there? Do you know the awful suffering and mental torment? A man's used to a drug and they cut him off it – cut him off it – till he goes raving mad for the lack of it and beats his head against the wall. That's what he does – your "forceful" doctor tortures people – tortures them – sends them to Hell – drives them mad . . .'

He was shaking violently. Suddenly he turned and left the room.

Sylvia Bassington-ffrench looked startled.

'What is the matter with Henry?' she said wonderingly. 'He seems very upset.'

Frankie and Roger dared not look at each other.

'He's not looked well all evening,' ventured Frankie.

'No. I noticed that. He's very moody lately. I wish he hadn't given up riding. Oh, by the way, Dr Nicholson invited Tommy over tomorrow, but I don't like him going there very much – not with all those queer nerve cases and dope-takers.'

'I don't suppose the doctor would allow him to come into contact with them,' said Roger. 'He seems very fond of children.'

'Yes, I think it's a disappointment he hasn't got any of his own. Probably to her, too. She looks very sad – and terribly delicate.'

'She's like a sad Madonna,' said Frankie.

'Yes, that describes her very well.'

'If Dr Nicholson is so fond of children I suppose he came to your children's party?' said Frankie carelessly.

'Unfortunately he was away for a day or two just then. I think he had to go to London for some conference.'

'I see.'

They went up to bed. Before she went to sleep, Frankie wrote to Bobby.

CHAPTER 15

A DISCOVERY

Bobby had had an irksome time. His forced inaction was exceedingly trying. He hated staying quietly in London and doing nothing.

He had been rung up on the telephone by George Arbuthnot who, in a few laconic words, told him that all had gone well. A couple of days later, he had a letter from Frankie, delivered to him by her maid, the letter having gone under cover to her at Lord Marchington's town house.

Since then he had heard nothing.

'Letter for you,' called out Badger.

Bobby came forward excitedly but the letter was one addressed in his father's handwriting, and postmarked Marchbolt.

At that moment, however, he caught sight of the neat blackgowned figure of Frankie's maid approaching down the Mews. Five minutes later he was tearing open Frankie's second letter.

Dear Bobby (wrote Frankie), *I think it's about time you came down. I've given them instructions at home that you're to have the Bentley whenever you ask for it. Get a chauffeur's livery – dark-green ours always are. Put it down to father at Harrods. It's best to be correct in details. Concentrate on making a good job of the moustache. It makes a frightful difference to anyone's face.*

Come down here and ask for me. You might bring me an ostensible note from Father. Report that the car is now in working order again. The garage here only holds two cars and as it's got the family Daimler and Roger Bassington-ffrench's two-seater in it, it is fortunately full up, so you will go to Staverley and put up there.

Get what local information you can when there – particularly about a Dr Nicholson who runs a place for dope patients. Several suspicious circumstances about him – he has a dark-blue Talbot saloon, he was away from home on the 16th when your beer was doctored, and he takes altogether too detailed an interest in the circumstances of my accident.

I think I've identified the corpse!!!

Au revoir, *my fellow sleuth.*
Love from your successfully concussed,
Frankie.
P.S. I shall post this myself.

Bobby's spirits rose with a bound.

Discarding his overalls and breaking the news of his immediate departure to Badger, he was about to hurry off when he remembered that he had not yet opened his father's letter. He did so with a rather qualified enthusiasm since the Vicar's letters were actuated by a spirit of duty rather than pleasure and breathed an atmosphere of Christian forbearance which was highly depressing.

The Vicar gave conscientious news of doings in Marchbolt, describing his own troubles with the organist and commenting on the unchristian spirit of one of his churchwardens. The rebinding of the hymn books was also touched upon. And the Vicar hoped that Bobby was sticking manfully to his job and trying to make good, and remained his ever affectionate father.

There was a postscript:

By the way, someone called who asked for your address in London. I was out at the time and he did not leave his name. Mrs Roberts describes him as a tall, stooping gentleman with pince-nez. He seemed very sorry to miss you and very anxious to see you again.

A tall, stooping man with pince-nez. Bobby ran over in his mind anyone of his acquaintance likely to fit that description but could think of nobody.

Suddenly a quick suspicion darted into his mind. Was this the forerunner of a new attempt upon his life? Were these mysterious enemies, or enemy, trying to track him down?

He sat still and did some serious thinking. They, whoever they were, had only just discovered that he had left the neighbourhood. All unsuspecting, Mrs Roberts had given his new address.

So that already they, whoever they were, might be keeping a watch upon the place. If he went out he would be followed – and just as things were at the moment that would never do.

'Badger,' said Bobby.

'Yes, old lad.'

'Come here.'

The next five minutes were spent in genuine hard work. At the end of ten minutes Badger could repeat his instructions by heart.

When he was word perfect, Bobby got into a two-seater Fiat dating from 1902 and drove dashingly down the Mews. He parked the Fiat in St James's Square and walked straight from there to his club. There he did some telephoning and a couple of hours later certain parcels were delivered to him. Finally, about half-past three, a chauffeur in dark green livery walked to St James's Square and went rapidly up to a large Bentley which had been parked there about half an hour previously. The parking attendant nodded to him – the gentleman who had left the car had remarked, stammering slightly as he did so, that his chauffeur would be fetching it shortly.

Bobby let in the clutch and drew neatly out. The abandoned Fiat still stood demurely awaiting its owner. Bobby, despite the intense discomfort of his upper lip, began to enjoy himself. He headed north, not south, and, before long, the powerful engine was forging ahead on the Great North Road.

It was only an extra precaution that he was taking. He was pretty sure that he was not being followed. Presently he turned off to the left and made his way by circuitous roads to Hampshire.

It was just after tea that the Bentley purred up the drive of Merroway Court, a stiff and correct chauffeur at the wheel.

'Hullo,' said Frankie lightly. 'There's the car.'

She went out to the front door. Sylvia and Roger came with her.

'Is everything all right, Hawkins?'

The chauffeur touched his cap.

'Yes, m'lady. She's been thoroughly overhauled.'

'That's all right, then.'

The chauffeur produced a note.

'From his lordship, m'lady.'

Frankie took it.

'You'll put up at the – what is it – Anglers' Arms in Staverley, Hawkins. I'll telephone in the morning if I want the car.'

'Very good, your ladyship.'

Bobby backed, turned and sped down the drive.

'I'm so sorry we haven't room here,' said Sylvia. 'It's a lovely car.'

'You get some pace out of that,' said Roger.

'I do,' admitted Frankie.

She was satisfied that no faintest quiver of recognition had shown on Roger's face. She would have been surprised if it had. She would not have recognized Bobby herself had she met him casually. The small moustache had a perfectly natural appearance, and that, with the stiff demeanour so uncharacteristic of the natural Bobby, completed the disguise enhanced by the chauffeur's livery.

The voice, too, had been excellent, and quite unlike Bobby's own. Frankie began to think that Bobby was far more talented than she had given him credit for being.

Meanwhile Bobby had successfully taken up his quarters at the Anglers' Arms.

It was up to him to create the part of Edward Hawkins, chauffeur to Lady Frances Derwent.

As to the behaviour of chauffeurs in private life, Bobby was singularly ill-informed, but he imagined that a certain haughtiness would not come amiss. He tried to feel himself a superior being and to act accordingly. The admiring attitude of various young women employed in the Anglers' Arms had a distinctly encouraging effect and he soon found that Frankie and her accident had provided the principal topic of conversation in Staverley ever since it had happened. Bobby unbent towards the landlord, a stout, genial person of the name of Thomas Askew, and permitted information to leak from him.

'Young Reeves, he was there and saw it happen,' declared Mr Askew.

Bobby blessed the natural mendacity of the young. The famous accident was now vouched for by an eye witness.

'Thought his last moment had come, he did,' went on Mr Askew. 'Straight for him down the hill it come – and then took the wall instead. A wonder the young lady wasn't killed.'

'Her ladyship takes some killing,' said Bobby.

'Had many accidents, has she?'

'She's been lucky,' said Bobby. 'But I assure you, Mr Askew, that when her ladyship's taken over the wheel from me as she sometimes does – well, I've made sure my last hour has come.'

Several persons present shook their heads wisely and said they didn't wonder and it's just what they would have thought.

'Very nice little place you have here, Mr Askew,' said Bobby kindly and condescendingly. 'Very nice and snug.'

Mr Askew expressed gratification.

'Merroway Court the only big place in the neighbourhood?'

'Well, there's the Grange, Mr Hawkins. Not that you'd call that a place exactly. There's no family living there. No, it had been empty for years until this American doctor took it.'

'An American doctor?'

'That's it – Nicholson his name is. And if you ask me, Mr Hawkins, there are some very queer goings on there.'

The barmaid at this point remarked that Dr Nicholson gave her the shivers, he did.

'Goings on, Mr Askew?' said Bobby. 'Now, what do you mean by goings on?'

Mr Askew shook his head darkly.

'There's those there that don't want to be there. Put away by their relations. I assure you, Mr Hawkins, the moanings and the shrieks and the groans that go on there you wouldn't believe.'

'Why don't the police interfere?'

'Oh, well, you see, it's supposed to be all right. Nerve cases, and such like. Loonies that aren't so very bad. The gentleman's a doctor and it's all right, so to speak –' Here the landlord buried his face in a pint pot and emerged again to shake his head in a very doubtful fashion.

'Ah!' said Bobby in a dark and meaning way. 'If we knew everything that went on in these places . . .'

And he, too, applied himself to a pewter pot.

The barmaid chimed in eagerly.

'That's what I say, Mr Hawkins. What goes on there? Why, one night a poor young creature escaped – in her nightgown she was – and the doctor and a couple of nurses out looking for her. "Oh! don't let them take me back!" That's what she was crying out. Pitiful it was. And about her being rich really and her relations having her put away. But they took her back, they did, and the doctor he explained that she'd got a persecution mania – that's what he called it. Kind of thinking everyone was against her. But I've often wondered – yes, I have. I've often wondered . . .'

'Ah!' said Mr Askew. 'It's easy enough to say –'

Somebody present said that there was no knowing what went on in places. And somebody else said that was right.

Finally the meeting broke up and Bobby announced his intention of going for a stroll before turning in.

The Grange was, he knew, on the other side of the village from Merroway Court, so he turned his footsteps in that direction. What he had heard that evening seemed to him worthy of attention. A lot of it could, of course, be discounted. Villages are usually prejudiced against newcomers, and still more so if the newcomer is of a different nationality. If Nicholson ran a place for curing drug takers, in all probability there would be strange sounds issuing from it – groans and even shrieks might be heard without any sinister reason for them, but all the same, the story of the escaping girl struck Bobby unpleasantly.

Supposing the Grange were really a place where people were kept against their will? A certain amount of genuine cases might be taken as camouflage.

At this point in his meditations Bobby arrived at a high wall with an entrance of wrought-iron gates. He stepped up to the gates and tried one gently. It was locked. Well, after all, why not?

And yet somehow, the touch of that locked gate gave him a faintly sinister feeling. The place was like a prison.

He moved a little father along the road measuring the wall with his eye. Would it be possible to climb over? The wall was smooth and high and presented no accommodating crannies. He shook his head. Suddenly he came upon a little door. Without much real hope he tried it. To his surprise it yielded. It was not locked.

'Bit of an oversight here,' thought Bobby with a grin.

He slipped through, closing the door softly behind him.

He found himself on a path leading through a shrubbery. He followed the path which twisted a good deal – in fact, it reminded Bobby of the one in *Alice Through the Looking Glass*.

Suddenly, without any warning, the path gave a sharp turn and emerged into an open space close to the house. It was a moonlit night and the space was clearly lit. Bobby had stepped full into the moonlight before he could stop himself.

At the same moment a woman's figure came round the corner of the house. She was treading very softly, glancing from side to side with – or so it seemed to the watching Bobby – the nervous alertness of a hunted animal. Suddenly she stopped dead and stood, swaying as though she would fall.

Bobby rushed forward and caught her. Her lips were white and it seemed to him that never had he seen such an awful fear on any human countenance.

'It's all right,' he said reassuringly in a very low voice. 'It's quite all right.'

The girl, for she was little more, moaned faintly, her eyelids half closed.

'I'm so frightened,' she murmured. 'I'm so terribly frightened.'

'What's the matter?' said Bobby.

The girl only shook her head and repeated faintly:

'I'm so frightened. I'm so horribly frightened.'

Suddenly some sound seemed to come to her ears. She sprang upright, away from Bobby. Then she turned to him.

'Go away,' she said. 'Go away at once.'

'I want to help you,' said Bobby.

'Do you?' She looked at him for a minute or two, a strange searching and moving glance. It was as though she explored his soul.

Then she shook her head.

'No one can help me.'

'I can,' said Bobby. 'I'd do anything. Tell me what it is that frightens you so.'

She shook her head.

'Not now. Oh! quick – they're coming! You can't help me unless you go now. At once – at once.'

Bobby yielded to her urgency.

With a whispered: 'I'm at the Anglers' Arms,' he plunged back along the path. The last he saw of her was an urgent gesture bidding him hurry.

Suddenly he heard footsteps on the path in front of him. Someone was coming along the path from the little door. Bobby plunged abruptly into the bushes at the side of the path.

He had not been mistaken. A man was coming along the path.

He passed close to Bobby but it was too dark for the young man to see his face.

When he had passed, Bobby resumed his retreat. He felt that he could do nothing more that night.

Anyway, his head was in a whirl.

For he had recognized the girl – recognized her beyond any possible doubt.

She was the original of the photograph which had so mysteriously disappeared.

CHAPTER 16

BOBBY BECOMES A SOLICITOR

'Mr Hawkins?'

'Yes,' said Bobby, his voice slightly muffled owing to a large mouthful of bacon and eggs.

'You're wanted on the telephone.'

Bobby took a hasty gulp of coffee, wiped his mouth and rose. The telephone was in a small dark passage. He took up the receiver.

'Hullo,' said Frankie's voice.

'Hullo, Frankie,' said Bobby incautiously.

'This is Lady Frances Derwent speaking,' said the voice coldly. 'Is that Hawkins?'

'Yes, m'lady.'

'I shall want the car at ten o'clock to take me up to London.'

'Very good, your ladyship.'

Bobby replaced the receiver.

'When does one say, "my lady", and when does one say, "your ladyship"?' he cogitated. 'I ought to know, but I don't. It's the sort of thing that will lead a real chauffeur or butler to catch me out.'

At the other end, Frankie hung up the receiver and turned to Roger Bassington-ffrench.

'It's a nuisance,' she observed lightly, 'to have to go up to London today. All owing to Father's fuss.'

'Still,' said Roger, 'you'll be back this evening?'

'Oh, yes!'

'I'd half thought of asking you if you'd give me a lift to town,' said Roger carelessly.

Frankie paused for an infinitesimal second before her answer – given with an apparent readiness.

'Why, of course,' she said.

'But on second thoughts I don't think I will go up today,' went on Roger. 'Henry's looking even odder than usual. Somehow I don't very much like leaving Sylvia alone with him.'

'I know,' said Frankie.

'Are you driving yourself?' asked Roger casually as they moved away from the telephone.

'Yes, but I shall take Hawkins. I've got some shopping to do as well and it's a nuisance if you're driving yourself – you can't leave the car anywhere.'

'Yes, of course.'

He said no more, but when the car came around, Bobby at the wheel very stiff and correct of demeanour, he came out on the doorstep to see her off.

'Goodbye,' said Frankie.

Under the circumstances she did not think of holding out a hand, but Roger took hers and held it a minute.

'You *are* coming back?' he said with curious insistence.

Frankie laughed.

'Of course. I only meant goodbye till this evening.'

'Don't have any more accidents.'

'I'll let Hawkins drive if you like.'

She sprang in beside Bobby, who touched his cap. The car moved off down the drive, Roger still standing on the step looking after it.

'Bobby,' said Frankie, 'do you think it possible that Roger might fall for me?'

'Has he?' inquired Bobby.

'Well, I just wondered.'

'I expect you know the symptoms pretty well,' said Bobby.

But he spoke absently. Frankie shot him a quick glance.

'Has anything – happened?' she asked.

'Yes, it has. Frankie, I've found the original of the photograph!'

'You mean – *the* one – the one you talked so much about – the one that was in the dead man's pocket?'

'Yes.'

'*Bobby!* I've got a few things to tell you, but nothing to this. Where did you find her?'

Bobby jerked his head back over his shoulder.

'In Dr Nicholson's nursing home.'

'Tell me.'

Carefully and meticulously Bobby described the events of the previous night. Frankie listened breathlessly.

'Then *we are* on the right track,' she said. 'And Dr Nicholson *is* mixed up in all this! I'm afraid of that man.'

'What is he like?'

'Oh! big and forceful – and he watches you. Very intently behind glasses. And you feel he knows all about you.'

'When did you meet him?'

'He came to dinner.'

She described the dinner party and Dr Nicholson's insistent dwelling on the details of her 'accident'.

'I felt he was suspicious,' she ended up.

'It's certainly queer his going into details like that,' said Bobby. 'What do you think is at the bottom of all this business, Frankie?'

'Well, I'm beginning to think that your suggestion of a dope gang, which I was so haughty about at the time, isn't such a bad guess after all.'

'With Dr Nicholson at the head of the gang?'

'Yes. This nursing home business would be a very good cloak for that sort of thing. He'd have a certain supply of drugs on the premises quite legitimately. While pretending to cure drug cases, he might really be supplying them with the stuff.'

'That seems plausible enough,' agreed Bobby.

'I haven't told you yet about Henry Bassington-ffrench.'

Bobby listened attentively to her description of her host's idiosyncracies.

'His wife doesn't suspect?'

'I'm sure she doesn't.'

'What is she like? Intelligent?'

'I never thought exactly. No, I suppose she isn't very. And yet in some ways she seems quite shrewd. A frank, pleasant woman.'

'And our Bassington-ffrench?'

'There I'm puzzled,' said Frankie slowly. 'Do you think, Bobby, that just possibly we might be all wrong about him?'

'Nonsense,' said Bobby. 'We worked it all out and decided that he must be the villain of the piece.'

'Because of the photograph?'

'Because of the photograph. No one else *could* have changed that photograph for the other.'

'I know,' said Frankie. 'But that one incident is all that we have against him.'

'It's quite enough.'

'I suppose so. And yet –'

'Well?'

'I don't know, but I have a queer sort of feeling that he's innocent – that he's not concerned in the matter at all.'

Bobby looked at her coldly.

'Did you say that he had fallen for you or that you had fallen for him?' he inquired politely.

Frankie flushed.

'Don't be so absurd, Bobby. I just wondered if there couldn't be some innocent explanation, that's all.'

'I don't see that there can be. Especially now that we've actually found the girl in the neighbourhood. That seems to clinch matters. If we only had some inkling as to who the dead man was –'

'Oh, but I have. I told you so in my letter. I'm nearly sure that the murdered man was somebody called Alan Carstairs.'

Once more she plunged into narrative.

'You know,' said Bobby, 'we really are getting on. Now we must try, more or less, to reconstruct the crime. Let's spread out our facts and see what sort of a job we can make of it.'

He paused for a moment and the car slackened speed as though in sympathy. Then he pressed his foot down once more on the accelerator and at the same time spoke.

'First, we'll assume that you are right about Alan Carstairs. He certainly fulfils the conditions. He's the right sort of man, he led a wandering life, he had very few friends and acquaintances in England, and if he disappeared he wasn't likely to be missed or sought after.

'So far, good. Alan Carstairs comes down to Staverley with these people – what did you say their name was –?'

'Rivington. There's a possible channel of inquiry there. In fact, I think we ought to follow it up.'

'We will. Very well, Carstairs comes down to Staverley with the Rivingtons. Now, is there anything in that?'

'You mean did he get them to bring him down here deliberately?'

'That's what I mean. Or was it just a casual chance? Was he brought down here by them and did he then come across the girl by accident just as I did? I presume he knew her before or he wouldn't have had her photograph on him.'

'The alternative being,' said Frankie thoughtfully, 'that he was already on the track of Nicholson and his gang.'

'And used the Rivingtons as a means of getting to this part of the world naturally?'

'That's quite a possible theory,' said Frankie. 'He may have been on the track of this gang.'

'Or simply on the track of the girl.'

'The girl?'

'Yes. She may have been abducted. He may have come over to England to find her.'

'Well, but if he had tracked her down to Staverley, why should he go off to Wales?'

'Obviously, there's a lot we don't know yet,' said Bobby.

'Evans,' said Frankie thoughtfully. 'We don't get any clues as to Evans. The Evans part of it must have to do with Wales.'

They were both silent for a moment or two. Then Frankie woke up to her surroundings.

'My dear, we're actually at Putney Hill. It seems like five minutes. Where are we going and what are we doing?'

'That's for you to say. I don't even know why we've come up to town.'

'The journey to town was only an excuse for getting a talk with you. I couldn't very well risk being seen walking the lanes at Staverley deep in conversation with my chauffeur. I used the pseudo-letter from Father as an excuse for driving up to town and talking to you on the way and even that was nearly wrecked by Bassington-ffrench coming too.'

'That would have torn it severely.'

'Not really. We'd have dropped him wherever he liked and then we'd have gone on to Brook Street and talked there. I think we'd better do that, anyway. Your garage place may be watched.'

Bobby agreed and related the episode of the inquiries made about him at Marchbolt.

'We'll go to the Derwents' town residence,' said Frankie. 'There's no one there but my maid and a couple of caretakers.'

They drove to Brook Street. Frankie rang the bell and was admitted, Bobby remaining outside. Presently Frankie opened the door again and beckoned him in. They went upstairs to the big drawing-room and pulled up some of the blinds and removed the swathing from one of the sofas.

'There's one other thing I forgot to tell you,' said Frankie. 'On the 16th, the day you were poisoned, Bassington-ffrench was at Staverley, but Nicholson was away – supposedly at a conference in London. And his car is a dark-blue Talbot.'

'And he has access to morphia,' said Bobby.

They exchanged significant glances.

'It's not exactly evidence, I suppose,' said Bobby, 'but it fits in nicely.'

Frankie went to a side table and returned with a telephone directory.

'What are you going to do?'

'I'm looking up the name Rivington.'

She turned pages rapidly.

'A. Rivington & Sons, Builders. B. A. C. Rivington, Dental Surgeon. D. Rivington, Shooters Hill, I think not. Miss Florence Rivington. Col. H. Rivington, D.S.O. – that's more like it – Tite Street, Chelsea.'

She continued her search.

'There's M. R. Rivington, Onslow Square. He's possible. And there's a William Rivington at Hampstead. I think Onslow Square and Tite Street are the most likely ones. The Rivingtons, Bobby, have got to be seen without delay.'

'I think you're right. But what are we going to say? Think up a few good lies, Frankie. I'm not much good at that sort of thing.'

Frankie reflected for a minute or two.

'I think,' she said, 'that'll you have to go. Do you feel you could be the junior partner of a solicitors' firm?'

That seems a most gentlemanly role,' said Bobby. 'I was afraid you might think of something much worse than that. All the same, it's not quite in character, is it?'

'How do you mean?'

'Well, solicitors never do make personal visits, do they? Surely they always write letters at six and eightpence a time, or else write and ask someone to keep an appointment at their office.'

'This particular firm of solicitors is unconventional,' said Frankie. 'Wait a minute.'

She left the room and returned with a card.

'*Mr Frederick Spragge*,' she said, handing it to Bobby. 'You are a young member of the firm of Spragge, Spragge, Jenkinson and Spragge, of Bloomsbury Square.'

'Did you invent that firm, Frankie?'

'Certainly not. They're Father's solicitors.'

'And suppose they have me up for impersonation?'

'That's all right. There isn't any young Spragge. The only Spragge is about a hundred, and anyway he eats out of my hand. I'll fix him if things go wrong. He's a great snob – he loves lords and dukes, however little money he makes out of them.'

'What about clothes? Shall I ring up Badger to bring some along?'

Frankie looked doubtful.

'I don't want to insult your clothes, Bobby,' she said. 'Or throw your poverty in your teeth, or anything like that. But will they carry conviction? I think, myself, that we'd better raid Father's wardrobe. His clothes won't fit you too badly.'

A quarter of an hour later, Bobby, attired in a morning coat and striped trousers of exquisitely correct cut and passable fit, stood surveying himself in Lord Marchington's pier glass.

'Your father does himself well in clothes,' he remarked graciously. 'With the might of Savile Row behind me, I feel a great increase of confidence.'

'I suppose you'll have to stick to your moustache,' said Frankie.

'It's sticking to me,' said Bobby. 'It's a work of art that couldn't be repeated in a hurry.'

'You'd better keep it, then. Though it's more legal-looking to be clean-shaven.'

'It's better than a beard,' said Bobby. 'Now, then, Frankie, do you think your father could lend me a hat?'

CHAPTER 17
MRS RIVINGTON TALKS

'Supposing,' said Bobby, pausing on the doorstep, 'that Mr M. R. Rivington of Onslow Square is himself a solicitor? That would be a blow.'

'You'd better try the Tite Street colonel first,' said Frankie. 'He won't know anything about solicitors.'

Accordingly, Bobby took a taxi to Tite Street. Colonel Rivington was out. Mrs Rivington, however, was at home. Bobby delivered over to the smart parlourmaid his card on which he had written: '*From Messrs Spragge, Spragge, Jenkinson & Spragge. Very Urgent.*'

The card and Lord Marchington's clothes produced their effect upon the parlourmaid. She did not for an instant suspect that Bobby had come to sell miniatures or tout for insurances. He was shown into a beautifully and expensively furnished drawing-room and presently Mrs Rivington, beautifully and expensively dressed and made up, came into the room.

'I must apologize for troubling you, Mrs Rivington,' said Bobby. 'But the matter was rather urgent and we wished to avoid the delay of letters.'

That any solicitor could ever wish to avoid delay seemed so transparently impossible that Bobby for a moment wondered anxiously whether Mrs Rivington would see through the pretence.

Mrs Rivington, however, was clearly a woman of more looks than brains who accepted things as they were presented to her.

'Oh, do sit down!' she said. 'I got the telephone message just now from your office saying that you were on your way here.'

Bobby mentally applauded Frankie for this last-minute flash of brilliance.

He sat down and endeavoured to look legal.

'It is about our client, Mr Alan Carstairs,' he said.

'Oh, yes?'

'He may have mentioned that we were acting for him.'

'Did he now? I believe he did,' said Mrs Rivington, opening very large blue eyes. She was clearly of a suggestible type. 'But of course, I know about you. You acted for Dolly Maltravers, didn't you, when she shot that dreadful dressmaker man? I suppose you know all the details?'

She looked at him with frank curiosity. It seemed to Bobby that Mrs Rivington was going to be easy meat.

'We know a lot that never comes into court,' he said, smiling.

'Oh, I suppose you must.' Mrs Rivington looked at him enviously. 'Tell me, did she really – I mean, was she dressed as that woman said?'

'The story was contradicted in court,' said Bobby solemnly. He slightly dropped the corner of his eyelid.

'Oh, I see,' breathed Mrs Rivington, enraptured.

'About Mr Carstairs,' said Bobby, feeling that he had now established friendly relations and could get on with his job. 'He left England very suddenly, as perhaps you know?'

Mrs Rivington shook her head.

'Has he left England? I didn't know. We haven't seen him for some time.'

'Did he tell you how long he expected to be over here?'

'He said he might be here for a week or two or it might be six months or a year.'

'Where was he staying?'

'At the Savoy.'

'And you saw him last – when?'

'Oh, about three weeks or a month ago. I can't remember.'

'You took him down to Staverley one day?'

'Of course! I believe that's the last time we saw him. He rang up to know when he could see us. He'd just arrived in London and Hubert was very put out because we were going up to Scotland the next day, and we were going down to Staverley to lunch and dining out with some dreadful people that we couldn't get rid of, and he wanted to see Carstairs because he liked him so much, and so I said: "My dear, let's take him down to the

Bassington-ffrenches with us. They won't mind." And we did. And, of course, they didn't.'

She came breathlessly to a pause.

'Did he tell you his reasons for being in England?' asked Bobby.

'No. Did he have any? Oh yes, I know. We thought it was something to do with that millionaire man, that friend of his, who had such a tragic death. Some doctor told him he had cancer and he killed himself. A very wicked thing for a doctor to do, don't you think so? And they're often quite wrong. Our doctor said the other day that my little girl had measles and it turned out to be a sort of heat rash. I told Hubert I should change him.'

Ignoring Mrs Rivington's treatment of doctors as though they were library books, Bobby returned to the point.

'Did Mr Carstairs know the Bassington-ffrenches?'

'Oh, no! But I think he liked them. Though he was very queer and moody on the way back. I suppose something that had been said must have upset him. He's a Canadian, you know, and I often think Canadians are so touchy.'

'You don't know what it was that upset him?'

'I haven't the least idea. The silliest things do it sometimes, don't they?'

'Did he take any walks in the neighbourhood?' asked Bobby.

'Oh, no! What a very odd idea!' She stared at him.

Bobby tried again.

'Was there a party? Did he meet any of the neighbours?'

'No, it was just ourselves and them. But it's odd your saying that –'

'Yes,' said Bobby eagerly, as she paused.

'Because he asked a most frightful lot of questions about some people who lived near there.'

'Do you remember the name?'

'No, I don't. It wasn't anyone very interesting – some doctor or other.'

'Dr Nicholson?'

'I believe that was the name. He wanted to know all about him and his wife and when they came there – all sorts of things. It seemed so odd when he didn't know them, and he wasn't a bit a curious man as a rule. But, of course, perhaps he was only making conversation, and couldn't think of anything to say. One does do things like that sometimes.'

Bobby agreed that one did and asked how the subject of the Nicholsons had come up, but that Mrs Rivington was unable to tell him. She had been out with Henry Bassington-ffrench in the garden and had come in to find the others discussing the Nicholsons.

So far, the conversation had proceeded easily, Bobby pumping the lady without any camouflage, but she now displayed a sudden curiosity.

'But what is it you want to know about Mr Carstairs?' she asked.

'I really wanted his address,' explained Bobby. 'As you know, we act for him and we've just had a rather important cable from New York – you know, there's rather a serious fluctuation in the dollar just now –'

Mrs Rivington nodded with desperate intelligence.

'And so,' continued Bobby rapidly, 'we wanted to get into touch with him – to get his instructions – and he hasn't left an address – and, having heard him mention he was a friend of yours, I thought you might possibly have news of him.'

'Oh, I see,' said Mrs Rivington, completely satisfied. 'What a pity. But he's always rather a vague man, I should think.'

'Oh, distinctly so,' said Bobby. 'Well,' he rose, 'I apologize for taking up so much of your time.'

'Oh, not at all,' said Mrs Rivington. 'And it's so interesting to know that Dolly Maltravers really did – as you say she did.'

'I said nothing at all,' said Bobby.

'Yes, but then lawyers are so discreet, aren't they?' said Mrs Rivington with a little gurgle of laughter.

'So that's all right,' thought Bobby, as he walked away down Tite Street. 'I seem to have taken Dolly Whatsername's character away for good, but I daresay she deserves it, and that charming idiot of a woman will never wonder why, if I wanted Carstairs' address, I didn't simply ring up and ask for it!'

Back in Brook Street he and Frankie discussed the matter from every angle.

'It looks as though it were really pure chance that took him to the Bassington-ffrenches,' said Frankie thoughtfully.

'I know. But evidently when he was down there some chance remark directed his attention to the Nicholsons.'

'So that, really, it is Nicholson who is at the heart of the mystery, not the Bassington-ffrenches?'

Bobby looked at her.

'Still intent on whitewashing your hero,' he inquired coldly.

'My dear, I'm only pointing out what it looks like. It's the mention of Nicholson and his nursing home that excited Carstairs. Being taken down to the Bassington-ffrenches was a pure matter of chance. You must admit that.'

'It seems like it.'

'Why only "seems"?'

'Well, there is just one other possibility. In some way, Carstairs may have found out that the Rivingtons were going down to lunch with the Bassington-ffrenches. He may have overheard some chance remark in a restaurant – at the Savoy, perhaps. So he rings them up, very urgent to see them, and what he hopes may happen does happen. They're very booked up and they suggest his coming down with them – their friends won't mind and they do so want to see him. That is possible, Frankie.'

'It is *possible*, I suppose. But it seems a very roundabout method of doing things.'

'No more roundabout than your accident,' said Bobby.

'My accident was vigorous direct action,' said Frankie coldly.

Bobby removed Lord Marchington's clothes and replaced them where he had found them. Then he donned his chauffeur's uniform once more and they were soon speeding back to Staverley.

'If Roger has fallen for me,' said Frankie demurely, 'he'll be pleased I've come back so soon. He'll think I can't bear to be away from him for long.'

'I'm not sure that you can bear it, either,' said Bobby. 'I've always heard that really dangerous criminals were singularly attractive.'

'Somehow I can't believe he is a criminal.'

'So you remarked before.'

'Well, I feel like that.'

'You can't get over the photograph.'

'Damn the photograph!' said Frankie.

Bobby drove up the drive in silence. Frankie sprang out and went into the house without a backward glance. Bobby drove away.

The house seemed very silent. Frankie glanced at the clock. It was half-past two.

'They don't expect me back for hours yet,' she thought. 'I wonder where they are?'

She opened the door of the library and went in, stopping suddenly on the threshold.

Dr Nicholson was sitting on the sofa, holding both Sylvia Bassington-ffrench's hands in his.

Sylvia jumped to her feet and came across the room towards Frankie.

'He's been telling me,' she said.

Her voice was stifled. She put both hands to her face as though to hide it from view.

'It's too terrible,' she sobbed, and, brushing past Frankie, she ran out of the room.

Dr Nicholson had risen. Frankie advanced a step or two towards him. His eyes, watchful as ever, met hers.

'Poor lady,' he said suavely. 'It has been a great shock to her.'

The muscles at the corner of his mouth twitched. For a moment or two Frankie fancied that he was amused. And then, quite suddenly, she realized that it was quite a different emotion.

The man was angry. He was holding himself in, hiding his anger behind a suave bland mask, but the emotion was there. It was all he could do to hold that emotion in.

There was a moment's pause.

'It was best that Mrs Bassington-ffrench should know the truth,' said the doctor. 'I want her to induce her husband to place himself in my hands.'

'I'm afraid,' said Frankie gently, 'that I interrupted you.' She paused. 'I came back sooner than I meant.'

CHAPTER 18

THE GIRL OF THE PHOTOGRAPH

On Bobby's return to the inn he was greeted with the information that someone was waiting to see him.

'It's a lady. You'll find her in Mr Askew's little sitting-room.'

Bobby made his way there slightly puzzled. Unless she had flown there on wings he could not see how Frankie could possibly have got to the Anglers' Arms ahead of him, and that his visitor could be anyone else but Frankie never occurred to him.

He opened the door of the small room which Mr Askew kept as his private sitting-room. Sitting bolt upright in a chair was a slender figure dressed in black – the girl of the photograph.

Bobby was so astonished that for a moment or two he could not speak. Then he noticed that the girl was terribly nervous. Her small hands were trembling and closed and unclosed themselves on the arm of the chair. She seemed too nervous even to speak, but her large eyes held a kind of terrified appeal.

'So it's you?' said Bobby at last. He shut the door behind him and came forward to the table.

Still the girl did not speak – still those large, terrified eyes looked into his. At last words came – a mere hoarse whisper.

'You said – you said – you'd help me. Perhaps I shouldn't have come –'

Here Bobby broke in, finding words and assurance at the same time.

'Shouldn't have come? Nonsense. You did quite right to come. Of course, you should have come. And I'll do anything – anything in the world – to help you. Don't be frightened. You're quite safe now.'

The colour rose a little in the girl's face. She said abruptly:

'Who are you? You're – you're – not a chauffeur. I mean, you may be a chauffeur, but you're not one really.'

Bobby understood her meaning in spite of the confused form of words in which she had cloaked them.

'One does all sorts of jobs nowadays,' he said. 'I used to be in the Navy. As a matter of fact, I'm not exactly a chauffeur –

but that doesn't matter now. But, anyway, I assure you you can trust me and – and tell me all about it.'

Her flush had deepened.

'You must think me mad,' she murmured. 'You must think me quite mad.'

'No, no.'

'Yes – coming here like this. But I was so frightened – so terribly frightened –' Her voice died away. Her eyes widened as though they saw some vision of terror.

Bobby seized her hand firmly.

'Look here,' he said, 'it's quite all right. Everything's going to be all right. You're safe now – with – with a friend. Nothing shall happen to you.'

He felt the answering pressure of her fingers.

'When you stepped out into the moonlight the other night,' she said in a low, hurried voice, 'it was – it was like a dream – a dream of deliverance. I didn't know who you were or where you came from, but it gave me hope and I determined to come and find you – and – tell you.'

'That's right,' said Bobby encouragingly. 'Tell me. Tell me everything.'

She drew her hand away suddenly.

'If I do, you'll think I'm mad – that I've gone wrong in my head from being in that place with those others.'

'No, I shan't. I shan't, really.'

'You will. It *sounds* mad.'

'I shall know it isn't. Tell me. Please tell me.'

She drew a little farther away from him, sitting very upright, her eyes staring straight in front of her.

'It's just this,' she said. 'I'm afraid I'm going to be murdered.'

Her voice was dry and hoarse. She was speaking with obvious self-restraint but her hands were trembling.

'Murdered?'

'Yes, that sounds mad, doesn't it? Like – what do they call it? – persecution mania.'

'No,' said Bobby. 'You don't sound mad at all – just frightened. Tell me, who wants to murder you and why?'

She was silent a minute or two, twisting and untwisting her hands. Then she said in a low voice:

'My husband.'

'Your husband?' Thoughts whirled round in Bobby's head: 'Who are you –' he said abruptly.

It was her turn to look surprised.

'Don't you know?'

'I haven't the least idea.'

She said: 'I'm Moira Nicholson. My husband is Dr Nicholson.'

'Then you're not a patient there?'

'A patient? Oh, no!' Her face darkened suddenly. 'I suppose you think I speak like one.'

'No, no, I didn't mean that at all.' He was at pains to reassure her. 'Honestly, I didn't mean it that way. I was only surprised at finding you married – and – all that. Now, go on with what you're telling me – about your husband wanting to murder you.'

'It sounds mad, I know. But it isn't – it isn't! I see it in his eyes when he looks at me. And queer things have happened – accidents.'

'Accidents?' said Bobby sharply.

'Yes. Oh! I know it sounds hysterical and as though I was making it all up –'

'Not a bit,' said Bobby. 'It sounds perfectly reasonable. Go on. About these accidents.'

'They were just accidents. He backed the car not seeing I was there – I just jumped aside in time – and some stuff that was in the wrong bottle – oh, stupid things – and things that people would think quite all right, but they weren't – they were *meant*. I know it. And it's wearing me out – watching for them – being on my guard – trying to save my life.'

She swallowed convulsively.

'Why does your husband want to do away with you?' asked Bobby.

Perhaps he hardly expected a definite answer – but the answer came promptly:

'Because he wants to marry Sylvia Bassington-ffrench.'

'What? But she's married already.'

'I know. But he's arranging for that.'

'How do you mean?'

'I don't know exactly. But I know that he's trying to get Mr Bassington-ffrench brought to the Grange as a patient.'

'And then?'

'I don't know, but I think something would happen.'

She shuddered.

'He's got some hold over Mr Bassington-ffrench. I don't know what it is.'

'Bassington-ffrench takes morphia,' said Bobby.

'Is that it? Jasper gives it to him, I suppose.'

'It comes by post.'

'Perhaps Jasper doesn't do it directly – he's very cunning. Mr Bassington-ffrench mayn't know it comes from Jasper – but I'm sure it does. And then Jasper would have him at the Grange and pretend to cure him – and once he was there –'

She paused and shivered.

'All sorts of things happen at the Grange,' she said. 'Queer things. People come there to get better – and they don't get better – they get worse.'

As she spoke, Bobby was aware of a glimpse into a strange, evil atmosphere. He felt something of the terror that had enveloped Moira Nicholson's life so long.

He said abruptly:

'You say your husband wants to marry Mrs Bassington-ffrench?'

Moira nodded.

'He's crazy about her.'

'And she?'

'I don't know,' said Moira slowly. 'I can't make up my mind. On the surface she seems fond of her husband and little boy and content and peaceful. She seems a very simple woman. But sometimes I fancy that she isn't so simple as she seems. I've even wondered sometimes whether she is an entirely different woman from what we all think she is . . . whether, perhaps, she isn't playing a part and playing it very well . . . But, really, I think, that's nonsense – foolish imagination on my part . . . When you've lived at a place like the Grange your mind gets distorted and you do begin imagining things.'

'What about the brother Roger?' asked Bobby.

'I don't know much about him. He's nice, I think, but he's the sort of person who would be very easily deceived. He's quite taken in by Jasper, I know. Jasper is working on him to persuade

Mr Bassington-ffrench to come to the Grange. I believe he thinks it's all his own idea.' She leaned forward suddenly and caught Bobby's sleeve. 'Don't let him come to the Grange,' she implored. 'If he does, something awful will happen. I know it will.'

Bobby was silent a minute or two, turning over the amazing story in his mind.

'How long have you been married to Nicholson?' he said at last.

'Just over a year –' She shivered.

'Haven't you ever thought of leaving him?'

'How could I? I've nowhere to go. I've no money. If anyone took me in, what sort of story could I tell? A fantastic tale that my husband wanted to murder me? Who would believe me?'

'Well, I believe you,' said Bobby.

He paused a moment, as though making up his mind to a certain course of action. Then he went on:

'Look here,' he said bluntly. 'I'm going to ask you a question straight out. Did you know a man called Alan Carstairs?'

He saw the colour come up in her cheeks.

'Why do you ask me that?'

'Because it's rather important that I should know. My idea is that you did know Alan Carstairs, that perhaps at some time or other you gave him your photograph.'

She was silent a moment, her eyes downcast. Then she lifted her head and looked him in the face.

'That's quite true,' she said.

'You knew him before you were married?'

'Yes.'

'Has he been down here to see you since you were married?'

She hesitated, then said:

'Yes, once.'

'About a month ago would that be?'

'Yes. I suppose it would be about a month.'

'He knew you were living down here?'

'I don't know how he knew – I hadn't told him. I had never even written to him since my marriage.'

'But he found out and came here to see you. Did your husband know that?'

'No.'

'You think not. But he might have known all the same?'

'I suppose he might, but he never said anything.'

'Did you discuss your husband at all with Carstairs? Did you tell him of your fears as to your safety?'

She shook her head.

'I hadn't begun to suspect then.'

'But you were unhappy?'

'Yes.'

'And you told him so?'

'No. I tried not to show in any way that my marriage hadn't been a success.'

'But he might have guessed it all the same,' said Bobby gently.

'I suppose he might,' she admitted in a low voice.

'Do you think – I don't know how to put it – but do you think that he knew anything about your husband – that he suspected, for instance, that this nursing home place mightn't be quite what it seemed to be?'

Her brows furrowed as she tried to think.

'It's possible,' she said at last. 'He asked one or two rather peculiar questions – but – no. I don't think he can really have known anything about it.'

Bobby was silent again for a few minutes. Then he said:

'Would you call your husband a jealous man?'

Rather to his surprise, she answered:

'Yes. Very jealous.'

'Jealous, for instance, of you.'

'You mean even though he doesn't care? But, yes, he would be jealous, just the same. I'm his property, you see. He's a queer man – a very queer man.'

She shivered.

Then she asked suddenly:

'You're not connected with the police in any way, are you?'

'I? Oh, no!'

'I wondered, I mean –'

Bobby looked down at his chauffeur's livery.

'It's rather a long story,' he said.

'You are Lady Frances Derwent's chauffeur, aren't you? So the landlord here said. I met her at dinner the other night.'

'I know.' He paused. 'We've got to get hold of her,' he said. 'And it's a bit difficult for me to do. Do you think you could ring up and ask to speak to her and then get her to come and meet you somewhere outdoors?'

'I suppose I could –' said Moira slowly.

'I know it must seem frightfully odd to you. But it won't when I've explained. We must get hold of Frankie as soon as possible. It's essential.'

Moira rose.

'Very well,' she said.

With her hand on the door-handle she hesitated.

'Alan,' she said, 'Alan Carstairs. Did you say you'd seen him?'

'I have seen him,' said Bobby slowly. 'But not lately.'

And he thought, with a shock:

'Of course – she doesn't know he's dead . . .'

He said:

'Ring up Lady Frances. Then I'll tell you everything.'

CHAPTER 19

A COUNCIL OF THREE

Moira returned a few minutes later.

'I got her,' she said. 'I've asked her to come and meet me at a little summer-house down near the river. She must have thought it very odd, but she said she'd come.'

'Good,' said Bobby. 'Now, just where is this place exactly?'

Moira described it carefully, and the way to get to it.

'That's all right,' said Bobby. 'You go first. I'll follow on.'

They adhered to this programme, Bobby lingering to have a word with Mr Askew.

'Odd thing,' he said casually, 'that lady, Mrs Nicholson, I used to work for an uncle of hers. Canadian gentleman.'

Moira's visit to him might, he felt, give rise to gossip, and the last thing he wanted was for gossip of that kind to get about and possibly find its way to Dr Nicholson's ears.

'So that's it, is it?' said Mr Askew. 'I rather wondered.'

'Yes,' said Bobby. 'She recognized me, and came along to hear what I was doing now. A nice, pleasant-spoken lady.'

'Very pleasant, indeed. She can't have much of a life living at the Grange.'

'It wouldn't be *my* fancy,' agreed Bobby.

Feeling that he had achieved his object, he strolled out into the village and with an aimless air betook himself in the direction indicated by Moira.

He reached the rendezvous successfully and found her there waiting for him. Frankie had not yet put in an appearance.

Moira's glance was frankly inquiring, and Bobby felt he must attempt the somewhat difficult task of explanation.

'There's an awful lot I've got to tell you,' he said, and stopped awkwardly.

'Yes?'

'To begin with,' said Bobby plunging, 'I'm not really a chauffeur, although I do work in a garage in London. And my name isn't Hawkins – it's Jones – Bobby Jones. I come from Marchbolt in Wales.'

Moira was listening attentively, but clearly the mention of Marchbolt meant nothing to her. Bobby set his teeth and went bravely to the heart of the matter.

'Look here, I'm afraid I'm going to give you rather a shock. This friend of yours – Alan Carstairs – he's, well – you've got to know – he's dead.'

He felt the start she gave and tactfully he averted his eyes from her face. Did she mind very much? Had she been – dash it all – keen on the fellow?

She was silent a moment or two, then she said in a low, thoughtful voice:

'So that's why he never came back? I wondered.'

Bobby ventured to steal a look at her. His spirits rose. She looked sad and thoughtful – but that was all.

'Tell me about it,' she said.

Bobby complied.

'He fell over the cliff at Marchbolt – the place where I live. I and the doctor there happened to be the ones to find him.' He paused and then added: 'He had your photograph in his pocket.'

'Did he?' She gave a sweet, rather sad smile. 'Dear Alan, he was – very faithful.'

There was silence for a moment or two and then she asked:

'When did this happen?'

'About a month ago. October 3rd to be exact.'

'That must have been just after he came down here.'

'Yes. Did he mention that he was going to Wales?'

She shook her head.

'You don't know anyone called Evans, do you?' said Bobby.

'Evans?' Moira frowned, trying to think. 'No, I don't think so. It's a very common name, of course, but I can't remember anybody. What is he?'

'That's just what we don't know. Oh! hullo, here's Frankie.'

Frankie came hurrying along the path. Her face, at the sight of Bobby and Mrs Nicholson sitting chatting together, was a study in conflicting expressions.

'Hullo, Frankie,' said Bobby. 'I'm glad you've come. We've got to have a great pow-wow. To begin with it's Mrs Nicholson who is the original of *the* photograph.'

'Oh!' said Frankie blankly.

She looked at Moira and suddenly laughed.

'My dear,' she said to Bobby, 'now I see why the sight of Mrs Cayman at the inquest was such a shock to you!'

'Exactly,' said Bobby.

What a fool he had been. However could he have imagined for one moment that any space of time could have turned a Moira Nicholson into an Amelia Cayman.

'Lord, what a fool I've been!' he exclaimed.

Moira was looking bewildered.

'There's such an awful lot to tell,' said Bobby, 'and I don't quite know how to put it all.'

He described the Caymans and their identification of the body.

'But I don't understand,' said Moira, bewildered. 'Whose body was it really, her brother's or Alan Carstairs?'

'That's where the dirty work comes in,' explained Bobby.

'And then,' continued Frankie, 'Bobby was poisoned.'

'Eight grains of morphia,' said Bobby reminiscently.

'Don't start on that,' said Frankie. 'You're capable of going on for hours on the subject and it's really very boring to other people. Let me explain.'

She took a long breath.

'You see,' she said, 'those Cayman people came to see Bobby after the inquest to ask him if the brother (supposed) had said anything before he died, and Bobby said, "No." But afterwards he remembered that he had said something about a man called Evans, so he wrote and told them so, and a few days afterwards he got a letter offering him a job in Peru or somewhere and when he wouldn't take it, the next thing was that someone put a lot of morphia –'

'Eight grains,' said Bobby.

'– in his beer. Only, having a most extraordinary inside or something, it didn't kill him. And so then we saw at once that Pritchard – or Carstairs, you know – must have been pushed over the cliff.'

'But why?' asked Moira.

'Don't you see? Why, it seems perfectly clear to us. I expect I haven't told it very well. Anyway, we decided that he had been and that Roger Bassington-ffrench had probably done it.'

'Roger Bassington-ffrench?' Moira spoke in tones of the liveliest amusement.

'We worked it out that way. You see, he was there at the time, and your photograph disappeared, and he seemed to be the only man who could have taken it.'

'I see,' said Moira thoughtfully.

'And then,' continued Frankie, 'I happened to have an accident just here. An amazing coincidence, wasn't it?' She looked hard at Bobby with an admonishing eye. 'So I telephoned to Bobby and suggested that he should come down here pretending to be my chauffeur and we'd look into the matter.'

'So now you see how it was,' said Bobby, accepting Frankie's one discreet departure from the truth. 'And the final climax was when last night I strolled into the grounds of the Grange and ran right into you – the original of the mysterious photograph.'

'You recognized me very quickly,' said Moira, with a faint smile.

'Yes,' said Bobby. 'I would have recognized the original of that photograph anywhere.'

For no particular reason, Moira blushed.

Then an idea seemed to strike her and she looked sharply from one to the other.

'Are you telling me the truth?' she asked. 'Is it really true that you came down here – by accident? Or did you come because – because' – her voice quavered in spite of herself – 'you suspected my husband?'

Bobby and Frankie looked at each other. Then Bobby said:

'I give you my word of honour that we'd never even heard of your husband till we came down here.'

'Oh, I see.' She turned to Frankie. 'I'm sorry, Lady Frances, but, you see, I remembered that evening when we came to dinner. Jasper went on and on at you – asking you things about your accident. I couldn't think why. But I think now that perhaps he suspected it wasn't genuine.'

'Well, if you really want to know, it wasn't,' said Frankie. 'Whoof – now I feel better! It was all camouflaged very carefully. But it was nothing to do with your husband. The whole thing was staged because we wanted to – to – what does one call it? – get a line on Roger Bassington-ffrench.'

'Roger?' Moira frowned and smiled perplexedly.

'It seems absurd,' she said frankly.

'All the same facts are facts,' said Bobby.

'Roger – oh, no.' She shook her head. 'He might be weak – or wild. He might get into debt, or get mixed up in a scandal – but pushing someone over a cliff – no, I simply can't imagine it.'

'Do you know,' said Frankie, 'I can't very well imagine it either.'

'But he must have taken that photograph,' said Bobby stubbornly. 'Listen, Mrs Nicholson, while I go over the facts.'

He did so slowly and carefully. When he had finished, she nodded her head comprehendingly.

'I see what you mean. It seems very queer.' She paused a minute and then said unexpectedly: 'Why don't you ask him?'

CHAPTER 20

COUNCIL OF TWO

For a moment, the bold simplicity of the question quite took their breath away. Both Frankie and Bobby started to speak at once:

'That's impossible –' began Bobby, just as Frankie said: 'That would never do.'

Then they both stopped dead as the possibilities of the idea sank in.

'You see,' said Moira eagerly, 'I do see what you mean. It does seem as though Roger *must* have taken that photograph, but I don't believe for one moment that he pushed Alan over. Why should he? He didn't even know him. They'd only met once – at lunch down here. They'd never come across each other in any way. There's no motive.'

'Then who *did* push him over?' asked Frankie bluntly.

A shadow crossed Moira's face.

'I don't know,' she said constrainedly.

'Look here,' said Bobby. 'Do you mind if I tell Frankie what you told me. About what you're afraid of.'

Moira turned her head away.

'If you like. But it sounds so melodramatic and hysterical. I can't believe it myself this minute.'

And indeed the bald statement, made unemotionally in the open air of the quiet English countryside, did seem curiously lacking in reality.

Moira got up abruptly.

'I really feel I've been terribly silly,' she said, her lip trembling. 'Please don't pay any attention to what I said, Mr Jones. It was just – nerves. Anyway, I must be going now. Goodbye.'

She moved rapidly away. Bobby sprang up to follow her, but Frankie pushed him firmly back.

'Stay there, idiot, leave this to me.'

She went rapidly off after Moira. She returned a few minutes later.

'Well?' queried Bobby anxiously.

'That's all right. I calmed her down. It was a bit hard on her having her private fears blurted out in front of her to a third person. I made her promise we'd have a meeting – all three of us – again soon. Now that you're not hampered by her being there, tell us all about it.'

Bobby did so. Frankie listened attentively. Then she said:

'It fits in with two things. First of all, I came back just now to find Nicholson holding both Sylvia Bassington-ffrench's hands

– and didn't he look daggers at me! If looks could kill I feel sure he'd have made me a corpse then and there.'

'What's the second thing?' asked Bobby.

'Oh, just an incident. Sylvia described how Moira's photograph had made a great impression on some stranger who had come to the house. Depend upon it, that was Carstairs. He recognized the photograph, Mrs Bassington-ffrench tells him that it is a portrait of a Mrs Nicholson, and that explains how he came to find out where she was. But you know, Bobby, I don't see yet where Nicholson comes in. Why should he want to do away with Alan Carstairs?'

'You think it was him and not Bassington-ffrench? Rather a coincidence if he and Bassington-ffrench should both be in Marchbolt on the same day.'

'Well, coincidences do happen. But if it was Nicholson, I don't yet see the motive. Was Carstairs on the track of Nicholson as the head of a dope gang? Or is your new lady friend the motive for the murder?'

'It might be both,' suggested Bobby. 'He may know that Carstairs and his wife had an interview, and he may have believed that his wife gave him away somehow.'

'Now, that is a possibility,' said Frankie. 'But the first thing is to make sure about Roger Bassington-ffrench. The only thing we've got against him is the photograph business. If he can clear that up satisfactorily –'

'You're going to tackle him on the subject? Frankie, is that wise? If he is the villain of the piece, as we decided he must be, it means that we're going to show him our hand.'

'Not quite – not the way I shall do it. After all, in every other way he's been perfectly straightforward and above board. We've taken that to be super-cunning – but suppose it just happens to be innocence? *If* he can explain the photograph – and I shall be watching him when he does explain – and if there's the least sign of hesitation of guilt I shall see it – as I say, *if* he can explain the photograph – then he may be a very valuable ally.'

'How do you mean, Frankie?'

'My dear, your little friend may be an emotional scare-monger who likes to exaggerate, but supposing she isn't – that all she says is gospel truth – that her husband wants to get rid of her and marry Sylvia. Don't you realize that, in that case, Henry Bassington-ffrench is in mortal danger too. At all costs we've got to prevent him being sent to the Grange. And at present Roger Bassington-ffrench is on Nicholson's side.'

'Good for you, Frankie,' said Bobby quietly. 'Go ahead with your plan.'

Frankie got up to go, but before departing she paused for a moment.

'Isn't it odd?' she said. 'We seem, somehow, to have got in between the covers of a book. We're in the middle of someone else's story. It's a frightfully queer feeling.'

'I know what you mean,' said Bobby. 'There is something rather uncanny about it. I should call it a play rather than a book. It's as though we'd walked on to the stage in the middle of the second act and we haven't really got parts in the play at all, but we have to pretend, and what makes it so frightfully hard is that we haven't the faintest idea what the first act was about.'

Frankie nodded eagerly.

'I'm not even so sure it's the second act – I think it's more like the third. Bobby, I'm sure we've got to go back a long way . . . And we've got to be quick because I fancy the play is frightfully near the final curtain.'

'With corpses strewn everywhere,' said Bobby. 'And what brought us into the show was a regular cue – five words – quite meaningless as far as we are concerned.'

'"*Why didn't they ask Evans?*" Isn't it odd, Bobby, that though we've found out a good deal and more and more characters come into the thing, we never get any nearer to the mysterious Evans?'

'I've got an idea about Evans. I've a feeling that Evans doesn't really matter at all – that although he's been the starting point as it were, yet in himself he's probably quite inessential. It will be like that story of Wells where a prince built a marvellous palace or temple round the tomb of his beloved. And when it was finished there was just one little thing that jarred. So he said: "Take it away." And the thing was actually the tomb itself.'

'Sometimes,' said Frankie, 'I don't believe there is an Evans.'

Saying which, she nodded to Bobby and retraced her steps towards the house.

CHAPTER 21

ROGER ANSWERS A QUESTION

Fortune favoured her, for she fell in with Roger not far from the house.

'Hullo,' he said. 'You're back early from London.'

'I wasn't in the mood for London,' said Frankie.

'Have you been to the house yet?' he asked. His face grew grave. 'Nicholson, I find, has been telling Sylvia the truth about poor old Henry. Poor girl, she's taken it hard. It seems she had absolutely no suspicion.'

'I know,' said Frankie. 'They were both together in the library when I came in. She was – very upset.'

'Look here, Frankie,' said Roger. 'Henry has absolutely got to be cured. It isn't as though this drug habit had a real hold on him. He hasn't been taking it so very long. And he's got every incentive in the world to make him keen on being cured – Sylvia, Tommy, his home. He's got to be made to see the position clearly. Nicholson is just the man to put the thing through. He was talking to me the other day. He's had some amazing successes – even with people who have been slaves for years to the beastly stuff. If Henry will only consent to go to the Grange –'

Frankie interrupted.

'Look here,' she said. 'There's something I want to ask you. Just a question. I hope you won't think I'm simply frightfully impertinent.'

'What is it?' asked Roger, his attention arrested.

'Do you mind telling me if you took a photograph out of that man's pocket – the one who fell over the cliff at Marchbolt?'

She was studying him closely, watching every detail of his expression. She was satisfied with what she saw.

Slight annoyance, a trace of embarrassment – no flash of guilt or dismay.

'Now, how on earth did you come to guess that?' he said. 'Or did Moira tell you – but, then, she doesn't know?'

'You did, then?'

'I suppose I'll have to admit it.'

'Why?'

Roger seemed embarrassed again.

'Well, look at it as I did. Here I am, mounting guard over a strange dead body. Something is sticking out of his pocket. I look at it. By an amazing coincidence it's the photograph of a woman I know – a married woman – and a woman who I guess is not too happily married. What's going to happen? An inquest. Publicity. Possibly the wretched girl's name in all the papers. I acted on impulse. Took the photo and tore it up. I daresay I acted wrongly, but Moira Nicholson is a nice little soul and I didn't want her to get landed in a mess.'

Frankie drew a deep breath.

'So that was it,' she said. 'If you only knew –'

'Knew what?' said Roger puzzled.

'I don't know that I can tell you just now,' said Frankie. 'I may later. It's all rather complicated. I can quite see why you took the photograph, but was there any objection to your saying you recognized the man? Oughtn't you to have told the police who he was?'

'Recognized him?' said Roger. He looked bewildered.

'How could I recognize him? I didn't know him.'

'But you'd met him down here – only about a week before.'

'My dear girl, are you quite mad?'

'Alan Carstairs – you did meet Alan Carstairs?'

'Ah, yes! Man who came down with the Rivingtons. But the dead man wasn't Alan Carstairs.'

'But he *was!*'

They stared at each other, then Frankie said with a renewal of suspicion:

'Surely you must have recognized him?'

'I never saw his face,' said Roger.

'What?'

'No. There was a handkerchief spread over it.'

Frankie stared at him. Suddenly she remembered that in Bobby's first account of the tragedy he had mentioned putting a handkerchief over the face of the dead man.

'You never thought of looking?' went on Frankie.

'No. Why should I?'

'Of course,' thought Frankie, 'if *I'd* found a photograph of somebody I knew in a dead person's pocket, I should simply have had to look at the person's face. How beautifully incurious men are!'

'Poor little thing,' she said. 'I'm so terribly sorry for her.'

'Who do you mean – Moira Nicholson? Why are you so sorry for her?'

'Because she's frightened,' said Frankie slowly.

'She always looks half scared to death. What is she frightened of?'

'Her husband.'

'I don't know that I'd care to be up against Jasper Nicholson myself,' admitted Roger.

'She's sure he's trying to murder her,' said Frankie abruptly.

'Oh, my dear!' He looked at her incredulously.

'Sit down,' said Frankie. 'I'm going to tell you a lot of things. I've got to prove to you that Dr Nicholson is a dangerous criminal.'

'A criminal?'

Roger's tone was frankly incredulous.

'Wait till you've heard the whole story.'

She gave him a clear and careful narrative of all that had occurred since the day Bobby and Dr Thomas had found the body. She only kept back the fact that her accident had not been genuine, but she let it appear that she had lingered at Merroway Court through her intense desire to get to the bottom of the mystery.

She could complain of no lack of interest on the part of her listener. Roger seemed quite fascinated by the story.

'Is this really true?' he demanded. 'All this about the fellow Jones being poisoned and all that?'

'Absolute gospel truth, my dear.'

'Sorry for my incredulity – but the facts do take a bit of swallowing, don't they?'

He was silent a minute, frowning.

'Look here,' he said at last. 'Fantastic as the whole thing sounds, I think you must be right in your first deduction. This man, Alex Pritchard, or Alan Carstairs, must have been murdered. If he wasn't there seems no point in the attack upon Jones. Whether the key word to the situation is the phrase "*Why didn't they ask Evans?*" or not doesn't seem to me to matter much since you've no clue to who Evans is or as to what he was to have been asked. Let's put it that the murderer or murderers assumed that Jones was in possession of some knowledge, whether he knew it himself or not, which was dangerous to them. So, accordingly, they tried to eliminate him, and probably would try again if they got on his track. So far that seems sense – but I don't see by what process of reasoning you fix on Nicholson as the criminal.'

'He's such a sinister man, and he's got a dark-blue Talbot and he was away from here on the day that Bobby was poisoned.'

'That's all pretty thin as evidence.'

'There are all the things Mrs Nicholson told Bobby.'

She recited them, and once again they sounded melodramatic and unsubstantial repeated aloud against the background of the peaceful English landscape.

Roger shrugged his shoulders.

'She thinks he supplies Henry with the drug – but that's pure conjecture, she's not a particle of evidence that he does so. She thinks he wants to get Henry to the Grange as a patient – well, that's a very natural wish for a doctor to have. A doctor wants as many patients as he can get. She thinks he's in love with Sylvia. Well, as to that, of course, I can't say.'

'If she thinks so, she's probably right,' interrupted Frankie. 'A woman would know all right about her own husband.'

'Well, granting that that's the case, it doesn't necessarily mean that the man's a dangerous criminal. Lots of respectable citizens fall in love with other people's wives.'

'There's her belief that he wants to murder her,' urged Frankie.

Roger looked at her quizzically.

'You take that seriously?'

'She believes it, anyhow.'

Roger nodded and lit a cigarette.

'The question is, how much attention to pay that belief of hers,' he said. 'It's a creepy sort of place, the Grange, full of queer customers. Living there would be inclined to upset a woman's balance, especially if she were of the timid nervous type.'

'Then you don't think it's true?'

'I don't say that. She probably believes quite honestly that he is trying to kill her – but is there any foundation in fact for that belief? There doesn't seem to be.'

Frankie remembered with curious clearness Moira saying, 'It's just nerves.' And somehow the mere fact that she had said that seemed to Frankie to point to the fact that it was not nerves, but she found it difficult to know how to explain her point of view to Roger.

Meanwhile the young man was going on:

'Mind you, if you could show that Nicholson had been in Marchbolt on the day of the cliff tragedy that would be very different, or if we could find any definite motive linking him with Carstairs, but it seems to me you're ignoring the real suspects.'

'What real suspects?'

'The – what did you call them – Haymans?'

'Caymans.'

'That's it. Now, they are undoubtedly in it up to the hilt. First, there's the false identification of the body. Then there's their insistence on the point of whether the poor fellow said anything before he died. And I think it's logical to assume, as you did, that the Buenos Aires offer came from, or was arranged for, by them.'

'It's a bit annoying,' said Frankie, 'to have the most strenuous efforts made to get you out of the way because you know something – and not to know yourself what the something you know is. Bother – what a mess one gets into with words.'

'Yes,' said Roger grimly, 'that was a mistake on their part. A mistake that it's going to take them all their time to remedy.'

'Oh!' cried Frankie. 'I've just thought of something. Up to now, you see, I've been assuming that the photograph of Mrs Cayman was substituted for the one of Moira Nicholson.'

'I can assure you,' said Roger gravely, 'that I have never treasured the likeness of a Mrs Cayman against my heart. She sounds a most repulsive creature.'

'Well, she was handsome in a way,' admitted Frankie. 'A sort of bold, coarse, vampish way. But the point is this: Carstairs must have had her photograph on him as well as Mrs Nicholson's.'

Roger nodded.

'And you think–' he suggested.

'I think one was love and the other was business! Carstairs was carrying about the Cayman's photograph for a reason. He wanted it identified by somebody, perhaps. Now, listen – what happens? Someone, the male Cayman perhaps, is following him and, seeing a good opportunity, steals up behind him in the mist and gives him a shove. Carstairs goes over the cliff with a startled cry. Male Cayman makes off as fast as he can; he doesn't know who may be about. We'll say that he doesn't know that Alan Carstairs is carrying about that photograph. What happens next? The photograph is published –'

'Consternation in the Cayman ménage,' said Roger helpfully.

'Exactly. What is to be done? The bold thing – grasp the nettle. Who knows Carstairs as Carstairs? Hardly anyone in this country. Down goes Mrs Cayman, weeping crocodile tears and recognizing body as that of a convenient brother. They also do a little hocus pocus of posting parcels to bolster up the walking-tour theory.'

'You know, Frankie. I think that's positively brilliant,' said Roger with admiration.

'I think it's pretty good myself,' said Frankie. 'And you're quite right. We ought to get busy on the track of the Caymans. I can't think why we haven't done so before.'

This was not quite true, since Frankie knew quite well the reason – namely that they had been on the track of Roger himself. However, she felt it would be tactless, just at this stage, to reveal the fact.

'What are we going to do about Mrs Nicholson?' she asked abruptly.

'What do you mean – do about her?'

'Well, the poor thing is terrified to death. I do think you're callous about her, Roger.'

'I'm not, really, but people who can't help themselves always irritate me.'

'Oh! but do be fair. What can she do? She's no money and nowhere to go.'

Roger said unexpectedly:

'If you were in her place, Frankie, you'd find something to do.'

'Oh!' Frankie was rather taken aback.

'Yes, you would. If you really thought somebody was trying to murder you, you wouldn't just stay there tamely waiting to be murdered. You'd run away and make a living somehow, or you'd murder the other person first! You'd do *something*.'

Frankie tried to think what she would do.

'I'd certainly do something,' she said thoughtfully.

'The truth of the matter is that you've got guts and she hasn't,' said Roger with decision.

Frankie felt complimented. Moira Nicholson was not really the type of woman she admired and she had also felt just slightly ruffled by Bobby's absorption in her. 'Bobby,' she thought to herself, 'likes them helpless.' And she remembered the curious fascination that the photograph had had for him from the start of the affair.

'Oh, well,' thought Frankie, 'at any rate, Roger's different.'

Roger, it was clear, did not like them helpless. Moira, on the other hand, clearly did not think very much of Roger. She had called him weak and had scouted the possibility of his having the guts to murder anyone. He was weak, perhaps – but undeniably he had charm. She had felt it from the first moment of arriving at Merroway Court.

Roger said quietly:

'If you liked, Frankie, you could make anything you chose of a man . . .'

Frankie felt a sudden little thrill – and at the same time an acute embarrassment. She changed the subject hastily.

'About your brother,' she said. 'Do you still think he should go to the Grange?'

CHAPTER 22

ANOTHER VICTIM

'No,' said Roger. 'I don't. After all, there are heaps of other places where he can be treated. The really important thing is to get Henry to agree.'

'Do you think that will be difficult?' asked Frankie.

'I'm afraid it may be. You heard him the other night. On the other hand, if we just catch him in the repentant mood, that's very different. Hullo – here comes Sylvia.'

Mrs Bassington-ffrench emerged from the house and looked about her, then seeing Roger and Frankie, she walked across the grass towards them.

They could see that she was looking terribly worried and strained.

'Roger,' she began, 'I've been looking for you everywhere.' Then, as Frankie made a movement to leave them – 'No, my dear, don't go. Of what use are concealments? In any case, I think you know all there is to know. You've suspected this business for some time, haven't you?'

Frankie nodded.

'While I've been blind – blind –' said Sylvia bitterly. 'Both of you saw what I never even suspected. I only wondered why Henry had changed so to all of us. It made me very unhappy, but I never suspected the reason.'

She paused, then went on again with a slight change of tone.

'As soon as Dr Nicholson had told me the truth, I went straight to Henry. I've only just left him now.' She paused, swallowing a sob.

'Roger – it's going to be all right. He's agreed. He will go to the Grange and put himself in Dr Nicholson's hands tomorrow.'

'Oh! no –' The exclamation came from Roger and Frankie simultaneously. Sylvia looked at them – astonished.

Roger spoke awkwardly.

'Do you know, Sylvia, I've been thinking it over, and I don't believe the Grange would be a good plan, after all.'

'You think he can fight it by himself?' asked Sylvia doubtfully.

'No, I don't. But there are other places – places not – so – well, not so near at hand. I'm convinced that staying in this district would be a mistake.'

'I'm sure of it,' said Frankie, coming to his rescue.

'Oh! I don't agree,' said Sylvia. 'I couldn't bear him to go away somewhere. And Dr Nicholson has been so kind and understanding. I shall feel happy about Henry being under his charge.'

'I thought you didn't like Nicholson, Sylvia,' said Roger.

'I've changed my mind.' She spoke simply. 'Nobody could have been nicer or kinder than he was this afternoon. My silly prejudice against him has quite vanished.'

There was a moment's silence. The position was awkward. Neither Roger nor Sylvia knew quite what to say next.

'Poor Henry,' said Sylvia. 'He broke down. He was terribly upset at my knowing. He agreed that he must fight this awful craving for my sake and Tommy's, but he said I hadn't a conception of what it meant. I suppose I haven't, though Dr Nicholson explained very fully. It becomes a kind of obsession – people aren't responsible for their actions – so he said. Oh, Roger, it seems so awful. But Dr Nicholson was really kind. I trust him.'

'All the same, I think it would be better –' began Roger.

Sylvia turned on him.

'I don't understand you, Roger. Why have you changed your mind? Half an hour ago you were all for Henry's going to the Grange.'

'Well – I've – I've had time to think the matter over since –'

Again Sylvia interrupted.

'Anyway, I've made up my mind. Henry shall go to the Grange and nowhere else.'

They confronted her in silence, then Roger said:

'Do you know, I think I will ring up Nicholson. He will be home now. I'd like – just to have a talk with him about matters.'

Without waiting for her reply he turned away and went rapidly into the house. The two women stood looking after him.

'I cannot understand Roger,' said Sylvia impatiently. 'About a quarter of an hour ago he was positively urging me to arrange for Henry to go to the Grange.'

Her tone held a distinct note of anger.

'All the same,' said Frankie, 'I agree with him. I'm sure I've read somewhere that people ought always to go for a cure somewhere far away from their homes.'

'I think that's just nonsense,' said Sylvia.

Frankie felt in a dilemma. Sylvia's unexpected obstinacy was making things difficult, and also she seemed suddenly to have become as violently pro-Nicholson as she formerly had been against him. It was very hard to know what arguments to use. Frankie considered telling the whole story to Sylvia – but would Sylvia believe it? Even Roger had not been very impressed by the theory of Dr Nicholson's guilt. Sylvia, with her new-found partisanship where the doctor was concerned, would probably be even less so. She might even go and repeat the whole thing to him. It was certainly difficult.

An aeroplane passed low overhead in the gathering dusk, filling the air with its loud beat of engines. Both Sylvia and Frankie stared up at it, glad of the respite it afforded, since neither of them quite knew what to say next. It gave Frankie time to collect her thoughts, and Sylvia time to recover from her fit of sudden anger.

As the aeroplane disappeared over the trees and its roar receded into the distance, Sylvia turned abruptly to Frankie.

'It's been so awful –' she said brokenly. 'And you all seem to want to send Henry far away from me.'

'No, no,' said Frankie. 'It wasn't that at all.'

She cast about for a minute.

'It was only that I thought he ought to have the best treatment. And I do think that Dr Nicholson is rather – well, rather a quack.'

'I don't believe it,' said Sylvia. 'I think he's a very clever man and just the kind of man Henry needs.'

She looked defiantly at Frankie. Frankie marvelled at the hold Dr Nicholson had acquired over her in such a short time. All her former distrust of the man seemed to have vanished completely.

At a loss what to say or do next, Frankie relapsed into silence. Presently Roger came out again from the house. He seemed slightly breathless.

'Nicholson isn't in yet,' he said. 'I left a message.'

'I don't see why you want to see Dr Nicholson so urgently,' said Sylvia. 'You suggested this plan, and it's all arranged and Henry has consented.'

'I think I've got some say in the matter, Sylvia,' said Roger gently. 'After all, I'm Henry's brother.'

'You suggested the plan yourself,' said Sylvia obstinately.

'Yes, but I've heard a few things about Nicholson since.'

'What things? Oh! I don't believe you.'

She bit her lip, turned away and plunged into the house.

Roger looked at Frankie.

'This is a bit awkward,' he said.

'Very awkward, indeed.'

'Once Sylvia has made her mind up she can be obstinate as the devil.'

'What are we going to do?'

They sat down again on the garden seat and went into the matter carefully. Roger agreed with Frankie that to tell the whole story to Sylvia would be a mistake. The best plan, in his opinion, would be to tackle the doctor.

'But what are you going to say exactly?'

'I don't know that I shall say much – but I shall hint a good deal. At any rate, I agree with you about one thing – Henry mustn't go to the Grange. Even if we come right out into the open, we've got to stop that.'

'We give the whole show away if we do,' Frankie reminded him.

'I know. That's why we've got to try everything else first. Curse Sylvia, why must she turn obstinate just at this minute?'

'It shows the power of the man,' Frankie said.

'Yes. You know, it inclines me to believe that, evidence or no evidence, you may be right about him after all – what's that?'

They both sprang up.

'It sounded like a shot,' said Frankie. 'From the house.'

They looked at each other, then raced towards the building. They went in by the french window of the drawing-room and passed through into the hall. Sylvia Bassington-ffrench was standing there, her face white as paper.

'Did you hear?' she said. 'It was a shot – from Henry's study.'

She swayed and Roger put an arm round her to steady her. Frankie went to the study door and turned the handle.

'It's locked,' she said.

'The window,' said Roger.

He deposited Sylvia, who was in a half-fainting condition, on a convenient settee and raced out again through the drawing-room, Frankie on his heels. They went round the house till they came to the study window. It was closed, but they put their faces close to the glass and peered in. The sun was setting and there was not much light – but they could see plainly enough.

Henry Bassington-ffrench was lying sprawled out across his desk. There was a bullet wound plainly visible in the temple and a revolver lay on the floor, where it had dropped from his hand.

'He's shot himself,' said Frankie. 'How ghastly! . . .'

'Stand back a little,' said Roger. 'I'm going to break the window.'

He wrapped his hand in his coat and struck the pane of glass a heavy blow that shattered it. Roger picked out the pieces carefully, then he and Frankie stepped into the room. As they did so, Mrs Bassington-ffrench and Dr Nicholson came hurrying along the terrace.

'Here's the doctor,' said Sylvia. 'He's just come. Has – has anything happened to Henry?'

Then she saw the sprawling figure and uttered a cry.

Roger stepped quickly out again through the window and Dr Nicholson thrust Sylvia into his arms.

'Take her away,' he said briefly. 'Look after her. Give her some brandy if she'll take it. Don't let her see more than you can help.'

He himself stepped through the window and joined Frankie. He shook his head slowly.

'This is a tragic business,' he said. 'Poor fellow. So he felt he couldn't face the music. Too bad. Too bad.'

He bent over the body then straightened himself up again.

'Nothing to be done. Death must have been instantaneous. I wonder if he wrote something first. They usually do.'

Frankie advanced till she stood beside them. A piece of paper with a few scrawled words on it, evidently freshly written, lay at Bassington-ffrench's elbow. Their purport was clear enough.

I feel this is the best way out, (Henry Bassington-ffrench had written). *This fatal habit has taken too great a hold on me for me to fight it now. Want to do the best I can for Sylvia – Sylvia and Tommy. God bless you both, my dears. Forgive me . . .*

Frankie felt a lump rise in her throat.

'We mustn't touch anything,' said Dr Nicholson. 'There will have to be an inquest, of course. We must ring up the police.'

In obedience to his gesture, Frankie went towards the door. Then she stopped.

'The key's not in the lock,' she said.

'No? Perhaps it's in his pocket.'

He knelt down, investigating delicately. From the dead man's coat pocket he drew out a key.

He tried it in the lock and it fitted. Together they passed out into the hall. Dr Nicholson went straight to the telephone.

Frankie, her knees shaking under her, felt suddenly sick.

CHAPTER 23

MOIRA DISAPPEARS

Frankie rang up Bobby about an hour later.

'Is that Hawkins? Hullo, Bobby – have you heard what has happened? You have. Quick, we must meet somewhere. Early tomorrow morning would be best, I think. I'll stroll out before breakfast. Say eight o'clock – the same place we met today.'

She rang off as Bobby uttered his third respectful 'Yes, your ladyship', for the benefit of any curious ears.

Bobby arrived at the rendezvous first, but Frankie did not keep him waiting long. She looked pale and upset.

'Hullo, Bobby, isn't it awful? I haven't been able to sleep all night.'

'I haven't heard any details,' said Bobby. 'Just that Mr Bassington-ffrench had shot himself. That's right, I suppose?'

'Yes. Sylvia had been talking to him – persuading him to agree to a course of treatment and he said he would. Afterwards, I suppose, his courage must have failed him. He went into his study, locked the door, wrote a few words on a sheet of paper – and – shot himself. Bobby, it's too ghastly. It's – it's grim.'

'I know,' said Bobby quietly.

They were both silent for a little.

'I shall have to leave today, of course,' said Frankie presently.

'Yes, I suppose you will. How is she – Mrs Bassington-ffrench, I mean?'

'She's collapsed, poor soul. I haven't seen her since we – we found the body. The shock to her must have been awful.'

Bobby nodded.

'You'd better bring the car round about eleven,' continued Frankie.

Bobby did not answer. Frankie looked at him impatiently.

'What's the matter with you, Bobby? You look as though you were miles away.'

'Sorry. As a matter of fact –'

'Yes?'

'Well, I was just wondering. I suppose – well, I suppose it's all right?'

'What do you mean – all right?'

'I mean it's quite certain that he *did* commit suicide?'

'Oh!' said Frankie. 'I see.' She thought a minute. 'Yes,' she said, 'it was suicide all right.'

'You're quite sure? You see, Frankie, we have Moira's word for it that Nicholson wanted two people out of the way. Well, *here's one of them gone.*'

Frankie thought again, but once more she shook her head.

'It must be suicide,' she said. 'I was in the garden with Roger when we heard the shot. We both ran straight in through the drawing-room to the hall. The study door was locked on the inside. We went round to the window. That was fastened also and Roger had to smash it. It wasn't till then that Nicholson appeared upon the scene.'

Bobby reflected upon this information.

'It looks all right,' he agreed. 'But Nicholson seems to have appeared on the scene very suddenly.'

'He'd left a stick behind earlier in the afternoon and had come back for it.'

Bobby was frowning with the process of thought.

'Listen, Frankie. Suppose that actually Nicholson shot Bassington-ffrench –'

'Having induced him first to write a suicide's letter of farewell?'

'I should think that would be the easiest thing in the world to fake. Any alteration in handwriting would be put down to agitation.'

'Yes, that's true. Go on with your theory.'

'Nicholson shoots Bassington-ffrench, leaves the farewell letter, and nips out locking the door – to appear again a few minutes later as though he had just arrived.'

Frankie shook her head regretfully.

'It's a good idea – but it won't work. To begin with, the key was in Henry Bassington-ffrench's pocket –'

'Who found it there?'

'Well, as a matter of fact, Nicholson did.'

'There you are. What's easier for him than to pretend to find it there.'

'I was watching him – remember. I'm sure the key was in the pocket.'

'That's what one says when one watches a conjurer. You *see* the rabbit being put into the hat! If Nicholson is a high-class criminal, a simple little bit of sleight of hand like that would be child's play to him.'

'Well, you may be right about that, but honestly, Bobby, the whole thing's impossible. Sylvia Bassington-ffrench was actually in the house when the shot was fired. The moment she heard it she ran out into the hall. If Nicholson had fired the shot and come out through the study door she would have been bound to see him. Besides, she told us that he actually came up the drive to the front door. She saw him coming as we ran round the house and went to meet him and brought him round to the study window. No, Bobby, I hate to say it, but the man has an alibi.'

'On principle, I distrust people who have alibis,' said Bobby.

'So do I. But I don't see how you can get round this one.'

'No. Sylvia Bassington-ffrench's word ought to be good enough.'

'Yes, indeed.'

'Well,' said Bobby with a sigh. 'I suppose we'll have to leave it at suicide. Poor devil. What's the next angle of attack, Frankie?'

'The Caymans,' said Frankie. 'I can't think how we've been so remiss as not to have looked them up before. You've kept the address Cayman wrote from, haven't you?'

'Yes. It's the same they gave at the inquest. 17 St Leonard's Gardens, Paddington.'

'Don't you agree that we've rather neglected that channel of inquiry?'

'Absolutely. All the same, you know, Frankie, I've got a very shrewd idea that you'll find the birds flown. I should imagine that the Caymans weren't exactly born yesterday.'

'Even if they have gone off, I may find out something about them.'

'Why – *I*?'

'Because, once again, I don't think you'd better appear in the matter. It's like coming down here when we thought Roger was the bad man of the show. You are known to them and I am not.'

'And how do your propose to make their acquaintance?' asked Bobby.

'I shall be something political,' said Frankie. 'Canvassing for the Conservative Party. I shall arrive with leaflets.'

'Good enough,' said Bobby. 'But, as I said before, I think you'll find the birds flown. Now there's another thing that requires to be thought of – Moira.'

'Goodness,' said Frankie, 'I'd forgotten all about her.'

'So I noticed,' said Bobby with a trace of coldness in his manner.

'You're right,' said Frankie thoughtfully. 'Something must be done about her.'

Bobby nodded. The strange haunting face came up before his eyes. There was something tragic about it. He had always felt that from the first moment when he had taken the photograph from Alan Carstairs' pocket.

'If you'd seen her that night when I first went to the Grange!' he said. 'She was crazy with fear – and I tell you, Frankie, *she's right*. It's not nerves or imagination, or anything like that. If Nicholson wants to marry Sylvia Bassington-ffrench, two obstacles have got to go. One's gone. I've a feeling that Moira's life is hanging by a hair and that any delay may be fatal.'

Frankie was sobered by the earnestness of his words.

'My dear, you're right,' she said. 'We must act quickly. What shall we do?'

'We must persuade her to leave the Grange – at once.'

Frankie nodded.

'I tell you what,' she said. 'She'd better go down to Wales – to the Castle. Heaven knows, she ought to be safe enough there.'

'If you can fix that, Frankie, nothing could be better.'

'Well, it's simple enough. Father never notices who goes or comes. He'll like Moira – nearly any man would – she's so feminine. It's extraordinary how men like helpless women.'

'I don't think Moira is particularly helpless,' said Bobby.

'Nonsense. She's like a little bird that sits and waits to be eaten by a snake without doing anything about it.'

'What could she do?'

'Heaps of things,' said Frankie vigorously.

'Well, I don't see it. She's got no money, no friends –'

'My dear, don't drone on as though you were recommending a case to the Girls' Friendly Society.'

'Sorry,' said Bobby.

There was an offended pause.

'Well,' said Frankie, recovering her temper. 'As you were. I think we'd better get on to this business as soon as possible.'

'So do I,' said Bobby. 'Really, Frankie, it's awfully decent of you to –'

'That's all right,' said Frankie interrupting him. 'I don't mind befriending the girl so long as you don't drivel on about her as though she had no hands or feet or tongue or brains.'

'I simply don't know what you mean,' said Bobby.

'Well, we needn't talk about it,' said Frankie. 'Now, my idea is that whatever we're going to do we'd better do it quickly. Is that a quotation?'

'It's a paraphrase of one. Go on, Lady Macbeth.'

'You know, I've always thought,' said Frankie, suddenly digressing wildly from the matter in hand, 'that Lady Macbeth incited Macbeth to do all those murders simply and solely because she was so frightfully bored with life – and incidentally with Macbeth. I'm sure he was one of those meek, inoffensive men who drive their wives distracted with boredom. But, having once committed a murder for the first time in his life, he felt the hell of a fine fellow and began to develop ego mania as a compensation for his former inferiority complex.'

'You ought to write a book on the subject, Frankie.'

'I can't spell. Now, where were we? Oh, yes, rescue of Moira. You'd better bring the car round at half-past ten. I'll drive over to the Grange, ask for Moira and, if Nicholson's there when I see her, I'll remind her of her promise to come and stay with me and carry her off then and there.'

'Excellent, Frankie. I'm glad we're not going to waste any time. I've a horror of another accident happening.'

'Half-past ten, then,' said Frankie.

By the time she got back to Merroway Court, it was half-past nine. Breakfast had just been brought in and Roger was pouring himself out some coffee. He looked ill and worn.

'Good morning,' said Frankie. 'I slept awfully badly. In the end I got up about seven and went for a walk.'

'I'm frightfully sorry you should have been let in for all this worry,' said Roger.

'How's Sylvia?'

'They gave her an opiate last night. She's still asleep, I believe. Poor girl, I'm most terribly sorry for her. She was simply devoted to Henry.'

'I know.'

Frankie paused and then explained her plans for departure.

'I suppose you'll have to go,' said Roger resentfully. 'The inquest's on Friday. I'll let you know if you're wanted for it. It all depends on the coroner.'

He swallowed a cup of coffee and a piece of toast and then went off to attend to the many things requiring his attention. Frankie felt very sorry for him. The amount of gossip and curiosity created by a suicide in a family she could imagine only too well. Tommy appeared and she devoted herself to amusing the child.

Bobby brought the car round at half-past ten; Frankie's luggage was brought down. She said goodbye to Tommy and left a note for Sylvia. The Bentley drove away.

They covered the distance to the Grange in a very short time. Frankie had never been there before and the big iron gates and the overgrown shrubbery depressed her spirits.

'It's a creepy place,' she observed. 'I don't wonder Moira gets the horrors here.'

They drove up to the front door and Bobby got down and rang the bell. It was not answered for some minutes. Finally a woman in nurse's kit opened it.

'Mrs Nicholson?' said Bobby.

The woman hesitated, then withdrew into the hall and opened the door wider. Frankie jumped out of the car and passed into the house. The door closed behind her. It had a nasty echoing clang as it shut. Frankie noticed that it had heavy bolts and bars across it. Quite irrationally she felt afraid – as though she was here, in this sinister house, a prisoner.

'Nonsense,' she told herself. 'Bobby's outside in the car. I've come here openly. Nothing can happen to me.' And, shaking off the ridiculous feeling, she followed the nurse upstairs and along a passage. The nurse threw open a door and Frankie passed into a small sitting-room daintily furnished with cheerful chintzes and flowers in the vases. Her spirits rose. Murmuring something, the nurse withdrew.

About five minutes passed and the door opened and Dr Nicholson came in.

Frankie was quite unable to control a slight nervous start, but she masked it by a welcoming smile and shook hands.

'Good morning,' she said.

'Good morning, Lady Frances. You have not come to bring me bad news of Mrs Bassington-ffrench, I hope?'

'She was still asleep when I left,' said Frankie.

'Poor lady. Her own doctor is, of course, looking after her.'

'Oh! yes.' She paused, then said: 'I'm sure you're busy. I mustn't take up your time, Dr Nicholson. I really called to see your wife.'

'To see Moira? That was very kind of you.'

Was it only fancy, or did the pale-blue eyes behind the strong glasses harden ever so slightly.

'Yes,' he repeated. 'That was very kind.'

'If she isn't up yet,' said Frankie, smiling pleasantly, 'I'll sit down and wait.'

'Oh! she's up,' said Dr Nicholson.

'Good,' said Frankie. 'I want to persuade her to come to me for a visit. She's practically promised to.' She smiled again.

'Why, now, that's really very kind of you, Lady Frances – very kind, indeed. I'm sure Moira would have enjoyed that very much.'

'Would have?' asked Frankie sharply.

Dr Nicholson smiled, showing his fine set of even white teeth.

'Unfortunately, my wife went away this morning.'

'Went away?' said Frankie blankly. 'Where?'

'Oh! just for a little change. You know what women are, Lady Frances. This is rather a gloomy place for a young woman. Occasionally Moira feels she must have a little excitement and then off she goes.'

'You don't know where she has gone?' said Frankie.

'London, I imagine. Shops and theatres. You know the sort of thing.'

Frankie felt that his smile was the most disagreeable thing she had ever come across.

'I am going up to London today,' she said lightly. 'Will you give me her address?'

'She usually stays at the Savoy,' said Dr Nicholson. 'But in any case I shall probably hear from her in a day or so. She's not a very good correspondent, I'm afraid, and I believe in perfect liberty between husband and wife. But I think the Savoy is the most likely place for you to find her.'

He held the door open and Frankie found herself shaking hands with him and being ushered to the front door. The nurse was standing there to let her out. The last thing Frankie heard was Dr Nicholson's voice, suave and, perhaps, just a trifle ironical.

'So very kind of you to think of asking my wife to stay, Lady Frances.'

CHAPTER 24

ON THE TRACK OF THE CAYMANS

Bobby had some ado to preserve his impassive chauffeur's demeanour as Frankie came out alone.

She said: 'Back to Staverly, Hawkins,' for the benefit of the nurse.

The car swept down the drive and out through the gates. Then, when they came to an empty bit of road, Bobby pulled up and looked inquiringly at his companion.

'What about it?' he asked.

Rather pale, Frankie replied:

'Bobby, I don't like it. Apparently, she's gone away.'

'Gone *away*? This morning?'

'Or last night.'

'Without a word to us?'

'Bobby, I just don't believe it. The man was lying – I'm sure of it.'

Bobby had gone very pale. He murmured:

'Too late! Idiots that we've been! We should never have let her go back there yesterday.'

'You don't think she's – dead, do you?' whispered Frankie in a shaky voice.

'No,' said Bobby in a violent voice, as though to reassure himself.

They were both silent for a minute or two, then Bobby stated his deductions in a calmer tone.

'She must be still alive, because of the disposing of the body and all that. Her death would have to seem natural and accidental. No, she's either been spirited away somewhere against her will, or else – and this is what I believe – she's still there.'

'At the Grange?'

'At the Grange.'

'Well,' said Frankie, 'what are we going to do?'

Bobby thought for a minute.

'I don't think you can do anything,' he said at last. 'You'd better go back to London. You suggested trying to trace the Caymans. Go on with that.'

'Oh, Bobby!'

'My dear, you can't be of any use down here. You're known – very well known by now. You've announced that you're going – what can you do? You can't stay on at Merroway. You can't come and stay at the Anglers' Arms. You'd set every tongue in the neighbourhood wagging. No, you must go. Nicholson may suspect, but he can't be *sure* that you know anything. You go back to town and I'll stay.'

'At the Anglers' Arms?'

'No, I think your chauffeur will now disappear. I shall take up my headquarters at Ambledever – that's ten miles away – and if Moira's still in that beastly house I shall find her.'

Frankie demurred a little.

'Bobby, you will be careful?'

'I shall be cunning as the serpent.'

With a rather heavy heart Frankie gave in. What Bobby said was certainly sensible enough. She herself could do no further good down here. Bobby drove her up to town and Frankie, letting herself into the Brook Street house, felt suddenly forlorn.

She was not one, however, to let the grass grow under her

feet. At three o'clock that afternoon, a fashionably but soberly dressed young woman with pince-nez and an earnest frown might have been seen approaching St Leonard's Gardens, a sheaf of pamphlets and papers in her hand.

St Leonard's Gardens, Paddington, was a distinctly gloomy collection of houses, most of them in a somewhat dilapidated condition. The place had a general air of having seen 'better days' a long time ago.

Frankie walked along, looking up at the numbers. Suddenly she came to a halt with a grimace of vexation.

No. 17 had a board up announcing that it was to be sold or let unfurnished.

Frankie immediately removed the pince-nez and the earnest air.

It seemed that the political canvasser would not be required.

The names of several house agents were given. Frankie selected two and wrote them down. Then, having determined on her plan of campaign, she proceeded to put it into action.

The first agents were Messrs. Gordon & Porter of Praed Street.

'Good morning,' said Frankie. 'I wonder if you can give me the address of a Mr Cayman? He was until recently at 17 St Leonard's Gardens.'

'That's right,' said the young man to whom Frankie had addressed herself. 'Only there a short time, though, wasn't he? We act for the owners, you see. Mr Cayman took it on a quarterly tenancy as he might have to take up a post abroad any moment. I believe he's actually done so.'

'Then you haven't got his address?'

'I'm afraid not. He settled up with us and that was all.'

'But he must have had some address originally when he took the house.'

'A hotel – I think it was the G.W.R., Paddington Station, you know.'

'References,' suggested Frankie.

'He paid the quarter's rent in advance and a deposit to cover the electric light and gas.'

'Oh!' said Frankie, feeling despairing.

She saw the young man looking rather curiously at her. House agents are adepts at summing up the 'class' of clients. He obviously found Frankie's interest in the Caymans rather unexpected.

'He owes me a good deal of money,' said Frankie mendaciously.

The young man's face immediately assumed a shocked expression.

Thoroughly sympathetic with beauty in distress, he hunted up files of correspondence and did all he could, but no trace of Mr Cayman's present or late abode could be found.

Frankie thanked him and departed. She took a taxi to the next firm of house agents. She wasted no time in repeating the process. The first agents were the ones who had let Cayman the house. These people would be merely concerned to let it again on behalf of the owner. Frankie asked for an order to view.

This time, to counteract the expression of surprise that she saw appear on the clerk's face, she explained that she wanted a cheap property to open as a hostel for girls. The surprised expression disappeared, and Frankie emerged with the key of 17 Leonard's Gardens, the keys of two more 'properties' which she had no wish to see, and an order to view yet a fourth.

It was a bit of luck, Frankie thought, that the clerk had not wished to accompany her, but perhaps they only did that when it was a question of a furnished tenancy.

The musty smell of a closed-up house assailed Frankie's nostrils as she unlocked and pushed open the front door of No. 17.

It was an unappetising house, cheaply decorated, and with blistered, dirty paint. Frankie went over it methodically from garret to basement. The house had not been cleaned up on departure. There were bits of string, old newspapers and some odd nails and tools. But of personal matter, Frankie could not find so much as the scrap of a torn-up letter.

The only thing that struck her as having a possible significance was an ABC railway guide which lay open on one of the window seats. There was nothing to indicate that any of the names of the open page were of special significance, but Frankie copied the lot down in a little note-book as a poor substitute for all she had hoped to find.

As far as tracing the Caymans was concerned, she had drawn a blank.

She consoled herself with the reflection that this was only to be expected. If Mr and Mrs Cayman were associated with the wrong side of the law they would take particularly good care that no one should be able to trace them. It was at least a kind of negative confirmatory evidence.

Still Frankie felt definitely disappointed as she handed back the keys to the house agents and uttered mendacious statements as to communicating with them in a few days.

She walked down towards the Park feeling rather depressed and wondered what on earth she was going to do next. These fruitless meditations were interrupted by a sharp and violent squall of rain. No taxi was in sight and Frankie hurriedly preserved a favourite hat by hurrying into the tube which was close at hand. She took a ticket to Piccadilly Circus and bought a couple of papers at the bookstall.

When she had entered the train – almost empty at this time of day – she resolutely banished thoughts of the vexing problem and, opening her paper, strove to concentrate her attention on its contents.

She read desultory snippets here and there.

Number of road deaths. Mysterious disappearance of a schoolgirl. Lady Peterhampton's party at Claridge's. Sir John Milkington's convalescence after his accident yachting – the *Astradora* – the famous yacht which had belonged to the late Mr John Savage, the millionaire. Was she an unlucky boat? The man who had designed her had met with a tragic death – Mr Savage had committed suicide – Sir John Milkington had just escaped death by a miracle.

Frankie lowered the paper, frowning in an effort of remembrance.

Twice before, the name of Mr John Savage had been mentioned – once by Sylvia Bassington-ffrench when she was speaking of Alan Carstairs, and once by Bobby when he was repeating the conversation he had had with Mrs Rivington.

Alan Carstairs had been a friend of John Savage's. Mrs Rivington had had a vague idea that Carstairs' presence in England had something to do with the death of Savage. Savage had – what was it? – he had committed suicide because he thought he had cancer.

Supposing – supposing Alan Carstairs had not been satisfied with the account of his friend's death. Supposing he had come over to inquire into the whole thing? Supposing that here, in the circumstances surrounding Savage's death – was the first act of the drama that she and Bobby were acting in.

'It's possible,' thought Frankie. 'Yes, it's possible.'

She thought deeply, wondering how best to attack this new phase of the matter. She had no idea as to who had been John Savage's friends or intimates.

Then an idea struck her – his will. If there had been something suspicious about the way he met his death, his will would give a possible clue.

Somewhere in London, Frankie knew, was a place where you went and read wills if you paid a shilling. But she couldn't remember where it was.

The train drew up at a station and Frankie saw that it was the British Museum. She had overshot Oxford Circus, where she meant to have changed, by two stations.

She jumped up and left the train. As she emerged into the street an idea came to her. Five minutes' walk brought her to the office of Messrs. Spragge, Spragge, Jenkinson & Spragge.

Frankie was received with deference and was at once ushered into the private fastness of Mr Spragge, the senior member of the firm.

Mr Spragge was exceedingly genial. He had a rich mellow persuasive voice which his aristocratic clients had found extremely soothing when they had come to him to be extricated from some mess. It was rumoured that Mr Spragge knew more discreditable secrets about noble families than any other man in London.

'This is a pleasure indeed, Lady Frances,' said Mr Spragge. 'Do sit down. Now are you sure that chair is quite comfortable? Yes, yes. The weather is very delightful just now, is it not? A St Martin's summer. And how is Lord Marchington? Well, I trust?'

Frankie answered these and other inquiries in a suitable manner.

Then Mr Spragge removed his pince-nez from his nose and became more definitely the legal guide and adviser.

'And now, Lady Frances,' he said. 'What is it gives me the

pleasure of seeing you in my – hm – dingy office this after-noon?'

'Blackmail?' said his eyebrows. 'Indiscreet letters? An entangle-ment with an undesirable young man? Sued by your dressmaker?'

But the eyebrows asked these questions in a very discreet manner as befitted a solicitor of Mr Spragge's experience and income.

'I want to look at a will,' said Frankie. 'And I don't know where you go and what you do. But there is somewhere you can pay a shilling, isn't there?'

'Somerset House,' said Mr Spragge. 'But what will is it? I think I can possibly tell you anything you want to know about – er – wills in your family. I may say that I believe our firm has had the honour of drawing them up for many years past.'

'It isn't a family will,' said Frankie.

'No?' said Mr Spragge.

And so strong was his almost hypnotic power of drawing confidences out of his clients that Frankie, who had not meant to do so, succumbed to the manner and told him.

'I wanted to see the will of Mr Savage – John Savage.'

'In-deed?' A very real astonishment showed in Mr Spragge's voice. He had not expected this. 'Now that is very extraordinary – very extraordinary indeed.'

There was something so unusual in his voice that Frankie looked at him in surprise.

'Really,' said Mr Spragge. 'Really, I do not know what to do. Perhaps, Lady Frances, you can give me your reasons for wanting to see that will?'

'No,' said Frankie slowly. 'I'm afraid I can't.'

It struck her that Mr Spragge was, for some reason, behaving quite unlike his usual benign omniscient self. He looked actually worried.

'I really believe,' said Mr Spragge, 'that I ought to warn you.'

'Warn me?' said Frankie.

'Yes. The indications are vague, very vague – but clearly there is something afoot. I would not, for the world, have you involved in any questionable business.'

As far as that went, Frankie could have told him that she

was already involved up to the neck in a business of which he would have decidedly disapproved. But she merely stared at him inquiringly.

'The whole thing is rather an extraordinary coincidence,' Mr Spragge was going on. 'Something is clearly afoot – clearly. But what it is I am not at present at liberty to say.'

Frankie continued to look inquiring.

'A piece of information has just come to my knowledge,' continued Mr Spragge. His chest swelled with indignation. 'I have been impersonated, Lady Frances. Deliberately impersonated. What do you say to that?'

But for just one panic-stricken minute Frankie could say nothing at all.

CHAPTER 25

MR SPRAGGE TALKS

At last she stammered:

'How did you find out?'

It was not at all what she meant to say. She could, in fact, have bitten out her tongue for stupidity a moment later, but the words had been said, and Mr Spragge would have been no lawyer had he failed to perceive that they contained an admission.

'So you know something of this business, Lady Frances?'

'Yes,' said Frankie.

She paused, drew a deep breath and said:

'The whole thing is really my doing, Mr Spragge.'

'I am amazed,' said Mr Spragge.

There was a struggle in his voice, the outraged lawyer was at war with the fatherly family solicitor.

'How did this come about?' he asked.

'It was just a joke,' said Frankie weakly. 'We – we wanted something to do.'

'And who,' demanded Mr Spragge, 'had the idea of passing himself off as Me?'

Frankie looked at him, her wits working once more, made a rapid decision.

'It was the young Duke of No –' She broke off: 'I really mustn't mention names. It isn't fair.'

But she knew that the tide had turned in her favour. It was doubtful if Mr Spragge could have forgiven a mere vicar's son such audacity, but his weakness for noble names led him to look softly on the impertinences of a duke. His benign manner returned.

'Oh! you Bright Young People – You Bright Young People,' he murmured, wagging a forefinger. 'What trouble you land yourselves in. You would be surprised, Lady Frances, at the amount of legal complication that may ensue from an apparently harmless practical joke determined upon on the spur of the moment. Just high spirits – but sometimes extremely difficult to settle out of court.'

'I think you're too marvellous, Mr Spragge,' said Frankie earnestly. 'I do, really. Not one person in a thousand would have taken it as you have done. I feel really terribly ashamed.'

'No, no, Lady Frances,' said Mr Spragge paternally.

'Oh, but I do. I suppose it was the Rivington woman – what exactly did she tell you?'

'I think I have the letter here. I opened it only half an hour ago.'

Frankie held out a hand and Mr Spragge put the letter into it with the air of one saying: 'There, see for yourself what your foolishness has led you into.'

Dear Mr Spragge (Mrs Rivington had written), *It's really too stupid of me, but I've just remembered something that might have helped you the day you called on me. Alan Carstairs mentioned that he was going to a place called Chipping Somerton. I don't know whether this will be any help to you.*

I was so interested in what you told me about the Maltravers case. With kind regards,

Yours sincerely,
Edith Rivington.

'You can see that the matter might have been very grave,' said Mr Spragge severely, but with a severity tempered by benevolence. 'I took it that some extremely questionable business was afoot.

Whether connected with the Maltravers case or with my client, Mr Carstairs –'

Frankie interrupted him.

'Was Alan Carstairs a client of yours?' she inquired excitedly.

'He was. He consulted me when he was last in England a month ago. You know Mr Carstairs, Lady Frances?'

'I think I may say I do,' said Frankie.

'A most attractive personality,' said Mr Spragge. 'He brought quite a breath of the – er – wide open spaces into my office.'

'He came to consult you about Mr Savage's will, didn't he?' said Frankie.

'Ah!' said Mr Spragge. 'So it was you who advised him to come to me? He couldn't remember just who it was. I'm sorry I couldn't do more for him.'

'Just what did you advise him to do?' asked Frankie. 'Or would it be unprofessional to tell me?'

'Not in this case,' said Mr Spragge smiling. 'My opinion was that there was nothing to be done – nothing, that is, unless Mr Savage's relatives were prepared to spend a lot of money on fighting the case – which I gather they were not prepared, or indeed in a position, to do. I never advise bringing a case into court unless there is every hope of success. The law, Lady Frances, is an uncertain animal. It has twists and turns that surprise the non-legal mind. Settle out of court has always been my motto.'

'The whole thing was very curious,' said Frankie thoughtfully.

She had a little of the sensation of walking barefoot over a floor covered with tin tacks. At any minute she might step on one – and the game would be up.

'Such cases are less uncommon than you might think,' said Mr Spragge.

'Cases of suicide?' inquired Frankie.

'No, no, I meant cases of undue influence. Mr Savage was a hard-headed business man, and yet he was clearly as wax in this woman's hands. I've no doubt she knew her business thoroughly.'

'I wish you'd tell me the whole story properly,' said Frankie boldly. 'Mr Carstairs was – well, was so heated, that I never seemed to get the thing clearly.'

'The case was extremely simple,' said Mr Spragge. 'I can run over the facts to you – they are accessible to everyone – so there is no objection to my doing so.'

'Then tell me all about it,' said Frankie.

'Mr Savage happened to be travelling back from the United States to England in November of last year. He was, as you know, an extremely wealthy man with no near relations. On this voyage he made the acquaintance of a certain lady – a – er – Mrs Templeton. Nothing much is known about Mrs Templeton except that she was a very good-looking woman and had a husband somewhere conveniently in the background.'

'The Caymans,' thought Frankie.

'These ocean trips are dangerous,' went on Mr Spragge, smiling and shaking his head. 'Mr Savage was clearly very much attracted. He accepted the lady's invitation to come down and stay at her little cottage at Chipping Somerton. Exactly how often he went there I have not been able to ascertain, but there is no doubt that he came more and more under this Mrs Templeton's influence.

'Then came the tragedy. Mr Savage had for some time been uneasy about his state of health. He feared that he might be suffering from a certain disease –'

'Cancer?' said Frankie.

'Well, yes, as a matter of fact, cancer. The subject became quite an obsession with him. He was staying with the Templetons at the time. They persuaded him to go up to London and consult a specialist. He did so. Now here, Lady Frances, I preserve an open mind. That specialist – a very distinguished man who has been at the top of his profession for many years – swore at the inquest that Mr Savage was not suffering from cancer and that he had told him so, but that Mr Savage was so obsessed by his own belief that he could not accept the truth when he was told it. Now, strictly without prejudice, Lady Frances, and knowing the medical profession, I think things may have gone a little differently.

'If Mr Savage's symptoms puzzled the doctor he may have spoken seriously, pulled a long face, spoken of certain expensive treatments and while reassuring him as to cancer yet have conveyed the impression that something was seriously wrong. Mr Savage, having heard that doctors usually conceal from a patient the fact that he *is* suffering from that disease, would interpret this according to his own lights. The doctor's reassuring words were *not* true – he *had* got the disease he thought he had.

'Anyway, Mr Savage came back to Chipping Somerton in a state of great mental distress. He saw ahead of him a painful and lingering death. I understand some members of his family had died of cancer and he determined not to go through what he had seen them suffer. He sent for a solicitor – a very reputable member of an eminently respectable firm – and the latter drew up a will there and then which Mr Savage signed and which he then delivered over to the solicitor for safe keeping. On that same evening Mr Savage took a large overdose of chloral, leaving a letter behind in which he explained that he preferred a quick and painless death to a long and painful one.

'By his will Mr Savage left the sum of seven hundred thousand pounds free of legacy duty to Mrs Templeton and the remainder to certain specified charities.'

Mr Spragge leaned back in his chair. He was now enjoying himself.

'The jury brought in the usual sympathetic verdict of Suicide while of Unsound Mind, but I do not think that we can argue from that that he was necessarily of unsound mind when he made the will. I do not think that any jury would take it so. The will was made in the presence of a solicitor in whose opinion the deceased was undoubtedly sane and in possession of his senses. Nor do I think we can prove undue influence. Mr Savage did not disinherit anyone near and dear to him – his only relatives were distant cousins whom he seldom saw. They actually lived in Australia, I believe.'

Mr Spragge paused.

'Mr Carstairs' contention was that such a will was completely uncharacteristic of Mr Savage. Mr Savage had no liking for organized charities and had always held very strong opinions as to money passing by blood relationship. However, Mr Carstairs had no documentary proof of these assertions and, as I pointed out to him, men change their opinions. In contesting such a will, there would be the charitable organizations to deal with as well as Mrs Templeton. Also, the will had been admitted to probate.'

'There was no fuss made at the time?' asked Frankie.

'As I say, Mr Savage's relatives were not living in this country and they knew very little about the matter. It was Mr Carstairs who took the matter up. He returned from a trip into the interior of Africa, gradually learnt the details of this business and came over to this country to see if something could be done about it. I was forced to tell him that in my view there was nothing to be done. Possession is nine points of the law, and Mrs Templeton was in possession. Moreover, she had left the country and gone, I believe, to the South of France to live. She refused to enter into any communication on the matter. I suggested getting counsel's opinion but Mr Carstairs decided that it was not necessary and took my view that there was nothing to be done – or, alternatively, that whatever might have been done at the time, and in my opinion that was exceedingly doubtful, it was now too late to do it.'

'I see,' said Frankie. 'And nobody knows anything about this Mrs Templeton?'

Mr Spragge shook his head and pursed his lips.

'A man like Mr Savage, with his knowledge of life, ought to have been less easily taken in – but –' Mr Spragge shook his head sadly as a vision of innumerable clients who ought to have known better and who had come to him to have their cases settled out of court passed across his mind.

Frankie rose.

'Men are extraordinary creatures,' she said.

She held out a hand.

'Goodbye, Mr Spragge,' she said. 'You've been wonderful – simply wonderful. I feel too ashamed.'

'You Bright Young People must be more careful,' said Mr Spragge, shaking his head at her.

'You've been an angel,' said Frankie.

She squeezed his hand fervently and departed.

Mr Spragge sat down again before his table.

He was thinking.

'The young Duke of –'

There were only two dukes who could be so described.

Which was it?

He picked up a *Peerage*.

CHAPTER 26

NOCTURNAL ADVENTURE

The inexplicable absence of Moira worried Bobby more than he cared to admit. He told himself repeatedly that it was absurd to jump to conclusions – that it was fantastic to imagine that Moira had been done away with in a house full of possible witnesses – that there was probably some perfectly simple explanation and that at the worst she could only be a prisoner in the Grange.

That she had left Staverley of her own free will Bobby did not for one minute believe. He was convinced that she would never have gone off like that without sending him a word of explanation. Besides, she had stated emphatically that she had nowhere to go.

No, the sinister Dr Nicholson was at the bottom of this. Somehow or other he must have become aware of Moira's activities and this was his counter move. Somewhere, within the sinister walls of the Grange, Moira was a prisoner, unable to communicate with the outside world.

But she might not remain a prisoner long. Bobby believed implicitly every word Moira had uttered. Her fears were neither the result of a vivid imagination not yet of nerves. They were simple stark truth.

Nicholson meant to get rid of his wife. Several times his plans had miscarried. Now, by communicating her fears to others, she had forced his hand. He must act quickly or not at all. Would he have the nerve to act?

Bobby believed he would. He must know that, even if these strangers had listened to his wife's fears, they had no evidence. Also, he would believe that he had only Frankie to deal with. It was possible that he had suspected her from the first – his pertinent questioning as to her 'accident' seemed to point to that – but as Lady Frances' chauffeur, Bobby did not believe that he himself was suspected of being anything other than he appeared to be.

Yes, Nicholson would act. Moira's body would probably be found in some district far from Staverley. It might, perhaps, be washed up by the sea. Or it might be found at the foot of a cliff. The thing would appear to be, Bobby was almost sure, an 'accident'. Nicholson specialized in accidents.

Nevertheless, Bobby believed that the planning and carrying out of such an accident would need time – not much time, but a certain amount. Nicholson's hand was being forced – he had to act quicker than he had anticipated. It seemed reasonable to suppose that twenty-four hours at least must elapse before he could put any plan into operation.

Before that interval had elapsed, Bobby meant to have found Moira if she were in the Grange.

After he had left Frankie in Brook Street, he started to put his plans into operation. He judged it wise to give the Mews a wide berth. For all he knew, a watch might be being kept on it. As Hawkins, he believed himself to be still unsuspected. Now Hawkins in turn was about to disappear.

That evening, a young man with a moustache, dressed in a cheap dark-blue suit, arrived at the bustling little town of Ambledever. The young man put up at an hotel near the station, registering as George Parker. Having deposited his suitcase there he strolled out and entered into negotiations for hiring a motorcycle.

At ten o'clock that evening a motor-cyclist in cap and goggles passed through the village of Staverley, and came to a halt at a deserted part of the road not far from the Grange.

Hastily shoving the bicycle behind some convenient bushes, Bobby looked up and down the road. It was quite deserted.

Then he sauntered along the wall till he came to the little door. As before, it was unlocked. With another look up and down the road to make sure he was not observed, Bobby slipped quietly inside. He put his hand into the pocket of his coat where a bulge showed the presence of his service revolver. The feel of it was reassuring.

Inside the grounds of the Grange everything seemed quiet.

Bobby grinned to himself as he recalled blood-curdling stories where the villain of the piece kept a cheetah or some excited beast of prey about the place to deal with intruders.

Dr Nicholson seemed content with mere bolts and bars and even there he seemed to be somewhat remiss. Bobby felt certain that that little door should not have been left open. As the villain of the piece, Dr Nicholson seemed regrettably care-less.

'No tame pythons,' thought Bobby. 'No cheetahs, no electrically-charged wires – the man is shamefully behind the times.'

He made these reflections more to cheer himself up than for any other reason. Every time he thought of Moira a queer constriction seemed to tighten around his heart.

Her face rose in the air before him – the trembling lips – the wide, terrified eyes. It was just about here he had first seen her in the flesh. A little thrill ran through him as he remembered how he had put his arm round her to steady her . . .

Moira – where was she now? What had that sinister doctor done with her? If only she were still alive . . .

'She must be,' said Bobby grimly between set lips. 'I'm not going to think anything else.'

He made a careful reconnaissance round the house. Some of the upstairs windows had lights in them and there was one lighted window on the ground floor.

Towards this window Bobby crept. The curtains were drawn across it, but there was a slight chink between them. Bobby put a knee on the window-sill and hoisted himself noiselessly up. He peered through the slits.

He could see a man's arm and shoulder moving along as though writing. Presently the man shifted his position and his profile came into view. It was Dr Nicholson.

It was a curious position. Quite unconscious that he was being watched, the doctor wrote steadily on. A queer sort of fascination stole over Bobby. The man was so near him that, but for the intervening glass, he could have stretched out his arm and touched him.

For the first time, Bobby felt, he was really seeing the man. It was a forceful profile, the big, bold nose, the jutting chin, the crisp, well-shaven line of the jaw. The ears, Bobby noted, were small and laid flat to the head and the lobe of the ear was actually joined to the cheek. He had an idea that ears like these were said to have some special significance.

The doctor wrote on – calm and unhurried. Now pausing for a moment or two as though to think of the right word – then setting to once more. His pen moved over the paper, precisely and evenly. Once he took off his prince-nez, polished them and put them on again.

At last with a sigh Bobby let himself slide noiselessly to the ground. From the look of it, Nicholson would be writing for some time to come. Now was the moment to gain admission to the house.

If Bobby could force an entrance by an upstairs window while the doctor was writing in his study he could explore the building at his leisure later in the night.

He made a circuit of the house again and singled out a window on the first floor. The sash was open at the top but there was no light in the room, so that it was probably unoccupied at the moment. Moreover, a very convenient tree seemed to promise an easy means of access.

In another minute, Bobby was swarming up the tree. All went well and he was just stretching out his hand to take a grip of the window ledge when an ominous crack came from the branch he was on and the next minute the bough, a rotten one, had snapped and Bobby was pitchforked head first into a clump of hydrangea bushes below, which fortunately broke his fall.

The window of Nicholson's study was farther along on the same side of the house. Bobby heard an exclamation in the doctor's voice and the window was flung up. Bobby, recovering from the first shock of his fall, sprang up, disentangled himself from the hydrangeas and bolted across the dark patch of shadow into the pathway leading to the little door. He went a short way along it, then dived into the bushes.

He heard the sound of voices and saw lights moving near the trampled and broken hydrangeas. Bobby kept still and held his breath. They might come along the path. If so, finding the door open, they would probably conclude that anyone had escaped that way and would not prosecute the search further.

However, the minutes passed and nobody came. Presently Bobby heard Nicholson's voice raised in a question. He did not hear the words but he heard an answer given in a hoarse, rather uneducated voice.

'All present and correct, sir. I've made the rounds.'

The sounds gradually died down, the lights disappeared. Everyone seemed to have returned to the house.

Very cautiously, Bobby came out of his hiding place. He emerged on to the path, listening. All was still. He took a step or two towards the house.

And then out of the darkness something struck him on the back of the neck. He fell forward . . . into darkness.

CHAPTER 27

'MY BROTHER WAS MURDERED'

On Friday morning the green Bentley drew up outside the Station Hotel at Ambledever.

Frankie had wired Bobby under the name they had agreed upon – George Parker – that she would be required to give evidence at the inquest on Henry Bassington-ffrench and would call in at Ambledever on the way down from London.

She had expected a wire in reply appointing some rendezvous, but nothing had come, so she had come to the hotel.

'Mr Parker, miss?' said the boots. 'I don't think there's any gentleman of that name stopping here, but I'll see.'

He returned a few minutes later.

'Came here Wednesday evening, miss. Left his bag and said he mightn't be in till late. His bag's still here but he hasn't been back to fetch it.'

Frankie felt suddenly rather sick. She clutched at a table for support. The man was looking at her sympathetically.

'Feeling bad, miss?' he inquired.

Frankie shook her head.

'It's all right,' she managed to say. 'He didn't leave any message?'

The man went away again and returned, shaking his head.

'There's a telegram come for him,' he said. 'That's all.'

He looked at her curiously.

'Anything I can do, miss?' he asked.

Frankie shook her head.

At the moment she only wanted to get away. She must have time to think what to do next.

'It's all right,' she said and, getting into the Bentley, she drove away.

The man nodded his head wisely as he looked after her.

'He's done a bunk, he has,' he said to himself. 'Disappointed her. Given her the slip. A fine rakish piece of goods she is. Wonder what he was like?'

He asked the young lady in the reception office, but the young lady couldn't remember.

'A couple of nobs,' said the boots wisely. 'Going to get married on the quiet – and he's hooked it.'

Meanwhile, Frankie was driving in the direction of Staverley, her mind a maze of conflicting emotions.

Why had Bobby not returned to the Station Hotel? There could only be two reasons: either he was on the trail – and that trail had taken him away somewhere, or else – or else something had gone wrong. The Bentley swerved dangerously. Frankie recovered control just in time.

She was being an idiot – imagining things. Of course, Bobby was all right. He was on the trail – that was all – on the trail.

But why, asked another voice, hadn't he sent her a word of reassurance?

That was more difficult to explain, but there were explanations. Difficult circumstances – no time or opportunity – Bobby would know that she, Frankie, wouldn't get the wind up about him. Everything was all right – bound to be.

The inquest passed like a dream. Roger was there and Sylvia – looking quite beautiful in her widow's weeds. She made an impressive figure and a moving one. Frankie found herself admiring her as though she were admiring a performance at a theatre.

The proceedings were very tactfully conducted. The Bassington-ffrenches were popular locally and everything was done to spare the feelings of the widow and the brother of the dead man.

Frankie and Roger gave their evidence – Dr Nicholson gave his – the dead man's farewell letter was produced. The thing seemed over in no time and the verdict given – 'Suicide while of Unsound Mind'.

The 'sympathetic' verdict, as Mr Spragge had called it.

The two events connected themselves in Frankie's mind.

Two suicides while of Unsound Mind. Was there – could there be a connection between them?

That this suicide was genuine enough she knew, for she had been on the scene. Bobby's theory of murder had had to be dismissed as untenable. Dr Nicholson's alibi was cast iron – vouched for by the widow herself.

Frankie and Dr Nicholson remained behind after the other people departed, the coroner having shaken hands with Sylvia and uttered a few words of sympathy.

'I think there are some letters for you, Frankie, dear,' said Sylvia. 'You won't mind if I leave you now and go and lie down. It's all been so awful.'

She shivered and left the room. Nicholson went with her, murmuring something about a sedative.

Frankie turned to Roger.

'Roger, Bobby's disappeared.'

'Disappeared?'

'Yes!'

'Where and how?'

Frankie explained in a few rapid words.

'And he's not been seen since?' said Roger.

'No. What do you think?'

'I don't like the sound of it,' said Roger slowly.

Frankie's heart sank.

'You don't think –?'

'Oh! it may be all right, but – sh, here comes Nicholson.'

The doctor entered the room with his noiseless tread. He was rubbing his hands together and smiling.

'That went off very well,' he said. 'Very well, indeed. Dr Davidson was most tactful and considerate. We may consider ourselves very lucky to have had him as our local coroner.'

'I suppose so,' said Frankie mechanically.

'It makes a lot of difference, Lady Frances. The conduct of an inquest is entirely in the hands of the coroner. He has wide powers. He can make things easy or difficult as he pleases. In this case everything went off perfectly.'

'A good stage performance, in fact,' said Frankie in a hard voice.

Nicholson looked at her in surprise.

'I know what Lady Frances is feeling,' said Roger. 'I feel the same. My brother was murdered, Dr Nicholson.'

He was standing behind the other and did not see, as Frankie did, the startled expression that sprang into the doctor's eyes.

'I mean what I say,' said Roger, interrupting Nicholson as he was about to reply. 'The law may not regard it as such, but murder it was. The criminal brutes who induced my brother to become a slave to that drug murdered him just as truly as if they had struck him down.'

He had moved a little and his angry eyes now looked straight into the doctor's.

'I mean to get even with them,' he said; and the words sounded like a threat.

Dr Nicholson's pale-blue eyes fell before his. He shook his head sadly.

'I cannot say I disagree with you,' he said. 'I know more about drug-taking than you do, Mr Bassington-ffrench. To induce a man to take drugs is indeed a most terrible crime.'

Ideas were whirling through Frankie's head – one idea in particular.

'It can't be,' she was saying to herself. 'That would be too monstrous. And yet – his whole alibi depends on her word. But in that case –'

She roused herself to find Nicholson speaking to her.

'You came down by car, Lady Frances? No accident this time?'

Frankie felt she simply hated that smile.

'No,' she said. 'I think it's a pity to go in too much for accidents – don't you?'

She wondered if she had imagined it, or whether his eyelids really flickered for a moment.

'Perhaps your chauffeur drove you this time?'

'My chauffeur,' said Frankie, 'has disappeared.'

She looked straight at Nicholson.

'Indeed?'

'He was last seen heading for the Grange,' went on Frankie.

Nicholson raised his eyebrows.

'Really? Have I – some attraction in the kitchen?' His voice sounded amused. 'I can hardly believe it.'

'At any rate that is where he was last seen,' said Frankie.

'You sound quite dramatic,' said Nicholson. 'Possibly you are paying too much attention to local gossip. Local gossip is very unreliable. I have heard the wildest stories.' He paused. His voice altered slightly in tone. 'I have even had a story brought to my ears that my wife and your chauffeur had been seen talking together down by the river.' Another pause. 'He was, I believe, a very superior young man, Lady Frances.'

'Is that it?' thought Frankie. 'Is he going to pretend that his wife has run off with my chauffeur? Is that his little game?'

Aloud she said:

'Hawkins is quite above the average chauffeur.'

'So it seems,' said Nicholson.

He turned to Roger.

'I must be going. Believe me, all my sympathies are with you and Mrs Bassington-ffrench.'

Roger went out into the hall with him. Frankie followed. On the hall table were a couple of letters addressed to her. One was a bill. The other –

Her heart gave a leap.

The other was in Bobby's handwriting.

Nicholson and Roger were on the doorstep.

She tore it open.

Dear Frankie (wrote Bobby), *I'm on the trail at last. Follow me as soon as possible to Chipping Somerton. You'd better come by train and not by car. The Bentley is too noticeable. The trains aren't too good but you can get there all right. You're to come to a house called Tudor Cottage. I'll explain to you just exactly how to find it. Don't ask the way.* (Here followed some minute directions.) *Have you got that clear? Don't tell* anyone. (This was heavily underlined.) No one at all.

    Yours ever,
    Bobby.

Frankie crushed the letter excitedly in the palm of her hand.

So it was all right.

Nothing dreadful had overtaken Bobby.

He was on the trail – and by a coincidence on the same trail as herself. She had been to Somerset House to look up the will of John Savage. Rose Emily Templeton was given as the wife of Edgar Templeton of Tudor Cottage, Chipping Somerton. And that again had fitted in with the open ABC in the St Leonard's Gardens house. Chipping Somerton had been one of the stations on the open page. The Caymans had gone to Chipping Somerton.

Everything was falling into place. They were nearing the end of the chase.

Roger Bassington-ffrench turned and came towards her.

'Anything interesting in your letter?' he inquired casually. For a moment Frankie hesitated. Surely Bobby had not meant Roger when he adjured her to tell nobody?

Then she remembered the heavy underlining – remembered, too, her own recent monstrous idea. If *that* were true, Roger might betray them both in all innocence. She dared not hint to him her own suspicions . . .

So she made up her mind and spoke.

'No,' she said. 'Nothing at all.'

She was to repent her decision bitterly before twenty-four hours had passed.

More than once in the course of the next few hours did she bitterly regret Bobby's dictum that the car was not to be used. Chipping Somerton was no very great distance as the crow flies but it involved changing three times, with a long dreary wait at a country station each time, and to one of Frankie's impatient temperament, this slow method of procedure was extremely hard to endure with fortitude.

Still, she felt bound to admit that there was something in what Bobby had said. The Bentley *was* a noticeable car.

Her excuses for leaving it at Merroway had been of the flimsiest order, but she had been unable to think of anything brilliant on the spur of the moment.

It was getting dark when Frankie's train, an extremely deliberate and thoughtful train, drew into the little station of Chipping Somerton. To Frankie it seemed more like midnight. The train seemed to her to have been ambling on for hours and hours.

It was just beginning to rain, too, which was additionally trying.

Frankie buttoned up her coat to her neck, took a last look at Bobby's letter by the light of the station lamp, got the directions clearly in her head and set off.

The instructions were quite easy to follow. Frankie saw the lights of the village ahead and turned off to the left up a lane which led steeply uphill. At the top of the lane she took the right-hand fork and presently saw the little cluster of houses that formed the village lying below her and a belt of pine trees ahead. Finally, she came to a neat wooden gate and, striking a match, saw Tudor Cottage written on it.

There was no one about. Frankie slipped up the latch and passed inside. She could make out the outlines of the house behind a belt of pine trees. She took up her post within the trees where she could get a clear view of the house. Then, heart beating a little faster, she gave the best imitation she could of the hoot of an owl. A few minutes passed and nothing happened. She repeated the call.

The door of the cottage opened and she saw a figure in chauffeur's dress peer cautiously out. Bobby! He made a beckoning gesture then withdrew inside, leaving the door ajar.

Frankie came out from the trees and up to the door. There was no light in any window. Everything was perfectly dark and silent.

Frankie stepped gingerly over the threshold into a dark hall. She stopped, peering about her.

'Bobby?' she whispered.

It was her nose that gave her warning. Where had she known that smell before – that heavy, sweet odour?

Just as her brain gave the answer 'Chloroform', strong arms seized her from behind. She opened her mouth to scream and a wet pad was clapped over it. The sweet, cloying smell filled her nostrils.

She fought desperately, twisting and turning, kicking. But it was of no avail. Despite the fight she put up, she felt herself succumbing. There was a drumming in her ears, she felt herself choking. And then she knew no more . . .

CHAPTER 28
....
AT THE ELEVENTH HOUR

When Frankie came to herself, the immediate reactions were depressing. There is nothing romantic about the after effects of chloroform. She was lying on an extremely hard wooden floor and her hands and feet were tied. She managed to roll herself over and her head nearly collided violently with a battered coal-box. Various distressing events then occurred.

A few minutes later, Frankie was able, if not to sit up, at least to take notice.

Close at hand she heard a faint groan. She peered about her. As far as she could make out, she seemed to be in a kind of attic. The only light came from a skylight in the roof, and at this moment there was very little of that. In a few minutes it would be quite dark. There were a few broken pictures lying against the wall, a dilapidated iron bed and some broken chairs, and the coal-scuttle before mentioned.

The groan seemed to have come from the corner.

Frankie's bonds were not very tight. They permitted motion of a somewhat crablike type. She wormed her way across the dusty floor.

'Bobby!' she ejaculated.

Bobby it was, also tied hand and foot. In addition, he had a piece of cloth bound round his mouth.

This he had almost succeeded in working loose. Frankie came to his assistance. In spite of being bound together, her hands were still of some use and a final vigorous pull with her teeth finally did the job.

Rather stiffly, Bobby managed to ejaculate:

'Frankie!'

'I'm glad we're together,' said Frankie. 'But it does look as though we'd been had for mugs.'

'I suppose,' said Bobby gloomily, 'it's what they call a "fair cop".'

'How did they get you?' demanded Frankie. 'Was it after you wrote that letter to me?'

'What letter? I never wrote any letter.'

'Oh! I see,' said Frankie, her eyes opening. 'What an idiot I have been! And all that stuff in it about not telling a soul.'

'Look here, Frankie, I'll tell you what happened to me and then you carry on the good work and tell me what happened to you.'

He described his adventures at the Grange and their sinister sequel.

'I came to in this beastly hole,' he said. 'There was some food and drink on a tray. I was frightfully hungry and I had some. I think it must have been doped for I fell asleep almost immediately. What day is it?'

'Friday.'

'And I was knocked out on Wednesday evening. Dash it all, I've been pretty well unconscious all the time. Now tell me what happened to you?'

Frankie recounted her adventures, beginning with the story she had heard from Mr Spragge and carrying on until she thought she recognized Bobby's figure in the doorway.

'And then they chloroformed me,' she finished. 'And oh, Bobby, I've just been sick in a coal-bucket!'

'I call that very resourceful of you, Frankie,' said Bobby approvingly. 'With your hands tied and everything? The thing is: what are we going to do now? We've had it our own way for a long time, but now the tables are turned.'

'If only I'd told Roger about your letter,' lamented Frankie. 'I did think of it and wavered – and then I decided to do exactly what you said and tell nobody at all.'

'With the result that no one knows where we are,' said Bobby gravely. 'Frankie, my dear, I'm afraid I've landed you in a mess.'

'We got a bit too sure of ourselves,' said Frankie sombrely.

'The only thing I can't make out is why they didn't knock us both on the head straightaway,' mused Bobby. 'I don't think Nicholson would stick at a little trifle like that.'

'He's got a plan,' said Frankie with a slight shiver.

'Well, we'd better have one, too. We've got to get out of this, Frankie. How are we going to do it?'

'We can shout,' said Frankie.

'Ye-es,' said Bobby. 'Somebody might be passing and hear.

But from the fact that Nicholson didn't gag you I should say that the chances in that direction are pretty poor. Your hands are more loosely tied than mine. Let's see if I can get them undone with my teeth.'

The next five minutes were spent in a struggle that did credit to Bobby's dentist.

'Extraordinary how easy these things sound in books,' he panted. 'I don't believe I'm making the slightest impression.'

'You are,' said Frankie. 'It's loosening. Look out! There's somebody coming.'

She rolled away from him. A step could be heard mounting a stair, a heavy, ponderous tread. A gleam of light appeared under the door. Then there was the sound of a key being turned in the lock. The door swung slowly open.

'And how are my two little birds?' said the voice of Dr Nicholson.

He carried a candle in one hand and, though he was wearing a hat pulled down over his eyes and a heavy overcoat with the collar turned up, his voice would have betrayed him anywhere. His eyes glittered palely behind the strong glasses.

He shook his head at them playfully.

'Unworthy of you, my dear young lady,' he said, 'to fall into the trap so easily.'

Neither Bobby nor Frankie made any reply. The honours of the situation so obviously lay with Nicholson that it was difficult to know what to say.

Nicholson put the candle down on a chair.

'At any rate,' he said, 'let me see if you are comfortable.'

He examined Bobby's fastenings, nodded his head approvingly and passed on to Frankie. There he shook his head.

'As they truly used to say to me in my youth,' he remarked, 'fingers were made before forks – and teeth were used before fingers. Your young friend's teeth, I see, have been active.'

A heavy, broken-backed oak chair was standing in a corner.

Nicholson picked up Frankie, deposited her on the chair and tied her securely to it.

'Not too uncomfortable, I trust?' he said. 'Well, it isn't for long.'

Frankie found her tongue.

'What are you going to do with us?' she demanded.

Nicholson walked to the door and picked up his candle.

'You taunted me, Lady Frances, with being too fond of accidents. Perhaps I am. At any rate, I am going to risk one more accident.'

'What do you mean?' said Bobby.

'Shall I tell you? Yes, I think I will. Lady Frances Derwent, driving her car, her chauffeur beside her, mistakes a turning and takes a disused road leading to a quarry. The car crashes over the edge. Lady Frances and her chauffeur are killed.'

There was a slight pause, then Bobby said:

'But we mightn't be. Plans go awry sometimes. One of yours did down in Wales.'

'Your tolerance of morphia was certainly very remarkable – and from our point of view – regrettable,' said Nicholson. 'But you need have no anxiety on my behalf this time. You and Lady Frances will be quite dead when your bodies are discovered.'

Bobby shivered in spite of himself. There had been a queer note in Nicholson's voice – it was the tone of an artist contemplating a masterpiece.

'He enjoys this,' thought Bobby. 'Really enjoys it.'

He was not going to give Nicholson further cause for enjoyment than he could help. He said in a casual tone of voice:

'You're making a mistake – especially where Lady Frances is concerned.'

'Yes,' said Frankie. 'In that very clever letter you forged you told me to tell nobody. Well, I made just one exception. I told Roger Bassington-ffrench. He knows all about you. If anything happens to us, he will know who is responsible for it. You'd better let us go and clear out of the country as fast as you can.'

Nicholson was silent for a moment. Then he said:

'A good bluff – but I call it.'

He turned to the door.

'What about your wife, you swine?' cried Bobby. 'Have you murdered her, too?'

'Moira is still alive,' said Nicholson. 'How much longer she will remain so, I do not really know. It depends on circumstances.'

He made them a mocking little bow.

'*Au revoir*,' he said. 'It will take me a couple of hours to complete my arrangements. You may enjoy talking the matter over. I shall not gag you unless it becomes necessary. You understand? Any calls for help and I return and deal with the matter.'

He went out and closed and locked the door behind him.

'It isn't true,' said Bobby. 'It can't be true. These things don't happen.'

But he could not help feeling that they were going to happen – and to him and Frankie.

'In books there's always an eleventh-hour rescue,' said Frankie, trying to speak hopefully.

But she was not feeling very hopeful. In fact, her morale was decidedly low.

'The whole thing's so impossible,' said Bobby as though pleading with someone. 'So fantastic. Nicholson himself was absolutely unreal. I wish an eleventh-hour rescue was possible, but I can't see who's going to rescue us.'

'If only I'd told Roger,' wailed Frankie.

'Perhaps in spite of everything, Nicholson believes you have,' suggested Bobby.

'No,' said Frankie. 'The suggestion didn't go down at all. The man's too damned clever.'

'He's been too clever for us,' said Bobby gloomily. 'Frankie, do you know what annoys me most about this business?'

'No. What?'

'That even now, when we're going to be hurled into the next world, we still don't know who Evans is.'

'Let's ask him,' said Frankie. 'You know – a last-minute boon. He can't refuse to tell us. I agree with you that I simply can't die without having my curiosity satisfied.'

There was a silence, then Bobby said:

'Do you think we ought to yell for help – a sort of last chance? It's about the only chance we've got.'

'Not yet,' said Frankie. 'In the first place, I don't believe anyone would hear – he'd never risk it otherwise – and in the second place, I feel I just can't bear waiting here to be killed without being able to speak or be spoken to. Let's leave shouting till the last possible moment. It's – it's so comforting having you to talk to.' Her voice wavered a little over the last words.

'I've got you into an awful mess, Frankie.'

'Oh! that's all right. You couldn't have kept me out. I wanted to come in. Bobby, do you think he'll really pull it off? Us, I mean.'

'I'm terribly afraid he will. He's so damnably efficient.'

'Bobby, do you believe now that it was he who killed Henry Bassington-ffrench?'

'If it were possible –'

'It is possible – granted one thing: *that Sylvia Bassington-ffrench is in it, too.*'

'Frankie!'

'I know. I was just as horrified when the idea occurred to me. But it fits. Why was Sylvia so dense about the morphia – why did she resist so obstinately when we wanted her to send her husband somewhere else instead of the Grange? And then she was in the house when the shot was fired –'

'She might have done it herself.'

'Oh! no, surely.'

'Yes, she might. And then have given the key of the study to Nicholson to put in Henry's pocket.'

'It's all crazy,' said Frankie in a hopeless voice. 'Like looking through a distorting mirror. All the people who seemed most all right are really all wrong – all the nice, everyday people. There ought to be some way of telling criminals – eyebrows or ears or something.'

'My God!' cried Bobby.

'What is it?'

'Frankie, that wasn't Nicholson who came here just now.'

'Have you gone quite mad? Who was it then?'

'I don't know – but it wasn't Nicholson. All along I felt there was something wrong, but couldn't spot it, and your saying ears has given me the clue. When I was watching Nicholson the other evening through the window I especially noticed his ears – the lobes are joined to the face. But this man tonight – his ears weren't like that.'

'But what does it mean?' Frankie asked hopelessly.

'This is a very clever actor impersonating Nicholson.'

'But why – and who could it be?'

'Bassington-ffrench,' breathed Bobby. '*Roger Bassington-ffrench!*

We spotted the right man at the beginning and then, like idiots, we went astray after red herrings.'

'Bassington-ffrench,' whispered Frankie. 'Bobby, you're right. It must be him. He was the only person there when I taunted Nicholson about accidents.'

'Then it really is all up,' said Bobby. 'I've still had a kind of sneaking hope that possibly Roger Bassington-ffrench might nose out our trail by some miracle but now the last hope's gone. Moira's a prisoner, you and I are tied hand and foot. Nobody else has the least idea where we are. The game's up, Frankie.'

As he finished speaking there was a sound overhead. The next minute, with a terrific crash, a heavy body fell through the skylight.

It was too dark to see anything.

'What the devil –' began Bobby.

From amidst a pile of broken glass, a voice spoke.

'B-b-b-bobby,' it said.

'Well, I'm damned!' said Bobby. 'It's Badger!'

CHAPTER 29
BADGER'S STORY

There was not a minute to be lost. Already sounds could be heard on the floor below.

'Quick, Badger, you fool!' said Bobby. 'Pull one of my boots off! Don't argue or ask questions! Haul it off somehow. Chuck it down in the middle there and crawl under that bed! *Quick*, I tell you!'

Steps were ascending the stairs. The key turned.

Nicholson – the pseudo Nicholson – stood in the doorway, candle in hand.

He saw Bobby and Frankie as he had left them, but in the middle of the floor was a pile of broken glass and in the middle of the broken glass was a boot!

Nicholson stared in amazement from the boot to Bobby. Bobby's left foot was bootless.

'Very clever, my young friend,' he said dryly. 'Extremely acrobatic.'

He came over to Bobby, examined the ropes that bound him and tied a couple of extra knots. He looked at him curiously.

'I wish I knew how you managed to throw that boot through the skylight. It seems almost incredible. A touch of the Houdini about you, my friend.'

He looked at them both, up at the broken skylight, then shrugging his shoulders, he left the room.

'Quick, Badger.'

Badger crawled out from under the bed. He had a pocket knife and with its aid he soon cut the other two free.

'That's better,' said Bobby, stretching himself. 'Whew! I'm stiff! Well, Frankie, what about our friend Nicholson?'

'You're right,' said Frankie. 'It's Roger Bassington-ffrench. Now that I *know* he's Roger playing the part of Nicholson I can *see* it. But it's a pretty good performance all the same.'

'Entirely voice and pince-nez,' said Bobby.

'I was at Oxford with a B-b-b-bassington-ffrench,' said Badger. 'M-m-m-marvellous actor. B-b-b-bad hat, though. B-b-b-bad business about forging his p-p-pater's n-n-n-name to a cheque. Old m-m-man hushed it up.'

In the minds of both Bobby and Frankie was the same thought. Badger, whom they had judged it wiser not to take into their confidence, could all along have given them valuable information!

'Forgery,' said Frankie thoughtfully. 'That letter from you, Bobby, was remarkably well done. I wonder how he knew your handwriting?'

'If he's in with the Caymans he probably saw my letter about the Evans business.'

The voice of Badger rose plaintively.

'W-w-w-what are we going to do next?' he inquired.

'We're going to take up a comfortable position behind this door,' said Bobby. 'And when our friend returns, which I imagine won't be for a little while yet, you and I are going to spring on him from behind and give him the surprise of his life. How about it, Badger? Are you game?'

'Oh! absolutely.'

'As for you, Frankie, when you hear his step you'd better get back on to your chair. He'll see you as soon as he opens the door and will come in without any suspicion.'

'All right,' said Frankie. 'And once you and Badger have got him down I'll join in and bite his ankles or something.'

'That's the true womanly spirit,' said Bobby approvingly. 'Now, let's all sit close together on the floor here and hear all about things. I want to know what miracle brought Badger through that skylight.'

'Well, you s-s-see,' said Badger, 'after you w-w-went off, I got into a bit of a m-m-mess.'

He paused. Gradually the story was extracted: a tale of liabilities, creditors and bailiffs – a typical Badger catastrophe. Bobby had gone off leaving no address, only saying that he was driving the Bentley down to Staverley. So to Staverley came Badger.

'I thought p-p-perhaps you m-m-might be able to let have a f-f-fiver,' he explained.

Bobby's heart smote him. To aid Badger in his enterprise he had come to London and had promptly deserted his post to go off sleuthing with Frankie. And even now the faithful Badger uttered no word of reproach.

Badger had no wish to endanger Bobby's mysterious enterprises, but he was of the opinion that a car like the green Bentley would not be difficult to find in a place the size of Staverley.

As a matter of fact, he came across the car before he got to Staverley, for it was standing outside a pub – empty.

'S-s-so I thought,' went on Badger, 'that I'd give you a little s-s-s-surprise, don't you know? There were some r-r-rugs and things in the b-b-back and nobody about. I g-g-got in and p-p-p-pulled them over me. I thought I'd give you the s-s-surprise of your life.'

What actually happened was that a chauffeur in green livery had emerged from the pub and that Badger, peering from his place of concealment, was thunderstruck to perceive that this chauffeur was not Bobby. He had an idea that the face was in some way familiar to him but couldn't place the man. The stranger got into the car and drove off.

Badger was in a predicament. He did not know what to do next. Explanations and apologies were difficult, and in any case it is not easy to explain to someone who is driving a car at sixty miles an hour. Badger decided to lie low and sneak out of the car when it stopped.

The car finally reached its destination – Tudor Cottage. The chauffeur drove it into the garage and left it there, but, on going out, he shut the garage doors. Badger was a prisoner. There was a small window at one side of the garage and through this about half an hour later Badger had observed Frankie's approach, her whistle and her admission into the house.

The whole business puzzled Badger greatly. He began to suspect that something was wrong. At any rate, he determined to have a look round for himself and see what it was all about.

With the help of some tools lying about in the garage he succeeded in picking the lock of the garage door and set out on a tour of inspection. The windows on the ground floor were all shuttered, but he thought that by getting on to the roof he might manage to have a look into some of the upper windows. The roof presented no difficulties. There was a convenient pipe running up the garage and from the garage roof to the roof of the cottage was an easy climb. In the course of his prowling, Badger had come upon the skylight. Nature and Badger's weight had done the rest.

Bobby drew a long breath as the narrative came to an end.

'All the same,' he said reverently, 'you are a miracle – a singularly beautiful miracle! But for you, Badger, my lad, Frankie and I would have been little corpses in about an hour's time.'

He gave Badger a condensed account of the activities of himself and Frankie. Towards the end he broke off.

'Someone's coming. Get to your post, Frankie. Now, then, this is where our play-acting Bassington-ffrench gets the surprise of his life.'

Frankie arranged herself in a depressed attitude on the broken chair. Badger and Bobby stood ready behind the door.

The steps came up the stairs, a line of candle-light showed underneath the door. The key was put in the lock and turned, the door swung open. The light of the candle disclosed Frankie drooping dejectedly on her chair. Their gaoler stepped through the doorway.

Then, joyously, Badger and Bobby sprang.

The proceedings were short and decisive. Taken utterly by surprise, the man was knocked down, the candle flew wide and was retrieved by Frankie, and a few seconds later the three friends stood looking down with malicious pleasure at a figure securely bound with the same ropes as had previously secured two of them.

'Good evening, Mr Bassington-ffrench,' said Bobby – and if the exultation in his voice was a little crude, who shall blame him? 'It's a nice night for the funeral.'

CHAPTER 30
ESCAPE

The man on the floor stared up at them. His pince-nez had flown off and so had his hat. There could be no further attempt at disguise. Slight traces of make-up were visible about the eyebrows, but otherwise the face was the pleasant, slightly vacuous face of Roger Bassington-ffrench.

He spoke in his own agreeable tenor voice, its note that of pleasant soliloquy.

'Very interesting,' he said. 'I really knew quite well that no man tied up as you were *could* have thrown a boot through that skylight. But because the boot was there among the broken glass I took it for cause and effect and assumed that, though it was impossible, the impossible had been achieved. An interesting light on the limitations of the brain.'

As nobody spoke, he went on still in the same reflective voice:

'So, after all, you've won the round. Most unexpected and extremely regrettable. I thought I'd got you all fooled nicely.'

'So you had,' said Frankie. 'You forged that letter from Bobby, I suppose?'

'I have a talent that way,' said Roger modestly.

'And Bobby?'

Lying on his back, smiling agreeably, Roger seemed to take a positive pleasure in enlightening them.

'I knew he'd go to the Grange. I only had to wait about in the bushes near the path. I was just behind him there when he retreated after rather clumsily falling off a tree. I let the hubbub die down and then got him neatly on the back of the neck with a sandbag. All I had to do was to carry him out to where my car was waiting, shove him in the dickey and drive him here. I was at home again before morning.'

'And Moira?' demanded Bobby. 'Did you entice her away somehow?'

Roger chuckled. The question seemed to amuse him.

'Forgery is a very useful art, my dear Jones,' he said.

'You swine,' said Bobby.

Frankie intervened. She was still full of curiosity, and their prisoner seemed in an obliging mood.

'Why did you pretend to be Dr Nicholson?' she asked.

'Why did I, now?' Roger seemed to be asking the question of himself. 'Partly, I think, the fun of seeing whether I could spoof you both. You were so very sure that poor old Nicholson was in it up to the neck.' He laughed and Frankie blushed. 'Just because he cross-questioned you a bit about the details of your accident – in his pompous way. It was an irritating fad of his – accuracy in details.'

'And really,' said Frankie slowly, 'he was quite innocent?'

'As a child unborn,' said Roger. 'But he did *me* a good turn. He drew my attention to that accident of yours. That and another incident made me realize that you mightn't be quite the innocent young thing you seemed to be. And then I was standing by you when you telephoned one morning and heard your chauffeur's voice say "Frankie". I've got pretty good hearing. I suggested coming up to town with you and you agreed – but you were very relieved when I changed my mind. After that –' He stopped and, as far as he was able, shrugged his bound shoulders. 'It was rather fun seeing you all get worked up about Nicholson. He's a harmless old ass, but he does look exactly like a scientific super-criminal on the films. I thought I might as well keep the deception up. After all, you never know. The best-laid plans go wrong, as my present predicament shows.'

'There's one thing you *must* tell me,' said Frankie. 'I've been driven nearly mad with curiosity. Who is Evans?'

'Oh!' said Bassington-ffrench. 'So you don't know that?'

He laughed – and laughed again.

'That's rather amusing,' he said. 'It shows what a fool one can be.'

'Meaning us?' asked Frankie.

'No,' said Roger. 'In this case, meaning me. Do you know, if you don't know who Evans is, I don't think I shall tell you. I'll keep that to myself as my own little secret.'

The position was a curious one. They had turned the tables on Bassington-ffrench and yet, in some peculiar way, he had robbed them of their triumph. Lying on the floor, bound and a prisoner, it was he who dominated the situation.

'And what are your plans now, may I ask?' he inquired.

Nobody had as yet evolved any plans. Bobby rather doubtfully murmured something about police.

'Much the best thing to do,' said Roger cheerfully. 'Ring them up and hand me over to them. The charge will be abduction, I suppose. I can't very well deny that.' He looked at Frankie. 'I shall plead a guilty passion.'

Frankie reddened.

'What about murder?' she asked.

'My dear, you haven't any evidence. Positively none. Think it over and you'll see you haven't.

'Badger,' said Bobby, 'you'd better stay here and keep an eye on him. I'll go down and ring the police.'

'You'd better be careful,' said Frankie. 'We don't know how many of them there may be in the house.'

'No one but me,' said Roger. 'I was carrying this through single-handed.'

'I'm not prepared to take your word for that,' said Bobby gruffly.

He bent over and tested the knots.

'He's all right,' he said. 'Safe as houses. We'd better all go down together. We can lock the door.'

'Terribly distrustful, aren't you, my dear chap,' said Roger. 'There's a pistol in my pocket if you'd like it. It may make you feel happier and it's certainly no good to me in my present position.'

Ignoring the other's mocking tone, Bobby bent down and extracted the weapon.

'Kind of you to mention it,' he said. 'If you want to know it does me me feel happier.'

'Good,' said Roger. 'It's loaded.'

Bobby took the candle and they filed out of the attic, leaving Roger lying on the floor. Bobby locked the door and put the key in his pocket. He held the pistol in his hand.

'I'll go first,' he said. 'We've got to be quite sure and not make a mess of things now.'

'He's a qu-qu-queer chap, isn't he?' said Badger with a jerk of his head backwards in the direction of the room they had left.

'He's a damned good loser,' said Frankie.

Even now she was not quite free from the charm of that very remarkable young man, Roger Bassington-ffrench.

A rather rickety flight of steps led down to the main landing. Everything was quiet. Bobby looked over the banisters. The telephone was in the hall below.

'We'd better look into these rooms first,' he said. 'We don't want to be taken in the rear.'

Badger flung open each door in turn. Of the four bedrooms, three were empty. In the fourth a slender figure was lying on the bed.

'It's Moira,' cried Frankie.

The others crowded in. Moira was lying like one dead, except that her breast moved up and down ever so slightly.

'Is she asleep?' asked Bobby.

'She's drugged I think,' said Frankie.

She looked round. A hypodermic syringe lay on a little enamel tray on a table near the window. There was also a little spirit lamp and a type of morphia hypodermic needle.

'She'll be all right, I think,' she said. 'But we ought to get a doctor.'

'Let's go down and telephone,' said Bobby.

They adjourned to the hall below. Frankie had a half fear that the telephone wires might be cut, but her fears proved quite unfounded. They got through to the police station quite easily, but found a good deal of difficulty in explaining matters. The local police station was highly disposed to regard the summons as a practical joke.

However, they were convinced at last, and Bobby replaced the receiver with a sigh. He had explained that they also wanted a doctor and the police constable promised to bring one along.

Ten minutes later a car arrived with an inspector and a constable and an elderly man who had his profession stamped all over him.

Bobby and Frankie received them and, after explaining matters once more in a somewhat perfunctory fashion, led the way to the attic. Bobby unlocked the door – then stood dumbfounded in the doorway. In the middle of the floor was a heap of severed ropes. Underneath the broken skylight a chair had been placed on the bed, which had been dragged out till it was under the skylight.

Of Roger Bassington-ffrench there was no sign.

Bobby, Badger and Frankie were dumbfounded.

'Talk of Houdini,' said Bobby. 'He must have out-Houdinied Houdini. How the devil did he cut these cords?'

'He must have had a knife in his pocket,' said Frankie.

'Even then, how could he get at it? Both hands were bound together behind his back.'

The inspector coughed. All his former doubts had returned. He was more strongly disposed than ever to regard the whole thing as a hoax.

Frankie and Bobby found themselves telling a long story which sounded more impossible every minute.

The doctor was their salvation.

On being taken to the room where Moira was lying, he declared at once that she had been drugged with morphia or some preparation of opium. He did not consider her condition serious and thought she would awake naturally in four or five hours' time.

He suggested taking her off then and there to a good nursing home in the neighbourhood.

To this Bobby and Frankie agreed, not seeing what else could be done. Having given their own names and addresses to the inspector, who appeared to disbelieve utterly in Frankie's, they themselves were allowed to leave Tudor Cottage and with the assistance of the inspector succeeded in gaining admission to the Seven Stars in the village.

Here, still feeling that they were regarded as criminals, they were only too thankful to go to their rooms – a double one for Bobby and Badger, and a very minute single one for Frankie.

A few minutes after they had all retired, a knock came on Bobby's door.

It was Frankie.

'I've thought of something,' she said. 'If that fool of a police inspector persists in thinking that we made all this up, at any rate I've got evidence that I was chloroformed.'

'Have you? Where?'

'In the coal-bucket,' said Frankie with decision.

CHAPTER 31

FRANKIE ASKS A QUESTION

Exhausted by all her adventures, Frankie slept late the next morning. It was half-past ten when she came down to the small coffee room to find Bobby waiting for her.

'Hullo, Frankie, here you are at last.'

'Don't be so horribly vigorous, my dear,' Frankie subsided into a chair.

'What will you have? They've got haddock and eggs and bacon and cold ham.'

'I shall have some toast and weak tea,' said Frankie, quelling him. 'What is the matter with you?'

'It must be the sandbagging,' said Bobby. 'It's probably broken up adhesions in the brain. I feel absolutely full of pep and vim and bright ideas and a longing to dash out and do things.'

'Well, why not dash?' said Frankie languidly.

'I have dashed, I've been with Inspector Hammond for the last half-hour. We'll have to let it go as a practical joke, Frankie, for the moment.'

'Oh, but, Bobby –'

'I said *for the moment*. We've got to get to the bottom of this, Frankie. We're on the right spot and all we've got to do is to get down to it. We don't want Roger Bassington-ffrench for abduction. We want him for murder.'

'And we'll get him,' said Frankie, with a revival of spirit.

'That's more like it,' said Bobby approvingly. 'Drink some more tea.'

'How's Moira?'

'Pretty bad. She came round in the most awful state of nerves. Scared stiff apparently. She's gone up to London – to a nursing home place in Queen's Gate. She says she'll feel safe there. She was terrified here.'

'She never did have much nerve,' said Frankie.

'Well, anyone might be scared stiff with a queer, cold-blooded murderer like Roger Bassington-ffrench loose in the neighbourhood.'

'He doesn't want to murder *her*. We're the ones he's after.'

'He's probably too busy taking care of himself to worry about us for the moment,' said Bobby. 'Now, Frankie, we've got to get down to it. The start of the whole thing must be John Savage's death and will. There's something wrong about it. Either that will was forged or Savage was murdered or something.'

'It's quite likely the will was forged if Bassington-ffrench was concerned,' said Frankie thoughtfully. 'Forgery seems to be his speciality.'

'It may have been forgery *and* murder. We've got to find out.' Frankie nodded.

'I've got the notes I made after looking at the will. The witnesses were Rose Chudleigh, cook, and Albert Mere, gardener. They ought to be quite easy to find. Then there are the lawyers who drew it up – Elford and Leigh – a very respectable firm as Mr Spragge said.'

'Right, we'll start from there. I think you'd better take the lawyers. You'll get more out of them than I would. I'll hunt up Rose Chudleigh and Albert Mere.'

'What about Badger?'

'Badger never gets up till lunch time – you needn't worry about him.'

'We must get his affairs straightened out for him sometime,' said Frankie. 'After all, he did save my life.'

'They'll soon get tangled again,' said Bobby. 'Oh! by the way, what do you think of this?'

He held out a dirty piece of cardboard for her inspection. It was a photograph.

'Mr Cayman,' said Frankie immediately. 'Where did you get it?'

'Last night. It had slipped down behind the telephone.'

'Then it seems pretty clear who Mr and Mrs Templeton were. Wait a minute.'

A waitress had just approached, bearing toast. Frankie displayed the photograph.

'Do you know who that is?' she asked.

The waitress regarded the photograph, her head a little on one side.

'Now, I've seen the gentleman – but I can't quite call to mind. Oh! yes, it's the gentleman who had Tudor Cottage – Mr Templeton. They've gone away now – somewhere abroad, I believe.'

'What sort of man was he?' asked Frankie.

'I really couldn't say. They didn't come down here very often – just weekends now and then. Nobody saw much of him. Mrs Templeton was a very nice lady. But they hadn't had Tudor Cottage very long – only about six months – when a very rich gentleman died and left Mrs Templeton all his money and they went to live abroad. They never sold Tudor Cottage, though. I think they sometimes lend it to people for weekends. But I don't suppose with all that money they'll ever come back here and live in it themselves.'

'They had a cook called Rose Chudleigh, didn't they?' asked Frankie.

But the girl seemed uninterested in cooks. Being left a fortune by a rich gentleman was what really stirred her imagination. In answer to Frankie's question she replied that she couldn't say, she was sure, and withdrew carrying an empty toast-rack.

'That's all plain sailing,' said Frankie. 'The Caymans have given up coming here, but they keep the place on for the convenience of the gang.'

They agreed to divide the labour as Bobby had suggested. Frankie went off in the Bentley, having smartened herself up by a few local purchases, and Bobby went off in quest of Albert Mere, the gardener.

They met at lunch time.

'Well?' demanded Bobby.

Frankie shook her head.

'Forgery's out of the question.' She spoke in a dispirited voice. 'I spent a long time with Mr Elford – he's rather an old dear. He'd got wind of our doings last night and was wild to hear a few details. I don't suppose they get much excitement down here.

Anyway, I soon got him eating out of my hand. Then I discussed the Savage case – pretended I'd met some of the Savage relations and that they'd hinted at forgery. At that my old dear bristled up – absolutely out of the question! It wasn't a question of letters or anything like that. He saw Mr Savage himself and Mr Savage insisted on the will being drawn up then and there. Mr Elford wanted to go away and do it properly – you know how they do – sheets and sheets all about nothing –'

'I don't know,' said Bobby. 'I've never made any wills.'

'I have – two. The second was this morning. I had to have some excuse for seeing a lawyer.'

'Who did you leave your money to?'

'You.'

'That was a bit thoughtless, wasn't it? If Roger Bassington-ffrench succeeded in bumping you off I should probably be hanged for it!'

'I never thought of that,' said Frankie. 'Well, as I was saying, Mr Savage was so nervous and wrought up that Mr Elford wrote out the will then and there and the servant and the gardener came and witnessed it, and Mr Elford took it away with him for safe keeping.'

'That does seem to knock out forgery,' agreed Bobby.

'I know. You can't have forgery when you've actually seen the man sign his name. As to the other business – murder, it's going to be hard to find out anything about that now. The doctor who was called in has died since. The man we saw last night is a new man – he's only been here about two months.'

'We seem to have rather an unfortunate number of deaths,' said Bobby.

'Why, who else is dead?'

'Albert Mere.'

'Do you think they've *all* been put out of the way?'

'That seems rather wholesale. We might give Albert Mere the benefit of the doubt – he was seventy-two, poor old man.'

'All right,' said Frankie. 'I'll allow you Natural Causes in his case. Any luck with Rose Chudleigh?'

'Yes. After she left the Templetons she went to the north of England to a place, but she's come back and married a man down here whom it seems she's been walking out with for the last seventeen years. Unfortunately she's a bit of a nitwit. She doesn't seem to remember anything about anyone. Perhaps you could do something with her.'

'I'll have a go,' said Frankie. 'I'm rather good with nitwits. Where's Badger, by the way?'

'Good Lord! I've forgotten all about him,' said Bobby. He got up and left the room, returning a few minutes later.

'He was still asleep,' he explained. 'He's getting up now. A chambermaid seems to have called him four times but it didn't make any impression.'

'Well, we'd better go and see the nitwit,' said Frankie, rising. 'And then I *must* buy a toothbrush and a nightgown and a sponge and a few other necessities of civilized existence. I was so close to Nature last night that I didn't think about any of them. I just stripped off my outer covering and fell upon the bed.'

'I know,' said Bobby. 'So did I.'

'Let's go and talk to Rose Chudleigh,' said Frankie.

Rose Chudleigh, now Mrs Pratt, lived in a small cottage that seemed to be overflowing with china dogs and furniture. Mrs Pratt herself was a bovine-looking woman of ample proportions, with fish-like eyes and every indication of adenoids.

'You see, I've come back,' said Bobby breezily.

Mrs Pratt breathed hard and looked at them both incuriously.

'We were so interested to hear that you had lived with Mrs Templeton,' explained Frankie.

'Yes, ma'am,' said Mrs Pratt.

'She's living abroad now, I believe,' continued Frankie, trying to give an impression of being an intimate of the family.

'I've heard so,' agreed Mrs Pratt.

'You were with her some time, weren't you?' asked Frankie.

'Were I which, ma'am?'

'With Mrs Templeton some time,' said Frankie, speaking slowly and clearly.

'I wouldn't say that, ma'am. Only two months.'

'Oh! I thought you'd been with her longer than that.'

'That was Gladys, ma'am. The house-parlourmaid. She was there six months.'

'There were two of you?'

'That's right. House-parlourmaid she was and I was cook.'

'You were there when Mr Savage died, weren't you?'

'I beg your pardon, ma'am.'

'You were there when Mr Savage died?'

'Mr Templeton didn't die – at least I haven't heard so. He went abroad.'

'Not Mr Templeton – Mr Savage,' said Bobby.

Mrs Pratt looked at him vacantly.

'The gentleman who left her all the money,' said Frankie.

A gleam of something like intelligence passed across Mrs Pratt's face.

'Oh! yes, ma'am, the gentleman there was the inquest on.'

'That's right,' said Frankie, delighted with her success. 'He used to come and stay quite often, didn't he?'

'I couldn't say as to that, ma'am. I'd only just come, you see. Gladys would know.'

'But you had to witness his will, didn't you?'

Mrs Pratt looked blank.

'You went and saw him sign a paper and you had to sign it, too.'

Again the gleam of intelligence.

'Yes, ma'am. Me and Albert. I'd never done such a thing before and I didn't like it. I said to Gladys I don't like signing a paper and that's a fact, and Gladys, she said it must be all right because Mr Elford was there and he was a very nice gentleman as well as being a lawyer.'

'What happened exactly?' asked Bobby.

'I beg your pardon, sir?'

'Who called you to sign your name?' asked Frankie.

'The mistress, sir. She came into the kitchen and said would I go outside and call Albert and would we both come up to the best bedroom (which she'd moved out of for Mr – the gentleman – the night before) and there was the gentleman sitting up in bed – he'd come back from London and gone straight to bed – and a very ill-looking gentleman he was. I hadn't seen him before. But he looked something ghastly, and Mr Elford was there, too, and he spoke very nice and said there was nothing to be afraid of and I was to sign my name where the gentleman had signed his, and I did and put "cook" after it and the address and Albert did the same and I went down to Gladys all of a tremble and said I'd never seen a gentleman look so like death, and Gladys said he'd looked all right the night before, and that it must have been something in London that had upset him. He'd gone up to London very early before anyone was up. And then I said about not liking to write my name to anything, and Gladys said it was all right because Mr Elford was there.'

'And Mr Savage – the gentleman died – when?'

'Next morning as ever was, ma'am. He shut himself up in his room that night and wouldn't let anyone go near him, and when Gladys called him in the morning he was all stiff and dead and a letter propped up by his bedside. "To the Coroner," it said. Oh! it gave Gladys a regular turn. And then there was an inquest and everything. About two months later Mrs Templeton told me she was going abroad to live. But she got me a very good place up north with big wages and she gave me a nice present and everything. A very nice lady, Mrs Templeton.'

Mrs Pratt was by now thoroughly enjoying her own loquacity. Frankie rose.

'Well,' she said. 'It's been very nice to hear all this.' She slipped a note out of her purse. 'You must let me leave you a – er – little present. I've taken up so much of your time.'

'Well, thank you kindly, I'm sure, ma'am. Good day to you and your good gentleman.'

Frankie blushed and retreated rather rapidly. Bobby followed her after a few minutes. He looked preoccupied.

'Well,' he said. 'We seem to have got at all she knows.'

'Yes,' said Frankie. 'And it hangs together. There seems no doubt that Savage *did* make that will, and I suppose his fear of cancer was genuine enough. They couldn't very well bribe a Harley Street doctor. I suppose they just took advantage of his having made that will to do away with him quickly before he changed his mind. But how we or anyone else can prove they did make away with him I can't see.'

'I know. We may suspect that Mrs T gave him "something to make him sleep", but we can't prove it. Bassington-ffrench may have forged the letter to the coroner, but that again we can't prove by now. I expect the letter is destroyed long ago after being put in as evidence at the inquest.'

'So we come back to the old problem – what on earth are Bassington-ffrench and Co. so afraid of our discovering?'

'Nothing strikes you as odd particularly?'

'No, I don't think so – at least only one thing. Why did Mrs Templeton send out for the gardener to come and witness the will when the house-parlourmaid was in the house. Why didn't they ask the parlourmaid?'

'It's odd your saying that, Frankie,' said Bobby.

His voice sounded so queer that Frankie looked at him in surprise.

'Why?'

'Because I stayed behind to ask Mrs Pratt for Gladys's name and address.'

'Well?'

'*The parlourmaid's name was Evans!*'

CHAPTER 32
EVANS

Frankie gasped.

Bobby's voice rose excitedly.

'You see, you've asked the same question that Carstairs asked. *Why didn't they ask the parlourmaid? Why didn't they ask Evans?*'

'Oh! Bobby, we're getting there at last!'

'The same thing must have struck Carstairs. He was nosing round, just as we were, looking for something fishy – and this point struck him just as it struck us. And, moreover, I believe he came to Wales for that reason. Gladys Evans is a Welsh name – Evans was probably a Welsh girl. He was following her to Marchbolt. And someone was following him – and so, he never got to her.'

'Why *didn't* they ask Evans?' said Frankie. 'There *must* be a reason. It's such a silly little point – and yet it's important. With a couple of maids in the house, why send out for a gardener?'

'Perhaps because both Chudleigh and Albert Mere were chumps, whereas Evans was rather a sharp girl.'

'It can't be only that. Mr Elford was there and he's quite shrewd. Oh! Bobby, the whole situation is there – I know it is.

If we could just get at the reason. Evans. Why Chudleigh and Mere and not Evans?'

Suddenly she stopped and put both hands over her eyes.

'It's coming,' she said. 'Just a sort of flicker. It'll come in a minute.'

She stayed dead still for a minute or two, then removed her hands and looked at her companion with an odd flicker in her eyes.

'Bobby,' she said, 'if you're staying in a house with two servants which do you tip?'

'The house-parlourmaid, of course,' said Bobby, surprised. 'One never tips a cook. One never sees her, for one thing.'

'No, and she never sees you. At least she might catch a glimpse of you if you were there some time. But a house-parlourmaid waits on you at dinner and calls you and hands you coffee.'

'What are you getting at, Frankie?'

'They couldn't have Evans witnessing that will – *because Evans would have known that it wasn't Mr Savage who was making it.*'

'Good Lord, Frankie, what do you mean? Who was it then?'

'Bassington-ffrench, of course! Don't you see, he impersonated Savage? I bet it was Bassington-ffrench who went to that doctor and made all that fuss about having cancer. Then the lawyer is sent for – a stranger who doesn't know Mr Savage but who will be able to swear that he saw Mr Savage sign that will and it's witnessed by two people, one of whom hadn't seen him before and the other an old man who was probably pretty blind and who probably had never seen Savage either. Now do you see?'

'But where was the real Savage all that time?'

'Oh! he arrived all right and then I suspect they drugged him and put him in the attic, perhaps, and kept him there for twelve hours while Bassington-ffrench did his impersonation stunt. Then he was put back in his bed and given chloral and Evans finds him dead in the morning.'

'My God, I believe you've hit it, Frankie. But can we prove it?'

'Yes – no – I don't know. Supposing Rose Chudleigh – Pratt, I mean – was shown a photograph of the real Savage? Would she be able to say, "that wasn't the man who signed the will"?'

'I doubt it,' said Bobby. 'She is such a nitwit.'

'Chosen for that purpose, I expect. But there's another thing. An expert ought to be able to detect that the signature is a forgery.'

'They didn't before.'

'Because nobody ever raised the question. There didn't seem any possible moment when the will *could* have been forged. But now it's different.'

'One thing we must do,' said Bobby. 'Find Evans. She may be able to tell us a lot. She was with the Templetons for six months, remember,'

Frankie groaned.

'That's going to make it even more difficult.'

'How about the post office?' suggested Bobby.

They were just passing it. In appearance it was more of a general store than a post office.

Frankie darted inside and opened the campaign. There was no one else in the shop except the postmistress – a young woman with an inquisitive nose.

Frankie bought a two-shilling book of stamps, commented on the weather and then said:

'But I expect you always have better weather here than we do in my part of the world. I live in Wales – Marchbolt. You wouldn't believe the rain we have.'

The young woman with the nose said that they had a good deal of rain themselves and last Bank Holiday it had rained something cruel.

Frankie said:

'There's someone in Marchbolt who comes from this part of the world. I wonder if you know her. Her name was Evans – Gladys Evans.'

The young woman was quite unsuspicious.

'Why, of course,' she said. She was in service here. At Tudor Cottage. But she didn't come from these parts. She came from Wales and she went back there and married – Roberts her name is now.'

'That's right,' said Frankie. 'You can't give me her address, I suppose? I borrowed a raincoat from her and forgot to give it back. If I had her address I'd post it to her.'

'Well now,' the other replied, 'I believe I can. I get a p.c. from her now and again. She and her husband have gone into service together. Wait a minute now.'

She went away and rummaged in a corner. Presently she returned with a piece of paper in her hand.

'Here you are,' she said, pushing it across the counter.

Bobby and Frankie read it together. It was the last thing in the world they expected.

> 'Mrs Roberts,
> The Vicarage,
> Marchbolt,
> Wales.'

CHAPTER 33

SENSATION IN THE ORIENT CAFÉ

How Bobby and Frankie got out of the post office without disgracing themselves neither of them ever knew.

Outside, with one accord, they looked at each other and shook with laugher.

'At the Vicarage – all the time!' gasped Bobby.

'And I looked through four hundred and eighty Evans,' lamented Frankie.

'*Now* I see why Bassington-ffrench was so amused when he realized we didn't know in the least who Evans was!'

'And of course it was dangerous from their point of view. You and Evans were actually under the same roof.'

'Come on,' said Bobby. 'Marchbolt's the next place.'

'Like where the rainbow ends,' said Frankie. 'Back to the dear old home.'

'Dash it all,' said Bobby, 'we must do something about Badger. Have you any money, Frankie?'

Frankie opened her bag and took out a handful of notes.

'Give these to him and tell him to make some arrangement with his creditors and that Father will buy the garage and put him in as manager.'

'All right,' said Bobby. 'The great thing is to get off quickly.'

'Why this frightful haste?'

'I don't know – but I've a feeling something might happen.'

'How awful. Let's go ever so quickly.'

'I'll settle Badger. You go and start the car.'

'I shall never buy that toothbrush,' said Frankie.

Five minutes saw them speeding out of Chipping Somerton. Bobby had no occasion to complain of lack of speed.

Nevertheless, Frankie suddenly said:

'Look here, Bobby, this isn't quick enough.'

Bobby glanced at the speedometer needle, which was, at the moment, registering eighty, and remarked dryly:

'I don't see what more we can do.'

'We can take an air taxi,' said Frankie. 'We're only about seven miles from Medeshot Aerodrome.'

'My dear girl!' said Bobby.

'If we do that we'll be home in a couple of hours.'

'Good,' said Bobby. 'Let's take an air taxi.'

The whole proceedings were beginning to take on the fantastic character of a dream. Why this wild hurry to get to Marchbolt? Bobby didn't know. He suspected that Frankie didn't know either. It was just a feeling.

At Medeshot Frankie asked for Mr Donald King and an untidy-looking young man was produced who appeared languidly surprised at the sight of her.

'Hullo, Frankie,' he said. 'I haven't seen you for an age. What do you want?'

'I want an air taxi,' said Frankie. 'You do that sort of thing, don't you?'

'Oh! yes. Where do you want to go?'

'I want to get home quickly,' said Frankie.

Mr Donald King raised his eyebrows.

'Is that all?' he asked.

'Not quite,' said Frankie. 'But it's the main idea.'

'Oh! well, we can soon fix you up.'

'I'll give you a cheque,' said Frankie.

Five minutes later they were off.

'Frankie,' said Bobby. 'Why are we doing this?'

'I haven't the faintest idea,' said Frankie. 'But I feel we must. Don't you?'

'Curiously enough, I do. But I don't know why. After all our Mrs Roberts won't fly away on a broomstick.'

'She might. Remember, we don't know what Bassington-ffrench is up to.'

'That's true,' said Bobby thoughtfully.

It was growing late when they reached their destination. The plane landed them in the Park and five minutes later Bobby and Frankie were driving into Marchbolt in Lord Marchington's Chrysler.

They pulled up outside the Vicarage gate, the Vicarage drive not lending itself to the turning of expensive cars.

Then jumping out they ran up the drive.

'I shall wake up soon,' thought Bobby. 'What are we doing and why?'

A slender figure was standing on the doorstep. Frankie and Bobby recognized her at the same minute.

'Moira!' cried Frankie.

Moira turned. She was swaying slightly.

'Oh! I'm so glad to see you. I don't know what to do.'

'But what on earth brings you here?'

'The same thing that has brought you, I expect.'

'You have found out who Evans is?' asked Bobby.

Moira nodded.

'Yes, it's a long story –'

'Come inside,' said Bobby.

But Moira shrank back.

'No, no,' she said hurriedly. 'Let's go somewhere and talk. There's something I must tell you – before we go into the house. Isn't there a café or some place like that in the town? Somewhere where we could go?'

'All right,' said Bobby, moving unwillingly away from the door. 'But why –'

Moira stamped her foot.

'You'll see when I tell you. Oh! do come. There's not a minute to lose.'

They yielded to her urgency. About half-way down the main street was the Orient Café – a somewhat grand name not borne out by the interior decoration. The three of them filed in. It was a slack moment – half-past six.

They sat down at a small table in the corner and Bobby ordered three coffees.

'Now then?' he said.

'Wait till she's brought the coffee,' said Moira.

The waitress returned and listlessly deposited three cups of tepid coffee in front of them.

'Now then,' said Bobby.

'I hardly know where to begin,' said Moira. 'It was in the train going to London. Really, the most amazing coincidence. I went along the corridor and –'

She broke off. Her seat faced the door and she leant forward, staring.

'He must have followed me,' she said.

'Who?' cried Frankie and Bobby together.

'Bassington-ffrench,' whispered Moira.

'You've seen him?'

'He's outside. I saw him with a woman with red hair.'

'Mrs Cayman,' cried Frankie.

She and Bobby jumped and ran to the door. A protest came from Moira but neither of them heeded it. They looked up and down the street but Bassington-ffrench was nowhere in sight.

Moira joined them.

'Has he gone?' she asked, her voice trembling. 'Oh! do be careful. He's dangerous – horribly dangerous.'

'He can't do anything so long as we're all together,' said Bobby.

'Brace up, Moira,' said Frankie. 'Don't be such a rabbit.'

'Well, we can't do anything for the moment,' said Bobby, leading the way back to the table. 'Go on with what you were telling us, Moira.'

He picked up his cup of coffee. Frankie lost her balance and fell against him and the coffee poured over the table.

'Sorry,' said Frankie.

She stretched over the adjoining table which was laid for possible diners. There was a cruet on it with two glass stoppered bottles containing oil and vinegar.

The oddity of Frankie's proceedings riveted Bobby's attention. She took the vinegar bottle, emptied out the vinegar into the slop bowl and began to pour coffee into it from her cup.

'Have you gone batty, Frankie?' asked Bobby. 'What the devil are you doing?'

'Taking a sample of this coffee for George Arbuthnot to analyse,' said Frankie.

She turned to Moira.

'*The game's up, Moira!* The whole thing came to me in a flash as we stood at the door just now! When I jogged Bobby's elbow and made him spill his coffee I saw your face. You put something in our cups when you sent us running to the door to look for Bassington-ffrench. The game's up, *Mrs Nicholson or Templeton or whatever you like to call yourself.*'

'Templeton?' cried Bobby.

'Look at her face,' cried Frankie. 'If she denies it ask her to come to the Vicarage and see if Mrs Roberts doesn't identify her.'

Bobby did look at her. He saw that face, that haunting, wistful face transformed by a demoniac rage. That beautiful mouth opened and a stream of foul and hideous curses poured out.

She fumbled in her handbag.

Bobby was still dazed but he acted in the nick of time.

It was his hand that struck the pistol up.

The bullet passed over Frankie's head and buried itself in the wall of the Orient Café.

For the first time in its history one of the waitresses hurried.

With a wild scream she shot out into the street calling: 'Help! Murder! Police!'

CHAPTER 34

LETTER FROM SOUTH AMERICA

It was some weeks later.

Frankie had just received a letter. It bore the stamp of one of the less well-known South American republics.

After reading it through, she passed it to Bobby.

It ran as follows:

> *Dear Frankie, Really, I congratulate you! You and your young naval friend have shattered the plans of a life-time. I had everything so nicely arranged.*

Would you really like to hear all about it? My lady friend has given me away so thoroughly (spite, I'm afraid – women are invariable spiteful!) that my most damaging admissions won't do me any further harm. Besides, I am starting life again. Roger Bassington-ffrench is dead.

I fancy I've always been what they call a 'wrong 'un'. Even at Oxford I had a little lapse. Stupid, because it was bound to be found out. The Pater didn't let me down. But he sent me to the Colonies.

I fell in with Moira and her lot fairly soon. She was the real thing. She was an accomplished criminal by the time she was fifteen. When I met her things were getting a bit too hot for her. The American police were on her trail.

She and I liked each other. We decided to make a match of it but we'd a few plans to carry through first.

To begin with, she married Nicholson. By doing so she removed herself to another world and the police lost sight of her. Nicholson was just coming over to England to start a place for nerve patients. He was looking for a suitable house to buy cheap. Moira got him on to the Grange.

She was still working in with her gang in the dope business. Without knowing it, Nicholson was very useful to her.

I had always had two ambitions. I wanted to be the owner of Merroway and I wanted to command an immense amount of money. A Bassington-ffrench played a great part in the reign of Charles II. Since then the family has dwindled down to mediocrity. I felt capable of playing a great part again. But I had to have money.

Moira made several trips across to Canada to 'see her people'. Nicholson adored her and believed anything she told him. Most men did. Owing to the complications of the drug business she travelled under various names. She was travelling as Mrs Templeton when she met Savage. She knew all about Savage and his enormous wealth and she went all out for him. He was attracted, but he wasn't attracted enough to lose his common sense.

However, we concocted a plan. You know pretty well the story of that. The man you know as Cayman acted the part of the unfeeling husband. Savage was induced to come down and stay at Tudor Cottage more than once. The third time he came our plans were laid. I needn't go into all that – you know it. The whole thing went with a bang. Moira cleared the money and went off ostensibly abroad – in reality back to Staverley and the Grange.

In the meantime, I was perfecting my own plans. Henry and young Tommy had to be got out of the way. I had bad luck over Tommy. A couple of perfectly good accidents went wrong. I wasn't going to fool about with accidents in Henry's case. He had a good deal of rheumatic pain after an accident in the hunting field. I introduced him to morphia. He took it in all good faith. Henry was a simple soul. He soon became an addict. Our plan was that he should go to the Grange for treatment and should there either 'commit suicide' or get hold of an overdose of morphia. Moira would do the business. I shouldn't be connected with it in any way.

And then that fool Carstairs began to be active. It seems that Savage had written him a line on board ship mentioning Mrs Templeton and even enclosing a snapshot of her. Carstairs went on a shooting trip soon afterwards. When he came back from the wilds and heard the news of Savage's death and will, he was frankly incredulous. The story didn't ring true to him. He was certain that Savage wasn't worried about his death and he didn't believe he had any special fear of cancer. Also the wording of the will sounded to him highly uncharacteristic. Savage was a hard-headed business man and while he might be quite ready to have an affair with a pretty woman, Carstairs didn't believe he would leave a vast sum of money to her and the rest to charity. The charity touch was my idea. It sounded so respectable and unfishy.

Carstairs came over here, determined to look into the business. He began to poke about.

And straightaway we had a piece of bad luck. Some friends brought him down to lunch and he saw a picture of Moira on the piano, and recognized it as the woman of the snapshot that Savage had sent him. He went down to Chipping Somerton and started to poke about there.

Moira and I began to get the wind up – I sometimes think unnecessarily. But Carstairs was a shrewd chap.

I went down to Chipping Somerton after him. He failed to trace the cook – Rose Chudleigh. She'd gone to the north, but he tracked down Evans, found out her married name and started off for Marchbolt.

Things were getting serious. If Evans identified Mrs Templeton and Mrs Nicholson as one and the same person matters were going to become difficult. Also, she'd been in the house some time and we weren't sure quite how much she might know.

I decided that Carstairs had got to be suppressed. He was making a serious nuisance of himself. Chance came to my aid. I was close behind him when the mist came up. I crept up nearer and a sudden push did the job.

But I was still in a dilemma. I didn't know what incriminating matter he might have on him. However, your young naval friend played into my hands very nicely. I was left alone with the body for a short time – quite enough for my purpose. He had a photograph of Moira – he'd got it from the photographers – presumably for identification. I removed that and any letters or identifying matter. Then I planted the photograph of one of the gang.

All went well. The pseudo sister and brother-in-law came down and identified him. All seemed to have gone off satisfactorily. And then your friend Bobby upset things. It seemed that Carstairs had recovered consciousness before he died and that he had been saying things. He'd mentioned Evans – and Evans was actually in service at the Vicarage.

I admit we were getting rattled by now. We lost our heads a bit. Moira insisted that he must be put out of the way. We tried one plan which failed. Then Moira said she'd see to it. She went down to Marchbolt in the car. She seized a chance very neatly – slipped some morphia into his beer when he was asleep. But the young devil didn't succumb. That was pure bad luck.

As I told you, it was Nicholson's cross-questioning that made me wonder if you were just what you seemed. But imagine the shock that Moira had when she was creeping out to meet me one evening and came face to face with Bobby! She recognized him at once – she'd had a good look when he was asleep that day. No wonder she was so scared she nearly passed out. Then she realized that it wasn't her he suspected and she rallied and played up.

She came to the inn and told him a few tall stories. He swallowed them like a lamb. She pretended that Alan Carstairs was an old lover and she piled it on thick about her fear of Nicholson. Also she did her best to disabuse you of your suspicions concerning me. I did the same to you and disparaged her as a weak, helpless creature

– Moira, who had the nerve to put any number of people out of the way without turning a hair!

The position was serious. We'd got the money. We were getting on well with the Henry plan. I was in no hurry for Tommy. I could afford to wait a bit. Nicholson could easily be got out of the way when the time came. But you and Bobby were a menace. You'd got your suspicions fixed on the Grange.

It may interest you to know that Henry didn't commit suicide. I killed him! When I was talking to you in the garden I saw there was no time to waste – and I went straight in and saw to things.

The aeroplane that came over gave me my chance. I went into the study, sat down by Henry who was writing and said: 'Look here, old man –' and shot him! The noise of the plane drowned the sound. Then I wrote a nice affecting letter, wiped off my fingerprints from the revolver, pressed Henry's hand round it and let it drop to the floor. I put the key of the study in Henry's pocket and went out, locking the door from the outside with the dining-room key which fits the lock.

I won't go into details of the neat little squib arrangement in the chimney which was timed to go off four minutes later.

Everything went beautifully. You and I were in the garden together and heard the 'shot'. A perfect suicide! The only person who laid himself open to suspicion was poor old Nicholson. The ass came back for a stick or something!

Of course Bobby's knight errantry was a bit difficult for Moira. So she just went off to the cottage. We fancied that Nicholson's explanation of his wife's absence would be sure to make you suspicious.

Where Moira really showed her mettle was at the cottage. She realized from the noise upstairs that I'd been knocked out, and she quickly injected a large dose of morphia into herself and lay down on the bed. After you all went down to telephone she nipped up to the attic and cut me free. Then the morphia took effect and by the time the doctor arrived she was genuinely off in a hypnotic sleep.

But all the same her nerve was going. She was afraid you'd get on to Evans and get the hang of how Savage's will and suicide was worked. Also she was afraid that Carstairs had written to Evans before he came to Marchbolt. She pretended to go up to a London nursing home. Instead, she hurried down to Marchbolt – and met *you on the doorstep! Then her one idea was to get you both out of the way. Her methods were crude to the last degree, but I believe she'd have got away with it. I doubt if the waitress would have been able to remember much about what the woman who came in with you was like. Moira would have got away back to London and lain low in a nursing home. With you and Bobby out of the way the whole thing would have died down.*

But you spotted her – and she lost her head. And then at the trial she dragged me into it!

Perhaps I was getting a little tired of her . . .

But I had no idea that she knew it.

You see, she had got the money – my money! Once I had married her I might have got tired of her. I like variety.

So here I am starting life again . . .

And all owing to you and that extremely objectionable young man Bobby Jones.

But I've no doubt I shall make good!

Or ought it to be bad, not good?

I haven't reformed yet.

But if at first you don't succeed, try, try, try again.

Goodbye, my dear – or, perhaps au revoir. *One never knows, does one?*

Your affectionate enemy, the bold, bad villain of the piece,
Roger Bassington-ffrench.

CHAPTER 35

NEWS FROM THE VICARAGE

Bobby handed back the letter and with a sigh Frankie took it.

'He's really a very remarkable person,' she said.

'You always had a fancy for him,' said Bobby coldly.

'He had charm,' said Frankie. 'So had Moira,' she added.

Bobby blushed.

'It was very queer that all the time the clue to the whole thing should have been in the Vicarage,' he said. 'You do know, don't you, Frankie, that Carstairs had actually written to Evans – to Mrs Roberts, that is?'

Frankie nodded.

'Telling her that he was coming to see her and that he wanted information about Mrs Templeton whom he had reason to believe was a dangerous international crook wanted by the police.

'And then when he's pushed over the cliff she doesn't put two and two together,' said Bobby bitterly.

'That's because the man who went over the cliff was Pritchard,' said Frankie. 'That identification was a very clever bit of work. If a man called Pritchard is pushed over, how *could* it be a man called Carstairs? That's how the ordinary mind works.'

'The funny thing is that she recognized Cayman,' went on Bobby. 'At least she caught a glimpse of him when Roberts was letting him in and asked him who it was. And he said it was Mr Cayman and she said, "Funny, he's the dead spit of a gentleman I used to be in service with."'

'Can you beat it?' said Frankie.

'Even Bassington-ffrench gave himself away once or twice,' she continued. 'But like an idiot I never spotted it.'

'Did he?'

'Yes, when Sylvia said that the picture in the paper was very like Carstairs he said there wasn't much likeness really – showing he'd seen the dead man. And then later he said to me that he never saw the dead man's face.'

'How on earth did you spot Moira, Frankie?'

'I think it was the description of Mrs Templeton,' said Frankie dreamily. 'Everyone said she was "such a nice lady". Now that didn't seem to fit with the Cayman woman. No servant would describe her a "nice lady". And then we got to the Vicarage and Moira was there and it suddenly came to me – *Suppose Moira was Mrs Templeton?*'

'Very bright of you.'

'I'm very sorry for Sylvia,' said Frankie. 'With Moira dragging Roger into it, it's been a terrible lot of publicity for her. But Dr Nicholson has stuck by her and I shouldn't be at all surprised if they ended by making a match of it.'

'Everything seems to have ended very fortunately,' said Bobby. 'Badger's doing well at the garage – thanks to your father, and also thanks to your father, I've got this perfectly marvellous job.'

'Is it a marvellous job?'

'Managing a coffee estate out in Kenya on a whacking big

screw? I should think so. It's just the sort of thing I used to dream about.'

He paused.

'People come out to Kenya a good deal on trips,' he said with intention.

'Quite a lot of people live out there,' said Frankie demurely.

'Oh! Frankie, you wouldn't?' He blushed, stammered, recovered himself. 'W-w-would you?'

'I would,' said Frankie. 'I mean, I will.'

'I've been keen about you always,' said Bobby in a stifled voice. 'I used to be miserable – knowing, I mean, that it was no good.'

'I suppose that's what made you so rude that day on the golf links?'

'Yes, I was feeling pretty grim.'

'H'm,' said Frankie. 'What about Moira?'

Bobby looked uncomfortable.

'Her face did sort of get me,' he admitted.

'It's a better face than mine,' said Frankie generously.

'It isn't – but it sort of "haunted" me. And then, when we were up in the attic and you were so plucky about things – well, Moira just faded out. I was hardly interested in what happened to her. It was *you* – only you. You were simply splendid! So frightfully plucky.'

'I wasn't feeling plucky inside,' said Frankie. 'I was all shaking. But I wanted you to admire me.'

'I did, darling. I do. I always have. I always shall. Are you sure you won't hate it out in Kenya?'

'I shall adore it. I was fed up with England.'

'Frankie.'

'Bobby.'

'If you will come in here,' said the Vicar, opening the door and ushering in the advance guard of the Dorcas Society.

He shut the door precipitately and apologized.

'My – er – one of my sons. He is – er – engaged.'

A member of the Dorcas Society said archly that it looked like it.

'A good boy,' said the Vicar. 'Inclined at one time not to take life seriously. But he has improved very much of late. He is going out to manage a coffee estate in Kenya.'

Said one member of the Dorcas Society to another in a whisper:

'Did you see? It was Lady Frances Derwent he was kissing?'

In an hour's time the news was all over Marchbolt.

MURDER IS EASY

Dedicated to
Rosalind and Susan
the first two critics of this book

CHAPTER I

A FELLOW-TRAVELLER

England!

England after many years!

How was he going to like it?

Luke Fitzwilliam asked himself that question as he walked down the gang-plank to the dock. It was present at the back of his mind all through the wait in the Customs' shed. It came suddenly to the fore when he was finally seated in the boat-train.

England on leave was one thing. Plenty of money to blue (to begin with anyway!), old friends to look up, meetings with other fellows home like himself – a carefree atmosphere of 'Well, it won't be long. Might as well enjoy myself! Soon be going back.'

But now there was no question of going back. No more of the hot stifling nights, no more blinding sun and tropical beauty of rich vegetation, no more lonely evenings reading and re-reading old copies of *The Times*.

Here he was, honourably retired on a pension, with some small private means of his own, a gentleman of leisure, come home to England. What was he going to do with himself?

England! England on a June day, with a grey sky and a sharp biting wind. Nothing welcoming about her on a day like this! And the people! Heavens, the people! Crowds of them, all with grey faces like the sky – anxious worried faces. The houses too, springing up everywhere like mushrooms. Nasty little houses! Revolting little houses! Chicken coops in the grandiose manner all over the countryside!

With an effort Luke Fitzwilliam averted his eyes from the landscape outside the railway carriage window and settled down to a perusal of the papers he had just bought. *The Times*, the *Daily Clarion* and *Punch*.

He started with the *Daily Clarion*. The *Clarion* was given over entirely to Epsom.

Luke thought: 'A pity we didn't get in yesterday. Haven't seen the Derby run since I was nineteen.'

He had drawn a horse in the Club sweep and he looked now to see what the *Clarion*'s racing correspondent thought of its chance. He found it dismissed contemptuously in a sentence.

'*Of the others, Jujube the II., Mark's Mile, Santony and Jerry Boy are hardly likely to qualify for a place. A likely outsider is –*'

But Luke paid no attention to the likely outsider. His eye had shifted to the betting. Jujube the II. was listed at a modest 40 to 1.

He glanced at his watch. A quarter to four. 'Well,' he thought. 'It's over now.' And he wished he'd had a bet on Clarigold who was the second favourite.

Then he opened *The Times* and became absorbed in more serious matters.

Not for long, however, for a fierce-looking colonel in the corner opposite was so incensed at what he himself had just read that he had to pass on his indignation to his fellow-passenger. A full half-hour passed before the colonel tired of saying what he thought about 'these damned Communist agitators, sir'.

The colonel died down at last and finally dropped off to sleep with his mouth open. Shortly afterwards the train slowed down and finally stopped. Luke looked out of the window. They were in a large empty-looking station with many platforms. He caught sight of a bookstall some way up the platform with a placard: DERBY RESULT. Luke opened the door, jumped out, and ran towards the bookstall. A moment later he was staring with a broad grin at a few smudged lines in the stop press.

> *Derby Result*
> *JUJUBE THE II.*
> *MAZEPPA*
> *CLARIGOLD*

Luke grinned broadly. A hundred pounds to blue! Good old Jujube the II., so scornfully dismissed by all the tipsters.

He folded the paper, still grinning to himself, and turned back – to face emptiness. In the excitement of Jujube the II.'s victory, his train had slipped out of the station unnoticed by him.

'When the devil did that train go out?' he demanded of a gloomy-looking porter.

The latter replied:

'What train? There hasn't been no train since the 3.14.'

'There was a train here just now. I got out of it. The boat express.'

The porter replied austerely:

'The boat express don't stop anywhere till London.'

'But it did,' Luke assured him. 'I got out of it.'

'No stop anywhere till London,' repeated the porter immovably.

'It stopped at this very platform and I got out of it, I tell you.'

Faced by facts, the porter changed his ground.

'You didn't ought to have done,' he said reproachfully. 'It don't stop here.'

'But it did.'

'That 'twas signal, that was. Signal against it. It didn't what you'd call "stop".'

'I'm not so good at these fine distinctions as you are,' said Luke. 'The point is, what do I do next?'

The porter, a man of slow ideas, repeated reproachfully: 'You didn't ought to have got out.'

'We'll admit that,' said Luke. 'The wrong is done, past all recall – weep we never so bitterly we can never bring back the dead past – Quoth the raven "Nevermore" – The moving finger writes; and having writ moves on, etc., etc., and so on and so forth. What I'm trying to get at is, what do you, a man experienced in the service of the railway company, advise me to do now?'

'You're asking what you'd better do?'

'That,' said Luke, 'is the idea. There are, I presume, trains that stop, really officially stop, here?'

'Reckon,' said the porter. 'You'd best go on by the 4.25.'

'If the 4.25 goes to London,' said Luke, 'the 4.25 is the train for me.'

Reassured on that point, Luke strolled up and down the

platform. A large board informed him that he was at Fenny Clayton Junction for Wychwood-under-Ashe, and presently a train consisting of one carriage pushed backwards by an antiquated little engine came slowly puffing in and deposited itself in a modest bay. Six or seven people alighted, and crossing over a bridge, came to join Luke on his platform. The gloomy porter suddenly awoke to life and began pushing about a large truck of crates and baskets, another porter joined him and began to rattle milk cans. Fenny Clayton awoke to life.

At last, with immense importance the London train came in. The third-class carriages were crowded, and of firsts there were only three and each one contained a traveller or travellers. Luke scrutinized each compartment. The first, a smoker, contained a gentleman of military aspect smoking a cigar. Luke felt he had had enough of Anglo-Indian colonels today. He passed on to the next one, which contained a tired-looking genteel young woman, possibly a nursery governess, and an active-looking small boy of about three. Luke passed on quickly. The next door was open and the carriage contained one passenger, an elderly lady. She reminded Luke slightly of one of his aunts, his Aunt Mildred, who had courageously allowed him to keep a grass snake when he was ten years old. Aunt Mildred had been decidedly a good aunt as aunts go. Luke entered the carriage and sat down.

After some five minutes of intense activity on the part of milk vans, luggage trucks and other excitements, the train moved slowly out of the station. Luke unfolded his paper and turned to such items of news as might interest a man who had already read his morning paper.

He did not hope to read it for long. Being a man of many aunts, he was fairly certain that the nice old lady in the corner did not propose to travel in silence to London.

He was right – a window that needed adjusting, dropped umbrella – and the way the old lady was telling him what a good train this was.

'Only an hour and ten minutes. That's very good, you know, very good indeed. Much better than the morning one. That takes an hour and forty minutes.'

She went on:

'Of course, nearly every one goes by the morning one. I mean, when it is the cheap day it's silly to go up in the afternoon. I meant to go up this morning, but Wonky Pooh was missing – that's my cat, a Persian, such a beauty only he's had a painful ear lately – and of course I couldn't leave home till he was found!'

Luke murmured:

'Of course not,' and let his eyes drop ostentatiously to his paper. But it was of no avail. The flood went on.

'So I just made the best of a bad job and took the afternoon train instead, and of course it's a blessing in one way because it's not so crowded – not that that matters when one is travelling first class. Of course, I don't usually do that. I mean, I should consider it an *extravagance*, what with taxes and one's dividends being less and servants' wages so much more and everything – but really I was so upset because you see, I'm going up on very important business, and I wanted to think out exactly what I was going to say – just quietly, you know –' Luke repressed a smile. 'And when there are people you know travelling up too – well, one can't be unfriendly – so I thought just for once, the expense was *quite permissible* – though I do think nowadays there is so much waste – and nobody saves or thinks of the future. One is sorry the seconds were ever abolished – it did make just that little difference.

'Of course,' she went on quickly, with a swift glance at Luke's bronzed face, 'I know soldiers on leave have to travel first class. I mean, being officers, it's expected of them –'

Luke sustained the inquisitive glance of a pair of bright twinkling eyes. He capitulated at once. It would come to it, he knew, in the end.

'I'm not a soldier,' he said.

'Oh, I'm sorry. I didn't mean – I just thought – you were so brown – perhaps home from the East on leave.'

'I'm home from the East,' said Luke. 'But not on leave.' He stalled off further researches with a bald statement. 'I'm a policeman.'

'In the police? Now really, that's very interesting. A dear friend of mine – *her* boy has just joined the Palestine police.'

'Mayang Straits,' said Luke, taking another short cut.

'Oh, dear – very interesting. Really, it's quite a coincidence – I mean, that you should be travelling in this carriage. Because, you see, this business I'm going up to town about – well, actually it is to Scotland Yard I'm going.'

'Really?' said Luke.

He thought to himself, 'Will she run down soon like a clock or will this go on all the way to London?' But he did not really mind very much, because he had been very fond of his Aunt Mildred, and he remembered how she had once stumped up a fiver in the nick of time. Besides, there was something very cosy and English about old ladies like this old lady and his Aunt Mildred. There was nothing at all like them in the Mayang Straits. They could be classed with plum pudding on Christmas Day and village cricket and open fireplaces with wood fires. The sort of things you appreciated a good deal when you hadn't got them and were on the other side of the world. (They were also the sort of thing you got very bored with when you had a good deal of them, but as has been already told, Luke had only landed in England three or four hours ago.)

The old lady was continuing happily:

'Yes, I meant to go up this morning – and then, as I told you, I was so worried about Wonky Pooh. But you don't think it will be too late, do you? I mean, there aren't any special office hours at Scotland Yard.'

'I don't think they close down at four or anything like that,' said Luke.

'No, of course, they couldn't, could they? I mean, somebody might want to report a serious crime at any minute, mightn't they?'

'Exactly,' said Luke.

For a moment the old lady relapsed into silence. She looked worried.

'I always think it's better to go right to the fountain-head,' she said at last. 'John Reed is quite a nice fellow – that's our constable in Wychwood – a very civil-spoken, pleasant man – but I don't feel, you know – that he would be quite the person to deal with anything serious. He's quite used to dealing with people who've drunk too much, or with exceeding the speed limit, or lighting-up time – or people who haven't taken out a dog licence – and perhaps with burglary even. But I don't think – I'm quite sure – he isn't the person to deal with *murder*!'

Luke's eyebrows rose.

'Murder?'

The old lady nodded vigorously.

'Yes, murder. You're surprised, I can see. I was myself at first . . . I really couldn't believe it. I thought I must be imagining things.'

'Are you quite sure you weren't?' Luke asked gently.

'Oh, no.' She shook her head positively. 'I might have been the first time, but not the second, or the third or the fourth. After that one *knows*.'

Luke said:

'Do you mean there have been – er – several murders?'

The quiet gentle voice replied:

'A good many, I'm afraid.'

She went on:

'That's why I thought it would be best to go straight to Scotland Yard and tell them about it. Don't *you* think that's the best thing to do?'

Luke looked at her thoughtfully, then he said:

'Why, yes – I think you're quite right.'

He thought to himself:

'They'll know how to deal with her. Probably get half a dozen old ladies a week coming in burbling about the amount of murders committed in their nice quiet country villages! There may be a special department for dealing with the old dears.'

And he saw in imagination a fatherly superintendent, or a good-looking young inspector, tactfully murmuring:

'Thank you, ma'am, very grateful to you, I'm sure. Now just go back and leave it all in our hands and don't worry any more about it.'

He smiled a little to himself at the picture. He thought:

'I wonder why they get these fancies? Deadly dull lives, I suppose – an unacknowledged craving for drama. Some old ladies, so I've heard, fancy every one is poisoning their food.'

He was roused from these meditations by the thin, gentle voice continuing:

'You know, I remember reading once – I think it was the Abercrombie case – of course *he'd* poisoned quite a lot of people before any suspicion was aroused – what was I saying? Oh, yes, somebody said that there was a look – a special look that he gave any one – and then very shortly afterwards that person would be taken ill. I didn't really believe that when I read about it – but it's true!'

'What's true?'

'The look on a person's face . . .'

Luke stared at her. She was trembling a little, and her nice pink cheeks had lost some of their colour.

'I saw it first with Amy Gibbs – and *she* died. And then it was Carter. And Tommy Pierce. But now – yesterday – it was Dr Humbleby – and he's such a *good* man – a *really* good man. Carter, of course, drank, and Tommy Pierce was a dreadfully cheeky impertinent little boy, and bullied the tiny boys, twisting their arms and pinching them. I didn't feel quite so badly about them, but Dr Humbleby's different. He *must* be saved. And the terrible thing is that if I went to him and told him about it he wouldn't believe me! He'd only laugh! And John Reed wouldn't believe me either. But at Scotland Yard it will be different. Because, naturally, they're *used* to crime there!'

She glanced out of the window.

'Oh, dear, we shall be in in a minute.' She fussed a little, opening and shutting her bag, collecting her umbrella.

'Thank you – thank you so much.' This to Luke as he picked the umbrella up for the second time. 'It's been such a *relief* talking to you – most kind of you, I'm sure – so glad you think I'm doing the right thing.'

Luke said kindly:

'I'm sure they'll give you good advice at Scotland Yard.'

'I really am most grateful.' She fumbled in her bag. 'My card – oh, dear, I only have one – I must keep that – for Scotland Yard –'

'Of course, of course –'

'But my name is Pinkerton.'

'Very suitable name, too, Miss Pinkerton,' said Luke, smiling, adding hastily as she looked a little bewildered, 'my name is Luke Fitzwilliam.'

As the train drew in to the platform he added:

'Can I get you a taxi?'

'Oh, no, thank you.' Miss Pinkerton seemed quite shocked at

the idea. 'I shall take the tube. That will take me to Trafalgar Square, and I shall walk down Whitehall.'

'Well, good luck,' said Luke.

Miss Pinkerton shook him warmly by the hand.

'So kind,' she murmured again. 'You know, just at first I thought you didn't believe me.'

Luke had the grace to blush.

'Well,' he said. 'So many murders! Rather hard to do a lot of murders and get away with it, eh?'

Miss Pinkerton shook her head.

She said earnestly:

'No, no, my dear boy, *that's* where you're wrong. It's very easy to kill – so long as no one suspects you. And you see, the person in question is just the last person any one *would* suspect!'

'Well, anyway, good luck,' said Luke.

Miss Pinkerton was swallowed up in the crowd. He himself went off in search of his luggage, thinking as he did so:

'Just a little bit batty? No, I don't think so. A vivid imagination, that's all. Hope they let her down lightly. Rather an old dear.'

CHAPTER 2

OBITUARY NOTICE

I

Jimmy Lorrimer was one of Luke's oldest friends. As a matter of course, Luke stayed with Jimmy as soon as he got to London. It was with Jimmy that he sallied forth on the evening of his arrival in search of amusement. It was Jimmy's coffee that he drank with an aching head the morning after, and it was Jimmy's voice that went unanswered while he read twice over a small insignificant paragraph in the morning paper.

'Sorry, Jimmy,' he said, coming to himself with a start.

'What were you absorbed in – the political situation?'

Luke grinned.

'No fear. No, it's rather queer – old pussy I travelled up with in the train yesterday got run over.'

'Probably trusted to a Belisha Beacon,' said Jimmy. 'How do you know it's her?'

'Of course, it mayn't be. But it's the same name – Pinkerton – she was knocked down and killed by a car as she was crossing Whitehall. The car didn't stop.'

'Nasty business,' said Jimmy.

'Yes, poor old bean. I'm sorry. She reminded me of my Aunt Mildred.'

'Whoever was driving that car will be for it. Bring it in manslaughter as likely as not. I tell you, I'm scared stiff of driving a car nowadays.'

'What have you got at present in the way of a car?'

'Ford V 8. I tell you, my boy –'

The conversation became severely mechanical.

Jimmy broke it off to ask:

'What the devil are you humming?'

Luke was humming to himself:

'*Fiddle de dee, fiddle de dee, the fly has married the bumble bee.*'

He apologized.

'Nursery rhyme remembered from my childhood. Can't think what put it into my head.'

II

It was over a week later that Luke, carelessly scanning the front page of *The Times*, gave a sudden startled exclamation.

'Well, I'm damned!'

Jimmy Lorrimer looked up.

'What's the matter?'

Luke did not answer. He was staring at a name in the printed column.

Jimmy repeated his question.

Luke raised his head and looked at his friend. His expression was so peculiar that Jimmy was quite taken aback.

'What's up, Luke? You look as though you'd seen a ghost.'

For a minute or two the other did not reply. He dropped the paper, strode to the window and back again. Jimmy watched him with increasing surprise.

Luke dropped into a chair and leaned forward.

'Jimmy, old son, do you remember my mentioning an old lady I travelled up to town with – the day I arrived in England?'

'The one you said reminded you of your Aunt Mildred? And then she got run over by a car?'

'That's the one. Listen, Jimmy. The old girl came out with a long rigmarole of how she was going up to Scotland Yard to tell them about a lot of murders. There was a murderer loose in her village – that's what it amounted to, and he's been doing some pretty rapid execution.'

'You didn't tell me she was batty,' said Jimmy.

'I didn't think she was.'

'Oh, come now, old boy, wholesale murder –'

Luke said impatiently:

'I didn't think she was off her head. I thought she was just letting her imagination run away with her like old ladies sometimes do.'

'Well, yes, I suppose that might have been it. But she was probably a bit touched as well, I should think.'

'Never mind what *you* think, Jimmy. At the moment, *I'm* telling *you*, see?'

'Oh, quite – quite – get on with it.'

'She was quite circumstantial, mentioned one or two victims by name and then explained that what had really rattled her was the fact that she knew who the next victim was going to be.'

'Yes?' said Jimmy encouragingly.

'Sometimes a name sticks in your head for some silly reason or other. This name stuck in mine because I linked it up with a silly nursery rhyme they used to sing to me when I was a kid. *Fiddle de dee, fiddle de dee, the fly has married the bumble bee.*'

'Very intellectual, I'm sure, but what's the point?'

'The point, my good ass, is that the man's name was Humbleby – Dr Humbleby. My old lady said Dr Humbleby would be the next, and she was distressed because he was "such a good man". The name stuck in my head because of the aforementioned rhyme.'

'Well?' said Jimmy.

'Well, look at this.'

Luke passed over the paper, his finger pressed against an entry in the column of deaths.

HUMBLEBY. – On June 13, suddenly, at his residence, Sandgate,

*Wychwood-under-Ashe, JOHN EDWARD HUMBLEBY, MD, beloved
husband of JESSIE ROSE HUMBLEBY. Funeral Friday. No flowers,
by request.*

'You see, Jimmy? That's the name and the place and he's a doctor.
What do you make of it?'

Jimmy took a moment or two to answer. His voice was serious
when he said at last rather uncertainly:

'I suppose it's just a damned odd coincidence.'

'Is it, Jimmy? Is it? Is that all it is?'

Luke began to walk up and down again.

'What else could it be?' asked Jimmy.

Luke wheeled round suddenly.

'Suppose that every word that dear bleating old sheep said
was *true*! Suppose that that fantastic story was just the plain
literal truth!'

'Oh, come now, old boy! That would be a bit thick! Things
like that don't happen.'

'What about the Abercrombie case? Wasn't he supposed to
have done away with a goodish few?'

'More than ever came out,' said Jimmy. 'A pal of mine had
a cousin who was the local coroner. I heard a bit through him.
They got Abercrombie for feeding the local vet with arsenic, then
they dug up his wife and she was full of it, and it's pretty certain
his brother-in-law went the same way – and that wasn't all, by
a long chalk. This pal of mine told me the unofficial view was
that Abercrombie had done away with at least fifteen people in
his time. *Fifteen!*'

'Exactly. So these things *do* happen!'

'Yes, but they don't happen often.'

'How do you know? They may happen a good deal oftener
than you suppose.'

'There speaks the police wallah! Can't you forget you're a
policeman now that you've retired into private life?'

'Once a policeman, always a policeman, I suppose,' said Luke.
'Now look here, Jimmy, supposing that before Abercrombie had
got so foolhardy as fairly to push his murders under the nose of
the police, some dear loquacious old spinster had just simply
guessed what he was up to and had trotted off to tell some one

in authority all about it. Do you suppose they'd have listened to her?'

Jimmy grinned.

'No fear!'

'Exactly. They'd have said she'd got bats in the belfry. Just as *you* said! Or they'd have said, "Too much imagination. Not enough to do." As *I* said! *And both of us, Jimmy, would have been wrong.*'

Lorrimer took a moment or two to consider, then he said:

'What's the position exactly – as it appears to you?'

Luke said slowly:

'The case stands like this. I was told a story – an improbable, but not an impossible story. One piece of evidence, the death of Dr Humbleby, supports that story. And there's one other significant fact. Miss Pinkerton was going to Scotland Yard with this improbable story of hers. *But she didn't get there.* She was run over and killed by a car that didn't stop.'

Jimmy objected.

'You don't know that she didn't get there. She might have been killed after her visit, not before.'

'She might have been, yes – but I don't think she was.'

'That's pure supposition. It boils down to this – you believe in this – this melodrama.'

Luke shook his head sharply.

'No, I don't say that. All I say is, there's a case for investigation.'

'In other words, *you* are going to Scotland Yard.'

'No, it hasn't come to that yet – not nearly. As you say, this man Humbleby's death may be merely a coincidence.'

'Then what, may I ask, is the idea?'

'The idea is to go down to this place and look into the matter.'

'So that's the idea, is it?'

'Don't you agree that that is the only sensible way to set about it?'

Jimmy stared at him, then he said:

'Are you *serious* about this business, Luke?'

'Absolutely.'

'Suppose the whole thing's a mare's nest?'

'That would be the best thing that could happen.'

'Yes, of course . . .' Jimmy frowned. 'But you don't think it is, do you?'

'My dear fellow, I'm keeping an open mind.' Jimmy was silent for a minute or two. Then he said:

'Got any plan? I mean, you'll have to have some *reason* for suddenly arriving in this place.'

'Yes, I suppose I shall.'

'No "suppose" about it. Do you realize what a small English country town is like? Any one new sticks out a mile!'

'I shall have to adopt a disguise,' said Luke with a sudden grin. 'What do you suggest? Artist? Hardly – I can't draw, let alone paint.'

'You could be a modern artist,' suggested Jimmy. 'Then that wouldn't matter.'

But Luke was intent on the matter in hand.

'An author? Do authors go to strange country inns to write? They might, I suppose. A fisherman, perhaps – but I'll have to find out if there's a handy river. An invalid ordered country air? I don't look the part, and anyway every one goes to a nursing home nowadays. I might be looking for a house in the neighbourhood. But that's not very good. Hang it all, Jimmy, there must be *some* plausible reason for a hearty stranger to descend upon an English village?'

Jimmy said:

'Wait a sec – give me that paper again.'

Taking it, he gave it a cursory glance and announced triumphantly:

'I thought so! Luke, old boy – to put it in a nutshell – I'll fix you OK. Everything's as easy as winking!'

Luke wheeled round.

'What?'

Jimmy was continuing with modest pride:

'I thought something struck a chord! Wychwood-under-Ashe. Of course! The very place!'

'Have you, by any chance, a pal who knows the coroner there?'

'Not this time. Better than that, my boy. Nature, as you know, has endowed me plentifully with aunts and cousins – my father having been one of a family of thirteen. Now listen to this: *I have a cousin in Wychwood-under-Ashe.*'

'Jimmy, you're a blinking marvel.'

'It is pretty good, isn't it?' said Jimmy modestly.

'Tell me about him.'

'It's a her. Her name's Bridget Conway. For the last two years she's been secretary to Lord Whitfield.'

'The man who owns those nasty little weekly papers?'

'That's right. Rather a nasty little man too! Pompous! He was born in Wychwood-under-Ashe, and being the kind of snob who rams his birth and breeding down your throat and glories in being self-made, he has returned to his home village, bought up the only big house in the neighbourhood (it belonged to Bridget's family originally, by the way) and is busy making the place into a "model estate".'

'And your cousin is his secretary?'

'She was,' said Jimmy darkly. 'Now she's gone one better! She's engaged to him!'

'Oh,' said Luke, rather taken aback.

'He's a catch, of course,' said Jimmy. 'Rolling in money. Bridget took rather a toss over some fellow – it pretty well knocked the romance out of her. I dare say this will pan out very well. She'll probably be kind of firm with him and he'll eat out of her hand.'

'And where do I come in?'

Jimmy replied promptly.

'You go down there to stay – you'd better be another cousin. Bridget's got so many that one more or less won't matter. I'll fix that up with her all right. She and I have always been pals. Now for your reason for going there – witchcraft, my boy.'

'Witchcraft?'

'Folklore, local superstitions – all that sort of thing. Wychwood-under-Ashe has got rather a reputation that way. One of the last places where they had a Witches' Sabbath – witches were still burnt there in the last century – all sorts of traditions. You're writing a book, see? Correlating the customs of the Mayang Straits and old English folklore – points of resemblance, etc. You know the sort of stuff. Go round with a notebook and interview the oldest inhabitant about local superstitions and customs. They're quite used to that sort of thing down there, and if you're staying at Ashe Manor it vouches for you.'

'What about Lord Whitfield?'

'He'll be all right. He's quite uneducated and completely credulous – actually believes things he reads in his own papers. Anyway Bridget will fix him. Bridget's all right. I'll answer for her.'

Luke drew a deep breath.

'Jimmy, old scout, it looks as though the thing is going to be easy. You're a wonder. If you can really fix up with your cousin –'

'That will be absolutely OK. Leave it to me.'

'I'm no end grateful to you.'

Jimmy said:

'All I ask is, if you're hunting down a homicidal murderer, let me be in at the death!'

He added sharply:

'What is it?'

Luke said slowly:

'Just something I remembered my old lady saying to me. I'd said to her that it was a bit thick to do a lot of murders and get away with it, and she answered that I was wrong – that it was very easy to kill . . .' He stopped, and then said slowly, 'I wonder if that's true, Jimmy? I wonder if it is –'

'What?'

'*Easy to kill . . .*'

CHAPTER 3

WITCH WITHOUT BROOMSTICK

I

The sun was shining when Luke came over the hill and down into the little country town of Wychwood-under-Ashe. He had bought a second-hand Standard Swallow, and he stopped for a moment on the brow of the hill and switched off the engine.

The summer day was warm and sunny. Below him was the village, singularly unspoilt by recent developments. It lay innocently and peacefully in the sunlight – mainly composed of a long straggling street that ran along under the overhanging brow of Ashe Ridge.

It seemed singularly remote, strangely untouched. Luke thought, 'I'm probably mad. The whole thing's fantastic.'

Had he really come here solemnly to hunt down a killer – simply on the strength of some garrulous ramblings on the part of an old lady, and a chance obituary notice?

He shook his head.

'Surely these things don't happen,' he murmured. 'Or – do they? Luke, my boy, it's up to you to find out if you're the world's most credulous prize ass, or if your policeman's nose has led you hot on the scent.'

He switched on the engine, threw in the gear and drove gently down the twisting road and so entered the main street.

Wychwood, as has been said, consists mainly of its one principal street. There were shops, small Georgian houses, prim and aristocratic, with whitened steps and polished knockers, there were picturesque cottages with flower gardens. There was an inn, the Bells and Motley, standing a little back from the street. There was a village green and a duck pond, and presiding over them a dignified Georgian house which Luke thought at first must be his destination, Ashe Manor. But on coming nearer he saw that there was a large painted board announcing that it was the Museum and Library. Farther on there was an anachronism, a large white modern building, austere and irrelevant to the cheerful haphazardness of the rest of the place. It was, Luke gathered, a local Institute and Lads' Club.

It was at this point that he stopped and asked the way to his destination.

He was told that Ashe Manor was about half a mile farther on – he would see the gates on his right.

Luke continued his course. He found the gates easily – they were of new and elaborate wrought-iron. He drove in, caught a gleam of red brick through the trees, and turned a corner of the drive to be stupefied by the appalling and incongruous castellated mass that greeted his eyes.

While he was contemplating the nightmare, the sun went in. He became suddenly conscious of the overlying menace of Ashe Ridge. There was a sudden sharp gust of wind, blowing back the leaves of the trees, and at that moment a girl came round the corner of the castellated mansion.

Her black hair was blown up off her head by the sudden gust and Luke was reminded of a picture he had once seen – Nevinson's 'Witch'. The long pale delicate face, the black hair flying up to the stars. He could see this girl on a broomstick flying up to the moon . . .

She came straight towards him.

'You must be Luke Fitzwilliam. I'm Bridget Conway.'

He took the hand she held out. He could see her now as she was – not in a sudden moment of fantasy. Tall, slender, a long delicate face with slightly hollow cheek-bones – ironic black brows – black eyes and hair. She was like a delicate etching, he thought – poignant and beautiful.

He had had an acknowledged picture at the back of his mind during his voyage home to England – a picture of an English girl flushed and sunburnt – stroking a horse's neck, stooping to weed a herbaceous border, sitting holding out her hands to the blaze of a wood fire. It had been a warm gracious vision . . .

Now – he didn't know if he liked Bridget Conway or not – but he knew that that secret picture wavered and broke up – became meaningless and foolish . . .

He said:

'How d'you do? I must apologize for wishing myself on you like this. Jimmy would have it that you wouldn't mind.'

'Oh, we don't. We're delighted.' She smiled, a sudden curving smile that brought the corners of her long mouth half-way up her cheeks. 'Jimmy and I always stand in together. And if you're writing a book on folklore this is a splendid place. All sorts of legends and picturesque spots.'

'Splendid,' said Luke.

They went together towards the house. Luke stole another glance at it. He discerned now traces of a sober Queen Anne dwelling overlaid and smothered by the florid magnificence. He remembered that Jimmy had mentioned the house as having originally belonged to Bridget's family. That, he thought grimly, was in its unadorned days. Stealing a glance at the line of her profile, at the long beautiful hands, he wondered.

She was about twenty-eight or -nine, he supposed. And she had brains. And she was one of those people about whom you knew absolutely nothing unless they chose that you should . . .

Inside, the house was comfortable and in good taste – the good taste of a first-class decorator. Bridget Conway led the way to a room with bookshelves and comfortable chairs where a tea table stood near the window with two people sitting by it.

She said:

'Gordon, this is Luke, a sort of cousin of a cousin of mine.'

Lord Whitfield was a small man with a semi-bald head. His face was round and ingenuous, with a pouting mouth and boiled gooseberry eyes. He was dressed in careless-looking country clothes. They were unkind to his figure, which ran mostly to stomach.

He greeted Luke with affability.

'Glad to see you – very glad. Just come back from the East, I hear? Interesting place. Writing a book, so Bridget tells me. They say too many books are written nowadays. I say no – always room for a good one.'

Bridget said, 'My aunt, Mrs Anstruther,' and Luke shook hands with a middle-aged woman with a rather foolish mouth.

Mrs Anstruther, as Luke soon learned, was devoted body and soul to gardening. She never talked of anything else, and her mind was constantly occupied by considerations of whether some rare plant was likely to do well in the place she intended to put it.

After acknowledging the introduction, she said now:

'You know, Gordon, the ideal spot for a rockery would be just beyond the rose garden, and then you could have the most marvellous water garden where the stream comes through that dip.'

Lord Whitfield stretched himself back in his chair.

'You fix all that with Bridget,' he said easily. 'Rock plants are niggly little things, I think – but that doesn't matter.'

Bridget said:

'Rock plants aren't sufficiently in the grand manner for you, Gordon.'

She poured out some tea for Luke and Lord Whitfield said placidly:

'That's right. They're not what I call good value for money. Little bits of flowers you can hardly see . . . I like a nice show in a conservatory, or some good beds of scarlet geraniums.'

Mrs Anstruther, who possessed *par excellence* the gift of continuing with her own subject undisturbed by that of anyone else, said:

'I believe those new rock roses would do perfectly in this climate,' and proceeded to immerse herself in catalogues.

Throwing his squat little figure back in his chair, Lord Whitfield sipped his tea and studied Luke appraisingly.

'So you write books,' he murmured.

Feeling slightly nervous, Luke was about to enter on explanations when he perceived that Lord Whitfield was not really seeking for information.

'I've often thought,' said his lordship complacently, 'that I'd like to write a book myself.'

'Yes?' said Luke.

'I *could*, mark you,' said Lord Whitfield. 'And a very interesting book it would be. I've come across a lot of interesting people. Trouble is, I haven't got the *time*. I'm a very busy man.'

'Of course. You must be.'

'You wouldn't believe what I've got on my shoulders,' said Lord Whitfield. 'I take a personal interest in each one of my publications. I consider that I'm responsible for moulding the public mind. Next week millions of people will be thinking and feeling just exactly what I've intended to make them feel and think. That's a very solemn thought. That means responsibility. Well, I don't mind responsibility. I'm not afraid of it. I can *do* with responsibility.'

Lord Whitfield swelled out his chest, attempted to draw in his stomach, and glared amiably at Luke.

Bridget Conway said lightly:

'You're a great man, Gordon. Have some more tea.'

Lord Whitfield replied simply:

'I *am* a great man. No, I won't have any more tea.'

Then, descending from his own Olympian heights to the level of more ordinary mortals, he inquired kindly of his guest:

'Know anybody round this part of the world?'

Luke shook his head. Then, on an impulse, and feeling that the sooner he began to get down to his job the better, he added:

'At least, there's a man here that I promised to look up – friend of friends of mine. Man called Humbleby. He's a doctor.'

'Oh!' Lord Whitfield struggled upright in his chair. 'Dr Humbleby? Pity.'

'What's a pity?'

'Died about a week ago,' said Lord Whitfield.

'Oh, dear,' said Luke. 'I'm sorry about that.'

'Don't think you'd have cared for him,' said Lord Whitfield. 'Opinionated, pestilential, muddle-headed old fool.'

'Which means,' put in Bridget, 'that he disagreed with Gordon.'

'Question of our water supply,' said Lord Whitfield. 'I may tell you, Mr Fitzwilliam, that I'm a public-spirited man. I've got the welfare of this town at heart. I was born here. Yes, born in this very town –'

With chagrin Luke perceived that they had left the topic of Dr Humbleby and had reverted to the topic of Lord Whitfield.

'I'm not ashamed of it and I don't care who knows it,' went on that gentleman. 'I had none of your natural advantages. My father kept a boot-shop – yes, a plain boot-shop. And I served in that shop when I was a young lad. I raised myself by my own efforts, Fitzwilliam – I determined to get out of the rut – and I *got* out of the rut! Perseverance, hard work and the help of God – that's what did it! That's what made me what I am today.'

Exhaustive details of Lord Whitfield's career were produced for Luke's benefit and the former wound up triumphantly:

'And here I am and the whole world's welcome to know how I've got here! I'm not ashamed of my beginnings – no, sir – I've come back here where I was born. Do you know what stands where my father's shop used to be? A fine building built and endowed by *me* – Institute, Boys' Clubs, everything tip-top and up to date. Employed the best architect in the country! I must say he's made a bare plain job of it – looks like a workhouse or a prison to me – but they say it's all right, so I suppose it must be.'

'Cheer up,' said Bridget. 'You had your own way over this house!'

Lord Whitfield chuckled appreciatively.

'Yes, they tried to put it over on me here! Carry out the original spirit of the building. No, I said, I'm going to *live* in the place, and I want something to *show* for my money! When one architect wouldn't do what I wanted I sacked him and got another. The fellow I got in the end understood my ideas pretty well.'

'He pandered to your worst flights of imagination,' said Bridget.

'She'd have liked the place left as it was,' said Lord Whitfield. He patted her arm. 'No use living in the past, my dear. Those old Georges didn't know much. I didn't want a plain red-brick house. I always had a fancy for a castle – and now I've got one!' He added, 'I know my taste isn't very classy, so I gave a good firm *carte blanche* to do the inside, and I must say they haven't done too badly – though some of it is a bit drab.'

'Well,' said Luke, a little at a loss for words, 'it's a great thing to know what you want.'

'And I usually get it too,' said the other, chuckling.

'You nearly didn't get your way about the water scheme,' Bridget reminded him.

'Oh, that!' said Lord Whitfield. 'Humbleby was a fool. These elderly men are inclined to be pig-headed. They won't listen to reason.'

'Dr Humbleby was rather an outspoken man, wasn't he?' Luke ventured. 'He made a good many enemies that way, I should imagine.'

'N-no, I don't know that I should say that,' demurred Lord Whitfield, rubbing his nose. 'Eh, Bridget?'

'He was very popular with every one, I always thought,' said Bridget. 'I only saw him when he came about my ankle that time, but I thought he was a dear.'

'Yes, he was popular enough on the whole,' admitted Lord Whitfield. 'Though I know one or two people who had it in for him. Pig-headedness again.'

'One or two of the people living here?'

Lord Whitfield nodded.

'Lots of little feuds and cliques in a place like this,' he said.

'Yes, I suppose so,' said Luke. He hesitated, uncertain of his next step.

'What sort of people live here mostly?' he queried.

It was rather a weak question, but he got an instant response.

'Relicts, mostly,' said Bridget. 'Clergymen's daughters and sisters and wives. Doctors' dittoes. About six women to every man.'

'But there are *some* men?' hazarded Luke.

'Oh, yes, there's Mr Abbot, the solicitor, and young Dr Thomas, Dr Humbleby's partner, and Mr Wake, the rector, and – who else is there, Gordon? Oh! Mr Ellsworthy, who keeps the antique shop and who is too, too terribly sweet! And Major Horton and his bulldogs.'

'There's somebody else I believe my friends mentioned as living down here,' said Luke. 'They said she was a nice old pussy but talked a lot.'

Bridget laughed. 'That applies to half the village!'

'What was the name now? I've got it. Pinkerton.'

Lord Whitfield said with a hoarse chuckle:

'Really, you've no luck! She's dead too. Got run over the other day in London. Killed outright.'

'You seem to have a lot of deaths here,' said Luke lightly.

Lord Whitfield bridled immediately.

'Not at all. One of the healthiest places in England. Can't count accidents. They may happen to anyone.'

But Bridget Conway said thoughtfully:

'As a matter of fact, Gordon, there *have* been a lot of deaths in the last year. They're always having funerals.'

'Nonsense, my dear.'

Luke said:

'Was Dr Humbleby's death an accident too?'

Lord Whitfield shook his head.

'Oh, no,' he said. 'Humbleby died of acute septicæmia. Just like a doctor. Scratched his finger with a rusty nail or something – paid no attention to it, and it turned septic. He was dead in three days.'

'Doctors are rather like that,' said Bridget. 'And of course, they're very liable to infection, I suppose, if they don't take care. It was sad, though. His wife was broken-hearted.'

'No good rebelling against the will of providence,' said Lord Whitfield easily.

II

'But was it the will of providence?' Luke asked himself later as
he changed into his dinner jacket. Septicæmia? Perhaps. A very
sudden death, though.

And there echoed through his head Bridget Conway's lightly
spoken words:

'*There have been a lot of deaths in the last year.*'

CHAPTER 4

....
LUKE MAKES A BEGINNING

Luke had thought out his plan of campaign with some care, and
prepared to put it into action without more ado when he came
down to breakfast the following morning.

The gardening aunt was not in evidence, but Lord Whitfield
was eating kidneys and drinking coffee, and Bridget Conway had
finished her meal and was standing at the window, looking out.

After good-mornings had been exchanged and Luke had sat
down with a plentifully heaped plate of eggs and bacon, he
began:

'I must get to work,' he said. 'Difficult thing is to induce people
to talk. You know what I mean – not people like you and –
er – Bridget.' (He remembered just in time not to say Miss
Conway.) 'You'd *tell* me anything you knew – but the trouble
is you wouldn't *know* the things I want to know – that is the local
superstitions. You'd hardly believe the amount of superstition that
still lingers in out-of-the-way parts of the world. Why, there's a
village in Devonshire. The rector had to remove some old granite
menhirs that stood by the church because the people persisted in
marching round them in some old ritual every time there was a
death. Extraordinary how old heathen rites persist.'

'Dare say you're right,' said Lord Whitfield. 'Education, that's
what people need. Did I tell you that I'd endowed a very fine
library here? Used to be the old manor house – was going for
a song – now it's one of the finest libraries –'

Luke firmly quelled the tendency of the conversation to turn
in the direction of Lord Whitfield's doings.

'Splendid,' he said heartily. 'Good work. You've evidently realized the background of old-world ignorance there is here. Of course, from my point of view, that's just what I want. Old customs – old wives' tales – hints of the old rituals such as –'

Here followed almost verbatim a page of a work that Luke had read up for the occasion.

'Deaths are the most hopeful line,' he ended. 'Burial rites and customs always survive longer than any others. Besides, for some reason or other, village people always like talking about deaths.'

'They enjoy funerals,' agreed Bridget from the window.

'I thought I'd make that my starting-point,' went on Luke. 'If I can get a list of recent demises in the parish, track down the relatives and get into conversation, I've no doubt I shall soon get a hint of what I'm after. Whom had I better get the data from – the parson?'

'Mr Wake would probably be very interested,' said Bridget. 'He's quite an old dear and a bit of an antiquary. He could give you a lot of stuff, I expect.'

Luke had a momentary qualm during which he hoped that the clergyman might not be so efficient an antiquary as to expose his own pretensions.

Aloud he said heartily:

'Good. You've no idea, I suppose, of likely people who've died during the last year.'

Bridget murmured:

'Let me see. Carter, of course. He was the landlord of the Seven Stars, that nasty little pub down by the river.'

'A drunken ruffian,' said Lord Whitfield. 'One of these socialistic, abusive brutes, a good riddance.'

'And Mrs Rose, the laundress,' went on Bridget. 'And little Tommy Pierce – he was a nasty little boy if you like. Oh, of course, and that girl Amy what's-her-name.'

Her voice changed slightly as she uttered the last name.

'Amy?' said Luke.

'Amy Gibbs. She was housemaid here and then she went to Miss Waynflete. There was an inquest on her.'

'Why?'

'Fool of a girl mixed up some bottles in the dark,' said Lord Whitfield.

'She took what she thought was cough mixture and it was hat paint,' explained Bridget.

Luke raised his eyebrows.

'Somewhat of a tragedy.'

Bridget said:

'There was some idea of her having done it on purpose. Some row with a young man.'

She spoke slowly – almost reluctantly.

There was a pause. Luke felt instinctively the presence of some unspoken feeling weighing down the atmosphere.

He thought:

'Amy Gibbs? Yes, that was one of the names old Miss Pinkerton mentioned.'

She had also mentioned a small boy – Tommy some one – of whom she had evidently held a low opinion (this, it seemed, was shared by Bridget!) And yes – he was almost sure – the name Carter had been spoken too.

Rising, he said lightly:

'Talking like this makes me feel rather ghoulish – as though I dabbled only in graveyards. Marriage customs are interesting too – but rather more difficult to introduce into conversation unconcernedly.'

'I should imagine that was likely,' said Bridget with a faint twitch of the lips.

'Ill-wishing or overlooking, there's another interesting subject,' went on Luke with a would-be show of enthusiasm. 'You often get that in these old-world places. Know of any gossip of that kind here?'

Lord Whitfield slowly shook his head. Bridget Conway said:

'We shouldn't be likely to hear of things like that –'

Luke took it up almost before she finished speaking.

'No doubt about it, I've got to move in lower social spheres to get what I want. I'll be off to the vicarage first and see what I can get there. After that perhaps a visit to the – Seven Stars, did you say? And what about the small boy of unpleasant habits? Did he leave any sorrowing relatives?'

'Mrs Pierce keeps a tobacco and paper shop in High Street.'

'That,' said Luke, 'is nothing less than providential. Well, I'll be on my way.'

With a swift graceful movement Bridget moved from the window.

'I think,' she said, 'I'll come with you, if you don't mind.'

'Of course not.'

He said it as heartily as possible, but he wondered if she had noticed that, just for a moment, he had been taken aback.

It would have been easier for him to handle an elderly antiquarian clergyman without an alert discerning intelligence by his side.

'Oh well,' he thought to himself. 'It's up to me to do my stuff convincingly.'

Bridget said:

'Will you just wait, Luke, while I change my shoes?'

Luke – the Christian name uttered so easily gave him a queer warm feeling. And yet what else could she have called him? Since she had agreed to Jimmy's scheme of cousinship she could hardly call him Mr Fitzwilliam. He thought suddenly and uneasily, 'What does she think of it all? In God's name what does she think?'

Queer that that had not worried him beforehand. Jimmy's cousin had just been a convenient abstraction – a lay figure. He had hardly visualized her, just accepted his friend's dictum that 'Bridget would be all right.'

He had thought of her – if he had thought of her at all – as a little blonde secretary person – astute enough to have captured a rich man's fancy.

Instead she had force, brains, a cool clear intelligence and he had no idea what she was thinking of him. He thought: *She's not an easy person to deceive.*

'I'm ready now.'

She had joined him so silently that he had not heard her approach. She wore no hat, and there was no net on her hair. As they stepped out from the house the wind, sweeping round the corner of the castellated monstrosity, caught her long black hair and whipped it into a sudden frenzy round her face.

She said smiling:

'You need me to show you the way.'

'It's very kind of you,' he answered punctiliously.

And wondered if he had imagined a sudden swiftly passing ironic smile.

Looking back at the battlements behind him, he said irritably: 'What an abomination! Couldn't anyone stop him?'

Bridget answered: 'An Englishman's house is his castle – literally so in Gordon's case! He adores it.'

Conscious that the remark was in bad taste, yet unable to control his tongue, he said:

'It's your old home, isn't it? Do you "adore" to see it the way it is now?'

She looked at him then – a steady slightly amused look it was.

'I hate to destroy the dramatic picture you are building up,' she murmured. 'But actually I left here when I was two and a half, so you see the old home motive doesn't apply. I can't even remember this place.'

'You're right,' said Luke. 'Forgive the lapse into film language.'

She laughed.

'Truth,' she said, 'is seldom romantic.'

And there was a sudden bitter scorn in her voice that startled him. He flushed a deep red under his tan, then realized suddenly that the bitterness had not been aimed at him. It was her own scorn and her own bitterness. Luke was wisely silent. But he wondered a good deal about Bridget Conway . . .

Five minutes brought them to the church and to the vicarage that adjoined it. They found the vicar in his study.

Alfred Wake was a small stooping old man with very mild blue eyes, and an absent-minded but courteous air. He seemed pleased but a little surprised by the visit.

'Mr Fitzwilliam is staying with us at Ashe Manor,' said Bridget, 'and he wants to consult you about a book he is writing.'

Mr Wake turned his mild inquiring eyes towards the younger man, and Luke plunged into explanations.

He was nervous – doubly so. Nervous in the first place because this man had no doubt a far deeper knowledge of folklore and superstitious rites and customs than one could acquire by merely hurriedly cramming from a haphazard collection of books. Secondly he was nervous because Bridget Conway was standing by listening.

Luke was relieved to find that Mr Wake's special interest was

Roman remains. He confessed gently that he knew very little of medieval folklore and witchcraft. He mentioned the existence of certain items in the history of Wychwood, offered to take Luke to the particular ledge of hill where it was said the Witches' Sabbaths had been held, but expressed himself regretful that he could add no special information of his own.

Inwardly much relieved, Luke expressed himself as somewhat disappointed, and then plunged into inquiries as to death-bed superstitions.

Mr Wake shook his head gently.

'I am afraid I should be the last person to know about those. My parishioners would be careful to keep anything unorthodox from my ears.'

'That's so, of course.'

'But I've no doubt, all the same, there *is* a lot of superstition still rife. These village communities are very backward.'

Luke plunged boldly.

'I've been asking Miss Conway for a list of all the recent deaths she could remember. I thought I might get at something that way. I suppose you could supply me with a list, so that I could pick out the likelies.'

'Yes – yes – that could be managed. Giles, our sexton, a good fellow but sadly deaf, could help you there. Let me see now. There have been a good many – a good many – a treacherous spring and a hard winter behind it – and then a good many accidents – quite a cycle of bad luck there seems to have been.'

'Sometimes,' said Luke, 'a cycle of bad luck is attributed to the presence of a particular person.'

'Yes, yes. The old story of Jonah. But I do not think there have been any strangers here – nobody, that is to say, outstanding in any way, and I've certainly never heard any rumour of such feeling – but then again, as I said, perhaps I shouldn't. Now let me see – quite recently we have had Dr Humbleby and poor Lavinia Pinkerton – a fine man, Dr Humbleby –'

Bridget put in:

'Mr Fitzwilliam knows friends of his.'

'Do you indeed? Very sad. His loss will be much felt. A man with many friends.'

'But surely a man with some enemies too,' said Luke. 'I'm

only going by what I've heard my friends say,' he went on hastily.

Mr Wake sighed.

'A man who spoke his mind – and a man who wasn't always very tactful, shall we say –' he shook his head. 'It does get people's backs up. But he was greatly beloved among the poorer classes.'

Luke said carelessly:

'You know I always feel that one of the most unpalatable facts to be faced in life, is the fact that every death that occurs means a gain to someone – I don't mean only financially.'

The vicar nodded thoughtfully.

'I see your meaning, yes. We read in an obituary notice that a man is regretted by everybody, but that can only be true very rarely I fear. In Dr Humbleby's case, there is no denying that his partner, Dr Thomas, will find his position very much improved by Dr Humbleby's death.'

'How is that?'

'Thomas, I believe, is a very capable fellow – certainly Humbleby always said so, but he didn't get on here very well. He was, I think, over-shadowed by Humbleby who was a man of very definite magnetism. Thomas appeared rather colourless in contrast. He didn't impress his patients at all. I think he worried over it, too, and that made him worse – more nervous and tongue-tied. As a matter of fact I've noticed an astonishing difference already. More aplomb – more personality. I think he feels a new confidence in himself. He and Humbleby didn't always agree, I believe. Thomas was all for newer methods of treatment and Humbleby preferred to stick to the old ways. There were clashes between them more than once – over that as well as over a matter nearer home – but there, I mustn't gossip –'

Bridget said softly and clearly:

'But I think Mr Fitzwilliam would like you to gossip!'

Luke shot her a quick disturbed look.

Mr Wake shook his head doubtfully, and then went on, smiling a little in deprecation.

'I am afraid one learns to take too much interest in one's neighbours' affairs. Rose Humbleby is a very pretty girl. One doesn't wonder that Geoffrey Thomas lost his heart. And of course Humbleby's point of view was quite understandable too – the girl is young and buried away here she hadn't much chance of seeing other men.'

'He objected?' said Luke.

'Very definitely. Said they were far too young. And of course young people resent being told that! There was a very definite coldness between the two men. But I must say that I'm sure Dr Thomas was deeply distressed at his partner's unexpected death.'

'Septicæmia, Lord Whitfield told me.'

'Yes – just a little scratch that got infected. Doctors run grave risks in the course of their profession, Mr Fitzwilliam.'

'They do indeed,' said Luke.

Mr Wake gave a sudden start.

'But I have wandered a long way from what we were talking about,' he said. 'A gossiping old man, I am afraid. We were speaking of the survival of pagan death customs and of recent deaths. There was Lavinia Pinkerton – one of our more kindly Church helpers. Then there was that poor girl, Amy Gibbs – you might discover something in your line there, Mr Fitzwilliam – there was just a suspicion, you know, that it might have been suicide – and there are certain rather eerie rites in connection with that type of death. There is an aunt – not, I fear, a very estimable woman, and not very much attached to her niece – but a great talker.'

'Valuable,' said Luke.

'Then there was Tommy Pierce – he was in the choir at one time – a beautiful treble – quite angelic – but not a very angelic boy otherwise, I am afraid. We had to get rid of him in the end, he made the other boys behave so badly. Poor lad, I'm afraid he was not very much liked anywhere. He was dismissed from the post office where we got him a job as telegraph boy. He was in Mr Abbot's office for a while, but there again he was dismissed very soon – interfered with some confidential papers, I believe. Then, of course, he was at Ashe Manor for a time, wasn't he, Miss Conway, as garden boy, and Lord Whitfield had to discharge him for gross impertinence. I was so sorry for his mother – a very decent hard-working soul. Miss Waynflete very kindly got him some odd window-cleaning work. Lord Whitfield objected at first, then suddenly he gave in – actually it was sad that he did so.'

'Why?'

'Because the boy was killed that way. He was cleaning the top windows of the library (the old Hall, you know) and tried some silly fooling – dancing on the window ledge or something of that sort – lost his balance, or else became dizzy, and fell. A nasty business! He never recovered consciousness and died a few hours after they got him to hospital.'

'Did any one see him fall?' asked Luke with interest.

'No. He was on the garden side – not the front of the house. They estimate he lay there for about half an hour before any one found him.'

'Who did find him?'

'Miss Pinkerton. You remember, the lady I mentioned just now who was unfortunately killed in a street accident the other day. Poor soul, she was terribly upset. A nasty experience! She had obtained permission to take a cutting of some plants and found the boy there lying where he had fallen.'

'It must have been a very unpleasant shock,' said Luke thoughtfully.

'A greater shock,' he thought to himself, 'than *you* know.'

'A young life cut short is a very sad thing,' said the old man, shaking his head. 'Tommy's faults may have been mainly due to high spirits.'

'He was a disgusting bully,' said Bridget. 'You know he was, Mr Wake. Always tormenting cats and stray puppies and pinching other little boys.'

'I know – I know.' Mr Wake shook his head sadly. 'But you know, my dear Miss Conway, sometimes cruelty is not so much innate as due to the fact that imagination is slow in ripening. That is why if you conceive of a grown man with the mentality of a child you realize that the cunning and brutality of a lunatic may be quite unrealized by the man himself. A lack of growth somewhere, that, I am convinced, is at the root of much of the cruelty and stupid brutality in the world today. One must put away childish things –'

He shook his head and spread out his hands.

Bridget said in a voice suddenly hoarse:

'Yes, you're right. I know what you mean. A man who is a child is the most frightening thing in the world . . .'

Luke looked at her with some curiosity. He was convinced that she was thinking of some particular person, and although Lord Whitfield was in some respects exceedingly childish, he did not believe she was thinking of him. Lord Whitfield was slightly ridiculous, but he was certainly not frightening.

Luke Fitzwilliam wondered very much whom the person Bridget was thinking of might be.

CHAPTER 5

VISIT TO MISS WAYNFLETE

Mr Wake murmured a few more names to himself.

'Let me see now – poor Mrs Rose, and old Bell and that child of the Elkins and Harry Carter – they're not all my people, you understand. Mrs Rose and Carter were dissenters. And that cold spell in March took off poor old Ben Stanbury at last – ninety-two he was.'

'Amy Gibbs died in April,' said Bridget.

'Yes, poor girl – a sad mistake to happen.'

Luke looked up to find Bridget watching him. She lowered her eyes quickly. He thought, with some annoyance:

'There's something here that I haven't got on to. Something to do with this girl Amy Gibbs.'

When they had taken leave of the vicar and were outside again, he said:

'Just who and what *was* Amy Gibbs?'

Bridget took a minute or two to answer. Then she said – and Luke noticed the slight constraint in her voice:

'Amy was one of the most inefficient housemaids I have ever known.'

'That's why she got the sack?'

'No. She stayed out after hours playing about with some young man. Gordon has very moral and old-fashioned views. Sin in his view does not take place until after eleven o'clock, but then it is rampant. So he gave the girl notice and she was impertinent about it!'

Luke asked: 'A good-looking girl?'

'Very good-looking.'

'She's the one who swallowed hat paint in mistake for cough mixture?'

'Yes.'

'Rather a stupid thing to do?' Luke hazarded.

'Very stupid.'

'Was she stupid?'

'No, she was quite a sharp girl.'

Luke stole a look at her. He was puzzled. Her replies were given in an even tone, without emphasis or even much interest. But behind what she said, there was, he felt convinced, something not put into words.

At that moment Bridget stopped to speak to a tall man who swept off his hat and greeted her with breezy heartiness.

Bridget, after a word or two, introduced Luke.

'This is my cousin, Mr Fitzwilliam, who is staying at the Manor. He's down here to write a book. This is Mr Abbot.'

Luke looked at Mr Abbot with some interest. This was the solicitor who had employed Tommy Pierce.

Luke had a somewhat illogical prejudice against lawyers in general – based on the grounds that so many politicians were recruited from their ranks. Also their cautious habit of not committing themselves annoyed him. Mr Abbot, however, was not at all the conventional type of lawyer, he was neither thin, spare, nor tight-lipped. He was a big florid man, dressed in tweeds with a hearty manner and a jovial effusiveness. There were little creases at the corners of his eyes, and the eyes themselves were more shrewd than one appreciated in a first casual glance.

'Writing a book, eh? Novel?'

'Folklore,' said Bridget.

'You've come to the right place for that,' said the lawyer. 'Wonderfully interesting part of the world here.'

'So I've been led to understand,' said Luke. 'I dare say you could help me a bit. You must come across curious old deeds – or know of some interesting surviving customs.'

'Well, I don't know about that – maybe – maybe –'

'Much belief in ghosts round here?' asked Luke.

'As to that I couldn't say – I really couldn't say.'

'No haunted houses?'

'No – I don't know of anything of that kind.'

'There's the child superstition, of course,' said Luke. 'Death of a boy child – a violent death that is – the boy always walks. Not a girl child – interesting that.'

'Very,' said Mr Abbot. 'I never heard that before.'

Since Luke had just invented it, that was hardly surprising.

'Seems there's a boy here – Tommy something – was in your office at one time. I've reason to believe they think that *he's* walking.'

Mr Abbot's red face turned slightly purple.

'Tommy Pierce? A good for nothing, prying, meddlesome jackanapes.'

'Spirits always seem to be mischievous. Good law-abiding citizens seldom trouble this world after they've left it.'

'Who's seen him – what's this story?'

'These things are difficult to pin down,' said Luke. 'People won't come out into the open with a statement. It's just in the air, so to speak.'

'Yes – yes, I suppose so.'

Luke changed the subject adroitly.

'The real person to get hold of is the local doctor. They hear a lot in the poorer cases they attend. All sorts of superstitions and charms – probably love philtres and all the rest of it.'

'You must get on to Thomas. Good fellow, Thomas, thoroughly up-to-date man. Not like poor old Humbleby.'

'Bit of a reactionary, wasn't he?'

'Absolutely pig-headed – a diehard of the worst description.'

'You had a real row over the water scheme, didn't you?' asked Bridget.

Again a rich ruddy glow suffused Abbot's face.

'Humbleby stood dead in the way of progress,' he said sharply. 'He held out against the scheme! He was pretty rude, too, in what he said. Didn't mince his words. Some of the things he said to me were positively actionable.'

Bridget murmured: 'But lawyers never go to law, do they? They know better.'

Abbot laughed immoderately. His anger subsided as quickly as it had arisen.

'Pretty good, Miss Bridget! And you're not far wrong. We who are in it know too much about law, ha, ha. Well, I must be getting along. Give me a call if you think I can help you in any way, Mr – er –'

'Fitzwilliam,' said Luke. 'Thanks, I will.'

As they walked on Bridget said:

'Your methods, I note, are to make statements and see what they provoke.'

'My methods,' said Luke, 'are not strictly truthful, if that is what you mean?'

'I've noticed that.'

A little uneasy, he hesitated what to say next. But before he could speak, she said:

'If you want to hear more about Amy Gibbs, I can take you to someone who could help you.'

'Who is that?'

'A Miss Waynflete. Amy went there after she left the Manor. She was there when she died.'

'Oh, I see –' he was a little taken aback. 'Well – thank you very much.'

'She lives just here.'

They were crossing the village green. Inclining her head in the direction of the big Georgian house that Luke had noticed the day before, Bridget said: 'That's Wych Hall. It's a library now.'

Adjoining the Hall was a little house that looked rather like a doll's house in proportion. Its steps were dazzlingly white, its knocker shone and its window curtains showed white and prim.

Bridget pushed open the gate and advanced to the steps.

As she did so the front door opened and an elderly woman came out.

She was, Luke thought, completely the country spinster. Her thin form was neatly dressed in a tweed coat and skirt and she wore a grey silk blouse with a cairngorm brooch. Her hat, a conscientious felt, sat squarely upon her well-shaped head. Her face was pleasant and her eyes, through their pince-nez, decidedly intelligent. She reminded Luke of those nimble black goats that one sees in Greece. Her eyes held just that quality of mild inquiring surprise.

'Good morning, Miss Waynflete,' said Bridget. 'This is Mr

Fitzwilliam.' Luke bowed. 'He's writing a book – about deaths and village customs and general gruesomeness.'

'Oh, dear,' said Miss Waynflete. 'How *very* interesting.'

And she beamed encouragingly upon him.

He was reminded of Miss Pinkerton.

'I thought,' said Bridget – and again he noted that curious flat tone in her voice – 'that you might tell him something about Amy.'

'Oh,' said Miss Waynflete. 'About Amy? Yes. About Amy Gibbs.'

He was conscious of a new factor in her expression. She seemed to be thoughtfully summing him up.

Then, as though coming to a decision, she drew back into the hall.

'Do come in,' she said. 'I can go out later. No, no,' in answer to a protest from Luke. 'I had really nothing urgent to do. Just a little unimportant domestic shopping.'

The small drawing-room was exquisitely neat and smelled faintly of burnt lavender. There were some Dresden china shepherds and shepherdesses on the mantelpiece, simpering sweetly. There were framed water-colours, two samplers, and three needlework pictures on the wall. There were some photographs of what were obviously nephews and nieces and some good furniture – a Chippendale desk, some little satinwood tables – and a hideous and rather uncomfortable Victorian sofa.

Miss Waynflete offered her guests chairs and then said apologetically:

'I'm afraid I don't smoke myself, so I have no cigarettes, but do please smoke if you like.'

Luke refused but Bridget promptly lighted a cigarette.

Sitting bolt upright in a chair with carved arms, Miss Waynflete studied her guest for a moment or two and then dropping her eyes as though satisfied, she said:

'You want to know about that poor girl Amy? The whole thing was very sad and caused me a great deal of distress. Such a tragic mistake.'

'Wasn't there some question of – suicide?' asked Luke.

Miss Waynflete shook her head.

'No, no, *that* I cannot believe for a moment. Amy was not at all that type.'

'What type was she?' asked Luke bluntly. 'I'd like to hear your account of her.'

Miss Waynflete said:

'Well, of course, she wasn't at *all* a good servant. But nowadays, really, one is thankful to get *anybody*. She was very slipshod over her work and always wanting to go out – well, of course she was young and girls *are* like that nowadays. They don't seem to realize that their time is their employer's.'

Luke looked properly sympathetic and Miss Waynflete proceeded to develop her theme.

'She wasn't the sort of girl I care for – rather a *bold* type though of course I wouldn't like to say much now that she's dead. One feels un-Christian – though really I don't think that that is a logical reason for suppressing the truth.'

Luke nodded. He realized that Miss Waynflete differed from Miss Pinkerton in having a more logical mind and better processes of thought.

'She was fond of admiration,' went on Miss Waynflete, 'and was inclined to think a lot of herself. Mr Ellsworthy – he keeps the new antique shop but he is actually a gentleman – he dabbles a little in water-colours and he had done one or two sketches of the girl's head – and I think, you know, that rather gave her *ideas*. She was inclined to quarrel with the young man she was engaged to – Jim Harvey. He's a mechanic at the garage and very fond of her.'

Miss Waynflete paused and then went on.

'I shall never forget that dreadful night. Amy had been out of sorts – a nasty cough and one thing and another (those silly cheap silk stockings they will wear and shoes with *paper* soles practically – of course they catch chills) and she'd been to the doctor that afternoon.'

Luke asked quickly:

'Dr Humbleby or Dr Thomas?'

'Dr Thomas. And he gave her the bottle of cough mixture that she brought back with her. Something quite harmless, a stock mixture, I believe. She went to bed early and it must have been about one in the morning when the noise began – an awful kind of choking scream. I got up and went to her door but it was locked on the inside. I called to her but couldn't get any answer. Cook was with me and we were both terribly upset. And then we went to the front door and luckily there was Reed (our constable) just passing on his beat, and we called to him. He went round the back of the house and managed to climb up on the outhouse roof, and as her window was open he got in quite easily that way and unlocked the door. Poor girl, it was terrible. They couldn't do anything for her, and she died in Hospital a few hours later.'

'And it was – what – hat paint?'

'Yes. Oxalic acid poisoning is what they called it. The bottle was about the same size as the cough linctus one. The latter was on her washstand and the hat paint was by her bed. She must have picked up the wrong bottle and put it by her in the dark ready to take if she felt badly. That was the theory at the inquest.'

Miss Waynflete stopped. Her intelligent goat's eyes looked at him, and he was aware that some particular significance lay behind them. He had the feeling that she was leaving some part of the story untold – and a stronger feeling that, for some reason, she wanted him to be aware of the fact.

There was a silence – a long and rather difficult silence. Luke felt like an actor who does not know his cue. He said rather weakly:

'And you don't think it was suicide?'

Miss Waynflete said promptly:

'Certainly not. If the girl had decided to make away with herself, she would have bought something probably. This was an old bottle of stuff that she must have had for years. And anyway, as I've told you, she wasn't that *kind* of girl.'

'So you think – what?' said Luke bluntly.

Miss Waynflete said:

'I think it was very unfortunate.'

She closed her lips and looked at him earnestly.

Just when Luke was feeling that he must try desperately to say something anticipated, a diversion occurred. There was a scratching at the door and a plaintive mew.

Miss Waynflete sprang up and went to open the door, where-upon a magnificent orange Persian walked in. He paused, looked disapprovingly at the visitor, and sprang upon the arm of Miss Waynflete's chair.

Miss Waynflete addressed him in a cooing voice.

'Why Wonky Pooh – where's my Wonky Pooh been all the morning?'

The name struck a chord of memory. Where had he heard something about a Persian cat called Wonky Pooh? He said:

'That's a very handsome cat. Have you had him long?'

Miss Waynflete shook her head.

'Oh, no, he belonged to an old friend of mine, Miss Pinkerton. She was run over by one of these horrid motor-cars and of course I couldn't have let Wonky Pooh go to strangers. Lavinia would have been most upset. She simply worshipped him – and he is very beautiful isn't he?'

Luke admired the cat gravely.

Miss Waynflete said: 'Be careful of his ears. They've been rather painful lately.'

Luke stroked the animal warily.

Bridget rose to her feet.

She said, 'We must be going.'

Miss Waynflete shook hands with Luke.

'Perhaps,' she said, 'I shall see you again before long.'

Luke said cheerfully: 'I hope so, I'm sure.'

He thought she looked puzzled and a little disappointed. Her gaze shifted to Bridget – a rapid look with a hint of interrogation in it. Luke felt that there was some understanding between the two women from which he was excluded. It annoyed him, but he promised himself to get to the bottom of it before long.

Miss Waynflete came out with them. Luke stood a minute on the top of the steps looking with approval on the untouched primness of the village-green and the duck pond.

'Marvellously unspoilt, this place,' he said.

Miss Waynflete's face lit up.

'Yes, indeed,' she said eagerly. 'Really it is still just as I remember it as a child. We lived in the Hall, you know. But when it came to my brother he did not care to live in it – indeed could not afford to do so, and it was put up for sale. A builder had made an offer and was, I believe, going to "develop the land", I think that was the phrase. Fortunately, Lord Whitfield stepped in and acquired the property and saved it. He turned the house into a library and museum – really it is practically untouched. I act as librarian twice a week there – unpaid, *of course* – and I can't tell you what a pleasure it is to be in the old place and know that it will not be vandalized. And really it *is* a perfect setting – you must visit our little museum one day, Mr Fitzwilliam. There are some quite interesting local exhibits.'

'I certainly shall make a point of doing so, Miss Waynflete.'

'Lord Whitfield has been a great benefactor to Wychwood,' said Miss Waynflete. 'It grieves me that there are people who are sadly ungrateful.'

Her lips pressed themselves together. Luke discreetly asked no questions. He said good-bye again.

When they were outside the gate Bridget said:

'Do you want to pursue further researches or shall we go home by way of the river? It's a pleasant walk.'

Luke answered promptly. He had no mind for further investigations with Bridget Conway standing by listening. He said:

'Go round by the river, by all means.'

They walked along the High Street. One of the last houses had a sign decorated in old gold lettering with the word Antiques on it. Luke paused and peered through one of the windows into the cool depths.

'Rather a nice slipware dish there,' he remarked. 'Do for an aunt of mine. Wonder how much they want for it?'

'Shall we go in and see?'

'Do you mind? I like pottering about antique shops. Sometimes one picks up a good bargain.'

'I doubt if you will here,' said Bridget dryly. 'Ellsworthy knows the value of his stuff pretty accurately, I should say.'

The door was open. In the hall were chairs and settees and dressers with china and pewter on them. Two rooms full of goods opened at either side.

Luke went into the room on the left and picked up the slipware dish. At the same moment a dim figure came forward from the back of the room where he had been sitting at a Queen Anne walnut desk.

'Ah, dear Miss Conway, what a pleasure to see you.'

'Good morning, Mr Ellsworthy.'

Mr Ellsworthy was a very exquisite young man dressed in a colour scheme of russet brown. He had a long pale face with a womanish mouth, long black artistic hair and a mincing walk.

Luke was introduced and Mr Ellsworthy immediately transferred his attention to him.

'Genuine old English slipware. Delicious, isn't it? I love my bits and pieces, you know, hate to sell them. It's always been my dream to live in the country and have a little shop. Marvellous place, Wychwood – it has atmosphere, if you know what I mean.'

'The artistic temperament,' murmured Bridget.

Ellsworthy turned on her with a flash of long white hands.

'Not that terrible phrase, Miss Conway. No – no, I implore you. Don't tell me I'm all arty and crafty – I couldn't bear it. Really, really, you know, I don't stock hand-woven tweeds and beaten pewter. I'm a tradesman, that's all, just a tradesman.'

'But you're really an artist, aren't you?' said Luke. 'I mean, you do water-colours, don't you?'

'Now who told you that?' cried Mr Ellsworthy, clasping his hands together. 'You know this place is really too marvellous – one simply can't keep a secret! That's what I like about it – it's so different from that inhuman you-mind-your-own-business-and-I-will-mind-mine of a city! Gossip and malice and scandal – all so delicious if one takes them in the right spirit!'

Luke contented himself with answering Mr Ellsworthy's question and paying no attention to the latter part of his remarks.

'Miss Waynflete told us that you had made several sketches of a girl – Amy Gibbs.'

'Oh, Amy,' said Mr Ellsworthy. He took a step backwards and set a beer mug rocking. He steadied it carefully. He said: 'Did I? Oh, yes, I suppose I did.'

His poise seemed somewhat shaken.

'She was a pretty girl,' said Bridget.

Mr Ellsworthy had recovered his aplomb.

'Oh, do you think so?' he asked. 'Very commonplace, I always thought. If you're interested in slipware,' he went on to Luke, 'I've got a couple of slipware birds – delicious things.'

Luke displayed a faint interest in the birds and then asked the price of the dish.

Ellsworthy named a figure.

'Thanks,' said Luke, 'but I don't think I'll deprive you of it after all.'

'I'm always relieved, you know,' said Ellsworthy, 'when I don't make a sale. Foolish of me, isn't it? Look here, I'll let you have it for a guinea less. You care for the stuff. I can see that – it makes all the difference. And after all, this *is* a shop!'

'No, thanks,' said Luke.

Mr Ellsworthy accompanied them out to the door, waving his hands – very unpleasant hands, Luke thought they were – the flesh seemed not so much white as faintly greenish.

'Nasty bit of goods, Mr Ellsworthy,' he remarked when he and Bridget were out of earshot.

'A nasty mind and nasty habits I should say,' said Bridget.

'Why does he really come to a place like this?'

'I believe he dabbles in black magic. Not quite black Masses but that sort of thing. The reputation of this place helps.'

Luke said rather awkwardly: 'Good lord – I suppose he's the kind of chap I really need. I ought to have talked to him on the subject.'

'Do you think so?' said Bridget. 'He knows a lot about it.'

Luke said rather uneasily:

'I'll look him up some other day.'

Bridget did not answer. They were out of the town now. She turned aside to follow a footpath and presently they came to the river.

There they passed a small man with a stiff moustache and protuberant eyes. He had three bulldogs with him to whom he was shouting hoarsely in turn. 'Nero, come here, sir. Nelly, leave it. Drop it, I tell you. Augustus – AUGUSTUS, I say –'

He broke off to raise his hat to Bridget, stared at Luke with what was evidently a devouring curiosity and passed on resuming his hoarse expostulations.

'Major Horton and his bulldogs?' quoted Luke.

'Quite right.'

'Haven't we seen practically every one of note in Wychwood this morning?'

'Practically.'

'I feel rather obtrusive,' said Luke. 'I suppose a stranger in an

English village is bound to stick out a mile,' he added ruefully, remembering Jimmy Lorrimer's remarks.

'Major Horton never disguises his curiosity very well,' said Bridget. 'He did stare, rather.'

'He's the sort of man you could tell was a Major anywhere,' said Luke rather viciously.

Bridget said abruptly: 'Shall we sit on the bank a bit? We've got lots of time.'

They sat on a fallen tree that made a convenient seat. Bridget went on:

'Yes, Major Horton is very military – has an orderly room manner. You'd hardly believe he was the most hen-pecked man in existence a year ago!'

'What, that fellow?'

'Yes. He had the most disagreeable woman for a wife that I've ever known. She had the money too, and never scrupled to underline the fact in public.'

'Poor brute – Horton, I mean.'

'He behaved very nicely to her – always the officer and gentleman. Personally, I wonder he didn't take a hatchet to her.'

'She wasn't popular, I gather.'

'Everybody disliked her. She snubbed Gordon and patronized me and made herself generally unpleasant wherever she went.'

'But I gather a merciful providence removed her?'

'Yes, about a year ago. Acute gastritis. She gave her husband, Dr Thomas and two nurses absolute Hell – but she died all right. The bulldogs brightened up at once.'

'Intelligent brutes!'

There was a silence. Bridget was idly picking at the long grass. Luke frowned at the opposite bank unseeingly. Once again the dreamlike quality of his mission obsessed him. How much was fact – how much imagination? Wasn't it bad for one to go about studying every fresh person you met as a potential murderer? Something degrading about that point of view.

'Damn it all,' thought Luke, 'I've been a policeman too long!'

He was brought out of his abstraction with a shock. Bridget's cold clear voice was speaking.

'Mr Fitzwilliam,' she said, 'just exactly why have you come down here?'

CHAPTER 6

HAT PAINT

Luke had been just in the act of applying a match to a cigarette. The unexpectedness of her remark momentarily paralysed his hand. He remained quite motionless for a second or two, the match burned down and scorched his fingers.

'Damn,' said Luke as he dropped the match and shook his hand vigorously. 'I beg your pardon. You gave me rather a nasty jolt.' He smiled ruefully.

'Did I?'

'Yes.' He sighed. 'Oh, well, I suppose any one of real intelligence was bound to see through me! That story of my writing a book on folklore didn't take you in for a moment, I suppose?'

'Not after I'd once seen you.'

'You believed it up to then?'

'Yes.'

'All the same it wasn't really a good story,' said Luke critically. 'I mean, any man might want to write a book, but the bit about coming down here and passing myself off as a cousin – I suppose that made you smell a rat?'

Bridget shook her head.

'No. I had an explanation for that – I thought I had, I mean. I presumed you were pretty hard up – a lot of my and Jimmy's friends are that – and I thought he suggested the cousin stunt so that – well, so that it would save your pride.'

'But when I arrived,' said Luke, 'my appearance immediately suggested such opulence that that explanation was out of the question?'

Her mouth curved in its slow smile.

'Oh, no,' she said. 'It wasn't that. It was simply that you were the wrong kind of person.'

'Not sufficient brains to write a book? Don't spare my feelings. I'd rather know.'

'You might write a book – but not that *kind* of book – old superstitions – delving into the past – not that sort of thing! You're not the kind of man to whom the past means much – perhaps not even the future – only just the present.'

'H'm – I see.' He made a wry face. 'Damn it all, you've made me nervous ever since I got here! You look so confoundedly intelligent.'

'I'm sorry,' said Bridget drily. 'What did you expect?'

'Well, I really hadn't thought about it.'

But she went on calmly:

'A fluffy little person – with just enough brains to realize her opportunities and marry her boss?'

Luke made a confused noise. She turned a cool amused glance on him.

'I quite understand. It's all right. I'm not annoyed.'

Luke chose effrontery.

'Well, perhaps, it was something faintly approaching that. But I didn't think much about it.'

She said slowly:

'No, you wouldn't. You don't cross your fences till you get to them.'

But Luke was despondent.

'Oh, I've no doubt I did my stuff pretty rottenly! Has Lord Whitfield seen through me too?'

'Oh, no. If you said you'd come down here to study the habits of water beetles and write a monograph about them, it would have been OK with Gordon. He's got a beautiful believing mind.'

'All the same I wasn't a bit convincing! I got rattled somehow.'

'I cramped your style,' said Bridget. 'I saw that. It rather amused me, I'm afraid.'

'Oh, it would! Women with any brains are usually cold-bloodedly cruel.'

Bridget murmured:

'One has to take one's pleasures as one can in this life!' She paused a minute, then said: 'Why are you down here, Mr Fitzwilliam?'

They had returned full circle to the original question. Luke had been aware that it must be so. In the last few seconds he had been trying to make up his mind. He looked up now and met her eyes – shrewd inquiring eyes that met his with a calm, steady gaze. There was a gravity in them which he had not quite expected to find there.

'It would be better, I think,' he said meditatively, 'not to tell you any more lies.'

'Much better.'

'But the truth's awkward . . . Look here, have you yourself formed any opinion – I mean has anything occurred to you about my being here?'

She nodded slowly and thoughtfully.

'What was your idea? Will you tell me? I fancy it may help somehow.'

Bridget said quietly:

'I had an idea that you came down here in connection with the death of that girl, Amy Gibbs.'

'That's it, then! That's what I saw – what I felt – whenever her name cropped up! I *knew* there was something. So you thought I came down about that?'

'Didn't you?'

'In a way – yes.'

He was silent – frowning. The girl beside him sat equally silent, not moving. She said nothing to disturb his train of thought.

He made up his mind.

'I've come down here on a wild goose chase – on a fantastical and probably quite absurd and melodramatic supposition. Amy Gibbs is part of that whole business. I'm interested to find out exactly how she died.'

'Yes, I thought so.'

'But dash it all – *why* did you think so? What is there about her death that – well – aroused your interest?'

Bridget said:

'I've thought – all along – that there was something wrong about it. That's why I took you to see Miss Waynflete.'

'Why?'

'Because she thinks so too.'

'Oh.' Luke thought back rapidly. He understood now the underlying suggestions of that intelligent spinster's manner. 'She thinks as you do – that there's something – odd about it?'

Bridget nodded.

'Why exactly?'

'Hat paint, to begin with.'

'What do you mean, hat paint?'

'Well, about twenty years ago, people *did* paint hats – one season you had a pink straw, next season a bottle of hat paint and it became dark blue – then perhaps another bottle and a black hat! But nowadays – hats are cheap – tawdry stuff to be thrown away when out of fashion.'

'Even girls of the class of Amy Gibbs?'

'I'd be more likely to paint a hat than she would! Thrift's gone out. And there's another thing. It was *red* hat paint.'

'Well?'

'And Amy Gibbs had red hair – carrots!'

'You mean it doesn't go together?'

Bridget nodded.

'You wouldn't wear a scarlet hat with carroty hair. It's the sort of thing a man wouldn't realize, but –'

Luke interrupted her with heavy significance.

'No – *a man* wouldn't realize that. It fits in – it all fits in.'

Bridget said:

'Jimmy has got some odd friends at Scotland Yard. You're not –'

Luke said quickly:

'I'm not an official detective – and I'm not a well-known private investigator with rooms in Baker Street, etc. I'm exactly what Jimmy told you I was – a retired policeman from the East. I'm homing in on this business because of an odd thing that happened in the train to London.'

He gave a brief synopsis of his conversation with Miss Pinkerton and the subsequent events which had brought about his presence in Wychwood.

'So you see,' he ended. 'It's fantastic! I'm looking for a certain man – a secret killer – a man here in Wychwood – probably well-known and respected. If Miss Pinkerton's right and you're right and Miss What's-'er-name is right – that man killed Amy Gibbs.'

Bridget said: 'I see.'

'It could have been done from outside, I suppose?'

'Yes, I think so,' said Bridget slowly. 'Reed, the constable, climbed up to her window by means of an outhouse. The window was open. It was a bit of a scramble, but a reasonably active man would find no real difficulty.'

'And having done that, he did what?'

'Substituted a bottle of hat paint for the cough linctus.'

'Hoping she'd do exactly what she did do – wake up, drink it off, and that every one would say she'd made a mistake or committed suicide?'

'Yes.'

'There was no suspicion of what they call in books, "foul play" at the inquest?'

'No.'

'Men again, I suppose – the hat paint point wasn't raised?'

'No.'

'But it occurred to you?'

'Yes.'

'And to Miss Waynflete? Have you discussed it together?'

Bridget smiled faintly:

'Oh, no – not in the sense you mean. I mean we haven't said anything right out. I don't really know how far the old pussy has gone in her own mind. I'd say she'd been just worried to start with – and gradually getting more so. She's quite intelligent, you know, went to Girton or wanted to, and was advanced when she was young. She's not got quite the woolly mind of most of the people down here.'

'Miss Pinkerton had rather a woolly mind I should imagine,' said Luke. 'That's why I never dreamed there was anything in her story to begin with.'

'She was pretty shrewd, I always thought,' said Bridget. 'Most of these rambling old dears are as sharp as nails in some ways. You said she mentioned other names?'

Luke nodded.

'Yes. A small boy – that was Tommy Pierce – I remembered the name as soon as I heard it. And I'm pretty sure that the man Carter came in too.'

'Carter, Tommy Pierce, Amy Gibbs, Dr Humbleby,' said Bridget thoughtfully. 'As you say, it's almost too fantastic to be true! Who on earth would want to kill all those people? They were all so different!'

Luke said:

'Any idea as to why anyone should want to do away with Amy Gibbs?'

Bridget shook her head.

'I can't imagine.'

'What about the man Carter? How did he die, by the way?'

'Fell into the river and was drowned. He was on his way home, it was a misty night and he was quite drunk. There's a footbridge with a rail on only one side. It was taken for granted that he missed his footing.'

'But someone *could* quite easily have given him a shove?'

'Oh, yes.'

'And somebody else could quite easily have given nasty little Tommy a push when he was window cleaning?'

'Again yes.'

'So it boils down to the fact that it's really quite easy to remove three human beings without anyone suspecting.'

'Miss Pinkerton suspected,' Bridget pointed out.

'So she did, bless her. *She* wasn't troubled with ideas of being too melodramatic, or of imagining things.'

'She often told me the world was a very wicked place.'

'And you smiled tolerantly, I suppose?'

'In a superior manner!'

'Anybody who can believe six impossible things before breakfast wins hands down at this game.'

Bridget nodded.

Luke said:

'I suppose it's no good my asking you if you've a hunch of any kind? There's no particular individual in Wychwood who gives you a creepy feeling down the spine, or who has strange pale eyes – or a queer maniacal giggle.'

'Everybody I've met in Wychwood appears to me to be eminently sane, respectable, and completely ordinary.'

'I was afraid you'd say that,' said Luke.

Bridget said:

'You think this man is definitely mad?'

'Oh, I should say so. A lunatic all right, but a cunning one. The last person you'd ever suggest – probably a pillar of society like a Bank Manager.'

'Mr Jones? I certainly can't imagine him committing wholesale murders.'

'Then he's probably the man we want.'

'It may be any one,' said Bridget. 'The butcher, the baker, the grocer, a farm labourer, a road-mender, or the man who delivers the milk.'

'It may be – yes – but I think the field is a little more restricted than that.'

'Why?'

'My Miss Pinkerton spoke of the look in his eyes when he was measuring up his next victim. From the way she spoke I got the impression – it's only an impression, mark you – that the man she was speaking of was at least her social equal. Of course, I may be wrong.'

'You're probably quite right! Those *nuances* of conversation can't be put down in black and white, but they're the sort of things one doesn't really make mistakes about.'

'You know,' said Luke, 'it's a great relief to have you knowing all about it.'

'It will probably cramp your style less, I agree. And I can probably help you.'

'Your help will be invaluable. You really mean to see it through?'

'Of course.'

Luke said with a sudden slight embarrassment:

'What about Lord Whitfield? Do you think –?'

'Naturally we don't tell Gordon anything about it!' said Bridget.

'You mean he wouldn't believe it?'

'Oh, he'd *believe* it! Gordon could believe anything! He'd probably be simply thrilled and insist on having half a dozen of his bright young men down to beat up the neighbourhood! He'd simply adore it!'

'That does rather rule it out,' agreed Luke.

'Yes, we can't allow him to have his simple pleasures, I'm afraid.'

Luke looked at her. He seemed about to say something then changed his mind. He looked instead at his watch.

'Yes,' said Bridget, 'we ought to be getting home.'

She got up. There was a sudden constraint between them as though Luke's unspoken words hovered uncomfortably in the air.

They walked home in silence.

CHAPTER 7

....

POSSIBILITIES

Luke sat in his bedroom. At lunch time he had sustained an interrogation by Mrs Anstruther as to what flowers he had had in his garden in the Mayang Straits. He had then been told what flowers would have done well there. He had also listened to further 'Talks to Young Men on the Subject of Myself' by Lord Whitfield. Now he was mercifully alone.

He took a sheet of paper and wrote down a series of names. It ran as follows:

> *Dr Thomas.*
> *Mr Abbot.*
> *Major Horton.*
> *Mr Ellsworthy.*
> *Mr Wake.*
> *Mr Jones.*
> *Amy's young man.*
> *The butcher, the baker, the candlestick maker, etc.*

He then took another sheet of paper and headed it VICTIMS. Under this heading, he wrote:

> *Amy Gibbs:*   *Poisoned.*
> *Tommy Pierce:*   *Pushed out of window.*
> *Harry Carter:*   *Shoved off footbridge (drunk? drugged?).*
> *Dr Humbleby:*   *Blood Poisoning.*
> *Miss Pinkerton:*   *Run down by car.*

He added:

> *Mrs Rose?*
> *Old Ben?*

And after a pause:

Mrs Horton?

He considered his lists, smoked awhile, then took up his pencil once more.

Dr Thomas: Possible case against him.
   Definite motive in the case of Dr Humbleby. Manner of
   latter's death suitable – namely, scientific poisoning by germs.
   Amy Gibbs visited him on afternoon of the day she died.
   (Anything between them? Blackmail?)
   Tommy Pierce? No connection known. (Did Tommy know of
   connection between him and Amy Gibbs?)
   Harry Carter? No connection known.
   Was Dr Thomas absent from Wychwood on the day Miss
   Pinkerton went to London?

Luke sighed and started a fresh heading:

Mr Abbot: Possible case against him.
   (Feel a lawyer is definitely a suspicious person. Possibly
   prejudice.) His personality, florid, genial, etc., would be
   definitely suspicious in a book – always suspect bluff genial
   men. Objection: this is not a book, but real life.
   Motive for murder of Dr Humbleby. Definite antagonism
   existed between them. H. defied Abbot. Sufficient motive for a
   deranged brain. Antagonism could have been easily noted by
   Miss Pinkerton.
   Tommy Pierce? Latter snooped among Abbot's papers. Did he
   find out something he shouldn't have known?
   Harry Carter? No definite connection.
   Amy Gibbs? No connection known. Hat paint quite suitable to
   Abbot's mentality – an old-fashioned mind. Was Abbot away
   from the village the day Miss Pinkerton was killed?

Major Horton: Possible case against him.
   No connection known with Amy Gibbs, Tommy Pierce
   or Carter.

What about Mrs Horton? Death sounds as though it might be arsenical poisoning. If so other murders might be result of that – blackmail? NB – Thomas was doctor in attendance. (Suspicious for Thomas again.)

Mr Ellsworthy: *Possible case against him.*
Nasty bit of goods – dabbles in black magic. Might be temperament of a blood-lust killer. Connection with Amy Gibbs. Any connection with Tommy Pierce? Carter? Nothing known. Humbleby? Might have tumbled to Ellsworthy's mental condition. Miss Pinkerton? Was Ellsworthy away from Wychwood when Miss Pinkerton was killed?

Mr Wake: *Possible case against him.*
Very unlikely. Possible religious mania? A mission to kill? Saintly old clergymen likely starters in books, but (as before) this is real life.
Note. Carter, Tommy, Amy all definitely unpleasant characters. Better removed by divine decree?

Mr Jones.
Data – none.
Amy's young man.
Probably every reason to kill Amy – but seems unlikely on general grounds.
The etceteras?
Don't fancy them.

He read through what he had written.
Then he shook his head.
He murmured softly:
'– which is absurd! How nicely Euclid put things.'
He tore up the lists and burnt them.
He said to himself:
'This job isn't going to be exactly easy.'

CHAPTER 8

DR THOMAS

Dr Thomas leant back in his chair, and passed a long delicate hand over his thick fair hair. He was a young man whose appearance was deceptive. Though he was over thirty, a casual glance would have put him down in the early twenties if not in his teens. His shock of rather unruly fair hair, his slightly startled expression and his pink and white complexion gave him an irresistibly school-boyish appearance. Immature as he might look, though, the diagnosis he had just pronounced on Luke's rheumatic knee agreed almost precisely with that delivered by an eminent Harley Street specialist only a week earlier.

'Thanks,' said Luke. 'Well, I'm relieved you think that electrical treatment will do the trick. I don't want to turn a cripple at my age.'

Dr Thomas smiled boyishly.

'Oh, I don't think there's any danger of that, Mr Fitzwilliam.'

'Well, you've relieved my mind,' said Luke. 'I was thinking of going to some specialist chap – but I'm sure there's no need now.'

Dr Thomas smiled again.

'Go if it makes your mind easier. After all, it's always a good thing to have an expert's opinion.'

'No, no, I've got full confidence in you.'

'Frankly, there is no complexity about the matter. If you take my advice, I am quite sure you will have no further trouble.'

'You've relieved my mind no end, doctor. Fancied I might be getting arthritis and would soon be all tied up in knots and unable to move.'

Dr Thomas shook his head with a slightly indulgent smile.

Luke said quickly:

'Men get the wind up pretty badly in these ways. I expect you find that? I often think a doctor must feel himself a "medicine man" – a kind of magician to most of his patients.'

'The element of faith enters in very largely.'

'I know. "The doctor says so" is a remark always uttered with something like reverence.'

Dr Thomas raised his shoulders.

'If one's patients only knew!' he murmured humorously.

Then he said:

'You're writing a book on magic, aren't you, Mr Fitzwilliam?'

'Now how did you know that?' exclaimed Luke, perhaps with somewhat overdone surprise.

Dr Thomas looked amused.

'Oh, my dear sir, news gets about very rapidly in a place like this. We have so little to talk about.'

'It probably gets exaggerated too. You'll be hearing I'm raising the local spirits and emulating the Witch of Endor.'

'Rather odd you should say that.'

'Why?'

'Well, the rumour has been going round that you had raised the ghost of Tommy Pierce.'

'Pierce? Pierce? Is that the small boy who fell out of a window?'

'Yes.'

'Now I wonder how – of course – I made some remark to the solicitor – what's his name, Abbot.'

'Yes, the story originated with Abbot.'

'Don't say I've converted a hard-boiled solicitor to a belief in ghosts?'

'You believe in ghosts yourself, then?'

'Your tone suggests that you do not, doctor. No, I wouldn't say I actually "believe in ghosts" – to put it crudely. But I have known curious phenomena in the case of sudden or violent death. But I'm more interested in the various superstitions pertaining to violent deaths – that a murdered man, for instance, can't rest in his grave. And the interesting belief that the blood of a murdered man flows if his murderer touches him. I wonder how that arose.'

'Very curious,' said Thomas. 'But I don't suppose many people remember that nowadays.'

'More than you would think. Of course, I don't suppose you have many murders down here – so it's hard to judge.'

Luke had smiled as he spoke, his eyes resting with seeming carelessness on the other's face. But Dr Thomas seemed quite unperturbed and smiled in return.

'No, I don't think we've had a murder for – oh, very many years – certainly not in my time.'

'No, this is a peaceful spot. Not conducive to foul play. Unless somebody pushed little Tommy What's-his-name out of the window.'

Luke laughed. Again Dr Thomas's smile came in answer – a natural smile full of boyish amusement.

'A lot of people would have been willing to wring that child's neck,' he said. 'But I don't think they actually got to the point of throwing him out of windows.'

'He seems to have been a thoroughly nasty child – the removal of him might have been conceived as a public duty.'

'It's a pity one can't apply that theory fairly often.'

'I've always thought a few wholesale murders would be beneficial to the community,' said Luke. 'A club bore, for instance, should be finished off with a poisoned liqueur brandy. Then there are the women who gush at you and tear all their dearest friends to pieces with their tongues. Backbiting spinsters. Inveterate diehards who oppose progress. If they were painlessly removed, what a difference it would make to social life!'

Dr Thomas's smile lengthened to a grin.

'In fact, you advocate crime on a grand scale?'

'Judicious elimination,' said Luke. 'Don't you agree that it would be beneficial?'

'Oh, undoubtedly.'

'Ah, but you're not being serious,' said Luke. 'Now I am. I haven't the respect for human life that the normal Englishman has. Any man who is a stumbling block on the way of progress ought to be eliminated – that's how I see it!'

Running his hand through his short fair hair, Dr Thomas said:

'Yes, but who is to be the judge of a man's fitness or unfitness?'

'That's the difficulty, of course,' Luke admitted.

'The Catholics would consider a Communist agitator unfit to live – the Communist agitator would sentence the priest to death as a purveyor of superstition, the doctor would eliminate the unhealthy man, the pacifist would condemn the soldier, and so on.'

'You'd have to have a scientific man as judge,' said Luke. 'Someone with an unbiased but highly specialized mind – a doctor, for instance. Come to that, I think you'd be a pretty good judge yourself, doctor.'

'Of unfitness to live?'

'Yes.'

Dr Thomas shook his head.

'My job is to make the unfit fit. Most of the time it's an uphill job, I'll admit.'

'Now just for the sake of argument,' said Luke. 'Take a man like the late Harry Carter –'

Dr Thomas said sharply:

'Carter? You mean the landlord of the Seven Stars?'

'Yes, that's the man. I never knew him myself, but my cousin, Miss Conway, was talking about him. He seems to have been a really thorough-going scoundrel.'

'Well,' said the other, 'he drank, of course. Ill-treated his wife, bullied his daughter. He was quarrelsome and abusive and had had a row with most people in the place.'

'In fact, the world is a better place without him?'

'One might be inclined to say so, I agree.'

'In fact, if somebody had given him a push and sent him into the river instead of his kindly electing to fall in of his own accord, that person would have been acting in the public interest?'

Dr Thomas said drily:

'These methods that you advocate – did you put them into practice in the – Mayang Straits, I think you said?'

Luke laughed.

'Oh, no, with me it's theory – not practice.'

'No, I do not think you are the stuff of which murderers are made.'

Luke asked:

'Why not? I've been frank enough in my views.'

'Exactly. Too frank.'

'You mean that if I were really the kind of man who takes the law into his own hands I shouldn't go about airing my views?'

'That was my meaning.'

'But it might be a kind of gospel with me. I might be a fanatic on the subject!'

'Even so, your sense of self-protection would be active.'

'In fact, when looking for a murderer, look out for a nice gentle wouldn't-hurt-a-fly type of man.'

'Slightly exaggerated perhaps,' said Dr Thomas, 'but not far from the truth.'

Luke said abruptly:

'Tell me – it interests me – have you ever come across a man whom you believed might be a murderer?'

Dr Thomas said sharply:

'Really – what an extraordinary question!'

'Is it? After all, a doctor must come across so many queer characters. He would be better able to detect – for instance – the signs of homicidal mania – in an early stage – before it's noticeable.'

Thomas said rather irritably:

'You have the general layman's idea of a homicidal maniac – a man who runs amok with a knife, a man more or less foaming at the mouth. Let me tell you a homicidal lunatic may be the most difficult thing on this earth to spot. To all seeming he may be exactly like everyone else – a man, per-haps, who is easily frightened – who may tell you, perhaps, that he has enemies. No more than that. A quiet, inoffensive fellow.'

'Is that really so?'

'Of course it's so. A homicidal lunatic often kills (as he thinks) in self-defence. But of course a lot of killers are ordinary sane fellows like you and me.'

'Doctor, you alarm me! Fancy if you should discover later that I have five or six nice quiet little killings to my credit.'

Dr Thomas smiled.

'I don't think it's very likely, Mr Fitzwilliam.'

'Don't you? I'll return the compliment. I don't believe you've got five or six murders to your credit either.'

Dr Thomas said cheerfully:

'You're not counting my professional failures.'

Both men laughed.

Luke got up and said good-bye.

'I'm afraid I've taken up a lot of your time,' he said apolo-getically.

'Oh, I'm not busy. Wychwood is a pretty healthy place. It's a pleasure to have a talk with someone from the outside world.'

'I was wondering –' said Luke and stopped.

'Yes?'

'Miss Conway told me when she sent me to you what a very – well – what a first-class man you were. I wondered if you didn't feel rather buried down here? Not much opportunity for talent.'

'Oh, general practice is a good beginning. It's valuable experience.'

'But you won't be content to stay in a rut all your life? Your late partner, Dr Humbleby, was an unambitious fellow, so I've heard – quite content with his practice here. He'd been here for a good many years, I believe?'

'Practically a lifetime.'

'He was sound but old-fashioned, so I hear.'

Dr Thomas said:

'At times he was difficult ... Very suspicious of modern innovations, but a good example of the old school of physicians.'

'Left a very pretty daughter, I'm told,' said Luke in jocular fashion.

He had the pleasure of seeing Dr Thomas's pale-pink countenance go a deep scarlet.

'Oh – er – yes,' he said.

Luke gazed at him kindly. He was pleased at the prospect of erasing Dr Thomas from his list of suspected persons.

The latter recovered his normal hue and said abruptly:

'Talking about crime just now, I can lend you rather a good book as you are interested in the subject! Translation from the German. Kreuzhammer on *Inferiority and Crime*.'

'Thank you,' said Luke.

Dr Thomas ran his finger along a shelf and drew out the book in question.

'Here you are. Some of the theories are rather startling – and of course they are only theories, but they are interesting. The early life of Menzheld, for instance, the Frankfurt butcher, as they called him, and the chapter on Anna Helm, the little nursemaid killer, are really extremely interesting.'

'She killed about a dozen of her charges before the authorities tumbled to it, I believe,' said Luke.

Dr Thomas nodded.

'Yes. She had a most sympathetic personality – devoted to children – and apparently quite genuinely heartbroken at each death. The psychology is amazing.'

'Amazing how these people get away with it,' said Luke.

He was on the doorstep now. Dr Thomas had come out with him.

'Not amazing really,' said Dr Thomas. 'It's quite easy, you know.'

'What is?'

'To get away with it.' He was smiling again – a charming, boyish smile. 'If you're careful. One just has to be careful – that's all! But a clever man *is* extremely careful not to make a slip. That's all there is to it.'

He smiled and went into the house.

Luke stood staring up the steps.

There had been something condescending in the doctor's smile. Throughout their conversation Luke had been conscious of himself as a man of full maturity and of Dr Thomas as a youthful and ingenuous young man.

Just for a moment he felt the roles reversed. The doctor's smile had been that of a grown-up amused by the cleverness of a child.

CHAPTER 9
MRS PIERCE TALKS

In the little shop in the High Street, Luke had bought a tin of cigarettes and today's copy of *Good Cheer*, the enterprising little weekly which provided Lord Whitfield with a good portion of his substantial income. Turning to the football competition, Luke, with a groan, gave forth the information that he had just failed to win a hundred and twenty pounds. Mrs Pierce was roused at once to sympathy and explained similar disappointments on the part of her husband. Friendly relations thus established, Luke found no difficulty in prolonging the conversation.

'A great interest in football Mr Pierce takes,' said Mr Pierce's spouse. 'Turns to it first of all in the news, he does. And as I say, many a disappointment he's had, but there, everybody can't win, that's what I say, and what I say is you can't go against luck.'

Luke concurred heartily in these sentiments, and proceeded to advance by an easy transition to a further profound statement that troubles never come singly.

'Ah, no, indeed, sir, that I *do* know.' Mrs Pierce sighed. 'And when a woman has a husband and eight children – six living and buried two, that is – well, she knows what trouble is, as you may say.'

'I suppose she does – oh, undoubtedly,' said Luke. 'You've – er – buried two, you say?'

'One no longer than a month ago,' said Mrs Pierce with a kind of melancholy enjoyment.

'Dear me, very sad.'

'It wasn't only sad, sir. It was a shock – that's what it was, a shock! I came all over queer, I did, when they broke it to me. Never having expected anything of that kind to happen to Tommy, as you might say, for when a boy's a trouble to you it doesn't come natural to think of him being took. Now my Emma Jane, a sweet little mite she was. "You'll never rear her." That's what they said. "She's too good to live." And it was true, sir. The Lord knows His own.'

Luke acknowledged the sentiment and strove to return from the subject of the saintly Emma Jane to that of the less saintly Tommy.

'Your boy died quite recently?' he said. 'An accident?'

'An accident it was, sir. Cleaning the windows of the old Hall, which is now the library, and he must have lost his balance and fell – from the top windows, that was.'

Mrs Pierce expatiated at some length on all the details of the accident.

'Wasn't there some story,' said Luke carelessly, 'of his having been seen dancing on the window-sill?'

Mrs Pierce said that boys would be boys – but no doubt it did give the major a turn, him being a fussy gentleman.

'Major Horton?'

'Yes, sir, the gentleman with the bulldogs. After the accident happened he chanced to mention having seen our Tommy acting very rash-like – and of course it does show that if something sudden had startled him he would have fallen easy enough. High spirits, sir, that was Tommy's trouble. A sore trial he's been to me in many ways,' she finished, 'but there it was, just high spirits – nothing but high spirits – such as any lad might have. There wasn't no real harm in him, as you might say.'

'No, no – I'm sure there wasn't, but sometimes, you know, Mrs Pierce, people – sober middle-aged people – find it hard to remember they've ever been young themselves.'

Mrs Pierce sighed.

'Very true those words are, sir. I can't help but hoping that some gentlemen I could name but won't will have taken it to heart the way they were hard upon the lad – just on account of his high spirits.'

'Played a few tricks upon his employers, did he?' asked Luke with an indulgent smile.

Mrs Pierce responded immediately.

'It was just his fun, sir, that was all. Tommy was always good at imitations. Make us hold our sides with laughing the way he'd mince about pretending to be that Mr Ellsworthy at the curio shop – or old Mr Hobbs, the churchwarden – and he was imitating his lordship up at the manor and the two under-gardeners laughing, when up came his lordship quiet-like and gave Tommy the sack on the spot – and naturally that was only to be expected, and quite right, and his lordship didn't bear malice afterwards, and helped Tommy to get another job.'

'But other people weren't so magnanimous, eh?' said Luke.

'That they were not, sir. Naming no names. And you'd never think it with Mr Abbot, so pleasant in his manner and always a kind word or a joke.'

'Tommy got into trouble with him?'

Mrs Pierce said:

'It's not, I'm sure, that the boy meant any harm . . . And after all, if papers are private and not meant to be looked at, they shouldn't be laid out on a table – that's what I say.'

'Oh, quite,' said Luke. 'Private papers in a lawyer's office ought to be kept in the safe.'

'That's right, sir. That's what I think, and Mr Pierce he

agrees with me. It's not even as though Tommy had read much of it.'

'What was it – a will?' asked Luke.

He judged (probably rightly) that a question as to what the document in question had been might make Mrs Pierce halt. But this direct question brought an instant response.

'Oh, no, sir, nothing of that kind. Nothing really important. Just a private letter it was – from a lady – and Tommy didn't even see who the lady was. All such a fuss about nothing – that's what I say.'

'Mr Abbot must be the sort of man who takes offence very easily,' said Luke.

'Well, it does seem so, doesn't it, sir? Although, as I say, he's always such a pleasant gentleman to speak to – always a joke or a cheery word. But it's true that I have heard he was a difficult man to get up against, and him and Dr Humbleby was daggers drawn, as the saying is, just before the poor gentleman died. And not a pleasant thought for Mr Abbot afterwards. For once there's a death one doesn't like to think there's been harsh words spoken and no chance of taking them back.'

Luke shook his head solemnly and murmured:

'Very true – very true.'

He went on:

'A bit of a coincidence – that. Hard words with Dr Humbleby and Dr Humbleby died – harsh treatment of your Tommy – and the boy dies! I should think that a double experience like that would tend to make Mr Abbot careful of his tongue in future.'

'Harry Carter, too, down at the Seven Stars,' said Mrs Pierce. 'Very sharp words passed between them only a week before Carter went and drowned himself – but one can't blame Mr Abbot for that. The abuse was all on Carter's side – went up to Mr Abbot's house, he did, being in liquor at the time, and shouting out the foulest language at the top of his voice. Poor Mrs Carter, she had a deal to put up with, and it must be owned Carter's death was a merciful release as far as she was concerned.'

'He left a daughter, too, didn't he?'

'Ah,' said Mrs Pierce. 'I'm never one to gossip.'

This was unexpected but promising. Luke pricked up his ears and waited.

'I don't say there was anything in it but talk. Lucy Carter's a fine-looking young woman in her way, and if it hadn't been for the difference in station I dare say no notice would have been taken. But talk there has been and you can't deny it – especially after Carter went right up to his house, shouting and swearing.'

Luke gathered the implications of this somewhat confused speech.

'Mr Abbot looks as though he'd appreciate a good-looking girl,' he said.

'It's often the way with gentlemen,' said Mrs Pierce. 'They don't mean anything by it – just a word or two in passing, but the gentry's the gentry and it gets noticed in consequence. It's only to be expected in a quiet place like this.'

'It's a very charming place,' said Luke. 'So unspoilt.'

'That's what artists always say, but I think we're a bit behind the times myself. Why, there's been no building here to speak of. Over at Ashevale, for instance, they've got a lovely lot of new houses, some of them with green roofs and stained-glass in the windows.'

Luke shuddered slightly.

'You've got a grand new institute here,' he said.

'They say it's a very fine building,' said Mrs Pierce, without great enthusiasm. 'Of course, his lordship's done a lot for the place. He means well, we all know that.'

'But you don't think his efforts are quite successful?' said Luke, amused.

'Well, of course, sir, he isn't really gentry – not like Miss Waynflete, for instance, and Miss Conway. Why, Lord Whitfield's father kept a boot-shop only a few doors from here. My mother remembers Gordon Ragg serving in the shop – remembers it as well as anything. Of course he's his lordship now and he's a rich man – but it's never the same, is it, sir?'

'Evidently not,' said Luke.

'You'll excuse me mentioning it, sir,' said Mrs Pierce. 'And of course I know you're staying at the manor and writing a book. But you're a cousin of Miss Bridget's, I know, and that's quite a different thing. Very pleased we shall be to have her back as mistress of Ashe Manor.'

'Rather,' said Luke. 'I'm sure you will.'

He paid for his cigarettes and paper with sudden abruptness.

He thought to himself:

'The personal element. One *must* keep that out of it! Hell, I'm here to track down a criminal. What does it matter who that black-haired witch marries or doesn't marry? She doesn't come into this . . .'

He walked slowly along the street. With an effort he thrust Bridget into the back of his mind.

'Now then,' he said to himself. 'Abbot. The case against Abbot. I've linked him up with three of the victims. He had a row with Humbleby, a row with Carter and a row with Tommy Pierce – and all three died. What about the girl Amy Gibbs? What was the private letter that infernal boy saw? Did he know who it was from? Or didn't he? He mayn't have said so to his mother. But suppose he *did*. Suppose Abbot thought it necessary to shut his mouth. It could be! That's all one can say about it. It could be! Not good enough!'

Luke quickened his pace, looking about him with sudden exasperation.

'This damned village – it's getting on my nerves. So smiling and peaceful – so innocent – and all the time this crazy streak of murder running through it. Or am I the crazy one? Was Lavinia Pinkerton crazy? After all, the whole thing *could* be coincidence – yes, Humbleby's death and all . . .'

He glanced back down the length of the High Street – and he was assailed by a strong feeling of unreality.

He said to himself:

'These things don't happen . . .'

Then he lifted his eyes to the long frowning line of Ashe Ridge – and at once the unreality passed. Ashe Ridge was real – it knew strange things – witchcraft and cruelty and forgotten blood lusts and evil rites . . .

He started. Two figures were walking along the side of the ridge. He recognized them easily – Bridget and Ellsworthy. The young man was gesticulating with those curious, unpleasant hands of his. His head was bent to Bridget's. They looked like two figures out of a dream. One felt that their feet made no sound as they sprang cat-like from turf to turf. He saw her black hair stream out behind her blown by the wind. Again that queer magic of hers held him.

'Bewitched, that's what I am, bewitched,' he said to himself.

He stood quite still – a queer numbed feeling spreading over him.

He thought to himself ruefully:

'Who's to break the spell? There's no one.'

CHAPTER 10
ROSE HUMBLEBY

A soft sound behind him made him turn sharply. A girl was standing there, a remarkably pretty girl with brown hair curling round her ears and rather timid-looking dark-blue eyes. She flushed a little with embarrassment before she spoke.

'Mr Fitzwilliam, isn't it?' she said.

'Yes. I –'

'I'm Rose Humbleby. Bridget told me that – that you knew some people who knew my father.'

Luke had the grace to flush slightly under his tan.

'It was a long time ago,' he said rather lamely. 'They – er – knew him as a young man – before he married.'

'Oh, I see.'

Rose Humbleby looked a little crestfallen. But she went on:

'You're writing a book, aren't you?'

'Yes. I'm making notes for one, that is. About local superstitions. All that sort of thing.'

'I see. It sounds frightfully interesting.'

'It will probably be as dull as ditch-water,' Luke assured her.

'Oh, no, I'm sure it won't.'

Luke smiled at her.

He thought:

'Our Dr Thomas is in luck!'

'There are people,' he said, 'who can make the most exciting subject unbearably boring. I'm afraid I'm one of them.'

'Oh, but why should you be?'

'I don't know. But the conviction is growing upon me.'

Rose Humbleby said:

'You might be one of the people who make dull subjects sound frightfully exciting!'

'Now that *is* a nice thought,' said Luke. 'Thank you for it.'

Rose Humbleby smiled back. Then she said:

'Do you believe in – in superstitions and all that?'

'That's a difficult question. It doesn't follow, you know. One can be interested in things one doesn't believe in.'

'Yes, I suppose so,' the girl sounded doubtful.

'Are you superstitious?'

'N-no – I don't think so. But I do think things come in – in waves.'

'Waves?'

'Waves of bad luck and good luck. I mean – I feel as though lately all Wychwood was under a spell of – of misfortune. Father dying – and Miss Pinkerton being run over, and that little boy who fell out of the window. I – I began to feel as though I hated this place – as though I *must* get away!'

Her breath came rather faster. Luke looked at her thoughtfully.

'So you feel like that?'

'Oh! I know it's silly. I suppose really it was poor daddy dying so unexpectedly – it was so horribly sudden.' She shivered. 'And then Miss Pinkerton. She said –'

The girl paused.

'What did she say? She was a delightful old lady, I thought – very like a rather special aunt of mine.'

'Oh, did you know her?' Rose's face lit up. 'I was very fond of her and she was devoted to daddy. But I've sometimes wondered if she was what the Scotch call "fey".'

'Why?'

'Because – it's so odd – she seemed quite afraid that something was going to happen to daddy. She almost *warned* me. Especially about accidents. And then that day – just before she went up to town – she was so odd in her manner – absolutely in a *dither*. I really do think, Mr Fitzwilliam, that she was one of those people who have second sight. I think she *knew* that something was going to happen to her. And she must have known that something was going to happen to daddy too. It's – it's rather frightening, that sort of thing!'

She moved a step nearer to him.

'There are times when one can foresee the future,' said Luke. 'It isn't always supernatural, though.'

'No, I suppose it's quite natural really – just a faculty that most people lack. All the same it – worries me –'

'You mustn't worry,' said Luke gently. 'Remember, it's all behind you now. It's no good going back over the past. It's the future one has to live for.'

'I know. But there's more, you see . . .' Rose hesitated. 'There was something – to do with your cousin.'

'My cousin? Bridget?'

'Yes. Miss Pinkerton was worried about her in some way. She was always asking me questions . . . I think she was afraid for her – too.'

Luke turned sharply, scanning the hillside. He had an unreasoning sense of fear. Bridget – alone with the man whose hands had that unhealthy hue of greenish decomposing flesh! Fancy – all fancy! Ellsworthy was only a harmless dilettante who played at shopkeeping.

As though reading his thoughts, Rose said:

'Do you like Mr Ellsworthy?'

'Emphatically no.'

'Geoffrey – Dr Thomas, you know, doesn't like him either.'

'And you?'

'Oh, no – I think he's dreadful.' She drew a little nearer. 'There's a lot of talk about him. I was told that he had some queer ceremony in the Witches' Meadow – a lot of his friends came down from London – frightfully queer-looking people. And Tommy Pierce was a kind of acolyte.'

'Tommy Pierce?' said Luke sharply.

'Yes. He had a surplice and a red cassock.'

'When was this?'

'Oh, some time ago – I think it was in March.'

'Tommy Pierce seems to have been mixed up in everything that ever took place in this village.'

Rose said:

'He was frightfully inquisitive. He always had to know what was going on.'

'He probably knew a bit too much in the end,' said Luke grimly.

Rose accepted the words at their face value.

'He was rather an odious little boy. He liked cutting up wasps and he teased dogs.'

'The kind of boy whose decease is hardly to be regretted!'

'No, I suppose not. It was terrible for his mother, though.'

'I gather she has five blessings left to console her. She's got a good tongue, that woman.'

'She does talk a lot, doesn't she?'

'After buying a few cigarettes from her, I feel I know the full history of every one in the place!'

Rose said ruefully:

'That's the worst of a place like this. Everybody knows everything about everybody else.'

'Oh, no,' said Luke.

She looked at him inquiringly.

Luke said with significance:

'No one human being knows the full truth about another human being.'

Rose's face grew grave. She gave a slight involuntary shiver.

'No,' she said slowly. 'I suppose that's true.'

'Not even one's nearest and dearest,' said Luke.

'Not even –' she stopped. 'Oh, I suppose you're right – but I wish you wouldn't say frightening things like that, Mr Fitzwilliam.'

'Does it frighten you?'

Slowly she nodded her head.

Then she turned abruptly.

'I must be going now. If – if you have nothing better to do – I mean if you could – do come and see us. Mother would – would like to see you because of your knowing friends of daddy's long ago.'

She walked slowly away down the road. Her head was bent a little as though some weight of care or perplexity bowed it down.

Luke stood looking after her. A sudden wave of solicitude swept over him. He felt a longing to shield and protect this girl.

From what? Asking himself the question, he shook his head with a momentary impatience at himself. It was true that Rose Humbleby had recently lost her father, but she had a mother, and she was engaged to be married to a decidedly attractive young man who was fully adequate to anything in the protection line. Then why should he, Luke Fitzwilliam, be assailed by this protection complex?

Good old sentimentality to the fore again, thought Luke. The protective male! Flourishing in the Victorian era, going strong in the Edwardian, and still showing signs of life despite what our friend Lord Whitfield would call the rush and strain of modern life!

'All the same,' he said to himself as he strolled on towards the looming mass of Ashe Ridge, 'I like that girl. She's much too good for Thomas – a cool, superior devil like that.'

A memory of the doctor's last smile on the doorstep recurred to him. Decidedly smug it had been! Complacent!

The sound of footsteps a little way ahead roused Luke from his slightly irritable meditations. He looked up to see young Mr Ellsworthy coming down the path from the hillside. His eyes were on the ground and he was smiling to himself. His expression struck Luke disagreeably. Ellsworthy was not so much walking as prancing – like a man who keeps time to some devilish little jig running in his brain. His smile was a strange secret contortion of the lips – it had a gleeful slyness that was definitely unpleasant.

Luke had stopped, and Ellsworthy was nearly abreast of him when he at last looked up. His eyes, malicious and dancing, met the other man's for just a minute before recognition came. Then, or so it seemed to Luke, a complete change came over the man. Where a minute before there had been the suggestion of a dancing satyr, there was now a somewhat effeminate and priggish young man.

'Oh, Mr Fitzwilliam, good-morning.'

'Good-morning,' said Luke. 'Have you been admiring the beauties of Nature?'

Mr Ellsworthy's long, pale hands flew up in a reproving gesture.

'Oh, no, no – oh, dear me, no. I abhor Nature. Such a coarse, unimaginative wench. I have always held that one cannot enjoy life until one has put Nature in her place.'

'And how do you propose to do that?'

'There are ways!' said Mr Ellsworthy. 'In a place like this, a delicious provincial spot, there are some most delectable amusements if one has the *goût* – the flair. I enjoy life, Mr Fitzwilliam.'

'So do I,' said Luke.

'*Mens sana in corpore sano*,' said Mr Ellsworthy. His tone was delicately ironic. 'I'm sure that's *so* true of you.'

'There are worse things,' said Luke.

'My dear fellow! Sanity is the one unbelievable bore. One must be mad – deliciously mad – perverted – slightly twisted – then one sees life from a new and entrancing angle.'

'The leper's squint,' suggested Luke.

'Ah, very good – very good – quite witty! But there's something in it, you know. An interesting angle of vision. But I mustn't detain you. You're having exercise – one must have exercise – the public school spirit!'

'As you say,' said Luke, and with a curt nod walked on.

He thought:

'I'm getting too darned imaginative. The fellow's just an ass, that's all.'

But some indefinable uneasiness drove his feet on faster. That queer, sly, triumphant smile that Ellsworthy had had on his face – was that just imagination on his, Luke's part? And his subsequent impression that it had been wiped off as though by a sponge the moment the other man caught sight of Luke coming towards him – what of that?

And with quickening uneasiness he thought:

'Bridget? Is she all right? They came up here together and he came back alone.'

He hurried on. The sun had come out while he was talking to Rose Humbleby. Now it had gone in again. The sky was dull and menacing, and wind came in sudden erratic little puffs. It was as though he had stepped out of normal everyday life into that queer half-world of enchantment, the consciousness of which had enveloped him ever since he came to Wychwood.

He turned a corner and came out on the flat ledge of green grass that had been pointed out to him from below and which went, he knew, by the name of the Witches' Meadow. It was here, so tradition had it, that the witches had held revelry on Walpurgis Night and Hallowe'en.

And then a quick wave of relief swept over him. Bridget was here. She sat with her back against a rock on the hillside. She was sitting bent over, her head in her hands.

He walked quickly over to her. Lovely springing turf strangely green and fresh.

He said:

'Bridget?'

Slowly she raised her face from her hands. Her face troubled him. She looked as though she were returning from some far-off world, as though she had difficulty in adjusting herself to the world of now and here.

Luke said – rather inadequately:

'I say – you're – you're all right, aren't you?'

It was a minute or two before she answered – as though she still had not quite come back from that far-off world that had held her. Luke felt that his words had to travel a long way before they reached her.

Then she said:

'Of course I'm all right. Why shouldn't I be?'

And now her voice was sharp and almost hostile.

Luke grinned.

'I'm hanged if I know. I got the wind up about you suddenly.'

'Why?'

'Mainly, I think, because of the melodramatic atmosphere in which I'm living at present. It makes me see things out of all proportion. If I lose sight of you for an hour or two I naturally assume that the next thing will be to find your gory corpse in a ditch. It would be in a play or a book.'

'Heroines are never killed,' said Bridget.

'No, but –'

Luke stopped – just in time.

'What were you going to say?'

'Nothing.'

Thank goodness he had just stopped himself in time. One couldn't very well say to an attractive young woman, 'But you're not the heroine.'

Bridget went on:

'They are abducted, imprisoned, left to die of sewer gas or be drowned in cellars – they are always in danger, but they don't ever die.'

'Nor even fade away,' said Luke.

He went on:

'So this is the Witches' Meadow?'

'Yes.'

He looked down at her.

'You only need a broomstick,' he said kindly.

'Thank you. Mr Ellsworthy said much the same.'

'I met him just now,' said Luke.

'Did you talk to him at all?'

'Yes. I think he tried to annoy me.'

'Did he succeed?'

'His methods were rather childish.' He paused and then went on abruptly. 'He's an odd sort of fellow. One minute you think he's just a mess – and then suddenly one wonders if there isn't a bit more to it than that.'

Bridget looked up at him.

'You've felt that too?'

'You agree then?'

'Yes.'

Luke waited.

Bridget said:

'There's something – odd about him. I've been wondering you know . . . I lay awake last night racking my brains. About the whole business. It seemed to me that if there was a – a killer about, *I* ought to know who it was! I mean, living down here and all that. I thought and I thought and it came to this – if there *is* a killer, he *must* definitely be mad.'

Thinking of what Dr Thomas had said, Luke asked:

'You don't think that a murderer can be as sane as you or I?'

'Not this kind of a murderer. As I see it, this murderer *must* be crazy. And that, you see, brought me straight to Ellsworthy. Of all the people down here, he's the only one who is definitely queer. He *is* queer, you can't get away from it!'

Luke said doubtfully:

'There are a good many of his sort, dilettanti, poseurs – usually quite harmless.'

'Yes. But I think there might be a little more than that. He's got such nasty hands.'

'You noticed that? Funny, I did too!'

'They're not just white – they're green.'

'They do give one that effect. All the same, you can't convict a man of being a murderer because of the colour of his flesh tints.'

'Oh, quite. What we want is evidence.'

'Evidence!' growled Luke. 'Just the one thing that's absolutely lacking. The man's been too careful. A *careful* murderer! A *careful* lunatic!'

'I've been trying to help,' said Bridget.

'With Ellsworthy, you mean?'

'Yes. I thought I could probably tackle him better than you could. I've made a beginning.'

'Tell me.'

'Well, it seems that he has a kind of little coterie – a band of nasty friends. They come down here from time to time and celebrate.'

'Do you mean what are called nameless orgies?'

'I don't know about nameless but certainly orgies. Actually it all sounds very silly and childish.'

'I suppose they worship the devil and do obscene dances.'

'Something of the kind. Apparently they get a kick out of it.'

'I can contribute something to this,' said Luke. 'Tommy Pierce took part in one of their ceremonies. He was an acolyte. He had a red cassock.'

'So he knew about it?'

'Yes. And that might explain his death.'

'You mean he talked about it?'

'Yes – or he may have tried a spot of quiet blackmail.'

Bridget said thoughtfully:

'I know it's all fantastic – but it doesn't seem quite so fantastic when applied to Ellsworthy as it does to anyone else.'

'No, I agree – the thing becomes just conceivable instead of being ludicrously unreal.'

'We've got a connection with two of the victims,' said Bridget. 'Tommy Pierce and Amy Gibbs.'

'Where do the publican and Humbleby come in?'

'At the moment they don't.'

'Not the publican. But I can imagine a motive for Humbleby's removal. He was a doctor and he may have tumbled to Ellsworthy's abnormal state.'

'Yes, that's possible.'

Then Bridget laughed.

'I did my stuff pretty well this morning. My psychic possibilities are grand, it seems, and when I told how one of my great-great-grandmothers had a near escape of being burnt for witchcraft my stock went soaring up. I rather think that I shall be invited to take part in the orgies at the next meeting of the Satanic Games whenever that may be.'

Luke said:

'Bridget, for God's sake, be careful.'

She looked at him, surprised. He got up.

'I met Humbleby's daughter just now. We were talking about Miss Pinkerton. And the Humbleby girl said that Miss Pinkerton had been worried about you.'

Bridget, in the act of rising, stopped as though frozen into immobility.

'What's that? Miss Pinkerton – worried – about *me*?'

'That's what Rose Humbleby said.'

'Rose Humbleby said that?'

'Yes.'

'What more did she say?'

'Nothing more.'

'Are you sure?'

'Quite sure.'

There was a pause, then Bridget said, 'I see.'

'Miss Pinkerton was worried about Humbleby and *he* died. Now I hear she was worried about *you* –'

Bridget laughed. She stood up and shook her head so that her long black hair flew out round her head.

'Don't worry,' she said. 'The devil looks after his own.'

CHAPTER 11

DOMESTIC LIFE OF MAJOR HORTON

Luke leaned back in his chair on the other side of the bank manager's table.

'Well, that seems very satisfactory,' he said. 'I'm afraid I've been taking up a lot of your time.'

Mr Jones waved a deprecating hand. His small, dark, plump face wore a happy expression.

'No, indeed, Mr Fitzwilliam. This is a quiet spot, you know. We are always glad to see a stranger.'

'It's a fascinating part of the world,' said Luke. 'Full of super-stitions.'

Mr Jones sighed and said it took a long time for education to eradicate superstition. Luke remarked that he thought education was too highly rated nowadays and Mr Jones was slightly shocked by the statement.

'Lord Whitfield,' he said, 'has been a handsome benefactor here. He realizes the disadvantages under which he himself suffered as a boy and is determined that the youth of today shall be better equipped.'

'Early disadvantages haven't prevented him from making a large fortune,' said Luke.

'No, he must have had ability – great ability.'

'Or luck,' said Luke.

Mr Jones looked rather shocked.

'Luck is the one thing that counts,' said Luke. 'Take a murderer, for example. Why does the successful murderer get away with it? Is it ability? Or is it sheer luck?'

Mr Jones admitted that it was probably luck.

Luke continued:

'Take a fellow like this man Carter, the landlord of one of your pubs. The fellow was probably drunk six nights out of seven – yet one night he goes and pitches himself off the footbridge into the river. Luck again.'

'Good luck for some people,' said the bank manager.

'You mean?'

'For his wife and daughter.'

'Oh, yes, of course.'

A clerk knocked and entered bearing papers. Luke gave two specimen signatures and was given a cheque-book. He rose.

'Well, I'm glad that's all fixed up. Had a bit of luck over the Derby this year. Did you?'

Mr Jones said smilingly that he was not a betting man. He added that Mrs Jones had very strong views on the subject of horse-racing.

'Then I suppose you didn't go to the Derby?'

'No indeed.'

'Anybody go to it from here?'

'Major Horton did. He's quite a keen racing man. And Mr Abbot usually takes the day off. He didn't back the winner, though.'

'I don't suppose many people did,' said Luke, and departed after the exchange of farewells.

He lit a cigarette as he emerged from the bank. Apart from the theory of the 'least likely person', he saw no reason for retaining Mr Jones on his list of suspects. The bank manager had shown no interesting reactions to Luke's test questions. It seemed quite impossible to visualize him as a murderer. Moreover, he had not been absent on Derby Day. Incidentally, Luke's visit had not been wasted, he had received two small items of information. Both Major Horton and Mr Abbot, the solicitor, had been away from Wychwood on Derby Day. Either of them, therefore, could have been in London at the time when Miss Pinkerton was run down by a car.

Although Luke did not now suspect Dr Thomas he felt he would be more satisfied if he knew for a fact that the latter had been at Wychwood engaged in his professional duties on that particular day. He made a mental note to verify that point.

Then there was Ellsworthy. Had Ellsworthy been in Wychwood on Derby Day? If he had, the presumption that he was the killer was correspondingly weakened. Although, Luke noted, it was possible that Miss Pinkerton's death had been neither more nor less than the accident that it was supposed to be.

But he rejected that theory. Her death was too opportune.

Luke got into his own car, which was standing by the kerb,

and drove in it to Pipwell's Garage, situated at the far end of the High Street.

There were various small matters in the car's running that he wanted to discuss. A good-looking young mechanic with a freckled face listened intelligently. The two men lifted the bonnet and became absorbed in a technical discussion.

A voice called:

'Jim, come here a minute.'

The freckled-faced mechanic obeyed.

Jim Harvey. That was right. Jim Harvey, Amy Gibbs's young man. He returned presently, apologizing, and conversation became technical once more. Luke agreed to leave the car there.

As he was about to leave he inquired casually:

'Do any good on the Derby this year?'

'No, sir. Backed Clarigold.'

'Can't be many people who backed Jujube the II.?'

'No, indeed, sir. I don't believe any of the papers even tipped it as an outside chance.'

Luke shook his head.

'Racing's an uncertain game. Ever seen the Derby run?'

'No, sir, wish I had. Asked for a day off this year. There was a cheap ticket up to town and down to Epsom, but the boss wouldn't hear of it. We were short-handed, as a matter of fact, and had a lot of work in that day.'

Luke nodded and took his departure.

Jim Harvey was crossed off his list. That pleasant-faced boy was not a secret killer, and it was not he who had run down Lavinia Pinkerton.

He strolled home by way of the river bank. Here, as once before, he encountered Major Horton and his dogs. The major was still in the same condition of apoplectic shouting. 'Augustus – Nelly – NELLY, I say. Nero – Nero – NERO.'

Again the protuberant eyes stared at Luke. But this time there was more to follow. Major Horton said:

'Excuse me. Mr Fitzwilliam, isn't it?'

'Yes.'

'Horton here – Major Horton. Believe I'm going to meet you tomorrow up at the Manor. Tennis party. Miss Conway very kindly asked me. Cousin of yours, isn't she?'

'Yes.'

'Thought so. Soon spot a new face down here, you know.'

Here a diversion occurred, the three bulldogs advancing upon a nondescript white mongrel.

'Augustus – Nero. Come here, sir – come here, I say.'

When Augustus and Nero had finally reluctantly obeyed the command, Major Horton returned to the conversation. Luke was patting Nelly, who was gazing up at him sentimentally.

'Nice bitch, that, isn't she?' said the major. 'I like bulldogs. I've always had 'em. Prefer 'em to any other breed. My place is just near here, come in and have a drink.'

Luke accepted and the two men walked together while Major Horton held forth on the subject of dogs and the inferiority of all other breeds to that which he himself preferred.

Luke heard of the prizes Nelly had won, of the infamous conduct of a judge in awarding Augustus merely a Highly Commended, and of the triumphs of Nero in the show ring.

By then they had turned in at the major's gate. He opened the front door, which was not locked, and the two men passed into the house. Leading the way into a small slightly doggy-smelling room lined with bookshelves, Major Horton busied himself with the drinks. Luke looked round him. There were photographs of dogs, copies of the *Field* and *Country Life* and a couple of well-worn arm-chairs. Silver cups were arranged round the bookcases. There was one oil painting over the mantelpiece.

'My wife,' said the major, looking up from the siphon and noting the direction of Luke's glance. 'Remarkable woman. A lot of character in her face, don't you think?'

'Yes, indeed,' said Luke, looking at the late Mrs Horton.

She was represented in a pink satin dress and was holding a bunch of lilies of the valley. Her brown hair was parted in the middle and her lips were pressed grimly together. Her eyes, of a cold grey, looked out ill-temperedly at the beholder.

'A remarkable woman,' said the major, handing a glass to Luke. 'She died over a year ago. I haven't been the same man since.'

'No?' said Luke, a little at a loss to know what to say.

'Sit down,' said the major, waving a hand towards one of the leather chairs.

He himself took the other one and sipping his whisky and soda, he went on:

'No, I haven't been the same man since.'

'You must miss her,' said Luke awkwardly.

Major Horton shook his head darkly.

'Fellow needs a wife to keep him up to scratch,' he said. 'Otherwise he gets slack – yes, slack. He lets himself go.'

'But surely –'

'My boy, I know what I'm talking about. Mind you, I'm not saying marriage doesn't come hard on a fellow at first. It does. Fellow says to himself, damn it all, he says, I can't call my soul my own! But he gets broken in. It's all discipline.'

Luke thought that Major Horton's married life must have been more like a military campaign than an idyll of domestic bliss.

'Women,' soliloquized the major, 'are a rum lot. It seems sometimes that there's no pleasing them. But by Jove, they keep a man up to the mark.'

Luke preserved a respectful silence.

'You married?' inquired the major.

'No.'

'Ah, well, you'll come to it. And mind you, my boy, there's nothing like it.'

'It's always cheering,' said Luke, 'to hear someone speak well of the marriage state. Especially in these days of easy divorce.'

'Pah!' said the major. 'Young people make me sick. No stamina – no endurance. They can't stand anything. No *fortitude!*'

Luke itched to ask why such exceptional fortitude should be needed, but he controlled himself.

'Mind you,' said the major, 'Lydia was a woman in a thousand – in a thousand! Every one here respected and looked up to her.'

'Yes?'

'She wouldn't stand any nonsense. She'd got a way of fixing a person with her eye – and the person wilted – just wilted. Some of these half-baked girls who call themselves servants nowadays. They think you'll put up with any insolence. Lydia soon showed them! Do you know we had fifteen cooks and house-parlourmaids in one year. *Fifteen!*'

Luke felt that this was hardly a tribute to Mrs Horton's domestic management, but since it seemed to strike his host differently he merely murmured some vague remark.

'Turned 'em out neck and crop, she did, if they didn't suit.'

'Was it always that way about?' asked Luke.

'Well, of course a lot of them walked out on us. A good riddance – that's what Lydia used to say!'

'A fine spirit,' said Luke, 'but wasn't it sometimes rather awkward?'

'Oh! I didn't mind turning to and putting my hand to things,' said Horton. 'I'm a pretty fair cook and I can lay a fire with any one. I've never cared for washing up but of course it's got to be done – you can't get away from that.'

Luke agreed that you couldn't. He asked whether Mrs Horton had been good at domestic work.

'I'm not the sort of fellow to let his wife wait on him,' said Major Horton. 'And anyway Lydia was far too delicate to do any housework.'

'She wasn't strong then?'

Major Horton shook his head.

'She had wonderful spirit. She wouldn't give in. But what that woman suffered! And no sympathy from the doctors either. Doctors are callous brutes. They only understand downright physical pain. Anything out of the ordinary is beyond most of them. Humbleby, for instance, every one seemed to *think* he was a good doctor.'

'You don't agree.'

'The man was an absolute ignoramus. Knew nothing of modern discoveries. Doubt if he'd ever heard of a neurosis! He understood measles and mumps and broken bones all right, I suppose. But nothing else. Had a row with him in the end. He didn't understand Lydia's case at all. I gave it him straight from the shoulder and he didn't like it. Got huffed and backed right out. Said I could send for any other doctor I chose. After that, we had Thomas.'

'You liked him better?'

'Altogether a much cleverer man. If any one could have pulled her through her last illness Thomas would have done it. As a matter of fact she was getting better, but she had a sudden relapse.'

'Was it painful?'

'H'm, yes. Gastritis. Acute pain – sickness – all the rest of it. How that poor woman suffered! She was a martyr if there ever was one. And a couple of hospital nurses in the house who were about as sympathetic as a brace of grandfather clocks! "The patient this" and "the patient that".' The major shook his head and drained his glass. 'Can't stand hospital nurses! So smug. Lydia insisted they were poisoning her. That wasn't true, of course – a regular sick fancy – lots of people have it, so Thomas said – but there was this much truth behind it – those women disliked her. That's the worst of women – always down on their own sex.'

'I suppose,' said Luke, feeling that he was putting it awkwardly but not seeing how to put it better, 'that Mrs Horton had a lot of devoted friends in Wychwood?'

'People were very kind,' said the major somewhat grudgingly. 'Whitfield sent down grapes and peaches from his hot-house. And the old tabbies used to come and sit with her. Honoria Waynflete and Lavinia Pinkerton.'

'Miss Pinkerton came often, did she?'

'Yes. Regular old maid – but a kind creature! Very worried about Lydia she was. Used to inquire into the diet and the medicines. All kindly meant, you know, but what I call a lot of *fuss*.'

Luke nodded comprehendingly.

'Can't stand fuss,' said the major. 'Too many women in this place. Difficult to get a decent game of golf.'

'What about the young fellow at the antique shop?' said Luke.

The major snorted:

'He doesn't play golf. Much too much of a Miss Nancy.'

'Has he been in Wychwood long?'

'About two years. Nasty sort of fellow. Hate those long-haired purring chaps. Funnily enough Lydia liked him. You can't trust women's judgement about men. They cotton to some amazing bounders. She even insisted on taking some patent quack nostrum of his. Stuff in a purple glass jar with signs of the Zodiac all over it! Supposed to be certain herbs picked at the full of the moon. Lot of tomfoolery, but women swallow that stuff – swallow it literally too – ha, ha!'

Luke said, feeling that he was changing the subject rather

abruptly, but correctly judging that Major Horton would not be aware of the fact:

'What sort of fellow is Abbot, the local solicitor? Pretty sound on the law? I've got to have some legal advice about something and I thought I might go to him.'

'They say he's pretty shrewd,' acknowledged Major Horton. 'I don't know. Matter of fact I've had a row with him. Not seen him since he came out here to make Lydia's will for her just before she died. In my opinion that man's a cad. But of course,' he added, 'that doesn't affect his ability as a lawyer.'

'No, of course not,' said Luke. 'He seems a quarrelsome sort of man, though. Seems to have fallen out with a good many people from what I hear.'

'Trouble with him is that he's so confoundedly touchy,' said Major Horton. 'Seems to think he's God Almighty and that any one who disagrees with him is committing *lèse-majesté*. Heard of his row with Humbleby?'

'They had a row, did they?'

'First-class row. Mind you, that doesn't surprise me. Humbleby was an opinionated ass! Still, there it is.'

'His death was very sad.'

'Humbleby's? Yes, I suppose it was. Lack of ordinary care. Blood poisoning's a damned dangerous thing. Always put iodine on a cut – I do! Simple precaution. Humbleby, who's a doctor, doesn't do anything of the sort. It just shows.'

Luke was not quite sure what it showed, but he let that pass. Glancing at his watch he got up.

Major Horton said:

'Getting on for lunch time? So it is. Well, glad to have had a chat with you. Does me good to see a man who's been about the world a bit. We must have a yarn some other time. Where was your show? Mayang Straits? Never been there. Hear you're writing a book. Superstitions and all that.'

'Yes – I –'

But Major Horton swept on.

'I can tell you several very interesting things. When I was in India, my boy –'

Luke escaped some ten minutes later after enduring the usual histories of fakirs, rope and mango tricks, dear to the retired Anglo-Indian.

As he stepped out into the open air, and heard the major's voice bellowing to Nero behind him, he marvelled at the miracle of married life. Major Horton seemed genuinely to regret a wife who, by all accounts, not excluding his own, must have been nearly allied to a man-eating tiger.

Or was it – Luke asked himself the question suddenly – was it an exceedingly clever bluff?

CHAPTER 12
PASSAGE OF ARMS

The afternoon of the tennis party was fortunately fine. Lord Whitfield was in his most genial mood, acting the part of the host with a good deal of enjoyment. He referred frequently to his humble origin. The players were eight in all. Lord Whitfield, Bridget, Luke, Rose Humbleby, Mr Abbot, Dr Thomas, Major Horton and Hetty Jones, a giggling young woman who was the daughter of the bank manager.

In the second set of the afternoon, Luke found himself partnering Bridget against Lord Whitfield and Rose Humbleby. Rose was a good player with a strong forehand drive and played in county matches. She atoned for Lord Whitfield's failures, and Bridget and Luke, who were neither of them particularly strong, made quite an even match of it. They were three games all, and then Luke found a streak of erratic brilliance and he and Bridget forged ahead to five–three.

It was then he observed that Lord Whitfield was losing his temper. He argued over a line ball, declared a serve to be a fault in spite of Rose's disclaimer, and displayed all the attributes of a peevish child. It was set point, but Bridget sent an easy shot into the net and immediately after served a double fault. Deuce. The next ball was returned down the middle line and as he prepared to take it he and his partner collided. Then Bridget served another double fault and the game was lost.

Bridget apologized. 'Sorry, I've gone to pieces.'

It seemed true enough. Bridget's shots were wild and she

seemed to be unable to do anything right. The set ended with Lord Whitfield and his partner victorious at the score of eight–six.

There was a momentary discussion as to the composition of the next set. In the end Rose played again with Mr Abbot as her partner against Dr Thomas and Miss Jones.

Lord Whitfield sat down, wiping his forehead and smiling complacently, his good humour quite restored. He began to talk to Major Horton on the subject of a series of articles on Fitness for Britain which one of his papers was starring.

Luke said to Bridget:

'Show me the kitchen garden.'

'Why the kitchen garden?'

'I have a feeling for cabbages.'

'Won't green peas do?'

'Green peas would be admirable.'

They walked away from the tennis court and came to the walled kitchen garden. It was empty of gardeners this Saturday afternoon and looked lazy and peaceful in the sunshine.

'Here are your peas,' said Bridget.

Luke paid no attention to the object of the visit. He said:

'Why the hell did you give them the set?'

Bridget's eyebrows went up a fraction.

'I'm sorry. I went to bits. My tennis is erratic.'

'Not so erratic as that! Those double faults of yours wouldn't deceive a child! And those wild shots – each of them half a mile out!'

Bridget said calmly:

'That's because I'm such a rotten tennis player. If I were a bit better I could perhaps have made it a bit more plausible! But as it is if I try to make a ball go just out, it's always on the line and all the good work still to do.'

'Oh, you admit it then?'

'Obvious, my dear Watson.'

'And the reason?'

'Equally obvious, I should have thought. Gordon doesn't like losing.'

'And what about me? Supposing I like to win?'

'I'm afraid, my dear Luke, that that isn't equally important.'

'Would you like to make your meaning just a little clearer still?'

'Certainly, if you like. One mustn't quarrel with one's bread and butter. Gordon is my bread and butter. You are not.'

Luke drew a deep breath. Then he exploded.

'What the hell do you mean by marrying that absurd little man? Why are you doing it?'

'Because as his secretary I get six pounds a week, and as his wife I shall get a hundred thousand settled on me, a jewel-case full of pearls and diamonds, a handsome allowance, and various perquisites of the married state!'

'But for somewhat different duties!'

Bridget said coldly:

'*Must* we have this melodramatic attitude towards every single thing in life? If you are contemplating a pretty picture of Gordon as an uxorious husband, you can wash it right out! Gordon, as you should have realized, is a small boy who has not quite grown up. What he needs is a mother, not a wife. Unfortunately his mother died when he was four years old. What he wants is someone at hand to whom he can brag, someone who will reassure him about himself and who is prepared to listen indefinitely to Lord Whitfield on the subject of Himself!'

'You've got a bitter tongue, haven't you?'

Bridget retorted sharply:

'I don't tell myself fairy stories if that's what you mean! I'm a young woman with a certain amount of intelligence, very moderate looks, and no money. I intend to earn an honest living. My job as Gordon's wife will be practically indistinguishable from my job as Gordon's secretary. After a year I doubt if he'll remember to kiss me good-night. The only difference is in the salary.'

They looked at each other. Both of them were pale with anger. Bridget said jeeringly:

'Go on. You're rather old-fashioned, aren't you, Mr Fitzwilliam? Hadn't you better trot out the old *clichés* – say that I'm selling myself for money – that's always a good one, I think!'

Luke said: 'You're a cold-blooded little devil!'

'That's better than being a hot-blooded little fool!'

'Is it?'

'Yes. I know.'

Luke sneered. 'What do you know?'

'I know what it is to care about a man! Did you ever meet Johnnie Cornish? I was engaged to him for three years. He was adorable – I cared like hell about him – cared so much that it *hurt*! Well, he threw me over and married a nice plump widow with a North-Country accent and three chins and an income of thirty thousand a year! That sort of thing rather cures one of romance, don't you think?'

Luke turned away with a sudden groan. He said:

'It might.'

'It did . . .'

There was a pause. The silence lay heavy between them. Bridget broke it at last. She said, but with a slight uncertainty in her tone:

'I hope you realize that you had no earthly right to speak to me as you did. You're staying in Gordon's house and it's damned bad taste!'

Luke recovered his composure.

'Isn't that rather a *cliché* too?' he inquired politely.

Bridget flushed. 'It's true, anyway!'

'It isn't. I had every right.'

'Nonsense!'

Luke looked at her. His face had a queer pallor, like a man who is suffering physical pain. He said:

'I *have* a right. I've the right of caring for you – what did you say just now? – of caring so much that it hurts!'

She drew back a step. She said: 'You –'

'Yes, funny, isn't it? The sort of thing that ought to give you a hearty laugh! I came down here to do a job of work and *you* came round the corner of that house and – how can I say it – put a spell on me! That's what it feels like. You mentioned fairy stories just now. I'm caught up in a fairy story! You've bewitched me. I've a feeling that if you pointed your finger at me and said: "Turn into a frog," I'd go hopping away with my eyes popping out of my head.'

He took a step nearer to her.

'I love you like hell, Bridget Conway. And, loving you like hell, you can't expect me to enjoy seeing you get married to a pot-bellied pompous little peer who loses his temper when he doesn't win at tennis.'

'What do you suggest I should do?'

'I suggest that you should marry me instead! But doubtless that suggestion will give rise to a lot of merry laughter.'

'The laughter is positively uproarious.'

'Exactly. Well, now we know where we are. Shall we return to the tennis court? Perhaps this time you will find me a partner who can play to win!'

'Really,' said Bridget sweetly, 'I believe you mind losing just as much as Gordon does!'

Luke caught her suddenly by the shoulders.

'You've got a devilish tongue, haven't you, Bridget?'

'I'm afraid you don't like me very much, Luke, however great your passion for me!'

'I don't think I like you at all.'

Bridget said, watching him:

'You meant to get married and settle down when you came home, didn't you?'

'Yes.'

'But not to someone like me?'

'I never thought of anyone in the least like you.'

'No – you wouldn't – I know your type. I know it exactly.'

'You are so clever, dear Bridget.'

'A really nice girl – thoroughly English – fond of the country and good with dogs . . . You probably visualized her in a tweed skirt stirring a log fire with the tip of her shoe.'

'The picture sounds most attractive.'

'I'm sure it does. Shall we return to the tennis court? You can play with Rose Humbleby. She's so good that you're practically certain to win.'

'Being old-fashioned I must allow you to have the last word.'

Again there was a pause. Then Luke took his hands slowly from her shoulders. They both stood uncertain as though something still unsaid lingered between them.

Then Bridget turned abruptly and led the way back. The next set was just ending. Rose protested against playing again.

'I've played two sets running.'

Bridget, however, insisted.

'I'm feeling tired. I don't want to play. You and Mr Fitzwilliam take on Miss Jones and Major Horton.'

But Rose continued to protest and in the end a men's four was arranged. Afterwards came tea.

Lord Whitfield conversed with Dr Thomas, describing at length and with great self-importance a visit he had recently paid to the Wellerman Kreitz Research Laboratories.

'I wanted to understand the trend of the latest scientific discoveries for myself,' he explained earnestly. 'I'm responsible for what my papers print. I feel that very keenly. This is a scientific age. Science must be made easily assimilable by the masses.'

'A little science might possibly be a dangerous thing,' said Dr Thomas with a slight shrug of his shoulders.

'Science in the home, that's what we have to aim at,' said Lord Whitfield. 'Science minded –'

'Test tube conscious,' said Bridget gravely.

'I was impressed,' said Lord Whitfield. 'Wellerman took me round himself, of course. I begged him to leave me to an underling, but he insisted.'

'Naturally,' said Luke.

Lord Whitfield looked gratified.

'And he explained everything most clearly – the culture – the serum – the whole principle of the thing. He agreed to contribute the first article in the series himself.'

Mrs Anstruther murmured:

'They use guinea-pigs, I believe – so cruel – though of course not so bad as dogs – or even cats.'

'Fellows who use dogs ought to be shot,' said Major Horton, hoarsely.

'I really believe, Horton,' said Mr Abbot, 'that you value canine life above human life.'

'Every time!' said the major. 'Dogs can't turn round on you like human beings can. Never get a nasty word from a dog.'

'Only a nasty tooth stuck into your leg,' said Mr Abbot. 'Eh, Horton?'

'Dogs are a good judge of character,' said Major Horton.

'One of your brutes nearly pinned me by the leg last week. What do you say to that, Horton?'

'Same as I said just now!'

Bridget interposed tactfully:

'What about some more tennis?'

A couple more sets were played. Then, as Rose Humbleby said good-bye, Luke appeared beside her.

'I'll see you home,' he said. 'And carry the tennis bat. You haven't got a car, have you?'

'No, but it's no distance.'

'I'd like a walk.'

He said no more, merely taking her racquet and shoes from her. They walked down the drive without speaking. Then Rose mentioned one or two trivial matters. Luke answered rather shortly but the girl did not seem to notice.

As they turned into the gate of her house, Luke's face cleared.

'I'm feeling better now,' he said.

'Were you feeling badly before?'

'Nice of you to pretend you didn't notice it. You've exorcised the brute's sulky temper, though. Funny, I feel as though I'd come out of a dark cloud into the sun.'

'So you have. There was a cloud over the sun when we left the Manor and now it's passed over.'

'So it's literally as well as figuratively. Well, well – the world's a good place after all.'

'Of course it is.'

'Miss Humbleby, may I be impertinent?'

'I'm sure you couldn't be.'

'Oh, don't be too sure of that. I wanted to say that I think Dr Thomas is a very lucky man.'

Rose blushed and smiled.

She said: 'So you've heard?'

'Was it supposed to be a secret? I'm so sorry.'

'Oh! Nothing is a secret in this place,' said Rose ruefully.

'So it is true – you and he are engaged?'

Rose nodded.

'Only – just now – we're not announcing it officially. You see, daddy was against it and it seems – well – unkind to – to blazon it abroad the moment he's dead.'

'Your father disapproved?'

'Well, not *disapproved* exactly. Oh, I suppose it did amount to that, really.'

Luke said gently:

'He thought you were too young?'

'That's what he said.'

Luke said acutely: 'But you think there was something more than that?'

Rose bent her head slowly and reluctantly.

'Yes – I'm afraid what it really amounted to was that daddy didn't – well, didn't really *like* Geoffrey.'

'They were antagonistic to each other?'

'It seemed like that sometimes . . . Of course, daddy was rather a prejudiced old dear.'

'And I suppose he was very fond of you and didn't like the thought of losing you?'

Rose assented but still with a shade of reservation in her manner.

'It went deeper than that?' asked Luke. 'He definitely didn't want Thomas as a husband for you?'

'No. You see – daddy and Geoffrey are so very unlike – and in some ways they clashed. Geoffrey was really very patient and good about it – but knowing daddy didn't like him made him even more reserved and shy in his manner, so that daddy really never got to know him any better.'

'Prejudices are very hard to combat,' said Luke.

'It was so completely unreasonable!'

'Your father didn't advance any reasons?'

'Oh, no. He couldn't! Naturally, I mean, there wasn't anything he could say against Geoffrey except that he didn't like him.'

'*I do not like thee, Dr Fell, the reason why I cannot tell.*'

'Exactly.'

'No tangible thing to get hold of? I mean, your Geoffrey doesn't drink or back horses?'

'Oh, no. I don't believe Geoffrey even knows what won the Derby.'

'That's funny,' said Luke. 'You know, I could swear I saw your Dr Thomas at Epsom on Derby Day.'

For a moment he was anxious lest he might already have mentioned that he only arrived in England on that day. But Rose responded at once quite unsuspiciously.

'You thought you saw Geoffrey at the Derby? Oh, no. He couldn't get away, for one thing. He was over at Ashewold nearly all that day at a difficult confinement case.'

'What a memory you've got!'

Rose laughed.

'I remember that, because he told me they called the baby Jujube as a nickname!'

Luke nodded abstractedly.

'Anyway,' said Rose, 'Geoffrey never goes to race meetings. He'd be bored to death.'

She added, in a different tone:

'Won't you – come in? I think mother would like to see you.'

'If you're sure of that?'

Rose led the way into a room where twilight hung rather sadly. A woman was sitting in an arm-chair in a curiously huddled up position.

'Mother, this is Mr Fitzwilliam.'

Mrs Humbleby gave a start and shook hands. Rose went quietly out of the room.

'I'm glad to see you, Mr Fitzwilliam. Some friends of yours knew my husband many years ago, so Rose tells me.'

'Yes, Mrs Humbleby.' He rather hated repeating the lie to the widowed woman, but there was no way out of it.

Mrs Humbleby said:

'I wish you could have met him. He was a fine man and a great doctor. He cured many people who had been given up as hopeless just by the strength of his personality.'

Luke said gently:

'I've heard a lot about him since I've been here. I know how much people thought of him.'

He could not see Mrs Humbleby's face very distinctly. Her voice was rather monotonous, but its very lack of feeling seemed to emphasize the fact that actually feeling was in her, strenuously held back.

She said rather unexpectedly:

'The world is a very wicked place, Mr Fitzwilliam. Do you know that?'

Luke was a little surprised.

'Yes, perhaps that may be.'

She insisted:

'No, but do you *know* it? It's important that. There's a lot of

480 · AGATHA CHRISTIE

wickedness about . . . One must be prepared – to fight it! John was. *He* knew. He was on the side of the right!'

Luke said gently:

'I'm sure he was.'

'He knew the wickedness there was in *this* place,' said Mrs Humbleby. 'He knew –'

She burst suddenly into tears.

Luke murmured:

'I'm so sorry –' and stopped.

She controlled herself as suddenly as she had lost control.

'You must forgive me,' she said. She held out her hand and he took it. 'Do come and see us while you are here,' she said. 'It would be so good for Rose. She likes you so much.'

'I like her. I think your daughter is the nicest girl I've met for a long time, Mrs Humbleby.'

'She's very good to me.'

'Dr Thomas is a very lucky man.'

'Yes.' Mrs Humbleby dropped his hand. Her voice had gone flat again. 'I don't know – it's all so difficult.'

Luke left her standing in the half gloom, her fingers nervously twisting and untwisting themselves.

As he walked home his mind went over various aspects of the conversation.

Dr Thomas had been absent from Wychwood for a good part of Derby Day. He had been absent in a car. Wychwood was thirty-five miles from London. Supposedly he had been attending a confinement case. Was there more than his word? The point, he supposed, could be verified. His mind went on to Mrs Humbleby.

What had she meant by her insistence on that phrase, '*There's a lot of wickedness about . . .*'?

Was she just nervous and overwrought by the shock of her husband's death? Or was there something more to it than that?

Did she perhaps know something? Something that Dr Humbleby had known before he died?

'I've got to go on with this,' said Luke to himself. 'I've got to go on.'

Resolutely he averted his mind from the passage of arms that had taken place between him and Bridget.

CHAPTER 13

MISS WAYNFLETE TALKS

On the following morning Luke came to a decision. He had, he felt, proceeded as far as he could with indirect inquiries. It was inevitable that sooner or later he would be forced into the open. He felt that the time had come to drop the book-writing camouflage and reveal that he had come to Wychwood with a definite aim in view.

In pursuance of this plan of campaign he decided to call upon Honoria Waynflete. Not only had he been favourably impressed by that middle-aged spinster's air of discretion and a certain shrewdness of outlook – but he fancied that she might have information that would help him. He believed that she had told him what she *knew*. He wanted to induce her to tell him what she might have *guessed*. He had a shrewd idea that Miss Waynflete's guesses might be fairly near the truth.

He called immediately after church.

Miss Waynflete received him in a matter-of-fact manner, showing no surprise at his call. As she sat down near him, her prim hands folded and her intelligent eyes – so like an amiable goat's – fixed on his face, he found little difficulty in coming to the object of his visit.

He said: 'I dare say you have guessed, Miss Waynflete, that the reason of my coming here is not merely to write a book on local customs?'

Miss Waynflete inclined her head and continued to listen.

Luke was not minded as yet to go into the full story. Miss Waynflete might be discreet – she certainly gave him the impression of being so – but where an elderly spinster was concerned Luke felt he could hardly rely on her resisting the temptation to confide an exciting story to one or two trusted cronies. He thereupon proposed to adopt a middle course.

'I am down here to inquire into the circumstances of the death of that poor girl, Amy Gibbs.'

Miss Waynflete said:

'You mean you have been sent down by the police?'

'Oh, no – I'm not a plain-clothes dick.' He added with a slightly humorous inflection, 'I'm afraid I'm that well-known character in fiction, the private investigator.'

'I see. Then it was Bridget Conway who brought you down here?'

Luke hesitated a moment. Then he decided to let it go at that. Without going into the whole Pinkerton story, it was difficult to account for his presence. Miss Waynflete was continuing, a note of gentle admiration in her voice.

'Bridget is so practical – so efficient! I'm afraid, if it had been left to *me*, I should have distrusted my own judgement – I mean, that if you are not absolutely sure of a thing, it is so difficult to commit yourself to a definite course of action.'

'But you are sure, aren't you?'

Miss Waynflete said gravely:

'No, indeed, Mr Fitzwilliam. It is not a thing one can be sure about! I mean, it *might* all be imagination. Living alone, with no one to consult or to talk to, one might easily become melodramatic and imagine things which had no foundation in fact.'

Luke assented readily to this statement, recognizing its inherent truth, but he added gently:

'But you are sure in your own mind?'

Even here Miss Waynflete showed a little reluctance.

'We are not talking at cross purposes, I hope?' she demurred.

Luke smiled.

'You would like me to put it in plain words? Very well. You do think that Amy Gibbs was murdered?'

Honoria Waynflete flinched a little at the crudity of the language. She said:

'I don't feel at all happy about her death. Not at all happy. The whole thing is profoundly unsatisfactory in my opinion.'

Luke said patiently:

'But you don't think her death was a natural one?'

'No.'

'You don't believe it was an accident?'

'It seems to me most improbable. There are so many –'

Luke cut her short.

'You don't think it was suicide?'

'Emphatically not.'

'Then,' said Luke gently, 'you *do* think that it was murder?'

Miss Waynflete hesitated, gulped, and bravely took the plunge.
'Yes,' she said. 'I do!'

'Good. Now we can get on with things.'

'But I have really no *evidence* on which to base that belief,'
Miss Waynflete explained anxiously. 'It is entirely an *idea*!'

'Quite so. This is a private conversation. We are merely
speaking about what we *think* and *suspect*. We *suspect* Amy
Gibbs was murdered. Who do we *think* murdered her?'

Miss Waynflete shook her head. She was looking very troubled.

Luke said, watching her:

'Who had reason to murder her?'

Miss Waynflete said slowly:

'She had had a quarrel, I believe, with her young man at the
garage, Jim Harvey – a most steady, superior young man. I know
one reads in the papers of young men attacking their sweethearts
and dreadful things like that, but I really can't believe that Jim
would do such a thing.'

Luke nodded.

Miss Waynflete went on.

'Besides, I can't believe that he would do it that way. Climb
up to her window and substitute a bottle of poison for the other
one with the cough mixture. I mean, that doesn't seem –'

Luke came to the rescue as she hesitated.

'It's not the act of an angry lover? I agree. In my opinion we
can wash Jim Harvey right out. Amy was killed (we're agreeing
she *was* killed) by someone who wanted to get her out of the way
and who planned the crime carefully so that it should appear to
be an accident. Now have you any idea – any *hunch* – shall we
put it like that? – who that person could be?'

Miss Waynflete said:

'No – really – no, I haven't the least idea!'

'Sure?'

'N-no – no, indeed.'

Luke looked at her thoughtfully. The denial, he felt, had not
rung quite true. He went on:

'You know of no motive?'

'No motive whatever.'

That was more emphatic.

'Had she been in many places in Wychwood?'

'She was with the Hortons for a year before going to Lord Whitfield.'

Luke summed up rapidly.

'It's like this, then. Somebody wanted that girl out of the way. From the given facts we assume that – first – it was a man and a man of moderately old-fashioned outlook (as shown by the hat paint touch), and secondly that it must have been a reasonably athletic man since it is clear he must have climbed up over the outhouse to the girl's window. You agree on those points?'

'Absolutely,' said Miss Waynflete.

'Do you mind if I go round and have a try myself?'

'Not at all. I think it is a very good idea.'

She led him out by a side door and round to the back yard. Luke managed to reach the outhouse roof without much trouble. From there he could easily raise the sash of the girl's window and with a slight effort hoist himself into the room. A few minutes later he rejoined Miss Waynflete on the path below, wiping his hands on his handkerchief.

'Actually it's easier than it looks,' he said. 'You want a certain amount of muscle, that's all. There were no signs on the sill or outside?'

Miss Waynflete shook her head.

'I don't think so. Of course the constable climbed up this way.'

'So that if there were any traces they would be taken to be his. How the police force assists the criminal! Well, that's that!'

Miss Waynflete led the way back to the house.

'Was Amy Gibbs a heavy sleeper?' he asked.

Miss Waynflete replied acidly:

'It was extremely difficult to get her up in the morning. Sometimes I would knock again and again, and call out to her before she answered. But then, you know, Mr Fitzwilliam, there's a saying there are none so deaf as those who will not hear!'

'That's true,' acknowledged Luke. 'Well, now, Miss Waynflete, we come to the question of *motive*. Starting with the most obvious one, do you think there was anything between that fellow Ellsworthy and the girl?' He added hastily, 'This is just your *opinion* I'm asking. Only that.'

'If it's a matter of opinion, I would say yes.'

Luke nodded.

'In your opinion, would the girl Amy have stuck at a spot of blackmail?'

'Again as a matter of opinion, I should say that that was quite possible.'

'Do you happen to know if she had much money in her possession at the time of her death?'

Miss Waynflete reflected.

'I do not think so. If she had had any unusual amount I think I should have heard about it.'

'And she hadn't launched into any unusual extravagance before she died?'

'I don't think so.'

'That rather militates against the blackmail theory. The victim usually pays once before he decides to proceed to extremes. There's another theory. The girl might *know* something.'

'What kind of thing?'

'She might have knowledge that was dangerous to someone here in Wychwood. We'll take a strictly hypothetical case. She'd been in service in a good many houses here. Supposing she came to know of something that would damage say, someone like Mr Abbot, professionally.'

'Mr Abbot?'

Luke said quickly:

'Or possibly some negligence or unprofessional conduct on the part of Dr Thomas.'

Miss Waynflete began, 'But surely –' and then stopped.

Luke went on:

'Amy Gibbs was housemaid, you said, in the Hortons' house at the time when Mrs Horton died.'

There was a moment's pause, then Miss Waynflete said:

'Will you tell me, Mr Fitzwilliam, why you bring the Hortons into this? Mrs Horton died over a year ago.'

'Yes, and the girl Amy was there at the time.'

'I see. What have the Hortons to do with it?'

'I don't know. I – just wondered. Mrs Horton died of acute gastritis, didn't she?'

'Yes.'

'Was her death at all unexpected?'

Miss Waynflete said slowly:

'It was to me. You see, she had been getting much better – seemed well on the road to recovery – and then she had a sudden relapse and died.'

'Was Dr Thomas surprised?'

'I don't know. I believe he was.'

'And the nurses, what did they say?'

'In my experience,' said Miss Waynflete, 'hospital nurses are never surprised at any case taking a turn for the worse! It is recovery that surprises them.'

'But her death surprised you?' Luke persisted.

'Yes. I had been with her only the day before, and she had seemed very much better, talked and seemed quite cheerful.'

'What did she think about her own illness?'

'She complained that the nurses were poisoning her. She had had one nurse sent away, but she said these two were just as bad!'

'I suppose you didn't pay much attention to that?'

'Well, no, I thought it was all part of the illness. And she was a very suspicious woman and – it may be unkind to say so – but she liked to make herself *important*. No doctor ever understood her case – and it was never anything simple – it must either be some very obscure disease or else somebody was "trying to get her out of the way".'

Luke tried to make his voice casual.

'She didn't suspect her husband of trying to do her in?'

'Oh, *no*, that idea never occurred to her!'

Miss Waynflete paused a minute, then she asked quietly:

'Is that what you think?'

Luke said slowly:

'Husbands have done that before and got away with it. Mrs Horton from all accounts was a woman any man might have longed to be rid of! And I understand that he came into a good deal of money on her death.'

'Yes, he did.'

'What do *you* think, Miss Waynflete?'

'You want my opinion?'

'Yes, just your opinion.'

Miss Waynflete said quietly and deliberately:

'In my opinion, Major Horton was quite devoted to his wife and would never have dreamed of doing such a thing.'

Luke looked at her and received the mild amber glance in reply. It did not waver.

'Well,' he said, 'I expect you're right. You'd probably know if it was the other way round.'

Miss Waynflete permitted herself a smile.

'We women are good observers, you think?'

'Absolutely first-class. Would Miss Pinkerton have agreed with you, do you think?'

'I don't think I ever heard Lavinia express an opinion.'

'What did she think about Amy Gibbs?'

Miss Waynflete frowned a little as though thinking.

'It's difficult to say. Lavinia had a very curious idea.'

'What idea?'

'She thought that there was something odd going on here in Wychwood.'

'She thought, for instance, that somebody pushed Tommy Pierce out of that window?'

Miss Waynflete stared at him in astonishment.

'How *did* you know that, Mr Fitzwilliam?'

'She told me so. Not in these words, but she gave me the general idea.'

Miss Waynflete leant forward, pink with excitement.

'When was this, Mr Fitzwilliam?'

Luke said quietly, 'The day she was killed. We travelled together to London.'

'What did she tell you exactly?'

'She told me that there had been too many deaths in Wychwood. She mentioned Amy Gibbs, and Tommy Pierce and that man Carter. She also said that Dr Humbleby would be the next to go.'

Miss Waynflete nodded slowly.

'Did she tell you who was responsible?'

'A man with a certain look in his eyes,' said Luke grimly. 'A look you couldn't mistake, according to her. She'd seen that look in his eye when he was talking to Humbleby. That's why she said Humbleby would be the next to go.'

'And he was,' whispered Miss Waynflete. 'Oh, dear. Oh, dear.'

She leaned back. Her eyes had a stricken look in them.

'Who was the man?' said Luke. 'Come now, Miss Waynflete, you know, you *must* know!'

'I don't. She didn't tell me.'

'But you can guess,' said Luke keenly. 'You've a very shrewd idea of who was in her mind.'

Reluctantly Miss Waynflete bowed her head.

'Then tell me.'

But Miss Waynflete shook her head energetically.

'No, indeed. You're asking me to do something that is highly improper! You're asking me to *guess* at what may – only *may*, mind you – have been in the mind of a friend *who is now dead*. I couldn't make an accusation of that kind!'

'It wouldn't be an accusation – only an opinion.'

But Miss Waynflete was unexpectedly firm.

'I've nothing to go on – nothing whatever,' she said. 'Lavinia never actually *said* anything to me. I may *think* she had a certain idea – but you see I might be entirely *wrong*. And then I should have misled you and perhaps serious consequences might ensue. It would be very wicked and unfair of me to mention a *name*. And I may be quite, quite wrong! In fact, I probably *am* wrong!'

And Miss Waynflete set her lips firmly and glared at Luke with a grim determination.

Luke knew how to accept defeat when he met it.

He realized that Miss Waynflete's sense of rectitude and something else more nebulous that he could not quite place were both against him.

He accepted defeat with a good grace and rose to say good-bye. He had every intention of returning to the charge later, but he allowed no hint of that to escape into his manner.

'You must do as you think right, of course,' he said. 'Thank you for the help you have given me.'

Miss Waynflete seemed to become a little less sure of herself as she accompanied him to the door.

'I hope you don't think,' she began, then changed the form of the sentence. 'If there is anything else I can do to help you, please, please let me know.'

'I will. You won't repeat this conversation, will you?'

'Of course not. I shan't say a word to anybody.'

Luke hoped that that was true.

'Give my love to Bridget,' said Miss Waynflete. 'She's such a handsome girl, isn't she? And clever too. I – I hope she will be happy.'

And as Luke looked a question, she added:

'Married to Lord Whitfield, I mean. Such a great difference in age.'

'Yes, there is.'

Miss Waynflete sighed.

'You know that I was engaged to him once,' she said unexpectedly.

Luke stared in astonishment. She was nodding her head and smiling rather sadly.

'A long time ago. He was such a promising boy. I had helped him, you know, to educate himself. And I was so proud of his – his spirit and the way he was determined to succeed.'

She sighed again.

'My people, of course, were scandalized. Class distinctions in those days were very strong.' She added after a minute or two, 'I've always followed his career with great interest. My people, I think, were wrong.'

Then, with a smile, she nodded a farewell and went back into the house.

Luke tried to collect his thoughts. He had placed Miss Waynflete as definitely 'old'. He realized now that she was probably still under sixty. Lord Whitfield must be well over fifty. She might, perhaps, be a year or two older than he, no more.

And he was going to marry Bridget. Bridget, who was twenty-eight. Bridget, who was young and alive . . .

'Oh, damn,' said Luke. 'Don't let me go on thinking of it. The job. Get on with the job.'

CHAPTER 14

MEDITATIONS OF LUKE

Mrs Church, Amy Gibbs's aunt, was definitely an unpleasant woman. Her sharp nose, shifty eyes, and her voluble tongue all alike filled Luke with nausea.

He adopted a curt manner with her and found it unexpectedly successful.

'What you've got to do,' he told her, 'is to answer my questions to the best of your ability. If you hold back anything or tamper with the truth the consequences may be extremely serious to you.'

'Yes, sir. I see. I'm sure I'm only too willing to tell you anything I can. I've never been mixed up with the police –'

'And you don't want to be,' finished Luke. 'Well, if you do as I've told you there won't be any question of that. I want to know all about your late niece – who her friends were – what money she had – anything she said that might be out of the way. We'll start with her friends. Who were they?'

Mrs Church leered at him slyly out of the corner of an unpleasant eye.

'You'll be meaning gentlemen, sir?'

'Had she any girl friends?'

'Well – hardly – not to speak of, sir. Of course there was girls she'd been in service with – but Amy didn't keep up with them much. You see –'

'She preferred the sterner sex. Go on. Tell me about that.'

'It was Jim Harvey down at the garage she was actually going with, sir. And a nice steady young fellow he was. "You couldn't do better," I've said to her many a time –'

Luke cut in:

'And the others?'

Again he got the sly look.

'I expect you're thinking of the gentleman who keeps the curiosity shop? I didn't like it myself, and I tell you that straight, sir! I've always been respectable and I don't hold with carryings on! But with what girls are nowadays it's no use speaking to them. They go their own way. And often they live to regret it.'

'Did Amy live to regret it?' asked Luke bluntly.

'No, sir – that I do *not* think.'

'She went to consult Dr Thomas on the day of her death. That wasn't the reason?'

'No, sir, I'm nearly sure it wasn't. Oh! I'd take my oath on it! Amy had been feeling ill and out of sorts, but it was just a bad cough and cold she had. It wasn't anything of the kind you suggest, I'm sure it wasn't, sir.'

'I'll take your word for that. How far had matters gone between her and Ellsworthy?'

Mrs Church leered.

'I couldn't exactly say, sir. Amy wasn't one for confiding in me.'

Luke said curtly:

'But they'd gone pretty far?'

Mrs Church said smoothly:

'The gentleman hasn't got at all a good reputation here, sir. All sorts of goings on. And friends down from town and many very queer happenings. Up in the Witches' Meadow in the middle of the night.'

'Did Amy go?'

'She did go once, sir, I believe. Stayed out all night and his lordship found out about it (she was at the Manor then) and spoke to her pretty sharp, and she sauced him back and he gave her notice for it, which was only to be expected.'

'Did she ever talk to you much about what went on in the places she was in?'

Mrs Church shook her head.

'Not very much, sir. More interested in her own doings, she was.'

'She was with Major and Mrs Horton for a while, wasn't she?'

'Nearly a year, sir.'

'Why did she leave?'

'Just to better herself. There was a place going at the Manor, and of course the wages was better there.'

Luke nodded.

'She was with the Hortons at the time of Mrs Horton's death?' he asked.

'Yes, sir. She grumbled a lot about that – with two hospital nurses in the house, and all the extra work nurses make, and the trays and one thing and another.'

'She wasn't with Mr Abbot, the lawyer, at all?'

'No, sir. Mr Abbot has a man and wife do for him. Amy did go to see him once at his office, but I don't know why.'

Luke stored away that small fact as possibly relevant. Since Mrs Church, however, clearly knew nothing more about it, he did not pursue the subject.

'Any other gentlemen in the town who were friends of hers?'

'Nothing that I'd care to repeat.'

'Come now, Mrs Church. I want the truth, remember.'

'It wasn't a gentleman, sir, very far from it. Demeaning herself, that's what it was, and so I told her.'

'Do you mind speaking more plainly, Mrs Church?'

'You'll have heard of the Seven Stars, sir? *Not* a good-class house, and the landlord, Harry Carter, a low-class fellow and half-seas over most of the time.'

'Amy was a friend of his?'

'She went a walk with him once or twice. I don't believe there was more in it than that. I don't indeed, sir.'

Luke nodded thoughtfully and changed the subject.

'Did you know a small boy, Tommy Pierce?'

'What? Mrs Pierce's son? Of course I did. Always up to mischief.'

'He ever see much of Amy?'

'Oh, no, sir. Amy would soon send him off with a flea in his ear if he tried any of his tricks on her.'

'Was she happy in her place with Miss Waynflete?'

'She found it a bit dull, sir, and the pay wasn't high. But of course after she'd been dismissed the way she was from Ashe Manor, it wasn't so easy to get another good place.'

'She could have gone away, I suppose?'

'To London, you mean?'

'Or some other part of the country?'

Mrs Church shook her head. She said slowly:

'Amy didn't want to leave Wychwood – not as things were.'

'How do you mean, *as things were*?'

'What with Jim and the gentleman at the curio shop.'

Luke nodded thoughtfully. Mrs Church went on:

'Miss Waynflete is a very nice lady, but very particular about brass and silver and everything being dusted and the mattresses turned. Amy wouldn't have put up with the fussing if she hadn't been enjoying herself in other ways.'

'I can imagine that,' said Luke drily.

He turned things over in his mind. He could see no further questions to ask. He was fairly certain that he had extracted all that Mrs Church knew. He decided on one last tentative attack.

'I dare say you can guess the reason of all these questions. The circumstances of Amy's death were rather mysterious. We're not entirely satisfied as to its being an accident. If not, you realize what it must have been.'

Mrs Church said with a certain ghoulish relish:

'Foul play!'

'Quite so. Now supposing your niece *did* meet with foul play, who do you think is likely to be responsible for her death?'

Mrs Church wiped her hands on her apron.

'There'd be a reward, as likely as not, for setting the police on the right track,' she inquired meaningly.

'There might be,' said Luke.

'I wouldn't like to say anything definite.' Mrs Church passed a hungry tongue over her thin lips. 'But the gentleman at the curio shop is a queer one. You'll remember the Castor case, sir – and how they found little bits of the poor girl pinned up all over Castor's seaside bungalow and how they found five or six other poor girls he'd served the same way. Maybe this Mr Ellsworthy is one of that kind?'

'That's your suggestion, is it?'

'Well, it might be that way, sir, mightn't it?'

Luke admitted that it might. Then he said:

'Was Ellsworthy away from here on the afternoon of Derby Day? That's a very important point.'

Mrs Church stared.

'Derby Day?'

'Yes – a fortnight ago last Wednesday.'

She shook her head.

'Really, I couldn't say as to that. He usually was away on Wednesdays – went up to town as often as not. It's early closing Wednesday, you see.'

'Oh,' said Luke. 'Early closing.'

He took his leave of Mrs Church, disregarding her insinuations that her time had been valuable and that she was therefore entitled to monetary compensation. He found himself disliking Mrs Church intensely. Nevertheless the conversation he had

had with her, though not strikingly illuminative in any way, had provided several suggestive small points.

He went over things carefully in his mind.

Yes, it still boiled down to those four people. Thomas, Abbot, Horton and Ellsworthy. The attitude of Miss Waynflete seemed to him to prove that.

Her distress and reluctance to mention a name. Surely that meant, that *must* mean, that the person in question was someone of standing in Wychwood, someone whom a chance insinuation might definitely injure. It tallied, too, with Miss Pinkerton's determination to take her suspicions to headquarters. The local police would ridicule her theory.

It was not a case of the butcher, the baker, the candlestick-maker. It was not a case of a mere garage mechanic. The person in question was one against whom an accusation of murder was a fantastic and, moreover, a serious matter.

There were four possible candidates. It was up to him to go carefully once more into the case against each one and make up his own mind.

First to examine the reluctance of Miss Waynflete. She was a conscientious and scrupulous person. She believed that she knew the man whom Miss Pinkerton had suspected, but it was, she pointed out, only a *belief* on her part. It was possible that she was mistaken.

Who was the person in Miss Waynflete's mind?

Miss Waynflete was distressed lest an accusation by her might injure an innocent man. Therefore the object of her suspicions *must* be a man of high standing, generally liked and respected by the community.

Therefore, Luke argued, that automatically barred out Ellsworthy. He was practically a stranger to Wychwood, his local reputation was bad, not good. Luke did not believe that, if Ellsworthy was the person in Miss Waynflete's mind, she would have had any objection to mentioning him. Therefore as far as Miss Waynflete was concerned, wash out Ellsworthy.

Now as to the others. Luke believed that he could also elimin-ate Major Horton. Miss Waynflete had rebutted with some warmth the suggestion that Horton might have poisoned his wife. If she had suspected him of later crimes, she would hardly have been so positive about his innocence of the death of Mrs Horton.

That left Dr Thomas and Mr Abbot. Both of them fulfilled the necessary requirements. They were men of high professional standing against whom no word of scandal had ever been uttered. They were, on the whole, both popular and well liked, and were known as men of integrity and rectitude.

Luke proceeded to another aspect of the matter. Could he, himself, eliminate Ellsworthy and Horton? Immediately he shook his head. It was not so simple. Miss Pinkerton had *known* – really known – who the man was. That was proved, in the first case by her own death, and in the second case, by the death of Dr Humbleby. But Miss Pinkerton had never actually mentioned a *name* to Honoria Waynflete. Therefore, though Miss Waynflete *thought* she knew, she might quite easily be wrong. We often *know* what other people are thinking – but sometimes we find out that we did not know after all – and have, in fact, made an egregious mistake!

Therefore the four candidates were still in the field. Miss Pinkerton was dead and could give no further assistance. It was up to Luke to do what he had done before, on the day after he came to Wychwood, weigh up the evidence and consider the probabilities.

He began with Ellsworthy. On the face of it Ellsworthy was the likeliest starter. He was abnormal and had possibly a perverted personality. He might quite easily be a 'lust killer'.

'Let's take it this way,' said Luke to himself. 'Suspect every one in turn. Ellsworthy, for instance. Let's say he's the killer! For the moment, let's take it quite definitely that I know that. Now we'll take the possible victims in chronological order. First, Mrs Horton. Difficult to see what motive Ellsworthy could have had for doing away with Mrs Horton. But there was a *means*. Horton spoke of some quack nostrum that she got from him and took. Some poison like arsenic could have been given that way. The question is – Why?

'Now the others. Amy Gibbs. Why did Ellsworthy kill Amy Gibbs? The obvious reason – she was being a nuisance! Threatened an action for breach of promise, perhaps? Or had she assisted at a midnight orgy? Did she threaten to talk? Lord

Whitfield has a good deal of influence in Wychwood and Lord Whitfield, according to Bridget, is a very moral man. He might have taken up the matter against Ellsworthy if the latter had been up to anything particularly obscene. So – exit Amy. Not, I think, a sadistic murder. The method employed is against that.

'Who's next – Carter? Why Carter? Unlikely *he* would know about midnight orgies (or did Amy tell him?). Was the pretty daughter mixed up in it? Did Ellsworthy start making love to her? (Must have a look at Lucy Carter.) Perhaps he was just abusive to Ellsworthy, and Ellsworthy in his cat-like feline way, resented it. If he'd already committed one or two murders he would be getting sufficiently callous to contemplate a killing for a very slight reason.

'Now Tommy Pierce. Why did Ellsworthy kill Tommy Pierce? Easy. Tommy had assisted at a midnight ritual of some kind. Tommy threatened to talk about it. Perhaps Tommy *was* talking about it. Shut Tommy's mouth.

'Dr Humbleby. Why did Ellsworthy kill Dr Humbleby? That's the easiest of the lot! Humbleby was a doctor and he'd noticed that Ellsworthy's mental balance was none too good. Probably was getting ready to do something about it. So Humbleby was doomed. There's a stumbling block there in the method. How did Ellsworthy ensure that Humbleby should die of blood poisoning? Or did Humbleby die of something else? Was the poisoned finger a coincidence?

'Last of all, Miss Pinkerton. Wednesday's early closing. Ellsworthy might have gone up to town that day. Has he a car, I wonder? Never seen him in one, but that proves nothing. He knew she'd suspected him and he was going to take no chances of Scotland Yard believing her story. Perhaps they already knew something about him then?

'That's the case against Ellsworthy! Now what is there *for* him? Well, for one thing, he's certainly not the man Miss Waynflete *thought* Miss Pinkerton meant. For another, he doesn't fit – quite – with my own vague impression. When she was talking I got a picture of a man – and it wasn't a man like Ellsworthy. The impression she gave me was of a very normal man – outwardly, that is – the kind of man nobody would suspect. Ellsworthy is the kind of man you *would* suspect. No, I got more the impression of a man like – Dr Thomas.

'Thomas, now. What about Thomas? I wiped him clean off the list after I'd had a chat with him. Nice unassuming fellow. But the whole point of this murderer – unless I've got the whole thing wrong – is that he would be a nice unassuming fellow. The last person you'd think ever would be a murderer! Which, of course, is exactly what one feels about Thomas.

'Now then, let's go through it all again. Why did Dr Thomas kill Amy Gibbs? Really, it seems most unlikely that he did! But she *did* go to see him that day, and he *did* give her that bottle of cough mixture. Suppose that was really oxalic acid. That would be very simple and clever! Who was called in, I wonder, when she was found poisoned – Humbleby or Thomas? If it was Thomas he might just come along with an old bottle of hat paint in his pocket, put it down unobtrusively on the table – and take off both bottles to be analysed as bold as brass! Something like that. It could be done if you were cool enough!

'Tommy Pierce? Again I can't see a likely motive. That's the difficulty with our Dr Thomas – *motive*. There's not even a crazy motive! Same with Carter. Why should Dr Thomas want to dispose of Carter? One can only assume that Amy, Tommy and the publican all knew something about Dr Thomas that it was unhealthy to know. Ah! Supposing now that that something was *the death of Mrs Horton*. Dr Thomas attended her. And she died of a rather unexpected relapse. He could have managed that easily enough. And Amy Gibbs, remember, was in the house at the time. She might have seen or heard something. That would account for *her*. Tommy Pierce, we have it on good authority, was a particularly inquisitive small boy. He *may* have got wise to something. Can't get Carter in. Amy Gibbs told him something. He may have repeated it in his cups, and Thomas may have decided to silence him too. All this, of course, is pure conjecture. But what else can one do?

'Now Humbleby. Ah! At last we come to a perfectly plausible murder. Adequate motive and ideal means! If Dr Thomas couldn't give his partner blood poisoning, no one could! He could reinfect the wound every time he dressed it! I wish the earlier killings were a little more plausible.

'Miss Pinkerton? She's more difficult, but there is one definite fact. Dr Thomas was not in Wychwood for at least a good part of the day. He gave out that he was attending a confinement. That may be. But the fact remains that he was away from Wychwood *in a car*.

'Is there anything else? Yes, just one thing. The look he gave me when I went away from the house the other day. Superior, condescending, the smile of a man who'd just led me up the garden path and knew it.'

Luke sighed, shook his head and went on with his reasoning.

'Abbot? He's the right kind of man too. Normal, well-to-do, respected, last sort of man, etc., etc. He's conceited, too, and confident. Murderers usually are! They've got over-weening conceit! Always think they'll get away with it. Amy Gibbs paid him a visit once. Why? What did she want to see him for? To get legal advice? Why? Or was it a personal matter? There's that mention of "a letter from a lady" that Tommy saw. Was that letter from Amy Gibbs? Or was it a letter written by Mrs Horton – a letter, perhaps, that Amy Gibbs had got hold of? What other lady could there be writing to Mr Abbot on a matter so private that he loses control when the office boy inadvertently sees it? What else can we think of re Amy Gibbs? The hat paint? Yes, right kind of old-fashioned touch – men like Abbot are usually well behind the times where women are concerned. The old-world style of philanderer! Tommy Pierce? Obvious – on account of the letter (really, it must have been a very damning letter!). Carter? Well, there was trouble about Carter's daughter. Abbot wasn't going to have a scandal – a low-down ruffianly halfwit like Carter dare to threaten him! He who had got away with two clever killings! Away with Mr Carter! Dark night and a well-directed push. Really, this killing business is almost too easy.

'Have I got the Abbot mentality? I think so. Nasty look in an old lady's eye. She's thinking things about him . . . Then, row with Humbleby. Old Humbleby daring to set himself against Abbot, the clever solicitor and murderer. The old fool – he little knows what's in store for him! *He's* for it! Daring to browbeat me!

'And then – what? Turning to catch Lavinia Pinkerton's eyes. And his own eyes falter – show a consciousness of guilt. He who was boasting of being unsuspected has definitely aroused suspicion. Miss Pinkerton knows his secret . . . She knows what he has done . . . Yes, but she can't have *proof*. But suppose she goes about looking for it . . . Suppose she talks . . . Suppose . . . He's quite a shrewd judge of character. He guesses what she will finally do. If she goes with this tale of hers to Scotland Yard they *may* believe her – they *may* start making inquiries. Something pretty desperate has got to be done. Has Abbot got a car or did he hire one in London? Anyway, he was away from here on Derby Day . . .'

Again Luke paused. He was so entering into the spirit of the thing that he found it hard to make a transition from one suspect to another. He had to wait a minute before he could force himself into the mood where he could visualize Major Horton as a successful murderer.

'Horton murdered his wife. Let's start with that! He had ample provocation and he gained considerably by her death. In order to carry it off successfully he had to make a good show of devotion. He's had to keep that up. Sometimes, shall we say, he overdoes it a bit?

'Very good, one murder successfully accomplished. Who's the next? Amy Gibbs. Yes, perfectly credible. Amy was in the house. She may have seen something – the major administering a soothing cup of beef-tea or gruel? She mayn't have realized the point of what she saw till some time later. The hat paint trick is the sort of thing that would occur to the major quite naturally – a very masculine man with little knowledge of women's fripperies.

'Amy Gibbs all serene and accounted for.

'The drunken Carter? Same suggestion as before. Amy told him something. Another straightforward murder.

'Now Tommy Pierce. We've got to fall back on his inquisitive nature. I suppose the letter in Abbot's office couldn't have been a complaint from Mrs Horton that her husband was trying to poison her? That's a wild suggestion, but it *might* be so. Anyway, the major becomes alive to the fact that Tommy is a menace, so Tommy joins Amy and Carter. All quite simple and straightforward and according to Cocker. Easy to kill? My God, yes.

'But now we come to something rather more difficult. Humbleby! Motive? Very obscure. Humbleby was attending Mrs Horton originally. Did he get puzzled by the illness, and did Horton influence his wife to change to the younger, more unsuspicious doctor? But if so, *what made Humbleby a danger so long after?* Difficult, that ... The manner of his death, too. A poisoned finger. Doesn't connect up with the major.

'Miss Pinkerton? That's perfectly possible. He has a car. I saw it. And he was away from Wychwood that day, supposedly gone to the Derby. It might be – yes. *Is* Horton a cold-blooded killer? Is he? Is he? I wish I knew ...'

Luke stared ahead of him. His brow was puckered with thought.

'It's one of them ... I don't *think* it's Ellsworthy – but it might be! He's the most obvious one! Thomas is wildly unlikely – if it weren't for the *manner* of Humbleby's death. That blood poisoning definitely points to a *medical* murderer! It *could* be Abbot – there's not as much evidence against him as against the others – but I can *see* him in the part, somehow ... Yes – he fits as the others don't. And it *could* be Horton! Bullied by his wife for years, feeling his insignificance – yes, it could be! But Miss Waynflete doesn't think it is, and she's no fool – and she knows the place and the people in it ...

'Which *does* she suspect, Abbot or Thomas? It must be one of these two ... If I tackled her outright – "Which of them is it?" – I'd get it out of her then, perhaps.

'But even then she might be wrong. There's no way of proving *her* right – like Miss Pinkerton proved herself. More evidence – that's what I want. If there were to be one more case – just one more – then I'd know –'

He stopped himself with a start.

'My God,' he said under his breath. 'What I'm asking for is *another murder* ...'

CHAPTER 15

IMPROPER CONDUCT OF A CHAUFFEUR

In the bar of the Seven Stars, Luke drank his pint and felt somewhat embarrassed. The stare of half a dozen bucolic pairs of eyes followed his least movement, and conversation had come to a standstill upon his entrance. Luke essayed a few comments of general interest such as the crops, the state of the weather, and football coupons, but to none did he get any response.

He was reduced to gallantry. The fine-looking girl behind the counter with her black hair and red cheeks he rightly judged to be Miss Lucy Carter.

His advances were received in a pleasant spirit. Miss Carter duly giggled and said, 'Go on with you! I'm sure you don't think nothing of the kind! That's telling!' – and other such rejoinders. But the performance was clearly mechanical.

Luke, seeing no advantage to be gained by remaining, finished his beer and departed. He walked along the path to where the river was spanned by a footbridge. He was standing looking at this when a quavering voice behind him said:

'That's it, mister, that's where old Harry went over.'

Luke turned to see one of his late fellow-drinkers, one who had been particularly unresponsive to the topic of crops, weather and coupons. He was now clearly about to enjoy himself as a guide to the macabre.

'Went over into the mud he did,' said the ancient labourer. 'Right into the mud and stuck in it head downwards.'

'Odd he should have fallen off here,' said Luke.

'He were drunk, he were,' said the rustic indulgently.

'Yes, but he must have come this way drunk many times before.'

'Most every night,' said the other. 'Always in liquor, Harry were.'

'Perhaps some one pushed him over,' said Luke, making the suggestion in a casual fashion.

'They might of,' the rustic agreed. 'But I don't know who'd go for to do that,' he added.

'He might have made a few enemies. He was fairly abusive when he was drunk, wasn't he?'

'His language was a treat to hear! Didn't mince his words, Harry didn't. But no one would go for to push a man what's drunk.'

Luke did not combat this statement. It was evidently regarded as wildly unsporting for advantage to be taken of a man's state of intoxication. The rustic had sounded quite shocked at the idea.

'Well,' he said vaguely, 'it was a sad business.'

'None so sad for his missus,' said the old man. 'Reckon her and Lucy haven't no call to be sad about it.'

'There may be other people who are glad to have him out of the way.'

The old man was vague about that.

'Maybe,' he said. 'But he didn't mean no harm, Harry didn't.'

On this epitaph for the late Mr Carter, they parted.

Luke bent his steps towards the old Hall. The library transacted its business in the two front rooms. Luke passed on to the back through a door which was labelled Museum. There he moved from case to case, studying the not very inspiring exhibits. Some Roman pottery and coins. Some South Sea curiosities, a Malay head-dress. Various Indian gods 'presented by Major Horton', together with a large and malevolent-looking Buddha, and a case of doubtful-looking Egyptian beads.

Luke wandered out again into the hall. There was no one about. He went quietly up the stairs. There was a room with magazines and papers there, and a room filled with non-fiction books.

Luke went a storey higher. Here were rooms filled with what he designated to himself as junk. Stuffed birds removed from the museum owing to the moth having attacked them, stacks of torn magazines and a room whose shelves were covered with out-of-date works of fiction and children's books.

Luke approached the window. Here it must have been that Tommy Price had sat, possibly whistling and occasionally rubbing a pane of glass vigorously when he heard anyone coming.

Somebody had come in. Tommy had shown his zeal – sitting half out of the window and polishing with zest. And then that somebody had come up to him, and while talking, had given a sudden sharp push.

Luke turned away. He walked down the stairs and stood a minute or two in the hall. Nobody had noticed him come in. Nobody had seen him go upstairs.

'*Anyone* might have done it!' said Luke. 'Easiest thing in the world.'

He heard footsteps coming from the direction of the library proper. Since he was an innocent man with no objection to being seen, he could remain where he was. If he had not wanted to be seen, how easy just to step back inside the door of the museum room!

Miss Waynflete came out from the library, a little pile of books under her arm. She was pulling on her gloves. She looked very happy and busy. When she saw him her face lit up and she exclaimed:

'Oh, Mr Fitzwilliam, have you been looking at the museum? I'm afraid there isn't very much there, really. Lord Whitfield is talking of getting us some really interesting exhibits.'

'Really?'

'Yes, something modern, you know, and up-to-date. Like they have at the Science Museum in London. He suggests a model aeroplane and a locomotive and some chemical things too.'

'That would, perhaps, brighten things up.'

'Yes, I don't think a museum should deal solely with the past, do you?'

'Perhaps not.'

'Then some food exhibits, too – calories and vitamins – all that sort of thing. Lord Whitfield is so keen on the Greater Fitness Campaign.'

'So he was saying the other night.'

'It's *the* thing at present, isn't it? Lord Whitfield was telling me how he'd been to the Wellerman Institute – and seen such a lot of germs and cultures and bacteria – it quite made me shiver. And he told me all about mosquitoes and sleeping sickness and something about a liver fluke that I'm afraid was a little too difficult for *me*.'

'It was probably too difficult for Lord Whitfield,' said Luke cheerfully. 'I'll bet he got it all wrong! You've got a much clearer brain than he has, Miss Waynflete.'

Miss Waynflete said sedately:

'That's very nice of you, Mr Fitzwilliam, but I'm afraid women are never quite such deep thinkers as men.'

Luke repressed a desire to criticize adversely Lord Whitfield's processes of thought. Instead he said:

'I did look into the museum but afterwards I went up to have a look at the top windows.'

'You mean where Tommy –' Miss Waynflete shivered. 'It's really very horrible.'

'Yes, it's not a nice thought. I've spent about an hour with Mrs Church – Amy's aunt – not a nice woman!'

'Not at all.'

'I had to take rather a strong line with her,' said Luke. 'I fancy she thinks I'm a kind of super policeman.'

He stopped as he noted a sudden change of expression on Miss Waynflete's face.

'Oh, Mr Fitzwilliam, do you think that was wise?'

Luke said:

'I don't really know. I think it was inevitable. The book story was wearing thin – I can't get much further on that. I had to ask the kind of questions that were directly to the point.'

Miss Waynflete shook her head – the troubled expression still on her face.

'In a place like this, you see – everything gets round so fast.'

'You mean that everybody will say "there goes the tec" as I walk down the street? I don't think that really matters now. In fact, I may get more that way.'

'I wasn't thinking of that.' Miss Waynflete sounded a little breathless. 'What I meant was – that *he'll* know. *He'll* realize that you're on his track.'

Luke said slowly:

'I suppose he will.'

Miss Waynflete said:

'But don't you see – that's horribly dangerous. *Horribly!*'

'You mean –' Luke grasped her point at last, 'you mean that the killer will have a crack at *me*?'

'Yes.'

'Funny,' said Luke. 'I never thought of that! I believe you're right, though. Well, that might be the best thing that could happen.'

Miss Waynflete said earnestly:

'I don't think you realize that he's – he's a very clever man. He's cautious, too! And remember, he's got a great deal of experience – perhaps more than *we* know.'

'Yes,' said Luke thoughtfully. 'That's probably true.'

Miss Waynflete exclaimed:

'Oh, I don't like it! Really, I feel quite *alarmed*!'

Luke said gently:

'You needn't worry. I shall be very much on my guard I can assure you. You see I've narrowed the possibilities down pretty closely. I've an idea at any rate who the killer might be . . .'

She looked up sharply.

Luke came a step nearer. He lowered his voice to a whisper:

'Miss Waynflete, if I were to ask you *which of two* men you considered the most likely – Dr Thomas or Mr Abbot – *what would you say?*'

'Oh –' said Miss Waynflete. Her hand flew to her breast. She stepped back. Her eyes met Luke's in an expression that puzzled him. They showed impatience and something closely allied to it that he could not quite place.

She said:

'I can't say anything –'

She turned away abruptly with a curious sound – half a sigh, half a sob.

Luke resigned himself.

'Are you going home?' he asked.

'No, I was going to take these books to Mrs Humbleby. That lies on your way back to the Manor. We might go part of the way together.'

'That will be very nice,' said Luke.

They went down the steps, turned to the left skirting the village green.

Luke looked back at the stately lines of the house they had left.

'It must have been a lovely house in your father's day,' he said.

Miss Waynflete sighed.

'Yes, we were all very happy there. I am so thankful it hasn't been pulled down. So many of the old houses are going.'

'I know. It's sad.'

'And really the new ones aren't nearly as well built.'

'I doubt if they will stand the test of time as well.'

'But of course,' said Miss Waynflete, 'the new ones *are* convenient – so labour-saving, and not such big draughty passages to scrub.'

Luke assented.

When they arrived at the gate of Dr Humbleby's house, Miss Waynflete hesitated and said:

'Such a beautiful evening. I think, if you don't mind, I will come a little farther. I am enjoying the air.'

Somewhat surprised, Luke expressed pleasure politely. It was hardly what he would have described as a beautiful evening. There was a strong wind blowing, turning back the leaves viciously on the trees. A storm, he thought, might come at any minute.

Miss Waynflete, however, clutching her hat with one hand, walked by his side with every appearance of enjoyment, talking as she went in little gasps.

It was a somewhat lonely lane they were taking, since from Dr Humbleby's house the shortest way to Ashe Manor was not by the main road, but by a side lane which led to one of the back gates of the Manor House. This gate was not of the same ornate ironwork but had two handsome gate pillars surmounted by two vast pink pineapples. Why pineapples, Luke had been unable to discover! But he gathered that to Lord Whitfield pineapples spelt distinction and good taste.

As they approached the gate the sound of voices raised in anger came to them. A moment later they came in sight of Lord Whitfield confronting a young man in chauffeur's uniform.

'You're fired,' Lord Whitfield was shouting. 'D'you hear? You're fired.'

'If you'd overlook it, m'lord – just this once.'

'No, I won't overlook it! Taking my car out. *My* car – and what's more you've been drinking – yes, you have, don't deny it! I've made it clear there are three things I won't have on my estate – one's drunkenness, another's immorality and the other's impertinence.'

Though the man was not actually drunk, he had had enough to loosen his tongue. His manner changed.

'You won't have this and you won't have that, you old bastard! *Your* estate! Think we don't all know your father kept a boot-shop down here? Makes us laugh ourselves sick, it does, seeing you strutting about as cock of the walk! Who are you, I'd like to know? You're no better than I am – that's what you are.'

Lord Whitfield turned purple.

'How dare you speak to me like that? How dare you?'

The young man took a threatening step forward.

'If you wasn't such a miserable pot-bellied little swine I'd give you a sock on the jaw – yes, I would.'

Lord Whitfield hastily retreated a step, tripped over a root and went down in a sitting position.

Luke had come up.

'Get out of here,' he said roughly to the chauffeur.

The latter regained sanity. He looked frightened.

'I'm sorry, sir. I don't know what came over me, I'm sure.'

'A couple of glasses too much, I should say,' said Luke.

He assisted Lord Whitfield to his feet.

'I – I beg your pardon, m'lord,' stammered the man.

'You'll be sorry for this, Rivers,' said Lord Whitfield.

His voice trembled with intense feeling.

The man hesitated a minute, then shambled away slowly.

Lord Whitfield exploded:

'Colossal impertinence! To me. Speaking to me like that. Something very serious will happen to that man! No respect – no proper sense of his station in life. When I think of what I do for these people – good wages – every comfort – a pension when they retire. The ingratitude – the base ingratitude . . .'

He choked with excitement, then perceived Miss Waynflete who was standing silently by.

'Is that you, Honoria? I'm deeply distressed you should have witnessed such a disgraceful scene. That man's language –'

'I'm afraid he wasn't quite himself, Lord Whitfield,' said Miss Waynflete primly.

'He was drunk, that's what he was, drunk!'

'Just a bit lit up,' said Luke.

'Do you know what he did?' Lord Whitfield looked from one to the other of them. 'Took out my car – *my* car! Thought I shouldn't be back so soon. Bridget drove me over to Lyne in the two-seater. And this fellow had the impertinence to take a girl – Lucy Carter, I believe – out in *my* car!'

Miss Waynflete said gently:

'A most improper thing to do.'

Lord Whitfield seemed a little comforted.

'Yes, wasn't it?'

'But I'm sure he'll regret it.'

'I shall see that he does!'

'You've dismissed him,' Miss Waynflete pointed out.

Lord Whitfield shook his head.

'He'll come to a bad end, that fellow.'

He threw back his shoulders.

'Come up to the house, Honoria, and have a glass of sherry.'

'Thank you, Lord Whitfield, but I must go to Mrs Humbleby with these books. Good-night, Mr Fitzwilliam. You'll be *quite* all right now.'

She gave him a smiling nod and walked briskly away. It was so much the attitude of a nurse who delivers a child at a party that Luke caught his breath as a sudden idea struck him. Was it possible that Miss Waynflete had accompanied him solely in order to protect him? The idea seemed ludicrous, but –

Lord Whitfield's voice interrupted his meditations.

'Very capable woman, Honoria Waynflete.'

'Very, I should think.'

Lord Whitfield began to walk towards the house. He moved rather stiffly and his hand went to his posterior and rubbed it gingerly.

Suddenly he chuckled.

'I was engaged to Honoria once – years ago. She was a nice-looking girl – not so skinny as she is today. Seems funny to think of now. Her people were the nobs of this place.'

'Yes?'

Lord Whitfield ruminated:

'Old Colonel Waynflete bossed the show. One had to come out and touch one's cap pretty sharp. One of the old school he was, and proud as Lucifer.'

He chuckled again.

'The fat was in the fire all right when Honoria announced she was going to marry me! Called herself a Radical, she did. Very earnest. Was all for abolishing class distinctions. She was a serious kind of girl.'

'So her family broke up the romance?'

Lord Whitfield rubbed his nose.

'Well – not exactly. Matter of fact we had a bit of a row over something. Blinking bird she had – one of those beastly twittering canaries – always hated them – bad business – wrung its neck. Well – no good dwelling on all that now. Let's forget it.'

He shook his shoulders like a man who throws off an unpleasant memory.

Then he said, rather jerkily:

'Don't think she's ever forgiven me. Well, perhaps it's only natural . . .'

'I think she's forgiven you all right,' said Luke.

Lord Whitfield brightened up.

'Do you? Glad of that. You know I respect Honoria. Capable woman *and* a lady! That still counts even in these days. She runs that library business very well.'

He looked up and his voice changed.

'Hallo,' he said. 'Here comes Bridget.'

CHAPTER 16

THE PINEAPPLE

Luke felt a tightening of his muscles as Bridget approached.

He had had no word alone with her since the day of the tennis party. By mutual consent they had avoided each other. He stole a glance at her now.

She looked provokingly calm, cool and indifferent.

She said lightly:

'I was beginning to wonder what on earth had become of you, Gordon?'

Lord Whitfield grunted:

'Had a bit of a dust up! That fellow Rivers had the impertinence to take the Rolls out this afternoon.'

'*Lèse-majesté*,' said Bridget.

'It's no good making a joke out of it, Bridget. The thing's serious. He took a girl out.'

'I don't suppose it would have given him any pleasure to go solemnly for a drive by himself!'

Lord Whitfield drew himself up.

'On my estate I'll have decent moral behaviour.'

'It isn't actually immoral to take a girl joy riding.'

'It is when it's *my* car.'

'That, of course, is worse than immorality! It practically amounts to blasphemy. But you can't cut out the sex stuff altogether, Gordon. The moon is at the full and it's actually Midsummer Eve.'

'Is it, by Jove?' said Luke.

Bridget threw him a glance.

'That seems to interest you?'

'It does.'

Bridget turned back to Lord Whitfield.

'Three extraordinary people have arrived at the Bells and Motley. Item one, a man with shorts, spectacles and a lovely plum-coloured silk shirt! Item two, a female with no eyebrows, dressed in a peplum, a pound of assorted sham Egyptian beads and sandals. Item three, a fat man in a lavender suit and co-respondent shoes. I suspect them of being friends of our Mr Ellsworthy! Says the gossip writer: "Someone has whispered that there will be gay doings in the Witches' Meadow tonight."'

Lord Whitfield turned purple and said:

'I won't have it!'

'You can't help it, darling. The Witches' Meadow is public property.'

'I won't have this irreligious mumbo jumbo going on down here! I'll expose it in *Scandals*.' He paused, then said, 'Remind me to make a note about that and get Siddely on to it. I must go up to town tomorrow.'

'Lord Whitfield's campaign against witchcraft,' said Bridget flippantly. 'Medieval superstitions still rife in quiet country village.'

Lord Whitfield stared at her with a puzzled frown, then he turned and went into the house.

Luke said pleasantly:

'You must do your stuff better than that, Bridget!'

'What do you mean?'

'It would be a pity if you lost your job! That hundred thousand isn't yours yet. Nor are the diamonds and pearls. I should wait until after the marriage ceremony to exercise your sarcastic gifts if I were you.'

Her glance met his coolly.

'You are so thoughtful, dear Luke. It's kind of you to take my future so much to heart!'

'Kindness and consideration have always been my strong points.'

'I hadn't noticed it.'

'No? You surprise me.'

Bridget twitched the leaf off a creeper. She said:

'What have you been doing today?'

'The usual spot of sleuthing.'

'Any results?'

'Yes and no, as the politicians say. By the way, have you got any tools in the house?'

'I expect so. What kind of tools?'

'Oh, any handy little gadgets. Perhaps I could inspect some.'

Ten minutes later Luke had made a selection from a cupboard shelf.

'That little lot will do nicely,' he said, slapping the pocket in which he had stowed them away.

'Are you thinking of doing a spot of forcing and entering?'

'Maybe.'

'You're very uncommunicative on the subject.'

'Well, after all, the situation bristles with difficulties. I'm in the hell of a position. After our little knock up on Saturday I suppose I ought to clear out of here.'

'To behave as a perfect gentleman, you should.'

'But since I'm convinced that I am pretty hot on the trail of a homicidal maniac, I'm more or less forced to remain. If you could think of any convincing reason for me to leave here and take up my quarters at the Bells and Motley, for goodness' sake trot it out.'

Bridget shook her head.

'That's not feasible – you being a cousin and all that. Besides, the inn is full of Mr Ellsworthy's friends. They only run to three guest rooms.'

'So I am forced to remain, painful as it must be for you.'

Bridget smiled sweetly at him.

'Not at all. I can always do with a few scalps to dangle.'

'That,' said Luke appreciatively, 'was a particularly dirty crack. What I admire about you, Bridget, is that you have practically no instincts of kindness. Well, well. The rejected lover will now go and change for dinner.'

The evening passed uneventfully. Luke won Lord Whitfield's approval even more deeply than before by the apparent absorbed interest with which he listened to the other's nightly discourse.

When they came into the drawing-room Bridget said:

'You men have been a long time.'

Luke replied:

'Lord Whitfield was being so interesting that the time passed like a flash. He was telling me how he founded his first newspaper.'

Mrs Anstruther said:

'These new little fruiting trees in pots are perfectly marvellous, I believe. You ought to try them along the terrace, Gordon.'

The conversation then proceeded on normal lines.

Luke retired early.

He did not, however, go to bed. He had other plans.

It was just striking twelve when he descended the stairs noise-lessly in tennis shoes, passed through the library and let himself out by a window.

The wind was still blowing in violent gusts interspersed with brief lulls. Clouds scudded across the sky, obliterating the moon so that darkness alternated with bright moonlight.

Luke made his way by a circuitous route to Mr Ellsworthy's establishment. He saw his way clear to doing a little investigation. He was fairly certain that Ellsworthy and his friends would be out together on this particular date. Midsummer Eve, Luke thought, was sure to be marked by some ceremony or other. Whilst this was in progress, it would be a good opportunity to search Mr Ellsworthy's house.

He climbed a couple of walls, got round to the back of the house, took the assorted tools from his pocket and selected a likely implement. He found a scullery window amenable to his efforts. A few minutes later he had slipped back the catch, raised the sash and hoisted himself over.

He had a torch in his pocket. He used it sparingly – a brief flash to show him his way and to avoid running into things.

In a quarter of an hour he had satisfied himself that the house was empty. The owner was out and abroad on his own affairs.

Luke smiled with satisfaction and settled down to his task.

He made a minute and thorough search of every available nook and corner. In a locked drawer, below two or three innocuous water-colour sketches, he came upon some artistic efforts which caused him to lift his eyebrows and whistle. Mr Ellsworthy's correspondence was unilluminating, but some of his books – those tucked away at the back of a cupboard – repaid attention.

Besides these, Luke accumulated three meagre but suggestive scraps of information. The first was a pencil scrawl in a little notebook. '*Settle with Tommy Pierce*' – the date being a couple of days before the boy's death. The second was a crayon sketch of Amy Gibbs with a furious red cross right across the face. The third was a bottle of cough mixture. None of these things were in any way conclusive, but taken together they might be considered as encouraging.

Luke was just restoring some final order, replacing things in their place, when he suddenly stiffened and switched off his torch.

He had heard the key inserted in the lock of a side door.

He stepped across to the door of the room he was in, and applied an eye to a crack. He hoped Ellsworthy, if it was he, would go straight upstairs.

The side door opened and Ellsworthy stepped in, switching on a hall light as he did so.

As he passed along the hall, Luke saw his face and caught his breath.

It was unrecognizable. There was foam on the lips, the eyes were alight with a strange mad exultation as he pranced along the hall in little dancing steps.

But what caused Luke to catch his breath was the sight of Ellsworthy's hands. They were stained a deep brownish red – the colour of dried blood . . .

He disappeared up the stairs. A moment later the light in the hall was extinguished.

Luke waited a little longer, then very cautiously he crept out of the hall, made his way to the scullery and left by the window. He looked up at the house, but it was dark and silent.

He drew a deep breath.

'My God,' he said, 'the fellow's mad all right! I wonder what he's up to? I'll swear that was blood on his hands!'

He made a detour round the village and returned to Ashe Manor by a roundabout route. It was as he was turning into the side lane that a sudden rustle of leaves made him swing round.

'Who's there?'

A tall figure wrapped in a dark cloak came out from the shadow of a tree. It looked so eerie that Luke felt his heart miss a beat. Then he recognized the long pale face under the hood.

'Bridget? How you startled me!'

She said sharply:

'Where have you been? I saw you go out.'

'And you followed me?'

'No. You'd gone too far. I've been waiting till you came back.'

'That was a damned silly thing to do,' Luke grumbled.

She repeated her question impatiently.

'Where have you been?'

Luke said gaily:

'Raiding our Mr Ellsworthy!'

Bridget caught her breath.

'Did you – find anything?'

'I don't know. I know a bit more about the swine – his pornographical tastes and all that, and there are three things that might be suggestive.'

She listened attentively as he recounted the result of his search.

'It's very slight evidence, though,' he ended. 'But, Bridget, just as I was leaving Ellsworthy came back. And I tell you this – the man's as mad as a hatter!'

'You really think so?'

'I saw his face – it was – unspeakable! God knows what he'd been up to! He was in a delirium of mad excitement. And his hands were stained. I'll swear with *blood*.'

Bridget shivered.

'Horrible . . .' she murmured.

Luke said irritably:

'You shouldn't have come out by yourself, Bridget. It was absolute madness. Somebody might have knocked you on the head.'

She laughed shakily.

'The same applies to you, my dear.'

'I can look after myself.'

'I'm pretty good at taking care of myself, too. Hard boiled, I should think you'd call me.'

A sharp gust of wind came. Luke said suddenly:

'Take off that hood thing.'

'Why?'

With an unexpected movement he snatched at her cloak and whipped it away. The wind caught her hair and blew it out straight up from her head. She stared at him, her breath coming fast.

Luke said:

'You certainly are incomplete without a broomstick, Bridget. That's how I saw you first.' He stared a minute longer and said, 'You're a cruel devil.'

With a sharp impatient sigh he tossed the cloak back to her.

'There – put it on. Let's get home.'

'Wait . . .'

'Why?'

She came up to him. She spoke in a low, rather breathless voice.

'Because I've got something to say to you – that's partly why I waited for you here – outside the Manor. I want to say it to you now – before we go inside – into Gordon's property . . .'

'Well?'

She gave a short, rather bitter laugh.

'Oh, it's quite simple. *You win*, Luke. That's all!'

He said sharply:

'What do you mean?'

'I mean that I've given up the idea of being Lady Whitfield.'

He took a step nearer.

'Is that true?' he demanded.

'Yes, Luke.'

'You'll marry me?'

'Yes.'

'Why, I wonder?'

'I don't know. You say such beastly things to me – and I seem to like it . . .'

He took her in his arms and kissed her. He said:

'It's a mad world!'

'Are you happy, Luke?'

'Not particularly.'

'Do you think you'll ever be happy with me?'

'I don't know. I'll risk it.'

'Yes – that's what I feel . . .'

He slipped his arm through hers.

'We're rather queer about all this, my sweet. Come along. Perhaps we shall be more normal in the morning.'

'Yes – it's rather frightening the way things happen to one . . .' She looked down and tugged him to a standstill. 'Luke – Luke – *what's that* . . . ?'

The moon had come out from the clouds. Luke looked down to where Bridget's shoe trembled by a huddled mass.

With a startled exclamation he dragged his arm free and knelt down. He looked from the shapeless heap to the gatepost above. The pineapple was gone.

He stood up at last. Bridget was standing, her hands pressed together on her mouth.

He said:

'It's the chauffeur – Rivers. He's dead . . .'

'That beastly stone thing – it's been loose for some time – I suppose it blew down on him?'

Luke shook his head.

'The wind wouldn't do a thing like that. Oh! that's what it's *meant* to look like – that's what it's *meant* to be – another accident! But it's a fake. *It's the killer again* . . .'

'No – no, Luke –'

'I tell you it is. Do you know what I felt on the back of his head – in with the stickiness and mess – *grains of sand*. There's no sand about here. I tell you, Bridget, somebody stood here and slugged him as he came through the gate back to his cottage. Then laid him down and rolled that pineapple thing down on top of him.'

Bridget said faintly:

'Luke – there's blood – on your hands . . .'

Luke said grimly:

'There was blood on someone else's hands. Do you know what I was thinking this afternoon – that if there were to be one more crime we'd surely know. And we *do* know! *Ellsworthy*! He was out tonight and he came in with blood on his hands capering and prancing and mad – drunk with the homicidal maniac's expression . . .'

Looking down, Bridget shivered and said in a low voice: 'Poor Rivers . . .'

Luke said pityingly:

'Yes, poor fellow. It's damnable bad luck. But this will be the last, Bridget! Now we *know*, we'll get him!'

He saw her sway and in two steps he had caught her in his arms.

She said in a small childlike voice:

'Luke, I'm frightened . . .'

He said, 'It's all over, darling. It's all over . . .'

She murmured:

'Be kind to me – please. I've been hurt so much.'

He said: 'We've hurt each other. We won't do that any more.'

CHAPTER 17

LORD WHITFIELD TALKS

Dr Thomas stared across his consulting-room desk at Luke.

'Remarkable,' he said. 'Remarkable! You are really *serious*, Mr Fitzwilliam?'

'Absolutely. I am convinced that Ellsworthy is a dangerous maniac.'

'I have not paid special attention to the man. I should say, though, that he is possibly an abnormal type.'

'I'd go a good deal further than that,' said Luke grimly.

'You seriously believe that this man Rivers was murdered?'

'I do. You noticed the grains of sand in the wound?'

Dr Thomas nodded.

'I looked out for them after your statement. I am bound to say that you were correct.'

'That makes it clear, does it not, that the accident was faked and that the man was killed by a blow from a sandbag – or at any rate was stunned by one.'

'Not necessarily.'

'What do you mean?'

Dr Thomas leaned back and joined his fingertips together.

'Supposing that this man Rivers had been lying out in a sandpit during the day – there are several about in this part of the world. That might account for grains of sand in the hair.'

'Man, I tell you he was murdered!'

'You may tell me so,' said Dr Thomas drily, 'but that doesn't make it a fact.'

Luke controlled his exasperation.

'I suppose you don't believe a word of what I'm telling you.'

Dr Thomas smiled, a kindly superior smile.

'You must admit, Mr Fitzwilliam, that it's rather a wild story. You assert that this man Ellsworthy has killed a servant girl, a small boy, a drunken publican, my own partner and finally this man Rivers.'

'You don't believe it?'

Dr Thomas shrugged his shoulders.

'I have some knowledge of Humbleby's case. It seems to me quite out of the question that Ellsworthy could have caused his death, and I really cannot see that you have any evidence at all that he did so.'

'I don't know how he managed it,' confessed Luke, 'but it all hangs together with Miss Pinkerton's story.'

'There again you assert that Ellsworthy followed her up to London and ran her down in a car. Again you haven't a shadow of proof that happened! It's all – well – romancing!'

Luke said sharply:

'Now that I know where I am it will be my business to get proofs. I'm going up to London tomorrow to see an old pal of mine. I saw in the paper two days ago that he'd been made Assistant Commissioner of Police. He knows me and he'll listen to what I have to say. One thing I'm sure of, he'll order a thorough investigation of the whole business.'

Dr Thomas stroked his chin thoughtfully.

'Well – no doubt that should be very satisfactory. If it turns out that you're mistaken –'

Luke interrupted him.

'You definitely don't believe a word of all this?'

'In wholesale murder?' Dr Thomas raised his eyebrows. 'Quite frankly, Mr Fitzwilliam, I don't. The thing is too fantastic.'

'Fantastic, perhaps. But it hangs together. You've got to admit it hangs together. Once you accept Miss Pinkerton's story as true.'

Dr Thomas was shaking his head. A slight smile came to his lips.

'If you knew some of these old maids as well as I do,' he murmured.

Luke rose, trying to control his annoyance.

'At any rate, you're well named,' he said. 'A doubting Thomas, if there ever was one!'

Thomas replied good-humouredly:

'Give me a few proofs, my dear fellow. That's all I ask. Not just a long melodramatic rigmarole based on what an old lady fancied she saw.'

'What old ladies fancy they see is very often right. My Aunt Mildred was positively uncanny! Have you got any aunts yourself, Thomas?'

'Well – er – no.'

'A mistake!' said Luke. 'Every man should have aunts. They illustrate the triumph of guesswork over logic. It is reserved for aunts to *know* that Mr A. is a rogue because he looks like a dishonest butler they once had. Other people say reasonably enough that a respectable man like Mr A. couldn't be a crook. The old ladies are right every time.'

Dr Thomas smiled his superior smile again.

Luke said, his exasperation mounting once more:

'Don't you realize that I'm a policeman myself? I'm not the complete amateur.'

Dr Thomas smiled and murmured:

'In the Mayang Straits!'

'Crime is crime even in the Mayang Straits.'

'Of course – of course.'

Luke left Dr Thomas's surgery in a state of suppressed irritation.

He joined Bridget, who said:

'Well, how did you get on?'

'He didn't believe me,' said Luke. 'Which, when you come to

think of it, is hardly surprising. It's a wild story with no proofs. Dr Thomas is emphatically *not* the sort of man who believes six impossible things before breakfast!'

'Will anybody believe you?'

'Probably not, but when I get hold of old Billy Bones tomorrow, the wheels will start turning. They'll check up on our long-haired friend, Ellsworthy, and in the end they're bound to get somewhere.'

Bridget said thoughtfully:

'We're coming out into the open very much, aren't we?'

'We've got to. We can't – we simply can't afford any more murders.'

Bridget shivered.

'For God's sake be careful, Luke.'

'I'm being careful all right. Don't walk near gates with pineapples on them, avoid the lonely wood at nightfall, watch out for your food and drink. I know all the ropes.'

'It's horrible feeling you're a marked man.'

'So long as you're not a marked woman, my sweet.'

'Perhaps I am.'

'I don't think so. But I don't intend to take risks! I'm watching over you like an old-fashioned guardian angel.'

'Is it any good saying anything to the police here?'

Luke considered.

'No, I don't think it is – better go straight to Scotland Yard.'

Bridget murmured:

'That's what Miss Pinkerton thought.'

'Yes, but *I* shall be watching out for trouble.'

Bridget said:

'I know what I'm going to do tomorrow. I shall march Gordon down to that brute's shop and make him buy things.'

'Thereby ensuring that our Mr Ellsworthy is not lying in ambush for me on the steps of Whitehall?'

'That's the idea.'

Luke said with some slight embarrassment: 'About Whitfield –'

Bridget said quickly:

'Let's leave it till you come back tomorrow. Then we'll have it out.'

'Will he be very cut up, do you think?'

'Well –' Bridget considered the question. 'He'll be annoyed.'

'Annoyed? Ye gods! Isn't that putting it a bit mildly?'

'No. Because you see Gordon doesn't *like* being annoyed! It upsets him!'

Luke said soberly, 'I feel rather uncomfortable about it all.'

That feeling was uppermost in his mind when he prepared that evening to listen for the twentieth time to Lord Whitfield on the subject of Lord Whitfield. It was, he admitted, a cad's trick to stay in a man's house and steal his fiancée. He still felt, however, that a pot-bellied, pompous, strutting little nincompoop like Lord Whitfield ought never to have aspired to Bridget at all!

But his conscience so far chastened him that he listened with an extra dose of fervent attention and in consequence made a thoroughly favourable impression on his host.

Lord Whitfield was in high good-humour this evening. The death of his erstwhile chauffeur seemed to have exhilarated rather than depressed him.

'Told you that fellow would come to a bad end,' he crowed, holding up a glass of port to the light and squinting through it. 'Didn't I tell you so yesterday evening?'

'You did, indeed, sir.'

'And you see I was right! It's amazing how often I'm right!'

'That must be splendid for you,' said Luke.

'I've had a wonderful life – yes, a wonderful life! My path's been smoothed clear before me. I've always had great faith and trust in Providence. That's the secret, Fitzwilliam, that's the secret.'

'Yes?'

'I'm a religious man. I believe in good and evil and eternal justice. There *is* such a thing as divine justice, Fitzwilliam, not a doubt of it!'

'I believe in justice, too,' said Luke.

Lord Whitfield, as usual, was not interested in the beliefs of other people.

'Do right by your Creator and your Creator will do right by you! I've always been an upright man. I've subscribed to charity, and I've made my money honestly. I'm not beholden to any man! I stand alone. You remember in the Bible how the patriarchs became prosperous, herds and flocks were added to them, and their enemies were smitten down!'

Luke stifled a yawn and said:

'Quite – quite.'

'It's remarkable – absolutely remarkable,' said Lord Whitfield. 'The way that a righteous man's enemies are struck down! Look at yesterday. That fellow abuses me – even goes so far as to try to raise his hand against me. And what happens? Where is he today?'

He paused rhetorically and then answered himself in an impressive voice:

'Dead! Struck down by divine wrath!'

Opening his eyes a little, Luke said:

'Rather an excessive punishment, perhaps, for a few hasty words uttered after a glass too much.'

Lord Whitfield shook his head.

'It's always like that! Retribution comes swiftly and terribly. And there's good authentic authority for it. Remember the children that mocked Elisha – how the bears came out and devoured them. That's the way things happen, Fitzwilliam.'

'I always thought that was rather unnecessarily vindictive.'

'No, no. You're looking at it the wrong way. Elisha was a great and holy man. No one could be suffered to mock at him and live! I understand that because of my own case!'

Luke looked puzzled.

Lord Whitfield lowered his voice.

'I could hardly believe it at first. *But it happened every time!* My enemies and detractors were cast down and exterminated.'

'Exterminated?'

Lord Whitfield nodded gently and sipped his port.

'Time after time. One case quite like Elisha – a little boy. I came upon him in the gardens here – he was employed by me then. Do you know what he was doing? He was giving an imitation of Me – of ME! *Mocking* me! Strutting up and down with an audience to watch him. Making fun of me on my own ground! *D'you know what happened to him?* Not ten days later he fell out of an upper window and was killed!

'Then there was that ruffian Carter – a drunkard and a man of evil tongue. He came here and abused me. What happened to him? A week later he was dead – drowned in the mud. There had been a servant girl, too. She lifted her voice and called me names. Her punishment soon came. She drank poison by mistake! I could tell you heaps more. Humbleby dared to oppose me over the Water scheme. *He* died of blood poisoning. Oh, it's been going on for years – Mrs Horton, for instance, was abominably rude to me and it wasn't long before *she* passed away.'

He paused and leaning forward passed the port decanter round to Luke.

'Yes,' he said. 'They all died. Amazing, isn't it?'

Luke stared at him. A monstrous, an incredible suspicion leapt into his mind! With new eyes, he stared at the small fat man who sat at the head of the table, who was gently nodding his head and whose light protuberant eyes met Luke's with a smiling insouciance.

A rush of disconnected memories flashed rapidly through Luke's brain. Major Horton saying 'Lord Whitfield was very kind. Sent down grapes and peaches from his hot-house.' It was Lord Whitfield who so graciously allowed Tommy Pierce to be employed on window-cleaning at the library. Lord Whitfield holding forth on his visit to the Wellerman Kreutz Institute with its serums and germ cultures just a short time before Dr Humbleby's death. Everything pointing plainly in one direction and he, fool that he had been, never even suspecting . . .

Lord Whitfield was still smiling. A quiet happy smile. He nodded his head gently at Luke.

'*They all die*,' said Lord Whitfield.

CHAPTER 18

CONFERENCE IN LONDON

Sir William Ossington, known to the cronies of earlier days as Billy Bones, stared incredulously at his friend.

'Didn't you have enough crime out in Mayang?' he asked plaintively. 'Have you got to come home and do our work for us here?'

'Crime in Mayang isn't on a wholesale basis,' said Luke. 'What I'm up against now is a man who's done a round half-dozen murders at least – and got away with it without a breath of suspicion!'

Sir William sighed.

'It does happen. What's his speciality – wives?'

'No, he's not that kind. He doesn't actually think he's God yet – but he soon will.'

'Mad?'

'Oh, unquestionably, I should say.'

'Ah! but he probably isn't legally mad. There's a difference, you know.'

'I should say he knows the nature and consequence of his acts,' said Luke.

'Exactly,' said Billy Bones.

'Well, don't let's quibble about legal technicalities. We're not nearly at that stage yet. Perhaps we never shall be. What I want from you, old boy, is a few facts. There was a street accident took place on Derby Day between five and six o'clock in the afternoon. Old lady run over in Whitehall and the car didn't stop. Her name was Lavinia Pinkerton. I want you to dig up all facts you can about that.'

Sir William sighed. 'I can soon get hold of that for you. Twenty minutes ought to do it.'

He was as good as his word. In less than that time Luke was talking to the police officer in charge of the matter.

'Yes, sir, I remember the details. I've got most of them written down here.' He indicated the sheet that Luke was studying. 'An inquest was held – Mr Satcherverell was the Coroner. Censure of the driver of the car.'

'Did you ever get him?'

'No, sir.'

'What make of car was it?'

'It seems pretty certain it was a Rolls – big car driven by a chauffeur. All witnesses unanimous on that point. Most people know a Rolls by sight.'

'You didn't get the number?'

'No, unfortunately, nobody thought to look at it. There was a note of a number FZX 4498 – but it was the wrong number, a woman spotted it and mentioned it to another woman who gave it to me. I don't know whether the second woman got it wrong but anyway it was no good.'

Luke asked sharply: 'How did you know it was no good?'

The young officer smiled.

'FZX 4498 is the number of Lord Whitfield's car. That car was standing outside Boomington House at the time in question and the chauffeur was having tea. He had a perfect alibi – no question of his being concerned and the car never left the building till 6.30 when his lordship came out.'

'I see,' said Luke.

'It's always the way, sir,' the man sighed, 'half the witnesses have disappeared before a constable can get there and take down particulars.'

Sir William nodded.

'We assumed it was probably a number not unlike that FZX 4498 – a number beginning probably with two fours. We did our best, but could not trace any car. We investigated several likely numbers but they could all give satisfactory accounts of themselves.'

Sir William looked at Luke questioningly.

Luke shook his head. Sir William said:

'Thanks, Bonner, that will do.'

When the man had gone out, Billy Bones looked inquiringly at his friend.

'What's it all about, Fitz?'

Luke sighed. 'It all tallies. Lavinia Pinkerton was coming up to blow the gaff – to tell the clever people at Scotland Yard all about the wicked murderer. I don't know whether you'd have listened to her – probably not –'

'We might,' said Sir William. 'Things do come through to us that way. Just hearsay and gossip – we don't neglect that sort of thing, I assure you.'

'That's what the murderer thought. He wasn't going to risk it. He eliminated Lavinia Pinkerton and although one woman was sharp enough to spot his number no one believed her.'

Billy Bones sprang upright in his chair.

'You don't mean –'

'Yes, I do. I'll bet you anything you like it was Whitfield who ran her down. I don't know how he managed it. The chauffeur was away at tea. Somehow or other, I suppose, he sneaked away putting on a chauffeur's coat and cap. But he *did it*, Billy!'

'Impossible!'

'Not at all. Lord Whitfield has committed at least seven murders to my certain knowledge and probably a lot more.'

'Impossible,' said Sir William again.

'My dear fellow, he practically boasted to me of it last night!'

'He's mad, then?'

'He's mad, all right, but he's a cunning devil. You'll have to go warily. Don't let him know we suspect him.'

Billy Bones murmured: 'Incredible . . .'

Luke said: 'But true!'

He laid a hand on his friend's shoulder.

'Look here, Billy, old son, we must get right down to this. Here are the facts.'

The two men talked long and earnestly.

On the following day Luke returned to Wychwood. He drove down early in the morning. He could have returned the night before but he felt a marked distaste for sleeping under Lord Whitfield's roof or accepting his hospitality under the circumstances.

On his way through Wychwood, he drew up his car at Miss Waynflete's house. The maid who opened the door stared at him in astonishment but showed him into the little dining-room where Miss Waynflete was sitting at breakfast.

She rose to receive him in some surprise.

He did not waste time. 'I must apologize for breaking in on you at this hour.'

He looked round. The maid had left the room, shutting the door. 'I'm going to ask you a question, Miss Waynflete. It's rather a personal one, but I think you will forgive me for asking it.'

'Please ask me anything you like. I am quite sure your reason for doing so will be a good one.'

'Thank you.'

He paused.

'I want to know exactly why you broke off your engagement to Lord Whitfield all those years ago.'

She had not expected that. The colour rose in her cheeks and one hand went to her breast.

'Has he told you anything?'

Luke replied: 'He told me there was something about a bird – a bird whose neck was wrung . . .'

'He said that?' Her voice was wondering. 'He *admitted* it? That's extraordinary!'

'Will you tell me, please.'

'Yes, I will tell you. But I beg that you will never speak of the matter to him – to Gordon. It is all past – all over and finished with – I don't want it – raked up.'

She looked at him appealingly.

Luke nodded.

'It is only for my personal satisfaction,' he said. 'I shall not repeat what you tell me.'

'Thank you.' She had recovered her composure. Her voice was quite steady as she went on. 'It was like this. I had a little canary – I was very fond of it – and – perhaps – rather silly about it – girls were, then. They were rather – well – coy about their pets. It must have been irritating to a man – I do realize that.'

'Yes,' said Luke as she paused.

'Gordon was jealous of the bird. He said one day quite ill-temperedly, "I believe you prefer that bird to me." And I, in the rather silly way girls went on in those days, laughed and held it up on my finger saying something like: "Of course I love you, dicky bird, better than a great silly boy! Of course I do!" Then – oh, it was frightening – Gordon snatched the bird from me and *wrung its neck*. It was such a shock – I shall never forget it!'

Her face had gone very pale.

'And so you broke off the engagement?' said Luke.

'Yes. I couldn't feel the same afterwards. You see, Mr Fitzwilliam –' she hesitated. 'It wasn't just the action – that *might* have been done in a fit of jealousy and temper – it was the awful feeling I had *that he'd enjoyed doing it* – it was *that* that frightened me!'

'Even long ago,' murmured Luke. 'Even in these days . . .'

She laid a hand on his arm.

'Mr Fitzwilliam –'

He met the frightened appeal in her eyes with a grave steady look.

'It is Lord Whitfield who committed all these murders!' he said. '*You've* known that all along, haven't you?'

She shook her head with vigour.

'Not *known* it! If I had *known* it, then – then of course I would have spoken out – no, it was just a *fear*.'

'And yet you never gave me a hint?'

She clasped her hands in a sudden anguish.

'How could I? How could I? I was fond of him once . . .'

'Yes,' said Luke gently. 'I see.'

She turned away, fumbled in her bag, and a small lace-edged handkerchief was pressed for a moment to her eyes. Then she turned back again, dry-eyed, dignified and composed.

'I am so glad,' she said, 'that Bridget has broken off her engagement. She is going to marry you instead, is she not?'

'Yes.'

'That will be much more suitable,' said Miss Waynflete rather primly.

Luke was unable to help smiling a little.

But Miss Waynflete's face grew grave and anxious. She leaned forward and once more laid a hand on his arm.

'But be very careful,' she said. 'Both of you must be very careful.'

'You mean – with Lord Whitfield?'

'Yes. It would be better not to tell him.'

Luke frowned. 'I don't think either of us would like the idea of that.'

'Oh! what does that matter? You don't seem to realize that he's *mad* – *mad*. He won't stand it – not for a moment! If anything happens to her –'

'Nothing shall happen to her!'

'Yes, I know – but *do* realize that you're not a match for him! He's so dreadfully cunning! Take her away at once – it's the only hope. Make her go abroad! You'd better both go abroad!'

Luke said slowly:

'It might be as well if she went. I shall stay.'

'I was afraid you would say that. But at any rate *get her away. At once*, mind!'

Luke nodded slowly.

'I think,' he said, 'that you're right.'

'I know I'm right! Get her away – *before it's too late*.'

CHAPTER 19
BROKEN ENGAGEMENT

Bridget heard Luke drive up. She came out on the steps to meet him.

She said without preamble:

'I've told him.'

'What?' Luke was taken aback.

His dismay was so patent that Bridget noticed it.

'Luke – what is it? You seem quite upset.'

He said slowly:

'I thought we agreed to wait until I came back.'

'I know, but I thought it was better to get it over. He was making plans – for our marriage – our honeymoon – all that! I simply *had* to tell him!'

She added – a touch of reproach in her voice:

'It was the only decent thing to do.'

He acknowledged it.

'From your point of view, yes. Oh, yes, I see that.'

'From every point of view I should have thought!'

Luke said slowly:

'There are times when one can't afford – decency!'

'Luke, what *do* you mean?'

He made an impatient gesture.

'I can't tell you now and here. How did Whitfield take it?'

Bridget said slowly:

'Extraordinarily well. Really extraordinarily well. I felt ashamed. I believe, Luke, that I've underestimated Gordon – just because he's rather pompous and occasionally futile. I believe really he's rather – well – a great little man!'

Luke nodded.

'Yes, possibly he is a great man – in ways we haven't suspected. Look here, Bridget, you must get out of here as soon as possible.'

'Naturally, I shall pack up my things and leave today. You might drive me up to town. I suppose we can't both go and stay at the Bells and Motley – that is, if the Ellsworthy contingent have left?'

Luke shook his head.

'No, you'd better go back to London. I'll explain presently. In the meantime I suppose I'd better see Whitfield.'

'I suppose it's the thing to do – it's all rather beastly, isn't it? I feel such a rotten little gold digger.'

Luke smiled at her.

'It was a fair enough bargain. You'd have played straight with him. Anyway, it's no use lamenting over things that are past and done with! I'll go in and see Whitfield now.'

He found Lord Whitfield striding up and down the drawing-room. He was outwardly calm, there was even a slight smile on his lips. But Luke noticed that a pulse in his temple was beating furiously.

He wheeled round as Luke entered.

'Oh! there you are, Fitzwilliam.'

Luke said:

'It's no good my saying I'm sorry for what I've done – that would be hypocritical! I admit that from your point of view I've behaved badly and I've very little to say in defence. These things happen.'

Lord Whitfield resumed his pacing.

'Quite – quite!' He waved a hand.

Luke went on:

'Bridget and I have treated you shamefully. But there it is! We care for each other – and there's nothing to be done about it – except tell you the truth and clear out.'

Lord Whitfield stopped. He looked at Luke with pale protuberant eyes.

'No,' he said, 'there's nothing you can do about it!'

There was a very curious tone in his voice. He stood looking at Luke, gently shaking his head as though in commiseration.

Luke said sharply: 'What do you mean?'

'There's nothing you can do!' said Lord Whitfield. 'It's too late!'

Luke took a step nearer him.

'Tell me what you mean.'

Lord Whitfield said unexpectedly:

'Ask Honoria Waynflete. *She'll* understand. *She* knows what happens. She spoke to me about it once!'

'What does she understand?'

Lord Whitfield said:

'*Evil doesn't go unpunished.* There must be justice! I'm sorry because I'm fond of Bridget. In a way I'm sorry for you both!'

Luke said:

'Are you threatening us?'

Lord Whitfield seemed genuinely shocked.

'No, no, my dear fellow. *I've* no feeling in the matter! When I did Bridget the honour to choose her as my wife, she accepted certain responsibilities. Now, she repudiates them – *but there's no going back in this life.* If you break laws you pay the penalty . . .'

Luke clenched both hands. He said:

'You mean that something is going to happen to Bridget? Now understand me, Whitfield, *nothing is going to happen to Bridget* – nor to me! If you attempt anything of that kind it's the finish. You'd better be careful! I know a good deal about you!'

'It's nothing to do with me,' said Lord Whitfield. 'I'm only the instrument of a higher Power. What that Power decrees happens!'

'I see you believe that,' said Luke.

'Because it's the truth! Anyone who goes against me pays the penalty. You and Bridget will be no exception.'

Luke said:

'That's where you're wrong. However long a run of luck may be, it breaks in the end. Yours is very near breaking now.'

Lord Whitfield said gently:

'My dear young man, you don't know who it is you're talking to. Nothing can touch *Me!*'

'Can't it? We'll see. You'd better watch your step, Whitfield.'

A little ripple of movement passed over the other. His voice had changed when he spoke.

'I've been very patient,' said Lord Whitfield. 'Don't strain my patience too far. Get out of here.'

'I'm going,' said Luke. 'As quick as I can. Remember that I've warned you.'

He turned on his heel and went quickly out of the room. He ran upstairs. He found Bridget in her room superintending the packing of her clothes by a housemaid.

'Ready soon?'

'In ten minutes.'

Her eyes asked a question which the presence of the maid prevented her from putting into words.

Luke gave a short nod.

He went to his own room and flung his things hurriedly into his suitcase.

He returned ten minutes later to find Bridget ready for departure.

'Shall we go now?'

'I'm ready.'

As they descended the staircase they met the butler ascending.

'Miss Waynflete has called to see you, miss.'

'Miss Waynflete? Where is she?'

'In the drawing-room with his lordship.'

Bridget went straight to the drawing-room, Luke close behind her.

Lord Whitfield was standing by the window talking to Miss Waynflete. He had a knife in his hand – a long slender blade.

'Perfect workmanship,' he was saying. 'One of my young men brought it back to me from Morocco where he'd been special correspondent. It's Moorish, of course, a Riff knife.' He drew a finger lovingly along the blade. 'What an edge!'

Miss Waynflete said sharply:

'Put it away, Gordon, for goodness' sake!'

He smiled and laid it down among a collection of other weapons on a table.

'I like the feel of it,' he said softly.

Miss Waynflete had lost some of her usual poise. She looked white and nervous.

'Ah, there you are, Bridget, my dear,' she said.

Lord Whitfield chuckled.

'Yes, there's Bridget. Make the most of her, Honoria. She won't be with us long.'

Miss Waynflete said, sharply:

'What d'you mean?'

'Mean? I mean she's going to London. That's right, isn't it? That's all I meant.'

He looked round at them all.

'I've got a bit of news for you, Honoria,' he said. 'Bridget isn't going to marry me after all. She prefers Fitzwilliam here. A queer thing, life. Well, I'll leave you to have your talk.'

He went out of the room, his hands jingling the coins in his pockets.

'Oh, dear –' said Miss Waynflete. 'Oh, dear –'

The deep distress in her voice was so noticeable that Bridget looked slightly surprised. She said uncomfortably:

'I'm sorry. I really am frightfully sorry.'

Miss Waynflete said:

'He's angry – he's frightfully angry – oh, dear, this is terrible. What are we going to do?'

Bridget stared.

'Do? What do you mean?'

Miss Waynflete said, including them both in her reproachful glance:

'You should never have told him!'

Bridget said:

'Nonsense. What else could we do?'

'You shouldn't have told him *now*. You should have waited till you'd got right away.'

Bridget said shortly:

'That's a matter of opinion. I think myself it's better to get unpleasant things over as quickly as possible.'

'Oh, my dear, if it were only a question of that –'

She stopped. Then her eyes asked a question of Luke.

Luke shook his head. His lips formed the words, 'Not yet.'

Miss Waynflete murmured, 'I see.'

Bridget said with some slight exasperation:

'Did you want to see me about something in particular, Miss Waynflete?'

'Well – yes. As a matter of fact I came to suggest that you should come and pay me a little visit. I thought – er – you might find it uncomfortable to remain on here and that you might want a few days to – er – well, mature your plans.'

'Thank you, Miss Waynflete, that was very kind of you.'

'You see, you'd be quite safe with me and –'

Bridget interrupted:

'*Safe?*'

Miss Waynflete, a little flustered, said hurriedly:

'Comfortable – that's what I meant – quite *comfortable* with me. I mean, not nearly so *luxurious* as here, naturally – but the hot water *is* hot and my little maid Emily really cooks quite nicely.'

'Oh, I'm sure everything would be lovely, Miss Waynflete,' said Bridget mechanically.

'But, of course, if you are going up to town, that is *much* better . . .'

Bridget said slowly:

'It's a little awkward. My aunt went off early to a flower show today. I haven't had a chance yet to tell her what has happened. I shall leave a note for her telling her I've gone up to the flat.'

'You're going to your aunt's flat in London?'

'Yes. There's no one there. But I can go out for meals.'

'You'll be alone in that flat? Oh, dear, I shouldn't do that. Not stay there *alone*.'

'Nobody will eat me,' said Bridget impatiently. 'Besides, my aunt will come up tomorrow.'

Miss Waynflete shook her head in a worried manner.

Luke said:

'Better go to a hotel.'

Bridget wheeled round on him.

'Why? What's the matter with you all? Why are you treating me as though I was an imbecile child?'

'No, no, dear,' protested Miss Waynflete. 'We just want you to be *careful* – that's all!'

'But why? Why? What's it all *about*?'

'Look here, Bridget,' said Luke. 'I want to have a talk with you. But I can't talk here. Come with me now in the car and we'll go somewhere quiet.'

He looked at Miss Waynflete.

'May we come to your house in about an hour's time? There are several things I want to say to you.'

'Please do. I will wait for you there.'

Luke put his hand on Bridget's arm. He gave a nod of thanks to Miss Waynflete.

He said: 'We'll pick up the luggage later. Come on.'

He led her out of the room and along the hall to the front door. He opened the door of the car. Bridget got in. Luke started the engine and drove rapidly down the drive. He gave a sigh of relief as they emerged from the iron gates.

'Thank God I've got you out of there safely,' he said.

'Have you gone quite mad, Luke? Why all this "hush hush – I can't tell you what I mean now" – business?'

Luke said grimly:

'Well, there are difficulties, you know, in explaining that a man's a murderer when you're actually under his roof!'

CHAPTER 20

WE'RE IN IT – TOGETHER

Bridget sat for a minute motionless beside him. She said:

'*Gordon?*'

Luke nodded.

'Gordon? *Gordon – a murderer?* Gordon *the* murderer? I never heard anything so ridiculous in all my life!'

'That's how it strikes you?'

'Yes, indeed. Why, Gordon wouldn't hurt a fly.'

Luke said grimly:

'That may be true. I don't know. But he certainly killed a canary bird, and I'm pretty certain he's killed a large number of human beings as well.'

'My dear Luke, I simply can't believe it!'

'I know,' said Luke. 'It does sound quite incredible. Why, he never even entered my head as a possible suspect until the night before last.'

Bridget protested:

'But I know all about Gordon! I know what he's *like*! He's really a sweet little man – pompous, yes, but rather pathetic really.'

Luke shook his head. 'You've got to readjust your ideas about him, Bridget.'

'It's no good, Luke, I simply can't believe it! What put such an absurd idea into your head? Why, two days ago you were quite positive it was Ellsworthy.'

Luke winced slightly.

'I know. I know. You probably think that tomorrow I shall suspect Thomas, and the day after I shall be convinced that it's

Horton I'm after! I'm not really so unbalanced as that. I admit the idea's completely startling when it first comes to you, but if you look into it a bit closer, you'll see that it all fits in remarkably well. No wonder Miss Pinkerton didn't dare to go to the local authorities. *She* knew they'd laugh at her! Scotland Yard was her only hope.'

'But what possible motive could Gordon have for all this killing business? Oh, it's all so *silly*!'

'I know. But don't you realize that Gordon Whitfield has a very exalted opinion of himself?'

Bridget said: 'He pretends to be very wonderful and very important. That's just inferiority complex, poor lamb!'

'Possibly that's at the root of the trouble. I don't know. But think, Bridget – just *think* a minute. Remember all the phrases you've used laughingly yourself about him – *lèse-majesté*, etc. Don't you realize that the man's ego is swollen out of all proportion? And it's allied with religion. My dear girl, the man's as mad as a hatter!'

Bridget thought for a minute.

She said at last: 'I still can't believe it. What evidence have you got, Luke?'

'Well, there are his own words. He told me, quite plainly and distinctly, the night before last, that anyone who opposed him in any way *always died*.'

'Go on.'

'I can't quite explain to you what I mean – but it was the way he said it. Quite calm and complacent and – how shall I put it? – quite *used* to the idea! He just sat there smiling to himself . . . It was uncanny and rather horrible, Bridget!'

'Go on.'

'Well, then he went on to give me a list of people who'd passed out because they'd incurred his sovereign displeasure! And, listen to this, Bridget, *the people he mentioned were Mrs Horton, Amy Gibbs, Tommy Pierce, Harry Carter, Humbleby, and that chauffeur fellow, Rivers.*'

Bridget was shaken at last. She went very pale.

'He mentioned those actual people?'

'Those actual people! *Now* do you believe?'

'Oh, God, I suppose I must . . . What were his reasons?'

'Horribly trivial – that's what made it so frightening. Mrs Horton had snubbed him, Tommy Pierce had done imitations of him and made the gardeners laugh, Harry Carter had abused him, Amy Gibbs had been grossly impertinent, Humbleby had dared to oppose him publicly, Rivers threatened him before me and Miss Waynflete –'

Bridget put her hands to her eyes.

'Horrible . . . Quite horrible . . .' she murmured.

'I know. Then there's some other outside evidence. The car that ran down Miss Pinkerton in London was a Rolls, *and its number was the number of Lord Whitfield's car.*'

'That definitely clinches it,' said Bridget slowly.

'Yes. The police thought the woman who gave them that number must have made a mistake. Mistake indeed!'

'I can understand that,' said Bridget. 'When it comes to a rich, powerful man like Lord Whitfield, naturally his story is the one to be believed!'

'Yes. One appreciates Miss Pinkerton's difficulty.'

Bridget said thoughtfully:

'Once or twice she said rather queer things to me. As though she were warning me against something . . . I didn't understand in the least at the time . . . I see now!'

'It all fits in,' said Luke. 'That's the way of it. At first one says (as you said), "Impossible!" and then once one accepts the idea, everything fits in! The grapes he sent to Mrs Horton – and she thought the nurses were poisoning her! And that visit of his to the Wellerman Kreutz Institute – somehow or other he must have got hold of some culture of germs and infected Humbleby.'

'I don't see how he managed that.'

'I don't either, *but the connection is there*. One can't get away from that.'

'No . . . As you say, it *fits*. And of course *he* could do things that other people couldn't! I mean he would be so completely above suspicion!'

'I think Miss Waynflete suspected. She mentioned that visit to the institute. Brought it into conversation quite casually – but I believe she hoped I'd act upon it.'

'She knew, then, all along?'

'She had a very strong suspicion. I think she was handicapped by having once been in love with him.'

Bridget nodded.

'Yes, that accounts for several things. Gordon told me they had once been engaged.'

'She wanted, you see, not to believe it was him. But she became more and more sure that it *was*. She tried to give me hints, but she couldn't bear to do anything outright against him! Women are odd creatures! I think, in a way, she still cares about him . . .'

'Even after he jilted her?'

'*She* jilted *him*. It was rather an ugly story. I'll tell you.'

He recounted the short, ugly episode. Bridget stared at him.

'Gordon did *that*?'

'Yes. Even in those days, you see, he can't have been normal!'

Bridget shivered and murmured:

'All those years ago . . . all those years . . .'

Luke said:

'He may have got rid of a lot more people than we shall ever know about! It's just the rapid succession of deaths lately that drew attention to him! As though he'd got reckless with success!'

Bridget nodded. She was silent for a minute or two, thinking, then she asked abruptly:

'What exactly did Miss Pinkerton say to you – in the train that day? How did she begin?'

Luke cast his mind back.

'Told me she was going to Scotland Yard, mentioned the village constable, said he was a nice fellow but not up to dealing with murder.'

'That was the first mention of the word?'

'Yes.'

'Go on.'

'Then she said, "*You're surprised, I can see. I was myself at first. I really couldn't believe it. I thought I must be imagining things.*"'

'And then?'

'I asked her if she was sure she wasn't – imagining things, I mean – and she said quite placidly, "*Oh, no! I might have been the first time, but not the second, or the third or the fourth. After that one knows.*"'

'Marvellous,' commented Bridget. 'Go on.'

'So of course I humoured her – said I was sure she was doing the right thing. I was an unbelieving Thomas if there ever was one!'

'I know. So easy to be wise after the event! I'd have felt the same, nice and superior to the poor old dame! How did the conversation go on?'

'Let me see – oh! she mentioned the Abercrombie case – you know, the Welsh poisoner. Said she hadn't really believed that there had been a look – a special look – that he gave his victims. But that she believed it now because she had seen it herself.'

'What words did she use exactly?'

Luke thought, creasing his brow.

'She said, still in that nice ladylike voice, "*Of course, I didn't really believe that when I read about it – but it's true.*" And I said, "What's true?" And she said, "*The look on a person's face.*" And by Jove, Bridget, the way she said that absolutely *got* me! Her quiet voice and the look on her face – like someone who had really seen something almost too horrible to speak about!'

'Go on, Luke. Tell me everything.'

'And then she enumerated the victims – Amy Gibbs and Carter and Tommy Pierce, and said that Tommy was a horrid boy and Carter drank. And then she said, "*But now – yesterday – it was Dr Humbleby – and he's such a good man – a really good man.*" And she said if she went to Humbleby and told him, he wouldn't believe her, he'd only laugh!'

Bridget gave a deep sigh.

'I see,' she said. 'I see.'

Luke looked at her.

'What is it, Bridget? What are you thinking of?'

'Something Mrs Humbleby once said. I wondered – no, never mind, go on. What was it she said to you right at the end?'

Luke repeated the words soberly. They had made an impression on him and he was not likely to forget them.

'I'd said it was difficult to get away with a lot of murders, and she answered, "*No, no, my dear boy, that's where you're wrong. It's very easy to kill – so long as no one suspects you. And you see, the person in question is just the last person any one would suspect . . .*"'

He was silent. Bridget said with a shiver:

'Easy to kill? Horribly easy – that's true enough! No wonder those words stuck in your mind, Luke. They'll stick in mine – all my life! A man like Gordon Whitfield – oh! of course it's easy.'

'It's not so easy to bring it home to him,' said Luke.

'Don't you think so? I've an idea I can help there.'

'Bridget, I forbid you –'

'You can't. One can't just sit back and play safe. I'm in this, Luke. It may be dangerous – yes, I'll admit that – but I've got to play my part.'

'Bridget –'

'I'm *in* this, Luke! I shall accept Miss Waynflete's invitation and stay down here.'

'My darling, I implore you –'

'It's dangerous for both of us. I know that. But we're in it, Luke – we're in it – together!'

CHAPTER 21

'O WHY DO YOU WALK THROUGH THE FIELDS IN GLOVES?'

The calm interior of Miss Waynflete's house was almost an anti-climax after that tense moment in the car.

Miss Waynflete received Bridget's acceptance of her invitation a little doubtfully, hastening, however, to reiterate her offer of hospitality by way of showing that her doubts were due to quite another cause than unwillingness to receive the girl.

Luke said:

'I really think it will be the best thing, since you are so kind, Miss Waynflete. I am staying at the Bells and Motley. I'd rather have Bridget under my eye than up in town. After all, remember what happened there before.'

Miss Waynflete said:

'You mean – Lavinia Pinkerton?'

'Yes. You would have said, wouldn't you, that any one would be quite safe in the middle of a crowded city.'

'You mean,' said Miss Waynflete, 'that any one's safety depends principally on the fact that nobody wishes to kill them?'

'Exactly. We have come to depend upon what has been called the goodwill of civilization.'

Miss Waynflete nodded her head thoughtfully.

Bridget said:

'How long have you known that – that Gordon was the killer, Miss Waynflete?'

Miss Waynflete sighed.

'That is a difficult question to answer, my dear. I suppose that I have been quite sure, in my inmost heart, for some time . . . But I did my best not to recognize that belief! You see, I didn't *want* to believe it and so I pretended to myself that it was a wicked and monstrous idea on my part.'

Luke said bluntly:

'Have you never been afraid – for yourself?'

Miss Waynflete considered.

'You mean that if Gordon had suspected that I knew, he would have found some means of getting rid of *me*?'

'Yes.'

Miss Waynflete said gently:

'I have, of course, been alive to that possibility . . . I tried to be – careful of myself. But I do not think that Gordon would have considered me a real menace.'

'Why?'

Miss Waynflete flushed a little.

'I don't think that Gordon would ever believe that I would do anything to – to bring him into danger.'

Luke said abruptly:

'You went as far, didn't you, as to warn him?'

'Yes. That is, I did hint to him that it was odd that anyone who displeased him should shortly meet with an accident.'

Bridget demanded:

'And what did he say?'

A worried expression passed over Miss Waynflete's face.

'He didn't react at all in the way I meant. He seemed – really it's most extraordinary! – he seemed *pleased* . . . He said, "So *you've* noticed that?" He quite – quite *preened* himself, if I may use that expression.'

'He's mad, of course,' said Luke.

Miss Waynflete agreed eagerly.

'Yes, indeed, there isn't any other explanation possible. He's not responsible for his acts.' She laid a hand on Luke's arm. 'They – they won't *hang* him, will they, Mr Fitzwilliam?'

'No, no. Send him to Broadmoor, I expect.'

Miss Waynflete sighed and leaned back.

'I'm so glad.'

Her eyes rested on Bridget, who was frowning down at the carpet.

Luke said:

'But we're a long way from all that still. I've notified the powers that be and I can say this much, they're prepared to take the matter seriously. But you must realize that we've got remarkably little evidence to go upon.'

'We'll get evidence,' said Bridget.

Miss Waynflete looked up at her. There was some quality in her expression that reminded Luke of someone or something that he had seen not long ago. He tried to pin down the elusive memory but failed.

Miss Waynflete said doubtfully:

'You are confident, my dear. Well, perhaps you are right.'

Luke said:

'I'll go along with the car, Bridget, and fetch your things from the Manor.'

Bridget said immediately:

'I'll come too.'

'I'd rather you didn't.'

'Yes, but I'd rather come.'

Luke said irritably:

'Don't do the mother and child act with me, Bridget! I refuse to be protected by you.'

Miss Waynflete murmured:

'I really think, Bridget, that it will be quite all right – in a car – and in daylight.'

Bridget gave a slightly shamefaced laugh.

'I'm being rather an idiot. This business gets on one's nerves.'

Luke said:

'Miss Waynflete protected me home the other night. Come now, Miss Waynflete, admit it! You did, didn't you?'

She admitted it, smiling.

'You see, Mr Fitzwilliam, you were so completely unsuspicious! And if Gordon Whitfield had really grasped the fact that you were down here to look into this business and for no other reason – well, it wasn't very safe. And that's a very lonely lane – *anything* might have happened!'

'Well, I'm alive to the danger now all right,' said Luke grimly. 'I shan't be caught napping, I can assure you.'

Miss Waynflete said anxiously:

'Remember, he is very cunning. And much cleverer than you would ever imagine! Really, a most ingenious mind.'

'I'm forewarned.'

'Men have courage – one knows that,' said Miss Waynflete, 'but they are more easily *deceived* than women.'

'That's true,' said Bridget.

Luke said:

'Seriously, Miss Waynflete, do you really think that I am in any danger? Do you think, in film parlance, that Lord Whitfield is really out to *get* me?'

Miss Waynflete hesitated.

'I think,' she said, 'that the principal danger is to Bridget. It is *her* rejection of him that is the supreme insult! I think that *after* he has dealt with Bridget he will turn his attention to *you*. But I think that undoubtedly he will try for her *first*.'

Luke groaned.

'I wish to goodness you'd go abroad – now – at once, Bridget.' Bridget's lips set themselves together.

'I'm not going.'

Miss Waynflete sighed.

'You are a brave creature, Bridget. I admire you.'

'You'd do the same in my place.'

'Well, perhaps.'

Bridget said, her voice dropping to a full, rich note:

'Luke and I are in this together.'

She went out with him to the door. Luke said:

'I'll give you a ring from the Bells and Motley when I'm safely out of the lion's den.'

'Yes, do.'

'My sweet, don't let's get all het up! Even the most accomplished murderers have to have a little time to mature their plans! I should say we're quite all right for a day or two. Superintendent Battle is coming down from London today. From then on Whitfield will be under observation.'

'In fact, everything is OK, and we can cut out the melodrama.'

Luke said gravely, laying a hand on her shoulder:

'Bridget, my sweet, you will oblige me by not doing anything *rash*!'

'Same to you, darling Luke.'

He squeezed her shoulder, jumped into the car and drove off.

Bridget returned to the sitting-room. Miss Waynflete was fussing a little in a gentle spinsterish manner.

'My dear, your room's not *quite* ready yet. Emily is seeing to it. Do you know what I'm going to do? I'm going to get you a nice cup of tea! It's just what you need after all these upsetting incidents.'

'It's frightfully kind of you, Miss Waynflete, but I really don't want any.'

What Bridget would have liked was a strong cocktail, mainly composed of gin, but she rightly judged that that form of refreshment was not likely to be forthcoming. She disliked tea intensely. It usually gave her indigestion. Miss Waynflete, however, had decided that tea was what her young guest needed. She bustled out of the room and reappeared about five minutes later, her face beaming, carrying a tray on which stood two dainty Dresden cups full of a fragrant, steaming beverage.

'Real Lapsang Souchong,' said Miss Waynflete proudly.

Bridget, who disliked China tea even more than Indian, gave a wan smile.

At that moment Emily, a small clumsy-looking girl with pronounced adenoids, appeared in the doorway and said:

'If you please, biss – did you bean the frilled billowcases?'

Miss Waynflete hurriedly left the room, and Bridget took advantage of the respite to pour her tea out of the window, narrowly escaping scalding Wonky Pooh, who was on the flower-bed below.

Wonky Pooh accepted her apologies, sprang up on the window-sill and proceeded to wind himself in and out over Bridget's shoulders, purring in an affected manner.

'Handsome!' said Bridget, drawing a hand down his back.

Wonky Pooh arched his tail and purred with redoubled vigour.

'Nice pussy,' said Bridget, tickling his ears.

Miss Waynflete returned at that minute.

'Dear me,' she exclaimed. 'Wonky Pooh has *quite* taken to you, hasn't he? He's so *standoffish* as a rule! Mind his ear, my dear, he's had a bad ear lately and it's still very painful.'

The injunction came too late. Bridget's hand had tweaked the painful ear. Wonky Pooh spat at her and retired, a mass of orange offended dignity.

'Oh, dear, has he scratched you?' cried Miss Waynflete.

'Nothing much,' said Bridget, sucking a diagonal scratch on the back of her hand.

'Shall I put some iodine on?'

'Oh, no, it's quite all right. Don't let's fuss.'

Miss Waynflete seemed a little disappointed. Feeling that she had been ungracious, Bridget said hastily:

'I wonder how long Luke will be?'

'Now don't worry, my dear. I'm sure Mr Fitzwilliam is well able to look after himself.'

'Oh, Luke's tough all right!'

At that moment the telephone rang. Bridget hurried to it. Luke's voice spoke.

'Hallo? That you, Bridget? I'm at the Bells and Motley. Can you wait for your traps till after lunch? Because Battle has arrived here – you know who I mean –'

'The superintendent man from Scotland Yard?'

'Yes. And he wants to have a talk with me right away.'

'That's all right by me. Bring my things round after lunch and tell me what he says about it all.'

'Right. So long, my sweet.'

'So long.'

Bridget replaced the receiver and retailed the conversation to Miss Waynflete. Then she yawned. A feeling of fatigue had succeeded her excitement.

Miss Waynflete noticed it.

'You're tired, my dear! You'd better lie down – no, perhaps that would be a bad thing just before lunch. I was just going to take some old clothes to a woman in a cottage not very far away

– quite a pretty walk over the fields. Perhaps you'd care to come with me? We'll just have time before lunch.'

Bridget agreed willingly.

They went out the back way. Miss Waynflete wore a straw hat and, to Bridget's amusement, had put on gloves.

'We might be going to Bond Street!' she thought to herself.

Miss Waynflete chatted pleasantly of various small village matters as they walked. They went across two fields, crossed a rough lane and then took a path leading through a ragged copse. The day was hot and Bridget found the shade of the trees pleasant.

Miss Waynflete suggested that they should sit down and rest a minute.

'It's really rather oppressively warm today, don't you think? I fancy there must be *thunder* about!'

Bridget acquiesced somewhat sleepily. She lay back against the bank – her eyes half-closed – some lines of poetry wandering through her brain.

> '*O why do you walk through the fields in gloves*
> *O fat white woman whom nobody loves?*'

But that wasn't quite right! Miss Waynflete wasn't fat. She amended the words to fit the case.

> '*O why do you walk through the fields in gloves,*
> *O lean grey woman whom nobody loves?*'

Miss Waynflete broke in upon her thoughts.

'You're very sleepy, dear, aren't you?'

The words were said in a gentle everyday tone, but something in them jerked Bridget's eyes suddenly open.

Miss Waynflete was leaning forward towards her. Her eyes were eager, her tongue passed gently over her lips. She repeated her question:

'You're *very* sleepy, aren't you?'

This time there was no mistaking the definite significance of the tone. A flash passed through Bridget's brain – a lightning flash of comprehension, succeeded by one of contempt at her own density!

She had suspected the truth – but it had been no more than a dim suspicion. She had meant, working quietly and secretly, to make sure. But not for one moment had she realized that anything was to be attempted against herself. She had, she thought, concealed her suspicions entirely. Nor would she have dreamed that anything would be contemplated so soon. Fool – seven times fool!

And she thought suddenly:

'The tea – there was something in the tea. *She doesn't know I never drank it.* Now's my chance! I must pretend! What stuff was it, I wonder? Poison? Or just sleeping stuff? She expects me to be sleepy – that's evident.'

She let her eyelids droop again. In what she hoped was a natural drowsy voice, she said:

'I do – frightfully . . . How funny! I don't know when I've felt so sleepy.'

Miss Waynflete nodded softly.

Bridget watched the older woman narrowly through her almost closed eyes.

She thought:

'I'm a match for her anyway! My muscles are pretty tough – she's a skinny frail old pussy. But I've got to make her *talk* – that's it – make her *talk*!'

Miss Waynflete was smiling. It was not a nice smile. It was sly and not very human.

Bridget thought:

'She's like a goat. God! how like a goat she is! A goat's always been an evil symbol! I see why now! I was right – I was right in that fantastic idea of mine! *Hell hath no fury like a woman scorned* . . . That was the start of it – it's all there.'

She murmured, and this time her voice held a definite note of apprehension.

'I don't know what's the matter with me . . . I feel so queer – so *very* queer!'

Miss Waynflete gave a swift glance round her. The spot was entirely desolate. It was too far from the village for a shout to be heard. There were no houses or cottages near. She began to fumble with the parcel she carried – the parcel that was supposed to contain old clothes. Apparently it did. The paper came apart, revealing a soft woolly garment. And still those gloved hands fumbled and fumbled.

'O why do you walk through the fields in gloves?'

'Yes – why? Why gloves?'

Of course! Of course! The whole thing so beautifully planned!

The wrapping fell aside. Carefully, Miss Waynflete extracted the knife, holding it very carefully so as not to obliterate the fingerprints which were already on it – where the short podgy fingers of Lord Whitfield had held it earlier that day in the drawing-room at Ashe Manor.

The Moorish knife with the sharp blade.

Bridget felt slightly sick. She must play for time – yes and she *must* make the woman talk – this lean, grey woman whom nobody loved. It ought not to be difficult – not really. Because she must want to talk, oh, so badly – and the only person she could ever talk to was someone like Bridget – someone who was going to be silenced for ever.

Bridget said – in a faint, thick voice:

'What's – that – knife?'

And then Miss Waynflete laughed.

It was a horrible laugh, soft and musical and ladylike, and quite inhuman. She said:

'It's for you, Bridget. For you! I've hated you, you know, for a very long time.'

Bridget said:

'Because I was going to marry Gordon Whitfield?'

Miss Waynflete nodded.

'You're clever. You're quite clever! This, you see, will be the crowning proof against him. You'll be found here, with your throat cut – and – *his* knife, and *his* fingerprints on the knife! Clever the way I asked to see it this morning!

'And then I slipped it into my bag wrapped in a handkerchief whilst you were upstairs. So easy! But the whole thing has been easy. I would hardly have believed it.'

Bridget said – still in the thick, muffled voice of a person heavily drugged:

'That's – because – you're – so – devilishly – clever . . .'

Miss Waynflete laughed her ladylike little laugh again. She said with a horrible kind of pride:

'Yes, I always had brains, even as a girl! But they wouldn't let me do anything . . . I had to stay at home – doing nothing. And then Gordon – just a common boot-maker's son, but he had ambition, I knew. I knew he would rise in the world. And he jilted me – jilted *me*! All because of that ridiculous business with the bird.'

Her hands made a queer gesture as though she were twisting something.

Again a wave of sickness passed over Bridget.

'Gordon Ragg daring to jilt *me* – Colonel Waynflete's daughter! I swore I'd pay him out for that! I used to think about it night after night . . . And then we got poorer and poorer. The house had to be sold. *He* bought it! He came along patronizing me, offering *me* a job in my own old home. How I hated him then! But I never showed my feelings. We were taught that as girls – a most valuable training. That, I always think, is where breeding tells.'

She was silent a minute. Bridget watched her, hardly daring to breathe lest she should stem the flow of words.

Miss Waynflete went on softly:

'All the time I was thinking and thinking . . . First of all I just thought of killing him. That's when I began to read up criminology – quietly, you know – in the library. And really I found my reading came in most *useful* more than once later. The door of Amy's room, for instance, turning the key in the lock from the outside with pincers after I'd changed the bottles by her bed. How she snored, that girl, quite disgusting, it was!'

She paused.

'Let me see, where was I?'

That gift which Bridget had cultivated, which had charmed Lord Whitfield, the gift of the perfect listener, stood her in good stead now. Honoria Waynflete might be a homicidal maniac but she was also something much more common than that. She was a human being who wanted to talk about herself. And with that class of human being Bridget was well fitted to cope.

She said, and her voice had exactly the right invitation in it:
'You meant at first to kill him –'

'Yes, but that didn't satisfy me – much too ordinary – it had to
be something better than just killing. And then I got this idea. It
just came to me. He should suffer for committing a lot of crimes of
which he was quite innocent. He should be a murderer! *He* should
be hanged for *my* crimes. Or else they'd say he was mad and he
would be shut up all his life . . . That might be even better.'

She giggled now. A horrible little giggle . . . Her eyes were
light and staring with queer elongated pupils.

'As I told you, I read a lot of books on crime. I chose my
victims carefully – there was not to be too much suspicion at
first. You see,' her voice deepened, 'I *enjoyed* the killing . . .
That disagreeable woman, Lydia Horton – she'd patronized me
– once she referred to me as an old maid. I was glad when Gordon
quarrelled with her. Two birds with one stone, I thought! *Such*
fun, sitting by her bedside and slipping the arsenic in her tea,
and then going out and telling the nurse how Mrs Horton had
complained of the bitter taste of Lord Whitfield's grapes! The
stupid woman never repeated that, which was such a pity.

'And then the others! As soon as I heard that Gordon had a
grievance against anyone, it was *so* easy to arrange for an accident!
And he was such a fool – such an incredible fool! I made him
believe that there was something very special about him! That
anyone who went against him suffered. He believed it quite
easily. Poor dear Gordon, he'd believe anything. So gullible!'

Bridget thought of herself saying to Luke scornfully:
'Gordon! He could believe anything!'

Easy? How easy! Poor pompous credulous little Gordon.

But she must learn more! Easy? This was easy too! She'd done
it as a secretary for years. Quietly encouraged her employers to
talk about themselves. And this woman wanted badly to talk, to
boast about her own cleverness.

Bridget murmured:
'But how did you manage it all? I don't see how you *could*.'

'Oh, it was *quite* easy! It just needed organization! When Amy
was discharged from the Manor I engaged her at once. I think the
hat paint idea was *quite* clever – and the door being locked on the
inside made *me* quite safe. But of course I was always safe because

I never had any *motive*, and you can't suspect any one of murder if there isn't a motive. Carter was quite easy too – he was lurching about in the fog and I caught up with him on the footbridge and gave him a quick push. I'm really very strong, you know.'

She paused and the soft horrible little giggle came again.

'The whole thing was such *fun*! I shall never forget Tommy's face when I pushed him off the window-sill that day. He hadn't the least idea . . .'

She leaned towards Bridget confidentially.

'People are really very stupid, you know. I'd never realized that before.'

Bridget said very softly:

'But then – you're unusually clever.'

'Yes – yes – perhaps you're right.'

Bridget said:

'Dr Humbleby – that must have been more difficult?'

'Yes, it was really amazing how that succeeded. It *might* not have worked, of course. But Gordon had been talking to everybody of his visit to the Wellerman Kreutz Institute, and I thought if I *could* manage it so that people remembered that visit and connected it afterwards. And Wonky Pooh's ear was really very nasty, a lot of discharge. I managed to run the point of my scissors into the doctor's hand, and then I was *so* distressed and insisted on putting on a dressing and bandaging it up. He didn't know the dressing had been infected first from Wonky Pooh's ear. Of course, it *mightn't* have worked – it was just a long shot. I was delighted when it did – especially as Wonky Pooh had been Lavinia's cat.'

Her face darkened.

'Lavinia Pinkerton! *She* guessed . . . It was she who found Tommy that day. And then when Gordon and old Dr Humbleby had that row, she caught me looking at Humbleby. I was off my guard. I was just wondering exactly how I'd do it . . . And she knew! I turned round to find her watching me and – I gave myself away. I saw that she knew. She couldn't prove anything, of course. I knew that. But I was afraid all the same someone might believe her. I was afraid they might believe her at Scotland Yard. I felt sure that was where she was going that day. I was in the same train and I followed her.

'The whole thing was so easy. She was on an island crossing Whitehall. I was close behind her. She never saw me. A big car came along and I shoved with all my might. I'm very strong! She went right down in front of it. I told the woman next to me I'd seen the number of the car and gave her the number of Gordon's Rolls. I hoped she'd repeat it to the police.

'It was lucky the car didn't stop. Some chauffeur joyriding without his master's knowledge, I suspect. Yes, I was lucky there. I'm always lucky. That scene the other day with Rivers, and Luke Fitzwilliam as witness. I've had such fun leading him along! Odd how difficult it was to make him suspect Gordon. But after Rivers's death he would be sure to do so. He must!

'And now – well, this will just finish the whole thing nicely.'

She got up and came towards Bridget. She said softly:

'Gordon jilted me! He was going to marry you. All my life I've been disappointed. I've had nothing – nothing at all . . .'

'*O lean grey woman whom nobody loves . . .*'

She was bending over her, smiling, with mad light eyes . . . The knife gleamed . . .

With all her youth and strength, Bridget sprang. Like a tiger-cat, she flung herself full force on the other woman, knocking her back, seizing her right wrist.

Taken by surprise, Honoria Waynflete fell back before the onslaught. But then, after a moment's inertia, she began to fight. In strength there was no comparison between them. Bridget was young and healthy with muscles toughened by games. Honoria Waynflete was a slender-built, frail creature.

But there was one factor on which Bridget had not reckoned. *Honoria Waynflete was mad.* Her strength was the strength of the insane. She fought like a devil and her insane strength was stronger than the sane muscled strength of Bridget. They swayed to and fro, and still Bridget strove to wrest the knife away from her, and still Honoria Waynflete hung on to it.

And then, little by little, the mad woman's strength began to prevail. Bridget cried out now:

'*Luke . . . Help . . . Help . . .*'

But she had no hope of help coming. She and Honoria Waynflete were alone. Alone in a dead world. With a supreme effort she wrenched the other's wrist back, and at last she heard the knife fall.

The next minute Honoria Waynflete's two hands had fastened round her neck in a maniac grasp, squeezing the life out of her. She gave one last choked cry . . .

CHAPTER 22

MRS HUMBLEBY SPEAKS

Luke was favourably impressed by the appearance of Superintendent Battle. He was a solid, comfortable-looking man with a broad red face and a large handsome moustache. He did not exactly express brilliance at a first glance, but a second glance was apt to make an observant person thoughtful, for Superintendent Battle's eye was unusually shrewd.

Luke did not make the mistake of underestimating him. He had met men of Battle's type before. He knew that they could be trusted, and that they invariably got results. He could not have wished for a better man to be put in charge of the case.

When they were alone together Luke said:

'You're rather a big noise to be sent down on a case like this?'

Superintendent Battle smiled.

'It may turn out to be a serious business, Mr Fitzwilliam. When a man like Lord Whitfield is concerned, we don't want to have any mistakes.'

'I appreciate that. Are you alone?'

'Oh, no. Got a detective-sergeant with me. He's at the other pub, the Seven Stars, and his job is to keep an eye on his lordship.'

'I see.'

Battle asked:

'In your opinion, Mr Fitzwilliam, there's no doubt whatever? You're pretty sure of your man?'

'On the facts I don't see that any alternative theory is possible. Do you want me to give you the facts?'

'I've had them, thank you, from Sir William.'

'Well, what do *you* think? I suppose it seems to you wildly unlikely that a man in Lord Whitfield's position should be a homicidal criminal?'

'Very few things seem unlikely to me,' said Superintendent Battle. 'Nothing's impossible in crime. That's what I've always said. If you were to tell me that a dear old maiden lady, or an archbishop, or a schoolgirl, was a dangerous criminal, I wouldn't say no. I'd look into the matter.'

'If you've heard the main facts of the case from Sir William, I'll just tell you what happened this morning,' said Luke.

He ran over briefly the main lines of his scene with Lord Whitfield. Superintendent Battle listened with a good deal of interest.

He said:

'You say he was fingering a knife. Did he make a special point of that knife, Mr Fitzwilliam? Was he threatening with it?'

'Not openly. He tested the edge in a rather nasty way – a kind of æsthetic pleasure about that that I didn't care about. Miss Waynflete felt the same, I believe.'

'That's the lady you spoke about – the one who's known Lord Whitfield all her life, and was once engaged to marry him?'

'That's right.'

Superintendent Battle said:

'I think you can make your mind easy about the young lady, Mr Fitzwilliam. I'll have someone put on to keep a sharp watch on her. With that, and with Jackson tailing his lordship, there ought to be no danger of anything happening.'

'You relieve my mind a good deal,' said Luke.

The superintendent nodded sympathetically.

'It's a nasty position for you, Mr Fitzwilliam. Worrying about Miss Conway. Mind you, I don't expect this will be an easy case. Lord Whitfield must be a pretty shrewd man. He will probably lie low for a good long while. That is, unless he's got to the last stage.'

'What do you call the last stage?'

'A kind of swollen egoism where a criminal thinks he simply can't be found out! He's too clever and everybody else is too stupid! Then, of course, we get him!'

Luke nodded. He rose.

'Well,' he said, 'I wish you luck. Let me help in any way I can.'

'Certainly.'

'There's nothing that you can suggest?'

Battle turned the question over in his mind.

'I don't think so. Not at the moment. I just want to get the general hang of things in the place. Perhaps I could have another word with you in the evening?'

'Rather.'

'I shall know better where we are then.'

Luke felt vaguely comforted and soothed. Many people had had that feeling after an interview with Superintendent Battle.

He glanced at his watch. Should he go round and see Bridget before lunch?

Better not, he thought. Miss Waynflete might feel that she had to ask him to stay for the meal, and it might disorganize her housekeeping. Middle-aged ladies, Luke knew from experience with aunts, were liable to be fussed over problems of housekeeping. He wondered if Miss Waynflete was an aunt? Probably.

He had strolled out to the door of the inn. A figure in black hurrying down the street stopped suddenly when she saw him.

'Mr Fitzwilliam.'

'Mrs Humbleby.'

He came forward and shook hands.

She said:

'I thought you had left?'

'No – only changed my quarters. I'm staying here now.'

'And Bridget? I heard she had left Ashe Manor?'

'Yes, she has.'

Mrs Humbleby sighed.

'I am so glad – so very glad she has gone right away from Wychwood.'

'Oh, she's still here. As a matter of fact, she's staying with Miss Waynflete.'

Mrs Humbleby moved back a step. Her face, Luke noted with surprise, looked extraordinarily distressed.

'Staying with Honoria Waynflete? Oh, but *why*?'

'Miss Waynflete very kindly asked her to stay for a few days.'

Mrs Humbleby gave a little shiver. She came close to Luke and laid a hand on his arm.

'Mr Fitzwilliam, I know I have no right to say anything – anything at all. I have had a lot of sorrow and grief lately and – perhaps – it makes me fanciful! These feelings of mine may be only sick fancies.'

Luke said gently:

'What feelings?'

'This conviction I have of – of *evil*!'

She looked timidly at Luke. Seeing that he merely bowed his head gravely and did not appear to question her statement, she went on:

'*So much wickedness* – that is the thought that is always with me – wickedness here in Wychwood. And that woman is at the bottom of it all. I am sure of it!'

Luke was mystified.

'What woman?'

Mrs Humbleby said:

'Honoria Waynflete is, I am sure, a very wicked woman! Oh, I see, you don't believe me! No one believed Lavinia Pinkerton either. *But we both felt it.* She, I think, knew more than I did . . . Remember, Mr Fitzwilliam, if a woman is not happy she is capable of terrible things.'

Luke said gently:

'That may be – yes.'

Mrs Humbleby said quickly:

'You don't believe me? Well, why should you? But I can't forget the day when John came home with his hand bound up from her house, though he pooh-poohed it and said it was only a scratch.'

She turned.

'Good-bye. Please forget what I have just said. I – I don't feel quite myself these days.'

Luke watched her go. He wondered why Mrs Humbleby called Honoria Waynflete a wicked woman. Had Dr Humbleby and Honoria Waynflete been friends, and was the doctor's wife jealous?

What had she said? 'Nobody believed Lavinia Pinkerton either.' Then Lavinia Pinkerton must have confided some of her suspicions to Mrs Humbleby.

With a rush the memory of the railway carriage came back, and the worried face of a nice old lady. He heard again an earnest voice saying, '*The look on a person's face.*' And the way her own face had changed as though she were seeing something very clearly in her mind. Just for a moment, he thought, her face had been quite different, the lips drawn back from the teeth and a queer, almost gloating look in her eyes.

He suddenly thought: *But I've seen someone look just like that – that same expression . . . Quite lately – when?* This morning! Of course! Miss Waynflete, when she was looking at Bridget in the drawing-room at the Manor.

And quite suddenly another memory assailed him. One of many years ago. His Aunt Mildred saying, 'She looked, you know, my dear, quite *half-witted*!' and just for a minute her own sane comfortable face had borne an imbecile, mindless expression . . .

Lavinia Pinkerton had been speaking of the look she had seen on a man's – no, a *person's* face. Was it possible that, just for a second, her vivid imagination had *reproduced the look that she saw – the look of a murderer looking at his next victim* . . .

Half unaware of what he was doing, Luke quickened his pace towards Miss Waynflete's house.

A voice in his brain was saying over and over again:

'Not a *man* – she never mentioned a *man* – *you* assumed it was a man because you were thinking of a man – but *she* never said so . . . Oh, God, am I quite mad? It isn't possible what I'm thinking . . . surely it isn't *possible* – it wouldn't make sense . . . But I *must* get to Bridget. I *must* know she's all right . . . Those eyes – those queer, light amber eyes. Oh, I'm mad! I must be mad! Whitfield's the criminal! He *must* be. He practically *said* so!'

And still, like a nightmare, he saw Miss Pinkerton's face in its momentary impersonation of something horrible and not quite sane.

The stunted little maid opened the door to him. A little startled by his vehemence, she said:

'The lady's gone out. Miss Waynflete told me so. I'll see if Miss Waynflete's in.'

He pushed past her, went into the drawing-room. Emily ran upstairs. She came down breathless.

'The mistress is out too.'

Luke took her by the shoulder.

'Which way? Where did they go?'

She gaped at him.

'They must have gone out by the back. I'd have seen them if they'd gone out frontways because the kitchen looks out there.'

She followed him as he raced out through the door into the tiny garden and out beyond. There was a man clipping a hedge. Luke went up to him and asked a question, striving to keep his voice normal.

The man said slowly:

'Two ladies? Yes. Some while since. I was having my dinner under the hedge. Reckon they didn't notice me.'

'*Which way did they go?*'

He strove desperately to make his voice normal. Yet the other's eyes opened a little wider as he replied slowly:

'Across them fields . . . Over that way. I don't know where after that.'

Luke thanked him and began to run. His strong feeling of urgency was deepened. He *must* catch up with them – he *must*! He might be quite mad. In all probability they were just taking an amicable stroll, but something in him clamoured for haste. More haste!

He crossed the two fields, stood hesitating in a country lane. Which way now?

And then he heard the call – faint, far away, but unmistakable . . .

'*Luke, help.*' And again, '*Luke . . .*'

Unerringly he plunged into the wood and ran in the direction from which the cry had come. There were more sounds now – scuffling – panting – a low gurgling cry.

He came through the trees in time to tear a mad woman's hands from her victim's throat, to hold her, struggling, foaming, cursing, till at last she gave a convulsive shudder and turned rigid in his grasp.

CHAPTER 23

....

NEW BEGINNING

'But I don't understand,' said Lord Whitfield. 'I don't understand.'

He strove to maintain his dignity, but beneath the pompous exterior a rather pitiable bewilderment was evident. He could hardly credit the extraordinary things that were being told him.

'It's like this, Lord Whitfield,' said Battle patiently. 'To begin with there is a touch of insanity in the family. We've found that out now. Often the way with these old families. I should say she had a predisposition that way. And then she was an ambitious lady – and she was thwarted. First her career and then her love affair.' He coughed. 'I understand it was *you* who jilted *her*?'

Lord Whitfield said stiffly:

'I don't like the term jilt.'

Superintendent Battle amended the phrase.

'It was you who terminated the engagement?'

'Well – yes.'

'Tell us why, Gordon,' said Bridget.

Lord Whitfield got rather red. He said:

'Oh, very well, if I must. Honoria had a canary. She was very fond of it. It used to take sugar from her lips. One day it pecked her violently instead. She was angry and picked it up – and – wrung its neck! I – I couldn't feel the same after that. I told her I thought we'd both made a mistake.'

Battle nodded. He said:

'That was the beginning of it! As she told Miss Conway, she turned her thoughts and her undoubted mental ability to one aim and purpose.'

Lord Whitfield said incredulously:

'To get *me* convicted as a murderer? I can't believe it.'

Bridget said, 'It's true, Gordon. You know, you were surprised yourself at the extraordinary way that everybody who annoyed you was instantly struck down.'

'There was a reason for that.'

'Honoria Waynflete was the reason,' said Bridget. 'Do get it into your head, Gordon, that it wasn't Providence that pushed

Tommy Pierce out of the window, and all the rest of them. It was Honoria.'

Lord Whitfield shook his head.

'It all seems to me quite incredible!' he said.

Battle said:

'You say you got a telephone message this morning?'

'Yes – about twelve o'clock. I was asked to go to the Shaw Wood at once as you, Bridget, had something to say to me. I was not to come by car but to walk.'

Battle nodded.

'Exactly. That would have been the finish. Miss Conway would have been found with her throat cut; and beside her *your* knife with *your* fingerprints on it! *And* you yourself would have been seen in the vicinity at the time! You wouldn't have had a leg to stand upon. Any jury in the world would have convicted you.'

'Me?' said Lord Whitfield, startled and distressed. 'Anyone would have believed a thing like that of Me?'

Bridget said gently:

'I didn't, Gordon. I never believed it.'

Lord Whitfield looked at her coldly, then he said stiffly:

'In view of my character and my standing in the county, I do not believe that anyone for one moment would have believed in such a monstrous charge!'

He went out with dignity and closed the door behind him.

Luke said:

'He'll never realize that he was really in danger!'

Then he said:

'Go on, Bridget, tell me how you came to suspect the Waynflete woman.'

Bridget explained:

'It was when you were telling me that Gordon was the killer. I couldn't believe it! You see, I knew him so *well*. I'd been his secretary for two years! I knew him in and out! I knew that he was pompous and petty and completely self-absorbed, but I knew, too, that he was a kindly person and almost absurdly tender-hearted. It worried him even to kill a wasp. That story about his killing Miss Waynflete's canary – it was all *wrong*. He just couldn't have done it. He'd told me once that he had jilted her. Now you insisted that it was *the other way about*. Well, that *might* be so! His pride might not have allowed him to admit that she had thrown him over. But not the canary story! That simply wasn't Gordon! He didn't even shoot because seeing things killed made him feel sick.

'So I simply knew that that part of the story was untrue. But if so, *Miss Waynflete must have lied*. And it was really, when you came to think of it, *a very extraordinary lie*! And I wondered suddenly if she'd told any more lies. She was a very proud woman – one could see that. To be thrown over must have hurt her pride horribly. It would probably make her feel very angry and revengeful against Lord Whitfield – especially, I felt, if he turned up again later all rich and prosperous and successful. I thought, "Yes, she'd probably enjoy helping to fix a crime upon him." And then a curious sort of whirling feeling came in my brain and I thought – but suppose *everything* she says is a lie – and I suddenly saw how easily a woman like that could make a fool of a man! And I thought, "It's fantastic, but suppose it was *she* who killed all these people and fed Gordon up with the idea that it was a kind of divine retribution!" It would be quite easy for her to make him believe that. As I told you once, Gordon would believe anything! And I thought, "*Could* she have done all those murders?" And I saw that she could! She could give a shove to a drunken man – and push a boy out of a window, and Amy Gibbs had died in her house. Mrs Horton, too – Honoria Waynflete used to go and sit with her when she was ill. Dr Humbleby was more difficult. I didn't know then that Wonky Pooh had a nasty septic ear and that she infected the dressing she put on his hand. Miss Pinkerton's death was even more difficult, because I couldn't imagine Miss Waynflete dressed up as a chauffeur driving a Rolls.

'And then, suddenly, I saw that that was the easiest of the lot! It was the old shove from behind – easily done in a crowd. The car didn't stop and she saw a fresh opportunity and told another woman she had seen the number of the car, and gave the number of Lord Whitfield's Rolls.

'Of course, all this only came very confusedly through my head. But if Gordon definitely *hadn't* done the murders – and I knew – yes, *knew* that he hadn't – well, who *had*? And the answer seemed quite clear. "*Someone who hates Gordon!*" Who hates Gordon? Honoria Waynflete, of course.

'And then I remembered that Miss Pinkerton had definitely spoken of a *man* as the killer. That knocked out all my beautiful theory, because, unless Miss Pinkerton was *right, she wouldn't have been killed* . . . So I got you to repeat exactly Miss Pinkerton's words and I soon discovered that she hadn't actually said "*man*" once. Then I felt that I was definitely on the right track! I decided to accept Miss Waynflete's invitation to stay with her and I resolved to try to ferret out the truth.'

'Without saying a word to me?' said Luke angrily.

'But, my sweet, you were so *sure* – and I wasn't sure a bit! It was all vague and doubtful. But I never dreamed that I was in any danger. I thought I'd have plenty of time . . .'

She shivered.

'Oh, Luke, it was horrible . . . Her eyes . . . And that dreadful, polite, inhuman laugh . . .'

Luke said with a slight shiver:

'I shan't forget how I only got there just in time.'

He turned to Battle. 'What's she like now?'

'Gone right over the edge,' said Battle. 'They do, you know. They can't face the shock of not having been as clever as they thought they were.'

Luke said ruefully:

'Well, I'm not much of a policeman! I never suspected Honoria Waynflete once. You'd have done better, Battle.'

'Maybe, sir, maybe not. You'll remember my saying that nothing's impossible in crime. I mentioned a maiden lady, I believe.'

'You also mentioned an archbishop and a schoolgirl! Am I to understand that you consider all these people as potential criminals?'

Battle's smile broadened to a grin.

'Anyone may be a criminal, sir, that's what I meant.'

'Except Gordon,' said Bridget. 'Luke, let's go and find him.'

They found Lord Whitfield in his study busily making notes.

'Gordon,' said Bridget in a small meek voice. 'Please, now that you know everything, will you forgive us?'

Lord Whitfield looked at her graciously.

'Certainly, my dear, certainly. I realize the truth. I was a busy man. I neglected you. The truth of the matter is as Kipling so wisely puts it: "He travels the fastest who travels alone. My path in life is a lonely one."' He squared his shoulders. 'I carry a big responsibility. I must carry it alone. For me there can be no companionship, no easing of the burden – I must go through life alone – till I drop by the wayside.'

Bridget said:

'Dear Gordon! You really are sweet!'

Lord Whitfield frowned.

'It is not a question of being sweet. Let us forget all this nonsense. I am a busy man.'

'I know you are.'

'I am arranging for a series of articles to start at once. Crimes committed by Women through the Ages.'

Bridget gazed at him with admiration.

'Gordon, I think that's a wonderful idea.'

Lord Whitfield puffed out his chest.

'So please leave me now. I must not be disturbed. I have a lot of work to get through.'

Luke and Bridget tiptoed from the room.

'But he really *is* sweet!' said Bridget.

'Bridget, I believe you were really fond of that man!'

'Do you know, Luke, I believe I was.'

Luke looked out of the window.

'I'll be glad to get away from Wychwood. I don't like this place. There's a lot of wickedness here, as Mrs Humbleby would say. I don't like the way Ashe Ridge broods over the village.'

'Talking of Ashe Ridge, what about Ellsworthy?'

Luke laughed a little shamefacedly.

'That blood on his hands?'

'Yes.'

'They'd sacrificed a white cock apparently!'

'How perfectly disgusting!'

'I think something unpleasant is going to happen to our Mr Ellsworthy. Battle is planning a little surprise.'

Bridget said:

'And poor Major Horton never even attempted to kill his wife, and Mr Abbot, I suppose, just had a compromising letter from a lady, and Dr Thomas is just a nice unassuming young doctor.'

'He's a superior ass!'

'You say that because you're jealous of his marrying Rose Humbleby.'

'She's much too good for him.'

'I always have felt you liked that girl better than me!'

'Darling, aren't you being rather absurd?'

'No, not really.'

She was silent a minute and then said:

'Luke, do you like me now?'

He made a movement towards her but she warded him off.

'I said *like*, Luke – not *love*.'

'Oh! I see . . . Yes, I do . . . I *like* you, Bridget, as well as loving you.'

Bridget said:

'I like you, Luke . . .'

They smiled at each other – a little timidly – like children who have made friends at a party.

Bridget said:

'Liking is more important than loving. It lasts. I want what is between us to last, Luke. I don't want us just to love each other and marry and get tired of each other and then want to marry someone else.'

'Oh! my dear Love, I know. You want reality. So do I. What's between us will last forever because it's founded on reality.'

'Is that true, Luke?'

'It's true, my sweet. That's why, I think, I was afraid of loving you.'

'I was afraid of loving you, too.'

'Are you afraid now?'

'No.'

He said:

'We've been close to Death for a long time. Now – that's over! Now – we'll begin to Live . . .'

AND THEN THERE WERE NONE

To Carlo and Mary
This is their book, dedicated to them
with much affection.

I

In the corner of a first-class smoking carriage, Mr Justice Wargrave, lately retired from the bench, puffed at a cigar and ran an interested eye through the political news in *The Times*.

He laid the paper down and glanced out of the window. They were running now through Somerset. He glanced at his watch – another two hours to go.

He went over in his mind all that had appeared in the papers about Soldier Island. There had been its original purchase by an American millionaire who was crazy about yachting – and an account of the luxurious modern house he had built on this little island off the Devon coast. The unfortunate fact that the new third wife of the American millionaire was a bad sailor had led to the subsequent putting up of the house and island for sale. Various glowing advertisements of it had appeared in the papers. Then came the first bald statement that it had been bought – by a Mr Owen. After that the rumours of the gossip writers had started. Soldier Island had really been bought by Miss Gabrielle Turl, the Hollywood film star! She wanted to spend some months there free from all publicity! *Busy Bee* had hinted delicately that it was to be an abode for Royalty??! *Mr Merryweather* had had it whispered to him that it had been bought for a honeymoon – Young Lord L— had surrendered to Cupid at last! *Jonas* knew for a *fact* that it had been purchased by the Admiralty with a view to carrying out some very hush-hush experiments!

Definitely, Soldier Island was news!

From his pocket Mr Justice Wargrave drew out a letter. The handwriting was practically illegible but words here and there stood out with unexpected clarity. *Dearest Lawrence . . . such years since I heard anything of you . . . must come to Soldier Island . . . the most enchanting place . . . so much to talk over . . . old days . . . communion with nature . . . bask in sunshine . . . 12.40 from*

Paddington . . . meet you at Oakbridge . . . and his correspondent signed herself with a flourish his *ever Constance Culmington*.

Mr Justice Wargrave cast back in his mind to remember when exactly he had last seen Lady Constance Culmington. It must be seven – no, eight years ago. She had then been going to Italy to bask in the sun and be at one with Nature and the *contadini*. Later, he had heard, she had proceeded to Syria where she proposed to bask in a yet stronger sun and live at one with Nature and the *bedouin*.

Constance Culmington, he reflected to himself, was exactly the sort of woman who *would* buy an island and surround herself with mystery! Nodding his head in gentle approval of his logic, Mr Justice Wargrave allowed his head to nod . . .

He slept . . .

II

Vera Claythorne, in a third-class carriage with five other travellers in it, leaned her head back and shut her eyes. How hot it was travelling by train today! It would be nice to get to the sea! Really a great piece of luck getting this job. When you wanted a holiday post it nearly always meant looking after a swarm of children – secretarial holiday posts were much more difficult to get. Even the agency hadn't held out much hope.

And then the letter had come.

'I have received your name from the Skilled Women's Agency together with their recommendation. I understand they know you personally. I shall be glad to pay you the salary you ask and shall expect you to take up your duties on August 8th. The train is the 12.40 from Paddington and you will be met at Oakbridge station. I enclose five £1 notes for expenses.

Yours truly,

Una Nancy Owen.'

And at the top was the stamped address, *Soldier Island, Sticklehaven, Devon . . .*

Soldier Island! Why, there had been nothing else in the papers lately! All sorts of hints and interesting rumours. Though probably they were mostly untrue. But the house had certainly been built by a millionaire and was said to be absolutely the last word in luxury.

Vera Claythorne, tired by a recent strenuous term at school, thought to herself, 'Being a games mistress in a third-class school isn't much of a catch . . . If only I could get a job at some *decent* school.'

And then, with a cold feeling round her heart, she thought: 'But I'm lucky to have even this. After all, people don't like a Coroner's Inquest, even if the Coroner *did* acquit me of all blame!'

He had even complimented her on her presence of mind and courage, she remembered. For an inquest it couldn't have gone better. And Mrs Hamilton had been kindness itself to her – only Hugo – *but she wouldn't think of Hugo!*

Suddenly, in spite of the heat in the carriage she shivered and wished she wasn't going to the sea. A picture rose clearly before her mind. *Cyril's head, bobbing up and down, swimming to the rock . . .* Up and down – up and down . . . And herself, swimming in easy practised strokes after him – cleaving her way through the water but knowing, only too surely, that she wouldn't be in time . . .

The sea – its deep warm blue – mornings spent lying out on the sands – Hugo – Hugo who had said he loved her . . .

She must *not* think of Hugo . . .

She opened her eyes and frowned across at the man opposite her. A tall man with a brown face, light eyes set rather close together and an arrogant, almost cruel mouth.

She thought to herself:

I bet he's been to some interesting parts of the world and seen some interesting things . . .

III

Philip Lombard, summing up the girl opposite in a mere flash of his quick moving eyes thought to himself:

'Quite attractive – a bit schoolmistressy perhaps.'

A cool customer, he should imagine – and one who could hold her own – in love or war. He'd rather like to take her on . . .

He frowned. No, cut out all that kind of stuff. This was business. He'd got to keep his mind on the job.

What exactly was up, he wondered? That little Jew had been damned mysterious.

'Take it or leave it, Captain Lombard.'

He had said thoughtfully:

'A hundred guineas, eh?'

He had said it in a casual way as though a hundred guineas was nothing to him. *A hundred guineas* when he was literally down to his last square meal! He had fancied, though, that the little Jew had not been deceived – that was the damnable part about Jews, you couldn't deceive them about money – they *knew*!

He said in the same casual tone:

'And you can't give me any further information?'

Mr Isaac Morris had shaken his little bald head very positively.

'No, Captain Lombard, the matter rests there. It is understood by my client that your reputation is that of a good man in a tight place. I am empowered to hand you one hundred guineas in return for which you will travel to Sticklehaven, Devon. The nearest station is Oakbridge, you will be met there and motored to Sticklehaven where a motor launch will convey you to Soldier Island. There you will hold yourself at the disposal of my client.'

Lombard had said abruptly:

'For how long?'

'Not longer than a week at most.'

Fingering his small moustache, Captain Lombard said:

'You understand I can't undertake anything – illegal?'

He had darted a very sharp glance at the other as he had spoken. There had been a very faint smile on the thick Semitic lips of Mr Morris as he answered gravely:

'If anything illegal is proposed, you will, of course, be at perfect liberty to withdraw.'

Damn the smooth little brute, he had smiled! It was as though he knew very well that in Lombard's past actions legality had not always been a *sine qua non* . . .

Lombard's own lips parted in a grin.

By Jove, he'd sailed pretty near the wind once or twice! But he'd always got away with it! There wasn't much he drew the line at really . . .

No, there wasn't much he'd draw the line at. He fancied that he was going to enjoy himself at Soldier Island . . .

IV

In a non-smoking carriage Miss Emily Brent sat very upright as was her custom. She was sixty-five and she did not approve of lounging. Her father, a Colonel of the old school, had been particular about deportment.

The present generation was shamelessly lax – in their carriage, *and in every other way* . . .

Enveloped in an aura of righteousness and unyielding principles, Miss Brent sat in her crowded third-class carriage and triumphed over its discomfort and its heat. Everyone made such a fuss over things nowadays! They wanted injections before they had teeth pulled – they took drugs if they couldn't sleep – they wanted easy chairs and cushions and the girls allowed their figures to slop about anyhow and lay about half naked on the beaches in summer.

Miss Brent's lips set closely. She would like to make an example of certain people.

She remembered last year's summer holiday. This year, however, it would be quite different. Soldier Island . . .

Mentally she re-read the letter which she had already read so many times.

> 'Dear Miss Brent,
>
> I do hope you remember me? We were together at Belhaven Guest House in August some years ago, and we seemed to have so much in common.
>
> I am starting a guest house of my own on an island off the coast of Devon. I think there is really an opening for a place where there is good plain cooking and a nice old-fashioned type of person. None of this nudity and gramophones half the night. I shall be very glad if you could see your way to spending your summer holiday on Soldier Island – quite free – as my guest. Would early in August suit you? Perhaps the 8th.
>
> Yours sincerely,
> U.N.O—.'

What was the name? The signature was rather difficult to read. Emily Brent thought impatiently: 'So many people write their signatures quite illegibly.'

She let her mind run back over the people at Belhaven. She had been there two summers running. There had been that nice middle-aged woman – Miss – Miss – now what *was* her name? – her father had been a Canon. And there had been a Mrs Olton – Ormen – No, surely it was *Oliver*! Yes – Oliver.

Soldier Island! There had been things in the paper about Soldier Island – something about a film star – or was it an American millionaire?

Of course often those places went very cheap – islands didn't suit everybody. They thought the idea was romantic but when they came to live there they realized the disadvantages and were only too glad to sell.

Emily Brent thought to herself: '*I shall be getting a free holiday at any rate.*'

With her income so much reduced and so many dividends not being paid, that was indeed something to take into consideration. If only she could remember a little more about Mrs – or was it Miss – Oliver?

V

General Macarthur looked out of the carriage window. The train was just coming into Exeter, where he had to change. Damnable, these slow branch line trains! This place, Soldier Island, was really no distance at all as the crow flies.

He hadn't got it clear who this fellow Owen was. A friend of Spoof Leggard's, apparently – and of Johnnie Dyer's.

'– *One or two of your old cronies are coming – would like to have a talk over old times.*'

Well, he'd enjoy a chat about old times. He'd had a fancy lately that fellows were rather fighting shy of him. All owing to that damned rumour! By God, it was pretty hard – nearly thirty years ago now! Armitage had talked, he supposed. Damned young pup! What did *he* know about it? Oh, well, no good brooding about these things! One fancied things sometimes – fancied a fellow was looking at you queerly.

This Soldier Island, now, he'd be interested to see it. A lot of gossip flying about. Looked as though there might be something in the rumour that the Admiralty or the War Office or the Air Force had got hold of it . . .

Young Elmer Robson, the American millionaire, had actually built the place. Spent thousands on it, so it was said. Every mortal luxury . . .

Exeter! And an hour to wait! And he didn't want to wait. He wanted to get on . . .

VI

Dr Armstrong was driving his Morris across Salisbury Plain. He was very tired . . . Success had its penalties. There had been a time when he had sat in his consulting room in Harley Street, correctly apparelled, surrounded with the most up to date appliances and the most luxurious furnishings and waited – waited through the empty days for his venture to succeed or fail . . .

Well, it had succeeded! He'd been lucky! Lucky *and* skilful of course. He was a good man at his job – but that wasn't enough for success. You had to have luck as well. And he'd had it! An accurate diagnosis, a couple of grateful women patients – women with money and position – and word had got about. 'You ought to try Armstrong – *quite* a young man – but *so* clever – Pam had been to all sorts of people for *years* and he put his finger on the trouble at once!' The ball had started rolling.

And now Dr Armstrong had definitely arrived. His days were full. He had little leisure. And so, on this August morning, he was glad that he was leaving London and going to be for some days on an island off the Devon coast. Not that it was exactly a holiday. The letter he had received had been rather vague in its terms, but there was nothing vague about the accompanying cheque. A whacking fee. These Owens must be rolling in money. Some little difficulty, it seemed, a husband who was worried about his wife's health and wanted a report on it without her being alarmed. She wouldn't hear of seeing a doctor. Her nerves –

Nerves! The doctor's eyebrows went up. These women and their nerves! Well, it was good for business after all. Half the women who consulted him had nothing the matter with them but boredom, but they wouldn't thank you for telling them so! And one could usually find something.

'A slightly uncommon condition of the (some long word)

nothing at all serious – but it needs just putting right. A simple treatment.'

Well, medicine was mostly faith-healing when it came to it. And he had a good manner – he could inspire hope and belief.

Lucky that he'd managed to pull himself together in time after that business ten – no, fifteen years ago. It had been a near thing, that! He'd been going to pieces. The shock had pulled him together. He'd cut out drink altogether. By Jove, it had been a near thing, though . . .

With a devastating ear-splitting blast on the horn an enormous Super-Sports Dalmain car rushed past him at eighty miles an hour. Dr Armstrong nearly went into the hedge. One of these young fools who tore round the country. He hated them. That had been a near shave, too. Damned young fool!

VII

Tony Marston, roaring down into Mere, thought to himself:

'The amount of cars crawling about the roads is frightful. Always something blocking your way. *And* they will drive in the middle of the road! Pretty hopeless driving in England, anyway . . . Not like France where you really *could* let out . . .'

Should he stop here for a drink, or push on? Heaps of time! Only another hundred miles and a bit to go. He'd have a gin and ginger beer. Fizzing hot day!

This island place ought to be rather good fun – if the weather lasted. Who *were* these Owens, he wondered? Rich and stinking, probably. Badger was rather good at nosing people like that out. Of course, he *had* to, poor old chap, with no money of his own . . .

Hope they'd do one well in drinks. Never knew with these fellows who'd made their money and weren't born to it. Pity that story about Gabrielle Turl having bought Soldier Island wasn't true. He'd like to have been in with that film star crowd.

Oh, well, he supposed there'd be a few girls there . . .

Coming out of the hotel, he stretched himself, yawned, looked up at the blue sky and climbed into the Dalmain.

Several young women looked at him admiringly – his six feet of well-proportioned body, his crisp hair, tanned face, and intensely blue eyes.

He let in the clutch with a roar and leapt up the narrow street. Old men and errand boys jumped for safety. The latter looked after the car admiringly.

Anthony Marston proceeded on his triumphal progress.

VIII

Mr Blore was in the slow train from Plymouth. There was only one other person in his carriage, an elderly seafaring gentleman with a bleary eye. At the present moment he had dropped off to sleep.

Mr Blore was writing carefully in a little notebook.

'That's the lot,' he muttered to himself. 'Emily Brent, Vera Claythorne, Dr Armstrong, Anthony Marston, old Justice Wargrave, Philip Lombard, General Macarthur, C.M.G., D.S.O. Man-servant and wife: Mr and Mrs Rogers.'

He closed the notebook and put it back in his pocket. He glanced over at the corner and the slumbering man.

'Had one over the eight,' diagnosed Mr Blore accurately.

He went over things carefully and conscientiously in his mind.

'Job ought to be easy enough,' he ruminated. 'Don't see how I can slip up on it. Hope I look all right.'

He stood up and scrutinized himself anxiously in the glass. The face reflected there was of a slightly military cast with a moustache. There was very little expression in it. The eyes were grey and set rather close together.

'Might be a Major,' said Mr Blore. 'No, I forgot. There's that old military gent. He'd spot me at once.'

'South Africa,' said Mr Blore, 'that's my line! None of these people have anything to do with South Africa, and I've just been reading that travel folder so I can talk about it all right.'

Fortunately there were all sorts and types of colonials. As a man of means from South Africa, Mr Blore felt that he could enter into any society unchallenged.

Soldier Island. He remembered Soldier Island as a boy . . . Smelly sort of rock covered with gulls – stood about a mile from the coast.

Funny idea to go and build a house on it! Awful in bad weather! But millionaires were full of whims!

The old man in the corner woke up and said:

'You can't never tell at sea – never!'

Mr Blore said soothingly, 'That's right. You can't.'

The old man hiccupped twice and said plaintively:

'There's a squall coming.'

Mr Blore said:

'No, no, mate, it's a lovely day.'

The old man said angrily:

'There's a squall ahead. I can *smell* it.'

'Maybe you're right,' said Mr Blore pacifically.

The train stopped at a station and the old fellow rose unsteadily.

'Thish where I get out.' He fumbled with the window. Mr Blore helped him.

The old man stood in the doorway. He raised a solemn hand and blinked his bleary eyes.

'Watch and pray,' he said. 'Watch and pray. The day of judgment is at hand.'

He collapsed through the doorway on to the platform. From a recumbent position he looked up at Mr Blore and said with immense dignity:

'I'm talking to *you*, young man. The day of judgment is very close at hand.'

Subsiding on to his seat Mr Blore thought to himself: He's nearer the day of judgment than I am!

But there, as it happens, he was wrong . . .

CHAPTER 2

I

Outside Oakbridge station a little group of people stood in momentary uncertainty. Behind them stood porters with suitcases. One of these called, 'Jim!'

The driver of one of the taxis stepped forward.

'You'm for Soldier Island, maybe?' he asked in a soft Devon voice. Four voices gave assent – and then immediately afterwards gave quick surreptitious glances at each other.

The driver said, addressing his remarks to Mr Justice Wargrave as the senior member of the party:

'There are two taxis here, sir. One of them must wait till the slow train from Exeter gets in – a matter of five minutes – there's one gentleman coming by that. Perhaps one of you wouldn't mind waiting? You'd be more comfortable that way.'

Vera Claythorne, her own secretarial position clear in her mind, spoke at once.

'I'll wait,' she said, 'if you will go on?' She looked at the other three, her glance and voice had that slight suggestion of command in it that comes from having occupied a position of authority. She might have been directing which tennis sets the girls were to play in.

Miss Brent said stiffly, 'Thank you,' bent her head and entered one of the taxis, the door of which the driver was holding open.

Mr Justice Wargrave followed her.

Captain Lombard said:

'I'll wait with Miss –'

'Claythorne,' said Vera.

'My name is Lombard, Philip Lombard.'

The porters were piling luggage on the taxi. Inside, Mr Justice Wargrave said with due legal caution:

'Beautiful weather we are having.'

Miss Brent said:

'Yes, indeed.'

A very distinguished old gentleman, she thought to herself. Quite unlike the usual type of man in seaside guest houses. Evidently Mrs or Miss Oliver had good connections . . .

Mr Justice Wargrave inquired:

'Do you know this part of the world well?'

'I have been to Cornwall and to Torquay, but this is my first visit to this part of Devon.'

The judge said:

'I also am unacquainted with this part of the world.'

The taxi drove off.

The driver of the second taxi said:

'Like to sit inside while you're waiting?'

Vera said decisively:

'Not at all.'

Captain Lombard smiled. He said:

'That sunny wall looks more attractive. Unless you'd rather go inside the station?'

'No, indeed. It's so delightful to get out of that stuffy train.'
He answered:

'Yes, travelling by train *is* rather trying in this weather.'

Vera said conventionally:

'I do hope it lasts – the weather, I mean. Our English summers are so treacherous.'

With a slight lack of originality Lombard asked:

'Do you know this part of the world well?'

'No, I've never been here before.' She added quickly, conscientiously determined to make her position clear at once, 'I haven't even seen my employer yet.'

'Your employer?'

'Yes, I'm Mrs Owen's secretary.'

'Oh, I see.' Just imperceptibly his manner changed. It was slightly more assured – easier in tone. He said: 'Isn't that rather unusual?'

Vera laughed.

'Oh, no, I don't think so. Her own secretary was suddenly taken ill and she wired to an agency for a substitute and they sent me.'

'So that was it. And suppose you don't like the post when you've got there?'

Vera laughed again.

'Oh, it's only temporary – a holiday post. I've got a permanent job at a girls' school. As a matter of fact, I'm frightfully thrilled at the prospect of seeing Soldier Island. There's been such a lot about it in the papers. Is it really very fascinating?'

Lombard said:

'I don't know. I haven't seen it.'

'Oh, really? The Owens are frightfully keen on it, I suppose. What are they like? Do tell me.'

Lombard thought: Awkward, this – am I supposed to have met them or not? He said quickly:

'There's a wasp crawling up your arm. No – keep quite still.' He made a convincing pounce. 'There. It's gone!'

'Oh, thank you. There are a lot of wasps about this summer.'

'Yes, I suppose it's the heat. Who are we waiting for, do you know?'

'I haven't the least idea.'

The loud drawn-out scream of an approaching train was heard. Lombard said:

'That will be the train now.'

It was a tall soldierly old man who appeared at the exit from the platform. His grey hair was clipped close and he had a neatly trimmed white moustache.

His porter, staggering slightly under the weight of the solid leather suitcase, indicated Vera and Lombard.

Vera came forward in a competent manner. She said:

'I am Mrs Owen's secretary. There is a car here waiting.' She added, 'This is Mr Lombard.'

The faded blue eyes, shrewd in spite of their age, sized up Lombard. For a moment a judgment showed in them – had there been any one to read it.

'Good-looking fellow. Something just a little wrong about him . . .'

The three of them got into the waiting taxi. They drove through the sleepy streets of little Oakbridge and continued about a mile on the main Plymouth road. Then they plunged into a maze of cross-country lanes, steep, green and narrow.

General Macarthur said:

'Don't know this part of Devon at all. My little place is in East Devon – just on the border-line of Dorset.'

Vera said:

'It really is lovely here. The hills and the red earth and everything so green and luscious-looking.'

Philip Lombard said critically:

'It's a bit shut in . . . I like open country myself. Where you can see what's coming . . .'

General Macarthur said to him:

'You've seen a bit of the world, I fancy?'

Lombard shrugged his shoulders disparagingly.

'I've knocked about here and there, sir.'

He thought to himself: 'He'll ask me now if I was old enough to be in the War. These old boys always do.'

But General Macarthur did not mention the War.

II

They came up over a steep hill and down a zigzag track to Sticklehaven – a mere cluster of cottages with a fishing boat or two drawn up on the beach.

Illuminated by the setting sun, they had their first glimpse of Soldier Island jutting up out of the sea to the south.

Vera said, surprised:

'It's a long way out.'

She had pictured it differently, close to shore, crowned with a beautiful white house. But there was no house visible, only the boldly silhouetted rock with its faint resemblance to a giant head. There was something sinister about it. She shivered faintly.

Outside a little inn, the Seven Stars, three people were sitting. There was the hunched elderly figure of the judge, the upright form of Miss Brent, and a third man – a big bluff man who came forward and introduced himself.

'Thought we might as well wait for you,' he said. 'Make one trip of it. Allow me to introduce myself. Name's Davis. Natal, South Africa's my natal spot, ha, ha!'

He laughed breezily.

Mr Justice Wargrave looked at him with active malevolence. He seemed to be wishing that he could order the court to be cleared. Miss Emily Brent was clearly not sure if she liked Colonials.

'Any one care for a little nip before we embark?' asked Mr Davis hospitably.

Nobody assenting to this proposition, Mr Davis turned and held up a finger.

'Mustn't delay, then. Our good host and hostess will be expecting us,' he said.

He might have noticed that a curious constraint came over the other members of the party. It was as though the mention of their host and hostess had a curiously paralysing effect upon the guests.

In response to Davis's beckoning finger, a man detached himself from a nearby wall against which he was leaning and came up to them. His rolling gait proclaimed him as a man of the sea. He had a weather-beaten face and dark eyes with a slightly evasive expression. He spoke in his soft Devon voice.

'Will you be ready to be starting for the island, ladies and gentlemen? The boat's waiting. There's two gentlemen coming by car but Mr Owen's orders was not to wait for them as they might arrive at any time.'

The party got up. Their guide led them along a small stone jetty. Alongside it a motor boat was lying.

Emily Brent said:

'That's a very small boat.'

The boat's owner said persuasively:

'She's a fine boat that, Ma'am. You could go to Plymouth in her as easy as winking.'

Mr Justice Wargrave said sharply:

'There are a good many of us.'

'She'd take double the number, sir.'

Philip Lombard said in his pleasant easy voice:

'It's quite all right. Glorious weather – no swell.'

Rather doubtfully, Miss Brent permitted herself to be helped into the boat. The others followed suit. There was as yet no fraternizing among the party. It was as though each member of it was puzzled by the other members.

They were just about to cast loose when their guide paused, boat-hook in hand.

Down the steep track into the village a car was coming. A car so fantastically powerful, so superlatively beautiful that it had all the nature of an apparition. At the wheel sat a young man, his hair blown back by the wind. In the blaze of the evening light he looked, not a man, but a young God, a Hero God out of some Northern Saga.

He touched the horn and a great roar of sound echoed from the rocks of the bay.

It was a fantastic moment. In it, Anthony Marston seemed to be something more than mortal. Afterwards more than one of those present remembered that moment.

III

Fred Narracott sat by the engine thinking to himself that this was a queer lot. Not at all his idea of what Mr Owen's guests were likely to be. He'd expected something altogether more classy. Togged up women and gentlemen in yachting costume and all very rich and important-looking.

Not at all like Mr Elmer Robson's parties. A faint grin came to Fred Narracott's lips as he remembered the millionaire's guests. That had been a party if you like – and the drink they'd got through!

This Mr Owen must be a very different sort of gentleman. Funny, it was, thought Fred, that he'd never yet set eyes on Owen – or his Missus either. Never been down here yet he hadn't. Everything ordered and paid for by that Mr Morris. Instructions always very clear and payment prompt, but it was odd, all the same. The papers said there was some mystery about Owen. Mr Narracott agreed with them.

Perhaps after all, it *was* Miss Gabrielle Turl who had bought the island. But that theory departed from him as he surveyed his passengers. Not this lot – none of them looked likely to have anything to do with a film star.

He summed them up dispassionately.

One old maid – the sour kind – he knew them well enough. She was a tartar he could bet. Old military gentleman – real Army look about him. Nice-looking young lady – but the ordinary kind, not glamorous – no Hollywood touch about her. That bluff cheery gent – *he* wasn't a real gentleman. Retired tradesman, that's what he is, thought Fred Narracott. The other gentleman, the lean hungry-looking gentleman with the quick eyes, he was a queer one, he was. Just possible he *might* have something to do with the pictures.

No, there was only one satisfactory passenger in the boat. The last gentleman, the one who had arrived in the car (and what a car! A car such as had never been seen in Sticklehaven before. Must have cost hundreds and hundreds, a car like that). He was the right kind. Born to money, he was. If the party had been all like him . . . he'd understand it . . .

Queer business when you came to think of it – the whole thing was queer – very queer . . .

IV

The boat churned its way round the rock. Now at last the house came into view. The south side of the island was quite different. It shelved gently down to the sea. The house was there facing south – low and square and modern-looking with rounded windows letting in all the light.

An exciting house – a house that lived up to expectation!

Fred Narracott shut off the engine, they nosed their way gently into a little natural inlet between rocks.

Philip Lombard said sharply:

'Must be difficult to land here in dirty weather.'

Fred Narracott said cheerfully:

'Can't land on Soldier Island when there's a south-easterly. Sometimes 'tis cut off for a week or more.'

Vera Claythorne thought:

'The catering must be very difficult. That's the worst of an island. All the domestic problems are so worrying.'

The boat grated against the rocks. Fred Narracott jumped out and he and Lombard helped the others to alight. Narracott made the boat fast to a ring in the rock. Then he led the way up steps cut in the cliff.

General Macarthur said:

'Ha! delightful spot!'

But he felt uneasy. Damned odd sort of place.

As the party ascended the steps and came out on a terrace above, their spirits revived. In the open doorway of the house a correct butler was awaiting them, and something about his gravity reassured them. And then the house itself was really most attractive, the view from the terrace magnificent . . .

The butler came forward bowing slightly. He was a tall lank man, grey-haired and very respectable. He said:

'Will you come this way, please.'

In the wide hall drinks stood ready. Rows of bottles. Anthony Marston's spirits cheered up a little. He'd just been thinking this was a rum kind of show. None of *his* lot! What could old Badger have been thinking about to let him in for this? However, the drinks were all right. Plenty of ice, too.

What was it the butler chap was saying?

Mr Owen – unfortunately delayed – unable to get here till tomorrow. Instructions – everything they wanted – if they would like to go to their rooms? . . . dinner would be at eight o'clock . . .

V

Vera had followed Mrs Rogers upstairs. The woman had thrown open a door at the end of a passage and Vera had walked into a delightful bedroom with a big window that opened wide upon the sea and another looking east. She uttered a quick exclamation of pleasure.

Mrs Rogers was saying:

'I hope you've got everything you want, Miss?'

Vera looked round. Her luggage had been brought up and had been unpacked. At one side of the room a door stood open into a pale blue-tiled bathroom.

She said quickly:

'Yes, everything, I think.'

'You'll ring the bell if you want anything, Miss?'

Mrs Rogers had a flat monotonous voice. Vera looked at her curiously. What a white bloodless ghost of a woman! Very respectable-looking, with her hair dragged back from her face and her black dress. Queer light eyes that shifted the whole time from place to place.

Vera thought:

'She looks frightened of her own shadow.'

Yes, that was it – frightened!

She looked like a woman who walked in mortal fear . . .

A little shiver passed down Vera's back. What on earth was the woman afraid of?

She said pleasantly:

'I'm Mrs Owen's new secretary. I expect you know that.'

Mrs Rogers said:

'No, Miss, I don't know anything. Just a list of the ladies and gentlemen and what rooms they were to have.'

Vera said:

'Mrs Owen didn't mention me?'

Mrs Rogers' eyelashes flickered.

'I haven't seen Mrs Owen – not yet. We only came here two days ago.'

Extraordinary people, these Owens, thought Vera. Aloud she said:

'What staff is there here?'

'Just me and Rogers, Miss.'

Vera frowned. Eight people in the house – ten with the host and hostess – and only one married couple to do for them.

Mrs Rogers said:

'I'm a good cook and Rogers is handy about the house. I didn't know, of course, that there was to be such a large party.'

Vera said:

'But you can manage?'

'Oh yes, Miss, I can manage. If there's to be large parties often perhaps Mrs Owen could get extra help in.'

Vera said, 'I expect so.'

Mrs Rogers turned to go. Her feet moved noiselessly over the ground. She drifted from the room like a shadow.

Vera went over to the window and sat down on the window seat. She was faintly disturbed. Everything – somehow – was a little queer. The absence of the Owens, the pale ghostlike Mrs Rogers. And the guests! Yes, the guests were queer, too. An oddly assorted party.

Vera thought:

'I wish I'd seen the Owens ... I wish I knew what they were like.'

She got up and walked restlessly about the room.

A perfect bedroom decorated throughout in the modern style. Off-white rugs on the gleaming parquet floor – faintly tinted walls – a long mirror surrounded by lights. A mantelpiece bare of ornaments save for an enormous block of white marble shaped like a bear, a piece of modern sculpture in which was inset a clock. Over it, in a gleaming chromium frame, was a big square of parchment – a poem.

She stood in front of the fireplace and read it. It was the old nursery rhyme that she remembered from her childhood days.

Ten little soldier boys went out to dine;
One choked his little self and then there were Nine.

Nine little soldier boys sat up very late;
One overslept himself and then there were Eight.

Eight little soldier boys travelling in Devon;
One said he'd stay there and then there were Seven.

Seven little soldier boys chopping up sticks;
One chopped himself in halves and then there were Six.

Six little soldier boys playing with a hive;
A bumble bee stung one and then there were Five.

Five little soldier boys going in for law;
One got in Chancery and then there were Four.

Four little soldier boys going out to sea;
A red herring swallowed one and then there were Three.

Three little soldier boys walking in the Zoo;
A big bear hugged one and then there were Two.

Two little soldier boys sitting in the sun;
One got frizzled up and then there was One.

One little soldier boy left all alone;
He went and hanged himself and then there were None.

Vera smiled. Of course! This was Soldier Island!

She went and sat again by the window looking out to sea.

How big the sea was! From here there was no land to be seen anywhere – just a vast expanse of blue water rippling in the evening sun.

The sea . . . So peaceful today – sometimes so cruel . . . The sea that dragged you down to its depths. Drowned . . . Found drowned . . . Drowned at sea . . . Drowned – drowned – drowned . . .

No, she wouldn't remember . . . She would *not* think of it! All that was over . . .

VI

Dr Armstrong came to Soldier Island just as the sun was sinking into the sea. On the way across he had chatted to the boatman – a local man. He was anxious to find out a little about these people who owned Soldier Island, but the man Narracott seemed curiously ill-informed, or perhaps unwilling to talk.

So Dr Armstrong chatted instead of the weather and of fishing.

He was tired after his long motor drive. His eyeballs ached. Driving west you were driving against the sun.

Yes, he was very tired. The sea and perfect peace – that was what he needed. He would like, really, to take a long holiday. But he couldn't afford to do that. He could afford it financially, of course, but he couldn't afford to drop out. You were soon forgotten nowadays. No, now that he had arrived, he must keep his nose to the grindstone.

He thought:

'All the same, this evening, I'll imagine to myself that I'm not going back – that I've done with London and Harley Street and all the rest of it.'

There was something magical about an island – the mere word suggested fantasy. You lost touch with the world – an island was a world of its own. A world, perhaps, from which you might never return.

He thought:

'I'm leaving my ordinary life behind me.'

And, smiling to himself, he began to make plans, fantastic plans for the future. He was still smiling when he walked up the rock-cut steps.

In a chair on the terrace an old gentleman was sitting and the sight of him was vaguely familiar to Dr Armstrong. Where had he seen that frog-like face, that tortoise-like neck, that hunched up attitude – yes and those pale shrewd little eyes? Of course – old Wargrave. He'd given evidence once before him. Always looked half-asleep, but was shrewd as could be when it came to a point of law. Had great power with a jury – it was said he could make their minds up for them any day of the week. He'd got one or two unlikely convictions out of them. A hanging judge, some people said.

Funny place to meet him . . . here – out of the world.

VII

Mr Justice Wargrave thought to himself:

'Armstrong? Remember him in the witness-box. Very correct and cautious. All doctors are damned fools. Harley Street ones are the worst of the lot.' And his mind dwelt malevolently on a recent interview he had had with a suave personage in that very street.

Aloud he grunted:

'Drinks are in the hall.'

Dr Armstrong said:

'I must go and pay my respects to my host and hostess.'

Mr Justice Wargrave closed his eyes again, looking decidedly reptilian, and said:

'You can't do that.'

Dr Armstrong was startled.

'Why not?'

The judge said:

'No host and hostess. Very curious state of affairs. Don't understand this place.'

Dr Armstrong stared at him for a minute. When he thought the old gentleman had actually gone to sleep, Wargrave said suddenly:

'D'you know Constance Culmington?'

'Er – no, I'm afraid I don't.'

'It's of no consequence,' said the judge. 'Very vague woman – and practically unreadable handwriting. I was just wondering if I'd come to the wrong house.'

Dr Armstrong shook his head and went on up to the house.

Mr Justice Wargrave reflected on the subject of Constance Culmington. Undependable like all women.

His mind went on to the two women in the house, the tight-lipped old maid and the girl. He didn't care for the girl, cold-blooded young hussy. No, three women, if you counted the Rogers woman. Odd creature, she looked scared to death. Respectable pair and knew their job.

Rogers coming out on the terrace that minute, the judge asked him:

'Is Lady Constance Culmington expected, do you know?'

Rogers stared at him.

'No, sir, not to my knowledge.'

The judge's eyebrows rose. But he only grunted.

He thought:

'Soldier Island, eh? There's a fly in the ointment.'

VIII

Anthony Marston was in his bath. He luxuriated in the steaming water. His limbs had felt cramped after his long drive. Very few thoughts passed through his head. Anthony was a creature of sensation – and of action.

He thought to himself:

'Must go through with it, I suppose,' and thereafter dismissed everything from his mind.

Warm steaming water – tired limbs – presently a shave – a cocktail – dinner.

And after –?

IX

Mr Blore was tying his tie. He wasn't very good at this sort of thing.

Did he look all right? He supposed so.

Nobody had been exactly cordial to him . . . Funny the way they all eyed each other – as though they *knew* . . .

Well, it was up to him.

He didn't mean to bungle his job.

He glanced up at the framed nursery rhyme over the mantelpiece.

Neat touch, having that there!

He thought:

Remember this island when I was a kid. Never thought I'd be doing this sort of a job in a house here. Good thing, perhaps, that one can't foresee the future.

X

General Macarthur was frowning to himself.

Damn it all, the whole thing was deuced odd! Not at all what he'd been led to expect . . .

For two pins he'd make an excuse and get away . . . Throw up the whole business . . .

But the motor-boat had gone back to the mainland.

He'd have to stay.

That fellow Lombard now, he was a queer chap.

Not straight. He'd swear the man wasn't straight.

XI

As the gong sounded, Philip Lombard came out of his room and walked to the head of the stairs. He moved like a panther, smoothly and noiselessly. There was something of the panther about him altogether. A beast of prey – pleasant to the eye.

He was smiling to himself.

A week – eh?

He was going to enjoy that week.

XII

In her bedroom, Emily Brent, dressed in black silk ready for dinner, was reading her Bible.

Her lips moved as she followed the words:

> 'The heathen are sunk down in the pit that they made: in the net which they hid is their own foot taken. The Lord is known by the judgment which he executeth: the wicked is snared in the work of his own hands. The wicked shall be turned into hell.'

Her lips tight closed. She shut the Bible.

Rising, she pinned a cairngorm brooch at her neck, and went down to dinner.

CHAPTER 3

I

Dinner was drawing to a close.

The food had been good, the wine perfect. Rogers waited well.

Every one was in better spirits. They had begun to talk to each other with more freedom and intimacy.

Mr Justice Wargrave, mellowed by the excellent port, was being amusing in a caustic fashion, Dr Armstrong and Tony Marston were listening to him. Miss Brent chatted to General Macarthur, they had discovered some mutual friends. Vera Claythorne was asking Mr Davis intelligent questions about South Africa. Mr Davis was quite fluent on the subject. Lombard listened to the conversation. Once or twice he looked up quickly, and his eyes narrowed. Now and then his eyes played round the table, studying the others.

Anthony Marston said suddenly:

'Quaint, these things, aren't they?'

In the centre of the round table, on a circular glass stand, were some little china figures.

'Soldiers,' said Tony. 'Soldier Island. I suppose that's the idea.'

Vera leaned forward.

'I wonder. How many are there? Ten?'

'Yes – ten there are.'

Vera cried:

'What fun! They're the ten little soldier boys of the nursery rhyme, I suppose. In my bedroom the rhyme is framed and hung up over the mantelpiece.'

Lombard said:

'In my room, too.'

'And mine.'

'And mine.'

Everybody joined in the chorus. Vera said:

'It's an amusing idea, isn't it?'

Mr Justice Wargrave grunted:

'Remarkably childish,' and helped himself to port.

Emily Brent looked at Vera Claythorne. Vera Claythorne looked at Miss Brent. The two women rose.

In the drawing-room the French windows were open on to the terrace and the sound of the sea murmuring against the rocks came up to them.

Emily Brent said, 'Pleasant sound.'

Vera said sharply, 'I hate it.'

Miss Brent's eyes looked at her in surprise. Vera flushed. She said, more composedly:

'I don't think this place would be very agreeable in a storm.'

Emily Brent agreed.

'I've no doubt the house is shut up in winter,' she said. 'You'd never get servants to stay here for one thing.'

Vera murmured:

'It must be difficult to get servants anyway.'

Emily Brent said:

'Mrs Oliver has been lucky to get these two. The woman's a good cook.'

Vera thought:

'Funny how elderly people always get names wrong.'

She said:

'Yes, I think Mrs Owen has been very lucky indeed.'

Emily Brent had brought a small piece of embroidery out of her bag. Now, as she was about to thread her needle, she paused.

She said sharply:

'Owen? Did you say Owen?'

'Yes.'

Emily Brent said sharply:

'I've never met anyone called Owen in my life.'

Vera stared.

'But surely –'

She did not finish her sentence. The door opened and the men joined them. Rogers followed them into the room with the coffee tray.

The judge came and sat down by Emily Brent. Armstrong came up to Vera. Tony Marston strolled to the open window. Blore studied with naïve surprise a statuette in brass – wondering perhaps if its bizarre angularities were really supposed to be the female figure. General Macarthur stood with his back to the mantelpiece. He pulled at his little white moustache. That had been a damned good dinner! His spirits were rising. Lombard turned over the pages of *Punch* that lay with other papers on a table by the wall.

Rogers went round with the coffee tray. The coffee was good – really black and very hot.

The whole party had dined well. They were satisfied with themselves and with life. The hands of the clock pointed to twenty minutes past nine. There was a silence – a comfortable replete silence.

Into that silence came The Voice. Without warning, inhuman, penetrating . . .

'Ladies and gentlemen! Silence please!'

Everyone was startled. They looked round – at each other, at the walls. Who was speaking?

The Voice went on – a high clear voice:

'*You are charged with the following indictments:*

'*Edward George Armstrong, that you did upon the 14th day of March, 1925, cause the death of Louisa Mary Clees.*

'*Emily Caroline Brent, that upon the 5th of November, 1931, you were responsible for the death of Beatrice Taylor.*

'*William Henry Blore, that you brought about the death of James Stephen Landor on October 10th, 1928.*

'*Vera Elizabeth Claythorne, that on the 11th day of August, 1935, you killed Cyril Ogilvie Hamilton.*

'*Philip Lombard, that upon a date in February, 1932, you were guilty of the death of twenty-one men, members of an East African tribe.*

'*John Gordon Macarthur, that on the 4th of January, 1917, you deliberately sent your wife's lover, Arthur Richmond, to his death.*

'*Anthony James Marston, that upon the 14th day of November last, you were guilty of the murder of John and Lucy Combes.*

'*Thomas Rogers and Ethel Rogers, that on the 6th of May, 1929, you brought about the death of Jennifer Brady.*

'*Lawrence John Wargrave, that upon the 10th day of June, 1930, you were guilty of the murder of Edward Seton.*

'*Prisoners at the bar, have you anything to say in your defence?*'

II

The voice had stopped.

There was a moment's petrified silence and then a resounding crash! Rogers had dropped the coffee tray!

At the same moment, from somewhere outside the room there came a scream and the sound of a thud.

Lombard was the first to move. He leapt to the door and flung it open. Outside, lying in a huddled mass, was Mrs Rogers.

Lombard called:

'Marston.'

Anthony sprang to help him. Between them, they lifted up the woman and carried her into the drawing-room.

Dr Armstrong came across quickly. He helped them to lift her on to the sofa and bent over her. He said quickly:

'It's nothing. She's fainted, that's all. She'll be round in a minute.'

Lombard said to Rogers:

'Get some brandy.'

Rogers, his face white, his hands shaking, murmured:

'Yes, sir,' and slipped quickly out of the room.

Vera cried out:

'*Who was that speaking?* Where was he? It sounded – it sounded –'

General Macarthur spluttered out:

'What's going on here? What kind of a practical joke was that?'

His hand was shaking. His shoulders sagged. He looked suddenly ten years older.

Blore was mopping his face with a handkerchief.

Only Mr Justice Wargrave and Miss Brent seemed comparatively unmoved. Emily Brent sat upright, her head held high. In both cheeks was a spot of hard colour. The judge sat in his habitual pose, his head sunk down into his neck. With one hand he gently scratched his ear. Only his eyes were active, darting round and round the room, puzzled, alert with intelligence.

Again it was Lombard who acted. Armstrong being busy with the collapsed woman, Lombard was free once more to take the initiative.

He said:

'That voice? It sounded as though it were in the room.'

Vera cried:

'*Who was it?* Who was it? It wasn't one of us.'

Like the judge, Lombard's eyes wandered slowly round the room. They rested a minute on the open window, then he shook his head decisively. Suddenly his eyes lighted up. He moved forward swiftly to where a door near the fireplace led into an adjoining room.

With a swift gesture, he caught the handle and flung the door open. He passed through and immediately uttered an exclamation of satisfaction.

He said:

'Ah, here we are.'

The others crowded after him. Only Miss Brent remained alone sitting erect in her chair.

Inside the second room a table had been brought up close to

the wall which adjoined the drawing-room. On the table was a gramophone – an old-fashioned type with a large trumpet attached. The mouth of the trumpet was against the wall, and Lombard, pushing it aside indicated where two or three small holes had been unobtrusively bored through the wall.

Adjusting the gramophone he replaced the needle on the record and immediately they heard again '*You are charged with the following indictments –*'

Vera cried:

'Turn it off! Turn it off! It's horrible!'

Lombard obeyed.

Dr Armstrong said, with a sigh of relief:

'A disgraceful and heartless practical joke, I suppose.'

The small clear voice of Mr Justice Wargrave murmured:

'So you think it's a joke, do you?'

The doctor stared at him.

'What else could it be?'

The hand of the judge gently stroked his upper lip.

He said:

'At the moment I'm not prepared to give an opinion.'

Anthony Marston broke in. He said:

'Look here, there's one thing you've forgotten. Who the devil turned the thing on and set it going?'

Wargrave murmured:

'Yes, I think we must inquire into that.'

He led the way back into the drawing-room. The others followed.

Rogers had just come in with a glass of brandy. Miss Brent was bending over the moaning form of Mrs Rogers.

Adroitly Rogers slipped between the two women.

'Allow me, Madam, I'll speak to her. Ethel – Ethel – it's all right. All right, do you hear? Pull yourself together.'

Mrs Rogers' breath came in quick gasps. Her eyes, staring frightened eyes, went round and round the ring of faces. There was urgency in Rogers' tone.

'Pull yourself together, Ethel.'

Dr Armstrong spoke to her soothingly:

'You'll be all right now, Mrs Rogers. Just a nasty turn.' She said:

'Did I faint, sir?'

'Yes.'

'It was the voice – that awful voice – *like a judgment* –'

Her face turned green again, her eyelids fluttered.

Dr Armstrong said sharply:

'Where's that brandy?'

Rogers had put it down on a little table. Someone handed it to the doctor and he bent over the gasping woman with it.

'Drink this, Mrs Rogers.'

She drank, choking a little and gasping. The spirit did her good. The colour returned to her face. She said:

'I'm all right now. It just – gave me a turn.'

Rogers said quickly:

'Of course it did. It gave me a turn, too. Fair made me drop that tray. Wicked lies, it was! I'd like to know –'

He was interrupted. It was only a cough – a dry little cough but it had the effect of stopping him in full cry. He stared at Mr Justice Wargrave and the latter coughed again. Then he said:

'Who put on that record on the gramophone. Was it you, Rogers?'

Rogers cried:

'I didn't know what it was. Before God, I didn't know what it was, sir. If I had I'd never have done it.'

The judge said dryly:

'That is probably true. But I think you'd better explain, Rogers.'

The butler wiped his face with a handkerchief. He said earnestly:

'I was just obeying orders, sir, that's all.'

'Whose orders?'

'Mr Owen's.'

Mr Justice Wargrave said:

'Let me get this quite clear. Mr Owen's orders were – what exactly?'

Rogers said:

'I was to put a record on the gramophone. I'd find the record in the drawer and my wife was to start the gramophone when I'd gone into the drawing-room with the coffee tray.'

The judge murmured:

'A very remarkable story.'

Rogers cried:

'It's the truth, sir. I swear to God it's the truth. I didn't know what it was – not for a moment. It had a name on it – I thought it was just a piece of music.'

Wargrave looked at Lombard.

'Was there a title on it?'

Lombard nodded. He grinned suddenly, showed his white pointed teeth. He said:

'Quite right, sir. It was entitled *Swan Song* . . .'

III

General Macarthur broke out suddenly. He exclaimed:

'The whole thing is preposterous – preposterous! Slinging accusations about like this! Something must be done about it. This fellow Owen whoever he is –'

Emily Brent interrupted. She said sharply:

'That's just it, who is he?'

The judge interposed. He spoke with the authority that a lifetime in the courts had given him. He said:

'That is exactly what we must go into very carefully. I should suggest that you get your wife to bed first of all, Rogers. Then come back here.'

'Yes, sir.'

Dr Armstrong said:

'I'll give you a hand, Rogers.'

Leaning on the two men, Mrs Rogers tottered out of the room. When they had gone Tony Marston said:

'Don't know about you, sir, but I could do with a drink.'

Lombard said:

'I agree.'

Tony said:

'I'll go and forage.'

He went out of the room.

He returned a second or two later.

'Found them all waiting on a tray outside ready to be brought in.'

He set down his burden carefully. The next minute or two was spent in dispensing drinks. General Macarthur had a stiff whisky and so did the judge. Every one felt the need of a stimulant. Only Emily Brent demanded and obtained a glass of water.

Dr Armstrong re-entered the room.

'She's all right,' he said. 'I've given her a sedative to take. What's that, a drink? I could do with one.'

Several of the men refilled their glasses. A moment or two later Rogers re-entered the room.

Mr Justice Wargrave took charge of the proceedings. The room became an impromptu court of law.

The judge said:

'Now then, Rogers, we must get to the bottom of this. Who is this Mr Owen?'

Rogers stared.

'He owns this place, sir.'

'I am aware of that fact. What I want you to tell me is what you yourself know about the man.'

Rogers shook his head.

'I can't say, sir. You see, I've never seen him.'

There was a faint stir in the room.

General Macarthur said:

'You've never seen him? What d'yer mean?'

'We've only been here just under a week, sir, my wife and I. We were engaged by letter, through an agency. The Regina Agency in Plymouth.'

Blore nodded.

'Old established firm,' he volunteered.

Wargrave said:

'Have you got that letter?'

'The letter engaging us? No, sir. I didn't keep it.'

'Go on with your story. You were engaged, as you say, by letter.'

'Yes, sir. We were to arrive on a certain day. We did. Everything was in order here. Plenty of food in stock and everything very nice. Just needed dusting and that.'

'What next?'

'Nothing, sir. We got orders – by letter again – to prepare the rooms for a house-party, and then yesterday by the afternoon post I got another letter from Mr Owen. It said he and Mrs Owen were detained and to do the best we could, and it gave the instructions about dinner and coffee and putting on the gramophone record.'

The judge said sharply:

'Surely you've got that letter?'

'Yes, sir, I've got it here.'

He produced it from a pocket. The judge took it.

'H'm,' he said. 'Headed Ritz Hotel and typewritten.'

With a quick movement Blore was beside him.

He said:

'If you'll just let me have a look.'

He twitched it out of the other's hand, and ran his eye over it. He murmured:

'Coronation machine. Quite new – no defects. Ensign paper – the most widely used make. You won't get anything out of that. Might be fingerprints, but I doubt it.'

Wargrave stared at him with sudden attention.

Anthony Marston was standing beside Blore looking over his shoulder. He said:

'Got some fancy Christian names, hasn't he? Ulick Norman Owen. Quite a mouthful.'

The old judge said with a slight start:

'I am obliged to you, Mr Marston. You have drawn my attention to a curious and suggestive point.'

He looked round at the others and thrusting his neck forward like an angry tortoise, he said:

'I think the time has come for us all to pool our information. It would be well, I think, for everybody to come forward with all the information they have regarding the owner of this house.' He paused and then went on: 'We are all his guests. I think it would be profitable if each one of us were to explain exactly how that came about.'

There was a moment's pause and then Emily Brent spoke with decision.

'There's something very peculiar about all this,' she said. 'I received a letter with a signature that was not very easy to read. It purported to be from a woman I had met at a certain summer resort two or three years ago. I took the name to be either Ogden or Oliver. I am acquainted with a Mrs Oliver and also with a Miss Ogden. I am quite certain that I have never met, or become friendly with any one of the name of Owen.'

Mr Justice Wargrave said:

'You have that letter, Miss Brent?'

'Yes, I will fetch it for you.'

She went away and returned a minute later with the letter. The judge read it. He said:

'I begin to understand . . . Miss Claythorne?'

Vera explained the circumstances of her secretarial engagement. The judge said:

'Marston?'

Anthony said:

'Got a wire. From a pal of mine. Badger Berkeley. Surprised me at the time because I had an idea the old horse had gone to Norway. Told me to roll up here.'

Again Wargrave nodded. He said:

'Dr Armstrong?'

'I was called in professionally.'

'I see. You had no previous acquaintanceship with the family?'

'No. A colleague of mine was mentioned in the letter.'

The judge said:

'To give verisimilitude . . . Yes, and that colleague, I presume, was momentarily out of touch with you?'

'Well – er – yes.'

Lombard, who had been staring at Blore, said suddenly:

'Look here, I've just thought of something –'

The judge lifted a hand.

'In a minute –'

'But I –'

'We will take one thing at a time, Mr Lombard. We are at present inquiring into the causes which have resulted in our being assembled here tonight. General Macarthur?'

Pulling at his moustache, the General muttered:

'Got a letter – from this fellow Owen – mentioned some old pals of mine who were to be here – hoped I'd excuse informal invitation. Haven't kept the letter, I'm afraid.'

Wargrave said: 'Mr Lombard?'

Lombard's brain had been active. Was he to come out in the open, or not? He made up his mind.

'Same sort of thing,' he said. 'Invitation, mention of mutual friends – I fell for it all right. I've torn up the letter.'

Mr Justice Wargrave turned his attention to Mr Blore. His forefinger stroked his upper lip and his voice was dangerously polite.

He said:

'Just now we had a somewhat disturbing experience. An apparently disembodied voice spoke to us all by name, uttering certain precise accusations against us. We will deal with those accusations presently. At the moment I am interested in a minor point. Amongst the names recited was that of William Henry Blore. But as far as we know there is no one named Blore amongst us. The name of Davis was *not* mentioned. What have you to say about that, Mr Davis?'

Blore said sulkily:

'Cat's out of the bag, it seems. I suppose I'd better admit that my name isn't Davis.'

'You are William Henry Blore?'

'That's right.'

'I will add something,' said Lombard. 'Not only are you here under a false name, Mr Blore, but in addition I've noticed this evening that you're a first-class liar. You claim to have come from Natal, South Africa. I know South Africa and Natal and I'm prepared to swear that you've never set foot in South Africa in your life.'

All eyes were turned on Blore. Angry suspicious eyes. Anthony Marston moved a step nearer to him. His fists clenched themselves.

'Now then, you swine,' he said. 'Any explanation?'

Blore flung back his head and set his square jaw.

'You gentlemen have got me wrong,' he said. 'I've got my credentials and you can see them. I'm an ex-CID man. I run a detective agency in Plymouth. I was put on this job.'

Mr Justice Wargrave asked:

'By whom?'

'This man Owen. Enclosed a handsome money order for expenses and instructed me as to what he wanted done. I was to join the house-party, posing as a guest. I was given all your names. I was to watch you all.'

'Any reason given?'

Blore said bitterly:

'Mrs Owen's jewels. Mrs Owen my foot! I don't believe there's any such person.'

Again the forefinger of the judge stroked his lip, this time appreciatively.

'Your conclusions are, I think, justified,' he said. 'Ulick Norman Owen! In Miss Brent's letter, though the signature of the surname is a mere scrawl the Christian names are reasonably clear – Una Nancy – in either case you notice, the same initials. Ulick Norman Owen – Una Nancy Owen – each time, that is to say, U. N. Owen. Or by a slight stretch of fancy, UNKNOWN!'

Vera cried:

'But this is fantastic – mad!'

The judge nodded gently.

He said:

'Oh, yes. I've no doubt in my own mind that we have been invited here by a madman – probably a dangerous homicidal lunatic.'

CHAPTER 4

I

There was a moment's silence. A silence of dismay and bewilderment. Then the judge's small clear voice took up the thread once more.

'We will now proceed to the next stage of our inquiry. First however, I will just add my own credentials to the list.'

He took a letter from his pocket and tossed it on to the table.

'This purports to be from an old friend of mine, Lady Constance Culmington. I have not seen her for some years. She went to the East. It is exactly the kind of vague incoherent letter she would write, urging me to join her here and referring to her host and hostess in the vaguest of terms. The same technique, you will observe. I only mention it because it agrees with the other evidence – from all of which emerges one interesting point. *Whoever it was who enticed us here, that person knows or has taken the trouble to find out a good deal about us all.* He, whoever he may be, is aware of my friendship for Lady Constance – and is familiar with her epistolary style. He knows something about Dr Armstrong's colleagues and their present whereabouts. He knows the nickname of Mr Marston's friend and the kind of telegrams he sends. He knows exactly where Miss Brent was two years ago for her holiday and the kind of people she met there. He knows all about General Macarthur's old cronies.'

He paused. Then he said:

'*He knows, you see, a good deal.* And out of his knowledge concerning us, he has made certain definite accusations.'

Immediately a babel broke out.

General Macarthur shouted:

'A pack of dam' lies! Slander!'

Vera cried out:

'It's iniquitous!' Her breath came fast. 'Wicked!'

Rogers said hoarsely:

'A lie – a wicked lie . . . we never did – neither of us . . .'

Anthony Marston growled:

'Don't know what the damned fool was getting at!'

The upraised hand of Mr Justice Wargrave calmed the tumult. He said, picking his words with care:

'I wish to say this. Our unknown friend accuses me of the murder of one Edward Seton. I remember Seton perfectly well. He came up before me for trial in June of the year 1930. He was charged with the murder of an elderly woman. He was very ably defended and made a good impression on the jury in the witness-box. Nevertheless, on the evidence, he was certainly guilty. I summed up accordingly, and the jury brought in a verdict of Guilty. In passing sentence of death I concurred with the verdict. An appeal was lodged on the grounds of misdirection. The appeal was rejected and the man was duly executed. I wish to say before you all that my conscience is perfectly clear on the matter. I did my duty and nothing more. I passed sentence on a rightly convicted murderer.'

Armstrong was remembering now. The Seton case! The verdict had come as a great surprise. He had met Matthews, KC on one of the days of the trial dining at a restaurant. Matthews had been confident. 'Not a doubt of the verdict. Acquittal practically certain.' And then afterwards he had heard comments: 'Judge was dead against him. Turned the jury right round and they brought him in guilty. Quite legal, though. Old Wargrave knows his law. It was almost as though he had a private down on the fellow.'

All these memories rushed through the doctor's mind. Before he could consider the wisdom of the question he had asked impulsively:

'Did you know Seton at all? I mean previous to the case.'

The hooded reptilian eyes met his. In a clear cold voice the judge said:

'I knew nothing of Seton previous to the case.'

Armstrong said to himself:

'The fellow's lying – I know he's lying.'

II

Vera Claythorne spoke in a trembling voice.

She said:

'I'd like to tell you. About that child – Cyril Hamilton. I was nursery governess to him. He was forbidden to swim out far. One day, when my attention was distracted, he started off. I swam after him . . . I couldn't get there in time . . . It was awful . . . But it wasn't my fault. At the inquest the Coroner exonerated me. And his mother – she was so kind. If even she didn't blame me, why should – why should this awful thing be said? It's not fair – not fair . . .'

She broke down, weeping bitterly.

General Macarthur patted her shoulder.

He said:

'There there, my dear. Of course it's not true. Fellow's a madman. A madman! Got a bee in his bonnet! Got hold of the wrong end of the stick all round.'

He stood erect, squaring his shoulders. He barked out:

'Best really to leave this sort of thing unanswered. However, feel I ought to say – no truth – no truth whatever in what he said about – er – young Arthur Richmond. Richmond was one of my officers. I sent him on a reconnaissance. He was killed. Natural course of events in wartime. Wish to say resent very much – slur on my wife. Best woman in the world. Absolutely – Cæsar's wife!'

General Macarthur sat down. His shaking hand pulled at his moustache. The effort to speak had cost him a good deal.

Lombard spoke. His eyes were amused. He said:

'About those natives –'

Marston said:

'What about them?'

Philip Lombard grinned.

'Story's quite true! I left 'em! Matter of self-preservation. We were lost in the bush. I and a couple of other fellows took what food there was and cleared out.'

General Macarthur said sternly:

'You abandoned your men – left them to starve?'

Lombard said:

'Not quite the act of a *pukka sahib*, I'm afraid. But self-preservation's a man's first duty. And natives don't mind dying, you know. They don't feel about it as Europeans do.'

Vera lifted her face from her hands. She said, staring at him:

'You left them – to *die*?'

Lombard answered:

'I left them to die.'

His amused eyes looked into her horrified ones.

Anthony Marston said in a slow puzzled voice:

'I've just been thinking – John and Lucy Combes. Must have been a couple of kids I ran over near Cambridge. Beastly bad luck.'

Mr Justice Wargrave said acidly:

'For them, or for you?'

Anthony said:

'Well, I was thinking – for me – but of course, you're right, sir, it was damned bad luck on them. Of course it was a pure accident. They rushed out of some cottage or other. I had my licence suspended for a year. Beastly nuisance.'

Dr Armstrong said warmly:

'This speeding's all wrong – all wrong! Young men like you are a danger to the community.'

Anthony shrugged his shoulders. He said:

'Speed's come to stay. English roads are hopeless, of course. Can't get up a decent pace on them.'

He looked round vaguely for his glass, picked it up off a table and went over to the side table and helped himself to another whisky and soda. He said over his shoulder:

'Well, anyway it wasn't my fault. Just an accident!'

III

The manservant, Rogers, had been moistening his lips and twisting his hands. He said now in a low deferential voice:

'If I might just say a word, sir.'

Lombard said:

'Go ahead, Rogers.'

Rogers cleared his throat and passed his tongue once more over his dry lips.

'There was a mention, sir, of me and Mrs Rogers. And of Miss Brady. There isn't a word of truth in it, sir. My wife and I were with Miss Brady till she died. She was always in poor health, sir, always from the time we came to her. There was a storm, sir, that night – the night she was taken bad. The telephone was out of order. We couldn't get the doctor to her. I went for him, sir, on foot. But he got there too late. We'd done everything possible for her, sir. Devoted to her, we were. Anyone will tell you the same. There was never a word said against us. Not a word.'

Lombard looked thoughtfully at the man's twitching face, his dry lips, the fright in his eyes. He remembered the crash of the falling coffee tray. He thought, but did not say: 'Oh yeah?'

Blore spoke – spoke in his hearty bullying official manner. He said:

'Came into a little something at her death, though? Eh?'

Rogers drew himself up. He said stiffly:

'Miss Brady left us a legacy in recognition of our faithful services. And why not, I'd like to know?'

Lombard said:

'What about yourself, Mr Blore?'

'What about me?'

'Your name was included in the list.'

Blore went purple.

'Landor, you mean? That was the bank robbery – London and Commercial.'

Mr Justice Wargrave stirred. He said:

'I remember. It didn't come before me, but I remember the case. Landor was convicted on your evidence. You were the police officer in charge of the case?'

Blore said:

'I was.'

'Landor got penal servitude for life and died on Dartmoor a year later. He was a delicate man.'

Blore said:

'He was a crook. It was he who knocked out the night watch-man. The case was quite clear against him.'

Wargrave said slowly:

'You were complimented, I think, on your able handling of the case.'

Blore said sulkily:

'I got my promotion.'

He added in a thick voice.

'I was only doing my duty.'

Lombard laughed – a sudden ringing laugh. He said:

'What a duty-loving law-abiding lot we all seem to be! Myself excepted. What about you, doctor – and your little professional mistake? Illegal operation, was it?'

Emily Brent glanced at him in sharp distaste and drew herself away a little.

Dr Armstrong, very much master of himself, shook his head good-humouredly.

'I'm at a loss to understand the matter,' he said. 'The name meant nothing to me when it was spoken. What was it – Clees? Close? I really can't remember having a patient of that name, or being connected with a death in any way. The thing's a complete mystery to me. Of course, it's a long time ago. It might possibly be one of my operation cases in hospital. They come too late, so many of these people. Then, when the patient dies, they always consider it's the surgeon's fault.'

He sighed, shaking his head.

He thought:

Drunk – that's what it was – drunk . . . And I operated! Nerves all to pieces – hands shaking. I killed her all right. Poor devil – elderly woman – simple job if I'd been sober. Lucky for me there's loyalty in our profession. The Sister knew, of course – but she held her tongue.

God, it gave me a shock! Pulled me up. But who could have known about it – after all these years?

IV

There was a silence in the room. Everybody was looking, covertly or openly, at Emily Brent. It was a minute or two before she became aware of the expectation. Her eyebrows rose on her narrow forehead. She said:

'Are you waiting for me to say something? I have nothing to say.'

The judge said: 'Nothing, Miss Brent?'

'Nothing.'

Her lips closed tightly.

The judge stroked his face. He said mildly:

'You reserve your defence?'

Miss Brent said coldly:

'There is no question of defence. I have always acted in accordance with the dictates of my conscience. I have nothing with which to reproach myself.'

There was an unsatisfied feeling in the air. But Emily Brent was not one to be swayed by public opinion. She sat unyielding.

The judge cleared his throat once or twice. Then he said: 'Our inquiry rests there. Now Rogers, who else is there on this island besides ourselves and you and your wife?'

'Nobody, sir. Nobody at all.'

'You're sure of that?'

'Quite sure, sir.'

Wargrave said:

'I am not yet clear as to the purpose of our Unknown host in getting us to assemble here. But in my opinion this person, whoever he may be, is not sane in the accepted sense of the word.

'He may be dangerous. In my opinion it would be well for us to leave this place as soon as possible. I suggest that we leave tonight.'

Rogers said:

'I beg your pardon, sir, but there's no boat on the island.'

'No boat at all?'

'No, sir.'

'How do you communicate with the mainland?'

'Fred Narracott, he comes over every morning, sir. He brings the bread and the milk and the post, and takes the orders.'

Mr Justice Wargrave said:

'Then in my opinion it would be well if we all left tomorrow morning as soon as Narracott's boat arrives.'

There was a chorus of agreement with only one dissentient voice. It was Anthony Marston who disagreed with the majority.

'A bit unsporting, what?' he said. 'Ought to ferret out the mystery before we go. Whole thing's like a detective story. Positively thrilling.'

The judge said acidly:

'At my time of life, I have no desire for "thrills" as you call them.'

Anthony said with a grin:

'The legal life's narrowing! I'm all for crime! Here's to it.'

He picked up his drink and drank it off at a gulp.

Too quickly, perhaps. He choked – choked badly. His face contorted, turned purple. He gasped for breath – then slid down off his chair, the glass falling from his hand.

CHAPTER 5

I

It was so sudden and so unexpected that it took every one's breath away. They remained stupidly staring at the crumpled figure on the ground.

Then Dr Armstrong jumped up and went over to him, kneeling beside him. When he raised his head his eyes were bewildered.

He said in a low awe-struck whisper:

'My God! he's dead.'

They didn't take it in. Not at once.

Dead? *Dead*? That young Norse God in the prime of his health and strength. Struck down all in a moment. Healthy young men didn't die like that, choking over a whisky and soda . . .

No, they couldn't take it in.

Dr Armstrong was peering into the dead man's face. He sniffed at the blue twisted lips. Then he picked up the glass from which Anthony Marston had been drinking.

General Macarthur said:

'Dead? D'you mean the fellow just choked and – and died?'

The physician said:

'You can call it choking if you like. He died of asphyxiation right enough.'

He was sniffing now at the glass. He dipped a finger into the dregs and very cautiously just touched the finger with the tip of his tongue.

His expression altered.

General Macarthur said:

'Never knew a man could die like that – just of a choking fit!'

Emily Brent said in a clear voice:

'In the midst of life we are in death.'

Dr Armstrong stood up. He said brusquely:

'No, a man doesn't die of a mere choking fit. Marston's death wasn't what we call a natural death.'

Vera said almost in a whisper:

'Was there – something – in the whisky?'

Armstrong nodded.

'Yes. Can't say exactly. Everything points to one of the cyanides. No distinctive smell of Prussic Acid, probably Potassium Cyanide. It acts pretty well instantaneously.'

The judge said sharply:

'It was in his glass?'

'Yes.'

The doctor strode to the table where the drinks were. He removed the stopper from the whisky and smelt and tasted it. Then he tasted the soda water. He shook his head.

'They're both all right.'

Lombard said:

'You mean – he must have put the stuff in his glass *himself*?'

Armstrong nodded with a curiously dissatisfied expression. He said:

'Seems like it.'

Blore said:

'Suicide, eh? That's a queer go.'

Vera said slowly:

'You'd never think that *he* would kill himself. He was so alive. He was – oh – enjoying himself! When he came down the hill in his car this evening he looked – he looked – oh I can't *explain*!'

But they knew what she meant. Anthony Marston, in the height of his youth and manhood, had seemed like a being who was immortal. And now, crumpled and broken, he lay on the floor.

Dr Armstrong said:

'Is there any possibility other than suicide?'

Slowly every one shook their heads. There could be no other explanation. The drinks themselves were untampered with. They had all seen Anthony Marston go across and help himself. It followed therefore that any cyanide in the drink must have been put there by Anthony Marston himself.

And yet – why should Anthony Marston commit suicide?

Blore said thoughtfully:

'You know, doctor, it doesn't seem right to me. I shouldn't have said Mr Marston was a suicidal type of gentleman.'

Armstrong answered:

'I agree.'

II

They had left it like that. What else was there to say?

Together Armstrong and Lombard had carried the inert body of Anthony Marston to his bedroom and had laid him there covered over with a sheet.

When they came downstairs again, the others were standing in a group, shivering a little, though the night was not cold.

Emily Brent said:

'We'd better go to bed. It's late.'

It was past twelve o'clock. The suggestion was a wise one – yet every one hesitated. It was as though they clung to each other's company for reassurance.

The judge said:

'Yes, we must get some sleep.'

Rogers said:

'I haven't cleared yet – in the dining-room.'

Lombard said curtly:

'Do it in the morning.'

Armstrong said to him:

'Is your wife all right?'

'I'll go and see, sir.'

He returned a minute or two later.

'Sleeping beautiful, she is.'

'Good,' said the doctor. 'Don't disturb her.'

'No, sir. I'll just put things straight in the dining-room and make sure everything's locked up right, and then I'll turn in.'

He went across the hall into the dining-room.

The others went upstairs, a slow unwilling procession.

If this had been an old house, with creaking wood, and dark shadows, and heavily panelled walls, there might have been an eerie feeling. But this house was the essence of modernity. There were no dark corners – no possible sliding panels – it was flooded with electric light – everything was new and bright and shining. There was nothing hidden in this house, nothing concealed. It had no atmosphere about it.

Somehow, that was the most frightening thing of all . . .

They exchanged good-nights on the upper landing. Each of them went into his or her own room, and each of them automatically, almost without conscious thought, locked the door . . .

III

In his pleasant softly tinted room, Mr Justice Wargrave removed his garments and prepared himself for bed.

He was thinking about Edward Seton.

He remembered Seton very well. His fair hair, his blue eyes, his habit of looking you straight in the face with a pleasant air of straightforwardness. That was what had made so good an impression on the jury.

Llewellyn, for the Crown, had bungled it a bit. He had been over-vehement, had tried to prove too much.

Matthews, on the other hand, for the Defence, had been good. His points had told. His cross-examinations had been deadly. His handling of his client in the witness-box had been masterly.

And Seton had come through the ordeal of cross-examination well. He had not got excited or over-vehement. The jury had been impressed. It had seemed to Matthews, perhaps, as though everything had been over bar the shouting.

The judge wound up his watch carefully and placed it by the bed.

He remembered exactly how he had felt sitting there – listening, making notes, appreciating everything, tabulating every scrap of evidence that told against the prisoner.

He'd enjoyed that case! Matthews' final speech had been first-class. Llewellyn, coming after it, had failed to remove the good impression that the defending counsel had made.

And then had come his own summing up . . .

Carefully, Mr Justice Wargrave removed his false teeth and dropped them into a glass of water. The shrunken lips fell in. It was a cruel mouth now, cruel and predatory.

Hooding his eyes, the judge smiled to himself.

He'd cooked Seton's goose all right!

With a slightly rheumatic grunt, he climbed into bed and turned out the electric light.

IV

Downstairs in the dining-room, Rogers stood puzzled.

He was staring at the china figures in the centre of the table.

He muttered to himself:

'That's a rum go! I could have sworn there were ten of them.'

V

General Macarthur tossed from side to side.

Sleep would not come to him.

In the darkness he kept seeing Arthur Richmond's face.

He'd liked Arthur – he'd been damned fond of Arthur. He'd been pleased that Leslie liked him too.

Leslie was so capricious. Lots of good fellows that Leslie would turn up her nose at and pronounce dull. 'Dull!' Just like that.

But she hadn't found Arthur Richmond dull. They'd got on well together from the beginning. They'd talked of plays and music and pictures together. She'd teased him, made fun of him, ragged him. And he, Macarthur, had been delighted at the thought that Leslie took quite a motherly interest in the boy.

Motherly indeed! Damn' fool not to remember that Richmond was twenty-eight to Leslie's twenty-nine.

He'd loved Leslie. He could see her now. Her heart-shaped face, and her dancing deep grey eyes, and the brown curling mass of her hair. He'd loved Leslie and he'd believed in her absolutely.

Out there in France, in the middle of all the hell of it, he'd sat thinking of her, taken her picture out of the breast pocket of his tunic.

And then – he'd found out!

It had come about exactly in the way things happened in books. The letter in the wrong envelope. She'd been writing to them both and she'd put her letter to Richmond in the envelope addressed to her husband. Even now, all these years after, he could feel the shock of it – the pain . . .

God, it had hurt!

And the business had been going on some time. The letter made that clear. Weekends! Richmond's last leave . . .

Leslie – Leslie and Arthur!

God damn the fellow! Damn his smiling face, his brisk 'Yes, sir.' Liar and hypocrite! Stealer of another man's wife!

It had gathered slowly – that cold murderous rage.

He'd managed to carry on as usual – to show nothing. He'd tried to make his manner to Richmond just the same.

Had he succeeded? He thought so. Richmond hadn't suspected. Inequalities of temper were easily accounted for out there, where men's nerves were continually snapping under the strain.

Only young Armitage had looked at him curiously once or twice. Quite a young chap, but he'd had perceptions, that boy.

Armitage, perhaps, had guessed – when the time came.

He'd sent Richmond deliberately to death. Only a miracle could have brought him through unhurt. That miracle didn't happen. Yes, he'd sent Richmond to his death and he wasn't sorry. It had been easy enough. Mistakes were being made all the time, officers being sent to death needlessly. All was confusion, panic. People might say afterwards 'Old Macarthur lost his nerve a bit, made some colossal blunders, sacrificed some of his best men.' They couldn't say more.

But young Armitage was different. He'd looked at his commanding officer very oddly. He'd known, perhaps, that Richmond was being deliberately sent to death.

(After the War was over – had Armitage talked?)

Leslie hadn't known. Leslie had wept for her lover (he supposed) but her weeping was over by the time he'd come back to

England. He'd never told her that he'd found her out. They'd gone on together – only, somehow, she hadn't seemed very real any more. And then, three or four years later she'd got double pneumonia and died.

That had been a long time ago. Fifteen years – sixteen years?

And he'd left the Army and come to live in Devon – bought the sort of little place he'd always meant to have. Nice neighbours – pleasant part of the world. There was a bit of shooting and fishing. He'd gone to church on Sundays. (But not the day that the lesson was read about David putting Uriah in the forefront of the battle. Somehow he couldn't face that. Gave him an uncomfortable feeling.)

Everybody had been very friendly. At first, that is. Later, he'd had an uneasy feeling that people were talking about him behind his back. They eyed him differently, somehow. As though they'd heard something – some lying rumour . . .

(Armitage? Supposing Armitage had talked.)

He'd avoided people after that – withdrawn into himself. Unpleasant to feel that people were discussing you.

And all so long ago. So – so purposeless now. Leslie had faded into the distance and Arthur Richmond too. Nothing of what had happened seemed to matter any more.

It made life lonely, though. He'd taken to shunning his old Army friends.

(If Armitage had talked, they'd know about it.)

And now – this evening – a hidden voice had blared out that old hidden story.

Had he dealt with it all right? Kept a stiff upper lip? Betrayed the right amount of feeling – indignation, disgust – but no guilt, no discomfiture? Difficult to tell.

Surely nobody could have taken the accusation seriously. There had been a pack of other nonsense, just as far-fetched. That charming girl – the voice had accused her of drowning a child! Idiotic! Some madman throwing crazy accusations about!

Emily Brent, too – actually a niece of old Tom Brent of the Regiment. It had accused *her* of murder! Any one could see with half an eye that the woman was as pious as could be – the kind that was hand and glove with parsons.

Damned curious business the whole thing! Crazy, nothing less.

Ever since they had got here – when was that? Why, damn it, it was only this afternoon! Seemed a good bit longer than that.

He thought: 'I wonder when we shall get away again.'

Tomorrow, of course, when the motor-boat came from the mainland.

Funny, just this minute he didn't want much to get away from the island . . . To go back to the mainland, back to his little house, back to all the troubles and worries. Through the open window he could hear the waves breaking on the rocks – a little louder now than earlier in the evening. Wind was getting up, too.

He thought: Peaceful sound. Peaceful place . . .

He thought: Best of an island is once you get there – you can't go any farther . . . you've come to the end of things . . .

He knew, suddenly, that he didn't want to leave the island.

VI

Vera Claythorne lay in bed, wide awake, staring up at the ceiling.

The light beside her was on. She was frightened of the dark. She was thinking:

'Hugo . . . Hugo . . . Why do I feel you're so near to me tonight? . . . Somewhere quite close . . .

'Where is he really? I don't know. I never shall know. He just went away – right away – out of my life.'

It was no good trying not to think of Hugo. He was close to her. She *had* to think of him – to remember . . .

Cornwall . . .

The black rocks, the smooth yellow sand. Mrs Hamilton, stout, good-humoured. Cyril, whining a little always, pulling at her hand.

'I want to swim out to the rock, Miss Claythorne. Why can't I swim out to the rock?'

Looking up – meeting Hugo's eyes watching her.

The evenings after Cyril was in bed . . .

'Come out for a stroll, Miss Claythorne.'

'I think perhaps I will.'

The decorous stroll down to the beach. The moonlight – the soft Atlantic air.

And then, Hugo's arms round her.

'*I love you. I love you. You know I love you, Vera?*'

Yes, she knew.

(Or thought she knew.)

'*I can't ask you to marry me. I've not got a penny. It's all I can do to keep myself. Queer, you know, once, for three months I had the chance of being a rich man to look forward to. Cyril wasn't born until three months after Maurice died. If he'd been a girl . . .*'

If the child had been a girl, Hugo would have come into everything. He'd been disappointed, he admitted.

'*I hadn't built on it, of course. But it was a bit of a knock. Oh well, luck's luck! Cyril's a nice kid. I'm awfully fond of him.*' And he was fond of him, too. Always ready to play games or amuse his small nephew. No rancour in Hugo's nature.

Cyril wasn't really strong. A puny child – no stamina. The kind of child, perhaps, who wouldn't live to grow up . . .

And then –?

'*Miss Claythorne, why can't I swim to the rock?*'

Irritating whiney repetition.

'*It's too far, Cyril.*'

'*But, Miss Claythorne . . .*'

Vera got up. She went to the dressing-table and swallowed three aspirins.

She thought:

'I wish I had some proper sleeping stuff.'

She thought:

'If *I* were doing away with myself I'd take an overdose of veronal – something like that – not cyanide!'

She shuddered as she remembered Anthony Marston's convulsed purple face.

As she passed the mantelpiece, she looked up at the framed doggerel.

'*Ten little soldier boys went out to dine;*
One choked his little self and then there were Nine.'

She thought to herself:

'It's horrible – *just like us this evening . . .*'

Why had Anthony Marston wanted to die?

She didn't want to die.

She couldn't imagine wanting to die . . .

Death was for – the other people . . .

CHAPTER 6

I

Dr Armstrong was dreaming . . .

It was very hot in the operating-room . . .

Surely they'd got the temperature too high? The sweat was rolling down his face. His hands were clammy. Difficult to hold the scalpel firmly . . .

How beautifully sharp it was . . .

Easy to do a murder with a knife like that. And of course he *was* doing a murder . . .

The woman's body looked different. It had been a large unwieldy body. This was a spare meagre body. And the face was hidden.

Who was it that he had to kill?

He couldn't remember. But he *must* know! Should he ask Sister?

Sister was watching him. No, he couldn't ask her. She was suspicious, he could see that.

But who was it on the operating-table?

They shouldn't have covered up the face like that . . .

If he could only see the face . . .

Ah! that was better. A young probationer was pulling off the handkerchief.

Emily Brent, of course. It was Emily Brent that he had to kill. How malicious her eyes were! Her lips were moving. What was she saying?

'*In the midst of life we are in death . . .*'

She was laughing now. No, nurse, don't put the handkerchief back. I've got to see. I've got to give the anaesthetic. Where's the ether? I must have brought the ether with me. What have you done with the ether, Sister? Châteauneuf-du-Pape? Yes, that will do quite as well.

Take the handkerchief away, nurse.

Of course! I knew it all the time! *It's Anthony Marston*! His face is purple and convulsed. But he's not dead – he's laughing. I tell you he's laughing! He's shaking the operating-table.

Look out, man, look out. Nurse, steady it – steady it –

With a start Dr Armstrong woke up. It was morning. Sunlight was pouring into the room.

And someone was leaning over him – shaking him. It was Rogers. Rogers, with a white face, saying: 'Doctor – doctor!'

Dr Armstrong woke up completely.

He sat up in bed. He said sharply:

'What is it?'

'It's the wife, doctor. *I can't get her to wake.* My God! I can't get her to wake. And – and she don't look right to me.'

Dr Armstrong was quick and efficient. He wrapped himself in his dressing-gown and followed Rogers.

He bent over the bed where the woman was lying peacefully on her side. He lifted the cold hand, raised the eyelid. It was some few minutes before he straightened himself and turned from the bed.

Rogers whispered:

'Is – she – is she –?'

He passed a tongue over dry lips.

Armstrong nodded.

'Yes, she's gone.'

His eyes rested thoughtfully on the man before him. Then they went to the table by the bed, to the washstand, then back to the sleeping woman.

Rogers said:

'Was it – was it – 'er 'eart, doctor?'

Dr Armstrong was a minute or two before replying. Then he said:

'What was her health like normally?'

Rogers said:

'She was a bit rheumaticky.'

'Any doctor been attending her recently?'

'Doctor?' Rogers stared. 'Not been to a doctor for years – neither of us.'

'You'd no reason to believe she suffered from heart trouble?'

'No, doctor. I never knew of anything.'

Armstrong said:

'Did she sleep well?'

Now Rogers' eyes evaded his. The man's hands came together and turned and twisted uneasily. He muttered:

'She didn't sleep extra well – no.'

The doctor said sharply:

'Did she take things to make her sleep?'

Rogers stared at him, surprised.

'Take things? To make her sleep? Not that I knew of. I'm sure she didn't.'

Armstrong went over to the washstand.

There were a certain number of bottles on it. Hair lotion, lavender water, cascara, glycerine of cucumber for the hands, a mouthwash, toothpaste and some Elliman's.

Rogers helped by pulling out the drawers of the dressing-table. From there they moved on to the chest of drawers. But there was no sign of sleeping draughts or tablets.

Rogers said:

'She didn't have nothing last night, sir, except what you gave her . . .'

II

When the gong sounded for breakfast at nine o'clock it found everyone up and awaiting the summons.

General Macarthur and the judge had been pacing the terrace outside, exchanging desultory comments on the political situation.

Vera Claythorne and Philip Lombard had been up to the summit of the island behind the house. There they had discovered William Henry Blore, standing staring at the mainland.

He said:

'No sign of that motor-boat yet. I've been watching for it.'

Vera said smiling:

'Devon's a sleepy county. Things are usually late.'

Philip Lombard was looking the other way, out to sea.

He said abruptly:

'What d'you think of the weather?'

Glancing up at the sky, Blore remarked:

'Looks all right to me.'

Lombard pursed up his mouth into a whistle.

He said:

'It will come on to blow before the day's out.'

Blore said:

'Squally – eh?'

From below them came the boom of a gong.

Philip Lombard said:

'Breakfast? Well, I could do with some.'

As they went down the steep slope Blore said to Lombard in a ruminating voice:

'You know, it beats me – why that young fellow wanted to do himself in! I've been worrying about it all night.'

Vera was a little ahead. Lombard hung back slightly. He said:

'Got any alternative theory?'

'I'd want some proof. Motive, to begin with. Well-off I should say he was.'

Emily Brent came out of the drawing-room window to meet them.

She said sharply:

'Is the boat coming?'

'Not yet,' said Vera.

They went into breakfast. There was a vast dish of eggs and bacon on the sideboard and tea and coffee.

Rogers held the door open for them to pass in, then shut it from the outside.

Emily Brent said:

'That man looks ill this morning.'

Dr Armstrong, who was standing by the window, cleared his throat. He said:

'You must excuse any – er – shortcomings this morning. Rogers has had to do the best he can for breakfast single-handed. Mrs Rogers has – er – not been able to carry on this morning.'

Emily Brent said sharply:

'What's the matter with the woman?'

Dr Armstrong said easily:

'Let us start our breakfast. The eggs will be cold. Afterwards, there are several matters I want to discuss with you all.'

They took the hint. Plates were filled, coffee and tea was poured. The meal began.

Discussion of the island was, by mutual consent, tabooed. They spoke instead in a desultory fashion of current events. The news from abroad, events in the world of sport, the latest reappearance of the Loch Ness monster.

Then, when plates were cleared, Dr Armstrong moved back his chair a little, cleared his throat importantly and spoke.

He said:

'I thought it better to wait until you had had your breakfast before telling you of a sad piece of news. Mrs Rogers died in her sleep.'

There were startled and shocked ejaculations.

Vera exclaimed:

'How awful! Two deaths on this island since we arrived!'

Mr Justice Wargrave, his eyes narrowed, said in his small precise clear voice:

'H'm – very remarkable – what was the cause of death?'

Armstrong shrugged his shoulders.

'Impossible to say offhand.'

'There must be an autopsy?'

'I certainly couldn't give a certificate. I have no knowledge whatsoever of the woman's state of health.'

Vera said:

'She was a very nervous-looking creature. And she had a shock last night. It might have been heart failure, I suppose?'

Dr Armstrong said dryly:

'Her heart certainly failed to beat – but what caused it to fail is the question.'

One word fell from Emily Brent. It fell hard and clear into the listening group.

'Conscience!' she said.

Armstrong turned to her.

'What exactly do you mean by that, Miss Brent?'

Emily Brent, her lips tight and hard, said:

'You all heard. She was accused, together with her husband, of having deliberately murdered her former employer – an old lady.'

'And you think?'

Emily Brent said:

'I think that that accusation was true. You all saw her last night. She broke down completely and fainted. The shock of having her wickedness brought home to her was too much for her. She literally died of fear.'

Dr Armstrong shook his head doubtfully.

'It is a possible theory,' he said. 'One cannot adopt it without more exact knowledge of her state of health. If there was cardiac weakness –'

Emily Brent said quietly:

'Call it if you prefer, an Act of God.'

Everyone looked shocked. Mr Blore said uneasily:

'That's carrying things a bit far, Miss Brent.'

She looked at them with shining eyes. Her chin went up. She said:

'You regard it as impossible that a sinner should be struck down by the wrath of God! I do not!'

The judge stroked his chin. He murmured in a slightly ironic voice:

'My dear lady, in my experience of ill-doing, Providence leaves the work of conviction and chastisement to us mortals – and the process is often fraught with difficulties. There are no short cuts.'

Emily Brent shrugged her shoulders.

Blore said sharply:

'What did she have to eat and drink last night after she went up to bed?'

Armstrong said:

'Nothing.'

'She didn't take anything? A cup of tea? A drink of water? I'll bet you she had a cup of tea. That sort always does.'

'Rogers assures me she had nothing whatsoever.'

'Ah,' said Blore. 'But he *might* say so!'

His tone was so significant that the doctor looked at him sharply.

Philip Lombard said:

'So that's your idea?'

Blore said aggressively:

'Well, why not? We all heard that accusation last night. Maybe sheer moonshine – just plain lunacy! On the other hand, it may not. Allow for the moment that it's true. Rogers and his Missus polished off that old lady. Well, where does that get you? They've been feeling quite safe and happy about it –'

Vera interrupted. In a low voice she said:

'No, I don't think Mrs Rogers ever felt safe.'

Blore looked slightly annoyed at the interruption.

'Just like a woman,' his glance said.

He resumed:

'That's as may be. Anyway there's no active danger to them as far as they know. Then, last night, some unknown lunatic spills the beans. What happens? The woman cracks – she goes to pieces. Notice how her husband hung over her as she was coming round. Not all husbandly solicitude! Not on your life! He was like a cat on hot bricks. Scared out of his life as to what she might say.

'And there's the position for you! They've done a murder and got away with it. But if the whole thing's going to be raked up, what's going to happen? Ten to one, the woman will give the show away. She hasn't got the nerve to stand up and brazen it out. She's a living danger to her husband, that's what she is. He's all right. *He*'ll lie with a straight face till kingdom comes – but he can't be sure of *her*! And if *she* goes to pieces, his neck's in danger! So he slips something into a cup of tea and makes sure that her mouth is shut permanently.'

Armstrong said slowly:

'There was no empty cup by her bedside – there was nothing there at all. I looked.'

Blore snorted.

'Of course there wouldn't be! First thing he'd do when she'd drunk it would be to take that cup and saucer away and wash it up carefully.'

There was a pause. Then General Macarthur said doubtfully:

'It may be so. But I should hardly think it possible that a man would do that – to his wife.'

Blore gave a short laugh.

He said:

'When a man's neck's in danger, he doesn't stop to think too much about sentiment.'

There was a pause. Before any one could speak, the door opened and Rogers came in.

He said, looking from one to the other:

'Is there anything more I can get you?'

Mr Justice Wargrave stirred a little in his chair. He asked:

'What time does the motor-boat usually come over?'

'Between seven and eight, sir. Sometimes it's a bit after eight. Don't know what Fred Narracott can be doing this morning. If he's ill he'd send his brother.'

Philip Lombard said:

'What's the time now?'

'Ten minutes to ten, sir.'

Lombard's eyebrows rose. He nodded slowly to himself.

Rogers waited a minute or two.

General Macarthur spoke suddenly and explosively:

'Sorry to hear about your wife, Rogers. Doctor's just been telling us.'

Rogers inclined his head.

'Yes, sir. Thank you, sir.'

He took up the empty bacon dish and went out.

Again there was a silence.

III

On the terrace outside Philip Lombard said:

'About this motor-boat –'

Blore looked at him.

Blore nodded his head.

He said:

'I know what you're thinking, Mr Lombard. I've asked myself the same question. Motor-boat ought to have been here nigh on two hours ago. It hasn't come? Why?'

'Found the answer?' asked Lombard.

'*It's not an accident* – that's what I say. It's part and parcel of the whole business. It's all bound up together.'

Philip Lombard said:

'It won't come, you think?'

A voice spoke behind him – a testy impatient voice.

'The motor-boat's not coming,' it said.

Blore turned his square shoulder slightly and viewed the last speaker thoughtfully.

'You think not too, General?'

General Macarthur said sharply:

'Of course it won't come. We're counting on the motor-boat to take us off the island. That's the meaning of the whole business.

We're not going to leave the island . . . None of us will ever leave . . . It's the end, you see – the end of everything . . .'

He hesitated, then he said in a low strange voice:

'That's peace – real peace. To come to the end – not to have to go on . . . Yes, peace . . .'

He turned abruptly and walked away. Along the terrace, then down the slope towards the sea – obliquely – to the end of the island where loose rocks went out into the water.

He walked a little unsteadily, like a man who was only half awake.

Blore said:

'There goes another one who's barmy! Looks as though it'll end with the whole lot going that way.'

Philip Lombard said:

'I don't fancy *you* will, Blore.'

The ex-Inspector laughed.

'It would take a lot to send me off my head.' He added dryly: 'And I don't think you'll be going that way either, Mr Lombard.'

Philip Lombard said:

'I feel quite sane at the minute, thank you.'

IV

Dr Armstrong came out on to the terrace. He stood there hesitating. To his left were Blore and Lombard. To his right was Wargrave, slowly pacing up and down, his head bent down.

Armstrong, after a moment of indecision, turned towards the latter.

But at that moment Rogers came quickly out of the house.

'Could I have a word with you, sir, please?'

Armstrong turned.

He was startled at what he saw.

Rogers' face was working. Its colour was greyish green. His hands shook.

It was such a contrast to his restraint of a few minutes ago that Armstrong was quite taken aback.

'Please sir, if I could have a word with you. Inside, sir.'

The doctor turned back and re-entered the house with the frenzied butler. He said:

'What's the matter, man, pull yourself together.'

'In here, sir, come in here.'

He opened the dining-room door. The doctor passed in. Rogers followed him and shut the door behind him.

'Well,' said Armstrong, 'what is it?'

The muscles of Rogers' throat were working. He was swallowing. He jerked out:

'There's things going on, sir, that I don't understand.'

Armstrong said sharply:

'Things? What things?'

'You'll think I'm crazy, sir. You'll say it isn't anything. But it's got to be explained, sir. It's got to be explained. Because it doesn't make any sense.'

'Well, man, tell me what it is. Don't go on talking in riddles.'

Rogers swallowed again.

He said:

'It's those little figures, sir. In the middle of the table. The little china figures. Ten of them, there were. I'll swear to that, ten of them.'

Armstrong said:

'Yes, ten. We counted them last night at dinner.'

Rogers came nearer.

'That's just it, sir. Last night, when I was clearing up, there wasn't but nine, sir. I noticed it and thought it queer. But that's all I thought. And now, sir, this morning. I didn't notice when I laid the breakfast. I was upset and all that.

'But now, sir, when I came to clear away. See for yourself if you don't believe me.

'*There's only eight, sir!* Only eight! It doesn't make sense, does it? *Only eight . . .*'

CHAPTER 7

I

After breakfast, Emily Brent had suggested to Vera Claythorne that they should walk to the summit again and watch for the boat. Vera had acquiesced.

The wind had freshened. Small white crests were appearing

on the sea. There were no fishing boats out – and no sign of the motor-boat.

The actual village of Sticklehaven could not be seen, only the hill above it, a jutting out cliff of red rock concealed the actual little bay.

Emily Brent said:

'The man who brought us out yesterday seemed a dependable sort of person. It is really very odd that he should be so late this morning.'

Vera did not answer. She was fighting down a rising feeling of panic.

She said to herself angrily:

'You must keep cool. This isn't like you. You've always had excellent nerves.'

Aloud she said after a minute or two:

'I wish he would come. I – I want to get away.'

Emily Brent said dryly:

'I've no doubt we all do.'

Vera said:

'It's all so extraordinary . . . There seems no – no meaning in it all.'

The elderly woman beside her said briskly:

'I'm very annoyed with myself for being so easily taken in. Really that letter is absurd when one comes to examine it. But I had no doubts at the time – none at all.'

Vera murmured mechanically: 'I suppose not.'

'One takes things for granted too much,' said Emily Brent.

Vera drew a deep shuddering breath.

She said:

'Do you really think – what you said at breakfast?'

'Be a little more precise, my dear. To what in particular are you referring?'

Vera said in a low voice:

'Do you really think that Rogers and his wife did away with that old lady?'

Emily Brent gazed thoughtfully out to sea. Then she said:

'Personally, I am quite sure of it. What do you think?'

'I don't know what to think.'

Emily Brent said:

'Everything goes to support the idea. The way the woman fainted. And the man dropped the coffee tray, remember. Then the way he spoke about it – it didn't ring true. Oh, yes, I'm afraid they did it.'

Vera said:

'The way she looked – scared of her own shadow! I've never seen a woman look so frightened . . . She must have been always haunted by it . . .'

Miss Brent murmured:

'I remember a text that hung in my nursery as a child. *"Be sure thy sin will find thee out."* It's very true, that. *Be sure thy sin will find thee out.*'

Vera scrambled to her feet. She said:

'But, Miss Brent – Miss Brent – in that case –'

'Yes, my dear?'

'The others? What about the others?'

'I don't quite understand you.'

'All the other accusations – they – *they* weren't true? But if it's true about the Rogerses –' She stopped, unable to make her chaotic thought clear.

Emily Brent's brow, which had been frowning perplexedly, cleared.

She said:

'Ah, I understand you now. Well, there is that Mr Lombard. He admits to having abandoned twenty men to their deaths.'

Vera said: 'They were only natives . . .'

Emily Brent said sharply:

'Black or white, they are our brothers.'

Vera thought:

'Our black brothers – our black brothers. Oh, I'm going to laugh. I'm hysterical. I'm not myself . . .'

Emily Brent continued thoughtfully.

'Of course, some of the other accusations were very far fetched and ridiculous. Against the judge, for instance, who was only doing his duty in his public capacity. And the ex-Scotland Yard man. My own case, too.'

She paused and then went on:

'Naturally, considering the circumstances, I was not going to say anything last night. It was not a fit subject to discuss before gentlemen.'

'No?'

Vera listened with interest. Miss Brent continued serenely.

'Beatrice Taylor was in service with me. *Not a nice girl* – as I found out too late. I was very much deceived in her. She had nice manners and was very clean and willing. I was very pleased with her. Of course, all that was the sheerest hypocrisy! She was a loose girl with no morals. Disgusting! It was some time before I found out that she was what they call "in trouble".' She paused, her delicate nose wrinkling itself in distaste. 'It was a great shock to me. Her parents were decent folk, too, who had brought her up very strictly. I'm glad to say they did not condone her behaviour.'

Vera said, staring at Miss Brent:

'What happened?'

'Naturally I did not keep her an hour under my roof. No one shall ever say that I condoned immorality.'

Vera said in a lower voice:

'What happened – to her?'

Miss Brent said:

'The abandoned creature, not content with having one sin on her conscience, committed a still graver sin. She took her own life.'

Vera whispered, horror-struck:

'She killed herself?'

'Yes, she threw herself into the river.'

Vera shivered.

She stared at the calm delicate profile of Miss Brent. She said:

'What did you feel like when you knew she'd done that? Weren't you sorry? Didn't you blame yourself?'

Emily Brent drew herself up.

'I? I had nothing with which to reproach myself.'

Vera said:

'But if your – hardness – drove her to it.'

Emily Brent said sharply:

'Her own action – her own sin – that was what drove her to it. If she had behaved like a decent modest young woman none of this would have happened.'

She turned her face to Vera. There was no self-reproach, no

uneasiness in those eyes. They were hard and self-righteous. Emily Brent sat on the summit of Soldier Island, encased in her own armour of virtue.

The little elderly spinster was no longer slightly ridiculous to Vera.

Suddenly – she was terrible.

II

Dr Armstrong came out of the dining-room and once more came out on the terrace.

The judge was sitting in a chair now, gazing placidly out to sea.

Lombard and Blore were over to the left, smoking but not talking.

As before, the doctor hesitated for a moment. His eye rested speculatively on Mr Justice Wargrave. He wanted to consult with someone. He was conscious of the judge's acute logical brain. But nevertheless, he wavered. Mr Justice Wargrave might have a good brain but he was an elderly man. At this juncture, Armstrong felt what was needed was a man of action.

He made up his mind.

'Lombard, can I speak to you for a minute?'

Philip started.

'Of course.'

The two men left the terrace. They strolled down the slope towards the water. When they were out of earshot Armstrong said:

'I want a consultation.'

Lombard's eyebrows went up. He said:

'My dear fellow, I've no medical knowledge.'

'No, no, I mean as to the general situation.'

'Oh, that's different.'

Armstrong said:

'Frankly, what do you think of the position?'

Lombard reflected a minute. Then he said:

'It's rather suggestive, isn't it?'

'What are your ideas on the subject of that woman? Do you accept Blore's theory?'

Philip puffed smoke into the air. He said:

'It's perfectly feasible – taken alone.'

'Exactly.'

Armstrong's tone sounded relieved. Philip Lombard was no fool.

The latter went on:

'That is, accepting the premise that Mr and Mrs Rogers have successfully got away with murder in their time. And I don't see why they shouldn't. What do you think they did exactly? Poisoned the old lady?'

Armstrong said slowly:

'It might be simpler than that. I asked Rogers this morning what this Miss Brady had suffered from. His answer was enlightening. I don't need to go into medical details, but in a certain form of cardiac trouble, amyl nitrite is used. When an attack comes on an ampoule of amyl nitrite is broken and it is inhaled. If amyl nitrite were withheld – well, the consequences might easily be fatal.'

Philip Lombard said thoughtfully:

'As simple as that. It must have been – rather tempting.'

The doctor nodded.

'Yes, no positive action. No arsenic to obtain and administer – nothing definite – just – negation! And Rogers hurried through the night to fetch a doctor and they both felt confident that no one could ever know.'

'And even if any one knew, nothing could ever be proved against them,' added Philip Lombard.

He frowned suddenly.

'Of course – that explains a good deal.'

Armstrong said, puzzled:

'I beg your pardon.'

Lombard said:

'I mean – it explains Soldier Island. There are crimes that cannot be brought home to their perpetrators. Instance the Rogerses'. Another instance, old Wargrave, who committed his murder strictly within the law.'

Armstrong said sharply: 'You believe that story?'

Philip Lombard smiled.

'Oh, yes, I believe it. Wargrave murdered Edward Seton all right, murdered him as surely as if he'd stuck a stiletto through him! But he was clever enough to do it from the judge's seat in wig and gown. So in the ordinary way you can't bring his little crime home to him.'

A sudden flash passed like lightning through Armstrong's mind.

'Murder in Hospital. Murder on the Operating-table. Safe – yes, safe as houses!'

Philip Lombard was saying:

'Hence – Mr Owen – hence – Soldier Island!'

Armstrong drew a deep breath.

'Now we're getting down to it. What's the real purpose of getting us all here?'

Philip Lombard said:

'What do *you* think?'

Armstrong said abruptly:

'Let's go back a minute to this woman's death. What are the possible theories? Rogers killed her because he was afraid she would give the show away. Second possibility: she lost her nerve and took an easy way out herself.'

Philip Lombard said:

'Suicide, eh?'

'What do you say to that?'

Lombard said:

'It could have been – yes – *if it hadn't been for Marston's death.* Two suicides within twelve hours is a little *too* much to swallow! And if you tell me that Anthony Marston, a young bull with no nerves and precious little brains, got the wind up over having mowed down a couple of kids and deliberately put himself out of the way – well, the idea's laughable! And anyway, how did he get hold of the stuff? From all I've ever heard, potassium cyanide isn't the kind of stuff you take about with you in your waistcoat pocket. But that's your line of country.'

Armstrong said:

'Nobody in their senses carries potassium cyanide. It might be done by someone who was going to take a wasps' nest.'

'The ardent gardener or landowner, in fact? Again, not Anthony Marston. It strikes me that that cyanide is going to need a bit of explaining. Either Anthony Marston meant to do away with himself before he came here, and therefore came prepared – or else –'

Armstrong prompted him.

'Or else?'

Philip Lombard grinned.

'Why make me say it? When it's on the tip of your own tongue. *Anthony Marston was murdered, of course.*'

III

Dr Armstrong drew a deep breath.

'And Mrs Rogers?'

Lombard said slowly:

'I could believe in Anthony's suicide (with difficulty) if it weren't for Mrs Rogers. I could believe in Mrs Rogers' suicide (easily) if it weren't for Anthony Marston. I can believe that Rogers put his wife out of the way – if it were not for the unexpected death of Anthony Marston. But what we need is a theory to explain two deaths following rapidly on each other.'

Armstrong said:

'I can perhaps give you some help towards that theory.'

And he repeated the facts that Rogers had given him about the disappearance of the two little china figures.

Lombard said:

'Yes, little china figures . . . There were certainly ten last night at dinner. And now there are eight, you say?'

Dr Armstrong recited:

'Ten little soldier boys going out to dine;
One went and choked himself and then there were Nine.

'Nine little soldier boys sat up very late;
One overslept himself and then there were Eight.'

The two men looked at each other. Philip Lombard grinned and flung away his cigarette.

'Fits too damned well to be a coincidence! Anthony Marston dies of asphyxiation or choking last night after dinner, and Mother Rogers oversleeps herself with a vengeance.'

'And therefore?' said Armstrong.

Lombard took him up.

'And therefore another kind of soldier. The Unknown Soldier! X! Mr Owen! U. N. Owen! One Unknown Lunatic at Large!'

'Ah!' Armstrong breathed a sigh of relief. 'You agree. But you see what it involves? Rogers swore that there was no one but ourselves and he and his wife on the island.'

'Rogers is wrong! Or possibly Rogers is lying!'

Armstrong shook his head.

'I don't think he's lying. The man's scared. He's scared nearly out of his senses.'

Philip Lombard nodded.

He said:

'No motor-boat this morning. That fits in. Mr Owen's little arrangements again to the fore. Soldier Island is to be isolated until Mr Owen has finished his job.'

Armstrong had gone pale. He said:

'You realize – the man must be a raving maniac!'

Philip Lombard said, and there was a new ring in his voice:

'There's one thing Mr Owen didn't realize.'

'What's that?'

'This island's more or less a bare rock. We shall make short work of searching it. We'll soon ferret out U. N. Owen, Esq.'

Dr Armstrong said warningly:

'He'll be dangerous.'

Philip Lombard laughed.

'Dangerous? Who's afraid of the big bad wolf? *I'*ll be dangerous when I get hold of him!'

He paused and said:

'We'd better rope in Blore to help us. He'll be a good man in a pinch. Better not tell the women. As for the others, the General's ga-ga, I think, and old Wargrave's forte is masterly inactivity. The three of us can attend to this job.'

CHAPTER 8

I

Blore was easily roped in. He expressed immediate agreement with their arguments.

'What you've said about those china figures, sir, makes all the difference. That's crazy, that is! There's only one thing. You don't think this Owen's idea might be to do the job by proxy, as it were?'

'Explain yourself, man.'

'Well, I mean like this. After the racket last night this young Marston gets the wind up and poisons himself. And Rogers, *he* gets the wind up too and bumps off his wife! All according to U.N.O's plan.'

Armstrong shook his head. He stressed the point about the cyanide. Blore agreed.

'Yes, I'd forgotten that. Not a natural thing to be carrying about with you. But how did it get into his drink, sir?'

Lombard said:

'I've been thinking about that. Marston had several drinks that night. Between the time he had his last one and the time he finished the one before it, there was quite a gap. During that time his glass was lying about on some table or other. I think – though I can't be sure, it was on the little table near the window. The window was open. Somebody could have slipped a dose of the cyanide into the glass.'

Blore said unbelievingly:

'Without our all seeing him, sir?'

Lombard said dryly:

'We were all – rather concerned elsewhere.'

Armstrong said slowly:

'That's true. We'd all been attacked. We were walking about, moving about the room. Arguing, indignant, intent on our own business. I think it *could* have been done . . .'

Blore shrugged his shoulders.

'Fact is, it must have been done! Now then, gentlemen, let's make a start. Nobody's got a revolver, by any chance? I suppose that's too much to hope for.'

Lombard said:

'I've got one.' He patted his pocket.

Blore's eyes opened very wide. He said in an over-casual tone:

'Always carry that about with you, sir?'

Lombard said:

'Usually. I've been in some tight places, you know.'

'Oh,' said Blore and added: 'Well, you've probably never been in a tighter place than you are today! If there's a lunatic hiding on this island, he's probably got a young arsenal on him – to say nothing of a knife or dagger or two.'

Armstrong coughed.

'You may be wrong there, Blore. Many homicidal lunatics are very quiet unassuming people. Delightful fellows.'

Blore said:

'I don't feel this one is going to be of that kind, Dr Armstrong.'

II

The three men started on their tour of the island.

It proved unexpectedly simple. On the north-west side, towards the coast, the cliffs fell sheer to the sea below, their surface unbroken.

On the rest of the island there were no trees and very little cover. The three men worked carefully and methodically, beating up and down from the highest point to the water's edge, narrowly scanning the least irregularity in the rock which might point to the entrance to a cave. But there were no caves.

They came at last, skirting the water's edge, to where General Macarthur sat looking out to sea. It was very peaceful here with the lap of the waves breaking over the rocks. The old man sat very upright, his eyes fixed on the horizon.

He paid no attention to the approach of the searchers. His oblivion of them made one at least faintly uncomfortable.

Blore thought to himself:

''Tisn't natural – looks as though he'd gone into a trance or something.'

He cleared his throat and said in a would-be conversational tone:

'Nice peaceful spot you've found for yourself, sir.'

The General frowned. He cast a quick look over his shoulder. He said:

'There is so little time – so little time. I really must insist that no one disturbs me.'

Blore said genially:

'We won't disturb you. We're just making a tour of the island so to speak. Just wondered, you know, if someone might be hiding on it.'

The General frowned and said:

'You don't understand – you don't understand at all. Please go away.'

Blore retreated. He said, as he joined the other two:

'He's crazy . . . It's no good talking to him.'

Lombard asked with some curiosity:

'What did he say?'

Blore shrugged his shoulders.

'Something about there being no time and that he didn't want to be disturbed.'

Dr Armstrong frowned.

He murmured:

'I wonder now . . .'

III

The search of the island was practically completed. The three men stood on the highest point looking over towards the mainland. There were no boats out. The wind was freshening.

Lombard said:

'No fishing boats out. There's a storm coming. Damned nuisance you can't see the village from here. We could signal or do something.'

Blore said:

'We might light a bonfire tonight.'

Lombard said, frowning:

'The devil of it is that that's all probably been provided for.'

'In what way, sir?'

'How do I know? Practical joke, perhaps. We're to be marooned here, no attention is to be paid to signals, etc. Possibly the village has been told there's a wager on. Some damn' fool story anyway.'

Blore said dubiously:

'Think they'd swallow that?'

Lombard said dryly:

'It's easier of belief than the truth! If the village were told that the island was to be isolated until Mr Unknown Owen had quietly murdered all his guests – do you think they'd believe that?'

Dr Armstrong said:

'There are moments when I can't believe it myself. And yet –'

Philip Lombard, his lips curling back from his teeth said:
'*And yet* – that's just it! You've said it, doctor!'

Blore was gazing down into the water.

He said:

'Nobody could have clambered down here, I suppose?'

Armstrong shook his head.

'I doubt it. It's pretty sheer. And where could he hide?'

Blore said:

'There might be a hole in the cliff. If we had a boat now, we could row round the island.'

Lombard said:

'If we had a boat, we'd all be halfway to the mainland by now!'

'True enough, sir.'

Lombard said suddenly:

'We can make sure of this cliff. There's only one place where there *could* be a recess – just a little to the right below here. If you fellows can get hold of a rope, you can let me down to make sure.'

Blore said:

'Might as well *be* sure. Though it seems absurd – on the face of it! I'll see if I can get hold of something.'

He started off briskly down to the house.

Lombard stared up at the sky. The clouds were beginning to mass themselves together. The wind was increasing.

He shot a sideways look at Armstrong. He said:

'You're very silent, doctor. What are you thinking?'

Armstrong said slowly:

'I was wondering exactly how mad old Macarthur was . . .'

IV

Vera had been restless all the morning. She had avoided Emily Brent with a kind of shuddering aversion.

Miss Brent herself had taken a chair just round the corner of the house so as to be out of the wind. She sat there knitting.

Every time Vera thought of her she seemed to see a pale drowned face with seaweed entangled in the hair . . . A face that had once been pretty – impudently pretty perhaps – and which was now beyond the reach of pity or terror.

And Emily Brent, placid and righteous, sat knitting.

On the main terrace, Mr Justice Wargrave sat huddled in a porter's chair. His head was poked down well into his neck.

When Vera looked at him, she saw a man standing in the dock – a young man with fair hair and blue eyes and a bewildered frightened face. Edward Seton. And in imagination she saw the judge's old hands put the black cap on his head and begin to pronounce sentence . . .

After a while Vera strolled slowly down to the sea. She walked along towards the extreme end of the island where an old man sat staring out to the horizon.

General Macarthur stirred at her approach. His head turned – there was a queer mixture of questioning and apprehension in his look. It startled her. He stared intently at her for a minute or two.

She thought to herself:

'How queer. It's almost as though he *knew* . . .'

He said:

'Ah, it's you! You've come . . .'

Vera sat down beside him. She said:

'Do you like sitting here looking out to sea?'

He nodded his head gently.

'Yes,' he said. 'It's pleasant. It's a good place, I think, to wait.'

'To wait?' said Vera sharply. 'What are you waiting for?'

He said gently:

'The end. But I think you know that, don't you? It's true, isn't it? We're all waiting for the end.'

She said unsteadily:

'What do you mean?'

General Macarthur said gravely:

'*None of us are going to leave the island.* That's the plan. You know it, of course, perfectly. What, perhaps, you can't understand is the relief!'

Vera said wonderingly:

'The relief?'

He said:

'Yes. Of course, you're very young . . . you haven't got to that yet. But it does come! The blessed relief when you know that you've done with it all – that you haven't got to carry the burden any longer. You'll feel that too, someday . . .'

Vera said hoarsely:

'I don't understand you.'

Her fingers worked spasmodically. She felt suddenly afraid of this quiet old soldier.

He said musingly:

'You see, I loved Leslie. I loved her very much . . .'

Vera said questioningly:

'Was Leslie your wife?'

'Yes, my wife . . . I loved her – and I was very proud of her. She was so pretty – and so gay.'

He was silent for a minute or two, then he said:

'Yes, I loved Leslie. That's why I did it.'

Vera said:

'You mean –' and paused.

General Macarthur nodded his head gently.

'It's not much good denying it now – not when we're all going to die. *I sent Richmond to his death.* I suppose, in a way, it was murder. Curious. *Murder* – and I've always been such a law-abiding man! But it didn't seem like that at the time. I had no regrets. "Serves him damned well right!" – that's what I thought. But afterwards –'

In a hard voice, Vera said:

'Well, afterwards?'

He shook his head vaguely. He looked puzzled and a little distressed.

'I don't know. I – don't know. It was all different, you see. I don't know if Leslie ever guessed . . . I don't think so. But, you see, I didn't know about her any more. She'd gone far away where I couldn't reach her. And then she died – and I was alone . . .'

Vera said:

'Alone – alone –' and the echo of her voice came back to her from the rocks.

General Macarthur said:

'You'll be glad, too, when the end comes.'

Vera got up. She said sharply:

'I don't know what you mean!'

He said:

'I *know*, my child. I *know* . . .'

'You don't. You don't understand at all . . .'

General Macarthur looked out to sea again. He seemed unconscious of her presence behind him.

He said very gently and softly:

'Leslie . . . ?'

V

When Blore returned from the house with a rope coiled over his arm, he found Armstrong where he had left him staring down into the depths.

Blore said breathlessly:

'Where's Mr Lombard?'

Armstrong said carelessly:

'Gone to test some theory or other. He'll be back in a minute. Look here, Blore, I'm worried.'

'I should say we were all worried.'

The doctor waved an impatient hand.

'Of course – of course. I don't mean it that way. I'm thinking of old Macarthur.'

'What about him, sir?'

Dr Armstrong said grimly:

'What we're looking for is a madman. *What price Macarthur?*'

Blore said incredulously:

'You mean he's homicidal?'

Armstrong said doubtfully:

'I shouldn't have said so. Not for a minute. But, of course, I'm not a specialist in mental diseases. I haven't really had any conversation with him – I haven't studied him from that point of view.'

Blore said doubtfully:

'Ga-ga, yes! But I wouldn't have said –'

Armstrong cut in with a slight effort as of a man who pulls himself together.

'You're probably right! Damn it all, there *must* be someone hiding on the island! Ah! here comes Lombard.'

They fastened the rope carefully.

Lombard said:

'I'll help myself all I can. Keep a lookout for a sudden strain on the rope.'

After a minute or two, while they stood together watching Lombard's progress, Blore said:

'Climbs like a cat, doesn't he?'

There was something odd in his voice.

Dr Armstrong said:

'I should think he must have done some mountaineering in his time.'

'Maybe.'

There was a silence and the ex-Inspector said:

'Funny sort of cove altogether. D'you know what I think?'

'What?'

'He's a wrong 'un!'

Armstrong said doubtfully:

'In what way?'

Blore grunted. Then he said:

'I don't know – exactly. But I wouldn't trust him a yard.'

Dr Armstrong said:

'I suppose he's led an adventurous life.'

Blore said:

'I bet some of his adventures have had to be kept pretty dark.' He paused and then went on: 'Did you happen to bring a revolver along with you, doctor?'

Armstrong stared.

'Me? Good Lord, no. Why should I?'

Blore said:

'*Why did Mr Lombard?*'

Armstrong said doubtfully:

'I suppose – habit.'

Blore snorted.

A sudden pull came on the rope. For some moments they had their hands full. Presently, when the strain relaxed, Blore said:

'There are habits *and* habits! Mr Lombard takes a revolver to out of the way places, right enough, *and* a primus and a sleeping-bag and a supply of bug powder no doubt! But habit wouldn't make him bring the whole outfit down here! It's only in books people carry revolvers around as a matter of course.'

Dr Armstrong shook his head perplexedly.

They leaned over and watched Lombard's progress. His search was thorough and they could see at once that it was futile.

Presently he came up over the edge of the cliff. He wiped the perspiration from his forehead.

'Well,' he said. 'We're up against it. It's the house or nowhere.'

VI

The house was easily searched. They went through the few outbuildings first and then turned their attention to the building itself. Mrs Rogers' yard measure discovered in the kitchen dresser assisted them. But there were no hidden spaces left unaccounted for. Everything was plain and straightforward, a modern structure devoid of concealments. They went through the ground floor first. As they mounted to the bedroom floor, they saw through the landing window Rogers carrying out a tray of cocktails to the terrace.

Philip Lombard said lightly:

'Wonderful animal, the good servant. Carries on with an impassive countenance.'

Armstrong said appreciatively:

'Rogers is a first-class butler, I'll say that for him!'

Blore said:

'His wife was a pretty good cook, too. That dinner – last night –'

They turned in to the first bedroom.

Five minutes later they faced each other on the landing. No one hiding – no possible hiding-place.

Blore said:

'There's a little stair here.'

Dr Armstrong said:

'It leads up to the servants' room.'

Blore said:

'There must be a place under the roof – for cisterns, water tank, etc. It's the best chance – and the only one!'

And it was then, as they stood there, that they heard the sound from above. A soft furtive footfall overhead.

They all heard it. Armstrong grasped Blore's arm. Lombard held up an admonitory finger.

'Quiet – listen.'

It came again – someone moving softly, furtively, overhead.

Armstrong whispered:

'He's actually in the bedroom itself. The room where Mrs Rogers' body is.'

Blore whispered back:

'Of course! Best hiding-place he could have chosen! Nobody likely to go there. Now then – quiet as you can.'

They crept stealthily upstairs.

On the little landing outside the door of the bedroom they paused again. Yes, someone was in the room. There was a faint creak from within.

Blore whispered:

'Now.'

He flung open the door and rushed in, the other two close behind him.

Then all three stopped dead.

Rogers was in the room, his hands full of garments.

VII

Blore recovered himself first. He said:

'Sorry – er – Rogers. Heard someone moving about in here, and thought – well –'

He stopped.

Rogers said:

'I'm sorry, gentlemen. I was just moving my things. I take it there will be no objection if I take one of the vacant guest chambers on the floor below? The smallest room.'

It was to Armstrong that he spoke and Armstrong replied:

'Of course. Of course. Get on with it.'

He avoided looking at the sheeted figure lying on the bed.

Rogers said:

'Thank you, sir.'

He went out of the room with his arm full of belongings and went down the stairs to the floor below.

Armstrong moved over to the bed and, lifting the sheet, looked down on the peaceful face of the dead woman. There was no fear there now. Just emptiness.

Armstrong said:

'Wish I'd got my stuff here. I'd like to know what drug it was.'

Then he turned to the other two.

'Let's get finished. I feel it in my bones we're not going to find anything.'

Blore was wrestling with the bolts of a low manhole.

He said:

'That chap moves damned quietly. A minute or two ago we saw him in the garden. None of us heard him come upstairs.'

Lombard said:

'I suppose that's why we assumed it must be a stranger moving about up here.'

Blore disappeared into a cavernous darkness. Lombard pulled a torch from his pocket and followed.

Five minutes later three men stood on an upper landing and looked at each other. They were dirty and festooned with cobwebs and their faces were grim.

There was no one on the island but their eight selves.

CHAPTER 9

I

Lombard said slowly:

'So we've been wrong – wrong all along! Built up a nightmare of superstition and fantasy all because of the coincidence of two deaths!'

Armstrong said gravely:

'And yet, you know, the argument holds. Hang it all, I'm a doctor, I know something about suicides. Anthony Marston wasn't a suicidal type.'

Lombard said doubtfully:

'It couldn't, I suppose, have been an accident?'

Blore snorted, unconvinced.

'Damned queer sort of accident,' he grunted.

There was a pause, then Blore said:

'About the woman –' and stopped.

'Mrs Rogers?'

'Yes. It's possible, isn't it, that that might have been an accident?'

Philip Lombard said:

'An accident? In what way?'

Blore looked slightly embarrassed. His red-brick face grew a little deeper in hue. He said, almost blurting out the words:

'Look here, doctor, you did give her some dope, you know.'

Armstrong stared at him.

'Dope? What do you mean?'

'Last night. You said yourself you'd given her something to make her sleep.'

'Oh that, yes. A harmless sedative.'

'What was it exactly?'

'I gave her a mild dose of trional. A perfectly harmless preparation.'

Blore grew redder still. He said:

'Look here – not to mince matters – you didn't give her an overdose, did you?'

Dr Armstrong said angrily:

'I don't know what you mean.'

Blore said:

'It's possible, isn't it, that you may have made a mistake? These things do happen once in a while.'

Armstrong said sharply:

'I did nothing of the sort. The suggestion is ridiculous.' He stopped and added in a cold biting tone: 'Or do you suggest that I gave her an overdose on purpose?'

Philip Lombard said quickly:

'Look here, you two, got to keep our heads. Don't let's start slinging accusations about.'

Blore said sullenly:

'I only suggested the doctor had made a mistake.'

Dr Armstrong smiled with an effort. He said, showing his teeth in a somewhat mirthless smile:

'Doctors can't afford to make mistakes of that kind, my friend.'

Blore said deliberately:

'It wouldn't be the first you've made – if that gramophone record is to be believed!'

Armstrong went white. Philip Lombard said quickly and angrily to Blore:

'What's the sense of making yourself offensive? We're all in the same boat. We've got to pull together. What about your own pretty little spot of perjury?'

Blore took a step forward, his hands clenched. He said in a thick voice:

'Perjury, be damned! That's a foul lie! You may try and shut me up, Mr Lombard, but there's things I want to know – and one of them is about *you*!'

Lombard's eyebrows rose.

'About me?'

'Yes. I want to know why you brought a revolver down here on a pleasant social visit?'

Lombard said:

'You do, do you?'

'Yes, I do, Mr Lombard.'

Lombard said unexpectedly:

'You know, Blore, you're not nearly such a fool as you look.'

'That's as may be. What about that revolver?'

Lombard smiled.

'I brought it because I expected to run into a spot of trouble.'

Blore said suspiciously:

'You didn't tell us that last night.'

Lombard shook his head.

'You were holding out on us?' Blore persisted.

'In a way, yes,' said Lombard.

'Well, come on, out with it.'

Lombard said slowly:

'I allowed you all to think that I was asked here in the same way as most of the others. That's not quite true. As a matter of fact I was approached by a little Jew-boy – Morris his name was. He offered me a hundred guineas to come down here and keep my eyes open – said I'd got a reputation for being a good man in a tight place.'

'Well?' Blore prompted impatiently.

Lombard said with a grin:

'That's all.'

Dr Armstrong said:

'But surely he told you more than that?'

'Oh no, he didn't. Just shut up like a clam. I could take it or leave it – those were his words. I was hard up. I took it.'

Blore looked unconvinced. He said:

'Why didn't you tell us all this last night?'

'My dear man –' Lombard shrugged eloquent shoulders. 'How was I to know that last night wasn't exactly the eventuality I was here to cope with? I lay low and told a non-committal story.'

Dr Armstrong said shrewdly:

'But now – you think differently?'

Lombard's face changed. It darkened and hardened. He said:

'Yes. I believe now that I'm in the same boat as the rest of you. That hundred guineas was just Mr Owen's little bit of cheese to get me into the trap along with the rest of you.'

He said slowly:

'*For we are in a trap* – I'll take my oath on that! Mrs Rogers' death! Tony Marston's! The disappearing soldier boys on the dinner-table! Oh yes, Mr Owen's hand is plainly seen – *but where the devil is Mr Owen himself*?'

Downstairs the gong pealed a solemn call to lunch.

II

Rogers was standing by the dining-room door. As the three men descended the stairs he moved a step or two forward. He said in a low anxious voice:

'I hope lunch will be satisfactory. There is cold ham and cold tongue, and I've boiled some potatoes. And there's cheese and biscuits, and some tinned fruits.'

Lombard said:

'Sounds all right. Stores are holding out, then?'

'There is plenty of food, sir – of a tinned variety. The larder is very well stocked. A necessity, that, I should say, sir, on an island where one may be cut off from the mainland for a considerable period.'

Lombard nodded.

Rogers murmured as he followed the three men into the dining-room:

'It worries me that Fred Narracott hasn't been over today. It's peculiarly unfortunate, as you might say.'

'Yes,' said Lombard, 'peculiarly unfortunate describes it very well.'

Miss Brent came into the room. She had just dropped a ball of wool and was carefully rewinding the end of it.

As she took her seat at table she remarked:

'The weather is changing. The wind is quite strong and there are white horses on the sea.'

Mr Justice Wargrave came in. He walked with a slow measured tread. He darted quick looks from under his bushy eyebrows at the other occupants of the dining-room. He said:

'You have had an active morning.'

There was a faint malicious pleasure in his voice.

Vera Claythorne hurried in. She was a little out of breath. She said quickly:

'I hope you didn't wait for me. Am I late?'

Emily Brent said:

'You're not the last. The General isn't here yet.'

They sat round the table.

Rogers addressed Miss Brent.

'Will you begin, Madam, or will you wait?'

Vera said:

'General Macarthur is sitting right down by the sea. I don't expect he would hear the gong there anyway' – she hesitated – 'he's a little vague today, I think.'

Rogers said quickly:

'I will go down and inform him luncheon is ready.'

Dr Armstrong jumped up.

'I'll go,' he said. 'You others start lunch.'

He left the room. Behind him he heard Rogers' voice.

'Will you take cold tongue or cold ham, Madam?'

III

The five people sitting round the table seemed to find conversation difficult. Outside, sudden gusts of wind came up and died away.

Vera shivered a little and said:

'There is a storm coming.'

Blore made a contribution to the discourse. He said conversationally:

'There was an old fellow in the train from Plymouth yesterday. *He* kept saying a storm was coming. Wonderful how they know weather, these old salts.'

Rogers went round the table collecting the meat plates.

Suddenly, with the plates held in his hands, he stopped.

He said in an odd scared voice:

'There's somebody running . . .'

They could all hear it – running feet along the terrace.

In that minute, they knew – knew without being told . . .

As by common accord, they all rose to their feet. They stood looking towards the door.

Dr Armstrong appeared, his breath coming fast.

He said:

'General Macarthur –'

'Dead!' The word burst from Vera explosively.

Armstrong said:

'Yes, he's dead . . .'

There was a pause – a long pause.

Seven people looked at each other and could find no words to say.

IV

The storm broke just as the old man's body was borne in through the door.

The others were standing in the hall.

There was a sudden hiss and roar as the rain came down.

As Blore and Armstrong passed up the stairs with their burden, Vera Claythorne turned suddenly and went into the deserted dining-room.

It was as they had left it. The sweet course stood ready on the sideboard untasted.

Vera went up to the table. She was there a minute or two later when Rogers came softly into the room.

He started when he saw her. Then his eyes asked a question.

He said:

'Oh, Miss, I – I just came to see . . .'

In a loud harsh voice that surprised herself Vera said:

'You're quite right, Rogers. Look for yourself. *There are only seven* . . .'

V

General Macarthur had been laid on his bed.

After making a last examination Armstrong left the room and came downstairs. He found the others assembled in the drawing-room.

Miss Brent was knitting. Vera Claythorne was standing by the window looking out at the hissing rain. Blore was sitting squarely in a chair, his hands on his knees. Lombard was walking restlessly up and down. At the far end of the room Mr Justice Wargrave was sitting in a grandfather chair. His eyes were half closed.

They opened as the doctor came into the room. He said in a clear penetrating voice:

'Well, doctor?'

Armstrong was very pale. He said:

'No question of heart failure or anything like that. Macarthur was hit with a life preserver or some such thing on the back of the head.'

A little murmur went round, but the clear voice of the judge was raised once more.

'Did you find the actual weapon used?'

'No.'

'Nevertheless you are sure of your facts?'

'I am quite sure.'

Mr Justice Wargrave said quietly:

'We know now exactly where we are.'

There was no doubt now who was in charge of the situation. This morning Wargrave had sat huddled in his chair on the terrace refraining from any overt activity. Now he assumed command with the ease born of a long habit of authority. He definitely presided over the court.

Clearing his throat, he once more spoke.

'This morning, gentlemen, whilst I was sitting on the terrace, I was an observer of your activities. There could be little doubt of your purpose. You were searching the island for an unknown murderer?'

'Quite right, sir,' said Philip Lombard.

The judge went on.

'You had come, doubtless, to the same conclusion that I had

– namely that the deaths of Anthony Marston and Mrs Rogers were neither accidental nor were they suicides. No doubt you also reached a certain conclusion as to the purpose of Mr Owen in enticing us to this island?'

Blore said hoarsely:

'He's a madman! A loony.'

The judge coughed.

'That almost certainly. But it hardly affects the issue. Our main preoccupation is this – to save our lives.'

Armstrong said in a trembling voice:

'There's no one on the island, I tell you. *No one!*'

The judge stroked his jaw.

He said gently:

'In the sense you mean, no. I came to that conclusion early this morning. I could have told you that your search would be fruitless. Nevertheless I am strongly of the opinion that "Mr Owen" (to give him the name he himself has adopted) *is* on the island. Very much so. Given the scheme in question which is neither more nor less than the execution of justice upon certain individuals for offences which the law cannot touch, *there is only one way in which that scheme could be accomplished.* Mr Owen could only come to the island in one way.

'It is perfectly clear. *Mr Owen is one of us . . .*'

VI

'Oh, no, no, no . . .'

It was Vera who burst out – almost in a moan. The judge turned a keen eye on her.

He said:

'My dear young lady, this is no time for refusing to look facts in the face. We are all in grave danger. One of us is U. N. Owen. And we do not know which of us. Of the ten people who came to this island three are definitely cleared. Anthony Marston, Mrs Rogers, and General Macarthur have gone beyond suspicion. There are seven of us left. Of those seven, one is, if I may so express myself, a bogus little soldier boy.'

He paused and looked round.

'Do I take it that you all agree?'

Armstrong said:

'It's fantastic – but I suppose you're right.'

Blore said:

'Not a doubt of it. And if you ask me, I've a very good idea –'

A quick gesture of Mr Justice Wargrave's hand stopped him. The judge said quietly:

'We will come to that presently. At the moment all I wish to establish is that we are in agreement on the facts.'

Emily Brent, still knitting, said:

'Your argument seems logical. I agree that one of us is possessed by a devil.'

Vera murmured:

'I can't believe it . . . I can't . . .'

Wargrave said:

'Lombard?'

'I agree, sir, absolutely.'

The judge nodded his head in a satisfied manner. He said:

'Now let us examine the evidence. To begin with, is there any reason for suspecting one particular person? Mr Blore, you have, I think, something to say.'

Blore was breathing hard. He said:

'Lombard's got a revolver. He didn't tell the truth – last night. He admits it.'

Philip Lombard smiled scornfully.

He said:

'I suppose I'd better explain again.'

He did so, telling the story briefly and succinctly.

Blore said sharply:

'What's to prove it? There's nothing to corroborate your story.'

The judge coughed.

'Unfortunately,' he said, 'we are all in that position. There is only our own word to go upon.'

He leaned forward.

'You have none of you yet grasped what a very peculiar situation this is. To my mind there is only one course of procedure to adopt. Is there any one whom we can definitely eliminate from suspicion on the evidence which is in our possession?'

Dr Armstrong said quickly:

'I, am a well-known professional man. The mere idea that I can be suspected of –'

Again a gesture of the judge's hand arrested a speaker before he finished his speech. Mr Justice Wargrave said in his small clear voice:

'I too, am a well-known person! But, my dear sir, that proves less than nothing! Doctors have gone mad before now. Judges have gone mad. So,' he added, looking at Blore, 'have policemen!'

Lombard said:

'At any rate, I suppose you'll leave the women out of it.'

The judge's eyebrows rose. He said in the famous 'acid' tones that Counsel knew so well:

'Do I understand you to assert that women are not subject to homicidal mania?'

Lombard said irritably:

'Of course not. But all the same, it hardly seems possible –'

He stopped. Mr Justice Wargrave still in the same thin sour voice addressed Armstrong.

'I take it, Dr Armstrong, that a woman would have been physically capable of striking the blow that killed poor Macarthur?'

The doctor said calmly:

'Perfectly capable – given a suitable instrument, such as a rubber truncheon or cosh.'

'It would require no undue exertion of force?'

'Not at all.'

Mr Justice Wargrave wriggled his tortoise-like neck. He said:

'The other two deaths have resulted from the administration of drugs. That, no one will dispute, is easily compassed by a person of the smallest physical strength.'

Vera cried angrily:

'I think you're mad!'

His eyes turned slowly till they rested on her. It was the dispassionate stare of a man well used to weighing humanity in the balance. She thought:

'He's just seeing me as a – as a specimen. And –' the thought came to her with real surprise, 'he doesn't like me much!'

In a measured tone the judge was saying:

'My dear young lady, do try and restrain your feelings. I am not accusing you.' He bowed to Miss Brent. 'I hope, Miss Brent, that you are not offended by my insistence that *all* of us are equally under suspicion?'

Emily Brent was knitting. She did not look up. In a cold voice she said:

'The idea that I should be accused of taking a fellow creature's life – not to speak of the lives of *three* fellow creatures – is of course, quite absurd to any one who knows anything of my character. But I quite appreciate the fact that we are all strangers to one another and that, in those circumstances, nobody can be exonerated without the fullest proof. There is, as I have said, a devil amongst us.'

The judge said:

'Then we are agreed. There can be no elimination on the ground of character or position alone.'

Lombard said: 'What about Rogers?'

The judge looked at him unblinkingly.

'What about him?'

Lombard said:

'Well, to my mind, Rogers seems pretty well ruled out.'

Mr Justice Wargrave said:

'Indeed, and on what grounds?'

Lombard said:

'He hasn't got the brains for one thing. And for another his wife was one of the victims.'

The judge's heavy eyebrows rose once more. He said:

'In my time, young man, several people have come before me accused of the murders of their wives – *and* have been found guilty.'

'Oh! I agree. Wife murder is perfectly possible – almost natural, let's say! But not this particular kind! I can believe in Rogers killing his wife because he was scared of her breaking down and giving him away, or because he'd taken a dislike to her, or because he wanted to link up with some nice little bit rather less long in the tooth. But I can't see him as the lunatic Mr Owen dealing out crazy justice and starting on his own wife for a crime they both committed.'

Mr Justice Wargrave said:

'You are assuming hearsay to be evidence. We do not know

that Rogers and his wife conspired to murder their employer. That may have been a false statement, made so that Rogers should appear to be in the same position as ourselves. Mrs Rogers' terror last night may have been due to the fact that she realized her husband was mentally unhinged.'

Lombard said:

'Well, have it your own way. U. N. Owen is one of us. No exceptions allowed. We all qualify.'

Mr Justice Wargrave said:

'My point is that there can be no exceptions allowed on the score of *character, position,* or *probability.* What we must now examine is the possibility of eliminating one or more persons on the *facts.* To put it simply, is there among us one or more persons who could not possibly have administered either cyanide to Anthony Marston, or an overdose of sleeping draught to Mrs Rogers, and who had no opportunity of striking the blow that killed General Macarthur?'

Blore's rather heavy face lit up. He leant forward.

'Now you're talking, sir!' he said. 'That's the stuff! Let's go into it. As regards young Marston I don't think there's anything to be done. It's already been suggested that someone from outside slipped something into the dregs of his glass before he refilled it for the last time. A person actually in the room could have done that even more easily. I can't remember if Rogers was in the room, but any of the rest of us could certainly have done it.'

He paused, then went on:

'Now take the woman Rogers. The people who stand out there are her husband and the doctor. Either of them could have done it as easy as winking –'

Armstrong sprang to his feet. He was trembling.

'I protest – this is absolutely uncalled for! I swear that the dose I gave the woman was perfectly –'

'Dr Armstrong.'

The small sour voice was compelling. The doctor stopped with a jerk in the middle of his sentence. The small cold voice went on:

'Your indignation is very natural. Nevertheless you must admit that the facts have got to be faced. Either you or Rogers *could* have administered a fatal dose with the greatest ease. Let us now consider the position of the other people present. What chance had I, had Inspector Blore, had Miss Brent, had Miss Claythorne, had Mr Lombard of administering poison? Can any one of us be completely and entirely eliminated?' He paused. 'I think not.'

Vera said angrily:

'I was nowhere near the woman! All of you can swear to that.'

Mr Justice Wargrave waited a minute, then he said:

'As far as my memory serves me the facts were these – will any one please correct me if I make a mis-statement? Mrs Rogers was lifted on to the sofa by Anthony Marston and Mr Lombard and Dr Armstrong went to her. He sent Rogers for brandy. There was then a question raised as to where the voice we had just heard had come from. We all went into the next room with the exception of Miss Brent who remained in this room – alone with the unconscious woman.'

A spot of colour came into Emily Brent's cheeks. She stopped knitting. She said:

'This is outrageous!'

The remorseless small voice went on:

'When we returned to this room, you, Miss Brent, were bending over the woman on the sofa.'

Emily Brent said:

'Is common humanity a criminal offence?'

Mr Justice Wargrave said:

'I am only establishing facts. Rogers then entered the room with the brandy which, of course, he could quite well have doctored before entering the room. The brandy was administered to the woman and shortly afterwards her husband and Dr Armstrong assisted her up to bed where Dr Armstrong gave her a sedative.'

Blore said:

'That's what happened. Absolutely. And that lets out the judge, Mr Lombard, myself and Miss Claythorne.'

His voice was loud and jubilant. Mr Justice Wargrave, bringing a cold eye to bear upon him, murmured:

'Ah, but does it? We must take into account *every possible eventuality*.'

Blore stared. He said:

'I don't get you.'

Mr Justice Wargrave said:

'Upstairs in her room, Mrs Rogers is lying in bed. The sedative that the doctor has given her begins to take effect. She is vaguely sleepy and acquiescent. Supposing that at that moment there is a tap on the door and someone enters bringing her, shall we say, a tablet, or a draught, with the message that "The doctor says you're to take this." Do you imagine for one minute that she would not have swallowed it obediently without thinking twice about it?'

There was a silence. Blore shifted his feet and frowned. Philip Lombard said:

'I don't believe in that story for a minute. Besides none of us left this room for hours afterwards. There was Marston's death and all the rest of it.'

The judge said:

'Someone could have left his or her bedroom – later.'

Lombard objected:

'But then Rogers would have been up there.'

Dr Armstrong stirred.

'No,' he said. 'Rogers went downstairs to clear up in the dining-room and pantry. Anyone could have gone up to the woman's bedroom then without being seen.'

Emily Brent said:

'Surely, doctor, the woman would have been fast asleep by then under the influence of the drug you had administered?'

'In all likelihood, yes. But it is not a certainty. Until you have prescribed for a patient more than once you cannot tell their reaction to different drugs. There is, sometimes, a considerable period before a sedative takes effect. It depends on the personal idiosyncrasy of the patient towards that particular drug.'

Lombard said:

'Of course you *would* say that, doctor. Suits your book – eh?'

Again Armstrong's face darkened with anger.

But again that passionless cold little voice stopped the words on his lips.

'No good result can come from recrimination. Facts are what we have to deal with. It is established, I think, that there is a possibility of such a thing as I have outlined occurring. I agree that its probability value is not high; though there again, it depends on who that person might have been. The appearance of Miss Brent or of Miss Claythorne on such an errand would have occasioned no surprise in the patient's mind. I agree that the appearance of myself, or of Mr Blore, or of Mr Lombard would have been, to say the least of it, unusual, but I still think the visit would have been received without the awakening of any real suspicion.'

Blore said:

'And that gets us – *where*?'

VII

Mr Justice Wargrave, stroking his lip and looking quite passionless and inhuman, said:

'We have now dealt with the second killing, and have established the fact that no one of us can be completely exonerated from suspicion.'

He paused and went on.

'We come now to the death of General Macarthur. That took place this morning. I will ask anyone who considers that he or she has an alibi to state it in so many words. I myself will state at once that I have no valid alibi. I spent the morning sitting on the terrace and meditating on the singular position in which we all find ourselves.

'I sat on that chair on the terrace for the whole morning until the gong went, but there were, I should imagine, several periods during the morning when I was quite unobserved and during which it would have been possible for me to walk down to the sea, kill the General, and return to my chair. There is only my word for the fact that I never left the terrace. In the circumstances that is not enough. There must be *proof*.'

Blore said:

'I was with Mr Lombard and Dr Armstrong all the morning. They'll bear me out.'

Dr Armstrong said:

'You went to the house for a rope.'

Blore said:

'Of course, I did. Went straight there and straight back. You know I did.'

Armstrong said:

'You were a long time . . .'

Blore turned crimson. He said:

'What the hell do you mean by that, Dr Armstrong?'

Armstrong repeated:

'I only said you were a long time.'

'Had to find it, didn't I? Can't lay your hands on a coil of rope all in a minute.'

Mr Justice Wargrave said:

'During Inspector Blore's absence, were you two gentlemen together?'

Armstrong said hotly:

'Certainly. That is, Lombard went off for a few minutes. I remained where I was.'

Lombard said with a smile:

'I wanted to test the possibilities of heliographing to the mainland. Wanted to find the best spot. I was only absent a minute or two.'

Armstrong nodded. He said:

'That's right. Not long enough to do a murder, I assure you.'

The judge said:

'Did either of you two glance at your watches?'

'Well, no.'

Philip Lombard said:

'I wasn't wearing one.'

The judge said evenly:

'A minute or two is a vague expression.'

He turned his head to the upright figure with the knitting lying on her lap.

'Miss Brent?'

Emily Brent said:

'I took a walk with Miss Claythorne up to the top of the island. Afterwards I sat on the terrace in the sun.'

The judge said:

'I don't think I noticed you there.'

'No, I was round the corner of the house to the east. It was out of the wind there.'

'And you sat there till lunch-time?'

'Yes.'

'Miss Claythorne?'

Vera answered readily and clearly:

'I was with Miss Brent early this morning. After that I wandered about a bit. Then I went down and talked to General Macarthur.'

Mr Justice Wargrave interrupted. He said:

'What time was that?'

Vera for the first time was vague. She said:

'I don't know. About an hour before lunch, I think – or it might have been less.'

Blore asked:

'Was it after we'd spoken to him or before?'

Vera said:

'I don't know. He – he was very queer.'

She shivered.

'In what way was he queer?' the judge wanted to know.

Vera said in a low voice:

'He said we were all going to die – he said he was waiting for the end. He – he frightened me . . .'

The judge nodded. He said:

'What did you do next?'

'I went back to the house. Then, just before lunch, I went out again and up behind the house. I've been terribly restless all day.'

Mr Justice Wargrave stroked his chin. He said:

'There remains Rogers. Though I doubt if his evidence will add anything to our sum of knowledge.'

Rogers, summoned before the court, had very little to tell. He had been busy all the morning about household duties and with the preparation of lunch. He had taken cocktails on to the terrace before lunch and had then gone up to remove his things from the attic to another room. He had not looked out of the window during the morning and had seen nothing that could have any bearing upon the death of General Macarthur. He would swear definitely that there had been eight china figures upon the dining-table when he laid the table for lunch.

At the conclusion of Rogers' evidence there was a pause.

Mr Justice Wargrave cleared his throat.

Lombard murmured to Vera Claythorne:

'The summing up will now take place!'

The judge said:

'We have inquired into the circumstances of these three deaths to the best of our ability. Whilst probability in some cases is against certain people being implicated, yet we cannot say definitely that any one person can be considered as cleared of all complicity. I reiterate my positive belief that of the seven persons assembled in this room one is a dangerous and probably insane criminal. There is no evidence before us as to who that person is. All we can do at the present juncture is to consider what measures we can take for communicating with the mainland for help, and in the event of help being delayed (as is only too possible given the state of the weather) what measures we must adopt to ensure our safety.

'I would ask you all to consider this carefully and to give me any suggestions that may occur to you. In the meantime I warn everybody to be upon his or her guard. So far the murderer has had an easy task, since his victims have been unsuspicious. From now on, it is our task to suspect each and every one amongst us. Forewarned is forearmed. Take no risks and be alert to danger. That is all.'

Philip Lombard murmured beneath his breath:

'The court will now adjourn . . .'

CHAPTER 10

I

'Do you believe it?' Vera asked.

She and Philip Lombard sat on the window-sill of the living-room. Outside the rain poured down and the wind howled in great shuddering gusts against the window-panes.

Philip Lombard cocked his head slightly on one side before answering. Then he said:

'You mean, do I believe that old Wargrave is right when he says it's one of us?'

'Yes.'

Philip Lombard said slowly:

'It's difficult to say. Logically, you know, he's right, and yet –'

Vera took the words out of his mouth.

'And yet it seems so incredible!'

Philip Lombard made a grimace.

'The whole thing's incredible! But after Macarthur's death there's no more doubt as to one thing. There's no question now of accidents or suicides. It's definitely murder. Three murders up to date.'

Vera shivered. She said:

'It's like some awful dream. I keep feeling that things like this *can't* happen!'

He said with understanding:

'I know. Presently a tap will come on the door, and early morning tea will be brought in.'

Vera said:

'Oh, how I wish that could happen!'

Philip Lombard said gravely:

'Yes, but it won't! We're all in the dream! And we've got to be pretty much upon our guard from now on.'

Vera said, lowering her voice:

'If – if it *is* one of them – which do you think it is?'

Philip Lombard grinned suddenly. He said:

'I take it you are excepting our two selves? Well, that's all right. I know very well that I'm not the murderer, and I don't fancy that there's anything insane about you, Vera. You strike me as being one of the sanest and most level-headed girls I've come across. I'd stake my reputation on your sanity.'

With a slightly wry smile, Vera said:

'Thank you.'

He said: 'Come now, Miss Vera Claythorne, aren't you going to return the compliment?'

Vera hesitated a minute, then she said:

'You've admitted, you know, that you don't hold human life particularly sacred, but all the same I can't see you as – as the man who dictated that gramophone record.'

Lombard said:

'Quite right. If I were to commit one or more murders it would be solely for what I could get out of them. This mass clearance isn't my line of country. Good, then we'll eliminate ourselves and concentrate on our five fellow prisoners. Which of them is U. N.

Owen. Well, at a guess, and with absolutely nothing to go upon, I'd plump for Wargrave!'

'Oh!' Vera sounded surprised. She thought a minute or two and then said, 'Why?'

'Hard to say exactly. But to begin with, he's an old man and he's been presiding over courts of law for years. That is to say, he's played God Almighty for a good many months every year. That must go to a man's head eventually. He gets to see himself as all powerful, as holding the power of life and death – and it's possible that his brain might snap and he might want to go one step farther and be Executioner and Judge Extraordinary.'

Vera said slowly:

'Yes, I suppose that's *possible* . . .'

Lombard said:

'Who do you plump for?'

Without any hesitation Vera answered:

'Dr Armstrong.'

Lombard gave a low whistle.

'The doctor, eh? You know, I should have put him last of all.'

Vera shook her head.

'Oh no! Two of the deaths have been poison. That rather points to a doctor. And then you can't get over the fact that the only thing we are absolutely certain Mrs Rogers had was the sleeping draught that *he* gave her.'

Lombard admitted:

'Yes, that's true.'

Vera persisted:

'If a doctor went mad, it would be a long time before any one suspected. And doctors overwork and have a lot of strain.'

Philip Lombard said:

'Yes, but I doubt if he could have killed Macarthur. He wouldn't have had time during that brief interval when I left him – not, that is, unless he fairly hared down there and back again, and I doubt if he's in good enough training to do that and show no signs of it.'

Vera said:

'He didn't do it then. He had an opportunity later.'

'When?'

'When he went down to call the General to lunch.'

Philip whistled again very softly. He said:

'So you think he did it then? Pretty cool thing to do.'

Vera said impatiently:

'What risk was there? He's the only person here with medical knowledge. He can swear the body's been dead at least an hour and who's to contradict him?'

Philip looked at her thoughtfully.

'You know,' he said, 'that's a clever idea of yours. I wonder –'

II

'Who is it, Mr Blore? That's what I want to know. Who is it?'

Rogers' face was working. His hands were clenched round the polishing leather that he held in his hand.

Ex-Inspector Blore said:

'Eh, my lad, that's the question!'

'One of us, 'is lordship said. Which one? That's what I want to know. Who's the fiend in 'uman form?'

'That,' said Blore, 'is what we all would like to know.'

Rogers said shrewdly:

'But you've got an idea, Mr Blore. You've got an idea, 'aven't you?'

'I may have an idea,' said Blore slowly. 'But that's a long way from being sure. I may be wrong. All I can say is that if I'm right the person in question is a very cool customer – a very cool customer indeed.'

Rogers wiped the perspiration from his forehead. He said hoarsely:

'It's like a bad dream, that's what it is.'

Blore said, looking at him curiously:

'Got any ideas yourself, Rogers?'

The butler shook his head. He said hoarsely:

'I don't know. I don't know at all. And that's what's frightening the life out of me. To have no idea . . .'

III

Dr Armstrong said violently:

'We must get out of here – we must – we must! At all costs!'

Mr Justice Wargrave looked thoughtfully out of the smoking-room window. He played with the cord of his eyeglasses. He said:

'I do not, of course, profess to be a weather prophet. But I should say that it is very unlikely that a boat could reach us – even if they knew of our plight – in under twenty-four hours – and even then only if the wind drops.'

Dr Armstrong dropped his head in his hands and groaned. He said:

'And in the meantime we may all be murdered in our beds?'

'I hope not,' said Mr Justice Wargrave. 'I intend to take every possible precaution against such a thing happening.'

It flashed across Dr Armstrong's mind that an old man like the judge was far more tenacious of life than a younger man would be. He had often marvelled at that fact in his professional career. Here was he, junior to the judge by perhaps twenty years, and yet with a vastly inferior sense of self-preservation.

Mr Justice Wargrave was thinking:

'Murdered in our beds! These doctors are all the same – they think in *clichés*. A thoroughly commonplace mind.'

The doctor said:

'There have been three victims already, remember.'

'Certainly. But you must remember that they were unprepared for the attack. We are forewarned.'

Dr Armstrong said bitterly:

'What can we do? Sooner or later –'

'I think,' said Mr Justice Wargrave, 'that there are several things we can do.'

Armstrong said:

'We've no idea, even, who it can be –'

The judge stroked his chin and murmured:

'Oh, you know, I wouldn't quite say that.'

Armstrong stared at him.

'Do you mean you *know*?'

Mr Justice Wargrave said cautiously:

'As regards actual evidence, such as is necessary in court, I admit that I have none. But it appears to me, reviewing the whole business, that one particular person is sufficiently clearly indicated. Yes, I think so.'

Armstrong stared at him.

He said:

'I don't understand.'

IV

Miss Brent was upstairs in her bedroom.

She took up her Bible and went to sit by the window.

She opened it. Then, after a minute's hesitation, she set it aside and went over to the dressing-table. From a drawer in it she took out a small black-covered notebook.

She opened it and began writing.

'A terrible thing has happened. General Macarthur is dead. (His cousin married Elsie MacPherson.) There is no doubt but that he was murdered. After luncheon the judge made us a most interesting speech. He is convinced that the murderer is one of us. That means that one of us is possessed by a devil. I had already suspected that. Which of us is it? They are all asking themselves that. I alone know . . .'

She sat for some time without moving. Her eyes grew vague and filmy. The pencil straggled drunkenly in her fingers. In shaking loose capitals she wrote:

THE MURDERER'S NAME IS BEATRICE TAYLOR . . .

Her eyes closed.

Suddenly, with a start, she awoke. She looked down at the notebook. With an angry exclamation she scored through the vague unevenly scrawled characters of the last sentence.

She said in a low voice:

'Did *I* write that? Did I? *I must be going mad . . .*'

V

The storm increased. The wind howled against the side of the house.

Everyone was in the living-room. They sat listlessly huddled together. And, surreptitiously, they watched each other.

When Rogers brought in the tea-tray, they all jumped. He said:

'Shall I draw the curtains? It would make it more cheerful like.'

Receiving an assent to this, the curtains were drawn and the lamps turned on. The room grew more cheerful. A little of the shadow lifted. Surely, by tomorrow, the storm would be over and someone would come – a boat would arrive . . .

Vera Claythorne said:

'Will you pour out tea, Miss Brent?'

The elder woman replied:

'No, you do it, dear. That teapot is so heavy. And I have lost two skeins of my grey knitting-wool. So annoying.'

Vera moved to the tea-table. There was a cheerful rattle and clink of china. Normality returned.

Tea! Bless ordinary everyday afternoon tea! Philip Lombard made a cheery remark. Blore responded. Dr Armstrong told a humorous story. Mr Justice Wargrave, who ordinarily hated tea, sipped approvingly.

Into this relaxed atmosphere came Rogers.

And Rogers was upset. He said nervously and at random:

'Excuse me, sir, but does any one know what's become of the bathroom curtain?'

Lombard's head went up with a jerk.

'The bathroom curtain? What the devil do you mean, Rogers?'

'It's gone, sir, clean vanished. I was going round drawing all the curtains and the one in the lav – bathroom wasn't there any longer.'

Mr Justice Wargrave asked:

'Was it there this morning?'

'Oh yes, sir.'

Blore said:

'What kind of a curtain was it?'

'Scarlet oilsilk, sir. It went with the scarlet tiles.'

Lombard said:

'And it's gone?'

'Gone, sir.'

They stared at each other.

Blore said heavily:

'Well – after all – what of it? It's mad – but so's everything else. Anyway it doesn't matter. You can't kill anybody with an oilsilk curtain. Forget about it.'

Rogers said:

'Yes, sir, thank you, sir.'

He went out shutting the door behind him.

Inside the room, the pall of fear had fallen anew.

Again, surreptitiously, they watched each other.

VI

Dinner came, was eaten, and cleared away. A simple meal, mostly out of tins.

Afterwards, in the living-room, the strain was almost too great to be borne.

At nine o'clock, Emily Brent rose to her feet.

She said:

'I'm going to bed.'

Vera said:

'I'll go to bed too.'

The two women went up the stairs and Lombard and Blore came with them. Standing at the top of the stairs, the two men watched the women go into their respective rooms and shut the doors. They heard the sound of two bolts being shot and the turning of two keys.

Blore said with a grin:

'No need to tell 'em to lock their doors!'

Lombard said:

'Well, *they*'re all right for the night, at any rate!'

He went down again and the other followed him.

VII

The four men went to bed an hour later. They went up together. Rogers, from the dining-room where he was setting the table for breakfast, saw them go up. He heard them pause on the landing above.

Then the judge's voice spoke.

'I need hardly advise you, gentlemen, to lock your doors.'

Blore said:

'And what's more, put a chair under the handle. There are ways of turning locks from the outside.'

Lombard murmured:

'My dear Blore, the trouble with you is you know too much!'

The judge said gravely:

'Good night, gentlemen. May we all meet safely in the morning!'

Rogers came out of the dining-room and slipped half-way up the stairs. He saw four figures pass through four doors and heard the turning of four locks and the shooting of four bolts.

He nodded his head.

'That's all right,' he muttered.

He went back into the dining-room. Yes, everything was ready for the morning. His eye lingered on the centre plaque of looking-glass and the seven little china figures.

A sudden grin transformed his face.

He murmured:

'I'll see no one plays tricks tonight, at any rate.'

Crossing the room he locked the door to the pantry. Then going through the other door to the hall he pulled the door to, locked it and slipped the key into his pocket.

Then, extinguishing the lights, he hurried up the stairs and into his new bedroom.

There was only one possible hiding-place in it, the tall wardrobe, and he looked into that immediately. Then, locking and bolting the door, he prepared for bed.

He said to himself:

'No more china-soldier tricks tonight. I've seen to that . . .'

CHAPTER 11

I

Philip Lombard had the habit of waking at daybreak. He did so on this particular morning. He raised himself on an elbow and listened. The wind had somewhat abated but was still blowing. He could hear no sound of rain . . .

At eight o'clock the wind was blowing more strongly, but Lombard did not hear it. He was asleep again.

At nine-thirty he was sitting on the edge of his bed looking at his watch. He put it to his ear. Then his lips drew back from his teeth in that curious wolf-like smile characteristic of the man.

He said very softly:

'I think the time has come to do something about this.'

At twenty-five minutes to ten he was tapping on the closed door of Blore's room.

The latter opened it cautiously. His hair was tousled and his eyes were still dim with sleep.

Philip Lombard said affably:

'Sleeping the clock round? Well, shows you've got an easy conscience.'

Blore said shortly:

'What's the matter?'

Lombard answered:

'Anybody called you – or brought you any tea? Do you know what time it is?'

Blore looked over his shoulder at a small travelling clock by his bedside.

He said:

'Twenty-five to ten. Wouldn't have believed I could have slept like that. Where's Rogers?'

Philip Lombard said:

'It's a case of echo answers where.'

'What d'you mean?' asked the other sharply.

Lombard said:

'I mean that Rogers is missing. He isn't in his room or anywhere else. And there's no kettle on and the kitchen fire isn't even lit.'

Blore swore under his breath. He said:

'Where the devil can he be? Out on the island somewhere? Wait till I get some clothes on. See if the others know anything.'

Philip Lombard nodded. He moved along the line of closed doors.

He found Armstrong up and nearly dressed. Mr Justice Wargrave, like Blore, had to be roused from sleep. Vera Claythorne was dressed. Emily Brent's room was empty.

The little party moved through the house. Rogers' room, as Philip Lombard had already ascertained, was untenanted. The bed had been slept in, and his razor and sponge and soap were wet.

Lombard said:

'He got up all right.'

Vera said in a low voice which she tried to make firm and assured:

'You don't think he's – hiding somewhere – waiting for us?'

Lombard said:

'My dear girl, I'm prepared to think anything of anyone! My advice is that we keep together until we find him.'

Armstrong said:

'He must be out on the island somewhere.'

Blore, who had joined them, dressed, but still unshaved, said:

'Where's Miss Brent got to – that's another mystery?'

But as they arrived in the hall, Emily Brent came in through the front door. She had on a mackintosh. She said:

'The sea is as high as ever. I shouldn't think any boat could put out today.'

Blore said:

'Have you been wandering about the island alone, Miss Brent? Don't you realize that that's an exceedingly foolish thing to do?'

Emily Brent said:

'I assure you, Mr Blore, that I kept an extremely sharp look out.'

Blore grunted. He said:

'Seen anything of Rogers?'

Miss Brent's eyebrows rose.

'Rogers? No, I haven't seen him this morning. Why?'

Mr Justice Wargrave, shaved, dressed and with his false teeth in position, came down the stairs. He moved to the open dining-room door. He said:

'Ha, laid the table for breakfast, I see.'

Lombard said:

'He might have done that last night.'

They all moved inside the room, looking at the neatly set plates and cutlery. At the row of cups on the sideboard. At the felt mats placed ready for the coffee urn.

It was Vera who saw it first. She caught the judge's arm and the grip of her athletic fingers made the old gentleman wince.

She cried out:

'The soldiers! Look!'

There were only six china figures in the middle of the table.

II

They found him shortly afterwards.

He was in the little wash-house across the yard. He had been chopping sticks in preparation for lighting the kitchen fire. The small chopper was still in his hand. A bigger chopper, a heavy affair, was leaning against the door – the metal of it stained a dull brown. It corresponded only too well with the deep wound in the back of Rogers' head . . .

III

'Perfectly clear,' said Armstrong. 'The murderer must have crept up behind him, swung the chopper once and brought it down on his head as he was bending over.'

Blore was busy on the handle of the chopper and the flour sifter from the kitchen.

Mr Justice Wargrave asked:

'Would it have needed great force, doctor?'

Armstrong said gravely:

'A woman could have done it if that's what you mean.' He gave a quick glance round. Vera Claythorne and Emily Brent had retired to the kitchen. 'The girl could have done it easily – she's an athletic type. In appearance Miss Brent is fragile-looking, but that type of woman has often a lot of wiry strength. And you must remember that anyone who's mentally unhinged has a good deal of unsuspected strength.'

The judge nodded thoughtfully.

Blore rose to his knees with a sigh. He said:

'No fingerprints. Handle was wiped afterwards.'

A sound of laughter was heard – they turned sharply. Vera Claythorne was standing in the yard. She cried out in a high shrill voice, shaken with wild bursts of laughter:

'Do they keep bees on this island? Tell me that. Where do we go for honey? Ha! ha!'

They stared at her uncomprehendingly. It was as though the sane well-balanced girl had gone mad before their eyes. She went on in that high unnatural voice:

'Don't stare like that! As though you thought I was mad. It's sane enough what I'm asking. Bees, hives, bees! Oh, don't you understand? Haven't you read that idiotic rhyme? It's up in all your bedrooms – put there for you to study! We might have come here straightaway if we'd had sense. *Seven little soldier boys chopping up sticks*. And the next verse. I know the whole thing by heart, I tell you! *Six little soldier boys playing with a hive*. And that's why I'm asking – do they keep bees on this island? – isn't it funny? – isn't it damned funny . . . ?'

She began laughing wildly again. Dr Armstrong strode forward. He raised his hand and struck her a flat blow on the cheek.

She gasped, hiccupped – and swallowed. She stood motionless a minute, then she said:

'Thank you . . . I'm all right now.'

Her voice was once more calm and controlled – the voice of the efficient games mistress.

She turned and went across the yard into the kitchen saying: 'Miss Brent and I are getting you breakfast. Can you – bring some sticks to light the fire?'

The marks of the doctor's hand stood out red on her cheek.

As she went into the kitchen Blore said:

'Well, you dealt with that all right, doctor.'

Armstrong said apologetically:

'Had to! We can't cope with hysteria on the top of everything else.'

Philip Lombard said:

'She's not a hysterical type.'

Armstrong agreed.

'Oh no. Good healthy sensible girl. Just the sudden shock. It might happen to anybody.'

Rogers had chopped a certain amount of firewood before he had been killed. They gathered it up and took it into the kitchen. Vera and Emily Brent were busy, Miss Brent was raking out the stove. Vera was cutting the rind off the bacon.

Emily Brent said:

'Thank you. We'll be as quick as we can – say half an hour to three-quarters. The kettle's got to boil.'

IV

Ex-Inspector Blore said in a low hoarse voice to Philip Lombard:

'Know what I'm thinking?'

Philip Lombard said:

'As you're just about to tell me, it's not worth the trouble of guessing.'

Ex-Inspector Blore was an earnest man. A light touch was incomprehensible to him. He went on heavily:

'There was a case in America. Old gentleman and his wife – both killed with an axe. Middle of the morning. Nobody in the house but the daughter and the maid. Maid, it was proved, couldn't have done it. Daughter was a respectable middle-aged spinster. Seemed incredible. So incredible that they acquitted her. But they never found any other explanation.' He paused. 'I thought of that when I saw the axe – and then when I went into the kitchen and saw her there so neat and calm. Hadn't turned a hair! That girl, coming all over hysterical – well, that's natural – the sort of thing you'd expect – don't you think so?'

Philip Lombard said laconically:

'It might be.'

Blore went on.

'But the other! So neat and prim – wrapped up in that apron – Mrs Rogers' apron, I suppose – saying: "Breakfast will be ready in half an hour or so." If you ask me that woman's as mad as a hatter! Lots of elderly spinsters go that way – I don't mean go in for homicide on the grand scale, but go queer in their heads. Unfortunately it's taken her this way. Religious mania – thinks she's God's instrument, something of that kind! She sits in her room, you know, reading her Bible.'

Philip Lombard sighed and said:

'That's hardly proof positive of an unbalanced mentality, Blore.'

But Blore went on, ploddingly, perseveringly:

'And then she was out – in her mackintosh, said she'd been down to look at the sea.'

The other shook his head.

He said:

'Rogers was killed as he was chopping firewood – that is to say first thing when he got up. The Brent wouldn't have needed to wander about outside for hours afterwards. If you ask me, the murderer of Rogers would take jolly good care to be rolled up in bed snoring.'

Blore said:

'You're missing the point, Mr Lombard. If the woman was innocent she'd be too dead scared to go wandering about by herself. She'd only do that *if she knew that she had nothing to fear.* That's to say *if she herself is the criminal.*'

Philip Lombard said:

'That's a good point . . . yes, I hadn't thought of that.'

He added with a faint grin:

'Glad you don't still suspect me.'

Blore said rather shamefacedly:

'I did start by thinking of you – that revolver – and the queer story you told – or didn't tell. But I've realized now that that was really a bit too obvious.' He paused and said: 'Hope you feel the same about me.'

Philip said thoughtfully:

'I may be wrong, of course, but I can't feel that you've got enough imagination for this job. All I can say is, if you're the criminal, you're a damned fine actor and I take my hat off to you.' He lowered his voice. 'Just between ourselves, Blore, and taking into account that we'll probably both be a couple of stiffs before another day is out, you did indulge in that spot of perjury, I suppose?'

Blore shifted uneasily from one foot to the other. He said at last:

'Doesn't seem to make much odds now. Oh well, here goes, Landor was innocent right enough. The gang had got me squared and between us we got him put away for a stretch. Mind you, I wouldn't admit this –'

'If there were any witnesses,' finished Lombard with a grin. 'It's just between you and me. Well, I hope you made a tidy bit out of it.'

'Didn't make what I should have done. Mean crowd, the Purcell gang. I got my promotion, though.'

'And Landor got penal servitude and died in prison.'

'I couldn't know he was going to die, could I?' demanded Blore.

'No, that was your bad luck.'

'Mine? His, you mean.'

'Yours, too. Because, as a result of it, it looks as though your own life is going to be cut unpleasantly short.'

'Me?' Blore stared at him. 'Do you think I'm going to go the way of Rogers and the rest of them? Not me! I'm watching out for myself pretty carefully, I can tell you.'

Lombard said:

'Oh well – I'm not a betting man. And anyway if you were dead I wouldn't get paid.'

'Look here, Mr Lombard, what do you mean?'

Philip Lombard showed his teeth. He said:

'I mean, my dear Blore, that in my opinion you haven't got a chance!'

'What?'

'Your lack of imagination is going to make you absolutely a sitting target. A criminal of the imagination of U. N. Owen can make rings round you any time he – or she – wants to.'

Blore's face went crimson. He demanded angrily:

'And what about you?'

Philip Lombard's face went hard and dangerous.

He said:

'I've a pretty good imagination of my own. I've been in tight places before now and got out of them! I think – I won't say more than that but I *think* I'll get out of this one.'

V

The eggs were in the frying-pan. Vera, toasting bread, thought to herself:

'Why did I make a hysterical fool of myself? That was a mistake. Keep calm, my girl, keep calm.'

After all, she'd always prided herself on her level-headedness!

'Miss Claythorne was wonderful – kept her head – started off swimming after Cyril at once.'

Why think of that now? All that was over – over . . . Cyril had disappeared long before she got near the rock. She had felt the current take her, sweeping her out to sea. She had let herself go with it – swimming quietly, floating – till the boat arrived at last . . .

They had praised her courage and her *sang-froid* . . .

But not Hugo. Hugo had just – looked at her . . .

God, how it hurt, even now, to think of Hugo . . .

Where was he? What was he doing? Was he engaged – married?

Emily Brent said sharply:

'Vera, that toast is burning.'

'Oh sorry, Miss Brent, so it is. How stupid of me.'

Emily Brent lifted out the last egg from the sizzling fat.

Vera, putting a fresh piece of bread on the toasting fork, said curiously:

'You're wonderfully calm, Miss Brent.'

Emily Brent said, pressing her lips together:

'I was brought up to keep my head and never to make a fuss.'

Vera thought mechanically:

'Repressed as a child . . . That accounts for a lot . . .'

She said:

'Aren't you afraid?'

She paused and then added:

'Or don't you mind dying?'

Dying! It was as though a sharp little gimlet had run into the solid congealed mess of Emily Brent's brain. Dying? But *she* wasn't going to die! The others would die – yes – but not she, Emily Brent. This girl didn't understand! Emily wasn't afraid, naturally – none of the Brents were afraid. All her people were

Service people. They faced death unflinchingly. They led upright lives just as she, Emily Brent, had led an upright life . . . She had never done anything to be ashamed of . . . And so, naturally, *she* wasn't going to die . . .

'*The Lord is mindful of his own.*' '*Thou shalt not be afraid for the terror by night; nor for the arrow that flieth by day . . .*' It was daylight now – there was no terror. '*We shall none of us leave this island.*' Who had said that? General Macarthur, of course, whose cousin had married Elsie MacPherson. He hadn't seemed to *care*. He had seemed – actually – to *welcome* the idea! Wicked! Almost impious to feel that way. Some people thought so little of death that they actually took their own lives. *Beatrice Taylor* . . . Last night she had dreamed of Beatrice – dreamt that she was outside pressing her face against the window and moaning, asking to be let in. But Emily Brent hadn't wanted to let her in. Because, if she did, something terrible would happen . . .

Emily came to herself with a start. That girl was looking at her very strangely. She said in a brisk voice:

'Everything's ready, isn't it? We'll take the breakfast in.'

VI

Breakfast was a curious meal. Every one was very polite.

'May I get you some more coffee, Miss Brent?'

'Miss Claythorne, a slice of ham?'

'Another piece of toast?'

Six people, all outwardly self-possessed and normal.

And within? Thoughts that ran round in a circle like squirrels in a cage . . .

'*What next? What next? Who? Which?*'

'*Would it work? I wonder. It's worth trying. If there's time. My God, if there's time . . .*'

'*Religious mania, that's the ticket . . . Looking at her, though, you can hardly believe it . . . Suppose I'm wrong . . .*'

'*It's crazy – everything's crazy. I'm going crazy. Wool disappearing – red silk curtains – it doesn't make sense. I can't get the hang of it . . .*'

'*The damned fool, he believed every word I said to him. It was easy . . . I must be careful, though, very careful.*'

'Six of those little china figures . . . only six – how many will there be by tonight? . . .'

'Who'll have the last egg?'

'Marmalade?'

'Thanks, can I cut you some bread?'

Six people, behaving normally at breakfast . . .

CHAPTER 12

I

The meal was over.

Mr Justice Wargrave cleared his throat. He said in a small authoritative voice:

'It would be advisable, I think, if we met to discuss the situation. Shall we say in half an hour's time in the drawing-room?'

Every one made a sound suggestive of agreement.

Vera began to pile plates together.

She said:

'I'll clear away and wash up.'

Philip Lombard said:

'We'll bring the stuff out to the pantry for you.'

'Thanks.'

Emily Brent, rising to her feet sat down again. She said:

'Oh dear.'

The judge said:

'Anything the matter, Miss Brent?'

Emily said apologetically:

'I'm sorry. I'd like to help Miss Claythorne, but I don't know how it is. I feel just a little giddy.'

'Giddy, eh?' Dr Armstrong came towards her. 'Quite natural. Delayed shock. I can give you something to –'

'No!'

The word burst from her lips like an exploding shell.

It took every one aback. Dr Armstrong flushed a deep red.

There was no mistaking the fear and suspicion in her face. He said stiffly:

'Just as you please, Miss Brent.'

She said:

'I don't wish to take anything – anything at all. I will just sit here quietly till the giddiness passes off.'

They finished clearing away the breakfast things.

Blore said:

'I'm a domestic sort of man. I'll give you a hand, Miss Claythorne.'

Vera said: 'Thank you.'

Emily Brent was left alone sitting in the dining-room.

For a while she heard a faint murmur of voices from the pantry.

The giddiness was passing. She felt drowsy now, as though she could easily go to sleep.

There was a buzzing in her ears – or was it a real buzzing in the room?

She thought:

'It's like a bee – a bumble bee.'

Presently she saw the bee. It was crawling up the window-pane.

Vera Claythorne had talked about bees this morning.

Bees and honey . . .

She liked honey. Honey in the comb, and strain it yourself through a muslin bag. Drip, drip, drip . . .

There was somebody in the room . . . somebody all wet and dripping . . . *Beatrice Taylor come from the river* . . .

She had only to turn her head and she would see her.

But she couldn't turn her head . . .

If she were to call out . . .

But she couldn't call out . . .

There was no one else in the house. She was all alone . . .

She heard footsteps – soft dragging footsteps coming up behind her. The stumbling footsteps of the drowned girl . . .

There was a wet dank smell in her nostrils . . .

On the window-pane the bee was buzzing – buzzing . . .

And then she felt the prick.

The bee sting on the side of her neck . . .

II

In the drawing-room they were waiting for Emily Brent.

Vera Claythorne said:

'Shall I go and fetch her?'

Blore said quickly:

'Just a minute.'

Vera sat down again. Every one looked inquiringly at Blore. He said:

'Look here, everybody, my opinion's this: we needn't look farther for the author of these deaths than the dining-room at this minute. I'd take my oath that woman's the one we're after!'

Armstrong said:

'And the motive?'

'Religious mania. What do you say, doctor?'

Armstrong said:

'It's perfectly possible. I've nothing to say against it. But of course we've no proof.'

Vera said:

'She was very odd in the kitchen when we were getting breakfast. Her eyes –' She shivered.

Lombard said:

'You can't judge her by that. We're all a bit off our heads by now!'

Blore said:

'There's another thing. She's the only one who wouldn't give an explanation after that gramophone record. Why? Because she hadn't any to give.'

Vera stirred in her chair. She said:

'That's not quite true. She told me – afterwards.'

Wargrave said:

'What did she tell you, Miss Claythorne?'

Vera repeated the story of Beatrice Taylor.

Mr Justice Wargrave observed:

'A perfectly straightforward story. I personally should have no difficulty in accepting it. Tell me, Miss Claythorne, did she appear to be troubled by a sense of guilt or a feeling of remorse for her attitude in the matter?'

'None whatever,' said Vera. 'She was completely unmoved.'

Blore said:

'Hearts as hard as flints, these righteous spinsters! Envy, mostly!'

Mr Justice Wargrave said:

'It is now five minutes to eleven. I think we should summon Miss Brent to join our conclave.'

Blore said:

'Aren't you going to take any action?'

The judge said:

'I fail to see what action we can take. Our suspicions are, at the moment, only suspicions. I will, however, ask Dr Armstrong to observe Miss Brent's demeanour very carefully. Let us now go into the dining-room.'

They found Emily Brent sitting in the chair in which they had left her. From behind they saw nothing amiss, except that she did not seem to hear their entrance into the room.

And then they saw her face – suffused with blood, with blue lips and starting eyes.

Blore said:

'My God, she's dead!'

III

The small quiet voice of Mr Justice Wargrave said:

'One more of us acquitted – too late!'

Armstrong was bent over the dead woman. He sniffed the lips, shook his head, peered into the eyelids.

Lombard said impatiently:

'How did she die, doctor? She was all right when we left her here!'

Armstrong's attention was riveted on a mark on the right side of the neck.

He said:

'That's the mark of a hypodermic syringe.'

There was a buzzing sound from the window. Vera cried:

'Look – a bee – *a bumble bee*. Remember what I said this morning!'

Armstrong said grimly:

'It wasn't that bee that stung her! A human hand held the syringe.'

The judge asked:

'What poison was injected?'

Armstrong answered:

'At a guess, one of the cyanides. Probably potassium cyanide, same as Anthony Marston. She must have died almost immediately by asphyxiation.'

Vera cried:

'But that *bee*? It can't be *coincidence*?'

Lombard said grimly:

'Oh no, it isn't coincidence! It's our murderer's touch of local colour! He's a playful beast. Likes to stick to his damnable nursery jingle as closely as possible!'

For the first time his voice was uneven, almost shrill. It was as though even his nerves, seasoned by a long career of hazards and dangerous undertakings, had given out at last.

He said violently:

'It's mad! – absolutely mad – we're all mad!'

The judge said calmly:

'We have still, I hope, our reasoning powers. *Did any one bring a hypodermic syringe to this house?*'

Dr Armstrong, straightening himself, said in a voice that was not too well assured:

'Yes, I did.'

Four pairs of eyes fastened on him. He braced himself against the deep hostile suspicion of those eyes. He said:

'Always travel with one. Most doctors do.'

Mr Justice Wargrave said calmly:

'Quite so. Will you tell us, doctor, where that syringe is now?'

'In the suitcase in my room.'

Wargrave said:

'We might, perhaps, verify that fact.'

The five of them went upstairs, a silent procession.

The contents of the suitcase were turned out on the floor.

The hypodermic syringe was not there.

IV

Armstrong said violently:

'Somebody must have taken it!'

There was silence in the room.

Armstrong stood with his back to the window. Four pairs of eyes were on him, black with suspicion and accusation. He looked from Wargrave to Vera and repeated helplessly – weakly:

'I tell you someone must have taken it.'

Blore was looking at Lombard who returned his gaze.

The judge said:

'There are five of us here in this room. *One of us is a murderer.* The position is fraught with grave danger. Everything must be done in order to safeguard the four of us who are innocent. I will now ask you, Dr Armstrong, what drugs you have in your possession.'

Armstrong replied:

'I have a small medicine case here. You can examine it. You will find some sleeping stuff – trional and sulphonal tablets – a packet of bromide, bicarbonate of soda, aspirin. Nothing else. I have no cyanide in my possession.'

The judge said:

'I have, myself, some sleeping tablets – sulphonal, I think they are. I presume they would be lethal if a sufficiently large dose were given. You, Mr Lombard, have in your possession a revolver.'

Philip Lombard said sharply:

'What if I have?'

'Only this. I propose that the doctor's supply of drugs, my own sulphonal tablets, your revolver and anything else of the nature of drugs or firearms should be collected together and placed in a safe place. That after this is done, we should each of us submit to a search – both of our persons and of our effects.'

Lombard said:

'I'm damned if I'll give up my revolver!'

Wargrave said sharply:

'Mr Lombard, you are a very strongly built and powerful young man, but ex-Inspector Blore is also a man of powerful physique. I do not know what the outcome of a struggle between you would be but I can tell you this. On Blore's side, assisting him to the best of our ability will be myself, Dr Armstrong and Miss Claythorne. You will appreciate therefore, that the odds against you if you choose to resist will be somewhat heavy.'

Lombard threw his head back. His teeth showed in what was almost a snarl.

'Oh, very well, then. Since you've got it all taped out.'

Mr Justice Wargrave nodded his head.

'You are a sensible young man. Where is this revolver of yours?'

'In the drawer of the table by my bed.'

'Good.'

'I'll fetch it.'

'I think it would be desirable if we went with you.'

Philip said with a smile that was still nearer a snarl:

'Suspicious devil, aren't you?'

They went along the corridor to Lombard's room.

Philip strode across to the bed-table and jerked open the drawer.

Then he recoiled with an oath.

The drawer of the bed-table was empty.

V

'Satisfied?' asked Lombard.

He had stripped to the skin and he and his room had been meticulously searched by the other three men. Vera Claythorne was outside in the corridor.

The search proceeded methodically. In turn, Armstrong, the judge, and Blore submitted to the same test.

The four men emerged from Blore's room and approached Vera. It was the judge who spoke.

'I hope you will understand, Miss Claythorne, that we can make no exceptions. That revolver must be found. You have, I presume, a bathing dress with you?'

Vera nodded.

'Then I will ask you to go into your room and put it on and then come out to us here.'

Vera went into her room and shut the door. She reappeared in under a minute dressed in a tight-fitting silk rucked bathing dress.

Wargrave nodded approval.

'Thank you, Miss Claythorne. Now if you will remain here, we will search your room.'

Vera waited patiently in the corridor until they emerged. Then she went in, dressed, and came out to where they were waiting.

The judge said:

'We are now assured of one thing. There are no lethal weapons or drugs in the possession of any of us five. That is one point to the good. We will now place the drugs in a safe place. There is, I think, a silver chest, is there not, in the pantry?'

Blore said:

'That's all very well, but who's to have the key? You, I suppose.'

Mr Justice Wargrave made no reply.

He went down to the pantry and the others followed him. There was a small case there designed for the purpose of holding silver and plate. By the judge's directions, the various drugs were placed in this and it was locked. Then, still on Wargrave's instructions, the chest was lifted into the plate cupboard and this in turn was locked. The judge then gave the key of the chest to Philip Lombard and the key of the cupboard to Blore.

He said:

'You two are the strongest physically. It would be difficult for either of you to get the key from the other. It would be impossible for any of us three to do so. To break open the cupboard – or the plate chest – would be a noisy and cumbersome proceeding and one which could hardly be carried out without attention being attracted to what was going on.'

He paused, then went on:

'We are still faced by one very grave problem. *What has become of Mr Lombard's revolver?*'

Blore said:

'Seems to me its owner is the most likely person to know that.'

A white dint showed in Philip Lombard's nostrils. He said:

'You damned pig-headed fool! I tell you it's been stolen from me!'

Wargrave asked:

'When did you see it last?'

'Last night. It was in the drawer when I went to bed – ready in case anything happened.'

The judge nodded.

He said:

'It must have been taken this morning during the confusion of searching for Rogers or after his dead body was discovered.'

Vera said:

'It must be hidden somewhere about the house. We must look for it.'

Mr Justice Wargrave's finger was stroking his chin. He said:

'I doubt if our search will result in anything. Our murderer has had plenty of time to devise a hiding-place. I do not fancy we shall find that revolver easily.'

Blore said forcefully:

'I don't know where the revolver is, but I'll bet I know where something else is – that hypodermic syringe. Follow me.'

He opened the front door and led the way round the house.

A little distance away from the dining-room window he found the syringe. Beside it was a smashed china figure – a sixth broken soldier boy.

Blore said in a satisfied voice:

'Only place it could be. After he'd killed her, he opened the window and threw out the syringe and picked up the china figure from the table and followed on with that.'

There were no prints on the syringe. It had been carefully wiped.

Vera said in a determined voice:

'Now let us look for the revolver.'

Mr Justice Wargrave said:

'By all means. But in doing so let us be careful to keep together. Remember, if we separate, the murderer gets his chance.'

They searched the house carefully from attic to cellars, but without result. The revolver was still missing.

CHAPTER 13

I

'One of us . . . One of us . . . One of us . . .'

Three words, endlessly repeated, dinning themselves hour after hour into receptive brains.

Five people – five frightened people. Five people who watched each other, who now hardly troubled to hide their state of nervous tension.

There was little pretence now – no formal veneer of conversation. They were five enemies linked together by a mutual instinct of self-preservation.

And all of them, suddenly, looked less like human beings. They were reverting to more bestial types. Like a wary old tortoise, Mr Justice Wargrave sat hunched up, his body motionless, his eyes keen and alert. Ex-Inspector Blore looked coarser and clumsier in build. His walk was that of a slow padding animal. His eyes were bloodshot. There was a look of mingled ferocity and stupidity about him. He was like a beast at bay ready to charge its pursuers. Philip Lombard's senses seemed heightened, rather than diminished. His ears reacted to the slightest sound. His step was lighter and quicker, his body was lithe and graceful. And he smiled often, his lips curling back from his long white teeth.

Vera Claythorne was very quiet. She sat most of the time huddled in a chair. Her eyes stared ahead of her into space. She looked dazed. She was like a bird that has dashed its head against glass and that has been picked up by a human hand. It crouches there, terrified, unable to move, hoping to save itself by its immobility.

Armstrong was in a pitiable condition of nerves. He twitched and his hands shook. He lighted cigarette after cigarette and stubbed them out almost immediately. The forced inaction of their position seemed to gall him more than the others. Every now and then he broke out into a torrent of nervous speech.

'We – we shouldn't just sit here doing nothing! There must be *something* – surely, surely there is *something* that we can do? If we lit a bonfire –?'

Blore said heavily:

'In this weather?'

The rain was pouring down again. The wind came in fitful gusts. The depressing sound of the pattering rain nearly drove them mad.

By tacit consent, they had adopted a plan of campaign. They all sat in the big drawing-room. Only one person left the room at a time. The other four waited till the fifth returned.

Lombard said:

'It's only a question of time. The weather will clear. Then we can do something – signal – light fires – make a raft – something!'

Armstrong said with a sudden cackle of laughter:

'A question of time – *time*? We can't afford time! We shall all be dead . . .'

Mr Justice Wargrave said and his small clear voice was heavy with passionate determination:

'Not if we are careful. *We must be very careful . . .*'

The midday meal had been duly eaten – but there had been no conventional formality about it. All five of them had gone to the kitchen. In the larder they had found a great store of tinned foods. They had opened a tin of tongue and two tins of fruit. They had eaten standing round the kitchen table. Then, herding close together, they had returned to the drawing-room – to sit there – sit, watching each other.

And by now the thoughts that ran through their brains were abnormal, feverish, diseased . . .

'It's Armstrong . . . I saw him looking at me sideways just then . . . his eyes are mad . . . quite mad . . . Perhaps he isn't a doctor at all . . . That's it, of course! . . . He's a lunatic, escaped from some doctor's house – pretending to be a doctor . . . It's true . . . shall I tell them? . . . Shall I scream out? . . . No, it won't do to put him on his guard . . . Besides he can seem so sane . . . What time is it? . . . Only a quarter past three! . . . Oh, God, I shall go mad myself . . . *Yes, it's Armstrong* . . . He's watching me now . . .'

'They won't get *me*! *I* can take care of myself . . . I've been in tight places before . . . Where the hell is that revolver? . . . Who took it? . . . Who's got it? . . . Nobody's got it – we know that. We were all searched . . . Nobody *can* have it . . . *But someone knows where it is . . .*'

'They're going mad ... They'll all go mad ... Afraid of death ... we're all afraid of death ... *I*'m afraid of death ... Yes, but that doesn't stop death coming ... *"The hearse is at the door, sir."* Where did I read that? The girl ... I'll watch the girl. Yes, I'll watch the girl ...'

'Twenty to four ... only twenty to four ... perhaps the clock has stopped ... I don't understand – no, I don't understand ... This sort of thing can't happen ... *it is happening* ... Why don't we wake up? Wake up – Judgment Day – no, not that! If only I could think ... My head – something's happening in my head – it's going to burst – it's going to split ... This sort of thing can't happen ... What's the time? Oh, God, it's only a quarter to four.'

'I must keep my head ... I must keep my head ... If only I keep my head ... It's all perfectly clear – all worked out. But nobody must suspect. It may do the trick. It must! Which one? That's the question – which one? I think – yes, I rather think – yes – *him*.'

When the clock struck five they all jumped.

Vera said:

'Does anyone – want tea?'

There was a moment's silence. Blore said:

'I'd like a cup.'

Vera rose. She said:

'I'll go and make it. You can all stay here.'

Mr Justice Wargrave said gently:

'I think, my dear young lady, we would all prefer to come and watch you make it.'

Vera stared, then gave a short rather hysterical laugh.

She said:

'Of course! You would!'

Five people went into the kitchen. Tea was made and drunk by Vera and Blore. The other three had whisky – opening a fresh bottle and using a siphon from a nailed up case.

The judge murmured with a reptilian smile:

'We must be very careful ...'

They went back again to the drawing-room. Although it was summer the room was dark. Lombard switched on the lights but they did not come on. He said:

'Of course! The engine's not been run today since Rogers hasn't been there to see to it.'

He hesitated and said:

'We could go out and get it going, I suppose.'

Mr Justice Wargrave said:

'There are packets of candles in the larder, I saw them, better use those.'

Lombard went out. The other four sat watching each other.

He came back with a box of candles and a pile of saucers. Five candles were lit and placed about the room.

The time was a quarter to six.

II

At twenty past six, Vera felt that to sit there longer was unbearable. She would go to her room and bathe her aching head and temples in cold water.

She got up and went towards the door. Then she remembered and came back and got a candle out of the box. She lighted it, let a little wax pour into a saucer and stuck the candle firmly to it. Then she went out of the room, shutting the door behind her and leaving the four men inside. She went up the stairs and along the passage to her room.

As she opened her door, she suddenly halted and stood stock still.

Her nostrils quivered.

The sea . . . The smell of the sea at St Tredennick.

That was it. She could not be mistaken. Of course, one smelt the sea on an island anyway, but this was different. It was the smell there had been on the beach that day – with the tide out and the rocks covered with seaweed drying in the sun.

'Can I swim out to the island, Miss Claythorne?'

'Why can't I swim out to the island? . . .'

Horrid whiney spoilt little brat! If it weren't for him, Hugo would be rich . . . able to marry the girl he loved . . .

Hugo . . .

Surely – surely – Hugo was beside her? No, waiting for her in the room . . .

She made a step forward. The draught from the window caught the flame of the candle. It flickered and went out . . .

In the dark she was suddenly afraid . . .

'Don't be a fool,' Vera Claythone urged herself. 'It's all right. The others are downstairs. All four of them. There's no one in the room. There can't be. You're imagining things, my girl.'

But that smell – that smell of the beach at St Tredennick . . . That wasn't imagined. *It was true.*

And there *was* someone in the room . . . She had heard something – surely she had heard something . . .

And then, as she stood there, listening – a cold, clammy hand touched her throat – a wet hand, smelling of the sea . . .

III

Vera screamed. She screamed and screamed – screams of the utmost terror – wild desperate cries for help.

She did not hear the sounds from below, of a chair being overturned, of a door opening, of men's feet running up the stairs. She was conscious only of supreme terror.

Then, restoring her sanity, lights flickered in the doorway – candles – men hurrying into the room.

'What the devil?' 'What's happened?' 'Good God, what is it?'

She shuddered, took a step forward, collapsed on the floor.

She was only half aware of someone bending over her, of someone forcing her head down between her knees.

Then at a sudden exclamation, a quick 'My God, look at that!' her senses returned. She opened her eyes and raised her head. She saw what it was the men with the candles were looking at.

A broad ribbon of wet seaweed was hanging down from the ceiling. It was that which in the darkness had swayed against her throat. It was that which she had taken for a clammy hand, a drowned hand come back from the dead to squeeze the life out of her!

She began to laugh hysterically. She said:

'It was seaweed – only seaweed – and that's what the smell was . . .'

And then the faintness came over her once more – waves upon waves of sickness. Again someone took her head and forced it between her knees.

Aeons of time seemed to pass. They were offering her something to drink – pressing the glass against her lips. She smelt brandy.

She was just about to gulp the spirit gratefully down when, suddenly, a warning note – like an alarm bell – sounded in her brain. She sat up, pushing the glass away.

She said sharply: 'Where did this come from?'

Blore's voice answered. He stared a minute before speaking. He said:

'I got it from downstairs.'

Vera cried:

'I won't drink it . . .'

There was a moment's silence, then Lombard laughed.

He said with appreciation:

'Good for you, Vera. You've got your wits about you – even if you have been scared half out of your life. I'll get a fresh bottle that hasn't been opened.'

He went swiftly out.

Vera said uncertainly:

'I'm all right now. I'll have some water.'

Armstrong supported her as she struggled to her feet. She went over to the basin, swaying and clutching at him for support. She let the cold tap run and then filled the glass.

Blore said resentfully:

'That brandy's all right.'

Armstrong said:

'How do you know?'

Blore said angrily:

'I didn't put anything in it. That's what you're getting at I suppose.'

Armstrong said:

'I'm not saying you did. You might have done, or someone might have tampered with the bottle for just this emergency.'

Lombard came swiftly back into the room.

He had a new bottle of brandy in his hands and a corkscrew.

He thrust the sealed bottle under Vera's nose.

'There you are, my girl. Absolutely no deception.' He peeled off the tin foil and drew the cork. 'Lucky there's a good supply of spirits in the house. Thoughtful of U. N. Owen.'

Vera shuddered violently.

Armstrong held the glass while Philip poured the brandy into it. He said:

'You'd better drink this, Miss Claythorne. You've had a nasty shock.'

Vera drank a little of the spirit. The colour came back to her face.

Philip Lombard said with a laugh:

'Well, here's one murder that hasn't gone according to plan!'

Vera said almost in a whisper:

'You think – that was what was meant?'

Lombard nodded.

'Expected you to pass out through fright! Some people would have, wouldn't they, doctor?'

Armstrong did not commit himself. He said doubtfully:

'H'm, impossible to say. Young healthy subject – no cardiac weakness. Unlikely. On the other hand –'

He picked up the glass of brandy that Blore had brought. He dipped a finger in it, tasted it gingerly. His expression did not alter. He said dubiously: 'H'm, tastes all right.'

Blore stepped forward angrily. He said:

'If you're saying that I tampered with that, I'll knock your ruddy block off.'

Vera, her wits revived by the brandy, made a diversion by saying:

'Where's the judge?'

The three men looked at each other.

'*That's odd* . . . Thought he came up with us.'

Blore said:

'*So did I* . . . What about it, doctor, you came up the stairs behind me?'

Armstrong said:

'I thought he was following me . . . Of course, he'd be bound to go slower than we did. He's an old man.'

They looked at each other again.

Lombard said:

'It's damned odd . . .'

Blore cried:

'We must look for him.'

He started for the door. The others followed him, Vera last.

As they went down the stairs Armstrong said over his shoulder:

'Of course he *may* have stayed in the living-room.'

They crossed the hall. Armstrong called out loudly:

'Wargrave, Wargrave, where are you?'

There was no answer. A deadly silence filled the house apart from the gentle patter of the rain.

Then in the entrance to the drawing-room door, Armstrong stopped dead. The others crowded up and looked over his shoulder.

Somebody cried out.

Mr Justice Wargrave was sitting in his high-backed chair at the end of the room. Two candles burnt on either side of him. But what shocked and startled the onlookers was the fact that he sat there robed in scarlet with a judge's wig upon his head . . .

Dr Armstrong motioned to the others to keep back. He himself walked across to the silent staring figure, reeling a little as he walked like a drunken man.

He bent forward, peering into the still face. Then, with a swift movement he raised the wig. It fell to the floor revealing the high bald forehead with, in the very middle, a round stained mark from which something had trickled.

Dr Armstrong lifted the lifeless hand and felt for the pulse. Then he turned to the others.

He said – and his voice was expressionless, dead, far away . . .

'*He's been shot . . .*'

Blore said:

'God – *the revolver!*'

The doctor said, still in the same lifeless voice:

'Got him through the head. Instantaneous.'

Vera stooped to the wig. She said, and her voice shook with horror:

'*Miss Brent's missing grey wool . . .*'

Blore said:

'And the scarlet curtain that was missing from the bathroom . . .'

Vera whispered:

'So this is what they wanted them for . . .'

Suddenly Philip Lombard laughed – a high unnatural laugh.

'*Five little soldier boys going in for law; one got in Chancery and then there were Four.* That's the end of Mr Bloody Justice Wargrave. No more pronouncing sentence for him! No more putting on of the black cap! Here's the last time *he*'ll ever sit in court! No more summing up and sending innocent men to death. How Edward Seton would laugh if he were here! God, how he'd laugh!'

His outburst shocked and startled the others.

Vera cried:

'Only this morning you said *he* was the one!'

Philip Lombard's face changed – sobered.

He said in a low voice:

'I know I did . . . Well, I was wrong. Here's one more of us who's been proved innocent – *too late!*'

CHAPTER 14

I

They had carried Mr Justice Wargrave up to his room and laid him on the bed.

Then they had come down again and had stood in the hall looking at each other.

Blore said heavily:

'What do we do now?'

Lombard said briskly:

'Have something to eat. We've got to eat, you know.'

Once again they went into the kitchen. Again they opened a tin of tongue. They ate mechanically, almost without tasting.

Vera said:

'I shall never eat tongue again.'

They finished the meal. They sat round the kitchen table staring at each other.

Blore said:

'Only four of us now . . . *Who'll be the next?*'

Armstrong stared. He said, almost mechanically:

'We must be very careful –' and stopped.

Blore nodded.

'That's what *he* said . . . and now he's dead!'

Armstrong said:

'How did it happen, I wonder?'

Lombard swore. He said:

'A damned clever doublecross! That stuff was planted in Miss Claythorne's room and it worked just as it was intended to. Everyone dashes up there thinking *she*'s being murdered. And so – in the confusion – someone – caught the old boy off his guard.'

Blore said:

'Why didn't anyone hear the shot?'

Lombard shook his head.

'Miss Claythorne was screaming, the wind was howling, we were running about and calling out. No, it wouldn't be heard.' He paused. 'But that trick's not going to work again. He'll have to try something else next.'

Blore said:

'He probably will.'

There was an unpleasant tone in his voice. The two men eyed each other.

Armstrong said:

'Four of us, and we don't know which . . .'

Blore said:

'*I* know . . .'

Vera said:

'I haven't the least doubt . . .'

Armstrong said slowly:

'I suppose I do know really . . .'

Philip Lombard said:

'I think I've got a pretty good idea now . . .'

Again they all looked at each other . . .

Vera staggered to her feet. She said:

'I feel awful. I must go to bed . . . I'm dead beat.'

Lombard said:

'Might as well. No good sitting watching each other.'

Blore said:

'*I*'ve no objection . . .'

The doctor murmured:

'The best thing to do – although I doubt if any of us will sleep.'

They moved to the door. Blore said:

'*I wonder where that revolver is now? . . .*'

II

They went up the stairs.

The next move was a little like a scene in a farce.

Each one of the four stood with a hand on his or her bedroom door handle. Then, as though at a signal, each one stepped into the room and pulled the door shut. There were sounds of bolts and locks, of the moving of furniture.

Four frightened people were barricaded in until morning.

III

Philip Lombard drew a breath of relief as he turned from adjusting a chair under the door handle.

He strolled across to the dressing-table.

By the light of the flickering candle he studied his face curiously.

He said softly to himself:

'Yes, this business has got you rattled all right.'

His sudden wolf-like smile flashed out.

He undressed quickly.

He went over to the bed, placing his wristwatch on the table by the bed.

Then he opened the drawer of the table.

He stood there, staring down at the revolver that was inside it . . .

IV

Vera Claythorne lay in bed.

The candle still burned beside her.

And yet she could not summon the courage to put it out.

She was afraid of the dark . . .

She told herself again and again: '*You're all right until morning. Nothing happened last night. Nothing will happen tonight. Nothing can happen. You're locked and bolted in. No one can come near you . . .*'

And she thought suddenly:

'Of course! I can stay here! Stay here locked in! Food doesn't really matter! I can stay here – safely – till help comes! Even if it's a day – or two days . . .'

Stay here. Yes, but could she stay here? Hour after hour –

with no one to speak to, with nothing to do but *think* . . .

She'd begin to think of Cornwall – of Hugo – of – of what she'd said to Cyril.

Horrid whiney little boy, always pestering her . . .

'Miss Claythorne, why can't I swim out to the rock? I can. I know I can.'

Was it her voice that had answered?

'Of course, you can, Cyril, really. I know that.'

'Can I go then, Miss Claythorne?'

'Well, you see, Cyril, your mother gets so nervous about you. I'll tell you what. Tomorrow you can swim out to the rock. I'll talk to your mother on the beach and distract her attention. And then, when she looks for you, there you'll be standing on the rock waving to her! It *will* be a surprise!'

'Oh, good egg, Miss Claythorne! That will be a lark!'

She'd said it now. Tomorrow! Hugo was going to Newquay. When he came back – it would be all over.

Yes, but supposing it wasn't? Supposing it went wrong? Cyril might be rescued in time. And then – then he'd say, *'Miss Claythorne said I could.'* Well, what of it? One must take *some* risk! If the worst happened she'd brazen it out. *'How can you tell such a wicked lie, Cyril? Of course, I never said any such thing!'* They'd believe her all right. Cyril often told stories. He was an untruthful child. Cyril would know, of course. But that didn't matter . . . and anyway nothing *would* go wrong. She'd pretend to swim out after him. But she'd arrive too late . . . Nobody would ever suspect . . .

Had Hugo suspected? Was that why he had looked at her in that queer far-off way? . . . Had Hugo known?

Was that why he had gone off after the inquest so hurriedly?

He hadn't answered the one letter she had written to him . . .

Hugo . . .

Vera turned restlessly in bed. No, no, she mustn't think of Hugo. It hurt too much! That was all over, over and done with . . . Hugo must be forgotten.

Why, this evening, had she suddenly felt that Hugo was in the room with her?

She stared up at the ceiling, stared at the big black hook in the middle of the room.

She'd never noticed that hook before.

The seaweed had hung from that.

She shivered as she remembered that cold clammy touch on her neck.

She didn't like that hook on the ceiling. It drew your eyes, fascinated you . . . a big black hook . . .

V

Ex-Inspector Blore sat on the side of his bed.

His small eyes, red-rimmed and bloodshot, were alert in the solid mass of his face. He was like a wild boar waiting to charge.

He felt no inclination to sleep.

The menace was coming very near now . . . Six out of ten!

For all his sagacity, for all his caution and astuteness, the old judge had gone the way of the rest.

Blore snorted with a kind of savage satisfaction.

What was it the old geezer had said?

'We must be very careful . . .'

Self-righteous smug old hypocrite. Sitting up in court feeling like God Almighty. He'd got his all right . . . No more being careful for him.

And now there were four of them. The girl, Lombard, Armstrong and himself.

Very soon another of them would go . . . But it wouldn't be William Henry Blore. He'd see to that all right.

(But the revolver . . . What about the revolver? That was the disturbing factor – the revolver!)

Blore sat on his bed, his brow furrowed, his little eyes creased and puckered while he pondered the problem of the revolver . . .

In the silence he could hear the clocks strike downstairs.

Midnight.

He relaxed a little now – even went so far as to lie down on his bed. But he did not undress.

He lay there thinking. Going over the whole business from the beginning, methodically, painstakingly, as he had been wont to do in his police officer days. It was thoroughness that paid in the end.

The candle was burning down. Looking to see if the matches

were within easy reach of his hand, he blew it out.

Strangely enough, he found the darkness disquieting. It was as though a thousand age-old fears woke and struggled for supremacy in his brain. Faces floated in the air – the judge's face crowned with that mockery of grey wool – the cold dead face of Mrs Rogers – the convulsed purple face of Anthony Marston.

Another face – pale, spectacled, with a small straw-coloured moustache.

A face that he had seen sometime or other – but when? Not on the island. No, much longer ago than that.

Funny that he couldn't put a name to it . . . Silly sort of face really – fellow looked a bit of a mug.

Of course!

It came to him with a real shock.

Landor!

Odd to think he'd completely forgotten what Landor looked like. Only yesterday he'd been trying to recall the fellow's face, and hadn't been able to.

And now here it was, every feature clear and distinct, as though he had seen it only yesterday.

Landor had had a wife – a thin slip of a woman with a worried face. There'd been a kid, too, a girl about fourteen. For the first time, he wondered what had become of them.

(The revolver. What had become of the revolver? That was much more important.)

The more he thought about it the more puzzled he was . . . He didn't understand this revolver business.

Somebody in the house had got that revolver . . .

Downstairs a clock struck one.

Blore's thoughts were cut short. He sat up on the bed, suddenly alert. For he had heard a sound – a very faint sound – somewhere outside his bedroom door.

There was someone moving about in the darkened house.

The perspiration broke out on his forehead. Who was it, moving secretly and silently along the corridors? Someone who was up to no good, he'd bet that!

Noiselessly, in spite of his heavy build, he dropped off the bed and with two strides was standing by the door listening.

But the sound did not come again. Nevertheless Blore was

convinced that he was not mistaken. He had heard a footfall just outside his door. The hair rose slightly on his scalp. He knew fear again . . .

Someone creeping about stealthily in the night.

He listened – but the sound was not repeated.

And now a new temptation assailed him. He wanted, desperately, to go out and investigate. If he could only see who it was prowling about in the darkness.

But to open his door would be the action of a fool. Very likely that was exactly what the other was waiting for. He might even have meant Blore to hear what he had heard, counting on him coming out to investigate.

Blore stood rigid – listening. He could hear sounds everywhere now, cracks, rustles, mysterious whispers – but his dogged, realistic brain knew them for what they were – the creations of his own heated imagination.

And then suddenly he heard something that was *not* imagination. Footsteps, very soft, very cautious, but plainly audible to a man listening with all his ears as Blore was listening.

They came softly along the corridor (both Lombard's and Armstrong's rooms were farther from the stairhead than his). They passed his door without hesitating or faltering.

And as they did so, Blore made up his mind.

He meant to see who it was! The footsteps had definitely passed his door going to the stairs. Where was the man going?

When Blore acted, he acted quickly, surprisingly so for a man who looked so heavy and slow. He tiptoed back to the bed, slipped matches into his pocket, detached the plug of the electric lamp by his bed and picked it up, winding the flex round it. It was a chromium affair with a heavy ebonite base – a useful weapon.

He sprinted noiselessly across the room, removed the chair from under the door handle and with precaution unlocked and unbolted the door. He stepped out into the corridor. There was a faint sound in the hall below. Blore ran noiselessly in his stockinged feet to the head of the stairs.

At that moment he realized why it was he had heard all these sounds so clearly. The wind had died down completely and the sky must have cleared. There was faint moonlight coming in through the landing window and it illuminated the hall below.

Blore had an instantaneous glimpse of a figure just passing out through the front door.

In the act of running down the stairs in pursuit, he paused.

Once again, he had nearly made a fool of himself! This was a trap, perhaps, to lure him out of the house!

But what the other man didn't realize was that he had made a mistake, had delivered himself neatly into Blore's hands.

For, of the three tenanted rooms upstairs, *one must now be empty*. All that had to be done was to ascertain *which*!

Blore went swiftly back along the corridor.

He paused first at Dr Armstrong's door and tapped. There was no answer.

He waited a minute, then went on to Philip Lombard's room.

Here the answer came at once.

'Who's there?'

'It's Blore. I don't think Armstrong is in his room. Wait a minute.'

He went on to the door at the end of the corridor. Here he tapped again.

'Miss Claythorne. Miss Claythorne.'

Vera's voice, startled, answered him.

'Who is it? What's the matter?'

'It's all right, Miss Claythorne. Wait a minute. I'll come back.'

He raced back to Lombard's room. The door opened as he did so. Lombard stood there. He held a candle in his left hand. He had pulled on his trousers over his pyjamas. His right hand rested in the pocket of his pyjama jacket. He said sharply:

'What the hell's all this?'

Blore explained rapidly. Lombard's eyes lit up.

'*Armstrong – eh?* So *he*'s our pigeon!' He moved along to Armstrong's door. 'Sorry, Blore, but I don't take anything on trust.'

He rapped sharply on the panel.

'Armstrong – Armstrong.'

There was no answer.

Lombard dropped to his knees and peered through the keyhole. He inserted his little finger gingerly into the lock.

He said:

'Key's not in the door on the inside.'

Blore said:

'That means he locked it on the outside and took it with him.'

Philip nodded.

'Ordinary precaution to take. *We'll get him, Blore* . . . This time, *we'll get him*! Half a second.'

He raced along to Vera's room.

'Vera.'

'Yes.'

'We're hunting Armstrong. He's out of his room. Whatever you do, *don't open your door*. Understand?'

'Yes, I understand.'

'If Armstrong comes along and says that I've been killed, or Blore's been killed, *pay no attention*. See? Only open your door *if both Blore and I speak to you*. Got that?'

Vera said:

'Yes. I'm not a complete fool.'

Lombard said:

'Good.'

He joined Blore. He said:

'And now – after him! The hunt's up!'

Blore said:

'We'd better be careful. He's got a revolver, remember.'

Philip Lombard racing down the stairs chuckled.

He said:

'That's where you're wrong.' He undid the front door, remarking, 'Latch pushed back – so he could get in again easily.'

He went on:

'I've got that revolver!' He took it half out of his pocket as he spoke. 'Found it put back in my drawer tonight.'

Blore stopped dead on the doorstep. His face changed. Philip Lombard saw it.

'Don't be a damned fool, Blore! I'm not going to shoot you! Go back and barricade yourself in if you like! I'm off after Armstrong.'

He started off into the moonlight. Blore, after a minute's hesitation, followed him.

He thought to himself:

'I suppose I'm asking for it. After all –'

After all he had tackled criminals armed with revolvers before now. Whatever else he lacked, Blore did not lack courage. Show him the danger and he would tackle it pluckily. He was not afraid of danger in the open, only of danger undefined and tinged with the supernatural.

VI

Vera, left to await results, got up and dressed.

She glanced over once or twice at the door. It was a good solid door. It was both bolted and locked and had an oak chair wedged under the handle.

It could not be broken open by force. Certainly not by Dr Armstrong. He was not a physically powerful man.

If she were Armstrong intent on murder, it was cunning that she would employ, not force.

She amused herself by reflecting on the means he might employ.

He might, as Philip had suggested, announce that one of the other two men was dead. Or he might possibly pretend to be mortally wounded himself, might drag himself groaning to her door.

There were other possibilities. He might inform her that the house was on fire. More, he might actually set the house on fire ... Yes, that would be a possibility. Lure the other two men out of the house, then, having previously laid a trail of petrol, he might set light to it. And she, like an idiot, would remain barricaded in her room until it was too late.

She crossed over to the window. Not too bad. At a pinch one could escape that way. It would mean a drop – but there was a handy flower-bed.

She sat down and picking up her diary began to write in it in a clear flowing hand.

One must pass the time.

Suddenly she stiffened to attention. She had heard a sound. It was, she thought, a sound like breaking glass. And it came from somewhere downstairs.

She listened hard, but the sound was not repeated.

She heard, or thought she heard, stealthy sounds of footsteps, the creak of stairs, the rustle of garments – but there was nothing definite and she concluded, as Blore had done earlier, that such sounds had their origin in her own imagination.

But presently she heard sounds of a more concrete nature. People moving about downstairs – the murmur of voices. Then the very decided sound of someone mounting the stairs – doors opening and shutting – feet going up to the attics overhead. More noises from there.

Finally the steps came along the passage. Lombard's voice said:

'Vera. You all right?'

'Yes. What happened?'

Blore's voice said:

'Will you let us in?'

Vera went to the door. She removed the chair, unlocked the door and slid back the bolt. She opened the door. The two men were breathing hard, their feet and the bottom of their trousers were soaking wet.

She said again:

'What's happened?'

Lombard said:

'*Armstrong's disappeared* . . .'

VII

Vera cried:

'What?'

Lombard said:

'Vanished clean off the island.'

Blore concurred:

'Vanished – that's the word! Like some damned conjuring trick.'

Vera said impatiently:

'Nonsense! He's hiding somewhere!'

Blore said:

'No, he isn't! I tell you, there's nowhere to hide on this island. It's as bare as your hand! There's moonlight outside. As clear as day it is. *And he's not to be found.*'

Vera said:

'He doubled back to the house.'

Blore said:

'We thought of that. We've searched the house, too. You must have heard us. *He's not here*, I tell you. He's gone – clean vanished, vamoosed . . .'

Vera said incredulously:

'I don't believe it.'

Lombard said:

'It's true, my dear.'

He paused and then said:

'There's one other little fact. A pane in the dining-room window has been smashed – *and there are only three little soldier boys on the table.*'

CHAPTER 15

I

Three people sat eating breakfast in the kitchen.

Outside, the sun shone. It was a lovely day. The storm was a thing of the past.

And with the change in the weather, a change had come in the mood of the prisoners on the island.

They felt now like people just awakening from a nightmare. There was danger, yes, but it was danger in daylight. That paralysing atmosphere of fear that had wrapped them round like a blanket yesterday while the wind howled outside was gone.

Lombard said:

'We'll try heliographing today with a mirror from the highest point of the island. Some bright lad wandering on the cliff will recognize SOS when he sees it, I hope. In the evening we could try a bonfire – only there isn't much wood – and anyway they might just think it was song and dance and merriment.'

Vera said:

'Surely someone can read Morse. And then they'll come to take us off. Long before this evening.'

Lombard said:

'The weather's cleared all right, but the sea hasn't gone down yet. Terrific swell on! They won't be able to get a boat near the island before tomorrow.'

Vera cried:

'Another night in this place!'

Lombard shrugged his shoulders.

'May as well face it! Twenty-four hours will do it, I think. If we can last out that, we'll be all right.'

Blore cleared his throat. He said:

'We'd better come to a clear understanding. *What's happened to Armstrong?*'

Lombard said:

'Well, we've got one piece of evidence. Only three little soldier boys left on the dinner-table. It looks as though Armstrong had got his quietus.'

Vera said:

'Then why haven't you found his dead body?'

Blore said:

'Exactly.'

Lombard shook his head. He said:

'It's damned odd – no getting over it.'

Blore said doubtfully:

'It might have been thrown into the sea.'

Lombard said sharply:

'By whom? You? Me? You saw him go out of the front door. You come along and find me in my room. We go out and search together. When the devil had I time to kill him and carry his body round the island?'

Blore said:

'I don't know. But I do know one thing.'

Lombard said:

'What's that?'

Blore said:

'The revolver. It was your revolver. It's in your possession now. There's nothing to show that it hasn't been in your possession all along.'

'Come now, Blore, we were all searched.'

'Yes, you'd hidden it away before that happened. Afterwards you just took it back again.'

'My good blockhead, I swear to you that it was put back in

my drawer. Greatest surprise I ever had in my life when I found it there.'

Blore said:

'You ask us to believe a thing like that! Why the devil should Armstrong, or anyone else for that matter, put it back?'

Lombard raised his shoulders hopelessly.

'I haven't the least idea. It's just crazy. The last thing one would expect. There seems no point in it.'

Blore agreed.

'No, there isn't. You might have thought of a better story.'

'Rather proof that I'm telling the truth, isn't it?'

'I don't look at it that way.'

Philip said:

'You wouldn't.'

Blore said:

'Look here, Mr Lombard, if you're an honest man, as you pretend –'

Philip murmured:

'When did I lay claims to being an honest man? No, indeed, I never said that.'

Blore went on stolidly:

'If you're speaking the truth – there's only one thing to be done. As long as you have that revolver, Miss Claythorne and I are at your mercy. The only fair thing is to put that revolver with the other things that are locked up – and you and I will hold the two keys still.'

Philip Lombard lit a cigarette.

As he puffed smoke, he said:

'Don't be an ass.'

'You won't agree to that?'

'No, I won't. That revolver's mine. I need it to defend myself – and I'm going to keep it.'

Blore said:

'In that case we're bound to come to one conclusion.'

'That I'm U. N. Owen? Think what you damned well please. But I'll ask you, if that's so, why I didn't pot you with the revolver last night? I could have, about twenty times over.'

Blore shook his head.

He said:

'I don't know – and that's a fact. You must have had some reason.'

Vera had taken no part in the discussion. She stirred now and said:

'I think you're both behaving like a pair of idiots.'

Lombard looked at her.

'What's this?'

Vera said:

'You've forgotten the nursery rhyme. Don't you see there's a clue there?'

She recited in a meaning voice:

'Four little soldier boys going out to sea;
A red herring swallowed one and then there were Three.'

She went on:

'*A red herring* – that's the vital clue. *Armstrong's not dead . . .* He took away the china soldier to make you think he was. You may say what you like – Armstrong's on the island still. His disappearance is just a red herring across the track . . .'

Lombard sat down again.

He said:

'You know, you may be right.'

Blore said:

'Yes, but if so, where is he? We've searched the place. Outside and inside.'

Vera said scornfully:

'We all searched for the revolver, didn't we, and couldn't find it? But it was somewhere all the time!'

Lombard murmured:

'There's a slight difference in size, my dear, between a man and a revolver.'

Vera said:

'I don't care – I'm sure I'm right.'

Blore murmured:

'Rather giving himself away, wasn't it? Actually mentioning a red herring in the verse. He could have written it up a bit different.'

Vera cried:

'But don't you *see*, he's *mad*? It's all mad! The whole thing of going by the rhyme is mad! Dressing up the judge, killing Rogers when he was chopping sticks – drugging Mrs Rogers so that she overslept herself – arranging for a bumble bee when Miss Brent died! It's like some horrible child playing a game. It's all got to fit in.'

Blore said:

'Yes, you're right.' He thought a minute. 'At any rate there's no zoo on the island. He'll have a bit of trouble getting over that.'

Vera cried:

'Don't you see? *We're the Zoo* . . . Last night, we were hardly human any more. *We're the Zoo* . . .'

II

They spent the morning on the cliffs, taking it in turns to flash a mirror at the mainland.

There were no signs that any one saw them. No answering signals. The day was fine, with a slight haze. Below, the sea heaved in a gigantic swell. There were no boats out.

They had made another abortive search of the island. There was no trace of the missing physician.

Vera looked up at the house from where they were standing.

She said, her breath coming with a slight catch in it:

'One feels safer here, out in the open . . . Don't let's go back into the house again.'

Lombard said:

'Not a bad idea. We're pretty safe here, no one can get at us without our seeing him a long time beforehand.'

Vera said:

'We'll stay here.'

Blore said:

'Have to pass the night somewhere. We'll have to go back to the house then.'

Vera shuddered.

'I can't bear it. I *can't* go through another night!'

Philip said:

'You'll be safe enough – locked in your room.'

Vera murmured: 'I suppose so.'

She stretched out her hands, murmuring:

'It's lovely – to feel the sun again . . .'

She thought:

'How odd . . . I'm almost happy. And yet I suppose I'm actually in danger . . . Somehow – now – nothing seems to matter . . . not in daylight . . . I feel full of power – I feel that I can't die . . .'

Blore was looking at his wristwatch. He said:

'It's two o'clock. What about lunch?'

Vera said obstinately:

'I'm not going back to the house. I'm going to stay here – in the open.'

'Oh come now, Miss Claythorne. Got to keep your strength up, you know.'

Vera said:

'If I even see a tinned tongue, I shall be sick! I don't want any food. People go days on end with nothing sometimes when they're on a diet.'

Blore said:

'Well, I need my meals regular. What about you, Mr Lombard?'

Philip said:

'You know, I don't relish the idea of tinned tongue particularly. I'll stay here with Miss Claythorne.'

Blore hesitated. Vera said:

'I shall be quite all right. I don't think he'll shoot me as soon as your back is turned if that's what you're afraid of.'

Blore said:

'It's all right if you say so. But we agreed we ought not to separate.'

Philip said:

'You're the one who wants to go into the lion's den. I'll come with you if you like.'

'No, you won't,' said Blore. 'You'll stay here.'

Philip laughed.

'So you're still afraid of me? Why, I could shoot you both this very minute if I liked.'

Blore said:

'Yes, but that wouldn't be according to plan. It's one at a time, and it's got to be done in a certain way.'

'Well,' said Philip, 'you seem to know all about it.'

'Of course,' said Blore, 'it's a bit jumpy going up to the house alone –'

Philip said softly:

'And therefore, *will I lend you my revolver*? Answer, no, I will *not*! Not quite so simple as that, thank you.'

Blore shrugged his shoulders and began to make his way up the steep slope to the house.

Lombard said softly:

'Feeding time at the Zoo! The animals are very regular in their habits!'

Vera said anxiously:

'Isn't it very risky, what he's doing?'

'In the sense you mean – no, I don't think it is! Armstrong's not armed, you know, and anyway Blore is twice a match for him in physique and he's very much on his guard. And anyway it's a sheer impossibility that Armstrong can be in the house. I *know* he's not there.'

'But – what other solution is there?'

Philip said softly:

'There's Blore.'

'Oh – do you really think –?'

'Listen, my girl. You heard Blore's story. You've got to admit that if it's true, *I can't possibly have had anything to do with Armstrong's disappearance*. His story clears me. *But it doesn't clear him*. We've only *his* word for it that he heard footsteps and saw a man going downstairs and out at the front door. The whole thing may be a lie. He may have got rid of Armstrong a couple of hours before that.'

'How?'

Lombard shrugged his shoulders.

'That we don't know. But if you ask me, we've only one danger to fear – and that danger is Blore! What do we know about the man? Less than nothing! All this ex-policeman story may be bunkum! He may be anybody – a mad millionaire – a crazy businessman – an escaped inmate of Broadmoor. One thing's certain. He *could* have done every one of these crimes.'

Vera had gone rather white. She said in a slightly breathless voice:

'And supposing he gets – us?'

Lombard said softly, patting the revolver in his pocket:

'I'm going to take very good care he doesn't.'

Then he looked at her curiously.

'Touching faith in me, haven't you, Vera? Quite sure I wouldn't shoot you?'

Vera said:

'One has got to trust someone . . . As a matter of fact I think you're wrong about Blore. I still think it's Armstrong.'

She turned to him suddenly:

'Don't you feel – all the time – that there's *someone*. Someone watching and waiting?'

Lombard said slowly:

'That's just nerves.'

Vera said eagerly:

'Then you *have* felt it?'

She shivered. She bent a little closer.

'Tell me – you don't think –' she broke off, went on: 'I read a story once – about two judges that came to a small American town – from the Supreme Court. They administered justice – Absolute Justice. *Because – they didn't come from this world at all . . .'*

Lombard raised his eyebrows.

He said:

'Heavenly visitants, eh? No, I don't believe in the supernatural. This business is human enough.'

Vera said in a low voice:

'Sometimes – I'm not sure . . .'

Lombard looked at her. He said:

'That's conscience . . .' After a moment's silence he said very quietly: 'So you *did* drown that kid after all?'

Vera said vehemently:

'I didn't! I didn't! You've no right to say that!'

He laughed easily.

'Oh yes, you did, my good girl! I don't know why. Can't imagine. There was a man in it probably. Was that it?'

A sudden feeling of lassitude, of intense weariness, spread over Vera's limbs. She said in a dull voice:

'Yes – there was a man in it . . .'

Lombard said softly:

'Thanks. That's what I wanted to know . . .'

Vera sat up suddenly. She exclaimed:

'What was that? It wasn't an earthquake?'

Lombard said:

'No, no. Queer, though – a thud shook the ground. And I thought – did you hear a sort of cry? I did.'

They stared up at the house.

Lombard said:

'It came from there. We'd better go up and see.'

'No, no, I'm not going.'

'Please yourself. I am.'

Vera said desperately:

'All right. I'll come with you.'

They walked up the slope to the house. The terrace was peaceful and innocuous-looking in the sunshine. They hesitated there a minute, then instead of entering by the front door, they made a cautious circuit of the house.

They found Blore. He was spreadeagled on the stone terrace on the east side, his head crushed and mangled by a great block of white marble.

Philip looked up. He said:

'Whose is that window just above?'

Vera said in a low shuddering voice:

'It's mine – and *that's the clock from my mantelpiece* . . . I remember now. It was – shaped like a bear.'

She repeated and her voice shook and quavered:

'It was shaped like a bear . . .'

III

Philip grasped her shoulder.

He said, and his voice was urgent and grim:

'This settles it. Armstrong is in hiding somewhere in that house. I'm going to get him.'

But Vera clung to him. She cried:

'Don't be a fool. It's *us* now! We're next! He *wants* us to look for him! He's *counting* on it!'

Philip stopped. He said thoughtfully:

'There's something in that.'

Vera cried:

'At any rate you do admit now I was right.'

He nodded.

'Yes – you win! It's Armstrong all right. But where the devil did he hide himself? We went over the place with a fine-tooth comb.'

Vera said urgently:

'If you didn't find him last night, you *won't find him now* . . . That's common sense.'

Lombard said reluctantly:

'Yes, but –'

'He must have prepared a secret place beforehand – naturally – of course it's just what he would do. You know, like a Priest's Hole in old manor houses.'

'This isn't an old house of that kind.'

'He could have had one made.'

Philip Lombard shook his head. He said:

'We measured the place – that first morning. I'll swear there's no space unaccounted for.'

Vera said:

'There must be . . .'

Lombard said:

'I'd like to see –'

Vera cried:

'Yes, you'd like to see! And he knows that! He's in there – waiting for you.'

Lombard said, half bringing out the revolver from his pocket:

'I've got this, you know.'

'You said Blore was all right – that he was more than a match for Armstrong. So he was physically, and he was on the look out too. But what you don't seem to realize is that Armstrong is *mad*! And a madman has all the advantages on his side. He's twice as cunning as any one sane can be.'

Lombard put back the revolver in his pocket. He said:

'Come on, then.'

IV

Lombard said at last:

'What are we going to do when night comes?'

Vera didn't answer. He went on accusingly:

'You haven't thought of that?'

She said helplessly:

'What *can* we do? Oh, my God, I'm *frightened* . . .'

Philip Lombard said thoughtfully:

'It's fine weather. There will be a moon. We must find a place – up by the top cliffs perhaps. We can sit there and wait for morning. *We mustn't go to sleep* . . . We must watch the whole time. And if any one comes up towards us, I shall shoot!'

He paused:

'You'll be cold, perhaps, in that thin dress?'

Vera said with a raucous laugh:

'Cold? I should be colder if I were dead!'

Philip Lombard said quietly:

'Yes, that's true . . .'

Vera moved restlessly.

She said:

'I shall go mad if I sit here any longer. Let's move about.'

'All right.'

They paced slowly up and down, along the line of the rocks overlooking the sea. The sun was dropping towards the west. The light was golden and mellow. It enveloped them in a golden glow.

Vera said, with a sudden nervous little giggle:

'Pity we can't have a bathe . . .'

Philip was looking down towards the sea. He said abruptly:

'What's that, there? You see – by that big rock? No – a little farther to the right.'

Vera stared. She said:

'It looks like somebody's clothes!'

'A bather, eh?' Lombard laughed. 'Queer. I suppose it's only seaweed.'

Vera said:

'Let's go and look.'

'It is clothes,' said Lombard as they drew nearer. 'A bundle of them. That's a boot. Come on, let's scramble along here.'

They scrambled over the rocks.

Vera stopped suddenly. She said:

'*It's not clothes – it's a man* . . .'

The man was wedged between two rocks, flung there by the tide earlier in the day.

Lombard and Vera reached it in a last scramble. They bent down.

A purple discoloured face – a hideous drowned face . . .
Lombard said:
'My God! it's *Armstrong . . .*'

CHAPTER 16

I

Aeons passed . . . worlds spun and whirled . . . Time was motionless . . . It stood still – it passed through a thousand ages . . .

No, it was only a minute or so . . .

Two people were standing looking down on a dead man . . .

Slowly, very slowly, Vera Claythorne and Philip Lombard lifted their heads and looked into each other's eyes . . .

II

Lombard laughed.

He said:

'So that's it, is it, Vera?'

Vera said:

'There's no one on the island – no one at all – *except* us two . . .'

Her voice was a whisper – nothing more.

Lombard said:

'Precisely. So we know where we are, don't we?'

Vera said:

'How was it worked – that trick with the marble bear?'

He shrugged his shoulders.

'A conjuring trick, my dear – a very good one . . .'

Their eyes met again.

Vera thought:

'Why did I never see his face properly before? A wolf – that's what it is – a wolf's face . . . Those horrible teeth . . .'

Lombard said, and his voice was a snarl – dangerous – menacing:

'This is the end, you understand. We've come to the truth now. *And it's the end . . .*'

Vera said quietly:

'I understand . . .'

She stared out to sea. General Macarthur had stared out to sea – when – only yesterday? Or was it the day before? He too had said, *'This is the end . . .'*

He had said it with acceptance – almost with welcome.

But to Vera the words – the thought – brought rebellion.

No, it should not be the end.

She looked down at the dead man. She said:

'Poor Dr Armstrong . . .'

Lombard sneered.

He said:

'What's this? Womanly pity?'

Vera said:

'Why not? Haven't *you* any pity?'

He said:

'I've no pity for you. Don't expect it!'

Vera looked down again at the body. She said:

'We must move him. Carry him up to the house.'

'To join the other victims, I suppose? All neat and tidy. As far as I'm concerned he can stay where he is.'

Vera said:

'At any rate let's get him out of the reach of the sea.'

Lombard laughed. He said:

'If you like.'

He bent – tugging at the body. Vera leaned against him, helping him. She pulled and tugged with all her might.

Lombard panted:

'Not such an easy job.'

They managed it, however, drawing the body clear of high water mark.

Lombard said as he straightened up:

'Satisfied?'

Vera said:

'Quite.'

Her tone warned him. He spun round. Even as he clapped his hand to his pocket he knew that he would find it empty.

She had moved a yard or two away and was facing him, revolver in hand.

Lombard said:

'So that's the reason for your womanly solicitude! You wanted to pick my pocket.'

She nodded.

She held it steadily and unwaveringly.

Death was very near to Philip Lombard now. It had never, he knew, been nearer.

Nevertheless he was not beaten yet.

He said authoritatively:

'Give that revolver to me.'

Vera laughed.

Lombard said:

'Come on, hand it over.'

His quick brain was working. Which way – which method – talk her over – lull her into security or a swift dash –

All his life Lombard had taken the risky way. He took it now.

He spoke slowly, argumentatively:

'Now look here, my dear girl, you just listen –'

And then he sprang. Quick as a panther – as any other feline creature . . .

Automatically Vera pressed the trigger . . .

Lombard's leaping body stayed poised in mid-spring then crashed heavily to the ground.

Vera came warily forward, the revolver ready in her hand.

But there was no need of caution.

Philip Lombard was dead – shot through the heart . . .

III

Relief possessed Vera – enormous exquisite relief.

At last it was over.

There was no more fear – no more steeling of her nerves . . .

She was alone on the island . . .

Alone with nine dead bodies . . .

But what did that matter? *She* was alive . . .

She sat there – exquisitely happy – exquisitely at peace . . .

No more fear . . .

IV

The sun was setting when Vera moved at last. Sheer reaction had kept her immobile. There had been no room in her for anything but the glorious sense of safety.

She realized now that she was hungry and sleepy. Principally sleepy. She wanted to throw herself on her bed and sleep and sleep and sleep . . .

Tomorrow, perhaps, they would come and rescue her – but she didn't really mind. She didn't mind staying here. Not now that she was alone . . .

Oh! blessed, blessed peace . . .

She got to her feet and glanced up at the house.

Nothing to be afraid of any longer! No terrors waiting for her! Just an ordinary well-built modern house. And yet, a little earlier in the day, she had not been able to look at it without shivering . . .

Fear – what a strange thing fear was . . .

Well, it was over now. She had conquered – had triumphed over the most deadly peril. By her own quick-wittedness and adroitness she had turned the tables on her would-be destroyer.

She began to walk up towards the house.

The sun was setting, the sky to the west was streaked with red and orange. It was beautiful and peaceful . . .

Vera thought:

'The whole thing might be a dream . . .'

How tired she was – terribly tired. Her limbs ached, her eyelids were dropping. Not to be afraid any more . . . To sleep. Sleep . . . sleep . . . sleep . . .

To sleep safely since she was alone on the island. One little soldier boy left all alone.

She smiled to herself.

She went in at the front door. The house, too, felt strangely peaceful.

Vera thought:

'Ordinarily one wouldn't care to sleep where there's a dead body in practically every bedroom!'

Should she go to the kitchen and get herself something to eat?

She hesitated a moment, then decided against it. She was really too tired . . .

She paused by the dining-room door. There were still three little china figures in the middle of the table.

Vera laughed.

She said:

'You're behind the times, my dears.'

She picked up two of them and tossed them out through the window. She heard them crash on the stone of the terrace.

The third little figure she picked up and held in her hand. She said:

'You can come with me. We've won, my dear! We've won!'

The hall was dim in the dying light.

Vera, the little soldier clasped in her hand, began to mount the stairs. Slowly, because her legs were suddenly very tired.

'One little soldier boy left all alone.' How did it end? Oh, yes! *'He got married and then there were none.'*

Married . . . Funny, how she suddenly got the feeling again that Hugo was in the house . . .

Very strong. Yes, Hugo was upstairs waiting for her.

Vera said to herself:

'Don't be a fool. You're so tired that you're imagining the most fantastic things . . .'

Slowly up the stairs . . .

At the top of them something fell from her hand making hardly any noise on the soft pile carpet. She did not notice that she had dropped the revolver. She was only conscious of clasping a little china figure.

How very quiet the house was. And yet – it didn't seem like an empty house . . .

Hugo, upstairs, waiting for her . . .

'One little soldier boy left all alone.' What was the last line again? Something about being married – or was it something else?

She had come now to the door of her room. Hugo was waiting for her inside – she was quite sure of it.

She opened the door . . .

She gave a gasp . . .

What was that – hanging from the hook in the ceiling? *A rope*

*with a noose all ready? And a chair to stand upon – a chair that
could be kicked away . . .*

That was what Hugo wanted . . .

And of course that was the last line of the rhyme.

'He went and hanged himself and then there were None . . .'

The little china figure fell from her hand. It rolled unheeded
and broke against the fender.

Like an automaton Vera moved forward. This was the end
– here where the cold wet hand (Cyril's hand, of course) had
touched her throat . . .

'You can go to the rock, Cyril . . .'

That was what murder was – as easy as that!

But afterwards you went on remembering . . .

She climbed up on the chair, her eyes staring in front of
her like a sleepwalker's . . . She adjusted the noose round
her neck.

Hugo was there to see she did what she had to do.

She kicked away the chair . . .

EPILOGUE

Sir Thomas Legge, Assistant Commissioner at Scotland Yard,
said irritably:

'But the whole thing's incredible!'

Inspector Maine said respectfully:

'I know, sir.'

The AC went on:

'Ten people dead on an island and not a living soul on it. It
doesn't make sense!'

Inspector Maine said stolidly:

'Nevertheless, it *happened*, sir.'

Sir Thomas Legge said:

'Dam' it all, Maine, somebody must have killed 'em.'

'That's just our problem, sir.'

'Nothing helpful in the doctor's report?'

'No, sir. Wargrave and Lombard were shot, the first through
the head, the second through the heart. Miss Brent and Marston
died of cyanide poisoning. Mrs Rogers died of an overdose of

chloral. Rogers' head was split open. Blore's head was crushed in. Armstrong died of drowning. Macarthur's skull was fractured by a blow on the back of the head and Vera Claythorne was hanged.'

The AC winced. He said:

'Nasty business – all of it.'

He considered for a minute or two. He said irritably:

'Do you mean to say that you haven't been able to get anything helpful out of the Sticklehaven people? Dash it, they must know something.'

Inspector Maine shrugged his shoulders.

'They're ordinary decent seafaring folk. They know that the island was bought by a man called Owen – and that's about all they do know.'

'Who provisioned the island and made all the necessary arrangements?'

'Man called Morris. Isaac Morris.'

'And what does he say about it all?'

'He can't say anything, sir, he's dead.'

The AC frowned.

'Do we know anything about this Morris?'

'Oh yes, sir, we know about him. He wasn't a very savoury gentleman, Mr Morris. He was implicated in that share-pushing fraud of Bennito's three years ago – we're sure of that though we can't prove it. And he was mixed up in the dope business. And again we can't prove it. He was a very careful man, Morris.'

'And he was behind this island business?'

'Yes, sir, he put through the sale – though he made it clear that he was buying Soldier Island for a third party, unnamed.'

'Surely there's something to be found out on the financial angle, there?'

Inspector Maine smiled.

'Not if you knew Morris! He can wangle figures until the best chartered accountant in the country wouldn't know if he was on his head or his heels! We've had a taste of that in the Bennito business. No, he covered his employer's tracks all right.'

The other man sighed. Inspector Maine went on:

'It was Morris who made all the arrangements down at Sticklehaven. Represented himself as acting for "Mr Owen".

And it was he who explained to the people down there that there was some experiment on – some bet about living on a "desert island" for a week – and that no notice was to be taken of any appeal for help from out there.'

Sir Thomas Legge stirred uneasily. He said:

'And you're telling me that those people didn't smell a rat? Not even then?'

Maine shrugged his shoulders. He said:

'You're forgetting, sir, that Soldier Island previously belonged to young Elmer Robson, the American. He had the most extraordinary parties down there. I've no doubt the local people's eyes fairly popped out over them. But they got used to it and they'd begun to feel that anything to do with Soldier Island would necessarily be incredible. It's natural, that, sir, when you come to think of it.'

The Assistant Commissioner admitted gloomily that he supposed it was.

Maine said:

'Fred Narracott – that's the man who took the party out there – did say one thing that was illuminating. He said he was surprised to see what sort of people these were. "Not at all like Mr Robson's parties." I think it was the fact that they were all so normal and so quiet that made him override Morris's orders and take out a boat to the island after he'd heard about the SOS signals.'

'When did he and the other men go?'

'The signals were seen by a party of boy scouts on the morning of the 11th. There was no possibility of getting out there that day. The men got there on the afternoon of the 12th at the first moment possible to run a boat ashore there. They're all quite positive that nobody could have left the island before they got there. There was a big sea on after the storm.'

'Couldn't someone have swum ashore?'

'It's over a mile to the coast and there were heavy seas and big breakers inshore. And there were a lot of people, boy scouts and others on the cliffs looking out towards the island and watching.'

The AC sighed. He said:

'What about that gramophone record you found in the house? Couldn't you get hold of anything there that might help?'

Inspector Maine said:

'I've been into that. It was supplied by a firm that do a lot of theatrical stuff and film effects. It was sent to U. N. Owen Esq., c/o Isaac Morris, and was understood to be required for the amateur performance of a hitherto unacted play. The typescript of it was returned with the record.'

Legge said:

'And what about the subject matter, eh?'

Inspector Maine said gravely:

'I'm coming to that, sir.'

He cleared his throat.

'I've investigated those accusations as thoroughly as I can.

'Starting with the Rogerses who were the first to arrive on the island. They were in service with a Miss Brady who died suddenly. Can't get anything definite out of the doctor who attended her. He says they certainly didn't poison her, or anything like that, but his personal belief is that there *was* some funny business – that she died as the result of neglect on their part. Says it's the sort of thing that's quite impossible to prove.

'Then there is Mr Justice Wargrave. That's OK. He was the judge who sentenced Seton.

'By the way, Seton was guilty – unmistakably guilty. Evidence turned up later, after he was hanged, which proved that beyond any shadow of doubt. But there was a good deal of comment at the time – nine people out of ten thought Seton was innocent and that the judge's summing up had been vindictive.

'The Claythorne girl, I find, was governess in a family where a death occurred by drowning. However, she doesn't seem to have had anything to do with it, and as a matter of fact she behaved very well, swam out to the rescue and was actually carried out to sea and only just rescued in time.'

'Go on,' said the AC with a sigh.

Maine took a deep breath.

'Dr Armstrong now. Well-known man. Had a consulting room in Harley Street. Absolutely straight and above board in his profession. Haven't been able to trace any record of an illegal operation or anything of that kind. It's true that there *was* a woman called Clees who was operated on by him way back in 1925 at Leithmore, when he was attached to the hospital there.

Peritonitis and she died on the operating table. Maybe he wasn't very skilful over the op – after all he hadn't much experience – but after all clumsiness isn't a criminal offence. There was certainly no motive.

'Then there's Miss Emily Brent. Girl, Beatrice Taylor, was in service with her. Got pregnant, was turned out by her mistress and went and drowned herself. Not a nice business – but again not criminal.'

'That,' said the AC, 'seems to be the point. U. N. Owen dealt with cases that the law couldn't touch.'

Maine went stolidly on with his list.

'Young Marston was a fairly reckless car driver – had his licence endorsed twice and he ought to have been prohibited from driving in my opinion. That's all there is to him. The two names John and Lucy Combes were those of two kids he knocked down and killed near Cambridge. Some friends of his gave evidence for him and he was let off with a fine.

'Can't find anything definite about General Macarthur. Fine record – war service – all the rest of it. Arthur Richmond was serving under him in France and was killed in action. No friction of any kind between him and the General. They were close friends as a matter of fact. There were some blunders made about that time – commanding officers sacrificed men unnecessarily – possibly this was a blunder of that kind.'

'Possibly,' said the AC.

'Now, Philip Lombard. Lombard has been mixed up in some very curious shows abroad. He's sailed very near the law once or twice. Got a reputation for daring and for not being over-scrupulous. Sort of fellow who might do several murders in some quiet out of the way spot.

'Then we come to Blore.' Maine hesitated. 'He of course was one of our lot.'

The other man stirred.

'Blore,' said the Assistant Commissioner forcibly, 'was a bad hat!'

'You think so, sir?'

The AC said:

'I always thought so. But he was clever enough to get away with it. It's my opinion that he committed black perjury in the

Landor case. I wasn't happy about it at the time. But I couldn't find anything. I put Harris on to it and *he* couldn't find anything but I'm still of the opinion that there was something to find if we'd known how to set about it. The man wasn't straight.'

There was a pause, then Sir Thomas Legge said:

'And Isaac Morris is dead, you say? When did he die?'

'I thought you'd soon come to that, sir. Isaac Morris died on the night of August 8th. Took an overdose of sleeping stuff – one of the barbiturates, I understand. There wasn't anything to show whether it was accident or suicide.'

Legge said slowly:

'Care to know what I think, Maine?'

'Perhaps I can guess, sir.'

Legge said heavily:

'That death of Morris's is a damned sight too opportune!'

Inspector Maine nodded. He said:

'I thought you'd say that, sir.'

The Assistant Commissioner brought down his fist with a bang on the table. He cried out:

'The whole thing's fantastic – impossible. Ten people killed on a bare rock of an island – and we don't know who did it, or why, or how.'

Maine coughed. He said:

'Well, it's not quite like that, sir. We do know *why*, more or less. Some fanatic with a bee in his bonnet about justice. He was out to get people who were beyond the reach of the law. He picked ten people – whether they were really guilty or not doesn't matter –'

The Commissioner stirred. He said sharply:

'Doesn't it? It seems to me –'

He stopped. Inspector Maine waited respectfully. With a sigh Legge shook his head.

'Carry on,' he said. 'Just for a minute I felt I'd got somewhere. Got, as it were, the clue to the thing. It's gone now. Go ahead with what you were saying.'

Maine went on:

'There were ten people to be – executed, let's say. They *were* executed. U. N. Owen accomplished his task. And somehow or other he spirited himself off that island into thin air.'

The AC said:

'First-class vanishing trick. But you know, Maine, there must be an explanation.'

Maine said:

'You're thinking, sir, that if the man wasn't on the island, he couldn't have left the island, and according to the account of the interested parties he never was on the island. Well, then the only explanation possible is that he was actually one of the ten.'

The AC nodded.

Maine said earnestly:

'We thought of that, sir. We went into it. Now, to begin with, we're not quite in the dark as to what happened on Soldier Island. Vera Claythorne kept a diary, so did Emily Brent. Old Wargrave made some notes – dry legal cryptic stuff, but quite clear. And Blore made notes too. All those accounts tally. The deaths occurred in this order. Marston, Mrs Rogers, Macarthur, Rogers, Miss Brent, Wargrave. After his death Vera Claythorne's diary states that Armstrong left the house in the night and that Blore and Lombard had gone after him. Blore has one more entry in his notebook. Just two words. "Armstrong disappeared."

'Now, sir, it seemed to me, taking everything into account, that we might find here a perfectly good solution. Armstrong was drowned, you remember. Granting that Armstrong was mad, what was to prevent him having killed off all the others and then committed suicide by throwing himself over the cliff, or perhaps while trying to swim to the mainland?

'That was a good solution – but it won't do. No, sir, it won't do. First of all there's the police surgeon's evidence. He got to the island early on the morning of August 13. He couldn't say much to help us. All he could say was that all the people had been dead at least thirty-six hours and probably a good deal longer. But he was fairly definite about Armstrong. Said he must have been from eight to ten hours in the water before his body was washed up. That works out at this, that Armstrong must have gone into the sea sometime during the night of the 10th–11th – and I'll explain why. We found the point where the body was washed up – it had been wedged between two rocks and there were bits of cloth, hair, etc., on them. It must have been deposited there at high water on the 11th – that's to say round about 11 o'clock a.m. After that, the storm subsided, and succeeding high water marks are considerably lower.

'You might say, I suppose, that Armstrong managed to polish off the other three *before* he went into the sea that night. But there's another point and one you can't get over. *Armstrong's body had been dragged above high water mark.* We found it well above the reach of any tide. And it was laid out straight on the ground – all neat and tidy.

'So that settles one point definitely. *Someone* was alive on the island *after Armstrong was dead.*'

He paused and then went on.

'And that leaves – just what exactly? Here's the position early on the morning of the 11th. Armstrong has "disappeared" (*drowned*). That leaves us three people. Lombard, Blore and Vera Claythorne. Lombard was shot. His body was down by the sea – near Armstrong's. Vera Claythorne was found hanged in her own bedroom. Blore's body was on the terrace. His head was crushed in by a heavy marble clock that it seems reasonable to suppose fell on him from the window above.'

The AC said sharply:

'Whose window?'

'Vera Claythorne's. Now, sir, let's take each of these cases separately. First Philip Lombard. Let's say *he* pushed over that lump of marble on to Blore – then he doped Vera Claythorne and strung her up. Lastly, he went down to the seashore and shot himself.

'But if so, *who took away the revolver from him?* For that revolver was found up in the house just inside the door at the top of the stairs – Wargrave's room.'

The AC said:

'Any fingerprints on it?'

'Yes, sir, Vera Claythorne's.'

'But, man alive, then –'

'I know what you're going to say, sir. That it was Vera Claythorne. That she shot Lombard, took the revolver back to the house, toppled the marble block on to Blore and then – hanged herself.

'And that's quite all right – up to a point. There's a chair in her bedroom and on the seat of it there are marks of seaweed same as on her shoes. Looks as though she stood on the chair, adjusted the rope round her neck and kicked away the chair.

'*But that chair wasn't found kicked over*. It was, like all the other chairs, neatly put back against the wall. That was done *after Vera Claythorne's death* – by *someone else*.

'That leaves us with Blore and if you tell me that after shooting Lombard and inducing Vera Claythorne to hang herself he then went out and pulled down a whacking great block of marble on himself by tying a string to it or something like that – well, I simply don't believe you. Men don't commit suicide that way – and what's more Blore wasn't that kind of man. *We* knew Blore – and he was not the man that you'd ever accuse of a desire for abstract justice.'

The Assistant Commissioner said:

'I agree.'

Inspector Maine said:

'And therefore, sir, there must have been *someone else* on the island. Someone who tidied up when the whole business was over. But where was he all the time – and where did he go to? The Sticklehaven people are absolutely certain that no one could have left the island before the rescue boat got there. But in that case –'

He stopped.

The Assistant Commissioner said:

'In that case –'

He sighed. He shook his head. He leaned forward.

'But in that case,' he said, '*who killed them?*'

A MANUSCRIPT DOCUMENT SENT TO SCOTLAND YARD BY THE MASTER OF THE *EMMA JANE* FISHING TRAWLER

From my earliest youth I realized that my nature was a mass of contradictions. I have, to begin with, an incurably romantic imagination. The practice of throwing a bottle into the sea with an important document inside was one that never failed to thrill me when reading adventure stories as a child. It thrills me still

– and for that reason I have adopted this course – writing my confession, enclosing it in a bottle, sealing the latter, and casting it into the waves. There is, I suppose, a hundred to one chance that my confession may be found – and then (or do I flatter myself?) a hitherto unsolved murder mystery will be explained.

I was born with other traits besides my romantic fancy. I have a definite sadistic delight in seeing or causing death. I remember experiments with wasps – with various garden pests . . . From an early age I knew very strongly the lust to kill.

But side by side with this went a contradictory trait – a strong sense of justice. It is abhorrent to me that an innocent person or creature should suffer or die by any act of mine. I have always felt strongly that right should prevail.

It may be understood – I think a psychologist would understand – that with my mental make-up being what it was, I adopted the law as a profession. The legal profession satisfied nearly all my instincts.

Crime and its punishment has always fascinated me. I enjoy reading every kind of detective story and thriller. I have devised for my own private amusement the most ingenious ways of carrying out a murder.

When in due course I came to preside over a court of law, that other secret instinct of mine was encouraged to develop. To see a wretched criminal squirming in the dock, suffering the tortures of the damned, as his doom came slowly and slowly nearer, was to me an exquisite pleasure. Mind you, I took no pleasure in seeing an *innocent* man there. On at least two occasions I stopped cases where to my mind the accused was palpably innocent, directing the jury that there was no case. Thanks, however, to the fairness and efficiency of our police force, the majority of the accused persons who have come before me to be tried for murder, have been guilty.

I will say here that such was the case with the man Edward Seton. His appearance and manner were misleading and he created a good impression on the jury. But not only the evidence, which was clear, though unspectacular, but my own knowledge of criminals told me without any doubt that the man had actually committed the crime with which he was charged, the brutal murder of an elderly woman who trusted him.

I have a reputation as a hanging judge, but that is unfair. I have always been strictly just and scrupulous in my summing up of a case.

All I have done is to protect the jury against the emotional effect of emotional appeals by some of our more emotional counsel. I have drawn their attention to the actual evidence.

For some years past I have been aware of a change within myself, a lessening of control – a desire to act instead of to judge.

I have wanted – let me admit it frankly – *to commit a murder myself*. I recognized this as the desire of the artist to express himself! I was, or could be, an artist in crime! My imagination, sternly checked by the exigencies of my profession, waxed secretly to colossal force.

I must – I must – I *must* – commit a murder! And what is more, it must be no ordinary murder! It must be a fantastical crime – something stupendous – out of the common! In that one respect, I have still, I think, an adolescent's imagination.

I wanted something theatrical, impossible!

I wanted to kill . . . Yes, I wanted to kill . . .

But – incongruous as it may seem to some – I was restrained and hampered by my innate sense of justice. The innocent must not suffer.

And then, quite suddenly, the idea came to me – started by a chance remark uttered during casual conversation. It was a doctor to whom I was talking – some ordinary undistinguished GP. He mentioned casually how often murder must be committed which the law was unable to touch.

And he instanced a particular case – that of an old lady, a patient of his who had recently died. He was, he said, himself convinced that her death was due to the withholding of a restorative drug by a married couple who attended on her and who stood to benefit very substantially by her death. That sort of thing, he explained, was quite impossible to prove, but he was nevertheless quite sure of it in his own mind. He added that there were many cases of a similar nature going on all the time – cases of deliberate murder – and all quite untouchable by the law.

That was the beginning of the whole thing. I suddenly saw

my way clear. And I determined to commit not one murder, but murder on a grand scale.

A childish rhyme of my infancy came back into my mind – the rhyme of the ten little soldier boys. It had fascinated me as a child of two – the inexorable diminishment – the sense of inevitability.

I began, secretly, to collect victims . . .

I will not take up space here by going into details of how this was accomplished. I had a certain routine line of conversation which I employed with nearly every one I met – and the results I got were really surprising. During the time I was in a nursing home I collected the case of Dr Armstrong – a violently teetotal Sister who attended on me being anxious to prove to me the evils of drink by recounting to me a case many years ago in hospital when a doctor under the influence of alcohol had killed a patient on whom he was operating. A careless question as to where the Sister in question had trained, etc., soon gave me the necessary data. I tracked down the doctor and the patient mentioned without difficulty.

A conversation between two old military gossips in my Club put me on the track of General Macarthur. A man who had recently returned from the Amazon gave me a devastating résumé of the activities of one Philip Lombard. An indignant memsahib in Majorca recounted the tale of the Puritan Emily Brent and her wretched servant girl. Anthony Marston I selected from a large group of people who had committed similar offences. His complete callousness and his inability to feel any responsibility for the lives he had taken made him, I considered, a type dangerous to the community and unfit to live. Ex-Inspector Blore came my way quite naturally, some of my professional brethren discussing the Landor case with freedom and vigour. I took a serious view of his offence. The police, as servants of the law, must be of a high order of integrity. For their word is perforce believed by virtue of their profession.

Finally there was the case of Vera Claythorne. It was when I was crossing the Atlantic. At a late hour one night the sole occupants of the smoking-room were myself and a good-looking young man called Hugo Hamilton.

Hugo Hamilton was unhappy. To assuage that unhappiness

he had taken a considerable quantity of drink. He was in the maudlin confidential stage. Without much hope of any result I automatically started my routine conversational gambit. The response was startling. I can remember his words now. He said:

'You're right. Murder isn't what most people think – giving someone a dollop of arsenic – pushing them over a cliff – that sort of stuff.' He leaned forward, thrusting his face into mine. He said, 'I've known a murderess – known her, I tell you. And what's more I was crazy about her . . . God help me, sometimes I think I still am . . . It's hell, I tell you – hell. You see, she did it more or less for me . . . Not that I ever dreamed . . . Women are fiends – absolute fiends – you wouldn't think a girl like that – a nice straight jolly girl – you wouldn't think she'd do that, would you? That she'd take a kid out to sea and let it drown – you wouldn't think a *woman* could do a thing like that?'

I said to him:

'Are you sure she did do it?'

He said and in saying it he seemed suddenly to sober up:

'I'm quite sure. Nobody else ever thought of it. But I knew the moment I looked at her – when I got back – after . . . And she knew I knew . . . What she didn't realize was that I loved that kid . . .'

He didn't say any more, but it was easy enough for me to trace back the story and reconstruct it.

I needed a tenth victim. I found him in a man named Morris. He was a shady little creature. Amongst other things he was a dope pedlar and he was responsible for inducing the daughter of friends of mine to take to drugs. She committed suicide at the age of twenty-one.

During all this time of search my plan had been gradually maturing in my mind. It was now complete and the coping stone to it was an interview I had with a doctor in Harley Street. I have mentioned that I underwent an operation. My interview in Harley Street told me that another operation would be useless. My medical adviser wrapped up the information very prettily, but I am accustomed to getting at the truth of a statement.

I did not tell the doctor of my decision – that my death should not be a slow and protracted one as it would be in the course of nature. No, my death should take place in a blaze of excitement. I would *live* before I died.

And now to the actual mechanics of the crime of Soldier Island. To acquire the island, using the man Morris to cover my tracks, was easy enough. He was an expert in that sort of thing. Tabulating the information I had collected about my prospective victims, I was able to concoct a suitable bait for each. None of my plans miscarried. All my guests arrived at Soldier Island on the 8th of August. The party included myself.

Morris was already accounted for. He suffered from indigestion. Before leaving London I gave him a capsule to take last thing at night which had, I said, done wonders for my own gastric juices. He accepted unhesitatingly – the man was a slight hypochondriac. I had no fear that he would leave any compromising documents or memoranda behind. He was not that sort of man.

The order of death upon the island had been subjected by me to special thought and care. There were, I considered, amongst my guests, varying degrees of guilt. Those whose guilt was the lightest should, I decided, pass out first, and not suffer the prolonged mental strain and fear that the more cold-blooded offenders were to suffer.

Anthony Marston and Mrs Rogers died first, the one instantaneously the other in a peaceful sleep. Marston, I recognized, was a type born without that feeling of moral responsibility which most of us have. He was amoral – pagan. Mrs Rogers, I had no doubt, had acted very largely under the influence of her husband.

I need not describe closely how those two met their deaths. The police will have been able to work that out quite easily. Potassium cyanide is easily obtained by householders for putting down wasps. I had some in my possession and it was easy to slip it into Marston's almost empty glass during the tense period after the gramophone recital.

I may say that I watched the faces of my guests closely during that indictment and I had no doubt whatever, after my long court experience, that one and all were guilty.

During recent bouts of pain, I had been ordered a sleeping draught – Chloral Hydrate. It had been easy for me to suppress this until I had a lethal amount in my possession. When Rogers brought up some brandy for his wife, he set it down on a table and in passing that table I put the stuff into the brandy. It was easy, for at that time suspicion had not begun to set in.

General Macarthur met his death quite painlessly. He did not hear me come up behind him. I had, of course, to choose my time for leaving the terrace very carefully, but everything was successful.

As I had anticipated, a search was made of the island and it was discovered that there was no one on it but our seven selves. That at once created an atmosphere of suspicion. According to my plan I should shortly need an ally. I selected Dr Armstrong for that part. He was a gullible sort of man, he knew me by sight and reputation and it was inconceivable to him that a man of my standing should actually be a murderer! All his suspicions were directed against Lombard and I pretended to concur in these. I hinted to him that I had a scheme by which it might be possible to trap the murderer into incriminating himself.

Though a search had been made of everyone's room, no search had as yet been made of the persons themselves. But that was bound to come soon.

I killed Rogers on the morning of August 10th. He was chopping sticks for lighting the fire and did not hear me approach. I found the key to the dining-room door in his pocket. He had locked it the night before.

In the confusion attending the finding of Rogers' body I slipped into Lombard's room and abstracted his revolver. I knew that he would have one with him – in fact I had instructed Morris to suggest as much when he interviewed him.

At breakfast I slipped my last dose of chloral into Miss Brent's coffee when I was refilling her cup. We left her in the dining-room. I slipped in there a little while later – she was nearly unconscious and it was easy to inject a strong solution of cyanide into her. The bumble bee business was really rather childish – but somehow, you know, it pleased me. I liked adhering as closely as possible to my nursery rhyme.

Immediately after this what I had already foreseen happened – indeed I believe I suggested it myself. We all submitted to a rigorous search. I had safely hidden away the revolver, and had no more cyanide or chloral in my possession.

It was then that I intimated to Armstrong that we must carry our plan into effect. It was simply this – *I* must appear to be the next victim. That would perhaps rattle the murderer – at any rate once I was supposed to be dead I could move about the house and spy upon the unknown murderer.

Armstrong was keen on the idea. We carried it out that evening. A little plaster of red mud on the forehead – the red curtain and the wool and the stage was set. The lights of the candles were very flickering and uncertain and the only person who would examine me closely was Armstrong.

It worked perfectly. Miss Claythorne screamed the house down when she found the seaweed which I had thoughtfully arranged in her room. They all rushed up, and I took up my pose of a murdered man.

The effect on them when they found me was all that could be desired. Armstrong acted his part in the most professional manner. They carried me upstairs and laid me on my bed. Nobody worried about me, they were all too deadly scared and terrified of each other.

I had a rendezvous with Armstrong outside the house at a quarter to two. I took him up a little way behind the house on the edge of the cliff. I said that here we could see if any one else approached us, and we should not be seen from the house as the bedrooms faced the other way. He was still quite unsuspicious – and yet he ought to have been warned – if he had only remembered the words of the nursery rhyme. 'A red herring swallowed one . . .' He took the red herring all right.

It was quite easy. I uttered an exclamation, leant over the cliff, told him to look, wasn't that the mouth of a cave? He leant right over. A quick vigorous push sent him off his balance and splash into the heaving sea below. I returned to the house. It must have been my footfall that Blore heard. A few minutes after I had returned to Armstrong's room I left it, this time making a certain amount of noise so that someone *should* hear me. I heard a door open as I got to the bottom of the stairs. They must have just glimpsed my figure as I went out of the front door.

It was a minute or two before they followed me. I had gone straight round the house and in at the dining-room window which I had left open. I shut the window and later I broke the glass. Then I went upstairs and laid myself out again on my bed.

I calculated that they would search the house again, but I did not think they would look closely at any of the corpses, a mere twitch aside of the sheet to satisfy themselves that it was not Armstrong masquerading as a body. This is exactly what occurred.

I forgot to say that I returned the revolver to Lombard's room. It may be of interest to someone to know where it was hidden during the search. There was a big pile of tinned food in the larder. I opened the bottommost of the tins – biscuits I think it contained, bedded in the revolver and replaced the strip of adhesive tape.

I calculated, and rightly, that no one would think of working their way through a pile of apparently untouched foodstuffs, especially as all the top tins were soldered.

The red curtain I had concealed by laying it flat on the seat of one of the drawing-room chairs under the chintz cover and the wool in the seat cushion, cutting a small hole.

And now came the moment that I had anticipated – three people who were so frightened of each other that anything might happen – *and one of them had a revolver*. I watched them from the windows of the house. When Blore came up alone I had the big marble clock poised ready. *Exit Blore* . . .

From my window I saw Vera Claythorne shoot Lombard. A daring and resourceful young woman. I always thought she was a match for him and more. As soon as that had happened I set the stage in her bedroom.

It was an interesting psychological experiment. Would the consciousness of her own guilt, the state of nervous tension consequent on having just shot a man, be sufficient, together with the hypnotic suggestion of the surroundings, to cause her to take her own life? I thought it would. I was right. Vera Claythorne hanged herself before my eyes where I stood in the shadow of the wardrobe.

And now for the last stage. I came forward, picked up the chair and set it against the wall. I looked for the revolver and found it at the top of the stairs where the girl had dropped it. I was careful to preserve her fingerprints on it.

And now?

I shall finish writing this. I shall enclose it and seal it in a bottle and I shall throw the bottle into the sea.

Why?

Yes, why?

It was my ambition to *invent* a murder mystery that no one could solve.

But no artist, I now realize, can be satisfied with art alone. There is a natural craving for recognition which cannot be gainsaid.

I have, let me confess it in all humility, a pitiful human wish that someone should know just how clever I have been . . .

In all this, I have assumed that the mystery of Soldier Island will remain unsolved. It may be, of course, that the police will be cleverer than I think. There are, after all, three clues. One: the police are perfectly aware that Edward Seton was guilty. They know, therefore, that one of the ten people on the island was not a murderer in any sense of the word, and it follows, paradoxically, that that person must logically be *the* murderer. The second clue lies in the seventh verse of the nursery rhyme. Armstrong's death is associated with a 'red herring' which he swallowed – or rather which resulted in swallowing him! That is to say that at that stage of the affair some hocus-pocus is clearly indicated – and that Armstrong was deceived by it and sent to his death. That might start a promising line of inquiry. For at that period there are only four persons and of those four I am clearly the only one likely to inspire him with confidence.

The third is symbolical. The manner of my death marking me on the forehead. The brand of Cain.

There is, I think, little more to say.

After entrusting my bottle and its message to the sea I shall go to my room and lay myself down on the bed. To my eyeglasses is attached what seems a length of fine black cord – but it is elastic cord. I shall lay the weight of the body on the glasses. The cord I shall loop round the door-handle and attach it, not too solidly, to the revolver. What I think will happen is this.

My hand, protected with a handkerchief, will press the trigger. My hand will fall to my side, the revolver, pulled by the elastic, will recoil to the door, jarred by the door-handle it will detach itself from the elastic and fall. The elastic, released, will hang down innocently from the eyeglasses on which my body *is* lying. A handkerchief lying on the floor will cause no comment whatever.

I shall be found, laid neatly on my bed, shot through the forehead in accordance with the record kept by my fellow victims. Times of death cannot be stated with any accuracy by the time our bodies are examined.

When the sea goes down, there will come from the mainland boats and men.

And they will find ten dead bodies and an unsolved problem on Soldier Island.

Signed:

Lawrence Wargrave.